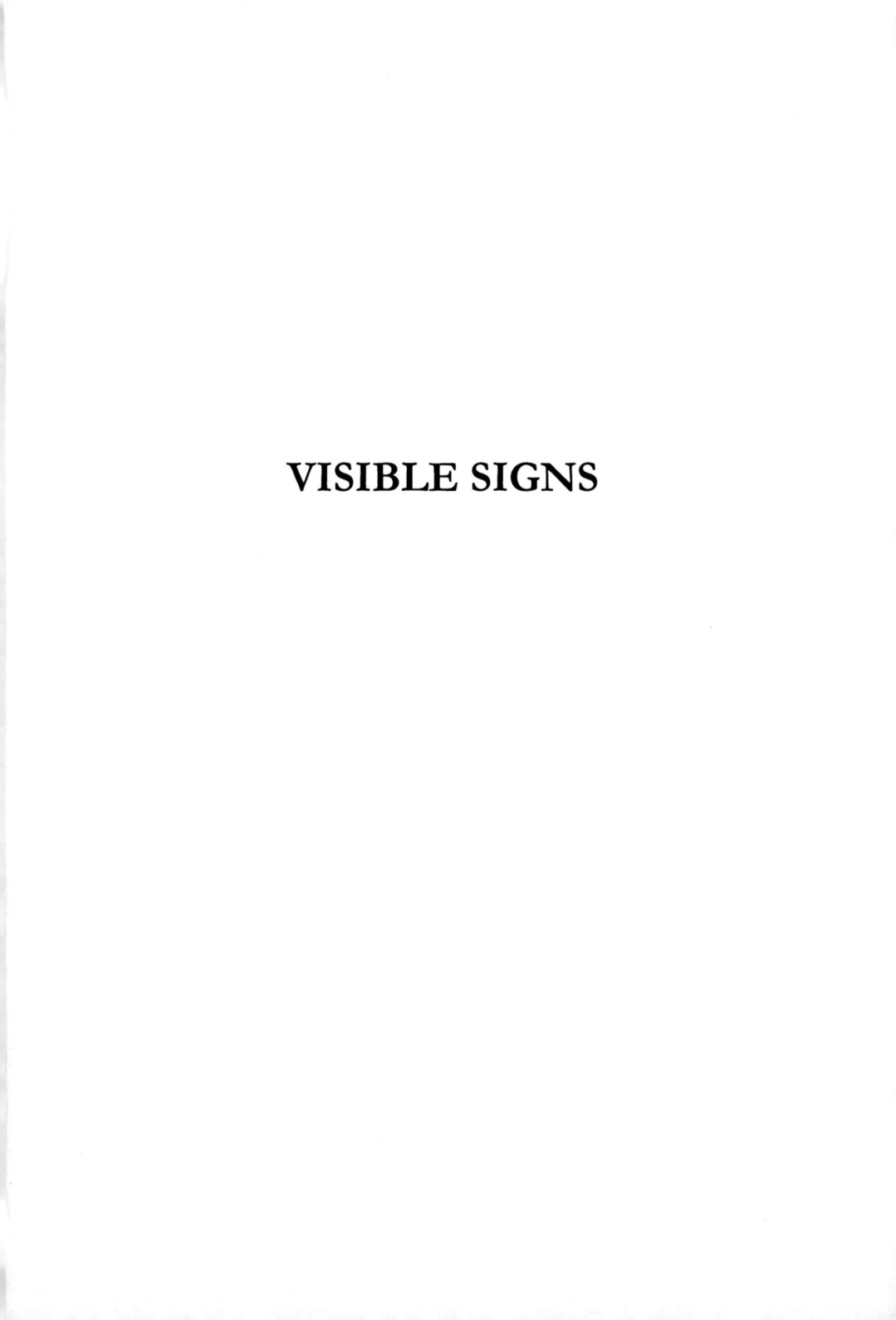

VISIBLE SIGNS

VISIBLE SIGNS

Heather Tosteson

Wising Up Press
Decatur, Georgia

Wising Up Press
P.O. Box 2122
Decatur, GA 30031-2122
www.universaltable.org

Copyright © 2007 by Heather Tosteson

All rights reserved. No part of this book may be used or reproduced in any manner whatsoever without written permission, except in the case of brief quotations embodied in critical articles or reviews.

This is a work of fiction. Names, characters, places, and incidents either are the product of the author's imagination or are used fictitiously. Any resemblance to actual persons, living or dead, events, or locales is entirely coincidental.

*Catologue-in-Publication data is on file with the Library of Congress.
LCCN: 2007936060*

Wising Up ISBN-13: 978-0-9796552-0-3

For Charlie,
who has been my steadfast companion in so many ways,
for what has been, and what will be...

ACKNOWLEDGEMENTS

I would particularly like to thank all my sisters in spirit, who, over the years, have supported me in my development as a writer and artist and as a spiritual seeker. I am especially grateful to how they have, by holding me in faith, all the many ones they represent, made it possible for me to hear and respond to my own. So, thank you thank you thank you for everything you are and everything you have given me over the years. I can't begin to repay you, but I can celebrate the worlds we have created together: Diane Jackson, Megan Krivchenia, Sybil Gilmar, Linda Yardney, Susan Mickelberry, Kat Meads, Tony Press, Mary Garland, Connie Veldink, Pat Hebert, Helen Moore, Patricia Mickelberry, Gerry Bassett, Janice Hume, Gladys Reynolds, Juarlyn Gaiter, Diane Rowley, Lorna Bozeman, Sue Gibbons, Barbara Alexander, Diane Grant, Mary Rose Bumpus, Marie Pappas, Norma Lauring, Marcia Klein, Sue Reynolds, Kim Hunt, Ruth Nejter, Karin Fleischer, Vyan Amedi, Lea Robinson, Lynnsay Buehler, Barbara Meinert, Martha Wright, Shahidah Mohamad, Betty Hasan-Amin, Mary Salaam, and Cindy Berg.

I would also like to acknowledge the people who have been part of our Antigua times: Tony Smith and José David Ovalle, Connie Erickson, Julio and Paula Carranza, and most especially Alicia Reyes de Barrios, of such generous spirit and luminous faith, who was my loyal guide to all the processions and *velaciones* in Antigua during Lent and Passion Week, 2000.

The support I received from Hambidge Center for the Arts over the years, and the various forms this book has taken, has been invaluable.

TABLE OF CONTENTS

SECTION I: THE WATCHERS

Friends in Passing (Ginger)	2
Chapter 1: Jam and Justice	4
After Life (Simon)	20
Chapter 2: Debilidad Humana	23
The Watchers (Mikela)	42
Chapter 3: Stealing	45
Without Warning (Ben)	71
Chapter 4: Echo Chamber	74

SECTION II: IN AND OUT OF THE BODY

Spiritual Life (Wilma)	92
Chapter 5: Truth	96
Girl in the Grip of God (Mikela)	100
Chapter 6: Life Drawing	106
Chess Master (Mamí Concepción)	134
Chapter 7: Lies	137
The Seeker (Marie)	148
Chapter 8: Lucid Dreams and Astral Travel	150
Chapter 9: Birth	179
Chapter 10: Wanton Kindness	187

SECTION III: THE ONLY SEAT IN THE ROOM

It Isn't What It Seems (Ben)   *196*
Chapter 11: Touch-Seeing   **202**
Living Until We Die (Ginger)   *243*
Chapter 12: Foster Care   **246**
Do Gooders (Mamí Concepción)   *273*
Chapter 13: Forethought   **279**
A God Ginny Can Worship (Simon)   *294*
Chapter 14: The Passion   **307**
The Child with Blue Eyes (Mikela)   *343*
Chapter 15: Judasina   **353**

SECTION IV: GOD IN THE ROUND

The Spirit of Adoption (Wilma)   *384*
Chapter 16: Burial   **391**
Chapter 17: Standing Firm   **412**
The Look (Gwen)   *422*
Chapter 18: Body Casting   **431**
Burning the Baby Snatchers (Mikela)   *451*
Chapter 19: Busqueda   **456**
Calling All the Spirits (Patricio)   *477*
Chapter 20: Asusto   **481**
God-in-the-Round (Ginger)   *498*
Chapter 21: The Visitation   **502**
Finding the Home That Won't Go (Natividad)   *514*

MIKELA'S LEGENDS

La Llorana   *519*
La Engañadora   *521*
The Woman Who Brought Disaster   *523*

For the word of God is quick and powerful and sharper than any two-edged sword, piercing even to the dividing asunder of soul and spirit, and of the joints and marrow, and is a discerner of your thoughts and intents of the heart. Neither is there any creature that is not manifest in her sight; but all things are naked and opened with the eyes of her with whom we have to do.

Hebrews 4: 12-13

Un Alma tienes no más, si la pierdes ¿qué háras?
Hermano Pedro de San José Betancur

ANTIGUA, GUATEMALA
2000

SECTION I
THE WATCHERS

You have searched me and known me.
You know me when I sit down and when I rise up;
you discern my thoughts from far away.
You search out my path and my lying down,
and are acquainted with all my ways.
Even before a word is on my tongue,
You know it completely.
You hem me in, behind and before,
and You lay your hand on me.
*   Psalm 139:1-5*

FRIENDS IN PASSING
(Ginger)

  Of course, I have Rosemary and she has me, and we'll probably have each other until the day one or the other of us dies. At our ages it takes too much energy to change our friends. But it's not like having a significant other. It's like having an insignificant other. Everything that matters most to one of us doesn't seem to register on the other's radar screen. For example, I say to Rosemary, "Today is the beginning of Advent," and she won't even pause for a second to register the remark, just puts a spoon in front of my lips, saying, "Taste this, will you? Do you think Wilma is skimping on the sugar in the tamarind juice. I told her four to one."
  Maybe we are such fast friends, for that we are, because our differences recall our childhoods. Not just that odd girl who lived next door who we played with for years until we went to school and realized we had some choice in our acquaintances. Both Rosemary and I had mothers who remained, until the days they died, more than a little wary of us. Not Mommy Dearest mothers by any means. Just separated from us by an unbridgeable temperamental gulf. They could never quite figure out how we'd been slipped into their nests. So, although they had all the appropriate instincts about preserving our lives, feeding and sheltering us until our wings were strong enough to carry us out into the wild, their hearts never opened to us in the way I've seen with some mothers and daughters where you can't be quite sure where one of them ends and the other begins. The ones, you know, you read about who bear their daughter's baby without thinking about it.
  Neither Rosemary nor I have that need for closeness or understanding from our

women friends. I think we may have had it with our last husbands and we cherish the memories but no longer have any dreams of having the experience repeated in this life. Listening to some of the women I know bare their souls to me or to each other, I think they find in their women friends a kind of closeness they've never known in their married lives. That feels more than a little sad to me. I like to have all my emotions—love and passion and comfort and closeness—in one place. It's a kind of efficiency or single-mindedness in me, I suppose. I guess it's what's brought me, at this time in my life, into such a passionate relationship with God.

Chapter 1
JAM AND JUSTICE

Sometimes, as she counted up her friends, massage clients and the members of the collective and all their current tribulations, Rosemary felt like a flustered shepherdess with a bad head for numbers. Someone was always wandering off bleating into the thickets, and Rosemary was always having to think who to send out to round them up again. Rosemary quite liked this image of herself—at least the staff, the sturdy shoes, the responsibility, the steep mountain slope, the view. At seventy-one, she thought happily, I may have at last found my true calling. One that was founded on humor and yearning and putting her autocratic nature to good use.

But sheep were such frightening creatures, really, with those strange eyes, so blank and quick simultaneously, and the way they seemed to become something more than themselves, less than themselves, whenever they started moving as one, like water. Why was it, she wondered, that we found it so difficult to believe, as Fra Lippo Lippi said in that poem by Robert Browning, that the world means, and it means intensely and it means good. Wasn't it that inability that drove us bleating, desperately singular, off into the thickets?

Actually, Rosemary thought, she was a herder of wild cats, who had a savage, unconscionable edge to their loneliness, a willingness to draw blood if their survival required it. It meant her strategies were different. One of them was just sipping coffee and appreciating their antics. The other was a little more cunning—scratching backs, but only when asked. Setting food out where it was readily visible. Looking the other way when necessary to lure them closer.

Funny, all these metaphors—how they made her think a little differently about herself, and God. Of course, she'd die rather than say a word of this to Ginger—who would just use it as proof that all her years of proselytizing had finally born fruit. Maybe it had, but not in the way Ginger expected. Rosemary certainly wasn't going to deny that having found her calling made her feel like she had a special bond with God and could see more and more often through Her eyes. What she realized when this happened is what a keen sense of humor God had, and what a powerful yearning for love, closeness, loyalty—not to Her exactly but to that belief that we are put here on this earth to mean and mean intensely and mean good.

Rosemary looked happily around her bright, clean bedroom, savoring the new coat of yellow-gold paint and how it set off Walt's last two landscapes—not to mention the hot pink bougainvillea pouring off the patio roof and snaking around the pillars. She did wish he could be with her now, in this new placid but deeply interested place she had discovered or received. There was no one she knew who would have appreciated more what it meant to her after all those years of her forties and fifties when she was locked in such furious battle, wresting meaning from an indifferent universe, wresting it from that sea of despair that seemed her deepest and most abiding reality. When it wasn't her own life she was fighting for, she fought for the lives of the children they took in. Such struggles they had had just to reach the ages they were when they came to them: Alicia at eleven, Byron at fourteen, Nefertiti at sixteen with a baby on the way, Valerie at twelve, Will at seventeen, David at ten.

She only wanted adolescents, she told the incredulous case workers. Because then all the worst damage had been done, there was no point in grieving or feeling responsible for creating a new world for them. It was a question of damage control, playing as well as one could the hand fate had dealt you. She wasn't a game player herself, but it felt like a good image—that or looking at the sparse supplies in the pantry and figuring out how to make the most interesting dinner possible out of them. It wasn't like Walt looking at the colors on his piece of plexiglass, willfully restricting his choices. These restrictions were more arbitrary, but intractable—an addicted mother, a demented grandmother, a father who couldn't keep his hands to himself, an embittering poverty so rich in things that it would pass for wealth where she was living now. When she and Walt moved to Antigua, she'd asked them all to come down and see her, but they were surprisingly small-minded, all her children, foster, step and whole. They didn't want to leave the certain perimeters of their own lives, however successful or unsuccessful. They didn't want to see her, or Walt for that matter, grow in ways they hadn't foretold.

Oh, she missed Walt so much, his natural broadmindedness, that dear little *oh* he breathed more and more lightly each time a new path opened up for them. She couldn't imagine what their lives would have been like if they had met each other any earlier. So much of their delight in each other came because of what they had known before—lousy spouses, years of solitude, meaningless riches or draining near poverty, alcoholism, cancer, the whole gamut. They didn't feel singled out by anything but their unexpected good fortune in finding each other when they did.

She was glad that they had had a full year in Antigua before Walt's stroke. They had spent a decade visiting in the summer, overseeing the building of the house. But only had four years together in it. Sometimes, in those last few months when he couldn't talk and he couldn't walk and only his eyes would follow her or Wilma around the house, she wasn't sure that he knew who she—or he—were anymore. But then she would come upon him and glimpse a look of such intelligence and acceptance that she began to weep for joy. It was then, at the age of sixty-six, that she found her solid ground—as if that sea of sorrow that had been the most pervasive reality of her life suddenly divided and an irresistible arc of sand beckoned. She still felt Walt was walking beside her there, enjoying the time it was taking them to reach the far shore, enjoying the miracle and quite at rest as well with what would come after.

The phone rang. She heard Wilma answer it and take a message. Rosemary never spoke to anyone until she had had her morning coffee and her meditation session in the garden. Smiling, already anticipant, Rosemary got out of bed and went to dress. Ginger, she wondered. Or Simon. One never knew who—or what. Who would have thought that as life simplified with age it became a pointillist painting, sharp points of appreciation. The smell of coffee coming from the kitchen, the sound of the fountain in the courtyard, the unexpected perspective she had on Walt's painting as she stood at her clothes rack meditating on what color spoke to her today, the promising buzzing of the bees in the trumpet flowers, Wilma's sweet murmur as she repeated whatever message she was given. Life, Rosemary thought, selecting a red dress and a mauve scarf, is waiting for me and finally, finally, I am ready for it.

"Wilma," she cried out, suddenly famished, "*Mi café por favor. Inmediatamente!*"

Rosemary's Spanish had, to put it kindly, lapses—but it was good enough for her to understand that Estella's husband had taken her jam money and used it for liquor, that Mariana's children, in their hunger, had eaten half of her portion of strawberry jam, that Soledad's one year old had worms and she had tried to use the jam as a medicine.

She led them all out onto the back patio behind the kitchen where four large baskets of mangoes sat ripening beside the sinks. The attitude she took was similar to the one she had with the foster children she and Walt had taken in over the years when they lived in the States. Every little bit helps—but only God knows how.

She called to Wilma, who came out of the kitchen reluctantly. She brought knives to peel and slice the mangoes and two buckets, one for the fruit and one for the peels. She thought Rosemary's project foolish and didn't waste a tittle of energy pretending otherwise.

"What do you expect me to do?" Rosemary had asked her once. "Just let people starve?"

"You're fattening them with false hopes," Wilma had said. "It's like feeding a starving child sweets when what she needs are milk and meat."

"Do you have any better suggestions?" Rosemary had asked her. "I'm open, but I have to do something."

She didn't force the women to come, for goodness sake. All she wanted to do was give them some options. Each month she tried something new. There was the month she had, at Ginger's suggestion, paid a carpenter to make a hundred small wooden crosses for the women to paint. She had thought they would sell them to the endless stream of missionary aid workers that came through the town, although the evangelicals found them suspiciously papist and the Catholics preferred their own tacky plastic rosaries. Ginger, bless her, bought most of them and shipped them back to her high Episcopalian friends with liberal sympathies.

There was the month she brought Lila's visiting daughter, a dress designer, in to suggest different cuts the women could give the blouses and skirts they tried to sell to tourists. The women had all looked blankly at Lila's daughter with her clear plastic bracelets, her dramatically geometric haircut, while she showed them how to make a pattern for a kimono or harem pants. They had all, over the centuries, mastered the rectangle—a long one for their skirt, two smaller, roughly tacked together panels for their blouses. They saw no need to expand their repertoire of cuts. Sewing wasn't really their thing. All their inventiveness was saved for the weaving itself—although inventiveness was perhaps the wrong word.

Just as options weren't exactly what the women hungered for, as Wilma constantly pointed out. They wanted food on their table, a sober mate, fields that he and their endlessly expanding crop of children could cultivate. They wanted someone to talk with as they wove.

But however hard working they were, they didn't have a true capitalist craving for novelty. Which is why, everywhere you went, you saw women weaving the same patterns or carrying on their heads the same high mound of chicken-shaped potholders, crocheted hats, little embroidered purses. They didn't seem to make any correlations between supply and demand—their level of production determined only by their time to weave, bead or sew and their ability to buy thread. But the blouses they made for themselves and then tried to sell to tourists had openings too small for a European's head, and the wide swatches of unfinished material bound by a woven belt that constituted the uniform skirt made tourists feel constrained and fat. How many people want to set up museum displays of old blouses, she asked them. They looked at her blankly, for they had never understood the tourist's interest in their clothes in the first place. What they had understood was the cash.

One month, she had bought beads and suggested they all practice creating new designs for their bracelets and necklaces. It was as successful as the crosses. The dress-making lesson.

"Senora Rosemary, just give them their pills and let them go," Wilma had scolded her.

It wasn't only the contraceptives, which Rosemary distributed on their departure, that kept the women coming every week, whatever Wilma said. Although Rosemary was at a loss to say what it was. It was their constant return that made Rosemary hopeful. Maybe next week, she could bring Ed from the expat church in to talk about marketing their mango chutney.

Oh, they frustrated and enticed her, these soft talking women with their ever present bundles of babies and wares. The contraceptives had been the result of the one clear request Rosemary had ever received from them. Rosemary had invited a nurse-missionary who had come to the expat church to come and talk about how to prevent intestinal infections in their children. But how, Estella, pregnant with her fifth child at age twenty-one, had asked, do you prevent the children themselves?

The other women had looked at her, shocked, a soft murmur running among them, but all of them had listened intently to the nurse's description of breast feeding as an effective contraceptive. Contingent, of course, on their having milk, Rosemary had broken in. What about family planning? But the nurse was Catholic and talked about the rhythms of the body like an astrologer talked about the portentous transits of the planets.

Rosemary was so miffed that she called the American Embassy and located someone over in USAID who linked her up with a UNICEF representative who linked her up with a local physician who told her contraceptives were available over the counter here if you only knew what to ask for. Rosemary had developed a close relationship with a pharmacy in the capital, where she regularly purchased large quantities of oral contraceptives, which she disbursed once a month with a lecture on how to take them, and, most importantly, how to hide them from your spouse.

If they just learned to make one new thing to sell that could cover the cost of the pills, Rosemary would feel she'd accomplished something. Which is not to say they would ever use the money for something as basic to their well-being as family planning. They wanted the pills, stood in line for them, answered Rosemary's questions on whether they understood how to take them, returned for refills, brought their mothers and sisters and daughters and friends to partake of the bounty. But it would never be a right for them, a necessity. Only a welcome, unanticipated stay of destiny.

Sometimes, when she thought about it, Rosemary just got wild. How long had it taken to break their will?

Rosemary thought of the funny little girl who had come over last Friday, Mikela, Concepción's protégé from the girls' home, making that fist of hers to show the bulge in her upper arm. Now she, Rosemary thought, had entrepreneurial verve. Maybe Rosemary should forget the mothers and concentrate on the little girls, who, by the age of three or four were already hoisting their baby brothers and sisters on their backs. They too deserved some options, didn't they?

"Today," she told the women, "we are making chutney. It is a special jam, very picante, from India. Foreigners will pay more for it than for other jams."

They all paused, knives in hands, watching her, listening impassively.

"How much?" Mariana asked. "How much more?"

They had never, Rosemary knew, bought jam off a shelf. But they all had incredible heads for numbers and were capable of adding and subtracting faster than Rosemary could form the sound of a single number in Spanish.

The price she gave made Mariana's eyes glisten. She turned her attention to the mango in her hand, rapidly and expertly peeling and slicing it and dropping it into the bucket.

The other women continued their work too, all of them talking in their soft, indecipherable dialect. Occasionally one of them would slide an infant off her back and lift her blouse and let it nurse, continuing the steady peeling, the humming conversation.

In the kitchen, Rosemary could hear Wilma angrily banging pots. Thank goodness that little girl was coming again this afternoon to help with the cleaning up. Wilma didn't mind the meetings of the collective, as long as they didn't take place in her kitchen.

Rosemary went in to see if she could appease her in any way.

"Do you want to double check the recipe with me?" Rosemary asked. She and Wilma had made the chutney last year for gifts for her friends in the States.

Wilma just scowled and pulled another large soup pot from the cupboard. She surveyed the supplies she had already set out—the brown sugar and hot peppers and quartered limes and ginger.

"Would you like to go and do something else?" Rosemary asked. "Shopping? Go out to lunch? I can keep an eye on everything—and that little girl will be coming to help with the cleaning up in the afternoon."

But Wilma wanted to make her presence, however irate, felt.

"You don't know where things are in here, Senora Rosemary."

And whose fault, Rosemary wanted to ask, was that? Wilma had come to stay with them after Walt had his stroke. Rosemary had relinquished all responsibility for the house to her so she could concentrate on Walt. She wondered if, after Walt's death, she had started the collective and her massage practice because she knew there was no way to reestablish her control over the housekeeping. Letting Wilma go had always been out of the question.

She had dedicated herself, instead, to disrupting all Wilma's careful domestic arrangements by this constant influx of friends, clients, collective. Wilma had, all told, handled the shift with aplomb. Their life, the last year of Walt's life, had been exceedingly quiet. Even if Rosemary lived in a ruckus for the rest of her life, she carried in the depths of her heart that hushed silence that was his sweet presence and the sorrow, so inextinguishable, of their leave-taking. Wilma was the only person who had shared that time with her and, beneath their daily friction, it was their indissoluble bond.

"Do not forget, Senora, that you have a client in an hour. I will see the women through this jam making."

Wilma smiled at Rosemary, her authority re-established. Rosemary had forgotten the massage appointment, forgotten the meeting of the collective when she'd made it. Well, there were some benefits of forgetfulness—and respite from Wilma's grim disapproval was certainly one of them.

It was Simon's new friend who was coming. Rosemary wandered off to see if she'd written her name down anywhere. She didn't seem, the one encounter Rosemary had had with her over at the restaurant in the plaza, to be a woman who made massage a regular part of her life. But Simon had said something about big life strains. Or was it a strained ligament? Both? She would know soon enough. It was amazing what people blurted out when they were touched. No one, Rosemary thought, should be a masseuse until they'd lived their own life nearly through—for it was the quality of the listening that was what allowed people to leave feeling lighter in their hearts, more at ease in their bodies, as if some essential internal weight of experience had become redistributed just by the laying on of compassionate but detached hands. But to listen like that, with your hands and heart as well as your mind, you really needed to have lived long enough to have very little surprise you.

When the doorbell rang, Rosemary went herself to open the door. All the women were now in the kitchen, stirring the large pots of braised onions and mangoes under Wilma's gruff but contented solitary authority.

The woman standing there was of medium height. Other than a faint crease between her eyebrows as she tried to see Rosemary's face through the grate, what struck Rosemary was the sleekness of her face. Not bony, exactly, just taut.

"Ah, Simon's friend," she said, hoping the woman would take the cue and introduce herself. Which she promptly did once Rosemary pulled the door open. She put out her hand in a very efficient way, as if highly practiced. Could she be a lawyer, Rosemary wondered. A politician who lost an election?

"Ginny Fox."

"Jenny?"

"Ginny. Short for Virginia. An accident of birth, the name. My parents were driving up the coast on their way home to Delaware when I arrived a month early. Personally, I think I would have preferred it if they had named me Richmond."

"Certainly better than Quantico or Newport News, I suppose."

Contained, Rosemary decided, was the adjective that might best describe her—from her sleek ash-blonde hair that just brushed her shoulders to the firm, athletic body dressed in jeans and a man's t-shirt. There was something about the angles of her face that seemed to cast off light. Her eyes were a clear, cool gray.

Behind them, they could hear the sound of laughter coming from the kitchen. Ginny looked a little puzzled.

"Am I interrupting anything?"

Rosemary explained about the collective as she led Ginny to the massage room. "Perhaps you'd like to meet them later. Now that Wilma's hit her stride, I'd hate to disrupt her."

"It feels indulgent to be coming here for a massage."

"Kindness, they say, begins at home." Rosemary switched on the light in the massage room and turned on her tape deck with its relaxing New Age tape. She noticed Ginny's limp. "Besides, it may not be an indulgence. Have you always had that limp?"

"No. I pulled a muscle or something when I was out running last week. That's when Simon called you. It's the cobblestones—can't have them interrupting my steady flow of beta-endorphins. Simon's line—not mine."

"I find movement, even at my age, deeply soothing," Rosemary said. She handed Ginny a sheet. "Why don't you get undressed and call me when you're ready. Along with your leg, do you have any other trouble spots?"

Ginny took the folded sheet in both hands, like an offering, or a flag at a military funeral. A look of distress crossed her face. Rosemary assumed it had to do with disrobing.

"Most of my clients leave their panties on but remove their bras."

Ginny nodded.

"Only your leg then?"

"And my shoulders and neck," Ginny said. "I think it was the bus ride, but I feel so tight I find it difficult to breathe."

"When you're ready, lie face down on the table and just give me a call. I'll be right outside the door."

As she waited, Rosemary lifted her face into the sun and let the light warm her face and then her hands. They were a ceremony, these massages. More satisfying to her than Sunday services. But there was always this moment of quiet just before she went in when Rosemary tried to open herself to what she had picked up from her client on arrival. Even if the client was an old friend, like Ginger, it helped to see them as someone new and unfamiliar. There was something interesting, something sleek and wild about Ginny that appealed to Rosemary, as if she were ready to pounce or take flight.

"Ready," Ginny called. She had a clear, pleasant voice—as cool and intact as everything else about her.

"Would you like music?" Rosemary asked. "And would you like scented oil or plain oil."

"Let's go for broke," Ginny said, her voice a little muffled because her face was resting in the donut-shaped head rest. "Music and scent."

Rosemary chose rosemary oil for its astringency, thinking that it went with everything she was picking up.

"Tell me immediately if anything feels uncomfortable," she said as she rubbed her large, knobby hands with the oil, then slowly drew the sheet down exposing Ginny's shoulders and upper back. She could see Ginny's body tense in anticipation, so began by just setting both her hands, thumbs touching, across Ginny's back like wings and letting them rest there for thirty seconds. She did the same with the back of Ginny's neck. She could feel how Ginny was imitating calm. She set her hands on the back of her head, just where the cervical vertebrae met the skull.

"Some clients prefer to talk, some don't. I'm comfortable with either. I'll assume you prefer silence unless you tell me different."

Ginny didn't, so Rosemary spent the next half hour speaking that other, subtle, wordless language that said so much.

There was something wary to the point of panic in Ginny's body, Rosemary discovered. And a discipline taut as wire that held her body perfectly, dissimulatingly still. For some reason Rosemary thought of the little girl who was coming this afternoon to help Wilma, what it had felt like to touch her tense little back and feel it begin to relax.

Untamed, she thought, but not savage. And, at the same time, they both had an intense sense of their own physical presence. Their bodies were their implements. She had been the same for much of her life—maybe that is why her hands seemed to move with such assurance, unfazed by the tenseness, the wariness.

She heard Walt, all those years ago, saying, "We all need to be touched, Rosemary. We all need to be loved." She had had no room, at forty-five, for love stories—and lived a passionate one for the rest of her life.

Oh, that last year of Walt's life, she tried, with her hands, to return to him everything he had taught her, all that she treasured from their twenty-one years together. She would massage his paralyzed leg and arm, looking into his large rheumy eyes, weeping as her hands steadily pressed and molded and cherished his insensible flesh.

It all goes, she thought, pressing her oil slick hands in bands across Ginny's back, the back of her legs. So there's no reason to hold back and every reason on earth to hold on. Only problem is we don't, until it is too late to do us much good.

The tape finished. She turned to change it, suggesting Ginny turn over on her back.

"It's a question of balance," she explained. "We never strain one muscle without putting strain on all. So its important to relax the muscles that are filling in as well." It's the closest she came to a philosophy of life, this intricate inter-relatedness of tendons and muscles, of desire and rebellion, mind and matter.

Ginny turned over slowly, almost sleepily, holding the sheet closely against her breasts. Her eyes held a trapped look now. Rosemary came over and stood at the head of the massage table, folding her hands carefully over Ginny's shoulders and letting them rest there.

"I want you to imagine that your body is a source of wisdom and healing," she said. "I want you to trust that it knows exactly what will help you, that it is safe to relax and let it take over."

Although she held her own head erect and looked out at the far wall, she could feel Ginny's eyes on her. There was something so bleak there, it didn't feel like trust. But was, Rosemary knew, if she could bear to take it in.

Rosemary closed her eyes and opened her own body to what her hands were learning.

Poor heart, she thought, her hands closing more warmly around Ginny's shoulders. Nowhere to go inside or out.

"Tell me about your running," she said, beginning to massage Ginny's shoulders gently. "How long have you been doing it? What are your goals?"

"My goal is never to have to stop."

"Then you're going to have to start listening to your body more. As it is now, it sure feels to me like you're tearing yourself up. Your body is far too tight."

"The only thing that eases the tension is running," Ginny said. "I *can't* stop."

Rosemary put her hands on Ginny's collar bone, pressing her fingers down slightly toward her chest. "Then don't. Until you can't possibly run anymore. But try to do it with a little tenderness. Your body is your home."

She cupped Ginny's head in her hands and pulled it gently back toward her, letting the cervical vertebrae expand. She could feel the tears snaking from Ginny's eyes around her ears and into her own hands, like an offering.

It was a wonderful thing, Rosemary thought, her own body going soft with wonder and thankfulness, to have found, at last, her own way of knowing God.

"Come and meet my women," Rosemary said to Ginny after she was dressed. She caught the look on Ginny's face and added, "I know that's not the politically correct way to refer to them. But even though we call what we have here a collective, and they have with great glee given themselves positions as president and vice-president and treasurer, I don't have any illusions that they would continue to meet without me. Sometimes I feel guilty, but then I remind myself no one is forcing them to come, they have a good time, and sometimes they make a little money from one project or another. They don't have to convert, like with the missionary groups, or use a past history of abuse or torture as their admission card, like with the human rights groups.

"And for me, having them all come together keeps me from establishing personal ties of obligation and dependency that would really feel uncomfortable. I keep my distance from their daily lives. We all like it that way."

As they neared the kitchen, Rosemary could swear she heard Wilma laughing, but when Wilma turned from the stove to see who was there, her face had its usual stern expression.

"We are almost finished," she said. She waved Rosemary and Ginny over toward the dining room table. Estella, a large ladle in her hand, was slowly pouring chutney into the glass jars.

"Do you want to explain to them that they'll get a better price if I shop them around to the specialty stores myself," Rosemary said to Wilma.

Ginny listened intently as Wilma explained. There was a telling silence among the women. They had all calculated their individual profit and, Rosemary had no doubt, spent it twice over.

"They might like to go with you," Ginny said. "Hear how you make your pitch so they can do it in the future."

"I was actually going to use barter and blackmail," Rosemary said. "Most of the store owners are my friends. They like massages. And they have their own pet projects they want me to invest in. Gardens of medicinal herbs. Helping the street children learn to read—like your pal Simon. You could come too," she said to Ginny. "You have a worldly flair to you that may convince them this isn't purely charity, that there may be some profit lurking somewhere. None of us is, in principle, opposed to profit."

"Flair?" Ginny said, looking down at her jeans and drab t-shirt.

"Class, dear. Let's just say you have class."

Ginny laughed, a rich laugh that was surprising in its spontaneity. She turned to the women and began talking, almost glibly, in Spanish. Wilma looked at Rosemary, raising her eyebrows, but nodded in approval at something Ginny said.

Rosemary closed her eyes, not trying to follow. She felt tired from the massage session, an emotional exhaustion more than a physical one. Walt used to complain of the same after a morning in his studio. "Who ever would believe seeing could be so taxing?" he would ask. Then he would take her hand after lunch and lead her back to their bedroom for a companionable siesta.

"Tell them I have a marketing expert willing to come talk with them," Rosemary said, not bothering to open her eyes.

"When?" Ginny asked.

"Next week," Rosemary said. "Possibly."

Ginny talked some more, then dug into her purse and pulled out a little notepad and pen and began to write something. She tore out the sheet and wrapped it around the glass jar.

"They're thinking labels are a good thing—ones that advertise the collective."

"They are?" Rosemary said. "Are you willing to help them?"

"Me?"

"I don't hear anyone else talking, dear," Rosemary said, her voice a little curt.

But Ginny's vitality left as quickly as it had come, leaving Rosemary remorseful as she watched Ginny fold up the little sheet of paper and look for a trash can to deposit it in, shrugging her shoulders as she did so. Wilma looked reprovingly at Rosemary. Rosemary closed her eyes again. I am an old woman, she thought. I am no longer accountable. But her discomfort was keen as a pin prick. She didn't want to be usurped.

The women were now all gathering their bundles. They each came, in that wonderfully polite way of theirs, to shake her hand, thank her for her kindness. She sat up straighter. The women were smart. They could see Ginny was only passing through but Rosemary was here for the duration.

While Wilma was showing the women out, Rosemary went to inspect the steaming jars of chutney. They smelled enticing. But then she remembered, paraffin. They'd forgotten to seal them.

"You don't know the mileage Wilma will get out of this. Even if it was her oversight," she told Ginny. She bent down and pulled a box of paraffin out from under the sink. "I had a friend bring this down from the States. The way they use candles here, you'd think it would be easy to find—but people looked at me as if I were sacrilegious for just asking. Candles are for God, not profitable perishables."

She filled a pan with water, then went through the dry goods to find a can she could open and empty to use as a melting pot. Rosemary noticed Ginny watching her with a look of amusement and uncertainty.

"I'd love to have your help with the labeling and marketing," Rosemary said. "But this is just brute labor. Let me let you out before I begin."

"I may be more suited for that right now," Ginny said. "My mind's not working so well these days."

Rosemary looked at her clear gray eyes, her keen face. "For a day," she said, "a week. But you have a future ahead of you. Anyone can see that. It's in your body language. Your quickness. You're a natural leader, dear."

"I had a future," Ginny said. "Now, as Simon tells me, I am just blessed with an after life."

"You're still a young woman," Rosemary said. She turned the stove off and led her out of the kitchen. Ginny winced at the bright sun.

"I'll be fifty this year."

"Just the right age to start a new stage," Rosemary said. "There are many people here who have, you know. After you start asking around, you won't feel so alone."

Ginny paused for a moment and looked at her directly, searching for something.

"I only know about you what you've told me," Rosemary said. "If you like, I can keep it that way."

Ginny closed her eyes, shuddered slightly. "I wish I could."

"You won't believe it, but there comes a time in your life when you're grateful for all of it—what you've learned, willingly or unwillingly, what you've fended off, what you've drawn real close. It's not like T. S. Eliot at all—that line of his about humans not being able to bear much reality. There comes a time when just having lived is justification enough. You would, if you could, live it all over."

As they crossed the courtyard, Wilma came up to them, followed by the little girl Concepción had sent. She glanced at Ginny and Rosemary, then ducked her head shyly. As Rosemary unbolted the door, Ginny stared back at the girl.

"Is she the daughter of one of the women in the collective?"

"No. A stray. Wilma's own well-calculated charity. But she's a bright, mesmerizing thing. I'm quite captivated. I'm sure she has quite a story to tell—although that doesn't mean we'll ever hear it. It's just interesting to speculate." She held Ginny's hand in hers and stroked it.

"Next week, then? Same time. Massage and then good works?"

Ginny nodded, then tucking her head down in a gesture strongly reminiscent of the little girl, walked quickly down the street. Rosemary watched her almost tenderly, remembering how she too, in her bad times, kept trying to rein her energy and power in, wanting to be for a day or a week, normal, muted, resigned. Of all the things she regretted in her life, she regretted that tamping down most. So useless, in the end.

Some of us, she thought contentedly as she closed the door, just need more air to breathe, more space to move, *more this*.

It didn't make life just, of course, but once you gave yourself over to it, it made life so rich you never wanted to relinquish it. But it was a difficult thing to trust, especially if you were a woman, this greed for existence. And you paid to reach that other place with all the grief your soul could suffer— and then more. The only way to know the suffering was unnecessary was to go through it. Why was that? Rosemary closed her eyes and listened to the fountain, remembering how large she felt, how free, as Ginny's tears collected in her waiting hands, drop by unwilling drop.

And then she heard a woman's voice, so rich and warm it thrilled her to the bone: *My power is in you. Use it.*

Rosemary stood there, letting the words reverberate through her. Later, she would wonder why she had no question about the rightness of what she'd heard. But she just lifted her face into the sun and let its heat begin to sing through her. She stretched her arms toward the ground, flexing her fingers. Through her half open eyes, her hands seemed to shiver with light. I want more time, she thought. But she knew, she really did, that, at last, she had enough.

Ginger would be green with envy, she thought contentedly, if she knew God was paying me house calls. It wasn't fair of course. She hadn't prayed for years on end, memorized the confession or the Nicene creed, mastered the niceties of those convoluted lectionaries. She didn't even have to endure the getting down on her knees or chewing that little paper wafer that always caught in her throat. It was all there, without her wanting it unduly.

Wisely, Rosemary, the voice said with a laugh, a faint trace of exasperation, but the same thrilling sweetness, biting as the chutney. *Use it wisely.*

AFTERLIFE
(Simon)

  Sometimes it seems to me the biggest problems we make for ourselves and for those around us are when we decide to be our brother's keeper. I can't believe David, my own brother, did what he did to her. Total mindfuck. And he had no idea. He thought he was freeing her. But all you have to do is look at her face and see what really happened. I'm not even sure he gets it yet. And I'm not going to check.
  There's not a word I can say to her that will make it better. I'm not my brother's keeper. Or his explicator. I don't think she can hear anything anyway. When your whole world has exploded, what use are words? That's a place I do know, in my gut, that place language can't touch. Where you just know. You just see. And know. And it doesn't matter anymore. You think it will last forever. It can last a hell of a long time. I should know. She should too. She kept me company there that whole year I lived in Boston before coming here. I'm grateful. Her company was probably the only company I could bear. Her intelligence like a cool hand on my forehead. Never breaking the silence. Leaving that up to me. But I knew when I did she would never diminish me by making it easier. By lying. By pity.
  But she never saw what came after. This wild and tranquil afterlife of mine. Maybe when she called me, she thought she was coming to join me in that other place, where one is just waiting for death as the only possible release. Maybe that earthly limbo was the only place she could imagine where she would feel safe.
  Instead she finds me here in Antigua with a new lease on life. I don't think that's what she's after right now. Anymore than I was in Boston. I just wanted it all to end. The

guilt. The anger. That sense of wasted possibility. A fatigue that felt like I was already ten feet under. No time, or energy, to change the balance sheet. "So what if you don't know what it was all for?," she asked me. "You think God has a mind as small as yours?"

She was right. Even if she'd hate to have it said back to her right now. We give God very little leash. Don't want God's responses to exceed our own sense of possibility or justice. We don't try to exercise the same control over life. It's always defying belief, and we accept that. But God, that's different. We want Him—or Her—safely contained, square and center in our imaginative field. That's how we feel real.

I don't know, truly, what real has to do with how Ginny feels now. She can't believe what's happened to her. She can't believe she didn't see it coming. And, right now, I think she'd rather die than not hold herself responsible. Uniquely and completely responsible.

I want to tell her just to get it over with and admit she believes God did it. That this catastrophe is God's righteous wrath. And if that's the case, why shouldn't she rethink their relationship, the way she has the one with David, the one with her church. Rethink! She'd look at me in that stunned, numb way. And she's right. What does thinking have to do with where she is now? She's like a sick animal, just trying to breathe with a minimum of energy, pain. Just trying to hang in there.

Like me a year ago. And here I am living happily in a state I would have called death before. It is an afterlife I'm in—and I'll be sad when it ends even though it doesn't fit in with anything I ever expected, or wanted, of life.

What do you do here? she asks me.

Observe, I tell her. Appreciate. Live the secret life of saints. Just like everyone else here. The women with their baskets of bright cloth going for nothing. The boys briskly rubbing their shoe brushes against their black palms, tidily packing their polishes and rags and brushes back into their wooden shoe shine boxes. The little girls in their sheath skirts and plastic sandals and embroidered blouses swaggering off to make a sale. Just grateful to be here another day.

But it took months to give up my stubbornness. To trust this. Some part of me really preferred death. I didn't like having to return to life like an animal, all my frames of meaning cracked, shattered. I hated not having any secrets from myself. Not having any defenses. I can pinpoint when it began to change for me. One morning I came out of my apartment and the volcano above the city was wreathed in a slipping circlet of cloud. I passed one of those ambiguous exterior walls, which look the same if you're a squatter or a millionaire, and the metal door was open. I could see an empty lot, a huge mound of gravel and bags of cement and these tiny sturdy men with mallets just laying into what had come before. I could feel the pleasure of that swing, of breathing in the dust. And I understood that's what it is to be human—to constantly be putting up adobe walls, tying plastic over cane. I was overjoyed at the busy relentlessness—how we're always trying to make new and better shelters, how, equally relentlessly, we're setting mallets to the old ones because they stand in our way and we have dreams, ambitions, drives. Wham! And then I looked down the street and saw the huge ruins and all that relentless activity seemed puny in comparison to a single meaningless, unintentional shudder of the earth that can fell enormous churches, level cities. Some part of me felt cheered that it was the same process, just on a bigger scale. There are so many churches that have fallen here.

So maybe Antigua is the place for Ginny to have come after all. Maybe, in time, she'll come to see what's happened to her as a natural catastrophe, not a moral cataclysm. I look back now with such a tenderness, such a fond attention to detail, to that time when I thought my life was over and I was engaged in the great accounting. I think about it now and I smile because I know, I can feel it streaming through every memory, how alive I was to my condition, how none of it was—how none of it had ever been—wasted. I see that terrible year, now, as my birth. But if you'd tried to tell me that then, I'd have had you put away.

That is what makes me undyingly loyal to Ginny. She never did. As a priest, a porta voz, a spokesperson for God, you would have thought, once or twice, she would have tried. But she stepped aside.

I wonder if this is what I'm being asked to do now. Not care so much whether she lives or dies. I'm not fooling myself. She really is on the cusp. But I think she has a little preference to how the balance falls or she wouldn't have looked me up. I want to be worthy of that trust, however unconscious it is, however faint. Not for her. For me.

Chapter 2
DEBILIDAD HUMANA

What drove Ginny was deeper than an impulse and even farther from a thought. She used the ticket the same day she bought it. There was no reason not to. She'd moved out of the rectory the second week in December and had put her few possessions in storage. Will's funeral was the 22nd, held with all possible pomp and circumstance at the cathedral in Chicago. She then flew to Naples, Florida, where she spent Christmas Day with her parents. On the 26th, she said good-bye and caught a plane to Miami. Her parents assumed, since she had never explained her situation, that she was returning to her job in Boston. If they had been other than who they were, they might have wondered what she was doing with them instead of officiating at her little church during one of the most important liturgical seasons in the year.

Instead, her mother was disappointed she wasn't joining them for their daily nine holes at the local country club. "I don't understand," she said as Ginny stood at the living room window watching for the cab she'd called to take her to the airport. "Why you can't show a little more flexibility?"

At the Miami airport, Ginny did. She looked at her ticket to Boston and thought, why in God's name am I doing this, and immediately tore the ticket up and threw it in the nearest trash bin. The dirty red plastic door to the trash bin swung back and forth as she paused, took a deep breath, and headed over to international flights. She didn't even think of Simon when she chose Guatemala. It was just the earliest available flight and she knew she needed to get out. Now.

Waiting for the plane, she bought a Central American guidebook in the bookstore. On the plane, she read the travel magazine and decided, equally rapidly, on the basis of their well-illustrated story, that the first thing she would do was head off to the Mayan pyramids tucked off in the jungle. She read through the guidebook to see how she might go about this and was relieved to find there was a night bus.

From the airport, she directed the driver to the appropriate bus company, where she bought an overnight ticket to the town closest to the pyramids. It was meant to be quite attractive, set on a little island in the middle of a large lake.

Ginny took a seat in the dirty waiting room of the bus company. She bought a coke and some potato chips, but let them sit unopened on top of her bags. Food felt completely irrelevant. So did sleep. So did emotion. So did thought. Motion, right now, was everything to her. Sweeter, by far, than prayer.

She stared blankly at the woman behind the ticket counter, at the buses roaring idly in the large loading bay that opened out from the interior door of the bus station. Outside on the street dusk was deepening. The street vendors were packing up their stands. Buses were pulling into and out of the other bus companies that lined the dingy street, accompanied by the indecipherable cries of the drivers and effacing clouds of pitch black exhaust.

Over the next two hours, couples and families gathered in the drab room, murmuring among themselves, opening their baskets and bright cloth bundles and drawing out tortillas and various fillings held in clear plastic bags that they scooped into the tortillas. Another American woman, in her sixties, came in and sat down at the far side of the room. She was accompanied by two small children, a girl and a boy, neither of whom looked American. She glanced briefly at Ginny, then concentrated on feeding the children with food she drew out of a large leather satchel.

When people rose and started moving out toward the loading bay, Ginny rose too, even though it was an hour before the time marked on her ticket. She slipped the can of coke and the chips in her bag. She thought about her visit to the large, immaculate bathroom in the airport, where the toilets flushed automatically when you stood up. There was no bathroom in the waiting room. She wondered where on the journey they might stop or whether her bladder was strong enough to last the twelve hours of the trip. She felt curious, but pleasantly indifferent to everything but getting herself on the right bus.

The other American woman was now collecting the children she'd come in with, who had been running up and down the aisles in the waiting room. Gripping them each firmly by the hand, she headed out toward the buses ahead of Ginny. She asked Ginny if she would be visiting the pyramids, and Ginny nodded.

"We'll be getting off earlier," she said, giving a nod toward the two children.

Ginny just nodded and smiled. She helped lift the small boy onto the steps of the bus, while the woman concentrated on the girl.

Seats were assigned, and she was relieved that hers was two rows ahead of the American woman and her two charges. The young girl already seated by the window in Ginny's assigned row gave her a bright smile which Ginny made herself return.

When she sat down in the aisle seat, having stored her knapsack in the rack above her, she immediately opened a murder mystery, one of four she had bought at the Miami airport along with the guidebook. She pulled her glasses out of her shirt pocket and began to read. The young woman next to her wriggled with impatience. She leaned out the window and bought sweets from one vendor, a plastic bag of cola from another. When, thirty minutes later, the bus started and the lights went out, she turned to Ginny and began to speak animatedly in Spanish.

"Do you understand?" she would ask on occasion and Ginny would promptly nod without saying anything but, "*Sí.*" She liked the girl's voice and demeanor, and the chance to practice her Spanish comprehension. Occasionally, she peered through the window to see what little she could see. Fast food signs. A big neon sign for the Kama Sutra Hotel. A tall, very American looking mall. And then the bus began a steep climb out of the city.

The girl was returning to see her family for the first time in five years. She had left when she was twelve to go work for a woman in the capital. This was very common, she said. She had several friends who had done the same. When she'd left her town, she'd thought she would see her friends in the city, but the capital was a very big and dangerous place and the woman she worked for lived far on the outskirts. There, she said, pointing to the lights scattered over the hillside. I lived up there. Now I work as a secretary. The woman I worked for was very kind to me and helped me go to school. Now another girl from my town works for her.

The American woman behind them was talking quite loudly in Spanish. Offering candies to the people around her as if they were loaves and fishes. Ginny felt a twinge of embarrassment, which deepened when the woman rose from her seat and came up to Ginny's seat. She put her hand on Ginny's shoulder to steady herself as she swung the open bag toward the young woman, who happily took several pieces of candy.

"Just one," the woman encouraged Ginny when she shook her head. "They don't stop for several hours. You didn't eat anything in the terminal either, and I know you were there longer than we were."

Ginny stared determinedly at the seatback in front of her, but, oblivious, the woman moved forward, offered her candies to the people in the next row, and then turned, leaning on their seat, to face Ginny.

"Would you like to come back and sit with me for awhile?" she asked in English. "Sometimes I enjoy being able to talk in English again—and I'd like to tell you a little about my orphanage. You might find it interesting. Honestly, I think everyone should find it interesting, but you know how that goes."

Ginny was preparing to say no, but found herself nodding and rising to her feet. "Of course," she said. "Would your little girl like to sit here?"

"She'd probably prefer to sit on one or our laps. She's a little clinger. In a few days, it should pass. I never try to fight it when they're like that. I just cling back and hope for the best."

When the woman slipped back into her seat, the little girl immediately curled up in her lap, wrapping her small arms tightly around the woman's neck as if the girl were a small monkey. The little girl had needed only one look at Ginny to know that Ginny didn't have a maternal bone in her body. Just watching the child's arms closing around the woman's neck made Ginny want to touch her own throat. But she resisted, just as she had resisted doing so in all the days since she had left the rectory and packed away her collars without acknowledging, even to herself, exactly what she was doing.

"Well," the woman said brightly as she rubbed her hand methodically over the little girl's straight black hair, "what would you like to know about me?"

By the time Ginny finally descended from the bus at eleven the next morning, dusty and slightly nauseous from the eight hours bucking over gutted, unpaved roads, she had learned how Florence Jones had come from Iowa with her husband Horace to direct an orphanage located in a small settlement in the jungle, how Florence had carried on after Horace's death by heart attack, how the children she collected on her regular trips to the capital flourished under her care and the clear strictures of Christian life. "Once they accept Jesus as their personal savior, it all follows quite quickly," she said with a sigh of pleasure. Ginny had learned as well how Silvia, the young woman returning to her family, had bought hair ornaments for her five sisters, a radio for her three brothers to share, a dress for her mother and rum for her papa. How she would be returning two nights later so that she would lose no wages, since the family needed them. Two of her younger sisters now had babies, she said a little sadly. Her time, she assured Ginny, would come.

And she'd learned that her bladder had, when deprived completely of liquids, substantial endurance—but not enough to protect her from the Dantean vision of the bathroom she'd entered at three in the morning, the memory of which, with its unflushed shit in the bowl and soiled paper and bloody tampax all over the floor, still made her want to gag.

Once off the bus and out of reach of its exhaust, she took a deep breath, slung her knapsack over her shoulder, and headed off across the causeway to the small town in the center of the lake. The red tiled roofs rose in jaunty tiers up the hillside. She thought she'd take a room in a hotel at the very top, but the thought of being alone in a hotel room both allured and terrified her. If I stop moving, she thought—and then the thought was there, movement or not, turning darkly as a dead star in the blankness that now was her mind. *Never. Never again. Gone.*

It wasn't until late the next afternoon at the pyramids when, enraged by the flash of her camera, the turkey lunged at her and slapped her with its unbelievably powerful wings that Ginny gave in and screamed, once, from the only true place left inside her, where there were no words, only pain without beginning or end. She returned, mortified, on the half-filled tourist van, the sound of her own voice and the laughter that followed echoing constantly. When she got to the hotel, she pulled out her address book and called Simon.

"Come," Simon said quietly when she told him where she was. "At once. Whether or not you know it, woman, you need a friend. And you have one. So come." He hung up before she had a chance to protest. So she didn't, rather did what he said.

Arrived, a day later, dirty, disheveled, numb. He opened his arms without hesitation and pulled her in. "Well," is all he said. "Well, well, well." Then he released her and showed her to her room and gave her a towel and a new bar of soap.

"When you're feeling a little more presentable," he said, "you'll find me out in the garden."

When she joined him, hair washed three times, wearing one of the clean t-shirts that he'd left on her bed, they sat sipping tea silently for two hours, watching the hummingbirds darting insatiably into the hibiscus and bougainvillea.

"Well," he said at last. "Don't you want to hear how I'm doing?"

Later, what Ginny would find most terrifying, out of everything that happened to her, was the sweetness that flooded, unbidden, through her limbs as they sat there, dappled by the afternoon sun, laughing. That she was still open to life, that there was something left, still, she could lose.

She never did tell Simon about the turkey, although he would have grasped instantly what it meant to her. That is probably why she didn't. She didn't tell him what had happened in Boston either, but he'd already heard about it all. Probably from David. He looked at her curiously, but didn't ask. What held him back was something deeper than tact, but it wasn't what would have set Ginny in motion again—pity. Now, when it was too late, she had impeccable instincts for what would destroy her.

"I'm glad you came," he said the next morning as he settled into his chair at the table set up in the middle of the small but lavish walled garden that was the pièce de résistance of his apartment. "I want you to stay as long as you like. Here with me if you're comfortable—or we can find you your own place if it starts to feel a little too close. I know you have a lot of sorting through to do, and much of that is best done alone. But this town is a good place to do it. And it's good to have a friend in calling distance. You know what I mean, close enough that all you have to do is whisper, 'Yo!'"

Ginny poured herself a second cup of coffee, then lifted her eyes to hold his. "I don't know where to begin," she said. "I've lost everything."

"Well," Simon said with a shrug, "welcome to the after life. I find it quite satisfying myself, although I never imagined I would. I'll take you on my little rounds today, just to give you a sense of my life here and then leave you to your own devices."

So Ginny went with Simon to the main plaza in town, where he sat on a bench near the fountain and fell into conversation with whomever sat next to him. A crowd of shoeshine boys jostled each other in their eagerness to shine his black leather running shoes. They looked at Ginny's white running shoes with ill-concealed disappointment. "You'll have to get another black pair if you expect to sit here with me very often," Simon told her.

The shoeshine boys knew that Simon kept a list of their names and rotated between them with scrupulous fairness. There were one or two of them who came up to Simon and shyly showed him worn, smudged pieces of paper on which they had written their names or a sentence about their family. Simon collected these gravely and gave them a coin and another piece of paper torn from a small notebook he carried in his shirt pocket. Their small hands, stained black with polish, smudged the pieces of paper as they folded them carefully and put them into the pockets of torn pants stiff with dirt. Simon told them, in Spanish, what he wanted them to write next.

The other boys all laughed and spoke among themselves in a soft indigenous dialect, but watched the interactions closely, especially the exchange of money. "How much?" they asked the boy who they had mocked only moments before.

"Once a school teacher, always a school teacher."

Ginny closed her eyes, the pain like a stabbing blow to her head. *Where did that leave her?*

Simon looked at her, hesitated, then said, "You lost your church, Ginny, not your faith. Remember that. When you can't, I'll remember it for you."

He rose briskly to his feet. "Come along. We need to accouter you. My clothes do nothing for you, dear."

Ginny looked down at the olive green t-shirt she was wearing over her only pair of jeans. Simon took her hands and drew her to her feet, staring deeply into her eyes. "Trust me, darling. Let yourself go."

"Your girlfriend?" one of the shoeshine boys asked.

"Why not?" Simon replied, putting his arm around Ginny.

Simon took Ginny on a tour of most of the small tourist stores in town to find some new clothes. "The indigenous have the mouth-watering clothes here, but its considered tacky for tourists to wear them, although you'll be hectored constantly to buy them."

"Anything, Simon," Ginny pleaded. "Just get it over with."

"You know how long I've waited for this moment, Gin. Can't you let me savor it?"

He chatted in Spanish with the girls who tended the stores, in English with the elderly expat owners, and selected a shirt here, pants there, and, more than once, a dress and insisted Ginny go and try them on. By the time they were through, Ginny owned several large gauzy cotton shirts, loose fitting pants and two floor length dresses that were, Simon assured her, as figure flattering as the robes she used to wear. Unwearied, he took her to the *mercado*, a huge rambling warren of tiny stores and fruit and vegetable stands, where he bought her black shoes, a straw hat, underwear, another pair of jeans, and a mammoth bouquet of flowers that he insisted she carry.

After lunch in a pleasant cafe back near the central plaza, all their bags mounded ostentatiously around them, Simon led a loudly protesting Ginny into an elegant store opening off the same courtyard as the restaurant. He selected a beautiful long flowing kimono coat made of scraps of hand-woven clothes that had once belonged to the indigenous. "I know you can make something of this metaphorically," Simon said. "And it definitely does something for you. Look in the mirror, dear."

"I don't recognize myself," Ginny said, looking at her reflection, the attractive flush in her cheeks, the clean drama of the vivid jacket.

"Being a stranger to yourself has a positive side, doesn't it," Simon said with a wink before turning to the cashier and handing over his charge card.

"You'll reimburse me for the others," he said when she started to object. "But this one is for me, Ginny. It's the least you can do."

"Simon," a hearty voice called out. "Is that you?"

"A tawdry imitation," Simon said. "Can't you tell?" He embraced a large woman with white hair falling from a loose bun. She wore a jacket very similar to the one Ginny now had on.

"My dear friend, Ginny Fox," Simon said, pulling Ginny over, seemingly oblivious to the resistance she put up. "Rosemary Kempe, my masseuse—among other things."

"Didn't see you at services yesterday," Rosemary said. "Will we see you next week? I wouldn't be asking, but Ginger has decided to flit off to see those astonishingly right-winged children of hers and is leaving me to conduct the services. Me! It's too much, I told her, what with the jam project—but she won't listen."

"Do you sing or play the organ?" she asked Ginny. "Do you ever go to church?"

Ginny looked at Simon, her eyes flicking desperately.

"Of course she does," Simon said. "We'll see you next week. Hand out prayer books for you, respond to the psalms. Bring some sweet things for coffee hour. What else?"

"I can't even find the damn lessons. That Episcopal prayer book Ginger is so fond of has all these ABC years. They make no sense. At our ages, we don't want such variety. Whose going to remember from one year to the next? I think I'm going to just go Quaker and have us sit in silence."

"We can do that, can't we, Gin?"

"Oh yes," Ginny said.

"Thank God," Rosemary said. "Some of the people in our little expat church are impossibly garrulous. They use any opportunity to share. My God, I want to tell them, is a grim old fellow. He wants to lead and have us blindly follow. He thinks we should, like good children, be seen and not heard. To be honest, I'm about as fond of Him as I was of my own father—which wasn't much, I can tell you. Silence is the only effective weapon against someone like that."

"If you feel that way, why do you go?" Ginny asked.

Startled, Rosemary looked at her, then said, simply, "Ginger. She would never let me hear the end of it if I didn't. It's the path of least resistance. If I show up, she comes and helps me with my projects glowing with the heady prospect of my conversion."

Rosemary leaned out and touched Ginny's shoulder. Ginny went rigid, and her left eye began furiously blinking again. It was a tic she couldn't control. It had started after the opening of David's show last summer, every time she recalled the painting. Rosemary looked directly into her eyes. She had enormous green eyes, startlingly clear.

"I didn't mean to offend you. I'm just blowing off steam. I do wish Ginger didn't take it so seriously, but since she does, if you wear your lovely jacket, I promise I won't wear mine. It looks much better on you, by the way. Very high priestess."

"I especially like the t-shirt with it," Simon said. "High priestess in army fatigues."

"A little décolleté might be interesting," Rosemary said, appraising Ginny with the same objectivity that Simon had shown all morning. Ginny was surprised to find that she didn't mind. There was something of the impartial curiosity of children in both of them. No wonder they were friends.

"See you Sunday," Simon said. He gave Rosemary a large hug. Then he removed the kimono coat from Ginny, neatly folding it and adding it to the other burgeoning bags. He handed Ginny the flowers that they had let refresh in the pool at the restaurant while they lunched and had left discreetly dripping outside the door of the dress shop. The water from the flowers continued to run in a steady stream down her legs as they walked back towards Simon's apartment, which was halfway between the central plaza and a large church that marked the end of the street. "Churches and ruins are the major landmarks here," Simon said. "We'll pick up a map at the travel agency when we go in. Then I'm taking a siesta and leaving you to entertain yourself." His apartment was at the back of an office building that contained a travel agency and two lawyers offices.

Once they were back in the apartment, Ginny found herself drifting quickly off to sleep as well, the bags scattered unopened around the room. She woke to the sound of the turkey slapping her in its dangerous embrace. Her thighs and hips, she had noticed as she changed clothes for Simon, were still bruised. It was a dream. It wasn't. It was a dream. It wasn't. Just like everything else about her life now. It doesn't matter if I reach my hands out, she thought. It doesn't matter if I make fists. I'm still in free fall.

The sound of the turkey slapping its large wings around her, her answering scream, woke Ginny every morning for the first week. Each time, the shame she felt was scalding, running across her neck, up to her ears. In an attempt to reduce the brutality of her re-entry into consciousness, Ginny forced herself every evening as she was drifting off to sleep, and again in the morning as soon as her eyelids registered light, to walk through that day at the pyramids from her waking to her falling into exhausted sleep. She started by looking around the small hotel room with its balcony looking down on the narrow curving street that led in a steep spiral down to the lake, the large wooden wardrobe in one corner, the three beds. Then she repeated the breakfast of sanka and thin white toast she had in the cafe before making her way to the lakeshore and crossing the causeway to catch the tourist van to the pyramids.

She climbed several pyramids in her mind, hesitating on the first one, where she suddenly wondered, four steps into her descent, whether she would be able to make her way down, the steps were so high and shallow, recalled how she had locked eyes with another woman, equally frozen and had said something in Spanish and they had smiled in intimate recognition and then had both started, warily, down again.

After that, Ginny had to climb every pyramid she came to—temple five, temple six. She had checked them off her map with a flourish. On one, she climbed a hill to reach it, then jogged down the steep steps in front. On another, the highest of all, she had climbed a rickety ladder tacked insecurely into the stones and joined a large crowd of tourists on a broad ledge. One could see for miles and miles out over the jungle, only the gray tips of the pyramids visible above the trees. The howls of the monkeys rose in waves all around them. A number of young people were sitting with their legs over the edge, breezily chatting and checking out the five story fall that enticed them. Ginny crowded back against the temple wall.

Beside her two young stoned American boys were reading from their journals. Or rather one was, and the other was saying, "Wow, man, that's really profound. I'm just never going to forget that journal of yours. God is the marijuana of the masses. Christ is their cocaine. Wow, man, that's really profound." Their laughter blended with the howls of the monkeys. "I must get down," Ginny thought. But she kept running into them everywhere, the next temple, the catacombs. Their laugher was mixed with that of the other tourists from the bus when the turkey slapped her.

The turkey. She had gone back to the entrance to find something to eat and to get away from the young men and the damp heat that felt like she was moving through water. She'd gone into the small museum, enjoying the cool emptiness, too tired at that point to take anything more in. She'd sat for half an hour looking out a plate glass window at splotchy lawn, more dirt than grass.

When she came out of the museum, she saw the turkeys parading across the lawn and she remembered the day she'd unknowingly taken little Victor, who had stowed away in the back of her car without her noticing, to the beach. When she discovered him, she had added an outing to the strawberry farm where they had a small petting zoo. While she was sitting beside the barn waiting for Victor to return from his pony ride, a turkey had stalked right up beside her before she was aware of it. Startled, she just stared into its chilly, mesmerizing eyes, that incredibly naked, warty skin pouring like water from its bright blue head to its pleated red neck, the skin running over the beak. She remembered all this, including the sermon she'd preached on her experience and its reception, and the chills started up again as they did whenever she brought Saint Peter's or the faces of anyone in her parish to mind.

Rebelling against the icy stream of fear and shame, she picked up her camera and studied the bird intently inside the lens, all those layers of meaning, of chance and circumstance, shivering there. A sickly turkey in the jungle. "It's over," she said to herself, willing her hands to steady themselves. "It doesn't matter what you think about it. It doesn't matter why. It's over, Ginny Fox, and there's not a damn thing you can do about it."

It was then she snapped the picture, the turkey's face so close in the telephoto lens that it filled the entire viewing screen. Then without warning the bird opened its wings and screamed and captured Ginny inside its vicious embrace and she couldn't help herself. She screamed back. It was like God answering her at last and she didn't, she really didn't, want to know. So that scream just floated out of her, loud as those waves of monkey cries washing over the pyramids.

A group of tourists on the dirt road beside the museum looked up and began laughing, as did the two boys who had dogged her since she'd seen them on the temple ledge. The driver of the tourist van came rushing over and beat the bird back with a branch he'd picked up, while Ginny just clutched her camera to her chest, the tears now running unchecked, uncheckable, down her hot grimy cheeks.

She had stared out the window all the way back to the little island town, screening herself off from the other passengers in the van with her loosened hair, but she couldn't check the tears. She tried to breathe as quietly and steadily as possible. She tried to block out the conversation of those two boys on the seat behind her, now discussing how to replenish their dwindling drug supply. On the seat in front of her, a minuscule couple, both indigenous, were holding hands. Standing, they would only reach midway between her elbow and shoulder. Their slender, perfect proportion made them look like dolls. They may have been fifteen or sixteen. The driver had stopped and picked them up along the side of the road. They were on their honeymoon, they said. They had decided it was a good time to visit the riches of their ancestors. The boy, a little larger than the girl, kept his arm protectively around her. Occasionally they would each look at the new wedding rings on their hands and exchange shy smiles. They were taking the bus back to the capital that evening.

Through the windows, Ginny saw the large airplane with the jaw of a shark that marked the garrison of the national guard. She noticed the young couple looked pointedly in the opposite direction when the driver pointed it out.

And all this time, the tears kept washing over her face and she kept breathing as steadily as she could and the sound of her own scream, if she listened, was always ready to start up again. "Dear God," she thought, the words forming at last, "Dear God, whatever is to become of me?"

Her own eyes reflected in the dirty window of the van stared back at her, stunned, bleak, submissive.

I will not leave you comfortless, I will come to you.

Ginny blinked and the image in the window steadied, then disappeared again.

"I never—" the voice inside her cried out. "I never—"

So what? A fact—as stunning as the swipe of those wings.

And then she was in her hotel room again, washing herself obsessively, washing the tears away only to have them begin again so she couldn't trust her voice, could just mimic using the phone to the man at the desk and walk blindly where he directed, and all the time she was dialing, talking to Simon, the tears came without her consent, just as they did the whole long trip back through the jungle on the bus the next day.

Ginny repeated the sequence every night and every morning, her thighs and buttocks still stinging with the wallop, her throat raw from the scream, but her cheeks scrupulously dry, her eyes taking everything in.

"Which do you prefer?" Simon said that evening as he dropped a bundle of booklets from the travel agency in her lap. "Good works, book learning, or pure escapism? We have volunteer opportunities, Spanish lessons, or weekends at health spas."

"Anything but Sunday services at the ex-pat church."

"Out of the generosity of my heart, I'll give you a raincheck this week—but then I insist on it. Think of it as your weekly stint in a hairshirt."

On Sunday, to ensure that Simon kept his word, Ginny slipped out of the apartment when the first church bells began ringing. She left a noncommittal note: Out walking. Don't wait. She headed in the opposite direction from the church at the end of the street, walking quickly down the empty streets, through the central plaza where people still slept in small cocoons on the porticos of the municipal buildings that surrounded the square. Soon she found herself in another square, where she sat down on a bench, settling her knapsack beside her, in which she had put water, a camera, and a notebook. At the far end of the park there was a large pool with an arched walkway along it in which were set small sinks. Already women were washing clothes there. Or their children. Or their hair. In the center of the park was a tall cross, with Jesus crucified on one side, Mary, open armed, on the other. When Ginny lifted her eyes, the green volcano loomed so close she felt crowded in.

Bells from a nearby church rang out again and again. A father, mother, and three teen-age girls in mini-skirts, heading quickly toward the sound of the bells. An old woman in a pink flowered housedress headed in the same direction. Picking up her knapsack, Ginny followed them, turning right and left through the narrow cobbled streets as they did, until they disappeared through the arched doorway into a larger cobbled courtyard that surrounded an enormous white church. Stands were set up against the walls of the courtyard, and, even at this early hour, the vendors were setting out their wares. The smell of incense drifted past Ginny where she stood, hesitating, in the street. She looked down at her clothes, her jeans and the long loose black shirt Simon had selected for her. The old woman seated by a large basket of tortillas, a small brazier burning beside her, smiled and nodded.

Several women and men moved around her to enter the arched

doorway and crossed the courtyard to the open doorway to the church. An acolyte with a brazier of incense stood at the door of the church and swung it out in large arcs over the courtyard, the smoke billowing out into the cool morning air in dense white streams, then turned at the touch of the priest and preceded him down the aisle.

Ginny walked slowly across the courtyard and entered the church. It was, even at six-thirty in the morning, filled with worshipers. Many of them were indigenous. Ginny walked along the left wall of the church a few feet, then slipped back around the column into an empty pew. The couple in front of her turned around briefly and nodded. The old man behind her buried his head more deeply in his hands. The opening hymn they sang had a lilting, childlike air to it, although the only words Ginny could make out were, *mi Señor*. There were no missals or hymnals in the pews, but people seemed to know the words to the song, know their prayers. Their meaning came to her in little snippets, several seconds after the words began, her comprehension imitating the echoes that blurred the voice of the priest. *Padre Nuestro*— Lord's Prayer. The Nicene creed. The confession.

The priest entered the pulpit and looked down at the congregation. He repeated the gospel story he had just read from Mark. A man with palsy was brought on a bier by four friends to a house where Jesus was preaching. The house was so crowded, they could not bring the sick man's pallet through, so the friends climbed on the roof and lowered him through a hole they made in the roof. When Jesus saw their faith, he said to the man with palsy, "Your sins are forgiven you."

"Which is easier," he asked the disapproving scribes, "to say to someone, 'Your sins are forgiven you.' Or 'Take up your bed and walk.'"

The priest was young, vigorous, attentive to his congregation, leaning forward and making eye contact. At times Ginny could understand his Spanish effortlessly, at times it was as if the sound was turned off in the church and all she could see were his gestures. The sick man needed to get near Jesus, to touch the hem of his garment. Why was that? Because we must know God in our hearts, in our bodies, for healing to happen. But we forget this. We are so interested in our lifestyle, in our independence. We cannot say we are sick, we are debilitated. We cannot say, even to Jesus, especially to Jesus, that we feel our weakness, our illness, is a state of sin. That it is caused by us. But until we do so, how can Jesus heal us?

The man with palsy could not come to Jesus on his own, he needed to be carried there by his friends. Friends who knew his weakness. But how many of us, with our friends, bring them to God for healing? How many of us, instead, shrug and say, "That's just the way it is with him." What would happen if we, instead, brought our friend to Jesus? How can we repent if we don't claim our sin, our *debilidad humana*? How can we repent if we do not know that God will forgive us, as we so often do not forgive our friends. Jesus says to the man with palsy, *Your sins are forgiven you.* Jesus says to the man with palsy, *Take up your bed and walk.*

"God has need of you from this day forward," the priest said, stretching out his hands to the congregation. "He has a need for every one of us, *from this day forward.* The sacrament of the eucharist reminds us of this, so as we come forward to take the host, let us hear Jesus saying to us, *Take up your bed, your debilidad humana, and walk. God has need of you from this minute on.*"

The couple in front of Ginny sat impassively through the sermon, although they joined in the hymn that followed. The old man in the pew behind her, his face invisible beneath his matted hair, his faded clothes smelling of dirt and urine, still murmured into his hands. The couple in front of her turned to shake her hand and exchange the peace, while the priest traveled up and down the pews greeting people.

When the priest held up the host, the church bells rang in wild cacophony for a full two minutes, during which time people began to walk up the aisle. Ginny bent her head and stared at her hands. She forced them open, turned them, crossed, palms up, and rested them in her lap. She felt as if she was floating, sinking. She felt as if the air had thinned without warning, even with the huge clouds of incense that followed the priests departure. As she slipped out of the church during the first stanza of the closing hymn, Ginny startled at the chill air on her cheeks. Her face was running with sweat.

Returning to the park, she chose a bench in the sunlight, and sat there breathing rapidly, both chilled to the bone and gleaming. She closed her eyes for a minute, listening to the church bells start up again in solemn, singular peals, like someone with palsy trying to walk.

She pulled her notebook from her knapsack and uncapped her pen.

She didn't know anymore who she was writing to. *I am as a woman with palsy who has never heard your name.* She saw them then, David and Will and Mr. Rufus Johnson and Simon, taking up the edges of the bier. She saw herself writhing on that bier, unable to get off by herself. When Jesus leaned toward her, all those people staring at her, lying naked on the pallet, he had the face of the young priest. "Your sins," he said, "are forgiven you."

I would rather die, Ginny wrote, *than live without you.*

I would rather die, Ginny wrote, *than accept what has happened to me.*

I would rather die, Ginny wrote, *than accept the full weight of my freedom.*

She closed the notebook and slipped it into her knapsack. She closed her eyes and felt the sun drying her face, the wind riffling her hair. When she startled awake, a half hour later, she felt first a wave of fear, then a wave of shame. What was happening to her? She never slept in front of anyone, and here she had drifted off for a full half hour in a park now humming with activity.

A young girl, with short straight black hair, crouched on her haunches in the grass about three feet from Ginny's bench watching her. She had a bright blue cloth tied across her back and knotted across her narrow chest.

"You are tired," she observed in Spanish.

"You have a camera?" she asked when Ginny didn't respond. "You pay me and I will let you take my picture."

Ginny stared at her, experiencing the same thinning of the air she had felt during the young priest's sermon, the same sense of sound coming in and out of focus.

"What is your name?" she asked.

"Mikela. And you?"

"Ginny."

The girl repeated, nodding, "She-knee."

"Are you from Germany?"

"The United States."

"For a quetzal, you may take my picture," she offered again.

Ginny unzipped the pocket where she'd put her camera, zipped closed the one that she had left opened when she drifted off. Thank goodness the little girl had been casing her out. She looked about seven or eight. She was dressed in a ladino dress but looked indigenous, except that her hair was cropped closer than Simon's.

"How old are you?"

"Ten."

"And you?"

"Very old," Ginny said. "Nearly five times as old as you."

"If that is true," the girl said, looking at her gravely, "you must be a very wise woman."

Ginny pulled some money from her pocket. "Go stand over there," she suggested to the girl, pointing to the large yellow pool where the women were gathered in their bright woven clothes. The girl looked at her rather drab dress with its small brown flowers, its drooping hem. She stared over at the women already working their looms, their wares neatly arranged on the grass along the borders of the park. Then she took a small fierce breath, put her hands on her hips, lifted her chin and stared straight at the camera, unsmiling.

Ginny brought the camera to her eye. The girl's eyes were so keen it unnerved her. The flash went off to balance the intense sun in the background, but the girl continued to stare at her unblinking.

"Your turn," Ginny said, handing the girl the camera.

Mikela stared into the lens, fascinated by her own reflection. She smiled. Ginny showed her the view finder was and the button to shoot. She immediately figured out how to work the zoom. She sent Ginny to sit on the bench again, crouching back down on her heels as she had been when Ginny woke to find her there. She sent the lens out and in several times, then shook her head. She came over to the bench and took Ginny by the hand and led her to stand by the tall cross in the middle of the park, had her look directly at the camera, while Jesus and Mary looked equally fixedly out to her right and left. She took the photo, then handed Ginny back her camera, and with it, the bills that Ginny had given her. When Ginny tried to give them back, she shook her head and danced out of reach.

"You are not from Germany?" she asked again.

"No," Ginny said. "Do you have a friend from Germany?"

But the girl had turned on her heels by then and was running across the grass.

It wasn't until Ginny returned to Simon's apartment that she realized her journal and pen had been stolen from her knapsack. Nothing else. Ginny's first response was to feel a little sick, exposed. It doesn't matter, she thought. No one here speaks English. It doesn't have my name on it. *No one knows.* And then her mind slipped to the little girl in the park gravely handing her back the worn bills, one by one. She saw the shape of the notebook clearly marked against the blue cloth on the girl's back as she turned to run off.

"It's a wonder she didn't take the camera too," she said to Simon when she described what had happened.

"I wonder what she needs it for," Simon said. "I wonder why she needed you to know what she was doing. She sat there a long time waiting for you to wake and see her, didn't she? And she made sure you took her picture."

When she fell asleep that night, Ginny did not dream of the jungle and the howls of the monkeys, the slap of the turkey. Rather she saw the small girl in the park gravely counting into her hand tattered and dirty bills before setting her carefully to stand beside the tall cross. She had Ginny stand under the crucifix. She had Ginny stand under Mary. Each time she made Ginny show her open hands with their sheaf of rag-soft, filthy money. "Smile," she told Ginny. And shot the camera, leaving Ginny blinded by the flash, hearing only the girl's heavy accent as she sang, in English, *She would rather die than dance. She would rather die than dance.*

THE WATCHERS
(Mikela)

We are everywhere, in every community. The watchers. The keepers of souls. I don't know how we recognize each other, but we do. And when we do, we feel known, at home.

I wonder sometimes if there was a time before I learned I had this gift. It seems as natural as breathing. But I know some weight in me lifts every time I find another one like me. I'm not complaining. Most of the time, the weight of my gift makes me feel safe. It makes the soles of my feet come alive and I feel all of one piece, grateful for the ground and the way it pushes back and gives me strength.

Many people believe that this gift is inherited. But not in a straight way, from father to son or mother to daughter. I like the idea that someone, a grandmother or uncle or great aunt, if they were still living, could look in my eyes and we would know each other for what we are.

My people also believe there need to be eight of us watchers of souls for the community to be safe. My community has been unsafe for as long as our memories, mine and my sister's and brothers' and my mother's and my father's. It's not that we watchers don't exist, but there aren't enough of us. That is why so many of my people have died at the hands of others.

My mother, when she threw my afterbirth in the river, gave a gift to others, but made her own world worse. We believe that where we bury the placenta and umbilical cord is our destiny. The umbilical cords of girls we bury inside the walls of our houses, so they will stay at home to help their families. But my mother threw my cord in the river, something done only with sons. So they will travel far and bring back riches. That is why so many of our young men set out for the States carrying their families with them in their hearts.

That is not why my mother threw my cord in the river. She did it so I might escape. She did it to make up for what she did to my sister Natividad when she dug her cord out of the wall and threw it away in the same river. She threw my sister's cord away in disgust, just the way she wanted to throw away all the memories of the past, of where my sister came from. My mother wanted to throw away her own gift for life. And she wanted to take it back. That is why, two years later, she threw my afterbirth in the river as well. She wanted to give me what she couldn't give herself. She didn't know about my gift. She didn't know that this meant I would wander wherever my sister went, keeping her soul, even when it left her body, safely in sight.

My mother dug Natividad's umbilical cord out of the wall with a sharp stick one morning when my father was out in the fields. My sister had only been alive six days. My mother could feel it all happening again, the soldiers, so many of them. She wanted to dig the memory out of her body, out of her house, the way they dug the babies out of the living mothers and threw them in the trees. She wanted release, but with every thrust of the stick into the crumbling clay, it was as if she were killing herself with her own hand. She felt it was the will of God that was driving her hand against the wall of her house. It felt like she was fighting for her life. And it felt like she was dying.

Every time the stick went in, her stomach tightened, the bleeding stopped. I believe at that moment my mother still loved my father but hated his hope, the way he thought if he just acted in the old ways, the old faith would come back. He knew where my sister came from. He knew that half of Natividad came from our mother. He thought sealing her cord away in the house would make my mother whole again. But my mother wouldn't have it.

So much depends on how we do a thing. I see my mother, my sister feeding at her breast, throwing that muddy knot into the river. Throwing it with all her strength, weeping and screaming without sound. Hating my sister's busy mouth. Hating the nipple she couldn't take out of it. And I can see my mother two years later, my sister on her back, me at her breast, doing the same thing—but with a completely different purpose. She was asking for forgiveness. She was giving me what she most wanted—freedom.

I am grateful that my mother made my choices for me. So when the time came to leave, I did it without worrying. I know I will never go back again. But I know, as well, that I take my gift with me. And I am free to use it here, now.

But I am not very old or wise. That is why I look for the others. I've found several so far. Mario, the shoe shine boy in the park, he is one of them. And there is a foreigner with gold hair who sits in the park some days, he is one of them. And the man *who pulls the cart from the park every evening filled with everything my people have made and cannot sell, he's one of them too. There are more here, I know because this town has many communities, and we watchers are in all of them. I wonder if the wanderers among us watchers wander between communities as well.*

Right now, my community is one person, my sister, Natividad, although I know soon there will be three of us. That is why I am looking for the other watchers. Natividad takes so much seeking, I know I will need help when the baby comes.

Chapter 3
STEALING

    Mikela liked waking in the dark to the shuffling and murmuring of the older girls in the next room. She could recognize who they were by the tones of their voices. Antonia always woke first and would whisper her friend Analisa awake gently, like a mother. Together they would go off to the showers, Analisa swearing at the smell several steps before she reached the bathrooms. But it was better than home, Mikela thought. Better than the capital.

    Her sister Natividad hadn't agreed with her, and only three months after the policeman had brought them here, Natividad had climbed up on Mikela's shoulders and slipped through the narrow opening in the window in the kitchen while the other girls were sleeping. Mikela had heard Natividad cry out as she landed on the ground, but Mikela didn't dare say anything. When Mikela met Natividad the next day on the way home from school as they had planned, she noticed her sister was limping badly. It was nothing, Natividad told her, compared to the yelling.

    Mikela wished Natividad had had more patience. The new Mamí, once she had been there for several weeks, stopped screaming so loudly or so often. She never yelled at the younger girls like Mikela. It was the older girls, who were twelve or thirteen and eager to be women she was so angry at. But when she yelled at Natividad, she hadn't known what she was doing or what would happen. Natividad was very quiet but very stubborn. Mikela could tell, as soon as Mamí Dolores started shouting, that Natividad went away somewhere inside herself, that the voice sounded too much like their mother for Natividad to stay in her body. But she hadn't expected Natividad to leave the girls' home, and Natividad hadn't expected Mikela to stay. Still, Natividad hadn't gone that far away and the mamís didn't know that she and Mikela met every day, or that Mikela knew she could go and join Natividad whenever she wanted to. Instead of the kitchen window Natividad had used to slip away, Mikela had found one in the bathroom that she could reach by standing on the faucets in the shower stall and pulling herself up over the edge of the window. She could get out without anyone else's help. Mikela was lucky that she was very strong—and also very quiet. She was much stronger than the other girls because she and Natividad came from the country. The girls from the city always complained about their work, but it was very little compared to the way things were for Mikela before she and Natividad ran away.

Natividad didn't like the way Mamí Dolores yelled at her and, even though Natividad was very smart, she didn't like the girls in her school, who made fun of the clothes she wore and the way she talked. Her voice still had the accent of their original language. Girls from the home stole, they said. That is why they were sent away from their families. And some of them sold themselves on the streets. It didn't matter that Mamí Concepción would tell them they were just jealous. "Many of you don't have people who welcome you home every day. Many of you don't know for sure there will be food on the table every evening. The girls in this home have a real home where they are never hungry and where they are always welcome." Mikela and her friend Juana had liked Mamí Concepción's fierce defense, but what the girls at the school said was true. The girls in the home stole—from each other and from their classmates. And if they liked the home it was because it *wasn't* home.

Some of the girls here, especially the ones who came from the capital, thought they were slaves here. They minded cleaning the bathrooms, doing the laundry, or making the meals in the large kitchen at the back of the home. But Mikela liked learning all these things—how to change the smell in the bathroom so it smelled like hope instead of fear, how to make the *atole* for breakfast or cake for dessert on their special days. Here they never cut firewood and carried it home on their heads or planted and picked corn or beans or walked miles before daylight to the mill to grind their corn for flour. Here the floors were stone and shone when she poured water over them.

Here the air wasn't filled with smoke, even in the kitchen, and she could see into the corners of every room. Here there were no ropes in the rafters and, except for Mamí Dolores, all the other mothers rarely raised their voices and, even more rarely, their hands. For it wasn't only her voice Mamí Dolores had raised against Natividad.

Mikela rolled on her side and nudged her friend Carmen who slept in the next bed. It was their week to help in the kitchen and the girls who went to school in the morning would be ready for their breakfast. They were impatient and yelled at Mikela and Carmen if they didn't bring the food quickly enough. Mikela thought they were funny and always laughed when they said things to her. But Carmen would start crying before long, so then Mikela would have to do all the carrying herself. She didn't like that. So, if she could have some of the food on the table before they came in, then they were less impatient, and Carmen wouldn't sit, weeping like a little baby, on Mamí Concepción's lap in the kitchen, while Mikela rushed back and forth by herself.

While Mikela waited for Carmen to dress, she pulled her knapsack from under her bed to make sure all her homework was ready. Natividad had helped her with it yesterday, but then Mikela had to copy it all over in her own writing or the teachers might know. Mikela could do her homework herself, but it made Natividad feel good to help her, and Mikela was worried about Natividad.

Natividad's body was very fat now, but her face and arms were very thin. Mikela stole food from the kitchens to take to her, but she knew Natividad shared it with her boyfriend, Pablo. Mikela thought Pablo probably asked nicely, but one time she saw a mark on her sister's arm. Since then, Mikela had been very careful to bring enough for two so there wouldn't be any more marks. Mikela didn't know, when the baby came, how she was going to be able to steal enough for all three of them.

Natividad didn't worry about food, though. What she wanted from Mikela was paper and pens—and these were getting even more difficult for Mikela to steal from the other girls' knapsacks at school. The stores kept their notebooks on shelves in the back of the store. Or inside a glass case where they could be seen but not touched. Either way, Mikela couldn't think of how she might take them without being seen. At school, she tried to steal from the older girls, especially the ones with the wooden cases because that meant they were in art or mechanical drawing classes and their paper was bigger and better for drawing. Even if they had drawn on one side, Natividad could use the other.

Natividad needed paper and pens more than bread, more than chicken, more than chocolate. Without them, she didn't know hunger at all because without her drawing Natividad could not come back into her body where she could feel thirst and hunger and hope. Where she could love her little sister. Mikela was going to make sure her own soul stayed deep inside her body, where it could eat and drink and grow big and strong. If paper and pens were the way to invite Natividad's soul back, Mikela was never going to stop finding ways to steal them. She wanted her sister's soul to grow big and strong too.

Yesterday, Mamí Concepción had suggested another way that Mikela might help Natividad, although she didn't know that was what she was doing. She thought she was helping Mikela, or really, she was helping her cousin Señora Wilma.

Mamí Concepción was the only mamí who was sad when Natividad escaped from the home. Mamí Dolores said very bad things about Natividad— that she was only interested in earning money by going with the men so she could breathe the glue. Really, Mamí Dolores was afraid that someone would learn that she had hit Natividad and then she might lose her job.

When Mamí Dolores talked this way, Mamí Maria Concepción would look at Mamí Dolores and shake her head. "Every girl here is our daughter," she would say. "Why are you talking about our children in this way, Dolores? You think if you paint them black you will look white? Why would a mother want to be whiter than her children?"

Mamí Concepción was not one of Mikela's people, but her skin was darker than Mikela's. Mamí Dolores' skin was very pale, like the Virgin's. She came from the capital, like Señora Evelina, the new director of the home. Mamí Dolores put on airs, that is what Mamí Concepción and Mamí Lina whispered to each other. Mamí Dolores only worked during the days, and she carried a leather satchel with her when she came. "Like a lawyer," Mamí Lina laughed.

All the mamís had children of their own who they went home to at night. Mamí Concepción and Mamí Lina spent the night at the home on alternate nights. Mikela liked knowing that there were nights when their children told themselves stories and made their own supper.

"You are a very hard worker," Mamí Concepción had told her several days ago. "Your people work very hard. It is in your blood, I think."

Mamí Concepción was very jolly with the girls and fierce when someone said something bad about them on the streets or in their schools, but she did not work very hard. She sat in a chair in the kitchen or out in the courtyard, praising the girls for the work they did, if, like Mikela, they were hard workers, or comforting them if, like Carmen, they started to cry. She would dance with the older girls, never asking them where they found their tapes—or even the player which belonged to three of the oldest girls.

Mikela didn't mind Mamí Concepción's laziness because her mind was busy thinking about the girls. She was the only Mamí who had asked Mikela where she came from, or had tried to talk to Natividad more than once or twice. Mamí Concepción would sit beside Natividad when she was drawing and study the pictures Natividad had made. Sometimes she would ask Natividad a question, but she wasn't bothered if Natividad didn't answer her. At first, Mikela answered for Natividad so Mamí Concepción would not stop looking. But Mamí Concepción just winked at her and said, "Go do your schoolwork now so you will have time to do some dancing. We are having a nice conversation, your sister and I."

Natividad and Mikela slept in different rooms. Mikela slept with the little girls, while Natividad slept with the older girls. Not the ones as old as Antonia and Analisa, who were almost finished with school, but the room with Paula and Soledad. They put the girls who had lived on the streets together in one room because they did not want the other girls to know what they had done there. But it made it impossible for Natividad to forget. That might have been why Natividad left.

The older girls, especially the ones in that room, sometimes did things with each other as well as with the men. Mamí Concepción stopped them when they tried to do things with the girls in Mikela's room. They had tried with Juana and Carmen, who had told Mamí Concepción. They had not troubled Mikela because she told them she had a knife under her pillow and she would use it. But the older girls, when Mamí Concepción asked them, said that Juana and Carmen were lying. Mamí Concepción then asked Natividad, but she said nothing. She had asked Mikela too, and Mikela told everything except about her lie about the knife.

So Mamí Concepción came in the next night and hid under the bed and when Paula and Soledad came again, she grabbed each of them by their ankles and pulled herself out from under the bed. It was funny because Mamí

Concepción was quite fat and got stuck a little as she pulled herself out. Her face was very dark with blood when she finally stood up.

"You are not to come into this room at night again," she said to them. But she didn't say it in an angry way, the way she talked back to the girls from the schools when they said bad things about the girls in the home.

Later Mikela heard her talking with Soledad and Paula. "It feels good to you," she said. "But it does not feel good to them. It doesn't matter if someone else did the same to you when you were their age and you enjoyed it. They have complained. If they do not want you to do it, it is a bad thing you are doing."

"And you, Mamí, can we play with you?" they asked. They were laughing, but there was something dangerous in their voices.

Mamí Concepción did not seem to notice, just laughed her loud warm laugh. "I have enough trouble with men," she said. "Why would I go doubling my misery?"

It was that night Natividad told Mikela to meet her in the kitchen and climbed on her shoulders and slipped away.

Mamí Concepción was the one who discovered Natividad had left. Natividad went to school in the mornings, and when she wasn't ready, Mamí Concepción went to look for her and saw that her bed was empty. She went to find Mikela, who was washing dishes in the kitchen.

"I know you know nothing about this," she said to Mikela. She sat on a chair by the sink and pulled Mikela toward her with both hands. Mamí Concepción's hands were very large and soft but stronger than Mikela expected. "Let me explain to you what will happen. I will need to tell Directora Evelina when she comes this morning. She will question you and also me and Mamí Dolores and all the girls who shared a room with your sister. She will want to know if Natividad spoke to anyone before leaving."

"Natividad only speaks at school when the teacher makes her."

"We know this. But Natividad came here, like you, because the police made her. She was too young to be doing the things she was doing. They sent her here instead of sending her to jail. They did it to protect her, but if she doesn't want this protection, they may want to punish her. We do not want that, do we?"

Mikela was afraid then, in a different way from how she and Natividad had been afraid in the capital. She knew Mamí Concepción was trying to tell her something under the words, but she wasn't sure she understood what it was. She knew it was important.

"Perhaps Natividad decided to go and visit a cousin in the country until the baby comes?" Mamí Concepción asked. "You do not know for sure, do you, that she hasn't."

Mikela shook her head, not sure what words were safe. She didn't know how Mamí Concepción knew about the baby growing inside Natividad. She had not known until she heard Paula and Soledad talking to Natividad one day a few weeks earlier when she went to her sister's room to ask her to help her with her homework.

"The only way your sister can come back to the home is without the baby. That may be why she decided to go stay with her cousin in the country. Perhaps the cousin in the country doesn't have any children and very much wants one."

Mamí Concepción had dark red lips and very quick eyes that kept watch over everything around her. As she talked to Mikela, she was also waving at Juana, who was still working in the kitchen. She made a joke with Paula and Soledad as they left for school.

"Your sister is a very smart girl, like you," she said. "If she would like, I can talk to the Mother Superior and see if, when she comes back from visiting her cousin, she can go to school with you there."

Soon after they came to the home, Mamí Concepción had taken Natividad to a private school and the Mother Superior had given Natividad tests. When she did well on them, Mamí Concepción brought Mikela for tests as well. The Mother Superior said they had only one scholarship and she was going to give it to Mikela because Natividad wouldn't talk. She thought there was something wrong with Natividad's thoughts, even though she was very smart. Mikela told them her sister's heart was heavy, that was all. She asked the Mother Superior to give the scholarship to Natividad. Mikela was younger, she explained. She could wait.

The Mother Superior shook her head firmly, although she had a wrinkle in her forehead as if she wasn't sure she was doing the right thing. Mikela started to talk to her again, but Natividad leaned over and whispered to her to take the scholarship. Mamí Concepción said the same thing. But if Natividad had taken it, would things have been different for her?

Natividad did not tell Mikela why she was leaving, but Mikela knew it was not just because of Mamí Dolores. It was also the girls in her room, especially Soledad and Paula. They watched Natividad undress at night and began to tease her about her belly. "You bring back some of what you're stealing," they told her. "We're not going to see you fatten up like a little pig and have us go hungry. Here," they said, imitating the voice of Directora Evelina, "we share and share alike."

"So," Mamí Concepción said, combing Mikela's hair with her fingers then flattening it with her palms, "we have understood each other, yes? We will tell the police not to worry about Natividad. We do not need to say very much because the police do not have very much patience. They do not like to spend their time looking for girls who have gone to visit their cousins, they would rather look for criminals."

"I know," Mikela said, and that was the end of that.

Mamí Concepción noticed when food was missing in the kitchen but she only gave Mikela a wink. She would tell Mikela to put the food away, then distract the other girls working in the kitchen with funny stories, while Mikela slipped a piece of cake or bread or meat under her skirt. Sometimes Mamí Concepción would leave pens and paper out for her, saying, "Mikela, you look like a creative girl. Would you like to go and write me a story?" She would never ask to see what Mikela had written, would just rub her head and say, "You are a special little thing. A world apart."

Today, after school, Mamí Concepción was going to take Mikela to visit her cousin Señora Wilma, who worked for a rich foreign woman. The rich woman had many projects she made with the poor women in the town, women who were indigenous, like Mikela. Indigenous was a word Mikela had learned at school. It meant the original people of a place. But Mikela wasn't from here, so she thought maybe she wasn't indigenous anymore. Few of her people were because of all the moving they did during the war. Even if she and Natividad went back to their old town, Mikela didn't know if they would be indigenous again. Could you be indigenous if you went away, even if it wasn't your idea to leave?

The rich woman made a lot of work for the poor women so they could earn some money. She also made a lot of work for Señora Wilma, who had to clean up after the poor women. Señora Wilma needed a little girl who was a hard worker to help her clean up after the rich woman.

"You are young," Mamí Concepción said, "but very smart and

diligent. The rich woman, Señora Rosemary, may pay you if you work hard. She will certainly pay you in food, and you could use a little fat on your bones. She may also let you spend the night there sometimes." Because you couldn't leave the home without permission, many girls thought it was a prison. It was a big privilege to have somewhere to go. Mikela understood this.

The rich woman's house was near Mikela's school, which was on the far side of the town from the home. Mikela could go there early in the morning before school or right after school and still be back home by supper. "No one needs to know," Mamí Concepción said.

Mikela understood that she was not to tell the other girls, especially Carmen who always complained of a stabbing hunger no matter how much she ate. Carmen wasn't a hard worker.

"It is my day off," Mamí Concepción said. "I will meet you there and introduce you."

When Mikela knocked on the big wooden gate in the afternoon, she could see the other girls from her school look at her curiously as they walked by. Mikela was the only girl from the home who went to this school. Most of the girls came from very rich families. Mikela wore the same uniform as the other girls, and she had cut her hair short, which the indigenous women never did, but the girls at school all knew she was different. Mikela always ran away from the school as fast as she could when the classes were over. She liked to run, but she was also in a hurry to see Natividad, who stayed with Pablo in a house near the *mercado*. But today, Mikela frowned at the other girls and pushed the bell again as Mamí Concepción had told her to do.

A woman said something in a language that Mikela did not know as she pulled open the little grated window high up on the door to see who was there. At first she didn't see Mikela. Mikela jumped up as high as she could waving her hands, and the woman laughed.

"Little one, what do you want?" she asked. "I'm not paying for the processions yet." She thought Mikela had come to beg for the church. She spoke in a very slow Spanish with time all mixed up.

"Señora Wilma," Mikela said. "Mamí Concepción sent me."

"Mamí Concepción?" the old woman repeated. Another woman said something to her and the old woman laughed again. "Oh, Concepción. Of course, come in."

When the door opened, two women stood there in a green courtyard. To the left, Mikela could see a small fountain—and directly behind them she could see an even larger courtyard through the open front door. She was, she decided, in a palace.

The old woman was very high with pale skin and even paler hair, the color of spiderwebs in the sun. "I am Señora Rosemary," she said to Mikela, leaning over and shaking her hand. "Any friend of Concepción's is a friend of mine. But you must tell her how good my Spanish is now. You may lie." She threw back her head and laughed again. She had a big loud laugh that made Mikela feel like she was inside a river, jostled by the water. Mikela liked the feeling.

"You can tell her yourself," said the other woman, who Mikela thought was Señora Wilma. "She is going to come in a little while to take the girl back."

"She looks so small," the old woman said. "Do you think she can really be a help to you?"

"I am strong," Mikela said. "That is why Mamí Concepción sent me. I am a very hard worker. See." She bent her arm and made a fist and tapped the big muscle in her upper arm.

"I like her spirit," the old woman said. "But she's in a school uniform. Don't you think she might find it difficult to do her school work too?"

Señora Wilma smiled at the old woman. "Of course not, Señora. You will help her. It will be another project for you. One that is cleaner than the jam."

"Come with me," she said to Mikela and walked quickly through the large door and out towards the even larger courtyard, then turned right and walked to the far side of the house and entered the kitchen. Señora Wilma was not as big as the rich foreign woman, but she had a very straight back and a force to her that made her seem almost as big. Mikela thought the two women liked each other but were both very stubborn.

"She does it just to torment me," Señora Wilma said, pausing at the door to the kitchen and looking around at all the dirty pots on the stove. There was a smell of burnt sugar. On the counters were many small jars with a deep red jam in them.

"Soon she will have me sitting down in the plaza with a big basket selling these," Señora Wilma said. "She'll make me wear native clothes and pretend I'm one of her women. She has no shame, Señora Rosemary, when she has a project."

Señora Wilma pulled a cloth from under the sink and handed it to

Mikela. "I will give you an hour. I want you to make this kitchen as clean as you possibly can. I will not tell you what to do. I want to see how good your eye is."

Mikela asked where the soap was and where the sinks for cleaning were and where the broom and mop were. After so many months at the home, she knew all the tasks she was supposed to do. After Señora Wilma showed her where these things were, she took the cloth Señora Wilma had given her and began to wipe the sugar off the counters. The counters were made of little squares of the same special stone they used in bathrooms, but these squares were a deep blue that made Mikela happy to touch. When Mikela didn't look up at Señora Wilma, but went to the *pila* for a pail of water, Señora Wilma disappeared. Mikela thought she was smiling.

When she came back to the empty kitchen, Mikela put her pail down and looked around her. She gave a little spin for pleasure. She liked this house. There was color everywhere. The blue counters, the red floor, and the yellow walls fed her eyes. There were racks for brightly colored dishes on the wall beside the eating table. There was a shelf covered with pitchers and cups with big red flowers painted on them.

There was a big yellow refrigerator humming in the corner. Mikela looked both ways and went to open it, but then stopped herself. She would wash the pots and pans first. Then she would wash the floor, and then just slide the refrigerator door open as she passed it. She had not changed out of her school uniform so that she could hide things under her skirt. Except when she was stealing, Mikela liked to wear the blue jeans the evangelicals brought to the home. They made her feel strong, like a boy.

She wouldn't, she decided, take any of the jam because she thought that Señora Wilma had probably counted up all the jars so she could scold the old Señora. Mikela felt a little sorry for the old Señora because Señora Wilma was probably very strict.

Mikela mopped the floor carefully and then dried it off with a cloth because this gave her a chance to open all the cupboards. There was so much food here Mikela thought even Carmen would stop complaining of hunger if she could just see it. There were bags of dried beans and dried chilis and glass jars of olives. There were bags of rice and flour and spaghetti. There were brown paper packages of chocolate. There were bags of sugar and salt. In the refrigerator, when Mikela peeked in, she found meat and cheese and lettuce and beets and broccoli and *chamote* and orange juice and cantaloupe and papaya and mangoes. There was milk. A little cloth napkin filled with tortillas.

Mikela felt dizzy. She didn't know what, or how much, she should hide under her skirt the first day.

"Nothing," Mamí Concepción said loudly from the doorway to the kitchen. "You will have nothing to concern yourself about, Wilma. I've watched her work at the home for several months and she is completely reliable. She actually seems to enjoy her tasks."

"Unbelievable," Señora Wilma said with a little cough. "You're sure you don't want to take her to your own house to help you a little?" Mikela understood she was teasing Mamí Concepción.

"She's a smart little thing as well," Mamí Concepción said. "Maybe Señora Rosemary will take an interest in her. You know there are no indigenous in the home except her. I thought it might be good to get her out from time to time. She had a sister there, but she ran away. I think there was a boyfriend hiding in the woods. She was pregnant. I think she probably knew we would have taken the baby from her.

"But Mikela is completely different. Seems to like the home just fine. Doesn't have any interest in boys—except in how to look like one. She won't let that hair of hers grow out—and you have no idea what persuasion it took to get her to sew herself a dress. She doesn't mind the uniform for school though. Her sister refused to change her *traje*, she wanted people to know where she came from. But when the Mother Superior offered to let Mikela wear a *corte* as part of her uniform, she just looked at her with this look that was far too old for a child and said, 'We are orphans, my sister and I. We have no people but each other.' But I'm sure she misses her customs and language."

Mikela stood up and both Mamí Concepción and Señora Wilma looked a little startled.

"You are not right," she told Mamí Concepción. "I do not miss my customs or my language. How can you miss something that is so deep inside you it will never go away?"

"Good question," Señora Rosemary said, coming into the kitchen through another door. Her arms were filled with flowers.

"Do you want to help me arrange these?" she asked Mikela.

"I was going to clean the refrigerator," Mikela said. Natividad couldn't eat hibiscus or lilies. Neither could she.

"Concepción," the old woman said as she put her flowers down and took the mamí's hands in both of hers and gave her a kiss on the cheek. "You've given up your language lessons completely?"

"Oh no," Mamí Concepción said. "I work at the home too because the salary is more regular. Smaller, but more regular. And it's night work, so it doesn't keep me from teaching—if there were any students."

For some reason Mikela had never imagined that Mamí Concepción did anything but come to the home and go back to her own house. She didn't know she worked so much with foreigners.

Mikela knew some foreigners were very dangerous, but she didn't feel the old woman was. But she wasn't sure she liked knowing that Mamí Concepción had a whole life she had no idea of, especially since Mamí Concepción was the only person who seemed to have any idea that Mikela might have a secret life too. If there are too many secret lives, the world can get very confusing.

"We will let you choose some food from the refrigerator to take with you once you have cleaned it," Señora Wilma said to Mikela. She ran her finger over the square blue stones on the counter and put her finger to her tongue. Mikela knew she was testing to see if it tasted sweet, but she could see from her face that it didn't.

"Food?" the old woman said. "Surely we're paying her in cash as well, Wilma?"

Mikela could see from the way Señora Wilma's back stiffened that she was going to get stubborn, so she said to Señora Rosemary, "Thank you so much. In the future, I would like to be paid in money as well as food. But today I was just showing Señora Wilma what I was able to do. It was an entrance exam, like at the school. The food is a gift, which I accept with much gratitude."

Señora Rosemary had enormous green eyes behind her thick glasses. In the river back home, there were stones of exactly the same color, although the stones whitened when they dried. Mikela had two hidden under her mattress. The old Señora put her hand on Mikela's shoulder. "Take whatever you like, dear. You've earned it."

But Señora Wilma chose the food for Mikela to take with her as Mikela set the food from the refrigerator on the counter. She was glad that Mamí Lina had shown her how to clean the refrigerator at the home so she didn't appear stupid. This was only the second refrigerator Mikela had seen.

This one was much whiter and cleaner than the one at the home.

As she chose the foods for Mikela, Señora Wilma and Mamí Concepción talked about how Mamí Concepción might get more students.

"Ask Señora Rosemary straight out to recommend people to you," she told Mamí Concepción. "She doesn't mind—and she is not subtle. So hints will not serve you. Stubborn, yes. Subtle, no."

"Ah, Wilma, what a waste of your talents then." Mamí Concepción laughed. She had known Señora Wilma since they were schoolgirls, she had told Mikela.

"She's a generous woman," Señora Wilma said, sounding a little angry with Mamí Concepción.

"I'm done," Mikela said. "Look how it shines with the light on."

Señora Wilma helped her return the food to the refrigerator. She handed Mikela a blue plastic bag, which was carefully tied at the top so Mikela couldn't peek. Mikela felt disappointed but happy as well. There would be many more days for her to pick and choose for herself once Señora Wilma became more comfortable with her and didn't watch her so closely.

Señora Wilma led them out of the kitchen. As they stood in the courtyard, Señora Rosemary came out of a small room on the far side of the patio. "So you're off, are you? Let me give you a little tour so you'll know what you're coming back to." She put her hand on Mikela's shoulder as she took her to each room in the house. There was a room where the poor women had their meetings. A room with a high table covered with brown leather with a white cloth lying over it. The old woman said she healed people with her hands, but she wasn't a *comadrina*. There was another room, a little house actually, set off away from the rest of the rooms. This was where Señora Rosemary's husband used to paint when he was alive.

"Maybe you will help me straighten it out one of these days," she said. Mikela felt a little river of joy run through her. When she went in, she would memorize everything she saw to tell Natividad, and then she would sneak what Natividad wanted out very carefully so no one would notice for a long time.

Mikela really didn't know very much about stealing. She knew it was a sin and also a little unjust to take what belonged to another. It was also necessary, all the girls in the home told you that. "Everyone else has so much," they would complain. "What about us? Who gives us anything?"

They had beds, school books, food every day. If it wasn't for

Natividad, Mikela wouldn't need anything. Soon, if she earned money like Señora Rosemary promised, she could buy Natividad her notebooks and paper at a store. She wasn't sure she wanted to have a secret life with everyone, which is what happened if you were a thief.

At the gate, Señora Rosemary waited with her for Mamí Concepción. "I think you're going to be a good addition here, my dear," she said. She stroked Mikela's back like she was a little girl. Mikela liked it but it made her feel scared too. At the home, she never let anyone, even Mamí Concepción, lay a hand on her.

Mamí Concepción didn't walk back with her to the home because it was her night off and it was too long a walk. "Just tell them you were at my house doing some errands for me," she said.

Mikela nodded and began to run. She had put the blue plastic bag inside her school knapsack and now the knapsack banged loudly against her back with every step. She hoped Señora Wilma had not given her anything that would break. She was careful to run two blocks in the direction of the home before changing direction and heading toward the mercado.

She didn't have very much time, so she banged very loudly on the door of the house where Natividad and Pablo slept at night, but no one answered. She went to the mercado and began to ask if anyone had seen them, but people just shrugged. A girl in dirty *traje*. A boy in a striped t-shirt and blue jeans. It could be anyone, they said. Mikela felt ready to cry. Natividad was not anyone. Natividad was beautiful, she wanted to tell them. When she smiled it was as if the sun had broken through the clouds. Her voice was as soft as the wind in the leaves of a mango tree.

But every day, it seemed harder to find Natividad. Many days, Natividad just wanted to sleep and would do so wherever she and Pablo went. Mikela thought that Natividad slept so much to forget her hunger, but sometimes she saw Pablo's nose running and this cloudy look in Natividad's eyes and wondered if they were breathing the glue again. Mikela knew that breathing glue was bad for her sister and bad for the baby. She didn't know if Natividad cared about the baby. Sometimes she thought Natividad didn't even know it was coming, even though Pablo would put his head on her stomach and listen to it moving, or Mikela would do the same. Maybe you only really believed it was true if you could hear it with your own ears. Natividad couldn't do that.

Mikela knocked again at the door of the house where Natividad and

Pablo usually slept. Finally an old man came out. He wore a long sleeved undershirt and old green pants. He had long hair that was very gray. He was the man who pulled the big wooden cart from the park each night with all the wares Mikela's people made to sell to the foreigners. He was very strong, like a horse.

"We sent them away," he told Mikela when she asked about her sister and Pablo. Mikela did not ask why. She knew.

"Do you have any idea where I might find them?"

The old man shrugged and started to close the door. He saw the tears in Mikela's eyes and politely looked away.

"Sometimes people sleep in the ruins. Your sister likes to draw. The last picture of hers I saw was of the ruin up beyond the church of San Francisco. Do you know the one?"

By then Mikela was running again, so she didn't answer. She needed to get to the home for dinner or she would be punished. But she needed to get the food to Natividad as well. She would sneak out in the evening, very late. Mamí Lina slept more soundly than Mamí Concepción, so she was sure she could get out without being noticed. But she didn't know how she would slip back in. She wanted to get back in. She didn't want to sleep on the streets again.

When she reached the home, Mikela had to ring the bell. Luckily Mamí Lina opened it. She did not punish her, just told Mikela to take her seat at the next seating in the dining room since her own group had already eaten. All dinner, Mikela kept trying to figure out how she might get back into the home once she'd left.

For her, it wasn't like Natividad. She liked the home. She like her school. She liked Señora Wilma and Señora Rosemary. She didn't want to escape, she just wanted to slip back and forth between her worlds without difficulty so she could do the work God had asked her to do. She could not live, she knew, without her sister. If Natividad needed paper and pens above everything, Mikela needed Natividad in the same way.

Mikela finally decided that she would take the food to Natividad on Saturday night because on Sunday morning many of the girls went to many different churches and it would be more likely that Mikela could slip back in unnoticed. She knew that none of the girls in her room would ever tell on her. They didn't dare. They were all a little afraid of Mikela, especially since she told that lie to Paula and Soledad about the knife. No one knew she was lying, not even her friend Juana. That was part of her secret life.

On Saturday during the day, Mikela talked Mamí Concepción into letting her leave the home for an hour to go running. They physical education teacher at her school had told them that they had no muscles, all except Mikela. She had told Mikela that she had a gift for speed and if she practiced her running regularly, she would be able to run races against girls in other schools. She was going to write Directora Evelina a letter asking her to let Mikela go running, but she was so busy she forgot.

Mamí Concepción looked at Mikela with a little smile all the time Mikela was talking, as if she didn't quite believe her but would let her go anyway. Mamí Concepción was always giving the girls permission to leave the home, sometimes just to go to the bakery if someone had sent them some money, or to have dinner with the evangelicals. All the girls liked to go to the evangelicals because they sang and also gave the girls big dinners after the services. They gave them clothes from America—tennis shoes and t-shirts and blue jeans. Mikela didn't go because she was worried that the Mother Superior might hear about it and take away her scholarship, although she wore the clothes the evangelicals gave away. Mamí Concepción was Catholic herself, but she understood that the evangelicals paid more attention to the girls, so she encouraged them to go. All except Mikela because Mamí Concepción wanted her to keep her scholarship too.

"Go on," she said. "But make sure you are back in an hour."

Mikela ran as fast as she possibly could down to the mercado. Often Natividad and Pablo stole fruit from the mercado and then sold it down at the plaza. Saturday was the busiest day at the mercado, so they often went there then because the marchantes couldn't keep such close watch. But Mikela couldn't find them. She decided to run up to the ruins the old man had seen in Natividad's drawing to see if she could find them there.

The ruins were on the very far side of the town, past the stone streets, where the dirt streets began. There were woods around the ruins, so they were easier to slip in and out of than some of the ruins in town. By the time Mikela reached them, she was breathing very hard. She called out for Natividad, but no one answered.

The ruins were used for a stage sometimes, so there were long benches leading down to them for people to sit and watch. Mikela pretended she was just looking as she walked by the benches, but she couldn't see Natividad anywhere. After she looked behind the ruin, which was only the front wall and bell tower of an old church, Mikela left a note written in the dirt under a tree near the corner where she had once seen Natividad sitting with Pablo and Tomás. The message was written with stones, sticks and leaves. When they made up their language, they though that they would only need three stones because they would never let more than three days pass without seeing each other. But recently, they were spending longer and longer apart.

Mikela left a stone on a leaf, scratching a moon and an M in the dirt as well to let Natividad know she would be back that night, but she didn't feel very sure at all that Natividad would find it. She wouldn't expect to find it here because she didn't know that Mikela knew where she had gone.

Mikela was a little angry at Natividad. She worked so hard to find her sister, but then Natividad would slip off again. She didn't leave messages for Mikela most of the time. This happened much more since Pablo had come with his friend Tomás to find them. If Pablo hadn't convinced Natividad she was safer with him, wouldn't she still be with Mikela? Wouldn't she be making it easier for Mikela to find her? Pablo was very proud of Natividad's stomach. "My woman," he said to his friend Tomás. Although Pablo was a little older than Natividad, he looked like a little boy. Mikela didn't think he could take better care of her sister than she could.

As she ran back to the home, Mikela thought about what she could do to help Natividad. She worried about what to do when Natividad was having the baby. Her mother gave birth to her brothers with the *comadrina's* help—but there was no one to help Natividad but Mikela. Mikela had never seen a baby born, only dogs and cats and goats. She expected all she had to do was catch the baby when it came out, but then when she thought about it more, she knew she needed a machete to cut the cord. She tried to talk about these things with Natividad, but Natividad just looked through her like she wasn't there. "Don't you think I know," she said. "Don't you think I already know?"

Mikela didn't know. She had asked the nurse who visited the home several times a week how babies were born. The nurse, Señora Vitalli, had looked at her carefully. "Why do you want to know?"

"I know it is different from how the Virgin had Jésus."

Señora Vitalli had laughed. "The birth was the same—just the method of conception was different."

"Is it any different from puppies or goats?" Mikela had persisted.

"Not very different," Señora Vitalli said, not looking so carefully at Mikela now.

But Mikela knew the *comadrina* had done things to her mother when she was giving birth to her brothers that no one did for goats and dogs and cats. She knew that goats and dogs didn't scream. She was afraid of Natividad screaming, afraid that someone might hear and take Natividad away. She would get a rag, Mikela decided, and fill up Natividad's mouth.

If only she could find her. She would look again tonight

When Mamí Concepción opened the door, she stood back a step and threw her hands up. "Just look at you," she said. "You're soaking wet."

"I ran and I ran and I ran," Mikela said. "Soon I will be the fastest girl in the school."

"As well as the most clever," Mamí Concepción said. "But only if you do your homework."

"Tonight?" Mikela asked, slipping around her.

"Of course not," Mamí said. "We'll have another sewing lesson instead. Why haven't I ever seen you wear your dress? You should be proud of it." Mikela shrugged and then leaned over, putting her hands on her knees, making her breath slow down like the teacher had shown her at school. She needed to save her energy for the night.

Mikela waited until the moon was shining in the middle of the courtyard before she slipped out of bed and went into the showers. She had rolled the brown dress Mamí Lina had her make into the blue cloth with the food for Natividad. She would put it on tomorrow to make it look like she was dressed for church. She dropped her bundle from the window first, then pulled herself up. But once she dragged herself over the window ledge, she realized she had a problem because the window was too narrow for her to turn around. She slipped back down and went out to the laundry line and took down one of the ropes. She went back and wound the rope around the pipe for the shower and threw the two ends out through the window. Then she pulled herself up again. When she pulled her head and arms through the window, she wrapped the rope around one wrist and slid her other hand down the rope, holding on tight. As her legs slipped through, she wrapped her feet in the rope then unwound her hands and climbed them up toward her feet. She imagined she was a monkey so she wouldn't think of falling. Once she had turned herself around by wrapping her wrists again and releasing her feet, she let herself drop to the ground and untied her wrists one by one. She pulled one end of the rope until it came free of the water pipe and fell down into her face. She rolled it up and put it in her carrying cloth.

Walking in the town at night was not like walking in the country—but it was not like walking in the capital either. She did not hear men hissing in the shadows. Mikela kept close to the walls of the houses and tried to walk very quietly. By the time she reached the ruins, her eyes and ears were tired from trying to see into the shadows and understand the sounds. She was hungry but tried not to think about it.

She could hear laughter as she climbed down past the benches toward the stage. She thought maybe she could hear Natividad, but then she wondered. Suddenly it felt more dangerous than the capital because she was all alone. In the capital, except for one night, she never lost sight of Natividad.

Mikela climbed up to the stage before the church doors. There were lights on the cross on the steeple, and on the one standing wall of the church, so she could see her own shadow spread out behind her and before. She felt safe and unsafe because she could see what was around her now but she could be seen too. Sometimes the police came here. If they found her, maybe they would think she breathed the glue too and put her in one of the homes run by foreigners. The government home, the one she was in, didn't want drug addicts. They only wanted girls whose parents had died or who had hurt them so much the girls ran away or some neighbor complained about the noise and the dirty bruises. Some girls they moved every month or two so their fathers wouldn't come and find them and kill them. Some fathers, even if they beat their children, didn't want them to go away. Nobody, Mikela knew, was looking for her or Natividad.

She ran along the edge of the lighted stage, keeping in the shadows as much possible as she followed the voices. She found Natividad sitting with Pablo and Tomás and two other boys at the foot of the tree where Mikela had left her message.

"What took you so long?" Natividad asked her. Her voice didn't sound familiar to Mikela. It was as if someone else was talking inside her.

This other spirit's voice was fast, where Natividad's voice was slow, hard where Natividad's voice was soft, and laughed after almost every word, where Natividad let huge pauses swallow her few words. There was a sweet smoke in the air and the boys were passing a cigarette around, each of them taking a big breath and holding it. Smoke was not good for Natividad's baby, so Mikela went over to her sister so she could blow the smoke away. But Natividad said, in the fast hard unfamiliar voice of the spirit that had taken her over, "Stop flapping the air like that, Mikela. You're not a bat."

Natividad pulled on Mikela's leg to make her sit. "Try some," she said, handing the cigarette to Mikela, but Mikela did not like the smell and gave it back to Pablo. She did not like the way Natividad held her breath, feeding this strange spirit inside her with the smoke.

Natividad tugged at the carrying cloth on Mikela's back. "What have you brought me?"

"Just food," Mikela said.

"Just food," Pablo said, grabbing the blue bag from Natividad. "Why not watches and batteries? Why not glue to mend our shoes?" He looked at his bare feet and laughed.

"The food is for Natividad," Mikela said. She tried to pull the bag back, but Pablo pulled at it too until the plastic tore and all the food tumbled on the ground, where Tomás and Pablo and the two other boys grabbed at it.

"Monkeys," Mikela said. She looked at all of them with disgust. "Greedy monkeys."

"Only food," Natividad repeated. But she took a tortilla from the ground where it had fallen and began to eat it without even brushing the dirt off. The spirit inside her was very hungry, Mikela could see, but she didn't want that spirit to grow big and strong in Natividad's body and keep Natividad's own soul away.

"Come with me," she said to her sister.

"You leave her alone," Pablo said, grabbing Mikela by the wrist and pulling her hand off Natividad's thin arm. "She's my woman."

"She's my sister,"

But Natividad moved closer to Pablo, still eating the tortilla.

"If you don't bring me things I can use, I can't see what use you are to me," Natividad said. Her voice was very cold.

"There is a house," Mikela said, "where there is a whole room filled with paper and paint."

"Liar," Pablo said.

But Mikela could see that Natividad stopped chewing for a second and listened. "If you meet me after school on Monday or Friday, I will show you," she said to Natividad. "But you will need to meet me alone."

"She doesn't go anywhere without me," Pablo said.

"Alone," Mikela said loudly. Pablo was a stupid boy. He wasn't a man. He had no rights. Why didn't Natividad understand this? Mikela wanted to kick dirt in his face. She wanted to hit him. But she knew there were too many of them and she knew the spirit that now filled Natividad would help them and not her little sister.

"I'm leaving," she said to her sister. "I have to get back to the home."

"Mamí's girl," the spirit inside Natividad sneered. "Little sister superior."

"Monday," Mikela told her. "Meet me in front of my school."

As she slipped back around the single wall of the ruined church, Mikela kept to the edges of the stage again. She hurried up the steps by the empty benches. She could tell by the moon that it would be quite awhile before light. She couldn't get back into the home and she couldn't stay with this girl who looked like Natividad but wasn't.

If she had brought paper and pens, she wondered would Natividad have come back to herself?

As she walked down the dirt road back toward the town, she wondered where she could hide until daylight. She thought she heard someone moving in the woods beside the road, so she started to run. If I keep running as fast as I can, she thought, I am invisible as the wind.

She flew down the cobblestone streets, her heart keeping time with her feet until she came to the church of San Francisco. This church was not a ruin. The courtyard was all covered with light from the streetlights, except right along the edges where the stalls were set up for her people to sell what they wove and carved. She found an empty stall and slipped into it after listening to see if she could hear anyone breathing. The priests let people sell here but insisted they sleep elsewhere. People understood about God needing some time to dream, but sometimes they disobeyed. Mikela knew some nights right after she had left the home, Natividad had hidden here. But Natividad had Pablo for company now. Tonight, Mikela had only herself. She lay along the wall so she could keep watch on the doorway. She kept herself in view of the saints rising up along the sides of the church, so they would know she was there, if only they would look closely. Sometimes, Mikela just wanted to close her eyes. Sometimes she wanted someone, even a statue, to watch over her too.

When the church bells rang, Mikela woke with a pounding heart. She imagined that she was inside the bell, hung by her feet, making the sound with her head as her body swung from side to side. She put her hands to her head to make the pain easier to bear. Moving deep into the corner of the stall, she pulled out her brown dress and pulled it on over her t-shirt. She untied her tennis shoes and slipped off her jeans and tied them back up in her carrying cloth. She put her shoes on again. She ran her fingers through her hair, then spit on them and tried to clean her face. If she went into the church, maybe the Mother Superior would see her and tell Mamí Concepción and Directora Evelina, and they would be so proud of her devotion they wouldn't wonder how she got out so early, or would assume that she had borrowed the key from Mamí Concepción's pocket. Only because of her devotion.

She waited in the stall until many people had passed across the courtyard into the church. When she came out of the stall, she did not look at the woman selling tortillas by the gateway. She would know Mikela had slept there against the priests' wishes. If only Mikela had woken a little earlier, she would have had a perfectly secret life.

In the church, Mikela sat in the very last row on the right side, so that the Mother Superior would be sure to see her if she came. But the Mother Superior didn't come. For a long time, she was the only one sitting in the back of the church, but after awhile more and more people slipped into the pews. Just after the priest passed in a cloud of incense, a foreign woman slipped along the other side of the church as quietly as Mikela had done. She had a secret life too, Mikela could tell by the way she moved, like she was trying to leave no footprints.

Mikela couldn't take her eyes off the foreign woman all through the service. The foreign woman didn't know the words to the prayers, not even the *Padre Nuestro* or the *Ave Maria* or the songs. But she listened to the priest's talk with her head turned to the right side as if she could only hear with one ear. Mikela had seen animals do that—cows and sheep in the field, or a cat in the house. They would get very still and listen, the ear acting like an extra eye.

The priest was talking about a man with palsy who needed friends to bring him to Jésus to be cured. Jésus was like the *curanderos* in her village, he had to talk to God first and then touch the people for the sickness to go. Mikela wondered about finding a *curandero* for Natividad, but she was afraid that if she took Natividad to a *curandero*, the *curandero* might say there was no way to help Natividad. Her soul had gone too far away. Mikela would not believe this. When she grew up, she would become a *curandera*. She would never make people like herself feel helpless.

We must keep hope for our friends, the priest said. We must bring those of us who need healing to Jésus. If Natividad had hurt her leg, Mikela would bring her to Jésus. If she was sad, she would bring her to the Virgin Dolores. But right now, Natividad needed something different, even if Mikela didn't know exactly what it was. Mikela felt she was listening, just like the foreign woman was, for something she couldn't see with her eyes or hear with her ears.

When the priest held the host up and the bells rang, Mikela wanted to cover her head again. She wondered if the foreign woman did too. The foreign woman sat so still and straight it was as is if she were only pretending to be there. Mikela stayed in her seat like the foreign woman did during communion. Mikela didn't need food any more than Natividad did—and those little white hosts just felt like paper in your mouth. It was Natividad who needed to feast on paper. Mikela was going to feed herself with the wind. But she was going to feed her sister too if she could. The foreign woman had a knapsack that looked very full. She slipped out of her seat when the foreign woman did.

Mikela followed the foreign woman to the park and watched her take a seat on a bench in the middle of the park. Mikela went up to the pila and stood at one of the sinks, watching the woman. She opened her knapsack and pulled out a notebook and pen and began to write.

God is watching over me, Mikela thought in relief as she watched the woman finish writing and put the notebook back in her pack but forget to zip it closed. The woman closed her eyes and her head again tilted to one side, but Mikela knew she was listening to her dreams now, something deep inside her.

Quietly, she made her way down the sidewalk toward the bench where the woman sat sleeping. In her mind, Mikela imagined slipping her hand into the knapsack and grabbing the notebook. She imagined it twice before she came to the bench, so when she made the motion, it felt very easy and quick. The woman didn't even move as Mikela's hand went into the red knapsack pocket and out again with the book. She slipped it inside the fold of her brown skirt as she quickly walked on down the sidewalk. At the end of the park, she crossed the street and kneeling down on the sidewalk with her face to the pink wall, pulled her blue carrying cloth from her back and opened it up and put the notebook inside. She tied the cloth around her again.

But instead of hurrying back to the home, she found herself returning to the bench where the foreign woman sat sleeping. Mikela felt like there was a string between them that was being pulled tighter and tighter. She knew God had something to do with this, but she wasn't sure how. "I'm not going to give the notebook back," she whispered to God. "I don't care if I go to hell. Natividad needs it more. You said, ask and you shall receive. I asked and now I am receiving and that's it."

Mikela felt the string pull her around the bench and stop about four feet from the foreign woman. She crouched down on the grass, studying her face. She had some lines around her eyes and her mouth, but other than that her face was very smooth. Her skin was very light. Her lips moved a little and Mikela could see her eyes moving back and forth under her lids. For some reason, watching the movement under her eyelids made Mikela feel as if she would cry. Instead, she got very still and tilted her head on the opposite side as that of the sleeping woman, so they could, between them, hear what was coming from either direction.

Mikela heard a woman's voice saying, *Daughter in spirit, daughter in deed. Call on me. Call on me.*

The voice sounded familiar to Mikela, although she had never heard it before. She knew it couldn't be God's voice because it was a woman's. She didn't think it was the Virgin's voice because it was too loud and strong. She thought the Virgin usually whispered.

Maybe, Mikela thought, the voice is coming from the foreigner's dreams. She decided she would wait a little longer to hear if it said anything more. It was a voice that made Mikela happy, and made her feel a little afraid too, just like Señora Rosemary's touch.

I love her so much, the voice said to Mikela. *Watch her for me.*

"But I have Natividad," Mikela said. "I have too much work to do already." She reached down and pulled at the grass with her fingers. She felt so tired, more tired than the woman sleeping in front of her.

You're not watching, the voice said.

What about me?, Mikela wondered. Who is watching me.

Look in front of you, the voice said. *You'll see.*

But all Mikela saw was the foreign woman with her head tilted to one side, her gold hair rippling and glinting in the morning sun like a fresh stream, her eyes moving back and forth in the darkness of her dreams, her lips forming words that never came to speech.

Wait until she wakes, the voice said.

Why me?, Mikela wondered, but settled back into the patch of sun, the heat feeling as comforting as the voice that whispered sweetly inside her, *Once there was a girl, Mikela, who was fast as the wind, as secret as a cat. God had great need of her from the day she was born of a woman born of a woman born of a woman.*

"I want to be a boy," Mikela said. "It's safer."

Don't interrupt, the voice said.

So Mikela did her best until the foreign woman opened her eyes and the thread between their dreams tore free and the voice stopped speaking.

WITHOUT WARNING
(Ben)

I have no idea how this happened.

Of course, I have a public explanation. I say it all the time. She received a wonderful grant that was too prestigious to give up—and it requires living out of the country for six months. She might have found my daughter Gwen's unexpected presence in our lives on a daily basis a little difficult to adjust to. I say that too.

But that doesn't answer the question of what happened to Lourdes, to us. Perhaps it was a mistake for her to have moved here to North Carolina after we married. We thought, because she was an artist and I am a chemist, that she was the more flexible. That may not be the case. It isn't easy, at our ages, to discover the deepest love we are capable of—something deeper by far than we ever imagined—so our whole value system goes crazy re-evaluating all those choices we made in the past. Then, on the other hand, there are all these losses that go with trying, at our ages, to make a safe real place in the world for all that wonder. The losses, for Lourdes, may have quickly obscured the gifts. At our ages, it is hard to trust your role in a love story.

Whenever I think of Lourdes these days, I think of her in her apartment in Boston, where she lived before I ever intruded on her life. Her apartment was like a secret shrine to everything she valued about herself. I could feel that as soon as she opened the door. I think she fell in love with me when she could see in my face and my body how completely, how quickly, I grasped that, responded to it.

I remember waking the first morning I slept over at Lourdes and finding her sitting on the window sill watching me. I couldn't see her face, only her silhouette. I remember how perfectly still she was, how held I felt myself to be in her unguarded attention.

"Has this really happened to us?" she asked at last.

"Yes."

"How?" She wasn't flirting. She wasn't asking for reassurance. She wasn't even expecting an answer. But she needed to release the question into the air where it seemed to shiver with life as the sunlight moved in and out of the pure white clouds dappling the intense blue sky.

"I've never made any room in my life for love."

"Never?"

"Not since I was a girl. Not the Adam and Eve, man-woman kind. I love my sons, but they're both grown. My art is my passion now. You can see that." She gestured at the walls of her bedroom. I can still remember the stillness inside her gesture, as if all time rested there.

I lay in her bed, the sheets down around my waist, letting her stare at me. I suppose it might have made someone else uncomfortable, especially when you reach my age, but I could tell from the way she looked at me and then at her paintings that she was trying me on in her imagination, that she was checking to see if there was anywhere I might fit into this landscape of hers. I knew that she was only interested in what was really there, that wishing and faking didn't have any place in this decision. At some level it wasn't even personal. After awhile, she noticed my own stillness and attention.

"You don't mind being looked at," she said, leaning back against the window and pulling her knees to her chest.

"I feel as if you can bring anyone alive just with your eyes."

I could see her shrink a little from the words, the idea.

"I feel safe in your eyes," I said. "I can't really explain it."

"I feel safe in your ears," she said after a pause. "I can't really explain it either."

What Lourdes was trying to tell me—something I immediately understood—was that I heard her silences. And I did. I found them deeply luxurious, exciting. I felt them all over.

And perhaps that was why Gwen's presence has proved to be such a disruption. It has deafened me to Lourdes' silences—which are, at the most fundamental level, Lourdes and my real language. Silence that has sight as its essential punctuation. It is a language that thrives on physical proximity. It's not the same at all over the phone. That's painfully obvious now, however many times I call.

When I asked Lourdes to marry me, four months after we met, she held my *eyes for the longest time. We were sitting in her bed. The wall we were facing had recently been painted blue in preparation for a new mural. Two figures, half worked in, a male and a female, nude, stood, hands clasped, in the far right corner. Light pencil markings covered the rest of the wall but would not resolve into distinct images. There was something wonderfully erotic in the unfinishedness.*

"I would have to give up this room," she said.

I didn't disagree, for even if I were to move to Boston, we would have needed larger quarters. But that wasn't exactly what she meant. It was that room, the whole history of her life in it, all the paintings that were layered onto the walls like an archaeologist's dream. It was pointless to suggest that she could paint the walls of her studio or of any bedroom we might share in the future.

There was something achingly complete in what she seemed to be saying. I have never felt so loved.

"I thought this was my destination," she said, looking around the room. Absently, she leaned over and pulled the sheet up over my chest to my underarms and smoothed it out. "But now I can see it was only a stage."

Did I really know what I was asking? Would one year, four—ten—have brought me any closer to knowing what would happen to her when she lost that room and everything that seemed to go with it?

Chapter 4
ECHO CHAMBER

"Just observe," the yoga teacher said. "Just observe. Observe how your body feels, whether it feels different from when you first came this evening. Where has tension gathered in it now? Where has it relaxed? Notice how your mind prefers some thoughts to others; your heart, some feelings; your body, some sensations. Don't try to control anything. Just observe. Observe how there is someone inside you watching who is not your sensations or your thoughts or your feelings. Tonight, let us close by saying Om for the watcher."

Lourdes, settling deeper into her sitting position, ready to wait this rather embarrassing part of the class out, was surprised to feel her belly expand, her mouth open, and a sound, melodious and sure, rise from her throat and meld with effortless harmony with the voices of the other women in the room.

This isn't me, Lourdes thought, some undercurrent of anxiety running through her but not strong enough to break through the sense of calm, so strong it was like a torpor, a fugue, that she'd built up through the yoga teacher's hypnotic invitation into the corpse pose and the quiet that came after. She felt her chest and stomach distend unintentionally and then release a third om. Lourdes thought, *I am watching the watcher inside me.* She felt almost giddy with the feel of the air humming around her heart and inside her closing mouth.

The teacher now led them in a healing meditation. They were to repeat, in expanding and contracting circles of implication, *May I know love. May you know love. May all beings know love. May all beings know love. May you know love. May I know love.* "Now," the teacher said, hold in mind someone special, speaking their name if you wish, and send them compassionate energy too." Lourdes tried unsuccessfully to bring her sons, Evan and Seth, to mind to screen off the faces of Ben, and then Gwen, which had flashed up immediately, then acceded to the inevitable. *Watch*, the voice she had been hearing for the past few weeks sounded so clearly in her mind she felt a shiver run down her spine. So she watched Ben and Gwen's faces as they talked to each other, their mouths moving inaudibly, their attention fixed exclusively on each other as if she didn't even exist. *Breathe*, the voice murmured, *Don't freeze, breathe.*

Lourdes let herself slip deeper, beneath their faces, beneath their inaudible words, back into the gold stillness the yoga teacher had created with the sweet resonance of her voice. Suddenly a laugh began to bubble up. I can't move, she thought. I can't open my eyes. My throat has shut. What on earth will they do with me? Woman frozen in lotus in foreign country. She thought of the woman she had seen a few days ago, her club feet tied together, a basket on her head, being lifted on and off a bus by the driver.

"*Namaste*," she heard the women murmuring. Her eyes took in the candles flickering throughout the small room where the women were crowded almost as close as they would on the local buses. The women had their hands pressed together at heart height and were nodding to each other.

"The light in me salutes the light in you," the yoga teacher translated. "*Namaste.*" The woman directly across the room from Lourdes, a small trim woman with short graying blonde hair, bowed to Lourdes. Lourdes bowed back. Her lips formed the strange word, but no sound came. Her bent legs were frozen to the mat. She felt the laugh building again, shifting into panic for a second, then subsiding into a gentle amusement and relief as the rhythm of acknowledgment took over. The woman to her left acknowledged her, then the woman on her right. Still speechless, Lourdes bowed and bobbed in return. I don't ever have to come back, she reassured herself. But she was as reluctant as the other women in the room to begin to move. What if she truly couldn't?

The teacher broke the trance, followed by the lithe woman on the far side of the room who had first saluted Lourdes. She looked vaguely familiar. Lourdes unfolded her legs and, after massaging her calves and ankles, climbed to her feet. She rolled up the turquoise rubber mat and carried it, along with the silk eye-bag and the canvas belt, over to the big duffle bag where they seemed to be regularly stored. She collected her shoes and socks and sweater and, seated on the stairs, began to dress. She watched the women below her, murmuring softly in the candle light, all of them, like her, slightly dazed.

She counted out the exact change, double checking the unfamiliar currency before she handed it to the teacher, who accepted it without looking at her, immersed now in an animated conversation with a tall redhead with a Southern accent. Lourdes turned to leave.

"Ve all valk together, yes?" a tall woman named Catarina said in a wonderfully deep and breathy French accent, gesturing toward all the women. Lourdes fell in, relieved. Except for the redhead who dangled car keys dangling from her fingers as she talked, all the other women in the class seemed to be, like Lourdes, dependent on their own two feet. As they headed down the street, they fell into two groups. Catarina, because of her long stride, walked with the two younger women, both healthy back-packers in their mid-twenties. From their accents, Lourdes thought they might be from Australia. The other trio included, along with Lourdes, the thin gray-blonde woman who sat opposite her in the class. Lourdes had the same uneasy sense of familiarity about her, but it refused to resolve. The other woman, Peggy, who introduced herself immediately, was even smaller but more muscular. One came to Lourdes' chin, the other to her shoulder, making her feel, as usual, cumbersome.

Peggy had a long bleached blonde page boy with heavy bangs over her broad forehead. Her manner was direct, her pace brisk. "I'm so glad I found this class. I can do my running by myself anywhere in the world, but for yoga, I need company. I know you're supposed to find it soothing to do it on your own, all that talk about one's 'practice', but I just get bored. Down dog, up cat. Cobra. I feel like a private zoo. I've seen you here before," she said to the graying blonde. "Your name is Marie, isn't it?"

The woman looked at her with an amused but distancing smile. Something, Lourdes surmised, about the unsophisticated nature of Americans.

"And you?" Peggy said, looking up at Lourdes. "Have I just missed running into you?" Her face was older than it had looked from a distance.

She must be Lourdes age or older. She waited for Lourdes to respond.

Lourdes felt the laughter and panic building simultaneously again. Other than Ben's weekly phone calls and a phrase uttered tentatively in the market or in one of the little *tiendas* near her house, Lourdes hadn't spoken in the last three weeks. She drew a deep breath and speculatively cleared her throat. At least the muscles seemed to work.

"My first class," she said. "I haven't been here very long."

"No one has," Marie said. "Yolande began these classes four months past when she arrived here. Who knows how long she will stay. There is much of the coming and the going in this town." Her voice had a slight indefinable accent, a little buzzing with her s's and th's that seemed to take place deep in her throat.

"Like me," Peggy said. "We try to come every year now, my husband and I. But we can never stay as long as we like. He went back a month ago, and for the first time I stayed on by myself because I'm retired and have the time. Are you here for awhile?" she asked Lourdes. "Are you by yourself?"

"Yes," Lourdes said. Her voice sounded surer, more resonant than she expected. As she lifted her arm to brush her hair back from her face, her still unfamiliar wedding ring glittered under the streetlight. She buried her fingers in her hair, then brought her hand quickly to her side.

They had reached the large street that ran by the market. Lourdes looked at the lined faces of the three older women, felt the contrast with their firm, vigorous bodies. Women of a certain age, she thought. Me too. And we're all waiting for wisdom, like a hot flash. The two young women with their heavy hiking boots and perfect skin shifted their weight impatiently.

"Here we go our separated ways," Catarina announced as she stepped off into the street, racing in front of a small rusted car with only one headlight. She was followed quickly by the two back-packers. With a brisk nod, Marie headed down the street in the opposite direction.

Peggy looked at Lourdes, opened her mouth to say something, then just bobbed her head and crossed the street. The sound of the buses on the cobblestones was a steady roar, but Lourdes could hear somewhere in the heart of it the fading murmurs of their voices. How quickly women set up those little affectional hums and let them die off again. She felt as if she might cry. She could see in her mind the number of streets she still needed to walk before reaching the house that attracted her and repelled her in equal measure.

She hadn't come here to make friends, she reminded herself. She'd come to paint. To recoup and move on. She stepped down from the high sidewalk and then stepped back as a car honked angrily, swerving around a truck and swerving back just as abruptly towards her. When, heart pounding, she reached the far side of the street, she found Peggy waiting for her.

"Would you like to come to my apartment for a cup of coffee?"

Lourdes hesitated, feeling both pleased and resentful. She needed to safeguard her solitude, didn't she? Wasn't that the whole point of being here? She didn't need to be a welcoming ear to someone else's life story. And these days she had nothing she could safely say about herself.

"Another day—"

"Ten minutes—" Peggy said.

The look on the other woman's face stopped Lourdes. What was she becoming, she wondered. A monster of self-absorption? "I'd love a cup of coffee," she answered. "I just don't want to impose. It will have to be fairly short because I'm expecting a phone call." She felt Peggy glance down at her hand, that astonishing gold band, but say nothing.

Peggy set off rapidly down the side street and stopped mid-block in front of a large wooden door. "Here we are," she said, turning the key effortlessly in the lock and pushing the door open. She waved at the small apartment whose inner window looked into a beautiful indoor patio. "Isn't it sweet? I just thought if I could show it to someone it would make me feel a little more grounded. I haven't spent so much time alone in years. It makes me feel weird."

"You'll have to come and see where I live," Lourdes was surprised to hear herself say. "I'm still trying to find my footing there—and may be still trying to the day I leave. Weird isn't all I'm feeling. I'm feeling dwarfed. It's too big for one person." She felt disloyal as she spoke. Peggy's apartment, with its bright, slightly cluttered kitchen, it's living room looking out onto a floodlit patio, seemed compact enough to relax in. Enclosed enough. This is what I should have held out for, she thought. I could rest here. Rest was definitely not what she was returning to.

"How long are you staying?" Peggy asked.

"At least six months. I have a fellowship whose only stipulation is that I do my art outside the U.S. I'm not even allowed to go back to visit."

"What made you choose to come here? Oh, that's silly. It's obvious why you would want to."

"Impulse. I got the fellowship at the last minute. I was on the waiting list. I didn't expect to get it at all but thought if I did I'd go to Europe. Then I saw a picture of one of the streets here in the travel section of our local newspaper. It looked familiar and strange at the same time, like a dream. I found it irresistible. Just the idea, you know, that something out there in the world could echo so closely the secret world inside your head—the one even you don't even know about half the time."

Peggy opened cabinets in the bright little kitchen and pulled down cups. "I'm not an artist. But I know when we came here, something clicked for Kevin and me too. We found it hard to explain to our friends back home in Portland. 'We feel at home there,' we tell them, and they look around at our pretty little town, where we've all lived for thirty years or more, and shrug and treat us gently as if we're in the earliest stages of Alzheimer's. If we didn't have each other, I bet we'd start doubting our responses. Kevin calls me every couple of days telling me how much he wants to be down here with me. And I tell him, much as I love it here, it just isn't the same without him. We married late, but now it's hard to imagine our lives without each other."

"This is good coffee," Lourdes said. She felt Peggy glancing at her ring again. I'll take it off when I get back, Lourdes thought. She closed both her hands around the cup, enjoying the heat. The weather here was surprisingly cold. She constantly wore the one pair of long underwear she had thrown into her suitcase on impulse just before zipping it up for the last time.

"Will you be at the Thursday class?" she asked, suddenly unbearably restless. "Perhaps I can invite you to my house after class."

"It's so dark. I hate to be an old lady about it, but could we meet one morning instead?"

They arranged for Saturday as Lourdes took her leave. She refused Peggy's offer to call a taxi. As she walked quickly along the cobblestone street, her feet seeking balance on the constantly shifting surface, Lourdes felt she was being followed but knew that it was only the echo of her own feet. There were advantages, she thought, to losing your hearing. She hadn't experienced them yet. For a painter, she had spent an unusual amount of time cultivating her sense of hearing. It was her livelihood. Or had been. And might be again. But it was not her soul.

How would you know? the voice asked her. *When have you used that gift to your own advantage? When, Lourdes, have you just listened to what you have to say to yourself?*

"I'm listening to you now," Lourdes murmured, quickening her pace. "How on earth can I listen to myself too?"

As Lourdes turned her key in the lock and tried to tease the tumbrels in the necessary little dance step she still hadn't mastered, she thought she heard the phone ring. She purposefully slowed down her movements. She looked with exaggerated ease to right and left as she started in with the key again. At the end of the street to her right, the spotlights lit the archway into the church yard and circular stained glass window set high in the church wall. On the other side of her, the streetlights illuminated the cobblestones and small promising patches of plaster walls of different colors, bougainvillea trailing over the red roofs. She heard someone approaching and turned her attention back to her task. Hearing the lock finally give, she quickly pushed the door open. She groped for the light switch over on her left as she closed and locked the door.

The phone started up again. She climbed the stairs with a stubborn measuredness, counting the rings as she did so. When it kept ringing, she walked over and picked it up.

"Veronica?" a man's voice asked in heavily accented English.

"There is no Veronica here," Lourdes said.

"No Veronica? Isn't this 59-82-03?"

"Yes. But no Veronica lives here now."

"She did not tell me she was leaving."

Nor, thought Lourdes, did Angie, Gertie, Sue, Pat or Wendy. The two apartments she now rattled around in seemed to have belonged to an endlessly shifting stream of attractive young women from the States and Europe. They taught in private schools in the capital and did their obviously active socializing in the small colonial town where Lourdes too had chosen to live. What interested her was how many of the young women there had been and how none of the young men who sought them ever apologized for disturbing her. Rather, like this one, they acted as if she were keeping something from them.

"You have her address?" the man asked. "Her phone number?"

"Nothing. I have never seen her."

She decided she would ask Simon tomorrow to find out the new phone number and address of the last resident. Better, she'd make one up herself. This couldn't have been what Simon meant by good female presences, could it? Giggles and margaritas and hot nights in the disco? Guys hungry for romance or a green card. Their lives struck Lourdes, the mood she was in, as rather sad. Aimless. Fielding all the calls, on the other hand, was just irritating.

"I cannot help you," she said again. "I don't know where they all went. I don't know why they left. Nor, frankly, do I care. They will not be here for the next six months, that I can guarantee you. Good night."

Within seconds, the phone began to ring again. She let it ring seven times, then, thinking it might be Ben, picked it up again. She didn't say anything.

"Veronica?" the man's voice asked again.

"No. No. No," Lourdes whispered as she dropped the receiver into its cradle. They always did this. Lourdes didn't know if it was that they didn't trust the phone company's connections or just couldn't believe their bad luck—or her. She didn't like feeling that she *was* their bad luck, but by the end of these conversations, she usually did.

These calls set a tone, both importunate and fantastic, she found difficult to shake.

You brought it with you, remember, the voice said. *A dream, you said. It felt like a dream.*

"Shut up," Lourdes said aloud. "Shut up. Shut up."

Her voice echoed across the balcony walkway and against the old stone wall that formed the far side of the airwell, enclosing the two apartments that Ben had insisted she rent. The outer walls of the house began to shudder as a large truck went past, the sound of it back-firing echoing like gunshots inside the house. She went to find her tape deck and put on a cello cassette, letting the sounds rumble through the house upstairs and downstairs.

She put a pan of water on the stove for tea and lit the water heater so she could take a shower—then tried the sink in the bathroom and realized the town water supply was already shut off for the night. What did it matter anyway, she thought. Who was there to notice? But she found the acrid scent of her own fear so troubling she dipped out some water from the large soup pot in which she stockpiled a nightly store of water and went into the bathroom to wash her face and underarms. As she was drying herself off, the phone rang again.

"Ben?" she asked as she picked it up.

"Who else?" he asked. "Where have you been? More importantly, what are you doing down there when I'm up here? God, do I miss you, Lourdes. What?" he yelled. "Excuse me," he said to Lourdes and covered the receiver.

Lourdes counted the seconds on her fingers. Stopping when she reached sixty. My tea, she thought, and started to set the receiver down, but Ben was back again, laughing.

"Sorry about that. Gwen just walked in. Pissed about the job interview. I guess she really doesn't want to be a manager at Hardees."

Couldn't it have waited? Lourdes thought. Or thought she thought, although for a second she felt it was that other voice speaking, the one that kept her almost constant company these days.

"Maybe we should talk some other time," she said.

"Now that I have you here, I don't want to let you go," Ben said. Lourdes reached out and touched her face reflected in one of the panes of glass in the window that looked out into the airwell. "Tell me how your work has been going, what you've been doing." She had, as she always did, an overwhelming urge to rest in Ben's kind voice, his interest.

"You first," she said

"Same old. Work is work. Gwen is still interviewing high and low. It's working out fairly well." He paused. "It's not really so comfortable. We haven't lived together in any continuous way since she was thirteen."

Lourdes couldn't help. Just the mention of Gwen's name and some dark space opened up inside her. She felt reassured by resistance of the cool glass under her fingertips as she steadily pressed the window open, pushing her own face out of sight.

"It's not the same without you here, Lourdes. I hope you're having a great time, but I want you back as soon as possible. I hope it's all right to say that."

Lourdes couldn't imagine opening her mouth, or, if she managed that, having sound come out. *Breathe,* the voice said to her. *Don't freeze, breathe.*

"I wonder if we can exchange e-mails this week. I'm feeling taciturn—for reasons having nothing to do with you. But I don't think either of us want to pay for vacant pauses."

"You're sure they're not pregnant ones?" Ben asked, his voice uncertain.

"Sure as sure can be," she said firmly. "I'm just trying to get into my work. And that isn't a very verbal place. Tonight I went to a yoga class and stopped and had coffee with one of the women from the class, so I'm just tired on top of that."

"A friend," Ben said. "I'm so pleased. I worry about you being too isolated down there."

"I'm not," Lourdes said. "She's just someone passing through. She leaves next week."

"You'll find other people."

The softness and condescension in Ben's voice, however unintentional, made her hot with anger. What was he doing, giving her, even here, her own life back.

"I'll e-mail you tomorrow, darling," she said evenly.

"I love you, Lourdes. Please take that in."

"Oh Ben," she said, and hung up as she heard her voice breaking. She waited a minute for the phone to ring again, and when it didn't, listened to her own voice inside her, saying, *Oh, Ben*. Trying to steady the sound, take the quaver, the crack out of it. She felt sick with remorse.

We reap, the voice said to her pleasantly, *what we owe*.

"How do you know?" Lourdes asked her. "How do *you* know."

"They say this house is filled with female spirits," Simon Goodall, the tall handsome blonde American expat who had located the apartments for them, told Lourdes, in an aside, after Ben had said, "It's a take," then, looking at her, corrected himself, "Isn't it, Lourdes?"

"Good ones?" Lourdes had asked.

"You'll have to ask them," Simon said. "But so far no one has complained."

Simon wasn't a realtor he'd told them when they'd fallen into conversation in the park. Just a connector. There was no finder's fee or anything involved. His reward was matching people with places that he thought might speak to them. His broad smile was both sweet and sly. Lourdes found it deeply appealing and wondered if he might pose for her sometime. He'd kind of fallen into this match-making since he came here a year ago, he'd explained. He'd seen a number of apartments before he'd settled on his own, had gotten a sense of the spaces, the owners, so when he met people wanting to settle in for a spell, he'd started taking them round. These apartments she lived in now weren't the only places he'd shown them. He'd taken them to an astonishing house set beside a ruin, owned by a reclusive—but charming, he assured Lourdes—French woman who had a large airy studio apartment over her garage that was sometimes available. The woman had opened the grate in her imposing wooden door, listened to Simon, then shook her head. Reluctantly, it seemed, since she stood there watching as the three of them turned and wandered off. Lourdes felt something click. That was where she had first seen the woman she sat opposite to in the yoga class, the small blonde with the slightly buzzing accent. Marie.

A small studio apartment deep inside a high walled garden would have been perfect, Lourdes thought as she took her mug of hot tea out onto the little patio. Why had she let Ben take over like that? Why hadn't she said anything when he'd said to Simon as they walked away from the French woman's house, "It would have been too small for Lourdes. She needs space to paint. She doesn't want to sleep with all those fumes." Maybe that's exactly what she did want—to be completely intoxicated with her work.

When Simon had shown them these apartments, Lourdes had been as charmed as Ben by the upstairs one with its dark steeply sloped ceiling in the living room, the multi-paned window onto the airwell and the doorless opening onto the balcony which gave access to the two bedrooms and small patio on the far side of the house. She'd loved the old stone wall that enclosed the whole building. She'd liked looking down into the patio below. She'd rather liked the idea of other people living below going about their own business. Lourdes free to listen or not as she pleased. But Ben had objected. For her, he said. She wouldn't be able to work with other people downstairs. They should take both apartments for privacy. It would give Lourdes twice as much space to paint in. And give Gwen a private place to stay when she came down with him at Easter. The private place, Lourdes gathered, was her studio space.

Why didn't Lourdes say something? Why didn't she say, "Let me tell you what I want."? Ben needed to feel they were doing this together. She'd been so abrupt about her decision to come here, letting him have his say about her living quarters seemed the least she could do. Besides, she couldn't bear to hear what she herself truly thought. When Ben said that about the second apartment, Lourdes felt some door inside her slam shut. She had no words for where it sent her. She would never paint there, she had quietly decided as she listened to Ben and Simon and the owner talk about rents. Not space she would have to relinquish to Ben's angry, accusatory daughter whenever she chose to visit. Let Ben think what he wanted to think. She knew Ben, when he asked about her painting, mentally placed her in the large living room of the lower apartment. But so far, she hadn't set foot in it since they viewed it together. She'd confined herself since she moved in to the upstairs apartment. Well, never having spent a night here he had no idea, none at all, of what the experience of living here was like.

Simon had mentioned female spirits, and the constant callers made implicit references, in their disappointed eagerness, to the warmth of all the women's bodies that had rotated for years through all these beds. But no one had said anything about the echoes, the eerie and inescapable maelstrom of sounds that eddied inside the airwell both day and night. By now, some of the sounds were familiar to her. The steady tread of a solitary runner when it was still pitch dark. Church bells that began to sound at six in the morning. The shuddering rumble of the cars and trucks passing over the cobblestones. But no one had told her that people talking on the street one story below could be heard with such clarity inside her bedroom that it was as if they were holding a conversation right beside her bed. And the telephone ringing in the house next door was louder than her own. She often went to answer it.

No one had mentioned the wild cat that clambered over the tile roofs and dropped from the stone wall onto her upstairs patio and crept across the balcony to the open living area where it ravaged whatever food had been left on the counters. The other night she had gotten up to use the bathroom and had almost stepped into a mound of vomit the cat had left, complete with half-gnawed chicken bone, in the open doorway to the living area. No one had mentioned, how could they, the icy stillness that filled Lourdes' body when she went into the second bedroom in the upstairs apartment and pulled out her paints and her first, newly stretched canvas, and felt an emptiness so deep she believed it would never resolve. No one had mentioned, how could they, this voice that had come, unbidden, to fill that emptiness.

More, the voice murmured. *You expected more, Lourdes.*

Lourdes put her mug down and stared at the stars. When she first moved in, she had loved this collapse of inside and outside. She had had no idea that the collapse would be internal as well, that within weeks she would want, more than anything in the world, a roof that covered her whole living space, doors that separated outside and in. Faces she could look deeply into when she heard voices speak.

What is it, the voice said again, *that you're so afraid to see?*

"I know what you're wanting," Lourdes said, closing her eyes against the stars and the thin sliver of moon. "I'm not going to give it to you."

Me, the voice continued smoothly. *You're afraid to see me. We both are.*

Lourdes put her hands over her ears, shaking her head. "Observe," she heard yoga teacher say, "Just observe. Don't try to control anything. Observe the one who is watching."

Me, the voice said contentedly. *Observe me.*

This voice, just like her time here, was a travesty of everything that Lourdes had hoped for herself, everything she had been so sure, only six months ago, she was moving toward.

What more did you expect? the voice asked. *Happiness? Bliss?*

By the time she arrived here at Christmas with Ben, Lourdes had one expectation left. To be alone. And now she was, and wasn't at all. Take this voice that she couldn't get rid of, whose tone could switch without warning from sweet to bitter, compassionate to loathing. Lourdes couldn't turn it off, anymore than she could control the loose and eerie transubstantiation of ambient sounds. Lourdes had spent most of her life exercising exquisite control over what she chose to hear, what she chose to screen out.

From the time she was eighteen until a year ago, when she married Ben and moved to North Carolina, Lourdes had worked as a court reporter. Every morning for almost thirty years, whatever was occurring in her life, she would sit on the bus that took her to a court house or lawyer's office emptying her mind of all the concerns and responses that defined her as a person. It was a discipline that resembled Eastern meditation practices but felt completely natural to her. It was something she had perfected as a child.

"This will be the most difficult skill to master," her first instructor had said. "You can't take your attention away from the person who is speaking. No matter what he or she is saying. And they will be saying some terrible things. You are a court reporter, after all. You'll be transcribing the testimony of murderers, robbers, women and children who have been raped, embezzlers, lawyers who are hungry for their next big fee, judges who have had a cocktail too many at lunchtime. There is no room here for your own opinions, your own responses. None of this has anything to do with you. Your job is simply to record the words each voice is saying. Court reporters are more accurate than tape recorders and video cameras—that is why they will never be replaced. They know when their attention wanders, their comprehension fails them. They know when their mental batteries go dead. So, although you may be exhausted at the end of the day from the concentration required, you will be able to sleep soundly knowing there will always be a need for your services."

"You never took it home with you?" Ben had asked her, both amazed and a little horrified by her description of her work. "You didn't find it dehumanizing?"

"It paid the rent," she said. But it did more than that. She had always liked her work—and for many of the reasons it bothered Ben. It created a safe place for her, a place without feeling or thought—only sensation. Where she was simply the sound of a stranger's voice resonating in her ear canal, the movement of her fingers transcribing those sounds into words. She was, unless she stopped the proceedings to have something repeated, completely invisible—and completely present in her senses, in her total attention to the stimuli she had selected. The reason court reporters were more accurate than tape recorders or video cameras was that they knew what to ignore, what *not* to record. They knew the rules.

Art too had rules—of attention, selection, deletion, self-effacement, of opening, without obstruction, to what was coming to you from outside. Even if what was coming to you from outside was an image of your own troubled heart. In this way, of course, it differed from her work as a court reporter because it recalled her to herself.

"This must have been so painful to paint," Ben had said of one of her paintings and she had let it pass, but recorded the word and when she returned to look at the painting, she tried to see if pain was a word that she would use to describe its content if not its creation. Relief, she had decided, was the world she would use. The painting—of a naked woman alone in the desert, holding a newborn infant to her breast, the baby's belly, like the mother's legs, still slick with blood—still filled her with relief when she looked at it. She had actually been thinking of resonances—between the color of the setting sun and their skin, between the rock formations and the woman's bent figure. *Hagar's Daughter* is what she had called the painting. The colors in it were still shocking to her in their intensity, so different from her previous palette. But it was the shock of hearing oneself say what one has been thinking in private for years. It was one of the slides she had submitted when she applied for the traveling fellowship—and the one the judges had mentioned in their acceptance letter. But it was an anomaly in her work and she had intentionally not included it in the several pages of slides she had brought down with her although she found herself bringing it to her mind at night now as a way of focusing herself in the echo chamber that was her current life.

A gun shot seemed to ring out from the patio on the first floor and, in spite of herself, Lourdes jumped. Fireworks, she reminded herself, waiting for the rest of the barrage. People here loved violent sound, found it exalting, at any hour of the day or night. Preferably explosion without light.

Before going into her bedroom, Lourdes paused at the door of the room she was using for her studio, but did not open it. Every day for a week, since she had finished stretching canvases, she had gone in, a little later each morning, and had stared at their perfect whiteness. She had never felt so afraid. It was all she had left now that her life with Ben was imploding, wasn't it, this new ability of hers she'd still not come to depend on completely? But Ben had become, without her really noticing, part of that experience. Her painting, for years the most private part of her life, had become, without her noticing it, a major subject of conversation between them. It was an intimacy she had never imagined—but one, once experienced, she understood she had hungered for with her whole being. And now, without knowing it, he was stripping that comfort away. Assuming, just like her art work, everything she was, everything *they* were, could just be painlessly packed away whenever his fully grown daughter appeared. As if her presence in their home, in their relationship, had nothing to do with her. And she was using her art against him. Accepting the fellowship without consulting him—as if these two parts of herself were now, once again, deeply opposed.

There didn't feel like there was a single thing in her life now that was trustworthy, that was truly one thing and not another. Her art, this wonderful richness that she'd discovered in herself as her sons grew older, was shallow. She couldn't make a mark on her sketch pads, on the canvas, because there was nothing in her head except this voice she couldn't control and which came out of nowhere, there was nothing in her heart but this numb darkness, no quickening of her senses. And no one she could turn to. No one she could blame.

Say her name, the voice said, sounding so close to her that Lourdes startled and shied back. *You're a big girl now. You can get it out.*

Sometimes there was something in the voice that reminded Lourdes of her mother Annie when Annie was smashed and coming in to have a little heart to heart with Lourdes and her sister Jacquie; sometimes it was Jacquie she was hearing—Jacquie at twenty, Jacquie at ten; sometimes it was Kate, her step-mother; sometimes it was her friend Lily, her next door neighbor all those years she was raising her sons, Seth and Evan; or Maxine, her neighbor in the first apartment she'd rented after her sons left. Sometimes, just like the voice was implying now, she heard Gwen, Ben's twenty-two year old daughter who, fierce with grief and expectation, had shown up on their doorstep without warning one morning in early October. Sometimes there were hints of completely new voices—the soft chup and churr of the speech of the women in the plaza talking in indecipherable indigenous dialects. But the voice was never hers. It was always female, but never her own. It couldn't leave her alone. She couldn't hear it, this was the worst part, without a violent response, both emotional and physical. Her heart would pound when she heard it, an excitement like a sickness, or her muscles would get ice-cold, almost paralyzed with dread.

Lourdes, who had emptied her mind religiously every morning for thirty years, who could select and record and never respond to endless stories in the courtroom, just heard the voice beginning to speak and felt herself deafened by the rush of her own blood. She couldn't share a single word of what she was going through. That she did know.

Who, it's true, would believe you?, the voice whispered.

Lourdes turned and went back into her living room. She could feel the flush in her cheeks, the rush of adrenaline. She collected the key to the downstairs apartment from the cracked Chinese bowl she'd tucked it in and stomped down the stairs, turning on all the light switches as she went.

She performed the same baffling back and forth with the lock to the downstairs apartment she had on the ones on the outside door. Finally the double lock gave and she pushed the door open. She turned on the light, then went to the window looking out on the patio and pushed it open. She opened the door and marched through, opening the doors to the other two rooms as well, leaving all the lights ablaze. She stood in the middle of the patio, her hands on her waist, arching back to look at the stars. She felt her anger dying down.

It's all yours, the voice said. *All this space. Why don't you use it? You've been holding yourself back for a long time.*

"I have not," Lourdes said.

Who do you think you're fooling?, the voice asked her with a sweetness that made Lourdes want to turn her cheek toward it, like a cat. *Who do you think can't bear the truth?* Didn't she sound like Annie then? And Ben. The conjunction was terrible. Lourdes knew better than to respond.

Leaving all the lights blazing, the doors ajar, she climbed back upstairs and locked herself into her small dark bedroom. She repeated, until she fell asleep, the chant from the yoga class, using her own voice to drown out everything around her, inside her, before and behind. And all the time she was speaking and all the time she was sleeping, someone she could not yet recognize watched and listened and felt, for her, compassion.

SECTION II
IN AND OUT OF THE BODY

Ask, and it shall be given; search and you shall find;
knock and the door shall be opened unto you.
For everyone who asks receives; everyone who searches finds;
and for everyone who knocks the door shall be opened.
For is there any mother among you, if her daughter
asks for a fish, will give her a snake instead of a fish?
Or if she asks for an egg, will give her a scorpion?
                                                Luke 11:9-12

SPIRITUAL LIFE
(Wilma)

Some days when I wake, I can barely make it to the kitchen, it is like moving through a waterfall the sound is so loud and so dense. Señora Rosemary hasn't the slightest inkling of the number of souls, corporeal and incorporeal, who watch her every move. Even if she did, it would not make her act more cautiously. Caution is not the Señora's way—and God blesses her for this, but from such a great distance, the angels and spirits of the crazy women from the past must come and surround her and keep her safe. She has no idea. For her, there is no one here but the ones she can see before her eyes—except, that is, for Señor Walter, with whom she has never stopped talking since the day they met. This is very good. It is through his sweet love that she knows what is waiting for her. Once you receive a deep love, even once, there is a space that God can enter and begin to expand into, slowly, very slowly, like a sweet sigh. It is this sigh that surrounds us when we die.

But Señora Rosemary does not always remember that what God promises her, he promises every other soul on earth too if they will only ask for it, open to it. Señora Rosemary sometimes acts as if she is God, that without her the world would surely go to the Devil. Señora Rosemary is acting very God-wild these days and she is shaking everyone up, living and dead.

The disturbance is everywhere in the house, there is no way to get away from it. There are the voices of the women in the Señora's collective and their jealous husbands and their children hungry for food and hope and dope. There is the voice of the Señora's friend, Señora Ginger, which is sometimes very clear and sometimes very faint as she slips back and forth between this life and the life to come. When she returns she brings with her the voices of all the other people Señora Rosemary has lost in her life. There are all the voices that the foreigners who visit the Señora for their massages bring with them, not to mention their own real voices, and their secret thoughts as they get swept up in the Señora's life (no one can avoid this, the Señora is like a tornado, drawing everyone in). And now there is that girl Mikela and the voices she is bringing with her—not just the voice of the mute sister who sings inside her mind or the baby who wails like the wind as he realizes that his birth is irresistible. But strange voices, her parents, the girls at the home, and voices that go back through the centuries, voices that go to Europe, voices that go deep into the jungles.

I can't be expected to keep all these people straight. I can't be expected to make them all welcome. I have enough spirits of my own to contend with.

Señora Rosemary looks at me suspiciously on those days when I am so tired of all the bustle and bother that I set the dishes down on the table with a force that jars the plates and silverware. She thinks I want to go back to the quiet days when the two of us spent all our time tending to the needs of the speechless Señor. She is mistaken.

God save me from Señora Rosemary's undivided attention! It is like a tidal wave, her attention. Pure force that sweeps up all in its path and, if we're lucky, carries it far off to sea, but just as often, slams it, with shattering power, groundward.

"My," Señora Rosemary says then, looking at the wanton destruction. "Oh my." She is often surprised, but never penitent. In this she is like a young girl. She is, above everything, curious. It is a sensation more powerful in her than guilt. She is Eve's direct descendant. Knowledge is what makes even the greatest loss tolerable.

"Who would have thought he would stay so close to me, Wilma, even after all these years?" she asked me just this morning. I knew she was talking about Señor Walter. "It's not just wish fulfillment, you know. I really do feel he is here."

"Well, I hope he is putting in a word of caution," I said.

"No." She stretched her arms over her head, waggling her fingers at the sun. "He is simply enjoying me."

The Señora misses Señor Walter, I have no doubt about this. But she is also fascinated by this new knowledge of hers that his existence has not ended with death, just transformed. However, she does not feel the same sense of interest and casual comfort when she thinks of Señora Ginger dying. No, Señora Rosemary is determined that her friend will live, whatever Señora Ginger's own wishes in the matter. Her plan is to keep the Señora Ginger so busy she has no time to make her housing arrangements in the next life.

"I won't hear of it," Señora Rosemary said just this morning. "Get on that plane and come back. What is another diagnosis going to do? You think the next one is going to say it's all a big mistake? You think he's going to suggest aggressive treatment at

your age? Think he cares, Ginger? Hah! But we do. You need to get yourself around people who care about you. We're going to lick this, Ginger, just not in conventional ways."

I'm sure the Señora Ginger felt just like me when the conversation was over. The need in Señora Rosemary's voice was so obvious, so sad and so sweet, and at the same time there was that tough bossiness that made you just want to go over and shake her and say, "Go ahead. Cry."

But that would not be Señora Rosemary. Instead, she turned and said to me, "We need to do some house cleaning and reorganizing, Wilma. I think Señora Ginger may be coming to live with us."

I asked her if we should clean out the room used by the collective or Señor Walter's painting cabaña.

"The guest room," she said. "Our lives aren't going to change a lot. We're just bringing Señora Ginger into the thick of it."

Ah, Señora Rosemary has no idea how thick that thick already is or how thick it is soon to become. She can't hear that newborn baby wailing in the wind, can't hear the baby's mother singing in the high clear voice of a little girl, Death of me. Death of me. She can't feel Mikela's fierce, fearless eyes casing out all the possibilities to plunder in this house.

It is not fair, I tell God, to have me sit watching a movie I cannot stop, cannot turn my eyes from, cannot affect.

"Pray," God tells me. "Pray to me about the pain you feel watching them blunder on alone. Pray to me about the pain you feel sitting on your hands and doing nothing. Pray to me about the pain you feel waiting to have your gifts recognized."

"I did not ask for this gift," I tell him.

"But it is a gift all the same. Sometimes it is more charged with joy, sometimes with sorrow. But it is always a gift. You must teach Mikela the same thing."

"She's a thief."

"And an agent of love. Who has she deprived with her thefts? You? Señora Rosemary? Who has she helped?"

"She'll get caught."

"And what will that mean for you, Wilma?"

"Why are you having me sit back?"

"Whoever said you couldn't clean the cabaña?"

When the Señora found me busy in the Señor's painting cabaña, she opened her mouth two or three times like a hooked fish swallowing deadly air. We have not unlocked it since he died six years ago.

"He would want us to put it to good use, to have some life flow through it. That

was what it was for him—a lively place, a sweet one," I said.

The Señora looked at all the paintings I had stacked against the wall, the half-used tubes of paints I had mounded on the table. For the second time in all the years I've known her, she began to cry. But when she turned to me, her face was glowing with relief.

"I see," is all she said. "I see."

Was she beginning to see the spirits with the same clarity with which I could hear them? Was she beginning to pick and choose between them so that she could begin to twine her will with God's—for not all our spirits help us get close to the Creator. Did she see now that she needed my help? She is not prepared for what that larcenous little girl will ask of her. She is not prepared for the death of her friend. She does not know how much she has yet to grow. How do the blind know what help the sighted can give them?

This old woman knows nothing, nothing, about me, I think crossly. She doesn't know the children I've lost, the careers I have had, the spirits who speak to me and through me.

"Start with yourself," God tells me. "Start with your own dead, Wilma. Why don't you ask me about them? You hunger to hear them. Why won't you open your ears?"

And hear the screams of so many lost souls?

"It is not your history alone, Wilma," God tells me. "It is your country's. It is the world's. It is replayed every day."

"Stop it," I tell him. "Why in hell don't you just stop it? What kind of person are you if you don't?"

"We are helpless without each other. Surely, at your age, you know that, Wilma," he answers.

I see, I tell him, and I wonder whether my face glows now like the stubborn Señora's. I see.

God help me. I see.

Chapter 5
TRUTH

Rosemary really didn't have any choice about letting Mikela go—even though Wilma, as usual, seemed to be expressing her doubt about Rosemary's judgment. Just once in her life Rosemary wanted a woman friend or companion who confirmed her rather than openly challenging her, like Ginger, or quietly undermining her with unvoiced doubts, like Wilma. She deserved better, really she did—considering how often her instincts proved true. Obviously, Wilma thought she was being too harsh with the girl and that it was muddled up in some way with missing Walt, but it wasn't.

She really couldn't tolerate lying or thieving. Never had. It was what she told her own children and her foster children. She had always had what they called now a zero tolerance policy. She wasn't going to change just because she was living in a country where lying and thieving were the norm. Just because it was the norm didn't mean it helped them. Just look at this country—using its peace funds to build soccer stadiums, prisoners bribing the directors of the prisons and walking nonchalantly free. You couldn't trust someone who did not tell you the truth. It left you no purchase, whatever the intention behind it was. And thieving just made people feel more and more deprived and entitled.

I've been there, she wanted to tell Wilma. You don't know what those foster children were like—or how it hurt me sometimes to stick to my principles. But I did. For them as much as me. I did it with my own children too.

But it was true that she did not tell Mikela the rules. She had just assumed, because Mikela was such a fierce little worker and had such an outspoken way about her, that Mikela instinctively understood.

Wilma thought that it was because Mikela took Walt's paints that Rosemary was having such a strong reaction. Wilma was free to have her own opinions, but she was wrong as Rosemary had already told her several times that morning. Wilma thought Rosemary idolized the objects in Walt's studio, that she wanted to leave it as a shrine. Wilma found this wasteful. If Rosemary put up a statue of the Virgin or of Jesus and lit some candles, maybe Wilma would let that space rest and collect dust and devotion. Why shouldn't every house have a useless room, one where we recollect ourselves, our pasts, our last hopes? But this was not the point, Rosemary reminded herself.

She didn't ask. That's what Rosemary was sticking at. All Mikela had had to do was ask.

"Would you if you were her?" Wilma had asked Rosemary when she tried to explain. "What would lead her to believe that you would say yes? It hurts to be refused. Even you, Señora, with all your privileges, you know that."

And then Wilma had looked meaningfully out at the cabaña that housed Walt's studio—for when Walt had had his second, more serious stroke and Rosemary realized that he would never paint again, possibly never talk again, she had gone out to the studio and had started to throw things, shouting at the top of her lungs at whatever power was out there that it was a liar and a thief. Setting her up. Filling her with hope. Snatching it back without warning. You stole my *hope*, she kept screaming.

Wilma had been working for them for eight months at that point. She had seen all the progress Rosemary and Walt had made, with Rosemary's massages and Walt's determination, and now it was all lost. More than anything, more than the use of this hands, his paintings, Rosemary missed Walt's voice, how it could make even the saddest truth bearable just by its timbre.

It was that kindness that she craved almost more than honesty—but of course she wanted them together, for one without the other was meaningless. Most of her life, Rosemary had felt that she had to choose between them, and always chose honesty, however brutal. Until she met Walt. But Walt was the one who taught her that the most difficult truth is that we want to be known, taken in, comforted in the bleakest reality. And that this need, met, doesn't falsify the experience. It makes it more balanced, more nuanced, more true. Sometimes Rosemary thought this was the essence of faith—to be able to be at rest in our bodies, in our vulnerabilities, even in situations of stress or chaos. Never to relinquish our need for love. She had learned that through Walt and never ever wanted to let it go. And, after the grief subsided, she learned she never would. Living or dead.

"All she had to do was ask," Rosemary had told Wilma. "Because if she doesn't, she will never know that her needs can be spoken, can be met."

"And you taught her that?" Wilma asked. *"Por favor, Señora!"*

"I said she could come back in a month, didn't I? She'll know how serious I am about this, but will know she can have a second chance."

"Who knows what can happen in a month," Wilma said, shrugging as if she couldn't be bothered.

Rosemary felt quite misunderstood—but wasn't that their history? Except of course with Walt. Wilma had put her arms around Rosemary that afternoon in the studio and had held her with surprising strength. "Trust me, Señora," she had said in a voice so sure and powerful Rosemary still remembered it although she had never heard it since. "You will never lose him, trust me."

Rosemary remained grateful to Wilma for that afternoon, for expressing what Rosemary herself did not dare to. Just as Rosemary was able to do that now for Ginger, telling her friend that they would see this through together, they wouldn't give up, no matter what the doctors said. Someone needed to tell Ginger that—even if Ginger didn't seem to realize it yet. Ginger seemed ready to give up without a fight—but Rosemary knew that wasn't right.

Rosemary didn't feel the same level of assurance about her treatment of Mikela. Perhaps Wilma was right and the girl wouldn't come back in a month. It wasn't the end of the world, of course. There were more than enough needy girls to take her place, equally deserving—they all were. That was the trouble, really.

But something about this particular girl had gotten in and snagged Rosemary—so she felt a real sense of loss thinking that she'd seen the last of her. The truth was, Rosemary didn't really want to tame her, she just wanted to establish a solid framework of mutual respect.

On whose terms? The voice asked her.

I'm getting too old, Rosemary thought, looking out from the kitchen table and seeing the door to Walt's studio yawning darkly at her.

You're never to old to learn to let go.

Is that a warning, Rosemary thought, sitting straighter and setting her cup down sharply on the table. Her heart was racing. I am *not* ready, she thought.

What's missing? the voice asked gently. *Walt's there. Ginger's getting ready to leave. Wilma can take or leave you. Your kids are never going to come and visit. Ginny seems like she could step right in and take over the collective. Really, Rosemary, what's keeping you?*

Greed, Rosemary thought, taking a deep breath and beginning to float a little on the sweet aroma of the asunción lilies.

Don't sell yourself short, the voice said. Rosemary felt a hand, as firm and knowing as Walt's, running across her shoulders and down her arms. *You have something left to give.*

You're just wearing me down, Rosemary said evenly. But I'm not going back on what I said. She can come back in a month, that's it.

I miss Walt, Rosemary thought. I miss him every day. It hurts like a rotten tooth. Each time he looked at me, I knew, really knew, I was the woman I most wanted to be.

Love, they say, is blind.

Not his. He just didn't let my faults define me. It made me feel so free. That's what I miss. His love made me feel free—his love made me free to give. It's not just men, but women as well, who dislike women with edges. We want women we can melt into. But what kind of love is it that forfeits integrity? We're *not* soft, under our muscles and skin we have hard bones that hold us upright, protect our hearts and lungs, that *define* us.

And sometimes make us feel imprisoned.

Whoever said I didn't want to be kind?

Whoever did? the voice said gently.

GIRL IN THE GRIP OF GOD
(Mikela)

  When my sister's soul leaves her body, she draws exactly what she sees without feeling. It is my job to take these images deep inside my own heart and give them meaning.

  When people look at Natividad's drawings, they are so astonished by the detail, they think nothing is missing, that that is meaning enough. But what meaning is there anywhere in the world if our soul isn't there to feel it for us?

  My people know that we must never be surprised by what life shows us. If we are startled, our souls may leave our bodies. Only the healers and witches know how to lure them back again.

  My sister has one drawing I carry with me all the time because I know it is an invitation to her soul. It is a drawing of a large hand holding onto a girl's ankles. Her feet are pointing toward the sky. That is all you can see in the picture. The hand at the bottom of the page, closing tightly over the girl's ankles. Like so many of my sister's drawings, this one takes a very small part of a scene and makes it as big as the paper before her. My sister could not have seen this in real life for what held her then was not a hand but a thick rope. The girl's ankles are crossed like Jésus' on the cross, but there are no nails. Only this strong hand around the ankles. And small perfect feet that point to heaven. This drawing is a prayer, and I carry it everywhere with me. He will never fail you, I want to tell her. See how closely he grips you. I am only telling her what she dares not tell herself. When her soul leaves her, only I can see her hope.

The day my sister and I left home for good, I came back early from the fields, leaving my brothers working with my father. I could hear my mother crying from the edge of the field. The woman next door was standing in her doorway watching me approach our house. She is a wise woman, a healer. Her name is Señora Mercedes. She made no move to go towards our house although I knew she could hear my mother. I began to run, afraid that the soldiers were with my mother again. Even though they say there is peace now in our country, there may never be peace for my people.

But what I saw when I entered the doorway to our house was worse than the soldiers. I made myself breathe very slowly and steadily because I did not want my soul to leave me. What use would I be to anyone then? I could feel the eyes of Señora Mercedes on my back, like two hands on my shoulders, sharing her courage with me. I knew I was facing a great mystery.

My mother had tied Natividad up by her heels and had tied the rope around the rafters. She was beating my sister with a broom. My sister's skirt was caught tight between her legs. Her hair hung nearly to the floor. My mother was weeping and beating her with a broom made of branches.

My sister's arms hung down from her shoulders as if she were diving into the river. The broom turned her round and round. My mother's motions were so very slow, I could almost imagine the branches were caressing my sister's shoulders. My mother was lost inside herself, just as my sister was. My mother was crying, but so regularly it was like a chant. A sigh escaped my sister with every beat of the broom.

My mother, as she lifted her arms, was whispering, "You will be the death of me. You will be the death of me." The branches swished against my sister's back. Her long black hair swung, barely visible in the dark corner. The light from the window caught my mother's rising arms. The light slashed between the adobe bricks as I turned my head.

I moved quietly across the room. I knew I mustn't startle either of them. I could see how closely God gripped them both: my sister by her ankles, my mother in the slowness of the strokes of the broom, the rhythm of her song. Death of me. Death of me.

Then Señora Mercedes was there beside me. I was able to slide my arms around my mother's waist and to pull her close to me. The broom fell from her hands and I kicked it away. I drew her over to the fire while Señora Mercedes untied my sister. Natividad covered her face with her hair as she rested her head on her knees. She was very ashamed. Señora Mercedes massaged her ankles so she would be able to stand.

My mother picked up the broom again and began sweeping the floor. "She should never have been born," she said, brushing the ashes from the morning fire into a neat circle.

My mother's face was blue with bruises. She had been beating Natividad that morning because our father had been beating her the night before and she believed it was Natividad's fault, that Natividad had turned our father against her.

What those who don't know them can't understand is that my mother's beating Natividad was a kind of love. She was trying to invite her own soul back. She was trying to cleanse them both. Natividad knew this. That is why her soul left her body, so her pain wouldn't stand in the way of our mother's prayer.

Señora Mercedes whispered to Natividad as she rubbed her ankles and feet. When I came close to listen, Señora Mercedes looked at me. "Mikela, you must go too to guide your sister." She dug into the pocket of her apron and handed me all the money she had. "You must both leave today before your father and your brothers come back."

Natividad and I both stared at our mother as she swept the dirt floor. She was only a shadow in a bright square of light. She was murmuring to herself. We couldn't tell if her words were threats or prayers. We were more afraid for her than we were for ourselves. We had no fear for ourselves. Natividad was not afraid because her soul had left her body, and all she could feel was the reassuring grip of the rope around her ankles as the world went black and she spun to the rhythm of my mother's curses and the scraping of the broom. I was not afraid because I could feel the hands of God closing around our little house as if around something very precious. Wherever we go, he will never let us forget each other.

Our mother hated Natividad because my sister is the child of rape and also because she believed Natividad has seen things she should not have. Things even our mother didn't understand. Natividad knew that on the nights that my father spent in the far fields, or down on the coast working on the plantations, my mother met a soldier under the pines on the other side of the river. Natividad knew my father would kill our mother if he knew for sure. She knew our mother met the soldier because my father already beat her because he knew she had left him in her heart. Our mother loved the soldier, but her love was a torment to her—she could not understand how it happened. She prayed to be freed of it, but she couldn't. The marks my father left on my mother's face and body were a kind of *prayer too. Natividad tried to tell our mother that, and she looked at Natividad as if she were mad. Perhaps we all were.*

Some days, when I heard what my father did to my mother after the beatings, I wished our house would collapse, that God would not have such a tight hold on all of us.

When we left that day, I knew what would happen. I could see Señora Mercedes preparing, gathering sticks and dry grass, as I helped Natividad fill her carrying cloth and then filled my own. With the fire she was making, Señora Mercedes was driving my parents out as if they were the bad spirits of the community. She was driving them out and saving their lives at the same time. She was sending them off in search of goodness again.

I knew she would tell my father that Natividad and I had tried to go into the house to save my mother's weaving. Our mother had tried to hold us back. Señora Mercedes had held my mother back as they had listened to our screams. I knew my father wouldn't question her. I knew my mother wouldn't contradict her.

Only my mother's lover, the soldier, would come and turn over the ashes in our yard with his gun, weeping. Señora Mercedes would watch him sadly. "You are her lost brother," she would say. "I'm so sorry. I have no idea where they went. They weren't from this village anyway."

Time is like water in a river, never returns in the same form. Soldiers beat my mother and opened her legs and made Natividad. My father opened my mother's legs and made me and my brothers. He made my brothers by force because by then he was sure my mother had betrayed him. She'd lost too many babies after me and that is always a sign that a woman has been unfaithful. The first time she lost a baby, he ignored it. But the second time, he went to the curandero, who told him the truth. Except it wasn't the truth. Anymore than it was the truth that Natividad was my father's daughter, although he would let people believe this if they wished.

Natividad had so many fathers she had none. Her beginning was a darkness thick as mud that my mother could not see or move through. It coated everything. My mother was fourteen when this happened. When she woke up, she was alone with so many corpses. She made her way to the village of her cousins because there was no one left in her own village. They were all dead or had hidden themselves away in the mountains. It was in this new village she met my father.

My father was much older than my mother. His first wife had died in childbirth. For many years my father and his first wife thought she could not have children, but then one day she was thick with child. My father was so happy and then he began to distrust her because she had been without children for so many years. He began to question her, first with words, then with his fists. Her family could not persuade him of his good fortune. When the baby was born dead and my father's wife died soon after, my father buried them both, but he would not give the child a name. She was a girl, like us.

I know this because before we left our village, the mother of the first wife would curse my sister and me if ever we passed by her house or met her in the market. For we have benefited from my father's guilt, but her daughter and granddaughter will never return to this earth. No action of my father will ever bring them back. No kindness my father ever did my mother could change the opinion of the mother of my father's first wife. When he began to beat my mother, the mother of his first wife did not see it as something new, rather a revelation of his true nature.

But my father, like everybody else, is a mix of good and cruel. He deserves his good deeds as much as his bad ones. My father married my mother because he wanted to give Natividad a name. He wanted to appease the spirits of his dead wife and his first daughter. He knew the darkness out of which Natividad was created. At that time, he believed that he and my mother could contain that darkness, just as the walls of their house could contain the afterbirth from my mother's womb. He thought love could make time run backwards.

I believe I was conceived in love, that there was a time when my mother shared my father's hopes. She would always look at Natividad with fear because she knew where she had come from. But she believed that with my birth the world had begun to right itself again.

Then she began to lose the babies. She was as confused as my father was. She went to the curandero, who told her she was aborting the ghosts of those soldiers. This made my mother almost crazy with fear. There were so many ghosts she would have to release with the rush of her own blood. My father, when he came near her, became one of them too. He could feel this and it made him crazy with anger. My father felt the same strange sorrow and disgust when he looked at my mother that she felt when she looked at Natividad. As if there was a terrible current catching both of them by the feet and dragging them deeper and deeper into a churning river.

It is a terrible thing to see one's guilt take form before you, to reach out towards it and know it isn't a spirit that can be driven off, that it is real flesh, that there is no way of getting rid of it that doesn't make you guilty all over again. My father understood this whenever he tried to approach my mother and feel himself become another in her eyes.

Someone he could not bear to recognize. Then she became, for him, his first wife all over again and he shook her and shook her, screaming at her unfaithfulness.

When my mother carried my brother Jésus to term, my father forgave her—but she did not forgive him. But it wasn't until after the birth of my brother Julio two years later that she met the soldier.

I knew about the soldier before Natividad did. I was the one who told her. I feel very guilty about this. But even if I hadn't, I'm not sure it would have made any difference. If it hadn't been this, my mother would have found another reason to beat my sister. That Natividad lived was an astonishment to my mother, just as astonishing as that she lived herself. My mother hated Natividad in just the same way she hated her own life and what happened to her. Natividad was proof that time runs in only one direction and that innocence was lost to my mother forever. My mother loved me because I was proof of the contrary.

I love Natividad as if we were one person, as if our hearts shared the same blood, our minds the same thoughts. When I look at Natividad's drawing of the two ankles held in a huge fist, I think of the two of us.

That is why I know where to go looking for Natividad's soul. That is why I know how to heal my mother's wounded mind so that she will not haunt us all our lives asking for forgiveness we can never give her. For just like time, guilt and innocence keep rushing away from where we stand now out towards the sea. They will never flow back.

I am not sorry my mother sought comfort in the arms of the soldier. I am not sorry she set Natividad and me free. I am not sorry Señora Mercedes set fire to my family's house and sent my mother and father and our two brothers off wandering again. I know that all these things happened so each of us could feel the pure force of time and the strength of God's hold on each of us. He will never let us drown.

Chapter 6
LIFE DRAWING

They had no hands. That was what made the images catch, sharp as fish hooks, in Lourdes's imagination so she didn't know who was doing the pulling, who was doing the resisting. She couldn't let them go without losing something of herself in the process.

But it was their scale that filled her with a tenderness so deep and instinctual that Lourdes couldn't separate it from the need to touch. They were three-quarters scale, all the baroque statues she saw in the churches and the museums that she had begun to frequent when she could no longer stand staring at her blank canvasses or her own blank mind.

It was Peggy who had gotten her started, surprisingly. When she had come for coffee, Lourdes had given her a tour of the apartments, beginning with the bottom floor. Peggy had exclaimed at the space, the plethora of showers, the rustic stone wall. Lourdes had led her upstairs, and, while the water for coffee was coming to a boil, showed her the bedroom and then, startling herself, she'd opened the door to the room she was using as a studio.

"There's nothing here but good intentions," she said, leaning against the door and staring at the canvases canted against each of the walls.

"It may be too soon," Peggy said after she had looked with a smile at all this raw ambition. "It seems to me you'd need to be absorbing your new environment—and that takes energy. It would be sort of a shame, though, to make exactly what you'd planned before coming, as if this new place didn't have the power to affect you. But what do I know about being an artist. I'm just a schoolteacher—or was. I always had trouble with making out my lesson plans before I'd met my students each year. How could I know how to proceed without taking them into account? To placate the authorities I'd draw up these pristine, generic plans, and then, the first two or three weeks of class, I'd spend most of my time just absorbing my students' personalities, their character as a class, and then I'd go back and revamp my plans completely.

"I know it was this second quality, not the first, that made me a good teacher. Learning about my students was where the life, the pleasure, were for me. When you have an idea for a painting, does it always come from inside you?"

Lourdes had looked again at the empty canvases, then looked at the small woman beside her as she closed the door. "I can't remember," she said.

But even as she spoke, it was as if the room she'd just shut the door on had entered her imagination. Empty Wishes might be its title. She felt a sense of pleasure as she began to imagine how she might paint it, the light of a vivid tropical morning making the canvases dissolve into glare.

"I guess that aversion to planning applies to travel too," Peggy continued. "I'm always surprised at people who take package tours, let someone else set their itinerary. Traveling for me means letting myself get a little lost, a little disoriented. Sometimes when friends come back from trips, I have this feeling that they went, snapped a photo, and came back. Nothing changed inside them. None of their preconceptions were challenged. I always come back a little hazy—like I'm carrying the sense traces of a dream back with me. The experience remains immediate, sensorily intense, not always comfortable—and not exactly real. Different smells, different colors, a different language. Different self."

"I wouldn't know. I haven't traveled very much. But what you're describing sounds a little like what it felt like to me when I discovered painting," Lourdes had answered, handing Peggy a cup of coffee and leading the way out to the upstairs patio where they could take advantage of the morning sun.

And Ben, the voice said. *You felt the same when you discovered him.*

Peggy segued, as if cued, into a description of her marriage to Kevin, something that had taken place fifteen years earlier, when she was in her early forties. "After all these years," she said, "it still feels surprising to me when I see him sipping his coffee across from me at the breakfast table." She glanced at Lourdes' ring and paused. "Would you like to walk?" she asked when Lourdes had not responded.

She's a gift, the voice had hissed. *Accept it.* Lourdes had risen so quickly she spilled her coffee.

Peggy took Lourdes to a small museum of colonial art that adjoined one of the fancier hotels in town, constructed on the ruins of an old monastery. It wasn't until later that Lourdes registered what she'd seen, when her dreams were filled with beckoning figures, their hands severed, small holes indicating where they could be attached again to the wrists, or their fingers all broken off at the first joints. The first morning, she had woken weeping, not just at the lost hands but at the clean look of anticipation on the woman's face. Was it Mary Magdalene? Some other saint? Mary, Mother of God? The Virgin of the Sorrows?

Lourdes suddenly knew what she needed to do, so every morning she went to one or another of the churches in the town to study the statuary. But it was the museums, with their old, maimed statues that really spoke to her, especially the first museum she visited with Peggy. She had such a craving to return, she felt almost naked. Certainly, after her third visit, the guards began to look at her a little askance. It was such a small museum, one visit would have been enough, they implied. So, she began to bring her sketch book although sketching wasn't what she really wanted to do. She wanted to touch.

The first time Lourdes left marks on her environment was when she moved into a one bedroom apartment near the art school after the boys had gone to college. She stopped being the sponge, the ear, the absorbent mother and began to express herself, to become the active principle.

Marking the walls in her first apartment was a similar process. Most of her sons' furniture and belongings were now in the apartment they were sharing in Amherst. This had been done at their own insistence, but Lourdes had raised no objections. Lourdes had, unknown to them, been fantasizing for much of the past two years about a single nearly monochromatic room with white rice paper shades, a futon, an easel, a small, low bureau, a low table with pillows to sit on. Even this kind of imagining was new to her. Lourdes listened so much—for her work, for her sons, she had had no idea what it meant, what it might feel like, to listen to herself. That was why the process, when it started, was so astonishing to her. There was something in there, full, incisive, enormously attractive to her. But she waited to begin living it out until her sons were in an apartment of their own, something enough like a home they wouldn't feel displaced.

She had ended up with a one bedroom apartment, rather than a studio, because she thought it would be better when Evan and Seth came back to visit. The apartment was on the fourth floor, tedious to walk up to, but with a wonderful view of the Fenway. The first thing she decided when she entered was that after she painted the walls stark white, she needed to paint every piece of furniture the deepest hues she could find for the pure pleasure of exploring color. So her minimalist vision immediately began to be compromised. But she didn't mind.

After having painted the walls and furniture, she pulled out her drawings and began to tack them to walls of her bedroom so that she could go to sleep to them, wake to them. When she did this, she felt something deeply exhibitionistic in her nature, some desire to be caught out, known. She also felt deeply comforted, clothed by their presence around her. She could keep the door closed, she assured herself. She could take them down. She wasn't so sure how a world of nudes would go over with her testosterone gorged sons—or their friends.

Instead of taking down her drawings, Lourdes for the most part chose to keep people out of her apartment. She socialized with old friends at their houses or at restaurants. Had coffee with people she met in the art school in the cafeteria or local coffee houses.

What was it that had driven her, finally, to mark the walls themselves, to start creating a world that couldn't be squirreled away in the back of a closet, couldn't be shrugged off as a hobby? The impulse had been half pleasure, half rage. The boys had come to spend several days at Christmas with her and had revealed to her that their father had been in touch with them. Had been in touch with them regularly since the previous year, as a matter fact. He had invited them to go out to Chicago and spend New Year's with him and his second family. He had also, after a lifetime of reneging on child support, offered to help them with their college fees, man to man. "No need," he'd told them, "to involve your mother."

That phrase had hooked in Lourdes' mind.
No need to involve me, she thought. *No need to involve me.*
She could see her sons exchanging knowing looks with each other after they told her. They didn't know what her response would be, that was why they had said nothing, but maybe they should have spoken up earlier. They hadn't been sure how things were developing and thought they'd wait until they had a clearer picture. *Man to man.* Lourdes did not release the careful expression of neutrality that froze her facial muscles until she saw the doors of the plane to Chicago close behind them. Her rage was as much at them as it was at her ex-husband George. All those dinners she'd prepared for Evan and Seth, when all they did was joke with each other and wonder why the milk had run out and what she was going to do about it. They weren't even being intentionally rude. All their lives, they had been a little world unto themselves. At some level, Lourdes had only existed as a service to them. You can't be rude to a service. You can only evaluate its adequacy. Milk? Where's the milk?

No need to involve me. Each time the phrase came, she wanted to cry out. Why hadn't it hurt at the time to be so profoundly ignored? Why had she felt contented watching them in their private world? Why hadn't she seen what they were becoming? But she hadn't—anymore than she had seen what their father was becoming so many years before. How he had looked at her, eight months into his first job, and said, "We've grown apart, Lourdes. There's nothing more to say." But she could hear what was being left unsaid. How he had looked away when she had picked up the wrong fork at his boss's house. How he'd flinched when she told his boss's wife that she had never gone to college—she had been too busy supporting him and the kids. He was ashamed of her, that was the real truth. Ashamed of the children she had brought into being, with no more participation from him than the Holy Ghost gave Mary.

Ashamed of them until now. Until he had his own career securely in place. Some wife of equivalent education. And Evan and Seth had been seen through all those arduous years of childhood and self-absorbed adolescence. Then he could accept his sons as young men who had been born from the head of Zeus. *No need to involve me.*

No indeed.

No indeed.

She had taken her drawings down from the walls before Evan and Seth came to visit that Christmas and had hidden them away, but when she got home from the airport, she pulled them out of the closet and spread them out on the bed. She could feel the past year, how she had wandered through that empty house she'd kept paying the mortgage on so the boys, especially Seth, would feel they had someplace dependable to come back to, someplace that bore their imprint. But not hers. That was what became disturbingly clear to her that year alone there—it would only take a few minutes to remove all visual traces of her. *No need to involve me.*

She looked around her new apartment. Took all the books and records and unwashed clothes Evan and Seth had left scattered around the living room and stuffed them in the living room closet. She stripped the sheets from the two futons and set them up again as couches. Then, feeling private at last, she returned to the bedroom and looked at her drawings again. It wasn't enough. A sheet of paper here or there. She needed a world. She closed the door to her bedroom even though no one was around. She felt she couldn't get private enough. She pulled down the shades.

Then she pulled out her pencil case and set it out on the bed. She chose some music and put it on her tape deck. And then she took her clothes off, every stitch, until she was as free as the models she had sketched for years.

No need to involve me.

Somewhere, floating in her consciousness, were all the rooms she had shared throughout her childhood with her younger sister, Jacquie. She could feel rather than see all the bright magazine clippings of movie stars and assassinated presidents and car wrecks and plane crashes her increasingly disturbed sister surrounded herself with, the perfect austerity of Lourdes own side of every room. She could feel the composure, a psychological equivalent of that physical starkness, she developed to provide the same simple comfort to those around her that a mirror would. She knew the comfort her quiet self-containment provided to Jacquie and their mother Annie because it was what she herself most deeply yearned for. She'd provided it to George, to her sons, a space where they could grow into themselves, expand into themselves. Her detachment was her biggest gift. Except that it hadn't been detachment. It had been the most intentional kind of self-effacement.

No need to involve me.

But it hadn't come without a cost. One that was far too high for her to bear alone. That was what she was learning. With a vengeance.

And one of those costs was the numbness she had woken to and gone to sleep to almost all her life. A state that helped her be the welcoming space that everyone wanted her to be. An accommodation that she was increasingly calling into question. That is why her response to her own drawings was so galvanic. She was waking herself up, filling herself up. She was no longer that quiet, absorbing body, that low comforting voice that took in her mother's drunken self-pity, or Jacquie's wild fantasies and paranoid hallucinations, or Evan and Seth's boyish miseries and triumphs.

To mark the walls on her bedroom was like coming to speech for her—not in the intimate whisper of her drawings—but something closer to a shout at first, and, as she continued, a song. That first night, she just drew with her pencil. She began with desert landscapes—ones that were presentiments, she now saw, of the world of her surprising painting of Hagar's daughter. All her figures, which were based on herself, blended into the shapes of the landscape, nearly impossible to retrieve if you didn't know what you were looking for. The height of the high ceilinged bedroom set the scale, so the figures were all slightly larger than life. She could lose herself in them, she thought with contentment as she climbed up on a chair to sketch them in. As the nights went on, Lourdes darkened the first faint tracings. Then she began to paint in her figures, suddenly eager to apply everything she was learning in her painting classes, but also just hungry for color, warmth, motion.

She was completely guided by her sensations. If the image hit her in the solar plexus, made her sex wet, the way a woman with her arms outstretched in ecstasy, dissolving into the crevice of a mountain pass did—she knew she needed to keep it, develop it. Whatever didn't evoke an intense sensual or emotional response, she painted over. She lived for her nights. When the boys came back from visiting their father a week later, she encouraged them to go back to school a little early, pleading course work for her art classes and a big court transcript to review. But the truth was, she couldn't bear keeping her bedroom door locked. She couldn't bear keeping what she was doing a secret in her own home.

Seth and Evan hadn't even really noticed. They were so busy catching up with their own friends home for the Christmas break, making their own social plans for their return to school, they didn't seem to register her eagerness to be rid of them. It wasn't, of course, just that she wanted to get back to her painting, it was that every time she looked at her two, tall, handsome, burly sons all she could hear was that stabbing phrase: *No need to involve me.* The only way she could stabilize the competing pressures so the phrase wouldn't keep tearing at her heart was to get away from their eyes and to keep immersing herself in that sensual illicit world that did involve her completely—where she drew figures she could lose herself in, could paint them up there, larger than life, using her fingers, her own skin to rub the color indelibly in. To wake every morning invited into a world that did have a place for her, an image she could grow into.

In the end, she slept in the living room because the colors were too intense, the experience too total and gripping for her to sleep inside it. But the bedroom became the place she went whenever she needed to hear herself think, for as the images formed on the wall, she could hear physical sensations in her body that slowly began to resolve into words. Simple ones at first. *No. More. Son of a bitch. Forget it.*

And then the phrases were less reactive. *I want to live inside this. Ears that don't hear our own hearts lie. My lips are sealed; my sex reveals. Mother love is terminal.*

I need to be.

Involve me.

Completely.

All through art school, she kept painting and repainting the bedroom in her apartment. There was always one blank wall waiting for her, hungry to take her in exactly as she had, by then, become.

"Art is my lover," she told Ben early after she'd met him. "I know that might sound overly dramatic, romantic, even kinky, but for me it's true. I don't need anyone or anything else when I'm painting."

"It hurts me to think about what that says of your life, Lourdes."

"It says I'm complete in myself."

"Well, I'm not. Don't think I'll ever be. Doesn't mean I don't love my work or my life—just that there's something missing if I don't have anyone to share it with."

She didn't know what that would feel like, Lourdes had thought, staring intently at this stocky white-haired man with his youthful face and invigorating but deeply restful intensity.

But now you do, the voice said, bringing Lourdes abruptly back to the big echoing apartment she now lived in alone. Ben's absence an ache in her vagina and uterus, what they called here her *matriz*, her matrix, so sharp it was like the first stages of a miscarriage. Her blank canvases were just as dismissing as the distance between the two of them. The numbness each day seemed to grow larger, last longer. It was a very, very old feeling and that is what made it so terrible. She couldn't tell where it came from, but she recognized it with every part of her mind, her body, her soul. It had a quality of inevitability to it that must have been the way Jesus felt on the cross when he realized that no one, especially not God, was going to answer him.

The religious image was strange to Lourdes who, in spite of her name, was devoid of religious upbringing. (She was named by the sisters at the Catholic hospital where here mother had abandoned her for a month after her birth, until guilt and a brief waltz with sobriety made Annie go back and collect her.) But, she assured herself, using the crucifixion as a metaphor was not the beginning of her own bout with the grandiose floridity of her sister's schizophrenia, rather the effect all the religious imagery she was absorbing willy nilly in her daily visits to the churches and museums here.

There were three statues she kept returning to in the small museum Peggy first took her to. One was a small boy kneeling, a chain attached to his right hand and to a column set on the left of the kneeling figure. There was a faint, terrifying line of blood crossing his forehead just below the hairline. The look on his face was intent, mesmerized. The sculpture was titled The Dream of the Christ Child.

"Oh, I hope he didn't know what was going to happen to him," Lourdes heard an elderly woman murmur to her husband, sliding her hand uneasily inside his arm as she spoke. "It would be too cruel, don't you think?"

Her husband, a beak-nosed, heavy set man with a pronounced stoop, patted her hand and drew her firmly away.

Lourdes stepped in with her sketch pad, carefully recording the fine red line across the unmarked forehead.

The other two statues were intriguing because they were the only images Lourdes had encountered that depicted God the Father. One was a pieta—but instead of the dead Jesus being held by his mother, he was held by his father. The dead Jesus still had the faintly erotic air of most of these images of parental loss—it was something about the arch of his back, the fall of his legs over the lap of his mourning parent.

The third statue that kept pulling her back was one of God the Father as the patriarch, seated on a throne, with a gilded triangular hat on his head, just like an Eastern Orthodox patriarch. His hands were held palms up, slightly cupped. The middle, ring and little fingers of both hands were broken off at the first joint. Inside the cupped hands hung the crossbar of a crucifix, from which hung a small, perfectly sculpted Christ. Throne of Grace. God's eyes coolly met Lourdes each time she approached. He seemed completely oblivious to the small half naked figure that hung from the cross. Every time Lourdes came near, she felt a surge of anger that made her want to talk back, insist that God look down, that he feel, goddamn it, what was going on inside the body of the mortified, betrayed miniature of the human condition.

No reason for the old autocrat to look so pleased with himself, now is there?

Lourdes didn't bother to answer—either that day in the museum or this one at home. She was doing her damnedest to freeze the voice out.

One way to do this was to keep on the move—in her thoughts but also physically.

She slipped her sketch pad and drawing materials into a knapsack and picked up the odd little drawing board she had purchased in the stationery store annex of the large, chaotic grocery store at the end of town, which seemed to be frequented, at any moment, by half the town. The drawing board had a wide shallow pocket built into the back where one could slide in completed drawings or blank paper. All the teenage school children carried these large awkward plywood briefcases to school each morning. Lourdes felt both foolish and acclimated when she bought one to use in the life drawing classes that she had recently started attending.

The sessions were held in the small art gallery inside the town's cultural center. Lourdes had learned about them through one of the discussions after yoga. Usually, the painter Maribel, who organized the sessions, came early to move art work and make room for the model and the spotlights and to hang sheets from the windows and over the glass door to the gallery so that the gardeners pruning and watering out on the patio wouldn't know what they were up to. There was something very soothing to Lourdes about the elaborate concealment and then the very natural ease of the models ambling naked around the room during their breaks, checking out the artists renditions of them as well as the paintings and sculptures currently on exhibit.

A fluctuating group of artists attended. Some were foreigners, both short and long-term residents, and also local painters. Lourdes, by the third week, realized she was now one of the regulars. So was Marie, the woman from her yoga class, who was the one who had mentioned the class to Lourdes when she learned she was an artist. Marie had a real gift for draftsmanship, which she took very lightly.

"I'm like a mirror," she would say with a shrug when someone paused, a little daunted, before one of her drawings. "I would give anything to bring a little more to the encounter. But it is as if my heart is a prisoner of my eye. And my eye is a little cold, a little callous, but very exact."

"Well, my heart," an older woman said with a snorting laugh of exasperation, "is a prisoner of my learning disabled hand."

"Don't look," the old woman said to the model who started her way. "You might take this personally and you shouldn't. You're not a hydrocephalic hunchback, Michelle."

"The self-judgment does not help us develop, Rosemary," Marie said.

"Another pose?" she would ask the model, ripping her most recent drawing from the pad and laying it face down on the floor. As if that made the rest of them feel more competent or relaxed. The tact, however kindly intended, wasn't necessary. One thing Lourdes liked about the group is that they all seemed comfortable with their own progress—or lack of it.

Today, Lourdes was the first person there, so eager had she been to leave the voice to its own devices. She had to knock on the door of the center and be admitted by one of the young gardeners. She studied the paintings of the most recent show. They were all in primary colors, flat. The compositions, which consisted of pieces of fruit and figures of the indigenous in equal scale, were slick in execution, and either pretentious or naïve in their blatant symbolism. Lourdes had the sense that they were derivative but she didn't know who the influences were. She didn't like the superciliousness in her own attitude. Who am I to judge? she thought, the image of her studio, the large pristine canvases still canted against three of the walls coming back to her with inexcusable clarity.

After twenty minutes, she was gathering her knapsack, ready to leave, when she heard a knock on the street door and then the sound of several voices, including Marie's and the old woman, Rosemary's, and the low hum of a man's voice that sounded familiar.

"I didn't know you were an artist," she said to Simon Goodall when he entered the gallery with the two women.

"I'm not," he said, leaning down and giving her a kiss on the cheek. "I'm the bod. Didn't you guess? There's nothing I won't do for love and money."

"So sorry," the attractive painter, Maribel, said in her usual breathless way as she came in right behind Rosemary and Marie. She was carrying a mound of blankets and beneath them, gripped her metal drawing box. "The model had a hangover. I must stop getting them from the bars. They are uninhibited but undependable. *Todavía*, when I called Marie to cancel, she suggested Simon, who has been kind enough to model for us before."

"I offered too," Rosemary, the older woman, said. Lourdes looked at her and realized she was serious. The idea intrigued her. After only three weeks, she was a little tired of these beautiful unblemished young women. The last one had a subtle resemblance to Ben's daughter, Gwen, which had made Lourdes increasingly anxious until, catching a certain stance, twist of the head, she understood the association.

"Perhaps next week," Maribel said. "Let's get our curtains up. It might shock the workers—all of us women drawing Simon."

"Or enliven their fantasies," Simon said. "Especially when they learn how much you girls are willing to fork out for the privilege." He helped move the large abstract sculpture in the center of the room over to the corner and laid out a grass mat on the tile floor, while Maribel unscrewed and extended the tripod stands for the spotlights.

"Ten one-minute poses, Simon. Then we'll do two ten-minute poses, then take a break."

Lourdes settled her drawing board on the back of a second plastic chair and clipped on her first piece of drawing paper.

Simon left to undress and re-entered the room in a large terry bathrobe and went to stand under the spotlights while Maribel readjusted them. Quietly, Lourdes sketched the two of them, this wonderful distortion of scale that humbled everyone who lived here, making the foreigners feel suddenly mammoth and awkward. And tender too, the same tenderness she felt toward the statues—an instinct that wasn't maternal, was deeper, more aboriginal. As if the world around us could be fitted inside us. Already she could feel that easing of tension in her forehead, something opening up in her solar plexus.

I've been too alone, she thought. I've been too wrapped up in myself. She let the keen pleasure she felt—at the rustle of paper, the chairs scraping across the floor, the intent expressions on Marie, Rosemary and Maribel's faces—build inside her.

She looked at Simon as he took his first pose—his hands high over his head, his right hip lifted and right foot arched, as if reaching for something just beyond his grasp. Quickly she caught the slants of his shoulders, hips, knees and ankles, the turn of his head. She abandoned the figure and began another as soon as Simon settled into his second pose, hands on knees, legs bent, head lifted.

Drawing for Lourdes was half visual, half kinesthetic, her own muscles imitating the posture of the model. She found herself slipping into the familiar trance that was what it meant to her—or had meant to her—to make art. There was a small steady rush of pleasure from her groin, a clearing in her mind. This emptying in her mind was quite similar to her preparation for court reporting, but that small rush of pleasure deep in her solar plexus was completely different. Implicating. Letting her know, with every stroke of her pencil or pastel or charcoal that this *did* involve her—and that she loved being drawn into this place where to see and to touch were one action. Where the absence of words wasn't an act of will, a renunciation, but a quieting, an opening up to something deeper and truer than language.

This was all it took to make her completely happy, she thought. A naked man taking odd poses before me, four women staring intently at their own blank paper, light diffusing through old stained sheets, the soft incomprehensible murmurs of the innocent gardeners pulling weeds and pruning bougainvillea. Her happiness came, she realized, from the intimacy and anonymity. She would not feel this free alone with a model. She would feel compelled to interact—while here she was both part and apart, invisible and included, engaged in an exciting and completely private and completely public and completely honest conversation with herself about the nature of the world around her. And her responses to it—they were there too in every stroke. A state as different as could be imagined from her work as a court reporter.

Whatever happens, she thought, she was not going back to that. She would sort potatoes or sell lingerie. Anything. And then she was out of the body state she craved and her sense of loss was so intense it brought tears to her eyes. She changed the paper on her drawing board and sat with her hands on her lap, encouraging her body to relax, her gaze to lose its focus, letting the small wash of pleasure begin again as her eye registered the intensity of the shadow along the underside of Simon's elbow and under his slightly bent leg as he lounged on the grass mat in his first extended pose.

All you have to do is give yourself over, the voice said. For a second, Lourdes experienced a sense of intense turmoil—as if the voice held echoes of both her mother in one of her fits of drunken sorrow and of Ben relaxing her deeper and deeper with just the sweet steadiness of his voice.

Not to them, the voice said. *To me*.

It was then that Lourdes understood how to bring the images that were haunting her into her drawings and something came quickly, engrossingly to life somewhere between her mind and her heart. Tenderly she slipped this knowledge into some special cherished space and turned her attention again to Simon in all his bony, gold tinted specificity, knowing—and this is where the rush of pleasure became most intense—that something more, something sure and deeply secret was waiting for her when she returned to the privacy of her own studio.

For the first time in six months, she began to feel hope.

Hard to admit it's back again, when you've been doing your damnedest not to admit to yourself it was gone.

Lourdes just smiled as she listened to the voice goading her. She could feel the painting beginning to take shape under her fingers. The voice couldn't touch that, whatever tack it took.

I'm your friend, Lourdes, the voice said. *Surely I have proved that to you by now.*

I can't wait to get home, Lourdes thought, imagining herself, step by step into her studio. The erotic surge she felt as she imagined the waiting canvas was like the sweetest promise.

On her way back to her apartment, Lourdes decided to sit for awhile in the park where the native women did their laundry and sold handicrafts. She wanted to savor her sense of anticipation—and her present. Lourdes liked the large semi-circular pool of water, fitted on its straight side with many sinks where women beat their beautiful traditional woven blouses or washed their dirty babies, dipping water from the standing pool with bright plastic bowls. She liked the hand looms with which the women bound themselves to the trees in the park, situating themselves so they could watch their wares and their children while they wove.

After a few minutes, Lourdes pulled out her sketch pad and began to sketch. If Lourdes drew, perhaps she wouldn't be inundated with requests to buy nuts, carved wooden masks, weavings of every imaginable shape and purpose. And perhaps the objects of her attention wouldn't feel as intruded upon as they might if she took a photo. She was especially taken with one family, a young girl of about five with a sharp chin and directive air who was showing her three year old sister how to strap their year old brother on her back, while the mother, a thin woman with a striking face, far more Aztec in its feature than Mayan, wove a bright red length of cloth. The glance she shared with her daughters was a wonderful blend of pride, fatigue, fondness and detachment.

Lourdes felt the warm breath on her neck before she heard the voice. A small girl in a plaid skirt and white pleated blouse and white kneesocks leaned her elbows on the back of the bench. She stared intently at Lourdes' drawing, then touched the paper gently with her rather grimy fingertips, exploring its unfamiliar texture.

"How much?"

"Nothing," Lourdes said. It was too difficult to explain in her nearly non-existent Spanish that this was only a sketch.

"I take, you give," the girl said.

Lourdes gestured with her charcoal to show the sketch wasn't finished. The girl settled in close beside her to wait. She inspected Lourdes' drawing board, pulling it up on her lap and starting to pull the paper out of the pocket. When Lourdes stopped her, the girl flashed her an exquisite smile. Her hair was very short, ragged, as if she had cut it herself with blunt scissors. She fixed her eyes on the family Lourdes had been drawing, an expression of intense interest on her face.

"What do you study?" Lourdes asked in Spanish, pointing at the girl's uniform and her worn blue knapsack.

The girl answered in Spanish, then mimed drawing and adding and subtracting and reading, when the inadequacy of Lourdes' Spanish became obvious. Then she just looked back and forth between Lourdes' drawing and the family who were serving as her models. She shook her head and pointed to the loom, indicating that Lourdes had shifted its location. Lourdes shrugged.

"Artistic license," she tried to say, then just tore the sketch from the pad and handed it to the little girl, who inspected it closely. She touched the charcoal gingerly with her finger, blowing the powder from the paper with a low, steady huffing as if she was starting a fire. Then she turned the sketch over and stared with equal intentness at the blank underside. She looked up at Lourdes with a radiant smile.

"Mine?"

"Yours," Lourdes said. She sat there watching the girl walk quickly away across the lawn. Her hips had that wonderful little swagger that the indigenous girls in their straight skirts had, something set in motion by the stillness of their shoulders and neck under the trays of goods they all carried insouciantly on their heads. It was carriage as much as features or clothing that defined the indigenous here. Maybe she isn't what she appears, Lourdes thought. Maybe she is passing.

Maybe we all are, the voice said.

Not you, Lourdes thought.

Try me, the voice said with her deep throaty laugh.

That's all I do, Lourdes thought wistfully.

As she stood up, Lourdes noticed the beauty salon across the street and on impulse decided to have her hair trimmed in honor of the dinner invitation for this evening she had just received from Simon. It was mentioning that only women would be present that made Lourdes think of the trim. Women were more demanding—or was it that they were more appreciative of the efforts they all took to keep themselves up.

When she walked into the small beauty salon, it seemed filled with people. As Lourdes turned to leave, a beautiful young woman approached and asked what she wanted. Lourdes pointed to her hair, took the ends in one hand and snipped at them with the other. The young woman nodded and gestured to the line of wooden chairs set in front of the open, barred window.

Lourdes, unable to say "another time" in Spanish, sat down to wait. The young woman went back to cutting the hair of a boy of about ten, while an older woman working at the chair next to her clipped the straight, shoulder length hair of a sedate looking girl of about eight. A third woman, stockier, her own hair neatly braided to her waist, tried to lift a small squirming girl into the last of the salon chairs.

"No," the girl said.

A middle-aged man sitting two seats down from Lourdes smiled encouragingly at the little girl, who set her feet more firmly on the floor, pushing her chest out. The father shrugged.

"She doesn't want," he said, in English. At first Lourdes thought he was speaking to the hairdresser, but then she realized from the uneasy scanning motion in his eyes, that he was talking to a fair-complexioned white haired man who had come to stand in the doorway smoking a cigarette.

"You tell her if she doesn't shut up I'll wop her one," the old man said in English. His voice was gruff and spoke of years of booze and tobacco. Lourdes should know. "I'm not having those kids back in the house until they look presentable."

The sedate little girl in the middle chair looked up and caught her father's eye in the mirror and smiled. She put a hand up and stroked her neatly turned hair. The boy kept his eyes glued on his knees.

"Her sister's getting her hair cut. Tell her to shut up and act like her sister," the old man said.

The hairdresser who was trying to quiet the screaming girl, looked up at the father and said, "*No quiere.*" She doesn't want.

"Don't care what the little bitch wants," the old man said to the father, stabbing out his cigarette with the toe of his white tennis shoes. "She does what I say or I'll beat the daylights our of her. Hear me?" He left.

Lourdes stared down at her hands, then off at the wall. I have to get out of here, she thought. She could feel rather than see the old man standing on the other side of the barred, open window behind her. She could smell the tobacco emanating from his clothes. The father gave her a placating smile as he went over to his small daughter, who was now wriggling determinedly down from the chair on her belly. He knelt down beside her trying to talk to her, but she kept yelling and shaking her head. "*Mi pelo. Mi pelo.*" *My* hair. *My* hair. Lourdes felt her hand go to her own hair automatically. I've got to get out of here, she thought again, but her muscles felt like lead.

The father gathered the little girl in his arms, but instead of heading back to his seat, he carried her over to the salon chair. When he tried to settle her into it, she began shaking with violent sobs. The hairdresser stood there with her arms folded over her chest, her expression unreadable. The other two hairdressers continued their ministrations to the other two children, not looking into the mirror, just focusing on their scissors, the gleaming black hair, their own brown hands.

The father grabbed the little girl as she began to wriggle off the seat again. He lifted her up and set her, more roughly now, into the seat. When she screamed and tried to escape again, he lifted her up and set her even more forcefully down on the seat. A third and a fourth time, he threw her forcefully down on the seat. Each time the little girl screamed fiercely and struggled out again.

Staring into the large mirror, Lourdes watched, her eyes as blank, her face as expressionless as the three hairdressers and the girl's older brother and sister. The father still wore his little appeasing smile.

Stop it, Lourdes thought. Someone has to stop this.

When the father threw the girl with both hands back onto the seat for the fifth time, suddenly the fight went out of her. She just sat there with a glazed look in her eyes, her head set at a slight angle. Once she was assured of the child's passivity, the hairdresser gently pulled a little cape around her shoulders. She lifted her hair up from her shoulders and gently began to brush it. As she did so, the chair turned, so Lourdes could see the girl's face clearly. The eyes terrified her, they were so blank.

Lourdes felt a dreadful sense of recognition.

You've been there, the voice said. *When are you coming back, Lourdes.*

This isn't about me, Lourdes answered back.

The white haired man came to the doorway, another lit cigarette in his hand. "About time," he said.

All three hairdressers bent their heads to the children. The little girls continued to stare out blankly into space, nothing in her body or face registering the presence of her grandfather.

This has happened more than once, Lourdes thought.

You should know, the voice said. Its tone was so tender it filled Lourdes with nausea.

Where did she go? Lourdes heard a small girl's voice inside her asking urgently.

Nobody's home, the voice said. *She's safe.*

"You don't know what you're saying," Lourdes said.

But you do, the voice answered.

Lourdes stared at her hands, beginning to draw them in her mind, centimeter by centimeter, loyal to every crack and crevice and curve.

"You?" the young woman asked, leaning over to catch Lourdes attention. She mimicked washing Lourdes hair, but Lourdes shook her head. Then she mimicked clipping Lourdes hair and gestured toward her chair. Lourdes thought at first she wouldn't be able to move, but the woman's eyes locked with hers, and they were so fierce, so insistent, that Lourdes could feel some energy, some will returning. For her entire haircut, she kept her eyes locked on the mole on the right side of the hairdresser's lips, so perfectly placed that it looked as if it could be painted on. She willed everything else in the mirror to dissolve, the doorway to the foyer, the open window. She did not look over to her left, even when the two hairdressers released their charges, although she could feel the father go over and lift the smallest girl from her seat and carry her gently out of the salon.

When Lourdes got home from the salon, she went immediately to her studio and pulled out one of the large sketch pads she had brought with her. She opened it, then closed it again, deciding that she needed to sit out on the little patio. She needed the clear sky above her, the glimpses of the trumpet-shaped flowers of the neighbors pomegranate tree. She needed, when she stood, to see the volcano sweeping the whole town into its embrace. The dim light in her studio reminded her too much of the light in the beauty salon.

The drawing she made showed the little girl's head aslant, arm resting on the armrests of the salon chair, her eyes dazed, her thumb in her mouth. A man's large hands were on her shoulders, the motion ambiguous as to whether he was lifting her up or throwing her down.

The next drawing was just of her face, the angle distressingly acute, as if her neck was broken, those big blank eyes which mirrored the figure of the hair dresser, with her arms crossed over chest, her hands gripping her elbows.

The next drawing showed the father lifting the little girl up to his shoulders in order to throw her down into the chair. The next moved out a little and showed the hairdresser with her arms crossed, the grandfather, smoking, reflected in the mirror, his confident figure framed by the doorway, the light emanating around him in rays.

And the last one showed Lourdes in the middle chair of the row of plastic chairs under the window, the three salon chairs, the father at the farthest one, lifting the little girl up to throw her, and an equal distance from Lourdes, the grandfather in the doorway, his shadow falling at her feet.

Throne of Grace, she kept titling them. Throne of Grace.

She set them all out on the concrete next to the wall of the patio, weighting each of them down with a stone. She kept staring at them, unable, yet, to feel anything. Holding herself heavy in her body so she wouldn't sink into the little girl's glazed eyes.

In her arms she could feel her sister's weight as a small child when Lourdes would hold her after one of her hysterical outbursts, the way Jacquie fixed her eyes on Lourdes face as her sister rocked her, their mother making her love-hungry ruckus with some man or another in the next room. "I'm here," Lourdes would keep murmuring to her. "I'm still here."

But were you? the voice asked. *Were you really, Lourdes? Weren't you just as lost as she was?*

It has to stop, Lourdes said, her body quietly rocking to that old rhythm. Somewhere it has to stop.

Like the almighty buck? the voice asked. *And always with you, Lourdes? Wasn't she just asking for it? It was only a haircut after all.*

"It was hers," Lourdes said. "Her hair. She used it to hide herself, to protect herself."

She saw the appeasing look on the father's face as he rose from the chair.

"Goddamn coward," Lourdes said, the tears beginning. "Goddamn coward."

Think of Isaac. There are precedents.

Lourdes shook her head, the tears streaming. But what was making her cry was the image of the bowl of her own clasped hands, the wedding ring, the way all of the fingers hinged, the numbness slowly flooding all her muscles, the pristine clarity with which her mind had recorded the dirty blue walls of the salon, the posters of the white women with their blonde windblown hairstyles, the intensity of the light and wind coming in through the window that opened onto the street, the demure lowering of the eyelids of the three hairdressers.

"Jesus Christ," she whispered. "*I* let it happen."

No, the voice said. *That's just the point. Then and now. You didn't. But that doesn't mean you're not sitting on the hot seat.*

Throne of Grace, Lourdes murmured, rocking, rocking, her arms numb again with the weight of her little sister.

We believe what we've got to believe, the voice said wearily. *Believe me.*

"Anything earth-shattering happen since I saw you this morning?" Simon asked, leaning down to give Lourdes a kiss on her cheek.

"Yes," Lourdes surprised herself by saying, surprised herself even more by breaking into tears.

"This sounds too interesting for words," Simon said, his voice a low murmur, as comforting as the arms he firmly closed around her. "You want to share it with everyone? You think it can wait until they leave? Or we can pretend to have a hot tryst in the bedroom and you can tell me all right now."

"Simon, control yourself," Rosemary called out imperiously. "I can see what you're up to from out here. She's barely set foot in the house and you're putting the make on her."

Simon lifted Lourdes heavy dark hair and set his lips to her ear. "My reputation is in your hands," he whispered.

Lourdes started laughing so hard she began choking.

"From foreplay to Heimlich. No one has ever said I'm not adaptable," Simon said as he turned Lourdes around to face the dark narrow hallway that led out to the garden.

Lourdes nodded to the three women who sat around a large black iron table. She knew two of the women—Marie from the yoga and drawing sessions, and the older woman from the drawing sessions, Rosemary. The third woman, a slender athletic looking woman with shoulder length blonde hair and astonishingly direct gray eyes was a stranger to her. Lourdes had furtively wiped her cheeks as she walked down the hall but she still felt as if her cheeks were grimy as a small child's. She fought off the impulse to wipe them again. Instead she put out her hand.

"We kiss here, dear," Rosemary corrected her. "Whatever our country of origin." She lifted her face and turned her cheek to Lourdes.

"Both cheeks if you're French like me," Marie said.

"But I'm fine with a handshake since I'm still acculturating," the third woman said, getting to her feet. "My name is Ginny Fox. I'm an old friend of Simon's." She had a fascinating voice, low but absolutely clear and resonant. Lourdes thought of the tones of wind chimes.

"Wine?" Simon asked. "Or would you prefer something milder in your condition?"

The three women looked at her inquisitively. "Wine would be fine," she told Simon. "It's not what it sounds like," she said to the women. "I don't know what got into me. Simon opened the door and asked how my day was going and I just broke into tears. It's not like me."

"He's had that effect on me too," Ginny said with a laugh. "Embarrassing as hell, isn't it?" She leaned back in her chair and looked up at Lourdes with a reassuringly cool expression.

"What happened?" Marie asked. "If you do not usually cry, something big must have occurréd."

"You think we might exchange professions, addresses, phone numbers before we start asking for the more intimate details of each other's lives," Simon said, setting one hand on Lourdes' shoulder as he handed her a glass of red wine with the other. He pulled up chairs for both of them.

"I can't stand the suspense," he said. "Tell us, Lourdes."

"It's something that happened at the beauty salon."

"They didn't get all the gray out?" Simon asked.

"Hush," Ginny Fox said.

"There was this family," Lourdes began. "This little girl." She felt her throat tighten.

Go on, the voice said. *Get it out. Get it out of you.*

I can't, Lourdes thought, staring blankly around her and feeling the tears beginning to roll down her cheeks.

"This isn't like me," she said again.

"Perimenopause," Rosemary said kindly. "If any of us are still strangers to it, it won't be for long."

"Excuse me?" Simon said.

"You're an honorary old bag," Rosemary said. "Act like it. Comfort her."

"What happened to this little girl?" Marie asked.

"She didn't want her hair cut. Her older brother and sister were already in two of the chairs and women were working on them. I was ready to leave and come back later, but one of the hairdressers was so insistent I take a seat, I just gave in. The little girl didn't want her hair cut. Their father was sitting two seats away from me. He kept looking at his daughter with this smile, you see, like he understood her. And he'd look at me with this kind of apologetic look. The little girl was shaking her head and saying, '*No quiero. No quiero.*' The father would have given in to her, but then this American man, an old man, came to the doorway smoking a cigarette and threatened the father, said he'd beat up the little girl if she didn't get her hair cut."

"What a bully—" Rosemary said.

"He meant it," Lourdes said. "It wasn't just words, he meant it. So the father started to throw the little girl into the chair. The hairdresser didn't want him to. No one wanted him to. He kept throwing her into the chair harder and harder—and then she just stopped fighting. She just left. She just left her body. And she sat there, her eyes so blank and empty, like a dead person, and the hairdresser cut her hair and the other hairdressers worked on the other children and the father came and sat back down on his seat and he smiled at me like I would understand."

Everyone at the table waited silently for her to continue. Lourdes finally lifted her eyes for the first time since she'd begun talking. The look on their faces was reassuring to her, both horrified and kind. She could feel herself beginning to breath regularly, deeply, for the first time since this had happened.

"The grandfather," she said, then choked. "He came back in. He saw the little girl like that and all he said was, 'About time,' and then he left again."

"We didn't *stop* him," Lourdes said. The bowl of her hands mesmerized her again. It looked so deep, the wave of her fingers so close nothing could slip through.

"Which one?" Ginny asked. "The father or the grandfather?"

"The father wouldn't have done what he did except for the grandfather," Lourdes said. "He was so afraid of the grandfather—"

"That he was an abusive bastard himself. Some excuse," Simon said.

"I want you to point him out to me," Rosemary said. "If he's American, I probably know him."

"He had a tattoo on his right arm," Lourdes said. "I didn't get a good look at it. But it's her face I can't get out of my mind. It's what happened to her that is haunting me. And the idea that this wasn't a one time thing, that it kept happening, keeps happening."

"It's a terrible thing to be little and filled with will," Marie said, taking a sip of her wine and setting the glass back down on the table and meditatively turning it around by its stem.

"It is a terrible thing to be driven out of your own body," Lourdes said.

"We come back," Rosemary said, putting her arm on Lourdes shoulder. "It's a kind of self-protection. It keeps us from losing ourselves forever."

"But at what cost?" Lourdes said, staring steadily at each of these unfamiliar faces. "That's what I can't seem to get over. At what fucking cost? I could have stopped it."

"How?" Ginny asked. "Attacking the father? The grandfather? Calling the police? You think in the long run she'd have been better off for that?"

"Yes," Simon said. "She'd have known people could object—that ultimately she wasn't helpless."

"I don't know what I would have done," Marie said. "It's not our country, after all. The father was from here, even if the grandfather was your countryman."

"We won't claim him," Simon said. "We'll pretend he's Australian or German."

"It was the look in her eyes," Lourdes said. "And the sound. The sound of her little body hitting the seat again and again. And the cigarette smoke. And the grandfather standing out there on the curb, staring out at the people in the park, like nothing out of the ordinary was happening."

"For him, it obviously wasn't." Puzzled, Lourdes looked at Ginny. "Out of the ordinary," she said.

"But for you, yes," Marie said reaching over and putting her hand over Lourdes. "Since you can't change this, how will you exorcise it?"

Is that what my drawing has always been, Lourdes wondered. An exorcism. All this time I thought it was an invitation.

You can't have one without the other, the voice said.

"Put wanted posters out," Rosemary said. "We'll let Marie be our forensic artist. Lourdes's drawings are too impressionistic."

"Maybe that will change," Marie said.

"It makes you realize how precious our will is," Ginny said gently. "That life without it isn't worth anything."

"She was conserving hers," Rosemary said firmly. "You must believe that, Lourdes. I had such a hard time with my foster children, letting them go back into their old environments, until I learned to love their defense mechanisms as much as I loved their spirits. Denial and dissociation bought them time. Time to become bigger, stronger. Time to learn something different about the world. Time to become good shepherds to their souls."

"All he was interested in really was pleasing," Lourdes said. "The father—that's all he cared about. That we would understand. That smile of his made me sick, but you know, I may have answered it. That is the most frightening thing of all, I might have given him the idea that what he did was all right."

"You can't turn the clock back," Marie said. "How will you move it forward, Lourdes?"

Lourdes looked at the French woman, something in her releasing as she stared into her stony blue eyes. She could feel rather than see her drawings laid out around her on the patio.

She's a picture of my own soul, Lourdes thought. I am almost fifty years old and that little girl is a picture of my own soul.

Hold her close, the voice said. *Love her like a mother who will never desert her.*

"I don't know," Lourdes said, still holding Marie's cool blue eyes.

"You will share with us your understanding, when it arises, no?"

Lourdes felt some pure energy building in her arms, her legs, making her lungs fill deeply. She wanted to go home immediately. She wanted to feel a piece of charcoal in her right hand, feel the texture of her sketch paper under the palm of her left, she wanted to let whatever this was that had been building in her go and go and go. The exhilaration she felt at the prospect was enormous. She folded it now into attention to the party.

"Thanks for listening," she said with a shrug. "Sorry for taking up so much of your time. It isn't like me."

"You have to stop saying that," Simon said. "I personally like hysterical, attention-grabbing women. They raise the energy level in any gathering. And you kept us distracted until the lasagna was done, so you served a useful social function."

Lourdes enjoyed the rest of the evening—Marie's stories of some of her tenants, Rosemary's description of the collective of indigenous women she directed. Although Ginny Fox didn't volunteer much information, there was something about her that appealed to Lourdes, something cool and stringent that separated wheat from chaff, right from wrong. What she liked most was how at rest she felt out there in Simon's garden, as if nothing terrible had happened. She had opened her heart—or had it torn open—and nothing terrible happened. The sound of the women's voices, Simon's voice like a steady undertow, rocked her, brought her back to herself. It reminded her of the comfort she felt at the sound of Seth and Evan's voices when they were young, how they consoled her, made her feel part of something. But this was different because these women wanted nothing from her—or if they did it was something that pleased Lourdes, some density, some complexity of being. They weren't asking her to be an empty vessel, a welcoming container for their own distress.

However comfortable she felt, she was the first to leave, the lure of her studio proving too strong for her. As Simon walked her to the door, she heard Rosemary saying, "Perhaps you can help me with my latest dilemma.

My new little maid is proving to be a kleptomaniac. I don't want to fire her, but I can't see any alternative."

"Thanks for coming," Simon said. "Even if you weren't yourself, I like the persona you presented. I think everyone did. Maybe you should let her out more often. Your first multiple."

Lourdes stepped back a second, her hands on his forearms, memorizing his features to use later that evening.

"I look forward to repaying your hospitality," she said.

"My calendar is your calendar."

"Good, because mine still looks pretty blank."

"But you're planning to remedy that, no?" Simon said, imitating perfectly Marie's wonderfully piercing stare.

"*Sí cómo no*," Lourdes said.

When she returned to the house, Lourdes went immediately to her studio. All night the drawings kept coming. There was a drawing of a little girl climbing into the chair, a faint line of blood wreathing her forehead. And another of Lourdes sitting with her eyes fixed on the bowl of her hands, the same fine wreath of blood marking her forehead, the drops falling into the liquid brimming inside her cupped hands. Then a drawing of a tall man, blonde like Simon, holding the little girl in his arms, but his hands are missing, there is only a sheer surface, the holes into which they need to be pegged. There is a drawing of the grandfather, his tattoo obvious on the arm that closes over the waist of the woman in a short shift who lies on his lap like Christ released from the cross. The woman's hands and feet are marked with stigmata, a wreath of roses around her brow, the blood from the thorns running gently down her face like tears. *God mourns what he has done*, Lourdes wrote.

You wish. Those guys never think twice. But don't give up. You're getting somewhere with these, Lourdes. Somewhere new.

"I know," Lourdes said, breathing in deeply, for the first time accepting the inevitability of this conversation. "Isn't it exciting."

It goes deeper than excitement, Lourdes. If you dare to know.

Home, Lourdes thought, the feeling of release spreading all through her. *It goes home.*

And for the first time since she arrived in Antigua, neither the thought, nor the reality, broke Lourdes' heart.

CHESS MASTER
(Mamí Concepción)

  What I love about the girls at the home is that they are so ruthless in their desires—whether it is for more bread, like Carmen; or for sex, like the girls who have been too long on the streets, like Paula and Soledad; or for self-sufficiency and for understanding, like this new indigenous girl, Mikela. What I like about the girls is I see myself in them and it pleases me and fills me with hope for all of us. That is what I used to feel when my daughter Marcela would come home, brooding on some little mystery: why lying could make us happy, perhaps, or why the Sisters talked about God as if he were a bully. I delighted in the waywardness of her mind. It made me happy—as if we were truly free in ways that we never imagined. But now my children have grown too conventional. They believe life is a question of divining, then minding, the rules—even when these rules deny their own experience. Why else, for example, would my daughter Marcela want to marry her muscle-bound, brain-dead novio? Why else is my son David coming up with a five-year career plan complete with goals and quotas in a country whose major accomplishment is walking backwards faster than its neighbors?

  My girls at the home, whatever good fortune comes their way, are never going to believe that good fortune came from following rules, or that it really had anything to do with them at all. They are, if you will, warped by life. I actually see them as freed by it—by all those events so beyond their control. The papas who would rather kill them and their mamas than let them go on and live their own lives—so they hide out with us, changing homes every month until their trail grows so cold their father finds another woman, makes *other children, and leaves them alone. Or the little indigenous girl who ran away, the one whose mother strung her to the rafters. Mikela's sister. You're never going to get her to believe that we are less dangerous to her than her own mama. And she has a point. At least her mother took her seriously enough to try to kill her. We just filled out our forms when she arrived, then let her slip through our fingers like water. A twelve year old with a belly like a small melon, pfft, through the window. Who's to say she isn't better off out there?*

I suppose I couldn't do what I do if I wasn't a faithful woman, if I didn't know that God meets us both coming and going. Otherwise, I might despair when a girl runs away. Or when they do cruel things to each other at night when we are not watching. But, I see all their actions as good tests for God. I have great confidence. I wonder what miracle he is going to work to set things right. I feel like I am watching a great chess master at work. All of us, the girls, me, the people of the town, the police, we are moving the black pieces, the castles and knights, the bishops and pawns. And God just yawns, or smiles, and slides his own piece in where it can't be dislodged. A madonna. A butterfly. A crucifix. A San Simón. We look at our pieces, then at the new ones he's invented—dismayed at the incongruity and also a little, secretly pleased. Who can call him on it? I like to watch his intelligence at work. I like knowing my only real job is to appreciate—his warmth, his sense of humor, his compassion.

Take those sisters, Mikela and Natividad for example. You could say their lives are tragic. The brutal poverty of both countryside and city. The crazy mother. Whatever led to the older sister being knocked up on the streets at twelve. The way little Mikela slips away at night to take her sister food and tried to keep her from sniffing glue. They way they have lost their own people and will never be taken in by mine.

Or you could say they are wonderful chess partners for God—Natividad with her wonderful ability to draw and her stubborn refusal to use any of the world's terms to make sense of what has happened to her; Mikela with a curiosity so pure it casts off light, whatever she looks at, her striking intelligence, and that determination that is almost holy to save her sister whatever rules she may have to break to do so. Don't you think God loves to make use of their gifts to check and checkmate their difficulties? Don't you think he loves the story he is making of their lives?

I believe it is my job to tell that story to them, to try to get them to see themselves as God may see them—valiant and ruthless and filled with a holy hardness that can, like diamond, scar glass and all that cheap complacence that surrounds us everywhere. Isn't that what my grandmother did for me? Telling me, every day, how the Señor had blessed her and my grandfather with my company. It was hard on my mother, she knew, to give me up. But she had insisted and what could my mother do but give in to her own mother? But now my mami had more children of her own, so everyone was satisfied. How many years did I live believing absolutely that story my grandmother told me about how I came to live with her? When I went to visit my mother and father and their four other children, I never wondered at my own situation. I was convinced I was special, chosen.

Who is to say my grandmother was lying—that her story was any less true than my mother and father's story? It was certainly more healing—and since when is it better to turn our backs on mercy? Perhaps I was made to enrich the days of my grandmother and grandfather, even if to do so meant that my mother needed, at seventeen, to become ill at the sight of me, to never be able to welcome me into the family she and my father began to build intentionally five years later, after they had finished their university careers. I was, and always will be, my mother's enormous error—and the sweetest surprise of my grandmother's life. Why would I choose to believe my mother's rationalizations over my grandmother's compassion? Why believe I was too difficult, sickly, willful—rather than that my mother so loved her mother she gave her a pearl without price? Given these experiences, why would I not embrace, always, the role of the outcast as the most privileged position, the most real, the one where God hums more continuously in our ears because we are sharper of hearing, more open of heart.

I love the girls in the home because they are more than survivors. They are God's wild legion. They know, through the fierceness of their hungers, that God has put them on this earth for a good reason, that he has need of each of them exactly as they are. He is never going to demean their suffering—or their hopes. When I feel, in my deepest heart, the joy of this reality, I know, down there where it will never leave me, that God is working the same miraculous transformation in my own life and I have what is almost a lust to be present, to see and appreciate what is happening all around me. To be, every day, more and more deeply surprised by life and God's great, good outwitting of that which maims, drains, damages and annihilates. I want to feel his hands on my shoulders, impelling me to step in sometime, somewhere, as he whispers check or checkmate. I want my whole body to ache with the knowledge that my existence is a gift, a good—just because it is a disruption, imposition, a shock to the intentions of those around me. I want my grandmother's world, the world of my children when they were small, the world of the wild girls in the home, to be the real ones—ones where I am, just as I am, a sweet surprise, a scandal.

Chapter 7
LIES

When Mikela found Natividad, she was going to tell her sister that Señora Rosemary had let her go because she had caught her carrying away some of the Señora's dead husband's paints. She was going to tell Natividad that she couldn't be thieving for her anymore.

"To steal from the living is one thing," Señora Wilma scolded her. "To steal from the dead, Mikela—"

"Is better," Mikela said. "They will not miss it. You tell me what the señora is going to do with these paints, this paper with big stains of mold. You told her yourself they were worthless." Mikela had spoken so boldly because if she didn't, she would cry. She felt so ashamed having seen the look in Señora Rosemary's eyes when the old woman came up behind her and set her hand on Mikela's shoulder as Mikela was opening the door to leave.

"*Mi amor*," the old woman said. "Do you have something you want to tell me?"

"I'll be back on Friday," Mikela had said, turning quickly back to the door.

"Just tell her to open her bags, Señora Rosemary," Señora Wilma had said. "She will not confess. It is not our way, except, sometimes with the *sacerdote* in the confessional. But usually not there either."

Señora Wilma leaned down and took the plastic bag from Mikela's hands. On the top were the fruits and breads Señora Wilma had given her.

"Señora Rosemary is missing some things of her husband's. I had put them aside for her."

This wasn't true. Señora Wilma had intended to throw them away when the old woman wasn't looking. She had told Mikela so herself. But at that moment, Mikela felt so sick in her heart and her stomach she had no words to defend herself. For Señora Wilma had not thrown the paints in the trash, she had just intended to. Mikela couldn't wait because she would not be back before the trash men and she wanted Natividad, not the trash men's children, to have those paints. She had ducked into the dead señor's little cabaña on her way out and had seen the paints still lying there, and she had just opened her bag and slipped them in under the fruit and the bread that Señora Wilma had given her. No one had see her. She was sure no one had seen her, but now it seems the two women had set her a test.

Now, Señora Wilma was pulling out of Mikela's bag the old crumpled tubes of paint and setting them down on the concrete. She also pulled out the pieces of paper Mikela had rolled into a tube even though they were dirty with mold and marked on one side.

"You should be ashamed, my child," she said. But the glance she gave Mikela wasn't really angry, rather curious—- as if she were trying to understand what kind of girl Mikela was.

The look Señora Rosemary gave her was worse—it was just sad, as if Mikela had become all of a sudden someone the Señora did not know. Never before had Mikela had the feeling of falling so fast and so low in someone's heart, like a stone.

"To steal from the living is one thing," Señora Wilma had scolded her. "To steal from the dead, Mikela—"

And Mikela found her words. But they made everything worse. Then Señora Wilma was angry, but she was also fair.

"She did not know their value to you Señora Rosemary. She did not do it to be cruel."

"Why *did* you do it?" Señora Rosemary asked. "Don't they buy you art materials for school?"

"The girls at the home," Mikela said. "They are always asking me to buy them something. They are so jealous that I have the privilege of working for you." Of course, the girls at the home didn't know. But Mikela was already a thief, why should she not be a liar too?

"You could have asked me," the Señora said. "Now I have no choice, you know. I can't tolerate theft. You can't come back here, my dear."

"Ever, Señora Rosemary?" Señora Wilma asked.

"For a month at least," Señora Rosemary said. "It's the principle, Mikela. I don't allow lying and I don't allow stealing. I can tolerate strong words, clumsy actions, even a little laziness—but never lying or stealing."

All Mikela could do was nod and keep her eyes on the floor. As soon as the big wooden doors closed behind her, the tears started down her cheeks. There were two things Mikela's people never forgave—being a woman of the streets and being a thief—and now she as well as Natividad were orphans of the worst kind. Now it was not only their own people but even the foreigners and the ladinos like Señora Wilma who would have nothing to do with her. They would tell Mamí Concepción and the Mother Superior. Mikela would be asked to leave the girls' home and the school. And all because she couldn't wait.

Mikela found herself moving blindly, her eyes streaming tears so salt they burned her skin, her empty hands closed into two tight fists in the center of which was only cold, damp air. She stumbled on in the direction of the park hoping that today she would be able to find Natividad there and that her sister's nose would not be running with the glue. She wished she could put her arms around her sister and bury her head in her sister's neck like a little girl. She wished she could find some comfort there. For even though we sin, we ache to be forgiven, just like Sister Carmen said.

But when she found Natividad, curled up in the corner of the yard where she and Pablo and Tomás slept, Mikela knew immediately she couldn't tell her sister what had happened. At first Mikela thought Natividad was sleepy from the glue. But Natividad's right eye was swollen shut and the left side of her face was too big. She looked like their mother after their father had let the drink capture his soul.

Mikela grabbed her sister by the arm. "We must go," she said. When Natividad mumbled something, Mikela just shook her as hard as she could. "This is not for you, it is for the baby that we do these things."

"It is because of the baby that Pablo—"

"Let's go," Mikela said. She no longer felt so sick with shame, but she felt very tired. She didn't know where she was going to take Natividad. It was already close to dark.

And then she thought of the ruins near the church of San Francisco.

They weren't so far away as the ones that Pablo and Tomás and their friends used. The boys did not visit the ruins near the church because there were people around all during the day selling food and weavings and rosaries and candles from the stalls that lined the courtyard of the church. They couldn't sniff their glue there or smoke their sweet cigarettes that made them so hungry or drink their rum.

The only problem was the woman who sold the tickets to the ruins and to the bathrooms. She would be suspicious of them going in at this hour, or at all, for it was not a place for people of the town, only tourists. She would be suspicious that Mikela could pay—and that her sister wore indigenous clothes while she wore the clothes of the ladina and had her hair cut short. She would also be suspicious of Natividad's swollen face, as would everyone they passed.

Mikela decided that the best thing to do was go into the church and wait until dark. No one would notice Natividad because it was the custom for their women to cover their heads in the church. That way, the only ones who would see Natividad's bruises were God and the Virgin of the Sorrows, *Virgen de Dolores*, and Jésus, (except that he often kept his eyes closed, his own sufferings were so great). Then, when it was dark, they could sneak into the ruins without the caretaker noticing.

So that is what they did, Mikela guiding Natividad down the quieter streets and keeping her arm around her sister. She knew they looked strange because the ladina and indigenous women were never friends—but that was better than people getting a close look at Natividad and thinking she was unloved or worthy of pity.

While Natividad sat in the back of the church, Mikela went outside and bought a yellow and a white candle. She took them over to light before the tomb of the good Hermano Pedro, who she had learned about in the school. He came with the conquistadors, but he did not do the terrible things the soldiers did. He did not see the indigenous as wild animals to be captured and caged or killed. He felt their hunger, shared their tears. Even now. Although he died hundreds and hundreds of years before, he was not completely a saint yet, but that was because the people in Rome were very slow and bureaucratic, just like their own government, Sister Carmen said with a laugh. Here, the people did not wait for Rome. They had too much need of the good brother's powers. The people here all knew personally of his powers, how he could cure the sick, especially children, how he could stick a branch in the ground and it would flower, his own faith was so large. Mikela lit a yellow candle for her sister, who was now an adult, and a white one for the baby, who had not yet come to this earth. They both needed protection. Mikela wondered if the baby's face was marked with bruises now, like Natividad's—and the thought made her feel so helpless and angry she began to cry. So she started to talk to the good Hermano Pedro and asked him, since he too had walked these streets as a man, since he had known hunger and sickness and death, what she should do for Natividad.

"She is my sister," Mikela kept telling the good brother. "I must help her. She thinks the glue will give her peace, but I do not believe this. She is lonely for her soul—but why would her soul wish to return to a body that has grown so crowded? Why would her soul wish to return to hunger and the pain of all those bruises? Why would her soul want to return to a mind that can remember how she lifted her skirts in the city—to a back that can still feel the scratches of our mother's broom—or to ears that still hear our mother singing, 'Death of me. Death of me.'"

Mikela kept talking and waving her hands and trying to explain to the good brother. She had to talk loudly and clearly and quickly so she could reach him where he was resting in his tomb. So many people came to him with their troubles, how else was Mikela to get herself noticed? And she needed to because it was just the same with Jésus and God—they were always surrounded by people clamoring for their attention—so the best thing was to engage the good intentions of one of the saints or the Holy Mother—because God and Jésus listened to them more because they were more important than a little girl like Mikela who was a thief and an orphan and a sinner.

"I am poor," she told the good brother. "And now I have no work and soon I may have no place to sleep and may not be able to return to school, but I promise you I will repay you ten times over for anything you do to help my sister. I will give you half of everything I ever earn. I will be your slave. Just help me keep her safe from whoever hit her and help me find a place to hide her until the baby comes. You have helped so many people, good brother, surely you can help me too."

And then, just as Mikela was opening her mouth to flatter the good brother some more, she felt a hand on her shoulder. A large hand. A woman's hand. An old woman's hand, covered with wrinkles. At first she thought it was Señora Rosemary come to forgive her.

"When I am very distressed in my heart, I go straight to God's

Mother," the Mother Superior said. "Not to the Virgin of Sorrows but the Virgin of the Sacred Heart, who is the advocate for all difficult and desperate causes. Perhaps you too could include her in your prayers. She never turns anyone away—and sometimes I feel she understands a little more quickly, with less explanation, what hurts the heart of a little girl or a grown woman. I am not saying our Hermano Pedro isn't powerful, just that she is too. Jésus cannot deny his mother anything."

Mikela nodded at what the Mother Superior said. She carefully kept her head turned away from the back of the church, where Natividad sat with her head covered with her old, torn rebozo.

"Isn't it time you were back at the home, my child?" the Mother Superior asked. "I was just straightening things after our class for the catechists. I know Mamí Concepción will be wondering where you are. And once we have given our prayers and our burdens to God, we need to go back to our lives with lightened hearts, secure that wiser minds and more agile hands are setting things to right."

So Mikela went and knelt at the small poster of the Virgin of the Sacred Heart, which was in a glass covered frame inside a little room filled with dusty plastic flowers. The room wasn't covered with metal plaques giving thanks for all the help she'd given. She was a ladina virgin—very pale, almost as pale as Señora Rosemary and her *extranjera* friends. Mikela thought the good Hermano Pedro might actually be a woman in disguise, just like Mikela had been disguised as a boy when she and Natividad lived in the city. If that was so, even if he was a Spaniard, he might understand her heart better than Jésus' mother, who never needed to pretend to be someone she wasn't. And the people had put up many metal plaques to his power—because only a saint who had walked these streets in the times of the conquistadors could understand how far the people who lived here could feel from God. God's mother couldn't understand that, could she? She could never feel so far from someone who had come from her own belly, could she?

"I hope you are not praying about your schoolwork, my child," the Mother Superior said, putting her hand on Mikela's shoulder again. It reminded Mikela of Señora Rosemary's gesture, but it did not feel so kind, for the Mother Superior's hands were heavier, like they carried God's judgment. "Your grades are the highest in your class. You are an example for your people. Before another month is past, we will move you to the next grade." The Mother Superior had done this once already because Mikela was a very quick learner.

    Mikela felt proud and angry at the Mother Superior's words and desperate to get back to Natividad. She was already planning how many blocks she would have to run away from the church in the direction of the girls' home in order to persuade the Mother Superior that she was really going there before it would be safe for her to turn back and return for Natividad. The fear that Natividad might leave and go back to Pablo turned Mikela's feet to wings and she ran faster than she had ever run before, running three blocks away from the church, then circling back. She caught Natividad on the corner and forced her to sit with her on the curb until they could slip into the church courtyard as the watchman was locking the far door to the courtyard. They hid in one of the empty stalls as he locked the other door.

    Mikela made Natividad wait for a long time before coming out of the stall. She listened very carefully to hear if the guard had locked himself in or out, but she heard no feet ringing on the cobblestones. Guards had shoes—just as she did, so they could not be very good thieves. They made too much noise. Mikela took her own shoes off and put them in her backpack and motioned for Natividad to take off her shoes as well and give them to her. Natividad looked rebellious, but Mikela insisted. Natividad now wore the plastic shoes from the market again. Something had happened to the heavy leather shoes they had given her at the girls' home, or perhaps Natividad thought those shoes, which their people never wore, might create suspicion and envy.

    Mikela took her sister by the hand and, staying in the shadows at the edge of the courtyard, they made their way toward the ruins. The front of the church was lit up brightly and Mikela could see all of the saints comfortably inside their little houses and she wished that she and Natividad each had a place that fit them so neatly, where they would never feel afraid. Mikela believed the saints never were afraid because they knew God was their close friend and would always help them—if not in this world (for most of the saints, she was learning in her school, had died most horrible deaths—just like her own people in the war), then in the next. Mikela wished her own life was one where she could be sure God was her friend—but God wasn't friends with people who lied or stole, for whatever reason, or who lifted their skirts in the capital, even if they were starving.

    Mikela wished God could be a little more understanding, but it was really too late to do anything about it. Maybe the Mother Superior was right and Mikela should start praying to the Virgin of Desperate Causes. Surely, she would have mercy on Natividad, even if she didn't have any left over for Mikela.

"*Dios te salve, Maria, llena era de gracias. El Señor es contigo, bendito eres entre todos las mujeres y bendito es el fruto de tu vientre, Jésus*," Mikela muttered to herself as she led Natividad into the entrance of the ruins. She had been there once before with her school and she tried to remember what it looked like. In her mind's eye, she could just remember many arches and broken walls, but when she tried to imagine her feet moving, she could find her way, even in the dark. The sudden sureness of her feet made her feel she was back in the country again, coming back from the fields .

"Slow down," Natividad said. "There may be holes here. Traps for soldiers."

Once, when their father had gone down to work on the coast at one of the sugar plantations, their mother made Natividad help her build a very deep trap near their house to capture any soldier or thief who might wander near. By then, their mother had met the soldier. Mikela thought she might have been trying to trick her own desire, not her family, with the trap. She remembered how Natividad had hated climbing down into that big hole and handing bucket after bucket of wet dirt and heavy stones up to Mikela or their mother. *Deeper*, is all their mother would say. When the hole got so deep their hands couldn't meet, Mikela tied a rope around the bucket and then wound the rope around a tree to help her pull the bucket out. She had to use the rope to help pull Natividad out at the end of the day too.

For months afterwards, Natividad would wake up crying because she dreamed she was in that pit and everyone had left, no one knew she was there. Their mother, she whispered to Mikela in the lowest voice she could, as if this were the worst part of the dream, had brought some banana leaves and palm branches and had set them over the top of the hole, so no one would ever know Natividad was there.

"Maybe she just didn't see you," Mikela would say.

"No," Natividad would whisper back. "She wanted me to die." And then she would sink back onto her mat so still that Mikela had to put her hand above her sister's face to make sure Natividad was still breathing.

"There are no traps here," she now said to Natividad. She made herself talk in a normal daylight voice, even though the tall shadows of the broken walls made her want to whisper. "I came here once before and I checked."

Natividad gripped Mikela's hand as she stumbled on a stone. "You're not going to leave me alone here, are you?"

"We'll find a safe place," Mikela said. "A place where you can sleep, where no one will find you. Tomorrow I will look for a better place. But I must go back to the girls' home or they will send the police out looking for me. If they find us together, they will punish you for leaving."

"What could they do?" Natividad said in a bored voice, which sounded just like Pablo. "They would just put me out in the street, where I live already."

"Mamí Concepción said they might put you in jail."

"It would be better than going back into the home."

"I don't want you to go very far from me, Natividad."

"The woman's prison is just across the street from the girls' home, Mikela. You could visit me often. You could join me there."

This made Mikela think about what might happen because of her thieving—but she blocked the thoughts out and concentrated on finding her footing on the path. Somewhere in her mind, her soul had drawn a map, making a perfect picture of the place in the ruins where Mikela could best hide Natividad. So all Mikela had to do was set her feet along the path she could see in her mind's eye. She was very grateful to her soul for being such a good friend to her and her sister, even if they didn't deserve it.

"We're almost here," she said, pulling Natividad out from under an arch and up a steep, grassy slope. "It's over to our right, the building I'm thinking about. It has a roof and some little rooms that no one goes into. You will be very safe from people and animals."

"I don't like being alone," Natividad said. "It's worse than anything."

"You're not alone," Mikela said. "The baby is with you always."

"What do *you* know, Mikela? What can you possibly know about that?" Natividad said in a strong, hissing voice. She scared Mikela, she was so alive, leaning toward her on the top of the hill. Her teeth gleamed in the moonlight, like the mouth of a wild dog.

"Trust me," Mikela said. "I will find you a place to stay, Natividad. One where the police will not find you. One where you are not alone. One where there are people who can help you when the baby comes." Mikela made her voice sound very steady and confident, although her mind was going very

very fast trying to imagine where she could possibly hide Natividad, how she could ever give her what she promised. But she must not be a liar to her sister. She would have to find these things.

Once Mikela had found the entrance to the building her soul had directed her to, her feet quickly took her to the small rooms that opened off on the left. She pulled her sister inside the one that was deepest into the ruin.

"Here is some food that the Señora Rosemary gave me. I will buy more food as soon as I can tomorrow, but it may not be until after school. Please do not leave, Natividad. You are safer here."

"Not safer from thieves and wild animals."

"But safer from Pablo, just as this town made us safer from the German, and the capital made us safer from our mother."

Something about the way Mikela was talking hurt Natividad so much she just put her hands around her knees and started rocking back and forth, sobbing. Even in the city, at the most terrible times, Natividad had never cried. Mikela knelt beside her and held her.

"Forgive me. Please forgive me. You are all I have. You and the baby."

But this just made Natividad sob harder. So Mikela put her arms around her sister and lay down with her and sang until Natividad was fast asleep. She sang songs she was learning in the church. Even after Natividad's breathing became very slow and steady, Mikela didn't get up for awhile.

She thought she could wait outside the home until the older girls who worked during the day came back from the night school. Mamí Concepción was on duty tonight, so maybe she would let Mikela in with the older girls. Mikela kissed her sister on her forehead and then started back toward the church, trying to make her mind run the map backwards, but it wasn't so good at that and she stumbled down a flight of stairs and stubbed her feet against several walls. Just as she reached the courtyard and saw the saints all luminous in their brightly lit little caves on the church wall, Mikela turned back. Mamí Concepción probably already knew about Mikela's thieving and had told the Directora. She wouldn't let Mikela in anyway. But more importantly, Mikela couldn't stand the idea of her sister sleeping all by herself in the little room in the ruins. Only if Mikela was there watching her would Natividad be safe. The image Mikela had of Natividad curled up on the dirt floor, the rebozo over her head to protect her face from the bats and the rats, felt too much like

Natividad's terrible dream of the hole their mother had made her build.

Mikela made her way quickly back to where her sister was sleeping and lay down beside her, folding her own body around her, closing her tight in her arms. Her hands lay flat on Natividad's big tummy, which moved continuously, as if she were feeling the back of someone crawling on their hands and knees under a rebozo. But the movement was also very slow and smooth, like someone diving in the sea. Mikela fell asleep with the feel of her sister's baby rubbing up through her skin to warm Mikela's own palms. She dreamt of strange animals swimming in the sea, more graceful than angels, the water holding them close, so close, just like the saints were held by the love of God.

THE SEEKER
(Marie)

Sometimes they come to me. I do not need to lift a finger. They ring my doorbell, and as soon as I slide the metal grate aside and peer through the bars, we recognize each other. It is that simple.

If the garage apartment is presently unoccupied, I smile and let them in. If it is occupied, I let them go, knowing someone else will come sooner or later. I've always felt quite easy about this, but last month when I saw Simon out there with his friend Ginny, I felt I'd done the wrong thing letting them go. I felt the same way six weeks earlier when Simon brought the other American, the one who is now in my yoga and drawing classes, Lourdes. I wonder if he and Patricó are in on this. That Patricó has asked him to disrupt my essential solitude. The woman, Lourdes, who came first wanted the apartment only for herself. Her husband was returning to the States. I thought about her too after I shut the grate and for several days was quite impatient with Gertrud, my current renter, for being so very twenty and German. I don't even like the Americans in general, so how strange that two of them, only weeks apart, set up this slight oscillation at first meeting.

I'm not a psychic. I don't believe in auras or energy flows or chakras, even though Patricó and I are so close and I stay with him often. I have made visits to San Simón, but that feels quite French to me—like taking my string bag to the mercado on Saturday and looking for the best bargains. But I do believe in chance, that it exceeds our imagination in directions both benign and destructive, and so, if we give ourselves up to it, it brings us back to ourselves, humbled, grateful, and happy to be home. I also believe the act of giving ourselves up like that enlarges our imagination so that the self we return to, however chastened, is larger for our departure and return. But when Simon brought these women, I questioned whether it was por azar as they say here. I did not give myself up to that possibility. And now I wonder why, for they stay in my mind these two.

I also believe in the power of recognition. Recognition is what makes these little journeys out of ourselves safe. We are assured, whatever happens, of meaning. It has taken me years to trust this capacity—to let the doors of my heart swing open freely, with a feeling of anticipation and interest.

I learned about the overwhelming power of chance when my only child, Colette, died twenty-five years ago. Childhood cancers are as random, brutal and senseless as the explosion that began our universe. With Colette's death, something in me changed so quickly, so completely, that both my husband and I had trouble taking it in. More difficulty than we did the overnight whitening of my hair once I heard her diagnosis. We made a family joke of that. It became me, Eduard said. But he didn't say that after Colette's death when I lost my powers of speech for long periods of time as well. For years, I fought off the implications of what had happened. Eduard did too. But it was true, I was a different person after Colette's last breath from the one I was holding her in her last hours.

I am not nostalgic for my dead child. I don't believe in an afterlife, a time when we will all be reunited. I don't feel remorse or recrimination for the years we didn't have together. She was nine when she died, so I had some idea of the woman she might have become. I would have liked her. We would have been friends I think. But at this point in my life I would be exactly where I am now whether she had lived or died.

Not necessarily this town, this country. But I would have divorced Eduard. I would have gone abroad. I would be a quiet woman with quick eyes who is more alive to the world inside her mind than the one outside her door. It would have taken me just as long to trust this sense of recognition, invitation.

It is difficult to be a skeptic and a mystic simultaneously, but I doubt, by nationality, temperament, and personal experience, I could be one without the other. What has taken me years is to learn how to bring these two impulses into harmonious collaboration. That is where recognition comes in, the collapse of inner and outer, when the world outside us just interests us in the simplest, most intimate way. When we see the smile of an unknown person on the outside of our grate, and we feel as if we had just taken a bite of the sweetest cake. Or we catch the eyes of another woman and it is like the welcome touch of cool water in our throat when we wake troubled from some chaotic and inconsequential dream.

Chapter 8
LUCID DREAMS AND ASTRAL TRAVEL

At first, Ginny thought she was in a bed, but then she felt the satin sides of the coffin against the back of her hands and arms, which were pressed down tightly against her sides. Will was leaning down over her.

"Boy, you really fucked up," he said, smiling his large white charismatic smile. "You sure didn't go halfway—not my Ginny-gin-gin. You should have taken some lessons from me." Will laughed, his mouth opening wide, so Ginny was staring straight down his clean red throat.

"What the hell," Ginny thought, waking abruptly, her heart racing. She heard her breath coming faster than it ever did when she was running and tried to bring it back under control. Her face was wet with sweat. She could still see the pain in Will's eyes, but it didn't change what she felt. She pulled the pillow up to her shoulders and leaned over and buried her face in it, letting her skin feel the soft caressing pressure, wiping the sweat from her forehead and under her eyes.

"Son of a bitch," she kept muttering as she brushed her face back and forth across the pillow. "Lessons from you. Son of a *bitch*, Will."

She quickly dressed in her running clothes, even though the sky wasn't yet blue. She needed to pound the distress out of her. Will was dead. The distance between them was permanent.

"You set yourself up, Ginny." Will had said to her. "Couldn't you have gotten it on with an engineer, my dear? Couldn't you have done it with a closeted nun? Someone, anyone, with just a smidgeon of discretion? Seems like you wanted to punish yourself."

"How would you know?" Ginny asked through gritted teeth as she pushed herself through that first wall of physical resistance.

She could smell the forced lilies in the cathedral in Chicago at Will's funeral, even stronger than the incense billowing from the censers. She could see Marcella standing up there in the pulpit reading her eulogy for her husband, so proud and controlled even in her grief. He had died of pneumonia allied with lung cancer, the obituary said. Who was going to contradict her?

"He owes me this," she had told Ginny. "I paid all our married life. Willingly, I'm not staying it wasn't willingly. But that doesn't make it any less of a debt."

Ginny had taken back the copy of her own eulogy that she had given to Marcella for comments. All her newly discovered home truths about Will were marked through with a thick red marker. "The rest of this is fine," Marcella said. "Those of us who experienced that side of Will, the complexity of his sexual nature, are the only ones in any position to speak of it. And out of respect for me, today no one will. Today we celebrate the man the world believed him to be, because he was that too. Is that clear?"

"Perfectly, Marcella."

"I loved him, Ginny. Don't lose sight of that. I knew him as well as anyone on this earth could—even you, my dear." Marcella's voice softened, and her brown hand rested gently on Ginny's shoulder. "Whatever it might appear like today, I don't simplify the man or the impact he had on my life or the lives of the other people who loved him and were loved by him. I sometimes think you paid the highest cost of all—and the saddest thing is you don't seem to know it."

But I do, Ginny thought, the sound of her feet colliding with the cobblestones echoed over and over again in the cool gray air. Lessons from you, Will! Lessons from you!

She spread her arms out like wings, just to be sure that the space was there, the empty air, for the feel of the satin sides of the coffin against the back of her hands was still so clear.

"I do not believe God has ever asked me to simplify my nature, rather to trust it and be true to it. I do not believe this disease is saying anything different," Will said when he told Ginny of his diagnosis.

"It is *my* choice," Marcella said. "I have a right to my privacy. Hypocrisy has nothing to do with it. Discretion is not the same as hypocrisy, Ginny."

"God isn't synonymous with social norms, Ginny."

Tell it, Will, she thought.

The church isn't synonymous with God, my dear, a woman's voice said so clearly that Ginny stumbled, looking around her with a sudden cooling of her blood. *Will isn't either.*

A small man dressed in torn green pants and a t-shirt crossed the street in front of her, his eyes trained on the cobblestones. He carried a huge bundle on his back, his head in rope traces to help him balance it. The volcano loomed nearly black against the pearly sky.

"You didn't believe, Ginny. You didn't believe God would let you be true to your own nature. If you had, wouldn't you have acted differently?" Will's voice was warm, so warm. Ginny felt, as she had all those years they worked together, comfortably enveloped in it. She had never felt invaded by Will, that is what she had loved about him. She felt so much herself around him, so intact.

Until now, the woman's voice said kindly. *He's really gotten to you now, hasn't he?*

I have to call Bob Althorpe and let him know I'm leaving the church, Ginny thought.

Why? the voice asked. *Why do you still feel you have to account to them for anything you do? You think they care, Ginny-gin-gin?*

But Ginny couldn't hear, the sound of her racing heart and her racing feet were both so loud inside her, and the images just wouldn't stop coming. Will's funeral, Bob Althorpe up there in his bishop's robes, his miter, giving Marcella's party line with total conviction. Four months earlier—Will and Bob and George Davidson at the meeting in Bob's office at the cathedral, all listening stone-faced to her own account of things. None of them had wanted to be alone with her. The meeting with the vestry, the senior warden, Mr. Rufus Johnson, crowing, literally crowing, with victory as he accepted her resignation. The last sermon before the whole congregation and the questions, without answers, that followed. The night of David's opening, walking into the museum and seeing her destruction walking toward her with an irresistible smile on her face. Doppelganger. And even so, the ache of longing that *was* David to her, how it made her want to cover her loins with her hands, it was so sharp.

I am doing it for me, Ginny told the voice. It has nothing to do with them. I'm doing it for me.

We believe what we need to believe, the voice said. *No one is going to stop you, Ginny.*

"Are you telling me to call or not to call?" Ginny asked.

"I'm suggesting maybe you should think on it over the weekend. It's waited this long, it can wait another few days."

"I don't think I'll change my mind," Ginny said, obscurely relieved by Simon's suggestion.

"It's not going to put a stop to anything, honey. I think you've got to stop expecting that."

"But it may free some energy if *I* say that I'm never going back."

"But you will be," Simon said. "In your mind if not your body. That's the bitch about being human—life may move in only one direction but until our brains short circuit with dementia, we're always going forward and back simultaneously. There's really not much we can do to stop it—we can just start thinking of it as a spiritual salsa step. Speaking of which, have you signed up for your dance classes yet? And what about another massage with Rosemary? I know you're having your aura read up at the lake." He laughed at Ginny's expression. "I do believe maybe I see some shooting stars inside that little black cloud you carry with you everywhere, but Patricó will be able to tell for sure."

Ginny was leaving soon to go with Marie up to the lake for a few days. Simon had pleaded other commitments, but really he and Ginny were eager for a little time away from each other. If she was going to stay on here, Ginny knew she would have to find a place of her own. And a purpose.

Healing, the voice said to her. *That should be obvious.*

"Under the circumstances, contrition isn't really a sufficient response—at least not to the vestry or the parish, Ginny," Bob Althorpe had said.

"And for you?" Ginny had asked.

"How the hell did you get yourself *into* this mess, Ginny?" he had exploded. "I did everything I could to help you. I didn't deserve this."

"You should have taken lessons from me, Ginny-gin-gin," Will said with his bone trembling laugh.

"I want you back, Will. You fucking hypocrite, I want you back," Ginny whispered.

"Say what?" Simon asked, pausing with the coffee pot in his hand, the cup half-filled.

"I need to pack," Ginny said. She pushed her chair back.

"Up there, they'll see it as channeling, my dear. Sanity depends so much on context, don't you think?"

"Every month I make my tour. I see it as a not-so-ordinaire pilgrimage," Marie said. "You'll see. But don't worry, you need not be religious to find it interesting."

She threw the car into gear and they started the astonishing jitterbug of any wheeled vehicle along the cobbled streets. "Think of the car ride as the deep muscle massage," Marie said. "It starts within your bones and shakes everything else out. It looses all a little so you will be more open to this country. It is like a little *temblor, an earthquake,* of the heart, no?"

But Ginny couldn't speak, her teeth were chattering so loudly.

"We will commence this not-so-ordinaire pilgrimage with a little douching of our aura at the Mutable Moon," Marie said, her voice suddenly steadying as they came to the end of the cobblestones and pulled out on the major road out of town. "Then tomorrow we will visit the God of firewater, tobacco and ready cash, Maximón, shop to cleanse our consciences, and then visit the church so the Trinity do not feel we ignores them."

"I'm not sure I believe in auras," Ginny said.

"I think it does not matter as long as the cleaner of the aura does. Then you are participating in a mystery—one that you may well be blind to, but that is often the way with mysteries, no? If the cleaner of the aura does not believe, that is different. Then you are being, what you call it, scammed. Tricked. But Patricó has a great belief, so we are in the sure hands."

Marie pulled out around the large green, purple and yellow school bus in front of them, then ducked back as an equally colorful school bus came roaring around the sharp curve on the narrow mountain road. Ginny yawned to hide her gasp. Behind them, a large pick-up truck pulled out as soon as the school bus passed and began to pass them and the bus ahead of them on yet another blind curve. Ginny yawned again.

Marie glanced over at her, noticing immediately how tightly Ginny was gripping her hands together. "The first step in this pilgrimage is to give yourself up to circumstances, especially the ones you are unable to control, such as the fate of this little car. You must not think of yourself as being in my hands, Ginny (Marie pronounced it like Genie). For you are not. You are in the hands of destiny, truly. *Bien sûr*, our new friendship cannot bear the pressure otherwise. You must keep in mind, the universe has seen fit to preserve me on this road for ten years now, and I come up many times a year. Why should the universe turn on me today?"

"You come to have your aura cleaned?" Ginny asked, forcing herself to unknot her hands and stretch the fingers out against her knees.

"It is very beautiful there—in a way that man have very little to do with. The beauty open me to everything else that happen. Wait, you'll see. It can be amusing, this cleansing. I am, you see, an agnostic about the forms God takes, but a credulous one."

"But isn't believing in everything equivalent to believing in nothing, finally?"

"No, I think not. I believe in the belief, you see. At our age, perhaps it is inevitable that the question poses itself, even if we do not pose it. It may help you to meet all these credulous people, even if what they believe is quite different, even *extrordinaire*. You, what do you believe?"

Marie glanced at her, then quickly turned her attention to another polychrome bus approaching and pick-up truck pulling out behind. "It won't be long now," she said soothingly as she slammed on the brakes and the accelerator almost simultaneously.

When they reached the lake, Marie drove them to a house in the middle of town which belonged to an old friend of hers. There they collected her friend's yardman, who accompanied them to the dock, where they left him with the keys to the car and rather cloudy plans for return, pulled on their knapsacks, and went down and took their places in a small blue boat which already looked as full as it could possibly be.

"*Falta dos más*," the captain said comfortably after they had squeezed themselves together into the last available seat. Marie sat by the plastic covered window, while Ginny rested with one buttock on the seat and one in the aisle, her position bolstered by the pressure from the thigh of the man on the opposite seat, who was equally precariously situated.

"Two more?" she asked Marie. "Is it possible?"

"Think of the abundance of a tin of sardines—so very many fishes in such a very little space. It is quite wonderful, no?"

The boat sank a few inches lower as a mother and child slipped on. The captain looked around and seemed satisfied that not an inch of space was going to waste. He started the motor. The woman and her daughter excused themselves and by some mystery of transubstantiation managed to slip between Ginny and the man who braced her. Pulling the girl on her lap, the woman balanced herself on the small spaces that still persisted on either seat in the row ahead of Ginny, where two tiny people already sat in each single seat. The mother's balance was astonishing; perhaps a sixteenth of each of her buttocks was suspended on the inch of seat available to her on either side of the aisle.

The child on her lap turned around and, kneeling, peered over her mother's shoulder at Ginny, a quick intelligence making her gaze move easily over everything that was happening on the dock as the motor started up, ropes were untied, and the boat backed away from the pier.

The water washed up over the heavy translucent plastic windows on either side. Ginny tried to remember the dramatic landscape just beyond the plastic windows. She took a deep breath and imagined she was being lifted on a pillow of air. The rhythms of the boat began to counterbalance the claustrophobia she was feeling at the press of so many bodies.

"Very *intime*, no?" Marie asked. "I hope you enjoy. If not, you may not enjoy India or China either."

"Perhaps not," Ginny said. Ginny in general needed to keep what Will used to call a criminal distance between herself and others. She kept her eyes fixed on the eyes of the little girl ahead of her. The sight of the huge volcanoes and the lake reflected there were replaced, as the girl shifted her head, with an equally clear image of the pilot standing, legs luxuriously spread, at the back of the boat. Ginny would look anywhere but at the close packed bodies around them.

The little girl leaned forward a little, her expression somber but intent.

"Do not look too closely," Marie murmured to Ginny. "People are sensitive to the interest of foreigners, especially middle-aged women. They think they may want to steal their babies."

"Not me," Ginny said. "I haven't a maternal bone in my body. Right now, I wish I had no bones at all."

By the time the boat had stopped five times, releasing ten passengers and taking on another fifteen, most of them sun-burnt, half-naked foreigners who crowded into the front of the boat despite the warnings of the captain about the uneven distribution of weight, Ginny had given up hope of ever being able to shift her hips, take a deep breath, or keep her precarious grip on the waves of hot panic that were pushing through her in time to the jarring progress of the boat.

"Here we are," Marie said as the boat pulled into the next cove. She had a discussion with the boat's captain about which dock she preferred. She pushed against Ginny, but this didn't seem to dislodge Ginny. Ginny's knees were, when finally released, pure jelly. The press of bodies, however, assured her that the only direction she could move in was up, which she did with the ease of a woman of a hundred.

Marie, disgustingly fresh, slipped out behind her and over the side of the boat, balancing lightly on the captain's hand as if they were dancing. She waited patiently as Ginny stumbled and righted herself, nearly pulling the captain off the boat. Ginny stood on the wooden dock, breathing loudly, feeling the planks of wood still rocking with the rhythm of the boat.

"If it doesn't interest you, the cleansing of the aura, you can always have a massage. I might suggest the Reiki, which does not involve so much the direct contact. It is the energy body that gets the massage, I believe." Marie waved to the captain as the boat turned around to leave the cove.

"It is a massage of my aura?" Ginny asked.

"Something *semblable*. We do not ask too much the explanation."

Marie headed briskly up the narrow dirt path that led from the reed marshes along the lakeside up into what appeared to be a dense jungle. Ginny concentrated on getting some feeling back in her feet and some mobility back in her hips.

"Patricio, *mon cheri*," Marie called out as they approached a tall wall of cane, above which Ginny could make out thatched roofs, a dash of intense blue. A sign, in blue and silver, identified the enclave as *The Mutable Moon, An Oasis for the Spirit*.

A huge, silver-bearded man with shoulder length brown hair met them at the gate to the compound with a roar of pleasure. "Marie! Marie! I thought you were going to be here for the second quarter, but you are too late."

"The moon may be mutable, but the phases of Patricio's course are inexorable," Marie said to Ginny. "This time around, we will learn only the wisdom of the third quarter. We will have a spiritual aperitif, no?"

"What would that be?" Ginny asked politely. "The wisdom of the third quarter?"

But the big man was swallowing Marie in an enormous embrace, nuzzling his bearded chin into the crook of her neck. His easy physicality shocked Ginny, but Marie did not seem to put up any resistance. Ginny found it a strange anomaly to Marie's general air of physical reserve, a reserve Ginny found very soothing and had thought was intrinsic to her personality.

"Patricio has known me as long as I have lived her," Marie said, emerging from his embrace, but still on point, the tips of her sandals digging into the mud. "He is my oldest friend. He is, as you can see, a stranger to restraint." She lifted her face up to him and laughed with delight.

"Which must be why I cannot get enough of you, Marie, for you have enough restraint for three, no?" Slowly Patricio let her feet rest again on the ground. He turned to Ginny. "We are attracted by our oppositions. It is chemical, this. It makes the strongest of bonds."

"Well, I have brought a friend as reserved as I am, so we will be like two little hydrogens to your oxygen, no? We will make the universal solvent."

"And where will that leave me?" A thin young man with a very low but melodious voice asked. He was as sleek as Patricio was ursine, wore rumpled linen to Patricio's denim.

"Byron, *mi amor*," Marie said, giving him a brisk kiss on either cheek. "Patricio's opposite—and inseparable companion," she said to Ginny.

Byron reached out his hand and rested it gently in Ginny's. He had surprisingly soft skin, and a smile that had a sweetness to it that Ginny responded to immediately.

"Come in, come in," he said. "We will settle you both into the House of the New Moon—it's the only one free now."

"Very well," Marie said. "It is a good thing to be blazers of the trail, no, Genie?"

"You will join us for lunch after you have rested a little?"

"But of course. And we will join you for the yoga this evening, Byron. Perhaps I can prevail upon Patricio to give our Genie just a little talk even though we are late. Perhaps then she will come back again, when she realizes what wonders you have in store for us."

Marie waved at Patricó as Byron led them across the dirt yard.

"He spoke this morning on lucid dreams and astral travel."

"Ah, one of my favorites. Do you think he might repeat a little."

"Or perhaps Ginny has some experiences of her own that she would like to share," Byron said politely.

"I feel mine would be too tame," Ginny said quickly. "I'd much prefer to listen."

"With Patricó that is the most compatible pattern," Byron said with a smile. He led them across the compound toward a blue cabin from whose thatched roof dandled silver slivers of new moons, like so many scimitars. Byron opened the door with a flourish to show a simple white room with two single beds set on either side. The lifted roof let light and air spill in. He turned on the fan.

"We listen to you too, *mi amor*," Marie said, touching Byron's arm as he turned to leave. "Perhaps a few days by yourself down at my place might be a good thing?" She waved him off, blowing him a kiss.

"They adore each other," she said as she slipped off her knapsack. "But sometimes people do not want all the time to be yin to another's yang. They want the freedom to be both."

"Or neither," Ginny said. She slipped her own knapsack off and lay down onto the thin mattress spread on a simple wooden platform. She stared contentedly up at the high thatch roof, breathing in the mold and also some incredibly sweet fragrance, perhaps the white flowers blooming on the bush outside the door. The room held the vestigial odor of incense as well. She closed her eyes and immediately re-experienced the jar and wallow of the boat. She opened her eyes, letting the nausea ease up. Was this what Marie meant by opening? she wondered. But she was asleep before her eyelashes touched her cheek.

Sister, do you believe you are truly called by God and his church to the priesthood?

For these and all my other sins which I cannot now remember, I am truly sorry.

Then flew one of the seraphims unto me having a live coal in his hand, which he had taken with the tongs from off the altar.

For these and all my other sins which I cannot now remember, I am truly sorry.

And he laid it upon my mouth and said, Lo, this hath touched thy lips; and thine iniquity is taken away, and thy sin is purged.

For these and all my other sins which I cannot now remember, I am truly sorry.

Also I heard the voice of the Lord saying, whom shall I send and who will go for us? Then I said, Here am I, send me.

For these and all my other sins which I cannot now remember, I am truly sorry.

Jerusalem hath grievously sinned; therefore she is removed: all that honored her despise her, because they have seen her nakedness: yea, she sigheth and turneth backward.

For these and all my other sins which I cannot now remember, I am truly sorry.

Her filthiness *is* in her skirts; she remembereth not her last end; therefore she came down wonderfully; she had no comforter.

And for the sins I cannot now remember, I am truly—

Let the whole world see and know that things which were cast down are being raised up, and things which had grown old are being made new, and that all things are brought to their perfection through—

O Lord, thou hast pleaded the causes of my soul; thou hast redeemed my life.

O Lord, thou hast seen my way; judge thou my cause.

Thou hast seen all their vengeance and all their imaginations against me.

The lips of those that rose up against me, and their device against me all the day.

Behold their sitting down and rising up; I *am* their music.

O God, I **am** *their music.*

"Yes, you are," Will said gently. "And I am your friend. Do you want to go through with this?"

"Just repeat the words that are written there, Will. The last thing I need are lessons from you."

"*She weepeth sore into the night, and her tears are on her cheeks; among all her lovers she hath none to comfort her; all her friends have dealt treacherously with her; they are become her enemies.*" Will's voice is so deep, so thick with pity, Ginny is afraid she will begin to convulse with sobs.

She tries to rise from her knees, but Marcela presses on one shoulder, Simon on the other. Ginny desperately twists her head away from the bright coal that Will holds out in the silver tongs.

"Swallow," he says kindly.
Can't you recognize the bread of life?
I *am* their music.
Where are your accusers?
Then I said, Here am I, send me.
And She did, the voice said. *She did.*

Ginny woke up fighting for air as if she were climbing up from the depths of the lake. Marie put her hand on her shoulder to orient her. "Ah," she said, "the spirits they are beginning to move you too, I believe. You talk with someone in your sleep. Don't worry," she added when she saw the look of alarm cross Ginny's face, "I do not drop the eaves. But it seems you talk with someone very close, someone you have the confidence with. Your face was very soft until the end."

"Soft?" Ginny asked.

"Perhaps you are ready now to learn more about life in the other dimensions and the metaphysics of the invisible world?"

Ginny touched her lips, where Will had set the live coal. They felt raw.

"A little burn of the sun?" Marie asked solicitously. "I have the salve." She dug in her bag and pulled out a small red tin. The waxy paste smelled like sandalwood.

"We will have lunch first," she went on. "We will let you place your feet down firm on the earth before we let Patricó send you traveling. Now, you must remember, Genie, that no one makes you go where you don't like. You have the control of your experience here.

"I do not mean anything against the beliefs of Patricó and Byron. They bring me the real peace in my life. Patricó loves to use me as example of the power of what he teach." Marie shrugged. "I do not mind. But me, I believe most purely in his capacity to love. Patricó heals with his big heart."

Ginny rubbed the salve over her lips, wincing.

"I had a friend for many years who had a heart big enough to hold the whole world, or so it seemed to me. I always felt so small, so stiff, in comparison. I loved being around him, I felt so safe, so embraced by his warmth."

"What happened to him?"

"He died three months ago."

"But before that," Marie said. "You talk to him in your sleep, no? There is something incomplete between you."

"I disappointed him and he closed his heart to me."

"Not for always. He comes back to visit you, no?"

"I miss him," Ginny blurted. She missed his voice and his laugh and the slight dryness of his brown skin, and the way he held up the host and broke it and opened her heart so many years ago—there had never been, would never be, anything like that in her life again.

"Coming?" Marie asked. "You look just a little flushed. The fresh air will do you good."

"The idea frightens many people," Patricío said. "They imagine it is like when you have the big fright and your soul leaps out of your body and watches helplessly what is happening to the poor body. You have had, I assume, this experience."

Ginny reluctantly put her spoon down. The cold cucumber soup was marvelous. It was a strange experience to be eating food deserving of an elegant French bistro in the bare, rather muddy yard of the compound, a few hens scratching in the dirt at the side of the kitchen cabaña.

Patricío leaned forward and stared intently into Ginny's eyes. It was a gaze that she felt deep inside her—too intense to be compassion but too accepting to be intrusive. His eyes were almost gold.

"There are very very few people who have not had this experience of having to throw their bodies to the dogs in order to save their souls. But this is a state of terrible division." He rapped down on the table with his knife. "Both the body and the soul object for they know, just like Siamese twins who share a single heart, that they cannot survive apart. People here call this *asusto*—soul shock. It may look like the state described in astral travel—but it is the opposite for there is no free will. The body cannot protect itself, the soul has no choice but to leave—but all its attention is turned toward the body. In this situation, the material world is more real—and completely uncontrollable. The soul is the only small pure space we can call home. In soul shock, the soul subsidizes the body. But in astral travel, our soul leaves the body of its own will. It is the body's job to watch for its return. The body subsidizes the soul."

"But astral travel?" Ginny asked. "It means you can travel through time? Visit the Spanish Inquisition or the Crucifixion?"

"Or another galaxy—or heaven, for that matter."

"Patricio doesn't believe in hell," Byron said, "or it would be on the list of possible destinations as well."

"You do?" Ginny asked.

"For a pacifist, my partner has a very war-like view of the universe," Patricio said. "Light struggles forever with the dark. There are evil spirits and good ones."

"They define each other, *mi amor*," Byron said with a shrug. "They are like your opposites, yes? They attract one to the other."

"I do not believe we move to greater suffering than we experience here in this world," Patricio said. "And astral travel is one of the ways we can carry that message to others through our deeds as well as our thoughts. For the astral world holds not only our souls but the projections of our thoughts as well. Here the worlds of imagination and experience show their similar natures, there is no difference between what we know and what we hope for."

"You do this?" Ginny asked. "On a regular basis?"

"I am not alone," Patricio said. "Sometimes Byron travels with me. Sometimes Marie."

"It's cheaper than Continental," Byron agreed. "And there's a greater choice of destinations."

"You wish to describe our experiences, Marie?" Patricio asked. He put his huge hand over her small, long-fingered one.

Marie looked directly at Ginny. Her eyes were, Ginny realized, the exact color of the lake. Marie seemed amused, curious about Ginny's responses.

"You have never wanted to leave your body and go visit people you were close to—people in your real life or in books?" she asked. "From the time I was a little girl, I felt a strong *besoin*, *ganas*, to be elsewhere. I would read about Christopher Columbus or Santa Teresa and I could feel that I had been put down in the wrong time. But I never felt I could remedy this. I felt this longing, this sense of being in the wrong place, was just part of the condition of the human. Then, when my daughter died, the feeling grew so strong in me that I needed to leave my life as I had known it. I couldn't stay there another moment. That was when I came here and met Patricio and Byron.

"I took one look at Marie and I just knew that we had been destined from the earliest times to meet each other," Patricio said.

"'Again!' is what he said to me. He just picked me up and swung me around as if I were his oldest friend. As if we were still children together. I should have been horrified—but it felt completely natural," Marie added.

"We channel as well," Byron said. "It allows us to be selective with our traveling, which is more tiring. Channeling is like having one of those little microphones that the parents use to listen to their children. It takes less energy—but the level of engagement is less."

"So you knew Marie in a past life too?" Ginny asked Byron. She felt her lips twitch and dearly wished that Simon were there to cue her.

"No, we start fresh the two of us." Byron winked at Marie. "The only history between us is what we make in the ten years since she arrive here. It is a good history, Marie, don't you agree?"

"But you and Patricio must have known each other forever."

"Oh yes. We have little grudges, little spites that go back to the first century. I was a Christian you see—and he was a Roman."

"Your death converted me—you were so irresistible up there on the cross before they set you aflame."

"You see, even now he avoids the enormity of what he did."

"Didn't I make it up to you in France in the fourteenth century? You weren't the one who had his head hacked off on the battlefield."

"You're right," Byron beamed. "I did the hacking. It was about time. I had more than a thousand years of anger stored up there!"

"Do you go back and try and sort out those old interactions?" Ginny was intrigued by the implications and couldn't wait to try the game out on Simon.

"Astral travel doesn't mean you can affect the past—you can just see it again at close quarters," Patricio said.

"That does sound hellish," Ginny said.

"Masochistic, yes," Patricio said, "but hellish, no. But that is why when we travel, we prefer to visit our friends in their past lives rather than our old selves."

"And you," Ginny said to Marie, "who do you go see?"

"I am, according to Patrició, masochistic. I only go to the one place. I go to the side of the bed of my daughter the night before we learned of her diagnosis, the night when I sat there filled with the gratefulness—for my beautiful girl, my sweet husband, my ordered life. So pleasant. So very pleasant. I was not complacent, you see. I knew what I had. I keep going back to that moment just to know that I was not ignorant of my bounty. I was not ignorant of the beauty of my daughter's life, even before we knew how short it was to be.

"Sometimes I believe she visits me as well. Some days I will be out in my garden or just sitting by the patio drinking my coffee and I will receive such a feeling of love and interest I don't know who else it could be who care for me so completely. I don't seem to be able to visit her in the present. Perhaps because I believe in neither heaven or hell. Just the now."

"But you believe in the lake," Ginny said.

Marie looked at her with eyes slightly closed, assessing something, then released a deep breath. "Yes," she said. She placed her hand over Ginny's. "I believe in the lake, in Patrició and Byron's friendship, in the restorative powers of their cuisine, and in the importance of trying to put ourselves one way or another in a spiritual world. I just prefer it to be this one."

"She will not try the parasails either," Patrició said sadly. "She is my dear friend and is a mystic—however much she disagrees—but she is a bourgeois mystic. This is a trial to me. It is on the verge of bad taste, you see."

"And you?" Byron asked Ginny. "If you were free, where would you go?"

"I don't know," Ginny said. "There are scenes I'd certainly *not* want to return to."

"Probably the ones where your soul left your body and your world got very small, no?" Patrició asked.

Ginny saw her naked body coming to meet her, moving out from the canvas, shimmering in the bright light, the steady murmur of conversation from the people obliviously sipping wine at the opening. She saw herself standing there in her black shirt and jacket, her collar. She heard the murmur of surprise as these strangers began to recognize her in all that magnified, magnetizing nakedness.

"Not exactly," she said.

"It is a gift," Patrició said. "A kind of charism if you will. Some people are spiritual homebodies. Others feel the risk is worth it."

"What risk is that?" Ginny asked. "I mean, if you can leap out of your body at will, you are pretty impervious to the slings and arrows of outrageous fortune aren't you?"

"If all our suffering were physical, my dear. But so little is. We don't escape our thoughts—on any plane. Our memories are all there, in the astral world, along with our dreams. And the dreams of all our incarnations."

"It sounds rather crowded," Ginny said. "Not to mention terrifying."

"You are leaving will out of it. You only voyage when you're ready to. The first time I went, I went looking for my mother to say those things that I could not say to her before she died. She was sitting in a chair exactly like the one in our house in Naples, arranging her favorite plastic flowers. 'At last,' she said when she saw me. As soon as I had said what I needed to say, she was free to ascend to her next level and I was much more tranquil in my own thoughts."

"Patricio feels that some of the dead stay in the lower astral planes waiting to reconcile. They come to us in our dreams, but we can't hear them clearly. They are not haunting us, really, just asking for release," Marie explained.

"Like your daughter," Patricio agreed.

"Yes," Marie said. "She needed to know that I would not die of grief. That I would have left her father anyway. That his new daughter with his second wife would never replace her. Since then, I have never sensed her there and it is a great relief to me. I go to visit with my own thoughts. That is as it should be."

"And me, Ginny-gin-gin, am I a ghost or an emanation of your own conscience?" Will asked.

Or a message from God, the voice asked.

"Is someone trying to reach you?" Patricio asked. "I saw a strange shimmering in your aura."

"And a shadow passed over your face," Byron said. "Perhaps you would like to spend a little time in the meditation house before the yoga?"

"I am also available for private spiritual direction," Patricio said. He laughed at Ginny's expression and reached across the table to hug her. "Everything in its good time. You will see."

"I believe I will have just a little massage," Marie said. "Is Juanita free?"

"Come with me," Byron said, giving Ginny a hand up from her chair. The cabaña he led her to had all the phases of the moon dangling from its thatched roof. Byron showed her where to leave her shoes, pressed the tips of three of the fingers of his right hand against her forehead, kissed her so lightly and gently on her cheek she did not even begin to withdraw.

It's time you began to thaw, the voice said. *Otherwise you're ripe for a meltdown.*

Is there no limit to your mixed metaphors? Ginny asked impatiently.

None, the voice said complacently.

I can't concentrate with you always breaking in this way, Ginny said.

What can I say? I've got as much right as you to be here.

I can't hear myself think.

That may be a good thing—until you have something good you can say.

I'm not complaining. Did I say I was complaining? Have I ever said I wasn't responsible for everything that has happened to me?

I rest my point, the voice said. *Just look at this, will you?*

The entry way to the meditation room was swagged with red sheets, like the opening of a womb. Warily, Ginny slipped between the silky, burgeoning walls. A flock of angels flew in formation above her. At the end of the birth canal, flanking the stairs which led down into the meditation room, stood two large wooden statues of angels wielding swords while being hugged to death by pythons.

The room Ginny entered was surprisingly luminous, its roof made of sheets of white plastic that produced an intense but diffuse light. In one corner was an Indian batik of Kali with her chastity belt of skulls. In the opposite corner, an enormous lingam, while a crucifix faced a tall stone pillar carved with Mayan glyphs. In the center of the room an open bible rested on a large metal Star of David. A candle was fitted into each of the angles of the star. Metal bowls with hammers were scattered around the room between the small white prayer pillows. A blackboard held the traces of Patricio's latest lecture—including a corpse-like figure and a wraith-like spirit snaking out of its belly and heading off through the sky.

"All we're missing are the Koran and a broomstick," Ginny muttered. She flinched at the echo of her voice. Simon was right, soon she was going to be certifiable. She couldn't tell when she was speaking aloud, when she was dreaming.

Or when you're revealing what you thought you were concealing.

Is this what it's come to? Ginny turned around, trying to face the source of the voice. All these little shards of belief. Is this is what is left to me?

I lost my church, Ginny said. I lost my calling. But I didn't lose my faith.

Who says, Ginny-gin-gin? Simon?

Ginny sat cross-legged on one of the white pillows. She reached out and picked up a small rubber-tipped hammer and tapped lightly against the side of one of the metal bowls. The sound was so rich it made her ribs resonate. She drew the bowl closer to her, setting it inside her crossed legs. She began to tap on it steadily, letting the echoes mount one inside the other. She closed her eyes and let herself dissolve inside the sound.

"I *am* their music," Ginny whispered, the tears streaming down her cheeks. "God help me, I *am* their music."

"I am," Ginny murmured, letting herself be rocked back and forth, in and out, by the weight of the air and the warmth of the sweet notes resounding in the bowl and in her flesh. "I *am* their music."

And mine, the voice said. *You're mine too.*

The birds broke into song at first light. Ginny lay there, half asleep, listening to a bird whose song sounded like water tumbling into a fountain. She stretched cautiously.

"Ooh," Marie sighed. "It never fails. I am always deceived by Byron's charm as a teacher, and for the next few days, I hobble around like an old woman. And you?"

Ginny too had thrown herself into Byron's vigorous yoga class, finding herself contorting in positions she had never dreamed were possible. Now she wiggled her toes cautiously, rolled her shoulders and clenched her fingers. She actually felt less used than she did after one of her runs.

"I think I'll be able to make it to the dock," she said, hoping that Marie would decide that they had had enough and could head back down to the city that she now considered home. No such luck.

"First we visit the Maximón. This early it will not be so like the sardine can, the boat. We will be more like the herrings."

"You look as if you had a good sleep," Patricío said to Ginny as they came to sit at one of the tables set out beside the kitchen. He put his hands on her shoulders and gently massaged them. "Byron work his magic?"

Ginny found herself leaning back into his hands. "Slept like a log for the first time in months. No astral travel," she added with a smile.

"But now you know you have the choice," Patricío said. "It is sometimes very soothing to know that we can say no. Then, in time, we can also say yes. I know you do not share our beliefs, but I also know you are a woman with a great faith. You must not be afraid of where it will take you." He pressed his hand down on the top of her head. "Thus spake Patricío," he intoned, then gave her a little pinch on the cheek and headed over to the next table, where a very tall woman in a flowing green robe and a shaved head sat sipping tea, the sunlight flashing off the rings she wore on every finger of every hand and the ten little diamonds pegged in each ear.

"This is your day of discernment, no?" Patricío murmured. "Remember you cannot force it, Mildred. It is a time when we all, men and women, must receive."

"And the two of you are trying your projection skills, yes?" he called to the two, fairly stoned-looking backpackers at the next table. "We try this, the first time, on dry land and without mind-altering substance."

"The young ones, they like to trip while they are out in those little dugouts," Byron explained. "We're tired of fishing them out of the lake."

"But they become good speakers for your near-death lecture, no?" Marie teased.

"I'll walk you down to the dock," Byron said. "Patricío will say his good-bye from the next astral plane."

Ginny found herself, after her eagerness to leave, strangely missing the Mutable Moon by the time they had seated themselves in the little launch. She waved at Byron as they headed out.

"It was not so usual for you, this experience?" Marie asked.

"Simon's been here?" Ginny asked.

"More than once. It is how we met. He is very close to Byron, you know. Sometimes it provokes a bit of a *crise*. But boys will be boys."

"He never mentioned it," Ginny said, a little put out. But how much room had she given Simon to describe anything about his own affectional life?

"You know this Maximón?" Marie asked.

Ginny shook her head. The boat lurched over the waves and she reached up and steadied herself against the roof. At least she had an entire seat to herself.

"A third of the town worships with Maximón, another third uses the Catholic church, and the others belong to the evangelicals. But the keepers of Maximón are the ones who are most eager for our money. Maximón needs his cigars and his rum—and so, I suspect, do his keepers. Many people go to look as a curiosity—but I feel that one needs to go there with a prayer. It feels more respectful."

"What do you pray for?"

"Oh, a good bank balance, low air fares to France, a change in the residence requirements. Maximón has big interest in the physical security. He is god of the appetites. I like that. It must be the bourgeois in me."

"Here we are." Marie patted Ginny's hand lightly. "Just the few waves rocking in our stomachs, not a big storm like yesterday."

A little indigenous girl met them as they walked in from the dock. She wore the typical straight skirt fastened by a little sash, a costume made jaunty by her insouciant ease in it. She held a rooster upside down by its feet.

"Maximón?" she asked. *"Diez?"*

"For two?" Marie began to bargain.

It's only ten in the morning, Ginny thought wearily. The fingers of the children plucking at her shirt for her attention felt as sharp as the beak of the rooster that dandled listlessly from the little girl's fist as she bargained with Marie. Pocketing the five Marie gave her, she pulled the rooster upright, tucked it in the crook of her arm, and headed at a trot down the side street to their left.

Ginny, obscurely perturbed by the rooster, the bartering, the black water running down the center of the unpaved road, and the brisk, voyeuristic tone of the adventure, found herself lagging behind. When she turned the corner onto an even narrower street with a wider channel of dirty water, neither Marie or the little girl were visible. She paused uncertainly. An old man in a dirty shirt peered drunkenly at her from a doorway. Down along the lakeside she could see women kneeling on the rocks and beating out their clothes.

"Genie," Marie called. "Come!" She waved from an adobe shack with a tin roof on the left side of the street. She was handing the little girl the last of the money she had promised her. When a man came out of the shack with a bowl, Marie looked at the rapidly retreating little girl and then shrugged and paid out an equal amount again.

"He is a god of material well-being, after all," Marie said. "Why shouldn't they engage in a little of the charge over, no?"

Reluctantly, Ginny followed her into the smoky room where a strange chest-high figure stood, its neck ringed with over a hundred neckties. A lit cigar was set in the mouth of its brown, mask-like face. A woman sat on the ground before the figure praying loudly and occasionally looking over her shoulder as if to assure herself of an audience. An older man in a red kerchief was counting up the money in the offering bowl, while another man was taking a swig from a small bottle of rum and handing it off to the man counting change.

This wasn't a religion, it was a tourist industry. But Marie seemed indifferent to the tawdry falseness. She leaned down and put more money in the alms bowl, then removed her knapsack and drew from one of its pockets a small bottle of rum and a set of cigars and laid them down in front of the totem. She pulled out some candles and walked over to a corner where a number of candles were already burning and squatted down and began lighting her own.

Quietly, Ginny began to back towards the exit. One of the men pulled the cigar out of the totem's mouth and began to smoke it quickly, blowing the smoke directly in Ginny's direction, his monotonous chanting blending in with that of the woman on the floor.

"See you outside," Ginny whispered to Marie, who just nodded, her attention still fixed on the candles she was lighting.

Ginny stood in the middle of the dirt patio trying to clear her head. The little girl who had earlier served as their guide plucked at her shirt and held up the rooster. *"Quiere?"* she asked. Ginny looked at her blankly and she mimicked twisting the bird's neck.

What have you to lose? the voice asked. *Isn't one live sacrifice much like another? Lamb of God. Rooster of Maximón.*

I want to go home, Ginny thought wildly, knowing as she did so how futile the desire was. There was no going back. Never any going back.

A hand pressed between her shoulder blades and Ginny jumped.

"A little strange all this?" Marie asked. "Come, we will do a little shopping to feel normal. Everyone all over the world shops when they can. Perhaps that is why I admire Maximón—the whole world buys and sells, why shouldn't we see this as an ultimate good, a god?"

"Here, lady, buy here," a woman called out to them as they turned the corner into the main street. The girl with the rooster was already guiding another pair of tourists back up the dirt road. They nodded, then cast their eyes down bashfully, as they passed Ginny and Marie.

"Here lady," another woman called from yet another stall filled with woven blouses and bedspreads and rebozos.

"You buy from us," two young girls said, coming quickly to either side of Marie and Ginny, so they were tightly flanked. Each girl carried a tray of beaded bracelets and wooden pencils with small hand-woven covers with birds and the name of the town on them.

"You no buy from her," the beautiful girl standing next to Ginny said. "You buy from me. I give better price."

"No thank you," Ginny said. "Maybe another day."

"Let's see what you have," Marie said fairly.

Ginny felt amazingly restless and bored, but the girls and Marie easily pawed their way through about thirty seemingly identical broad beaded bracelets.

"You don't mind?" Marie asked. "This is the business of life here, you know. These two girls, they speak to me with their energy. They amuse, but are a little brutal. We will not be free if we do not buy. They will follow us everywhere. You might like this necklace." She held out a black and white beaded collar.

"Or this one?" She held out a red one with a pattern of turquoise diamonds. "A little vulgar, perhaps, but sometimes we need the glitz, no? And for Simon, maybe this one with the green back and the bolts of thunder?"

"And for you?" Ginny asked, but Marie had set about bargaining the girls down, with much laughter and repartee, to a price a third of what they'd originally suggested.

"*D'accord?*" Marie asked, waving the necklace and bracelet in her hand like an auctioneer. The two girls nodded, holding their hands out for the money Marie carefully counted into them.

"When I first come here, in my sorrow time, I had no interest in nothing. I take the boat with Patrició and Byron and we come here and I am like the zombie with my blind eyes. Patrició do with me what I do with you now. He take me by the hand and make me touch everything. He say if I am not completely awake in this life, I can never be awake in the others either. 'And looking,' he told me, 'means touching, it means wanting, here and there, just a little, Marie.'

"I think now he had the right. These things we buy are a way of talking. We buy a necklace because we want to hide something—a mole maybe, or those rings of age that make us look like the elephants. Or we buy it because it is beautiful and we think that beauty will radiate from us, we will have the aura that says, good taste, interesting person, talk with me. And why not? Why not buy if we have the money? For the girls or their mothers or their little sisters work hard to make the necklaces and the weavings and if they give us a little pleasure, within the reason, are we not all joining a little more fully in the life?"

"I wouldn't know," Ginny said. "I wore a uniform for years. I've gotten out of the habit of thinking what to wear. Simon bought my clothes when I first arrived here. It's another kind of uniform, I suppose, but I like it." She looked down at her long loose red shirt and flowing black pants, which, although wrinkled from having been worn for two days, still looked dramatic. "But I can't say that it's me—or not me, for that matter."

"And your uniform before? Was that you—or a professional necessity?"

"I thought it was me. Now, I don't know. I don't recognize myself without it—and I don't think, these days, I would recognize myself with it either."

"Perhaps it is like the shell of the crab they call the pilgrim, the anchorite?"

"Hermit crab?"

"Perfect for its time—but then the crab must find another throw me down shell to fill. It feels a little sad this. It is a good thing, I think, to be clothed in good intentions that are our very own. A red necklace. A turquoise skirt. An open or defiant heart pinned, right there, on the sleeve."

Marie looked down at her slim faded jeans, her little jean jacket and white shirt. "This is my uniform," she said. "Patricío and Byron chose it for me many years ago. Now it fits me like a second skin. But every day I put it on with purpose. It says not too much, not too little. It says my skin is thin and sensitive in the sun, so it needs the protection of the heavy material. It says, by the *je-ne-sais-quoi* of its fit," she wriggled her hips a little, "that I am French, and my jewelry says, every day, that I am not. And you, if you could choose a new uniform of your very own, not just receive it like the pilgrim crab from someone else, what would it be?"

She stood waiting patiently for Ginny to answer, but Ginny started looking studiously through all the different woven blouses with their little grids of hand embroidered birds or machine appliquéd flowers. Who, Ginny wondered, would she be able to give them to? She really didn't know a woman she was close to. It stood out here, where you almost never saw a woman alone, they were always accompanied by children, mothers, sisters, friends, husbands. Even in these stores and stalls there was always more than one.

"This is beautiful," she said, lifting a heavily woven blouse of deep blues and greens from the pile. A tiny woman in an even more heavily woven red blouse and red skirt was bobbing at Ginny's elbow as soon as her fingers closed around the cloth. "*Cuánto quiere pagar?*" she asked. How much do you want to pay. "*Dígame, Señora.*"

"Let her speak first," Marie coached. "You can almost always get a price down by half. So start a bit below where you want to end up."

Don't, for a minute, think this is beneath you, the voice said. *You need some give, Ginny. You need some take.*

By the time Ginny had danced the woman down to two thirds her original price (the woman had paused momentarily to apply her baby to her breast, but returned immediately to the cajoling sally of bids), Ginny was flushed with triumph. The cloth hung, nearly forgotten, in her hands. Ginny looked down, expecting the cloth to look tawdry now that the excitement was beginning to ebb, but it didn't. The deep colors glowed under her fingers. She liked the heavy feel of the material. "Yes," she said, nodding happily and holding the cloth out to be bagged, thus closing the deal.

Even Marie's smile, which seemed both mocking and kind, pleased her. "It is very *intime*, is it not, this back and forth, back and forth?"

"I don't know," Ginny said. "All I know is I liked it—and I like the blouse although I have no idea who I can give it to."

"Ah, you are laying up a supply of generosity," Marie said. "That is not a bad thing."

The first thing Ginny heard was the song of the birds that fluttered down from the high wooden eaves and swooped in and out of the open doors. The next thing that caught her attention were the statues set in groups along the narrow, waist-high ledge that ran the length of both sides of the church. The different groups of statues were all dressed in clothes of different patterned material. The costumes gave a wry look to the baroque wooden statues. Christ in a tropical pink flowered shirt did not seem to find the cross so heavy, while Saint John, in blue paisley, seemed less inclined to helplessly scan the heavens for direction.

It took her a little longer to hear the sound of the women praying in the chapel to the right of the main altar, the sound of their voices fused so easily with the sound of the birds, the murmur of the women coming into the church from the plaza, pulling their colorful rebozos over their heads as they entered, wiping their hands on the frilled aprons they used as cash registers. Once she heard the women at prayer, Ginny felt an intense need to approach so she could make out the words. Marie was still studying the statuary and merely nodded as Ginny indicated she was going to explore further.

Ginny had to fight off an impulse to walk all the way around the church so that her curiosity wouldn't be so evident. She didn't know why her attraction made her feel so exposed. No one else was giving her a second thought. They were used to tourists wandering in and out of their church at whim.

She took a seat on one of the pews in the main church, from which she could see the recessed chapel where the women were still gathering, even though it was already filled with kneeling women. One of them would call out a line and the rest would join together in the refrain. Then another woman would call out again and the rest would murmur their response. From here, Ginny could make out none of the words, only the mesmerizing rhythm.

Ginny slipped to her knees on the prayer bench so she wouldn't be so noticeable. Women continued to enter from the market and to leave, their rebozos sliding on and off their gleaming black hair with casual grace.

So intime, the voice murmured, *this back and forth, back and forth, no?*

Don't you want to join in, Ginny-gin-gin?

Ginny closed her eyes and just listened to the sound of the voices washing back and forth. The wave of grief that lifted her up was so intense she almost cried out. *Never again.*

Never again? the voice asked. *How can you say that, Ginny-gin-gin? Why don't you say, Never before! This has never happened to you before. This is new. Listen. Your future may be singing here.*

I want you, Ginny thought desperately. I want to be yours again.

A man's voice began to intrude. Ginny opened her eyes and saw an old man dressed in knee-length white pants and a double-breasted green coat with brass buttons. He was lighting a long yellow candle from a match and melting its base and fixing it on the ledge beside a bust of Jesus. The bust sported a pale green flowered cravat. The man set a handful of orange candles on the ledge. He leaned his elbow on the ledge as he looked over at Jesus and began to talk to him in his own language.

An old woman, her white hair in a long braid, sat on the floor nearby. Her head was covered with a rebozo like the women in the chapel, but she held another dozen or more yellow candles in her lap, and the old man seemed to include her in the sweep of his arm as he chatted with his Savior. He touched Jesus' shoulder, man to man, and looked attentively into his face while he explained in his beautiful soft churring language whatever had brought him here. He didn't raise his voice to be heard over the women, nor did he lower it so as not to interfere.

The old man, nodding at something he seemed to have heard, took another candle from the stash he'd set on the ledge and lit it and fixed it on the other side of Jesus. He went back to his discussion. He had a serious but relaxed expression on his face, as if he were sure that, man to man, shoulder to shoulder, they could set things right. He touched Jesus lightly on the cheek, then touched his own forehead and chest, making the sign of the cross. He leaned down and placed all his remaining candles in a colorful cloth he had earlier spread out on the floor. He walked over to the old woman and gathered her candles and put them too in his cloth. Then he walked off toward the central altar. The old woman rose slowly from her knees and followed him. They both knelt in front of the main altar while he held up his bundle of candles and offered another payer.

"The *Ave Maria*? That is what has you so fascinated?" Marie asked Ginny as she slipped in beside her, knelt briefly on the prayer bench, crossed herself and reseated herself. "You are familiar with this, of course? They are perhaps making a novena to the Virgin. It can go on for a long time. You are not Catholic?"

"These days, I'm nothing," Ginny said. "I just like the sound."

"Listen as long as you want. I will wait for you outside." Marie set her hand lightly on Ginny's.

Ginny waited for the rhythm of the women's voices to build up inside her again and absorb the sound of Maria's boots ringing on the stone floor.

Here is the question of the year, Ginny-gin-gin. Did you ever talk to God like you didn't have to apologize for having eyes, a mind, and a body of your own?

"God blessed my flesh, sweetheart. He blessed my wild and crazy crazy heart."

Hers, the voice chided Will. *We're talking about hers now.*

Ginny rose to her feet, genuflected as she crossed before the altar, and made her way out of the church passing by the chapel where the old man now waved a handful of long white candles. As Ginny stood, trying to find her balance in the endless surge and fall of the conversation inside her, the old man spoke first to the dead Christ in the glass sarcophagus, blanketed in sequins, then walked back and stared up into the downcast gaze of the crucified Christ, his loins too covered with sequins. He touched the nail in Christ's crossed feet gently with one hand, gesturing with the candles with the other. The old and young women looked off in opposite directions. The boy fiddled with his fingers; his mother put out her hand to quiet him. The old man came over and waved his candles over the boy, calling out, this time in Spanish, something about *malos espiritus*. The mother and old woman nodded and the boy looked contentedly down at his innocently laced fingers as the old man confidently brushed the threat from the air.

Let it in, Ginny-gin-gin. Let it in. What's always been missing. It's not something terrible. But it's everything. It's you, Ginny. What's been missing is you.

No, Ginny said, making her way out of the church. I know you. I know you for who you are.

"Are you sure?" Will whispered. "Are you sure, sweetheart?"

As she emerged into the blinding sunlight and paused, blinking, women passed her as they went in and out of the church, the vivid rebozos sliding up and falling back from their long, gleaming hair. They moved around her easily, as if she were a tree, a lamppost, a different order of existence.

"And this," Marie asked, "it was perhaps the most strange of all?"

But the most strange of all was the mad banging at Marie's door just after they'd pulled into her garage and were unpacking their knapsacks and the produce Marie had bought on their way back from the lake. When Ginny went to answer the door, she found the little girl who had stolen her notebook in the park a month ago, the one who now worked for Rosemary, hopping back and forth from one foot to the other. She held her gripped hands up toward Ginny as if she were praying.

"*Por amor de Dios,*" the girl said, "*ayúdennos.*" For the love of God, help us.

Chapter 9
BIRTH

In the morning, Mikela decided that she would not go to school because she did not believe Natividad would stay in the ruins by herself. She decided it wasn't safe to go out herself and get Natividad some tortillas for the gatekeeper might already be at her post. So Mikela fed Natividad another mango and the last of the bread, even though she was hungry for it too.

She thought about the hot sweet *atole* she would have drunk at the home before going to school, how it covered her throat and her stomach and made them feel quiet and content. She thought about her school, how it felt to set her two pencils in a neat row, point to eraser, in the little trough at the top of her desk. How she liked that moment when Sister Carmen finished erasing the board—even if there was nothing written on it, the sister always erased the board—and turned to the class and announced what they would learn that day. Often the other girls would squirm in their seats or yawn, but this was always a wonderful moment for Mikela because she liked learning new things—about almost anything. She liked learning about the lives of the saints—and every day in the church she learned about another saint who worked miracles or suffered terrible things all for the love of God. Suffering seemed as important as working miracles for the Sisters, but Mikela thought the miracles were better, and she kept a list in her notebook of saints who would come help you in different situations. San Francisco de Assisi and Santa Clara were two. And San Antonio de Padua. And Santa Barbara.

But that was not all they learned. They learned the rules of *castellaño* and they learned about the government and about how their bodies worked and about fishes and frogs and monkeys and sentences and nouns and additions and subtractions—but the girls at the school could never add half as fast as her own people did at the mercado.

Today Mikela was sure the Mother Superior would be standing at the front door when Mikela arrived and in her eyes would be a look that would hurt Mikela even more than the look of Señora Rosemary because in it she would see something of the sadness of the Holy Mother that was so very very deep and Mikela would feel like she was a sword in the Mother Superior's chest.

Mikela didn't want that. She did not like being a disappointment to anyone, not to Natividad or to Señora Rosemary or Mamí Concepción or the Mother Superior or to God. She felt more than a little angry that there was no way she could avoid this. If only people could see how important Natividad was to her, that there was no kindness they could do for Mikela that meant anything if it didn't help her sister too. And if only Natividad could see that sometimes she made it hard for Mikela to help her.

"I was not myself yesterday," Natividad said, swallowing her last bite of bread without having offered Mikela the smallest little piece. Mikela had told her to eat it all, but even so, it would have been nice if she had offered, like she used to in the capital no matter how hungry she was. "Now I am all right and I am going to leave here, Mikela, and go find Pablo and ask his forgiveness."

"For what?"

"He says he didn't know I had lifted my skirts for the men in the capital. That he thought this baby could only be his."

"He is a cruel and stupid boy," Mikela said. "He is not old enough to be a father."

"I cannot say he isn't the father," Natividad said. "I cannot say he is." She yawned, but it was not because she was tired. Like their mother, there had been too many men for Natividad to know exactly who had made themselves at home inside her. But Natividad, just like the Virgin, was responsible for whoever grew inside her.

Mikela thought again about the baby having bruises on its face as blue as the ones on Natividad's face, and it made her very sad and stubborn. She was not going to let Natividad go back and live with Pablo. It was a terrible thing to bruise someone who had not been born yet. Natividad never drew anymore—and it wasn't because Mikela didn't bring her paper and pens. Hadn't Mikela given her just a few days ago that thick white paper from the *extranjera* that was only drawn on one side. Because Natividad wasn't drawing, Mikela often had no idea where to find her, even when her sister was sitting right in front of her.

But how was Mikela going to keep her promise to Natividad of a place where she would not be alone and where people might help her with the baby? Somewhere in the back of her mind, she had thought if she worked hard enough for Señora Rosemary and Señora Wilma, they might help her. Or the nurse, Señora Vitalli, at the girls' home—who was Italian and just gave her time to the girls because she had a very big heart. Or Mamí Concepción. But now, because of what she herself had done, this was impossible.

"We must be careful not to let the gardeners see us," she told Natividad. "At least not until other people come. We must stay away from where they are working." She brushed the dirt in their little room to make it look as if they had never been there. "But there is no reason we need to sit in the dark all day. We can go over under the trees and study from my school books. And when some tourists come, maybe we can follow them and slip outside with them without the gatekeeper noticing."

So she and Natividad sat up on the hill hidden behind the trunk of a large tree and began to study Mikela's lessons for the day. But Natividad would not concentrate very hard. She would stop and put her hand on her stomach and move her head. It was as if she were always listening for something very far away. Maybe their ancestors were trying to reach her, to give her some good advice. Mikela always waited until Natividad turned her head, then she would begin again.

Finally, Natividad did not bring her attention back to their work by herself, even though Mikela waited for a long time. Her sister's lips were moving slightly as if she were answering one of their ancestors, although Mikela could not understand what her sister was saying. Mikela felt very impatient with her sister. She also felt hungry. She concentrated on her school books by herself.

Then she felt Natividad move, but when she lifted her own head, she saw Natividad was staring at the wet ground around her. She felt ashamed for her sister. But Natividad did not look ashamed. She looked very surprised. She touched the wet ground with the tips of her fingers and then lifted her dirty fingers to her nose and smelled them.

Then Mikela understood what was happening. She felt very frightened because there were no *comadrinas* in this town that she knew of. Although she had asked Señora Vitalli how women had babies, the nurse had said that was not for little girls to worry themselves about. Mikela tried to remember what had happened with her mother, but neither she nor Natividad had been allowed anywhere near her mother when she was giving birth to Jésus and Jorge.

"Come," she said to Natividad. She quickly put her books in her knapsack and zipped it shut and put it on her back. She grabbed her sister's hand and tried to make her stand up, but Natividad just sat there, putting her fingers to the ground and then to her nose as if what she smelled there might act on her like the glue and take her to a peaceful place.

Mikela went around her sister and put her hands under her arms. She thought she heard people talking, and she knew she had to hurry and hide Natividad back in their room before anyone saw them. She put her arms under Natividad's and pulled up with all her strength.

"Help me, Natividad," she said. "If anyone sees you, they will take you to the hospital. Maybe they will take the baby away from you."

Natividad just smiled at Mikela as if the liquid she had smelled on her hands had a power like the glue. Mikela was angry at her, just like she felt when Natividad was sniffing the glue. She did not like to see her sister act like a stupid person.

Mikela pinched Natividad hard on the back to make her pay attention. "Hurry," she said. "Get up."

Finally Natividad obeyed her. When she stood up, Mikela saw that her skirt was all wet with blood. She put her arm around her sister, trying to make sure her own skirt didn't get dirty—for that would make it difficult to go get help. Maybe she should go back to the home and get Señora Vitalli. That is what she would do. Perhaps the Señora would help Natividad. Perhaps she would let Mikela work as her maid to pay her back.

Mikela hurried her sister down the back side of the slope, then up a flight of stairs and down another until they were able to enter the building with the roof from the far side. Mikela could hear tourists walking loudly along the roof of the ruins on the other side of the lawn.

She hurried Natividad back toward the room where they had spent the night. She made her sister lie down so she would be invisible to anyone who might look into the small arched opening on the far side of the building. For these were not really rooms, more like little stalls for sheep and goats. Natividad lay down on her side on the ground, her knees up to her stomach. She was breathing very hard. When Mikela lay down behind her and put her arms around her as she had in the night, she could feel her sister's stomach get very hard under her own hands, like it was made of metal. She could hear Natividad begin to sob with the pain.

"Soon," Mikela said. "Soon the baby will come out and you will feel better."

Natividad began to rock herself back and forth like a little baby when it is sad. She didn't open her eyes or answer her sister.

But the baby didn't come and didn't come. When Mikela looked out through the arches, the sun was so high it cast no shadows, then the shadows began to fall in the opposite direction. Natividad's stomach would get hard and she would sob with the pain. Mikela gave her the rebozo to bite down on and choke off the sound so no one would hear her. Mikela had never thought so many tourists came to the ruins, but again and again she heard voices and had to tell Natividad to bite down harder on the rebozo so she wouldn't give them away.

But then, late in the afternoon, Natividad's body began to run with sweat and she began calling out for their mother like a little girl and rocking back and forth and she wouldn't bite down on the rebozo anymore and Mikela knew something terrible was happening to her sister and to the baby inside her. She knew she had to find some help for her sister.

She would go to Señora Rosemary and Señora Wilma. She would beg for them to help her. They were old women, even if they weren't *comadrinas*. Perhaps they would know what to do. But as she got up to leave, Natividad screamed out and grabbed at her hand.

"Don't leave me alone," she cried. "Don't leave me alone down here."

Mikela understood that her sister was dreaming that she was down at the bottom of the trap they had dug to help their mother.

"I will be back soon," Mikela said. She pulled her hand out of her sister's grasp. She knew she was not smart enough to do this alone. She would go to the hospital with Señora Rosemary and get a doctor. Señora Rosemary would not let the doctor steal the baby. However disappointed she was in Mikela, Señora Rosemary would help Natividad the way she helped the women in her collective because they wore the clothes of the indigenous.

Mikela slipped out of the building and ran across the lawn without looking around her. She got to the bottom of the next stairs when she heard Natividad screaming so loud it sounded like someone had started a fire at her feet. She turned back. She was crying. She didn't know what to do. She saw a tall *extranjera* looking down at her from the top of the ruins. She was the artist woman who had given Mikela one of her drawings. She looked over at the building where Natividad was hiding as if she had heard Natividad screaming. Then she saw Mikela and smiled, recognizing her. But then her face became very serious and she started down the stairs. Mikela didn't know what to do, whether it was better just to run to see Natividad or ask the woman for help. She was not a bad woman, Mikela knew that. But she did not speak Spanish.

Mikela ran up to meet her and pulled on her hands. She pointed over to the building where Natividad was. She had to go and get her sister quiet or the police would come. She pulled harder on the woman's hands. *"Ayúdenos, por favor,"* she said.

Mikela ran back to the building, pulling the woman with her. Natividad was now squatting down, her back to the wall. Her hair was all loose over her face and she looked like a crazy person. She had the rebozo between her teeth and was biting down on it and shaking her head, trying to keep quiet. Mikela could see that her sister was trying to keep quiet.

The *extranjera* gasped and knelt down beside Natividad. She put one of her hands on Natividad's stomach and the other on her head.

"How long?" she asked Mikela. *"Cuánto tiempo?"*

"Dando luz," Mikela explained. *"Mi hermana esta dando luz."*

"Luz?" the woman asked, puzzled.

"Bebé," Mikela said. *"Ayúdenos."*

"Hospital," the woman said, but Mikela shook her head.

"Puedes leer?" the woman asked. She pulled a notebook from the bag buckled around her waist and wrote down some names and addresses. "Señora Rosemary,' she said and pointed at the first address. "Señora Marie," she said and pointed at the second address. *"Hablan español. Ayuda."* She wrote a little more on the paper, then stopped. *"Explica por favor. Ambulancia."*

Mikela shook her head at the ambulance, but she took the piece of paper the woman gave her and began to run. But as she was leaving the last hallway of the ruin, she heard Natividad scream so loudly she felt her own knees buckle. She couldn't leave her sister. She ran back.

The *extranjera* had taken off her sister's skirt and spread it across the ground like a blanket. Her sister did not seem to feel her nakedness. She was lying on her back with her knees up. The foreign woman was on her knees before her sister. She had her hands down between Natividad's legs.

She was saying things in a language that did not make sense to Mikela, but it sounded like Señora Rosemary's language. The sound of her voice, though, was very kind and soft, like she was sighing. The sound made Mikela's heart slow down its beating a little.

Natividad just stared at the woman, a look on her face that hurt Mikela in a place so deep that she thought she would die. It was the look that Natividad should have had on her face when their mother was beating her, when the man with the blue eyes was doing what he did to her in the capital, but she hadn't. It was a look of such fear and such sadness and at the same time Natividad was hanging onto the sound of the *extranjera*'s voice, holding on to the look in her eyes as if she were at the bottom of the trap and someone had drawn the leaves away and was looking down at her and lowering a rope.

"Shhh," the woman said. "Shhhh." A sound like the sea, like a mother hushing a little baby.

And then her sister closed her eyes and her mouth made a terrible shape as if she were screaming but no sound came.

But the foreign woman was smiling, slipping her hands inside Natividad's most private place. She was stealing the baby, and Mikela couldn't stop her. Not yet.

Mikela stood in the middle of the doorway so that when the woman stood up with the baby in her arms, ready to take it away, Mikela could grab it back. It was *their* baby, hers and Natividad's.

Her sister was making a terrible sound as if she didn't know that Mikela was there ready to protect her. She was panting like a sick dog, so fast, so fast. The sound made Mikela dizzy.

The foreign woman kept making that hushing sound and smiling at Natividad. And then she was moving back on her knees, pulling the baby out of Natividad, all blue and red and wet, very wet.

The woman held the baby close to her, not worrying about her clothes. She lowered the baby to her own lap and took her skirt and began to wipe the baby's face. She held the baby to her chest again and began to press on its back and then a little sound began to come from it and Mikela let out an even bigger sound that sounded like a sob but it wasn't sadness she was feeling.

She moved over to the foreign woman and put out her hands to take the baby.

"*Nuestro bebé,*" she said. "*Nuestro, no suyo.*" *Our* baby. *Ours*, not yours.

The woman looked at her with a little smile and patted the ground beside her. "*Siéntese,*" she said. "*Más seguro.*" Sit down, it's safer.

So Mikela did, and the woman put the baby in her arms and Mikela held it so close to her she could feel its little chest move against her own and she felt the tears come because she knew that finally God had come to them in a form that could save her sister.

Chapter 10
WANTON KINDNESS

When Wilma came hurrying in late in the afternoon with Ginny Fox to ask her help with Mikela's sister, Rosemary was more flexible that anyone imagined she would be. But she didn't, immediately, offer to take the girls in. Them or their progeny.

For it was clear as soon as she and Wilma arrived at Lourdes's apartments that the baby belonged equally to Mikela and her strange, mute sister. Any decision made would have to include Mikela—and her month's probation wasn't even started yet. But Rosemary kept these thoughts to herself.

Marie and Lourdes were settling the little mother, Natividad, and her even tinier infant in a large double bed in the downstairs apartment. Lourdes had dressed the girl in a clean t-shirt, which came almost to her ankles. Marie was fashioning a diaper out of a dishcloth under the very strict observation of Mikela, who seemed to feel that she was the only one who could safely touch the newborn. Once Marie had finished winding the dishcloth through the baby's legs, Mikela pulled the baby close to her and crawled up on the bed and curled in beside her sister, pressing the baby between them. Her sister didn't turn around, even when the baby began to cry.

"Can a child of that age breastfeed?" Lourdes asked.

"We may have to teach her," Marie said. "The response doesn't seem instinctual with her, although I can't imagine an indigenous girl her age who hasn't watched her mother nursing all her life." She knelt down by the bed, looking at Natividad, who kept her eyes determinedly closed. Very gently she put her hand on her forehead and left it there. Rosemary could see a very delicate relaxation begin, an easing of the mask-like tension in her face. Mikela, curved around her sister like a spoon, began to hum a little song to the baby, whose cries just got louder.

"Don't you think we should get a doctor to check on them both?" Lourdes asked. "Marie helped me with the placenta, but we know nothing about birth—except for having our own children. I don't trust us, frankly, and am not going to feel at rest until we have someone in here to look at them."

Rosemary looked around at the five of them. "Seems to me there are a fair number of people here to look at her—and after her. Women here give birth unassisted all the time. But if you want to call someone, call a midwife. I know one who will come and see them here. It may be less frightening to them. Where is your telephone?"

"She's very afraid that the baby will be taken away," Lourdes said. "Even with my limited Spanish, I could get that."

"You mean the little sister," Marie asked, not removing her eyes from the young mother's face. "This one seems to be somewhere else."

"Her name is Mikela," Rosemary said. "The sister."

"You know her?" Lourdes asked in surprise.

"She's my little sneak thief," Rosemary said. "The one I told you about last week."

"Señora, *por favor*," Wilma said. "You said you would give her a second chance."

"She's been working as our maid for the last month. She lives at the girls' home," Rosemary explained to Marie and Lourdes.

"Maybe they belong there now," Lourdes said.

"From what I understand, the sister ran away some months ago. But they never mentioned she was pregnant. Wilma, do you think they would take the two of them in?"

"We can call Concepción," Wilma said a little dubiously.

"*Por favor*," Mikela said, sitting up with both arms crossed over the baby's back. "*Ayúdennos.*" She began to talk so rapidly that Rosemary couldn't get everything, although Marie and Wilma kept nodding as Mikela spoke.

The doorbell rang and immediately Mikela slipped under the sheet, pulling it over her sister's head as well as her own.

It was Ginny bringing paper diapers and plastic bottles and formula. And Simon, who looked amused when he joined the group gathered in the bedroom staring down at the three little forms hidden under the sheets.

"This has mythic overtones," he said, "I just can't locate them yet."

"I don't see how we've all gotten involved in this," Lourdes said. "And I'm not sure what we need to do in the future. But right now, I think the mother needs medical attention and sleep. And the baby needs food. I don't mind keeping them here for awhile until we can figure out what to do. I have all this space going to waste."

"It's obvious," Rosemary said. "We have to find someone to adopt the baby and give that little girl back her life."

"Or find a place for the two of them together. She may want the child," Marie said.

"Mikela does, that's clear," Señora Wilma said.

The baby began to cry more loudly, its voice and Mikela's increasingly desperate consolations both muffled by the sheet.

"How are we going to get the mother to bond with the baby?" Lourdes asked.

"Get three quarters of us out of here," Simon suggested. "And the sister?"

"Do not separate them," Wilma spoke up surprisingly forcefully. "It is better right now to treat them as if they were one person—all three."

For some reason, the quiet consensus was that Rosemary was the one most fitted to try to get the baby nursing. Rosemary gave Wilma directions to the birthing clinic to pick up Sally Marshall. She chose a foreigner because a local midwife would probably feel she needed to do something bureaucratic. Sally's loyalty lay first and foremost with the mother. She knew what to ignore.

Just as Rosemary did, whatever Wilma might think.

Once everyone had left the room, Rosemary began to talk to the girls. First to Mikela in her serviceable but inelegant Spanish. Rosemary sat on the edge of the bed, at its foot, her hands folded in her lap. She spoke out into the room at large.

"We are going to help your sister," Rosemary told her. "We are going to help her take care of her baby. But to do this, you will need to let me touch the baby, Mikela."

"*Nuestro nene*," Mikela said. "*No suyo.*" *Our* baby. Not yours.

"Of course," Rosemary reassured her. "But the baby is crying with hunger, Mikela. He must eat. We must teach your sister to feed him. To do this, I will need your help." Rosemary could feel Mikela moving under the sheet, but she didn't look over at her.

"I know your sister does not talk," Rosemary said. "But does she hear?"

Mikela pulled the sheet down slightly. "She hears me. She talks to me. She is not a stupid girl. She is a very brave girl. She is a mother. She will defend her baby."

"I'm sure she will, but she does not need to now because no one here will harm the baby." Slowly Rosemary turned around to look at Mikela. The baby nuzzled, moaning, at Mikela's soiled white shirt. Mikela was still in her school uniform. Rosemary wondered if she had changed clothes since she had last left Rosemary's house. She knew Wilma and Concepción had been consulting regularly on the phone and Wilma had been repeating to Concepción, "Wait. I have a feeling about this. Don't do anything yet. It will all arrange itself." As if Wilma had some inside track.

God bless the reflexive, Rosemary had thought as she listened to Wilma, irritated that Wilma never shared the content of the conversations with her, rather used them as a fairly obvious way to increase the pressure. But Wilma had had *la razón*, the reason, Rosemary had to concede. Here was Mikela safe and sound and fiercer than ever. And Rosemary was right where Wilma had wanted her to be. Feeling guilty.

"What I need for you to do is help me introduce the baby to your sister," Rosemary said. "Your sister trusts you. I can see that. Even when she does not trust anyone else, she trusts you. If you introduce her to the baby, maybe she will trust the baby too.

"Will you let me hold the baby while you explain to your sister that we are going to help her and the baby, that she has nothing to be afraid of. I am going to teach her how to feed the baby. Can you tell her that?"

Mikela, still clutching the baby, leaned over and whispered to her sister in their native language. When her sister didn't move, Mikela sat up, clutching the baby to her chest. Her eyes began to fill with tears.

"We will help your sister," Rosemary said. "Don't be afraid."

"She is not a stupid girl. She is very brave, my sister," Mikela said, rocking back and forth with the baby netted in her tiny, wiry arms.

"But can she hear you?" Rosemary asked.

"She is not there now," Mikela said. "Natividad went away. It took too long for the baby to come. She thought she was lost in the trap and no one was coming. I was there, but she forgets."

"She is a very brave girl," Rosemary agreed. "She is a mother. She has you to help her. What happens to her when you touch her when she has gone away?"

"Sometimes she comes back. But sometimes it is worse."

"If we put the baby close to her, do you think she may come back?"

Mikela fixed her brown eyes on Rosemary's face. Her chin trembled.

"I think your sister might like that," Rosemary said. "Really I do." She stretched her hands out, palms up, as if to accept the baby. Slowly Mikela uncrossed her arms and let the baby draw a little more air. She inched across the bed toward Rosemary, but Rosemary shook her head.

"You hold the baby. I will try to get your sister to turn over so she will look at the baby."

Rosemary pulled a chair up beside Mikela's sister.

"What is her name?"

"Natividad."

"Fitting," Rosemary said. She leaned over and put her hands on Natividad's shoulders and let them rest there. She closed her eyes to get a feel for where the girl was.

"*Es curandera?*" Mikela asked. Are you a healer? Rosemary felt a little aggrieved at the disbelief in the girl's voice.

But she didn't let Mikela's doubt throw her. She concentrated on sending energy through her palms into the muscles of that traumatized little body. She let her anger pulse through as well, anger at how tiny the child was, how frail, how unfair it was that before she'd even discovered her own body, it was indentured to another. She could feel the girl begin to relax under her hands, even move a little closer to that energy. So strange, really, that the same energy that drove people away when Rosemary opened her mouth was what made her touch so eminently dependable. People knew there was a real person there and that made them feel safe.

I am who I am, the voice said pleasantly. *And you are too. It's your strength,*

Rosemary.

Wasn't that what I was telling you before? Rosemary asked.
I thought you were talking about edges then. This seems more like a caress.
Same difference, Rosemary said, smarting.
I don't want to distract you. Just wanted you to know I'm here when your own power supplies run a little low.

"They're frightening," Rosemary whispered to Natividad as she slowly moved her hands a few inches down her back and then let them rest again. "Babies are frightening. They are so red and their mouths open and it seems like they will devour us. Their hands are like the hands of ghosts. They can set up storms inside us. Cyclones. Earthquakes. *I* know. I really do. Most women do, even if they never speak of it. It isn't easy being food for another, really it isn't. It's all right to take your time."

Rosemary kept her voice low and monotonous, letting the words come as they wished. She slowly moved her outspread hands down to the girl's lower back, letting them rest there like the pages of an open book, her voice keeping up its subversive but melodious chant.

"Many of us feel we just can't do this—we can't take this little whirlwind of hunger and hurt and hold it close to our hearts." Slowly Rosemary began to shift the girl onto her side so she faced the center of the bed, where her sister knelt with the baby in her arms. Rosemary motioned to Mikela to set the baby down on the bed. She edged off her chair onto the edge of the bed so that Natividad's body could rest against hers. She closed Natividad's unresisting hand in both of hers, chafing it slightly.

It barely fills my palm, Rosemary thought with dismay, continuing to chafe it until it began to feel as warm as her own skin. She set the girl's hand flat on the sheet, tracing the flattened fingers one by one.

"We aren't prisoners," she crooned. "We can choose who we love. Who we push away. That's what makes motherhood valuable. It's something we can choose. It doesn't feel like that, no one talks about it that way, but it's true. Every mother is a creation of her own will. Whatever anyone may tell you. We choose, we *always* choose to love. And to *be* loved. Sometimes that is all that we seem to have left to us. The choice not to feel, *not* to open again, *not* to accept. I wouldn't blame you, little one. I really wouldn't. If you wanted to push that little creature off the end of the bed and the ends of the earth. Why wouldn't you? Here he is eating up your future before you've even had a good look at it."

Mikela was watching Rosemary with a look of total fascination and hope. *"Es curandera?"* she asked again. Are you a healer?

Rosemary leaned down and held Natividad tightly in her arms, weeping as if her heart would break. She felt the way she had when she'd lost Walt—or when she'd first met him and had to let go of all that anger, all that resistance, to let him in.

"Either way," she murmured to Natividad, "either way, we're here. It will be all right. It will all arrange itself. Either way, it will arrange itself.*"*

"She is not the baby," Mikela said loudly. "She is a brave girl. She is a mother. Her baby is right here."

"Touch him with your eyes," Rosemary whispered to Natividad. "Only with your eyes."

Even though she spoke in English, the girl seemed to understand and her eyes flickered open, caught a glimpse of Mikela's lively face, the baby that rested braced between her hands.

"Now your fingers," Rosemary said. "Touch him with your fingertips." She lifted Natividad's hand and drew it toward the baby, pausing an inch above the baby's flailing legs. Slowly the girl lowered her hand on to the baby's belly. As if recognizing her touch, the baby quieted.

"I knew," Mikela whispered. "I knew you would come back." But Mikela's lips kept trembling until she caught her lower lip in her teeth.

Natividad felt the baby gently with her fingertips, first with her eyes closed and then with her eyes opened. Her expression never varied, but Rosemary could sense the opening in Natividad's body and something deep in Rosemary began to relax as she could feel that some kind of connection between the mother and child was possible.

"She feeds the baby now?" Mikela asked, patting her own flat chest.

"If she chooses," Rosemary said. "We have bottles if she doesn't. Either way, *todo arreglaré.*"

"She must," Mikela said sternly. "It is her duty. She is like the Virgin. God depends on her."

Natividad smiled at her sister's voice—not only the sternness but the sad undercurrent of desperation that Mikela couldn't control. She looked into Mikela's face as she drew the baby toward her. Rosemary gently lifted Natividad's t-shirt and brought the baby's lips to Natividad's tiny breast buds. Natividad continued to look at her sister, but she pulled the baby closer to her and drew up her knees to create a small cave to contain him.

Gently, Rosemary kept rubbing her back while the baby mouthed at the dry nipple. "Either way, either way," she repeated. *"Todo arreglaré."*

Mikela inched closer, slipping her hand under the baby's head so that its lips could close more tightly around Natividad's nipple.

For a moment, it seemed as if the room lifted and fell with the rhythm of Rosemary's breath, which was the rhythm of Natividad's and Mikela's, a silence broken only by the busy suckling of the baby.

You see, the voice said gently, so gently, *you do have something left to give. And more than one person eager to receive it.*

It shouldn't *be,* Rosemary thought crossly. None of this should be happening.

But it is, the voice said. *Isn't that just the way of things. They're always defying our sense of justice, right and wrong, either way, todo arreglaré if we just open ourselves up to the ocean.*

Poppycock, Rosemary thought, but she couldn't seem to mobilize any anger. The little girls kept, even now, that easy rhythm of breath she had established for them. They returned it to her as if it were their own creation.

SECTION III
THE ONLY SEAT IN THE ROOM

True, it is an interruption of our ordinary tasks; we do lay down our work as though it were a day of rest when the penitent is alone before you in self-accusation. This is indeed an interruption. But it is an interruption that searches back into its very beginnings that it might bind up anew that which sin has separated, that in its grief it might atone for lost time, that in its anxiety it might bring to completion that which lies before it.

S. Kierkegaard

IT ISN'T WHAT IT SEEMS
(Ben)

The question now is not trying to regain what we lost—but trying to go forward. That's why I encouraged Lourdes to take the grant. Why I've insisted Gwen come down to visit as well. Now that Cristina is dead, Lourdes and I are all Gwen has.

Gwen and Lourdes would both correct me if they could. I am all that Gwen has, they would both tell me. But I just can't seem to accept that. I see them as having so much to give each other. We don't have to call it a family. I look into my daughter's eyes and I see something back there that sends a jolt of anguish right through me. Something similar sits in the back of Lourdes' gaze as well. I could never name it. All I know is that it waits, and it has a purity and a weight and a sorrow and a joy to it that makes me feel I am in the presence of something truly terrible and desirable. Something a believing man would call Holy. I'm a secular Jew, a chemist—and a believer. I know the Holy when I feel myself held in its unremitting gaze. I would not necessarily call it loving, but irresistibly compelling.

"She needs me," I told Gwen when I let her know I was going down earlier than I had originally planned to see Lourdes.

"Why shouldn't she?" Gwen, who alternates between a terrified girl of thirteen and a world-weary woman of fifty, asked me. She was setting the table. I noticed how she removed her knife and fork and spoon and realigned them. How she held the spoon in front of her and then blew on it and rubbed some imperceptible tarnish from it. "Wives need their husbands."

Gwen has never forgiven me for leaving Cristina. Leaving her, my brother and sister try to correct me. But they're wrong. Gwen can't forgive me for leaving Cristina to her care. She's told me that again and again in the past few months.

"I didn't know enough," she will say. "If I'd known more, maybe I could have gotten her more involved—- gotten her out of the house more."

I had no idea what a recluse Cristina had become. Her phone calls—which never let up even with the divorce—were always raucous and argumentative, as if she'd just come in from a heavy evening at the local bar. Of course, I worried about Gwen, but I knew I'd never be able to get custody. If I did, that would mean sacrificing Gwen's relationship with her mother because Cristina would never have stood for so much disloyalty. Gwen seemed like such a balanced young teenager, mature above her years.

"What did you know," she yells at me now. "You just packed your bags and cleared your mind and it's as if she never was."

"It's not that simple," I tell her. "It's never that simple. You're a smart girl. You know that."

"I know how long it took her to die," Gwen said.

Cristina had been diagnosed with breast cancer. Treatable breast cancer, Gwen likes to remind me. But she stockpiled her four prescriptions for xanax and her three prescriptions for valium and took them both with a quart of Wild Turkey one evening when Gwen had stayed late at college to study. Or so Gwen still claims—although there is a young man who calls here regularly, and who she refuses to speak to at all. He may have had some small role in her absence. I'm not accusing my daughter. I think she's blameless in the matter of her mother's death. I think I am too. Gwen doesn't share my views.

"She started dying the day the moving men came to ship your things to North Carolina and take ours over to that little condo," Gwen said. "Nine years is a long time to take to die."

"Or live," I tell her. "Your mother had lots of opportunities to get over me." Even while I was still in the picture, goddamnit, I want to say—but thank God still have not. Suffering silently or alone was not Cristina's way. Not, Gwen will be quick to remind me, until the very end. I don't believe in such last minute transformations in character. I believe she died expecting Gwen to be there weeping uncontrollably at the end. And I hate her for it. Forgive me, I hate her for it.

"She was the one who asked me to leave, Gwen."

I look at my angry, unfamiliar daughter and wonder if her presence really is what has ended my marriage to Lourdes? I feel very disloyal when I think this. Gwen was, for thirteen years, the miracle glue in my marriage to her mother. It was Gwen I came home to, not Cristina. And Cristina never, for a second, missed that—or forgave me for it.

Just as Gwen never forgave me when she realized that one of the reasons for my frequent visits to Boston area once she started college was not just work but also Lourdes. Right after I introduced them for the first time, two months after meeting Lourdes, Gwen got Cristina to call me up at Lourdes' apartment and bawl me out for misleading Gwen about the purposes for my visits. "She thought you were working up to a reconciliation, you fucking bastard," Cristina said. "Why did you lead her on that way?"

Lourdes listened without expression as I tried to placate Cristina. When I hung up the phone, she asked me how Cristina had learned the phone number.

"The phone directory," I said, unwilling to implicate Gwen.

Lourdes handed me the phone book. "Where?" she asked. It was the first time I realized Lourdes' number was unlisted.

The next time I came to visit, Lourdes had changed her phone number and had bought me a cell phone on which to receive personal calls. That response was—and is—so much Lourdes. No discussion, just this rapid analysis and then a solution that I can either take or leave. When I tried to explain about Cristina, she just shrugged.

"I want to feel comfortable answering the phone in my own apartment. Her phone manners leave far too much to be desired." There was something about how Lourdes spoke that made me realize it really was a take it or leave it matter.

"Gwen and her mother are very protective of one another," I said.

"You don't need to explain anything, Ben," Lourdes said. "I've taken the steps I need to take care of myself."

But was taking an unexpected windfall grant and heading off for a country she'd never even seen before really what Lourdes needed to do to take care of herself when Gwen showed up on our doorstep in October with four large suitcases and a battered cardboard box containing a microwave and a coffee maker?

It didn't help that the first thing Gwen did was push past Lourdes without a word and throw herself in my arms. "I can't do it," she sobbed. "I've tried, but I just can't do it, Daddy."

The it she couldn't do was finish her last year in college. She was at that point living in a dorm—because I had strongly recommended that she not live on alone in the condo she'd shared with Cristina all the way through college in order to extend Cristina's alimony beyond Gwen's high school years. We'd invited Gwen down to spend some weeks with us right after Cristina's funeral, but the situation was so awkward for both of them that Gwen announced she preferred to have her cousin Ruth, my sister Naomi's eldest daughter, come and stay with her in Boston for the rest of the summer. Lourdes and I decided I should fly up and visit her every two weeks. Gwen was the one who said the visits were too frequent. She was also the one who wanted to stay on in the condo by herself.

"She's twenty-two," Lourdes said when I brought up the advisability of a dorm. "Surely she has some sense of what is best for her."

"There's twenty-two and twenty-two," I said.

"Twenty-two is what life asks of you," Lourdes shrugged. At seventeen, she'd been on her own with responsibility for her younger sister. By twenty-two, Lourdes was a mother twice over. Her mother had died when she was thirteen. You would have thought this would have created some sympathy in her for Gwen's loss. But all these encounters with Gwen after Cristina's death showed a hardness to Lourdes I had never imagined. Perhaps she hadn't either. Perhaps it frightened her so much, some central confidence just guttered out.

All I know is that four weeks after Gwen came to live with us in October, Lourdes accepted her traveling fellowship. A take it or leave it solution.

My sister Naomi, who likes Lourdes, thinks she was just trying to be helpful. Buying all of us some time. Gwen, I believe, is as conflicted about successfully running her step-mother off as she would have been about having to live with her—and neither of these conflicts holds a candle to her ambivalence about her own mother's death.

I try to get Gwen to concentrate on her own life, to find some work that might help her decide on a career path after college. (She's majoring in literature, which has few empirical applications. She's obviously not scientifically inclined. And doesn't seem to have the right temperament for a service job.) I haven't set an ultimatum, but I think she understands when Lourdes returns, she will need to leave.

Gwen has rage about my leaving Cristina and guilt about her own role in Cristina's death—but I have my own guilts and areas of responsibility I will not assume. I don't want Gwen ever to be dependent on me the way she was on her mother. And certainly not the way her mother was on me. I have never met anyone else in my life who disliked me as much as Cristina did—or persisted in having such an inextinguishable set of expectations for me either. I know that people watching the way Gwen interacts with me right now might wonder—but I know what motivates Gwen, however similar her behaviors are to her mother's, is worlds apart from Cristina's lethal push-pull. There are people who just have a fault line where their soul should be. It doesn't matter how much love you pour in—it just seeps away.

I know Lourdes looks at Gwen and believes she is Cristina's twin. And something about that is so painful she shuts down completely, as if all the life in her just poured out, pfft, just like that. Lourdes may have a fault line too. The difference is she doesn't ask for more. What's gone is gone. I hate it. It terrifies me, actually. It violates everything I believe in and care about. I'm a positive man. I like to feel that things, however difficult, can be set right. But Lourdes has made it clear that I am not to be part of the solution. For her.

And probably not for Gwen either. I look at my angry, guilt-ridden, beautiful, lost, tenacious and promising daughter and I think, deep inside her she has my heart, she has my soul, and she knows exactly what she grieves for and what can and can't be consoled.

I know deep down there she doesn't want to keep Lourdes away from me forever.

I know, just as the two of them do, that I would do almost anything not to be in a position where I might have to choose.

But if you were, I hear a voice whisper to me whenever I hang up the phone after another difficult phone call with Lourdes, if you were, the voice says again and it sounds a little like Lourdes' voice, a little like Cristina's, a little like Gwen's, we all know exactly who you would choose.

They're right. I do know. I would choose Lourdes.

But I don't know whether Lourdes, even more than I, could survive my making that choice.

So, when Lourdes told me in this last phone call about the little girls, I really knew, you see, what was at stake, what still is, if she decides she can't keep them. There are some things you can't explain in words. Your can't really explain why—because there may be no explanation. You just know that suddenly, without warning, you stand in the uncharted minefield of someone's essential being.

When I promised Lourdes I would be her partner in sickness and in health, I also meant (although she can't bear to put me to the test anymore than I can bear to do the same to her) I would be her partner in those places—so undesired and unexpected—where the past swallows the present and the present gives birth to the past and hell, hell itself, would be easier.

"Tomorrow," I told her just an hour ago. "Tomorrow you will be in my arms again. Tomorrow my world will have color again. Tomorrow my world will have heat and texture and light."

There was a silence, and then she said, "And Gwen. Have her plans changed too?"

The weight of each word made me breathless. My daughter. My dear daughter.

"The first week is ours, ours alone," I told her. "I don't intend to share you with anyone. I want you to be forewarned."

"Oh Ben," she said. I wanted to help her shoulder the weight of the word. If I only could.

"I know what I'm asking of you," I told her, two years ago as she smoothed the sheets up over me.

But did I? Do we ever? Would it have stopped me?

"I need you," I told her. "I need you the way other men need bread and water, sunlight and rain. I need you the way saints need God."

Chapter 11
TOUCH-SEEING

In just a month, Lourdes' life had transformed from maddening but self-selected solitude to a constant open house. She woke worrying about feeding schedules and tutorials, listening for the sound of Mikela and Natividad murmuring in that melodious but incomprehensible language of theirs, relishing the music as a living pulse to her day. Without much discussion, they had all quickly settled into a routine. Ginny and Simon came over after breakfast to tutor Natividad and Mikela. Lourdes would take the baby upstairs to her studio so the girls could concentrate. Later, Rosemary would come and do massage therapy with Natividad and the baby, while Señora Wilma or her cousin, Mamí Concepción, who worked in one of the language schools and also at the girls home where Mikela had been, would give Lourdes emergency Spanish lessons. In the afternoon, Marie Toussaint would come and spell Lourdes for awhile so she could either walk or get down to serious work in her studio. For, astonishing as it seemed, in all this hubbub, Lourdes' imagination was flourishing.

Lourdes' drawings were becoming very large and sculptural. Larger than life. It was something about holding the baby, all the touch, beginning to see again through her fingers again, just like infants do. Mothers. She was learning about the girls' lives through her Spanish lessons with Mamí Concepción. The images from the girls' stories spoke to Lourdes in a way that she did not quite understand, as if they *belonged* to her at the deepest level. It wasn't just the image of Natividad strung up by her feet, her mother beating her with a broom. It was this terrible picture she called *Mother of God*—of a beautiful young woman being systematically raped by soldiers and lawyers and priests and foreigners. For where, they all wondered, had those blue eyes come from? And how much trauma did they represent? How many generations?

Lourdes found the images of the girls' lives mixed with disturbing ease with the images of the statues that had already started filling her imagination since coming to Antigua. But this translation between the images of the saints and real life wasn't restricted to the girls. Lourdes would wake at night and *see* Rosemary with all the detail she had in the one drawing class where Rosemary had modeled. The image that came to Lourdes wasn't warm, nurturing, rather of a stern God with a divine plan. Lourdes drew the old woman, nude, sitting in a large wingback chair, the miniature girls suspended in her grip, rigid with resistance. Each girl had an arm wrapped around her sister's shoulders, the other arm outstretched stiff as a cross piece, palm raised at right angles to the arm as if to fend off the relentless press of destiny. They were naked except for a red *rebozo* tied across their chests, their exposed pubises childishly bare of hair. The baby peered from between their heads, the red cloth that bound him to them binding the two girls to each other as well. She drew Ginger, carried on a bier by Marie and Rosemary and Lourdes and Ginny, like the cripple who was lowered through the roof for Jesus' touch. But they were lowering Ginger into an artist's studio, where Natividad, baby forgotten at her breast, sat before an easel, charcoal in hand.

The slightest thing could set an image off: a song Mikela had learned in school, a phrase of Marie's. As she drew, Lourdes felt a sweet relief, as if she was letting herself be carried down a fast moving river toward the sea. She felt as she had in her first apartment, intensely alive and fascinated but at the same time furtive, as if this sense of sureness and delight could only lead to disaster.

What do you take me for? the voice asked her. *A sadist? A tease?*

This has nothing to do with you, Lourdes said. She rubbed the charcoal drawing with a kleenex and then her fingertips, deepening the contour of the legs of the woman, hands and feet still showing the stigmata of nails, who lay unresisting in her father's arms. The expression on God-the-Father's face bothered her intensely, until she realized that she had somehow captured the gentleness in Ben's expression, something that made this image even more troubling to her than the image of the old woman holding the crucifix made of the two little Indian girls.

Of course it bothers you, the voice said warmly. *Love bothers you. Pleasure bothers you.*

Lourdes closed her eyes in frustration. If only she could drown her out. Especially now. She felt a hot breath on her neck, realer than real, one that brought with it a wave of sexual excitement and then an equally intense wave of fear. She opened her eyes immediately, but the strange mix of sensations and associations wouldn't stop, the images they evoked combining in crazy ways. Ben's hand on her thigh, the warm release as his fingers just grazed her labia, she was so ready for him. And then an image of her mother Annie, the self-satisfaction on her face as she came out of her bedroom and stared down her dour daughters. "It's not for you to say. When you're older, you'll understand. You won't be so quick to judge." Grabbing Lourdes' shoulder, turning her back to face her, and Lourdes seeing in her mother's face those same competing waves of pleasure and terror. "I love you, baby. Don't judge me. Whatever you do, don't judge me." The feel of her mother's shoulders inside her arms, her mother's breasts against her chest. Her mother's shoulders rocking with guilty sobs. Lourdes' hands memorizing, memorizing, memorizing. Even then, at ten, Lourdes was taller than her mother. She could feel her mother's heart beating directly against her own chest, hollow as a drum. Nothing, no one, home.

It was logical, she assured herself, to have it all come back. She was Natividad's age when her mother had died and she and her sister had to make their own way. She had Mikela's fierce loyalty toward her own sister Jacquie. But whatever Lourdes told herself, she wasn't really a thinking being these days. She was litmus. A holding cell for lost sensations, personalities desperate for embodiment.

She tried to draw Annie from memory, hoping to slow the process down, bring it out into the open. But when she tried, she was surprised and a little horrified to see Marie Toussaint's small, slim frame take shape under the sweep of her pastels. Marie's mouth was open in song, her hands clasped, palms flat and fingers splayed, at a right angle to her breast bone, just as they did the namaste salute in yoga class. *The Mother Who Sings for Herself*, the voice said, and Lourdes obediently penciled the phrase on the margin of the drawing.

She returned to her blasphemous images. Simon and Ginny hammering God-the-Father to a cross. God was the awful grandfather she'd seen at the hairdressing salon. A cigar drooped from his lips. His hand was raised to strike, but Simon had the spike ready and Ginny, standing behind the cross, had gripped the old man's waist with both her hands. He wasn't going anywhere. But Lourdes was. Already the next image was forming under her charcoal.

A woman seen only in profile, forming out of wet clay a manikin, so beautiful, so chastely sexed, inside her large, arthritic hands.

God's Boy Toy? the voice suggested.

Love, Lourdes wrote.

The drawings shocked her and also filled her with elation. Her whole body felt alive, anticipant, just as she had when she'd first met Ben, or, years before that, when she'd started drawing for the first time. What was different here was that she could maintain the state without conflict amid all the fervor around her. She didn't need to be an isolate to be an artist.

"Who *are* these people answering the phone," Ben asked her in exasperation when he called unexpectedly late in the afternoon. Ginny and Simon had stopped by to help with homework and Lourdes had raced upstairs to her studio to take advantage of the brief reprieve. She left it up to them to answer the phone or let it ring—since it could as well be for them as for her.

"It's too difficult to go into," Lourdes said.

"You haven't forgotten we're coming down to visit you soon."

"There's plenty of space here."

"I'm glad you're not feeling isolated, but—"

"I miss you too," she said. Seconds too late.

As soon as she hung up, Lourdes went downstairs. She always did after her calls with Ben, she felt so guilty and unsettled. She would hold the baby while Mikela helped Natividad with the homework Simon had assigned them. Or she would chat with Simon or Ginny if they were still around. It was those moments, the baby nuzzling aimlessly over her chest, her body quieting with the touch of his lips, his little kneading hands, that opened her heart to Ben. Too late, always too late. The despair wasn't there as long as she held the baby. She would watch the two little girls seated at the table, their dark heads gleaming under the overhead light, Mikela's impatience flashing as Natividad's attention wandered. She would look fondly at these new friends of hers, Simon and Ginny, who stood behind the girls, correcting a word, a sum. "Maybe," she mused, her breath matching the rhythm of the sleeping child, "maybe. . ." She never let the thought, the urge go any further.

This afternoon when she went down, she found Mikela alone in the patio washing their clothes. When Lourdes asked her where Natividad and the baby were, she appeared not to hear. She just threw their clothes against the side of the sink beating out dirt and suds.

Lourdes went to the front door to see if perhaps Natividad and the baby were coming back from a little outing to the church at the end of the street. The girl was so frail and the baby so robust, they discouraged her from going any farther without a companion. Simon and Ginny, planning the girls' next lessons, didn't look up as she passed the table.

When she opened the door, she didn't see Natividad immediately, focused as she was on the doorway to the churchyard in the distance. Not until her foot tucked itself into the girl's side. She had missed the baby by an inch or two. Lourdes knelt down immediately, taking the girl and the baby into her arms. Terrified, she lifted Natividad's head—and saw the cloudy eyes and the runny nose. Stoned. As stoned as Jacquie had been the night Lourdes told her to leave the house immediately and never come back.

Lourdes didn't say that to Natividad. But she called her by her own sister's name. When she played the scene over in her mind later, she could hear her own voice saying, over and over again, "Jacquie, what have you done to yourself? Oh, baby, what have you done?" There was a sense of shame at her mistake, at these crazy words she couldn't stop saying. And then the rage, the unbearable rage because she could hear her own son, Seth, crying helplessly in his crib in the far bedroom. It wasn't Seth. A man now. It wasn't Jacquie, dead sixteen years. It was only Miguel, Mikela's archangel, muffled in the folds of a red rebozo.

Lourdes concentrated on untying the cloth. "Oh baby," she kept saying, "what have you done." Once she had the baby free, she held him close to her as she crouched on her heels, letting Natividad slip back down on the doorsill. Lourdes couldn't move. Natividad, her head propped on the doorframe, watched her without blinking. Lourdes couldn't look away. She could feel Miguel's little heart beating inside her hands. They knew each other, she and Natividad. They looked into each others eyes and they knew each other. Lourdes didn't dare let go of the baby. She didn't dare move another muscle.

Mikela had come out of the apartment, alerted by the street noise. She saw immediately what had happened and tried to take the baby from Lourdes. When she couldn't get Lourdes to respond to her or give her the baby, she went for Simon and Ginny. They put Natividad to sleep once they were assured she was out of her stupor—just in her usual inarticulate daze. Mikela kept talking fiercely to her sister, and kept trying to take the baby from Lourdes. Simon ordered in a pizza and did not leave until he and Ginny had settled Mikela and the baby down for the night as well. He had to take the baby from Lourdes himself. Mikela, he promised her, would be an equally fierce guardian. From who, his eyes asked sadly.

Natividad lay curled in a fetal position on a small mattress in the other downstairs bedroom, her head covered in a blanket. She hadn't moved since Simon had lifted her up off the doorsill and carried her back into the house, except to turn her head when Mikela slapped her. Twelve years old. An old tragic story Lourdes wanted no part in. She knew, she'd always known, how it would end. What had she been thinking? What in heaven's name had she been thinking?

Once Ginny and Simon left, Lourdes went up to her own apartment and slipped miserably under the covers of her own bed. The phone seemed to ring all around her, down in the girls' apartment, in the house next door, everywhere but her own living room. It stopped, began again. The fourth time, Mikela called up to her, *"Señora, por favor, contéstalo. Estás molestando los sueños del nene."* Answer. You're bothering the baby's dreams. Although she was standing, hands officiously on her hips, down in the patio below, she too sounded as if she were right beside Lourdes' bed.

So, reluctantly, Lourdes contested.

"Where have you been?" Ben asked. "Never mind. I have great news."

"Five days," Lourdes said slowly. "You're both coming in five days?"

"Gwen's sticking to her original schedule. That means we can go off on a second honeymoon. I've been checking the guidebooks. The lake sounds great."

"But the girls," Lourdes said.

"What girls?"

"What do you mean?" she asked, genuinely puzzled. How could she have forgotten that she hadn't told Ben about Natividad and Mikela? Couldn't. Her responses to them had been so natural, so accepting they made an awkward mirror to her responses to Gwen. She had known she needed to keep the situation from him. And tonight she couldn't tell him because the terrible mix of emotions she felt toward Natividad were far too close to those she had for Gwen for her to describe them, or even, in the privacy of her mind, bear the resonance.

"Five days is fine," she said. "I'll make some reservations if you have particular hotels in mind."

"Why don't you ask your new friends," he said quietly, obviously disappointed by her absence of enthusiasm.

Too late. Always too late, the voice murmured.

Lourdes shook her head and gripped the phone receiver more tightly. "I'm just a little disoriented. You woke me up. I've been working so hard on my drawings, I've worked up a sleep debt, and I thought I'd pay it off tonight. I want you to come Ben."

"Soon, then."

You can't remember his touch, the voice said. *How can you call it love if you can't remember his touch?*

I can too, Lourdes reprimanded her. I can remember it every time I hold the baby.

Is that why you want to send them away? You can't bear to remember?

But Lourdes wasn't listening. She was under the covers again. Her hand reaching out and touching Natividad's cheek. Her hand reaching out and touching Jacquie's cheek. Her fingers grazing Annie's face, so still and white and untroubled, in the coffin. Ben's face the night she decided to leave. She could see their eyes, open, closed, feel the temperature of their skin, see her own hands, so round with youth, so tried, now, by chemicals and age—touching. Seeing. Touch-seeing.

Lourdes imagined Seth or Evan in her arms, her fingers cupping a busy mouth and bringing it to her breast. The sweet stability of the rocking chair.

What are you going to title it, Lourdes? This world where you are a perfect stranger to rage? And love, Lourdes. A perfect stranger to love.

"I have to have a plan," Lourdes blurted to Marie as soon as she opened the door to her the following morning.

"Pressed a few of the buttons, no?" Marie asked. "Simon called to tell me of the how do you do yesterday. I will talk with the girl today—she will be more awake. I will take the baby for a little walk. You go and do your beautiful work."

Lourdes didn't expect that she could, but she did. She drew herself on four large sheets of paper, a terrifying, towering figure, reaching, reaching, with her broom, as the girl turned and turned. *My Future*, Lourdes wrote.

Don't be afraid, the voice said. *Even if it is, you both will live.*

Simon and Ginny and Marie seemed understanding when Lourdes told them of her decision. But when she tried to explain her decision to Concepción, she encountered a determined blankness.

"My husband," she finally said. "I have no choice. I must first attend to him. We must find some other place for the girls to stay."

"Of course," Concepción said gravely. But her faintly contemptuous look made Lourdes wild with a simple, pulsing anger.

"I don't even *know* these children," Lourdes said. "I just happened upon them one afternoon in the ruins. Wrong place. Wrong time." Even as she spoke, she wanted to correct herself.

"No one is saying you haven't been generous," Concepción said.

But no one was stepping up as Lourdes stepped back. Not Ginny. Not Simon. Not Marie. Finally, reluctantly, Lourdes called Rosemary.

"There's no point in beating around the bush. I really need your help."

What Lourdes didn't make clear in the phone call was that she needed Rosemary's help fast. Very fast. That evening, she looked at the girls quietly seated at the dining room table waiting for their food. She knew she couldn't sit like this with them again. Not for even one more evening.

They are not safe with me. Although it held her the way the other voice did, it had to be her own voice, didn't it? For that voice called her *you*, not *I*, not *me*.

They're still children, she thought as she handed them their bowls of stew. Although their eyes watched her warily, their bodies still knew how to rest. Oh, she wanted to shake them, warn them somehow. *Cuidado*. Watch out. That knowledge couldn't go deep enough. It could never go deep enough. She picked up her spoon and they both imitated her.

"*Sabroso*," Mikela said after she took a sip. "*Muy sabroso.*" She looked meaningfully at Natividad, who stared blankly at a point somewhere above Lourdes' head. There is nothing sadder than a twelve year old girl with a drug hangover, but Lourdes didn't feel an ounce of sympathy at that minute. She wanted to take Natividad by the shoulders, force her face as close to the girl as possible and hiss at her, scream at her, demand her attention. Just as Annie, in a drunken rage, used to do with Lourdes and Jacquie if they every tried to close her out. But even as Lourdes saw herself, *felt* herself, approaching the girl in this way, she could also feel the complete passivity of Natividad's little body, and a compassion so deep in herself it made her crazy with sorrow and anger. So much anger.

Lourdes had never imagined herself capable of such anger—unless it was directed at helping or protecting someone else. Now it wasn't. For *was* she really trying to protect Miguel, safely asleep in his little box? Wasn't he watched over night and day by Mikela and this wonderful group of people, all drawn to the situation by forces out of their control?

Lourdes was protecting something, something as precious to her *as* her own children, or her sister when Jacquie was a child, but what *was* it? If she didn't get a handle on it soon, something terrible was going to happen. She knew that as surely as she knew her own name or the feel of a piece of charcoal in her hand, the sound it made connecting with paper.

The girls sipped their soup, their eyes fixed on her, the white showing beneath the brown irises since Lourdes, still standing by the stove, was so much bigger than they. Is this how Annie felt? Lourdes wondered. Is this what it felt like to sit down and eat with Jacquie and me every day? Is this what it felt like to be seen as a monster? She could feel a trap door opening in her belly. She could smell ice and dust and mold. She sat down and took a sip of soup, trying to draw in the aroma of oregano and thyme and bay leaf with which she had flavored it. She looked up and stared at the two girls. Their black hair gleamed in the lamplight as they bent over their spoons. I have to get them out of here. For their sakes. They're not safe. They're not safe.

From who? The voice asked. *They're not safe from who, Lourdes?*

She drew a deep breath and looked out at the air well, the stars appearing in the sky, the light from her studio edging the leaves of the pomegranate tree, the lights from the patio below edging all the old stones of the back wall of the courtyard.

"Do you have homework? *Hay tareas?*" she asked Mikela, who nodded her head. With Concepción's intervention, she was back in school.

The little girl touched her sister's arm, prompting Natividad to give Mikela her half-full soup bowl so Mikela could carry it to the sink. They never asked for seconds. Never asked for salt. Drank their milk with more curiosity than relish.

"You can leave the baby with me," Lourdes said in her poor Spanish. It came out as a command, and she could see Mikela's back stiffen, see the way her eyes darted over to the large cardboard box set beside the couch, where Lourdes insisted they leave the baby while they ate.

Lourdes forced herself to smile. She stood up and went over, shadowed by Mikela, and lifted the box up. Natividad, oblivious, was standing at the sink washing their dishes. The smell coming from Mikela was acrid she was so afraid, and at that Lourdes heart dissolved.

"You're a good girl," she told Mikela. "A smart girl. You take good care of your sister and your nephew. You work very hard to take care of them, don't you."

Mikela looked at her, assessing the tone of Lourdes' voice since she didn't understand her words. She looked over to her sister as if to include her in Lourdes' tone, but with the glance, Lourdes' anger began to build again. She walked over to the sink with the box in her arms, and reached a finger out to touch Natividad's shoulder. Natividad stilled as soon she felt Lourdes' fingertip. Lourdes had never seen such stillness. It broke her heart and made her want to kill.

There, the voice said. *It's out now. You can never take it back. It makes you want to kill. A twelve year old girl, Lourdes.*

Lourdes squinted her eyes, as if that could drown out the sound. She mimicked going downstairs and Natividad, after drying her hands carefully on the dish towel, followed her, as did Mikela.

Just after Lourdes set the baby, still sleeping in his box, on the table, the phone upstairs rang.

Lourdes pulled their door shut with a loud bang before racing upstairs. Don't let it stop, she thought, as she ran up the last few steps and threw herself toward the couch.

"Is that you?"

"Who else?" Ben asked.

"Oh, any of a half dozen locals—Marie or Simon or Ginny or Rosemary, not to mention Concepción or Wilma."

"You've built quite a life for yourself in just three months."

"Built implies intention, and this just happened. But I need to fill you in, Ben." She told him about the girls, the baby, the labor, the drugs. She didn't wait for his responses.

"I had no idea," he said when she finally came to a stop. "You gave me no idea. But you can't be expected to take all this on by yourself. You went down there to make art, not to start a halfway house."

"I have help," Lourdes said. "People come every day."

"You can't bring them home with you, Lourdes," Ben said gently.

"I never said I wanted to, did I?"

"You're smitten with the baby and the little sister."

"Sucked in," Lourdes said.

"What can I do to help?"

"Back me up. Tell me I need to find another place for them to stay."

"Because I'm your macho man and I come first?" He laughed. "I don't think you need any excuse, Lourdes. Your asking them to move on would make sense to anyone. They've been staying there for almost five weeks, haven't they? Total strangers. And I had no idea. Absolutely no idea."

"They've gotten to me," Lourdes said. "In ways I can't explain, can't understand. I don't want to get away from them, really, just what they're opening up in me." Lourdes had never explained her childhood to Ben. Estranged was the word she had chosen. It wasn't a word that fit very easily with this hurtling sense of pressure and dread.

"I don't know how to stop it, Ben. Something got set in motion and I don't know how to stop it."

"All because the kid sniffed glue?" he asked.

At that moment Lourdes felt a stab of hatred toward him. I am going crazy, she thought. I can't get the words out fast enough. I can't get the feelings to match.

"I feel like something terrible is going to happen and I don't know how to protect us,' she said and started to sob. Lourdes had not cried since the day Annie died—not when she learned that Jacquie was never going to get well, not when she sent her away, or heard the news of her death, not when George left her, not when she left Ben.

"I wish I weren't so far away," Ben said. "I wish I could hold you."

But who could hold Lourdes as she was now, shaking so hard her teeth were clicking against each other.

"Don't hang up," Ben said. "Whatever you do, don't hang up on me, Lourdes. Keep talking. Keep your eyes fixed on something in the room, a lamp, a table." Where had he learned to talk like this, Lourdes wondered. Was she changing places with his crazy dead wife?

Why not? the voice asked. *Why don't you change places with everyone you hate, Lourdes? Be on the receiving end for once in your life.*

That's the only place I've ever been, Lourdes thought. The receiving end.

"Keep talking," Ben said. "Sweetheart, keep talking to me. Tell me what you're so afraid of having happen. You're afraid they'll feel abandoned, those two little girls? You think the people around there will judge you? How *can* they? You already told me none of them are racing up to take your place."

"You don't understand."

"But I'm trying. I want you to stay in touch with me. Day or night. This is *your* time, darling, no one else's. Time to stretch your wings. To find yourself as an artist."

Lourdes wrapped her arms around herself trying to stop the shaking.

"Nothing you've told me does anything but fill me with admiration," Ben said. "You delivered the baby, for God's sake. And then you've taken them in for weeks, organized a battalion of acquaintances to help. But it wasn't planned, none of it was planned. You're not one of those single women or childless couples who move down there to adopt. Can't you just hook them up with one of them?"

Lourdes kept her eyes on the lamp, just as Ben had suggested. She could see the dust, the omnipresent dust, coating its rim. She reached her hand out and began to make small swift strokes in it, covering the base with the semblance of feathers. "They don't want to go away. They don't want to be separated."

"But maybe it's for the best," Ben said softly. "Maybe it will let each of them get what they need."

"They need each other," Lourdes said, able now, with those words, to breathe regularly again.

"Just as I need you," Ben said. "And you need me. I'm coming as soon as I can."

"It's all right," Lourdes said. "I just lost if for a little."

"No, it's not. It's not all right between us. It's not all right down there. Just listen to yourself."

"Who are you to judge?" Lourdes screamed. She caught herself immediately. "I didn't mean that. I didn't meant for that sound to come out of my mouth. But really, who *are* you to judge."

"Try love," Ben said. "Change the word to love. That is a question I can easily answer—and I'm going to do so as soon as I can. In person."

The next morning, when Rosemary showed up, Natividad was alert enough to let her in and bring her upstairs. Lourdes was in her studio working on her huge drawing. She didn't hide it from them. How could she? It took up an entire wall. Natividad came up to it and began to study the strokes. Rosemary stood at the door, her hands supporting her lower back as she took in the scale.

"Do you have any idea what you are trying to tell yourself?"

"Not the least," Lourdes said briskly. "That's why I need to have you help me. I need a little distance from all this."

"You said you wanted to take a trip."

"It's more than that," Lourdes said. "Ben's coming, yes, and then his daughter, Gwen. But I don't think I'm the one to keep the girls. I have the space, I know that."

"But you may not have the psychic room?" The older woman stared uncompromisingly at Lourdes. Lourdes closed her eyes, but instead of feeling Rosemary's glance as burning, it felt remarkably cool, soothing.

"There are things you don't know about me. Things Ben doesn't know about me. Things even I don't understand." She felt herself begin to rock a little back and forth and then felt small hands wrap around either side of her waist, steadying her. When she opened her eyes, she couldn't see Natividad, who stood directly behind her, her hands still gripping Lourdes' waist.

"When do you want me to take them?" Rosemary asked.

"Today. As soon as possible."

"For how long?"

"I can't say."

"I can't do it permanently. I'm too old. And I have my friend. She isn't well."

"I don't know who else to ask," Lourdes said.

"You've asked everyone else?"

Lourdes shook her head, smiled. "No. I knew I needed to start with you. And it's a relief these days to know I know something."

"I'll do what I can," Rosemary said.

Lourdes heard a scuffing sound behind her and turned to see Natividad erasing one of the waves in the girl's hair, tossed here and there with the beatings of the broom. Slowly, Natividad penciled in another line. The baby's cries rose through the air well, magnified, enveloping. A girl's high voice from the street filled the room with flirtatious laughter.

"She's forgotten the baby," Rosemary said.

She and Lourdes watched Natividad stand back and then approach the large drawing again. Then they turned and went downstairs to comfort the baby. Natividad didn't seem to notice their movements until they reached the door, when she turned to them, a delicate smile on her lips. "*Maravilloso*," she said. "*Como la vida—pero más grande.*"

"Marvelous," Rosemary translated, putting her arm around Lourdes. "Like life—but bigger."

When Ben arrived three days later, Lourdes went to the airport by herself to meet him. The decrepit taxi coughed so badly up the steep slope into the capital that she tried to dismiss it at the airport. But the driver stood his ground, assuring her the taxi was *muy seguro*, that it could return to Antigua without difficulty, and he was far more trustworthy than these unscrupulous capitalinos.

Lourdes signaled to Ben in the crowd moving through the arrival gate that they would meet him outside. When they reached him, he was looking thoroughly baffled as three different cab drivers held out their arms to take his bag. Her driver, wagging his head officiously at the other cab drivers, took Ben's bag.

"I see we are in good hands," Ben murmured as he followed the driver through the crowds. Ben kept his arm wrapped tightly around Lourdes waist as if he thought she might be lost without warning in the crowd.

"A survivor," Ben pronounced with a laugh when he arrived at the battered hulk. He set his suitcase on top of the two by four set across the middle of the trunk space to provide some stability to the rusting floor, rocked it a little for balance, then shrugged.

As soon as they were in the car, he held Lourdes close to him again. She held his face away from her with both her hands and looked into his warm brown eyes. "I didn't realize," she said at last.

"But now you do," he said, his face settling into a look so somber it tore at her heart.

"Yes," she said. "I do." And then she drew him close to her, desperate to relieve the doubt she saw so clearly mirrored there.

The very first time Ben made love to her, Lourdes felt such a profound sense of homecoming, she knew her world could never return to what it had been. Some absolutely new possibility that was also absolutely familiar had been introduced. She would never be able to forget it. She watched curiously as powerful emotions that were impossible to name washed over her again and again.

Through the window in her bedroom, the apricot glow of the streetlights reflected off the overcast night sky. Exactly how many minutes, she wondered, does it take to change your world forever? Is the transformation greater with pleasure or with pain?

She ran her hand down his chest, through his thick white chest hair, into the gray pubic hair, over his slack, still damp penis. Her hands couldn't stop tracing his outline, running from hip to shoulder, from waist to foot as she knelt to observe him more closely. Why this man and not another? He was about her height, burly in the chest, but with surprisingly thin but muscular legs, which gave him a little of the delicacy and force of Picasso's bulls. But then you added Ben's warm, deeply lined, attractive face with its heavy nose and full lips and brown eyes that always seemed to shine with understanding and that sense of power and delicacy became something else again.

So how have we ended up like this, Lourdes wondered, turning to face Ben's back in the lumpy double bed in her bedroom in a country where her own tongue was as foreign as the feelings Ben had introduced her to three years before. She ran her hands along Ben's shoulder and down his side, savoring the amazing silkiness of his skin to her touch. She couldn't stop the way her body softened and opened just at the feel of his skin, the sound of his breathing. When Ben turned to her, she was ready, so ready.

"I should never have let you come here without me." He kissed her cheek.

An explosion rocked the house. Ben grabbed her close. "My god, what is it? Another coup?"

"It may be a saint's day," Lourdes said as several more firecrackers exploded, a passing truck began to racket along the cobblestones.

Sitting upright, Ben reached around for his robe. By the time he located it, the first peal of the church bells was sounding. The early morning runner pounded by. One of the feral cats slunk along the far wall of the patio and leaped onto the roof of the adjoining house, rattling the tiles and loosing an angry howl as it landed.

"Relax," Lourdes said. "This is an average morning. It's cold out there. Close the door and entertain me."

"You never *told* me," Ben said. He peered disbelievingly down the air well to the patio and then up at the sky. "You might as well be living on the street."

"It might be quieter," Lourdes agreed.

"How have you put up with it?" He came in and closed the door. He sat down on the edge of the bed, shaking his head.

"We signed a lease," she reminded him. "I meant to suggest you bring earplugs. It's such an auditory assault, it has taken on its own metaphorical I-don't-know-what. I can't go as far as to say I like it—but it defines my experience here, that's for sure."

"I feel terrible," Ben said as he slipped back under the blanket. "I've been imagining you having a wonderfully tranquil time, completely focused on your work."

"Now you can see why it wouldn't bother me to have the apartment below filled with people," Lourdes said. "At least I could see where some of the sound was coming from."

"When do I get to meet them," Ben asked.

"The little girls or the friends who helped me?" Lourdes was now looking for her caftan, which had slid halfway under the bed and came up gritty with dust. Anything that touched the floor did, no matter how many times she swept. She slipped the caftan over her head and moved out of Ben's reach.

"I'll go and start some coffee."

"It's still dark. There's no hurry is there?"

But Lourdes was already opening the door and stepping out on the balcony, peering along its length to see what damage the cats had done in the night.

"I'll bring the coffee back. Stay there."

Lourdes took her time making the coffee. The unfamiliar tears poured down her cheeks the second she pulled the bedroom door closed. The insides of her hands could still feel the sweet texture of his skin—better than the texture of paper or pastels or charcoal or the first glaze of underpainting.

You've missed him, Lourdes. That's all it is. You've missed him.

And I'll miss him more before this is over, she thought, and found her legs giving out under her. She sat on the floor of the kitchen leaning against the cabinets, trying to control the gasps that were rocking her body.

Who says you have to give him up?

You don't know what you're talking about, Lourdes whispered. You really don't know what you're talking about.

She pressed the heels of her hands into her eye sockets trying to stop these crazy, crazy tears.

How many years has it been since you let yourself give in?

I know, Lourdes thought. Be quiet. I *know* you.

"You should have called me." Ben quietly rested his hands on her head. She could feel his legs on either side of her. She rested her head against one of them, pulling her hands away from her eyes, giving up all pretense of being able to stop the tears. She took the hand he offered her and rose to her feet.

"I can't stop myself. I'm so sorry."

Ben held her. "You're going about this all wrong. Don't think about stopping. Think about doing more. Cry *more*, Lourdes. Suffer *more*. I'll join you."

He pulled her back down to the floor and buried his head in his hands, rocking and wailing in a surprisingly convincing simulation of grief. Lourdes sat back and watched him, her eyes suddenly dry. She began to laugh.

"Where did you learn that?"

"My father used to try it all the time with my brother. It never worked with him. Never worked with Gwen—or her mother. But I've always had my hopes that someday someone would appreciate my father's oppositional wisdom."

Ben's gentle smile broadened then disappeared. "I am here, Lourdes."

"If I knew what was happening, I would tell you," she said. "I should have warned you—asked you not to come, maybe."

"Who else should be with you when you're having a hard time?"

You really don't want to test this any farther, Lourdes.

Is that what I'm doing, Lourdes wondered. Testing?

"Let's make that coffee and take it back to bed and begin all over again." Lourdes climbed to her feet.

She made coffee in a colander, the way the locals did. But the coffee went untasted, and Ben's promise untested. As soon as they were under the covers again, their hands sought each other and found each other and all they wanted was more and then more of the same.

They caught the sun's dramatic decline in brief, vertiginous glimpses as they made an even more dramatic descent themselves along the tortuous mountain road. Just as the sun was setting over the lake, they arrived, slightly queasy, at the hotel Ben had chosen sight unseen from the guidebook. It was at lakeside, down a long, unkempt dirt road. Ben insisted they watch the sun set completely before they registered. The desk clerk stood in the doorway to the office smiling brightly and nodding every time one or the other of them glanced his way. He had something shiny rubbed into his hair and several silver teeth. His face was smooth as a ten year old boy's. When they walked out on the lawn to watch the last colors flood over the water, Lourdes noticed the absence of any lights in the hotel rooms.

"Could we possibly be the only people here?"

"How romantic," Ben said.

"Cash," the young clerk said as he dangled their room key in front of them. "We only take the cash, not the VISA or the American Express."

"And dinner?" Ben asked.

"You will excuse us," the clerk said, with a smile as big and white and silver as his sneakers. "We do not have the cook this day, but we can call him to come and make the breakfast."

"The other guests," Lourdes said. "Where do they eat? There are other guests, aren't there?"

"Of course, Señora. They arrive in no times. See—they have made the reservations." He pushed the register toward her, covering whatever was or wasn't written there with his hand as he did so.

"And where will you advise them to go for dinner?" Ben asked.

"How far away is the town?" Lourdes asked. She had been so mesmerized by their plummeting descent down the mountain, she had just greeted the sign for the hotel with a sigh of relief and hadn't looked beyond. The sky was now a pitchy black. Pfft. Just like that. She never got over how quickly night descended here.

"I call taxi," the clerk assured them. "I advise the taxista where you go. Good restaurant."

"I'm not sure this is a great idea," Lourdes said.

"It's an adventure. I've always wanted a hotel to myself."

"You keep the lights on?" Lourdes asked the clerk as he lifted her bag to take to their room on the third floor, chosen by Ben for the view. She looked at the few wistful lights along the walkway. Forty watts was being optimistic. There were stories, Concepción had assured her, that she didn't want to know. Everywhere but especially up here by the lake. But that was long ago, she said. Before the girls were born. Wilma wouldn't come up here—the spirits were too busy. But Lourdes, of course, was not so sensitive. And she had her man, didn't she.

"All night," she asked. "You leave them on all night?"

"*Claro que sí*. And we have the guard. It is very secure here," the clerk said.

"And of course, you have those other guests who are arriving any minute now," Lourdes added as she reluctantly followed the two men up the dim stairs.

"A working fireplace," Ben said with satisfaction as he entered the room. "We couldn't have made a better choice." The room had a louvered wooden door out to the balcony, which Ben immediately opened, raising his arms to embrace the dark, star dazzled sky.

"The lights in the halls, they are left on all night?" Lourdes asked the clerk again. "And you will be here as well?"

"The guard he pass the night here," the clerk said. He turned his attention to Ben. "You like the room, yes? The wood for fire." He and Ben nodded approvingly at the tall stack of logs by the corner fireplace. He nodded again several times and then turned and ran down the cement stairs, his tennis shoes making an unpleasant sticking sound. Lourdes closed the door.

Ben stepped out onto the balcony. "Oh my God, darling, come and look at this, will you. We're going to have an incredible view in the morning. We have an incredible view now." He stared blissfully down at the tar-black lake, up at the even darker tar-black sky, now covered with a dense mantle of stars, the lights of the town winking far in the distance.

"They call it the *Vía Láctea* in Spanish," Lourdes said at last.

Ben put his hand on her shoulder. "I wish you'd relax. It's a world of our own."

"I'd feel safer if there were other people here."

"Trust me—no one will fight harder for your honor."

"It's not a joke, Ben. It makes me uneasy." As uneasy as she had felt in the apartment until the girls came.

"You're just hungry. Let me wash my face and we'll go down and call a taxi."

"You think he'd call me one if I asked for it—or does he only respond to pricks?"

"Come again?" Ben said.

"Señor. He said he'd call a taxi if the señor asked."

"It's just the custom, Lourdes." Ben went into the bathroom and turned the water on and dipped a washcloth in it.

"I don't like it. It made me feel completely invisible," Lourdes said loudly. She decided against brushing her hair or even looking at her face in the bathroom mirror.

The taxi driver they finally located after leaving the restaurant looked a little disbelieving when they told him where they were staying. He asked them twice if they were sure it was open.

"We have a room," Ben said firmly. He put his arm around Lourdes and waited for the driver to start the motor.

"Far ago, my cousin, he work at your hotel," the taxi driver said. He pulled out with a squeal.

"And now?" Lourdes asked.

"He die," the taxi driver said.

"At the hotel?" Lourdes asked.

"Soldiers," the driver said. "Before the peace. Many people here, they did not have the good luck. Me, I am evangelical. I accept Jesus Christ as my personality savior. My wife, she give up her old clothes." He turned and turned and turned again, down dirt roads and paved ones.

"I feel as if I'm missing something here," Ben said. "All I'm really clear about is his brother didn't die at the hotel."

The taxi took to the winding highway as if leaving town, then, after a few minutes, turned off toward the lake, rattled along the dirt road, and turned into the driveway to the hotel. Lourdes still couldn't get a sense of how far they were from civilization. The sides of the large building glowed dimly at those points where four weak light bulbs lit the length of the walkway.

"He said he'll pick us up at eight tomorrow morning. He has another cousin, a live one, who works at a hotel on the other side of town. He swears they have at least six guests there."

"Eight o'clock," she repeated as the taxi began to pull out from between them.

"Seven?" Ben asked. "Six? I'll barricade the door, Lourdes, I promise."

He came over and pulled her into his arms. "The air, the smell of the water, the mountains. It doesn't remind me of anything I know. It makes me feel very free. A fresh start."

"Where do you think the guard is?" Lourdes asked as they walked toward the office, their shadows huge but almost indistinguishable from the pervasive dark.

"It must have been very grand once," Ben said. "These tiles are beautiful. And you can't have a more fantastic setting. And the luxury—a fireplace in every room."

Lourdes stopped outside the office. "There are no lights on in the hallways, Ben. He promised, the little twerp. I'm not going up there until the guard has turned the lights on—in all the halls as well as the stairwell."

She sat down on a bench. Ben went into the office, then came out and started to walk out onto the lawn.

"*Cuidado*," a voice barked out, and a short heavy-set figure emerged from the side of the hotel with an automatic rifle slung over his shoulder, the muzzle dragging along the grass.

"Great," Lourdes said. "Just great. I can't tell you how safe I feel."

"I thought you'd feel reassured," Ben said backing up toward Lourdes, his hands raised, casually, palms up, at chest height. "You want to do the talking?"

The man, when he stood under the light, looked even more forbidding. His nose was broken and a think scar gleamed whitely under his right cheekbone.

"*Habla inglés?*" Lourdes asked him.

"But of course," he said. "You are the *huespedes, sí?* I get you for the keys. Third floor." He disappeared into the office and returned with a key. He nodded briskly at Lourdes, pulling back as she reached out for the key.

"And the lights?" Lourdes asked. "On all three floors. All night."

"No," the guard said. "I will turn on until you arrive to your room. By then I *apagar* them all. It cost much when there is no peoples."

"We're no peoples?" Lourdes asked.

"It is my job—the defense. You just trust me, lady. See?" he said. He twitched the rifle so its nose scraped the concrete walk.

"I think this is where I need to step in," Ben said. He put his arm around Lourdes. "My wife is afraid of the dark. She finds it isolated here. Can't we have the lights on to go to our room."

"I already says the yes," the guard said. "I go with you. No danger. All is *seguro*. I have the *confianza*."

"Let's just get up there, ok. It's late. We didn't get very much sleep last night."

Lourdes withdrew from Ben's embrace and refused the hand he reached back toward her as he obediently followed the guard, who had decided to carry his gun with the muzzle pointed up to keep it from clanging on the stairs.

"Here we are," Ben called out heartily when he reached the landing to the third floor. Grudgingly, the guard switched on the hall light. Ben reached out for the door key and the guard handed it over. By the time Lourdes reached the landing, Ben had the door open.

The guard lounged insolently against the stair rail. "Your husband, he take good care of you, lady. No problem."

"In an emergency, I want to be able to get out of here. I want to be able to leave."

The guard shrugged and started down the stairs.

"I want to be able to *see* to get out of here," Lourdes said.

"It is all decided," the guard said, waving the barrel of his rifle lazily through the air. "It is my job the protection."

"I *will* turn those lights back on," Lourdes said as she closed the door to their room. She could hear the guard flipping switches as he descended, his heavy boots ringing on the stairs. "As many times as he turns them off."

"What's gotten into you, Lourdes? We really are safe here," Ben said. "You're just tired. Slip into bed and I'll build us a fire."

Lourdes lay on the bed with her arms crossed over her chest. All my life, she thought, I've been able to make myself safe. I've been able to take care of myself.

Too late now, the voice said.

"Don't touch me," Lourdes said, shutting her eyes. "Whatever you do, don't touch me right now, Ben Silver."

"I wonder what I can use for starter," Ben said after a pause.

For a terrible second, Lourdes could see herself ripping her drawings apart into fine strips and handing them over to him, her rage, her crazy rage, destroying everything.

You have to trust someone, the voice said. *Who is it going to be?*

I'm falling apart, Lourdes thought.

When do you think it began—when he came into the picture or when you ran from it? The satisfaction in her voice made Lourdes sick.

Please shut up, Lourdes pleaded. Please just shut up.

"Aha," Ben said. "Today's newspaper. I can't read it anyway." He began to tear the paper in long strips, crumpling them all together and putting them on the floor of the fireplace. He set the logs over a lattice of kindling.

Lourdes lay back on the bed and closed her eyes again. She heard the rasp of the match. She could feel the light of the burning paper on her lids, her retinas swarming with complementary colors. Soon she could smell the tart resinous smell of the pine kindling. Then she began to cough—and opened her eyes to see Ben throwing the balcony door open as well as the door to the dark stairwell.

"Just give it a second." Ben flapped his jacket at the chimney trying to force the billows of smoke back into the fireplace. The smoke snaked over his shoulders and around his hips. Her eyes began to burn, then water.

"I think I may come out with you and admire the view."

Ben turned, his white hair standing on end, his face sagging with dismay.

"I wanted to seduce you, Lourdes. I wanted you to feel safe. I wanted this to feel like a second honeymoon."

"I would have settled for warm," Lourdes said. "Better yet, inhabited. There are ghosts in this country. The only thing that quiets them is life. Lots of life."

Instead of going out on the balcony, she walked over to the big wooden door to the hall and opened it to create a cross current. At the far end of the hall, she could see the lake as a faint luminescence against the dark archway. Standing at the stairwell, she peered down into total darkness. Out of perversity the guard had even turned off the walkway lights.

"Success," Ben crowed. "It's begun to draw. Now you'll love me again."

Sooty, coughing and delighted, he stood in the doorway, his silhouette visible against the tide of white smoke. "You will come back in, won't you, Lourdes. I gave you my word. I will protect you."

Lourdes felt the anger building again. She leaned farther over the stairwell trying to see if she could catch even a glimmer of light.

"I see you out there," Ben said. "I'm coming to get you at the count of ten. *Uno. Dos. Tres. Quatro.* I can't wait. Or count any higher in Spanish." He walked across the hall, but paused behind her as if he were afraid any pressure from him might send her tumbling over the stair rail. When she turned, he closed her in his arms and stepped back firmly.

"You scared me, Lourdes. Don't do that again."

"Want to try the balcony?" she asked with a laugh.

Ben looked sadly at the room still heavily blanketed in smoke. "I fucked up. I admit it. We may need to take the bedding out on the balcony. It couldn't be any colder—and the air is certainly clearer."

Suddenly the smoke in Lourdes' head cleared and she could see him, so tired, so very tired. A little dash of ash on his right temple and all over his fingertips. She brought them to her lips.

He held her away from him with his other hand, his fingers gripping her hip. "My life will never be the same if you leave me, Lourdes. I'll always know what I'm missing."

"No one has said anything about leaving, have they?" Lourdes suddenly felt numb. How had they gotten here without warning.

"We haven't needed to, have we? I wake up to an empty bed. You do too. That says something pretty clearly in my book."

"It's late," Lourdes said.

"Do you want me to throw cold water on our fire?"

Lourdes ran her fingers lightly up Ben's arm. He cupped her face in his hands and held her eyes. "All you have to do is tell me, Lourdes."

"I would rather die," Annie yelled. "You hear me, Lourdes, baby? You hear me, Jacquie? I would rather die than have him take you away from me."

Pete was Jacquie's daddy. Maybe he was Lourdes' too—although he and Annie never seemed too sure. Pete didn't fight to see Lourdes the way he fought to see Jacquie. If he fought less, maybe Annie wouldn't be so angry at him. It wasn't as if she didn't leave them most weekends. Just not with Pete.

"It's one night," he said. His face was very red and he smelled of liquor, just like Annie.

"You're always trying to turn them against me. I know your kind, Pete Stevens."

"You know all kinds, Annie. No one's questioning that."

"In front of my children. Defaming me," Annie screamed.

Lourdes went over and turned the radio on. She walked back to the bathroom and turned on the bath. The neighbors might call the police again. They did that when Annie got too noisy. She'd promised not to yell anymore because last time a woman came from social services.

"Never," Lourdes had told the woman when she came to the house one afternoon when Annie was out. "Our mommy never yells at us." The woman had on stockings with a run up the side of her right leg. She wrote down every word Lourdes said and then silently read it to herself. She had very black hair pulled in a bun and very red lipstick that ran over her lips like she didn't know yet how to color inside the lines. Jacquie went over and sat near her. Jacquie liked it when people read to her. Now that Lourdes was in school, sometimes she read her own books to Jacquie. See Spot run. See Spot run.

"I can see you love your mommy very much," the social worker said to Lourdes.

"Me too," Jacquie said as she squirmed closer to her. "I love mommy too."

Lourdes held herself perfectly still. The social worker hadn't known which one of them was lying, the neighbor or Lourdes. Lourdes held the social worker's eyes as if she were the most honest girl in the world. Inside her, it was perfectly quiet, just as it would be when she was working in the courtroom as a reporter. Her concentration was perfect

The social worker finally dropped her eyes. She believed Lourdes and went away. She left a card with Lourdes with her phone number on it, but Annie found it. She threw it away after waving it in front of Lourdes with an angry face but not saying a single word. That was worse than her yelling. Lourdes never knew what Annie would do when she was in a quiet rage. Sometimes she didn't come back for days. Lourdes told Annie that all the social worker's questions were about the yelling and Annie seemed to understand, but here she was, a week later, doing it all again. Soon she would be crying. Lourdes hoped so. Annie cried loudly, but it wasn't as loud as the yelling.

"We love you, Mommy," she said when she came back into the room where Pete and Annie stood, hands on hips, frowning at each other, their mouths half open as if they were both ready to take a bite out of each other. "We love you best," Lourdes said. But Annie didn't even look at her. She just opened her mouth very wide to say something louder and meaner to Pete. Lourdes took Jacquie's hand and pulled her sister back into the bathroom with her and shut and locked the door.

"The water makes a music," she told her sister.

If they couldn't hear, maybe the neighbors wouldn't either.

Annie banged on the door to the bathroom, but Lourdes didn't open it. The steam was so thick, Jacquie and Lourdes had to wave their arms to see each other. It felt like the clouds in heaven would, Lourdes thought. Wet and heavy and hot. The white changed everything.

"You come out right this minute," Annie yelled, "or I won't let you go with your daddy."

"We don't love Pete," Jacquie murmured. "Only love Annie. Only love Annie."

"And Lourdes," Lourdes told her sister, drawing her into her lap, holding Jacquie's head to her chest the way a mother should.

That was the last time they saw Pete—until Annie really did die. Then it wasn't of Annie's choosing, their leaving. It wasn't of Pete's choosing, their coming. What Lourdes and Jacquie felt had nothing to do with choosing, never would.

Oh how Lourdes longed, those years with Pete and his second wife Kate and her kids, for the sound of Annie's voice, so deep and hoarse and invincible and sadder than any voice in the world had any right to be.

Are you talking about me? the voice asked. And suddenly, it was all there. All of it.

Lourdes had tried so hard, their years together, to drown out the sound of Annie's voice with the sound of the bathwater splashing in the sink, the sound of the radio, the sound of her own voice reading to Jacquie, or singing her to sleep at night. And then once Annie was gone for good, Annie's voice was all Lourdes listened for.

Can it ever be gone for good until you and Jacquie are?

"What are you suggesting?" Lourdes cried. "What in God's name are you suggesting?"

"Sorry," Ben said, taking his hand away from her breast.

She wanted to say something. Lourdes knew she wanted to say something, but her voice had gone and, if her life depended on it, she could not have moved a muscle.

"What have I done to you?" Ben asked, his voice sadder than any voice had any right to be. "My darling, what have I done to you?"

Lourdes woke to a blast of cool air, a stream of light.

"See," Ben said. "Danger. Drama. Glamour. Indescribable beauty. We survived it all, my love. But the shower, I hate to tell you, is cold."

They turned down the desk clerk's eager offer to locate a cook for a personal visit, as well as his offer to call a taxi. Seated on their suitcases, they waited twenty-five minutes for their driver of the night before to appear. The taxi driver's other cousin seemed not to have accepted Jesus as his personality savior, for he appeared at the front door of the rather small, dark hotel at the far end of town in a dramatic scarf and black wool shorts and a vivid red shirt. The cousin was desolated. The hotel was full. Italians. They had decided to stay another night. There was another hotel, very nice, in the center of town. Very big. City people stayed there. They had hot water and spoke English. And there was a little pension where the young tourists with the backpacks and the long hair stayed.

They decided on the big hotel with the high retaining wall and four cars in the parking lot. They checked in, stored their bags, and headed down to the wharf to buy ferry tickets to Santiago Atitlán, the town on the far side of the lake that Marie, Ginny, Simon and Rosemary had suggested they visit.

"I feel like the Pied Piper of Hamlin." Ben looked around, his hand fluttering around his face as if trying to see through a swarm of insects, a mist. Now, not only were they followed by all the young men selling ferry tickets but also by a stream of tiny girls in soiled, intricately embroidered blouses and straight skirts, trays of pot holders and purses on their heads, and a dozen or more bead necklaces on each forearm.

"Your little girls, do they look like this?" Ben asked.

"They're older," Lourdes said. "The younger one has taken to conventional dress."

"And accepted Jesus Christ as her personality savior?" Ben asked.

"I don't think so. She goes to Catholic school. She may just want to fit in." Even as Lourdes spoke, she could see Mikela staring back at her, the baby tied to her back, her dowdy, brown flowered dress hiked up in the rear, her strong little arms dangling out of the too large puffed sleeves, her short, boyish black hair standing on end. Those quietly calculating eyes that traveled over the bedroom and the patio as she followed Rosemary out the door of Lourdes' house, her few belongings tumbled onto a worn blue plastic bag that Rosemary insisted Lourdes search before they left. Why had she let Rosemary shame them both that way? Lourdes had insisted Mikela take the English dictionary, extra paper for school. A suitcase to carry her possessions. It even occurred to Lourdes to give the girl the battered vanity case she used to store her paints. Annie's vanity case. She only had to take one brief look at Mikela's stoic face to know it was a gesture whose quixotic largesse would match its irrelevance. Annie's pale blue vanity case was an ugly, dented, stained and precious fetish. It's cover was thick now with dabs of paint and gesso and, a constant feature in all her studios, it was so familiar and indispensable Lourdes could forget its origins. Until. Until.

"They're special, those two little girls. When you meet them, you'll feel it. So is the baby—if you can have a gift after only two months on this planet."

"Past life," Ben said. "I was reading about it in the guidebook. They have a place along the lake where they channel. What do you think?"

"I believe in letting sleeping dogs and past lives lie," Lourdes said. Then, suddenly exasperated, she turned to the tormenting swarm of children. "*Por favor! No vamos a comprar nada hoy,*" she said sternly. We're not going to buy anything today.

"A lot of work went into those," Ben said, staring down at all the trays of pot holders and purses bobbing beneath them. "I want to reward it."

Lourdes caught his hand. "Don't."

"Why you not let him buy?" the little girl cried. "We hungry, lady. We hungry."

As they reached the end of the cobbled street that led to the town beach and ferry launch, she firmly waved the children off and tugged Ben toward the sand. The young men who had followed them through town leaped down the rock embankment and came to stand in front of them just beside the jetty.

"Now you buy?"

Lourdes shrugged. Ben pulled out his money belt and handed them a large bill. They looked at it dubiously.

"*Voy a cambiarlo,*" a little boy said eagerly. I'll go change it.

Lourdes dug in her purse for smaller bills. "We don't need change," she said to the little boy.

Ben reached out to pat the boy on the head, but Lourdes stopped him. "Never touch the children here," she warned him. "Didn't they tell you that in the guidebook?"

"How did you deliver a baby then?"

The young men handed them their tickets and they joined the line of tourists.

"Her little sister was watching all the time to make sure I didn't run off with it. It was sad, really. Still is. She's convinced someone wants to make off with the baby. I think she's getting sick keeping watch all the time."

"How old is she?"

"Ten, I think. It's hard to know. They're all so tiny. And of course she'll lie if she thinks it will help her. I think her older sister's twelve."

"The mother."

"Well the younger one is the caretaker. The older one I'd call the giver of birth and the younger one the giver of life."

And you, Lourdes, in your life—which one are you?

They sat out on the back deck, Ben's arms wrapped tightly around her, the rocking of the boat steady as the rhythm of a cradle.

"I look forward to meeting the girls," Ben said. "I feel when I do I'll know you better."

But what will he know, Lourdes? Lourdes didn't understand how a voice so low and melodious could be so spiteful.

"It was all chance," Lourdes said. "My being at the ruins that afternoon. Mikela having run away from the girls' home. Everything. What can chance tell you about me?"

She closed her eyes and let the hum of the engine become one with the light, everything emptying out of her except the reality of that vibration and the thin skin that separated chance from destiny, love from loss, inside from out.

"This is heaven," Ben murmured into her hair. "And to believe we just stumbled upon it."

Like thousands of other tourists a year, the voice said tartly.

Lourdes laughed and settled deeper into Ben's embrace.

Just for a moment, she assured the voice. Just to really let myself know what I'm letting go of.

Life itself, the voice murmured. *But it's your choice. It's always—and only—your choice, Lourdes.*

By the time Ben and Lourdes had climbed a few short blocks toward the Santiago Atitlán, they were clinging to each other for protection. Lourdes spied a store that sold skirt material and went inside to buy two lengths for Natividad. She chose a blue denim-like material that she had seen worn by women in Antigua and also a wonderful red material threaded with gold, which seemed distinctive to the women here. When she came out of the store, Ben was ringed by girls. Ben held up two identical bracelets in his hand. "You and Gwen might like these."

"Why don't you choose two different designs," Lourdes said. She spoke softly, but her voice still sounded hollow to her. She forced her way into the ring of young women, took Ben by the arm, and urged him upwards toward the church.

As soon as she entered the church, Lourdes could feel she was on to something. Perhaps it was the comical statues along the walls in their waistcoats and cravats of brightly patterned materials. Or the birds swooping down from the rafters. Or the women entering, pulling on their *rebozos* and hurrying over to one of the side chapels where they all knelt and began to recite something impossible to hear over the sound of the men gathered at the entrance on the left side of the church, who were hammering at the concrete floor.

"I think I'll meet you outside," Ben said. "We Jews, however secular, find Jesus, especially in these graphic forms, a little off-putting. But take your time. I know it's important for your work."

"And it's noisy," he yelled as he stepped away.

Ben had not yet seen Lourdes' new work. Lourdes had told him she wanted to save it for their return when they would have plenty of time to look at it. But she had mentioned her growing fascination with the religious statues. If Ben thought the statues in this church were hard going, so foppishly costumed, what would he think of the images in her drawings? Lourdes realized it mattered to her. It really mattered to her.

She passed the side door where the men were gathered hammering and laughing and sat down in one of the front rows, oddly pleased with the cacophony of the hammering and the recitative of the women in the chapel over to the right of the main altar, a haunting echo.

A woman walked down the central aisle to the main altar. She knelt down and opened a brightly colored cloth and pulled out a handful of white candles and a handful of red ones. She waved them in front of the altar, talking in a low voice.

"*Mi Señor*," she said. "*Dios mio. Madre de dios.*" And then continued talking in a language similar to the one that Mikela and Natividad used, her voice like a turbulent stream. Was this where the girls had come from? Lourdes wondered. There was something about this woman which seemed to fit into the world of images that were taking shape in her studio. The woman lit a candle and then began to melt the wax at the bottom of each of the candles to glue them to the floor in front of her. She sat back on her heels, the lit candle in her hands, continuing her incomprehensible but bitter, unbearably bitter, lamentations.

The men hammered louderr. The woman raised her voice in response. She began to light the candles, calling out in her own language and occasionally in Spanish. *"Dios mio. Madre de Dios. Cristo. Cristo."* Lourdes had the sense that everything that was taking place outside her was also taking place inside her, that she *was* the church. She didn't dare look over at the woman as her voice grew louder.

The woman beat her chest and screamed. Then bowed her face to the floor.

I have to get out of here, Lourdes thought. But her feet were glued to the floor.

You know that scream, Lourdes. You've carried it inside you all your life.

I am not crazy.

Neither is she, the voice said. She sounded like the woman beating the floor right beside Lourdes' pew. She sounded like Lourdes. She sounded like Annie. Like Ginny. Like Marie. Like Rosemary. She spoke softly. Loudly. Lourdes couldn't tell anymore. She wasn't sure whether she was hearing the sounds of wings beating the air or hair sweeping the floor, or fire taking root in the wood, or the shattering of stone as the men swung their sledge hammers breaking open the concrete floor.

"No," the woman cried, raising her face and then bending it, her loose hair spreading around her like oil. *"Dios mio. No. No. No."*

Lourdes found her own hands clutched to her chest, her face raised, her mouth open.

You can go now, the voice said. It was pleasantly cool. A little cruel. A little condescending. *Just so you know, Lourdes. Just so you know what we're all capable of—you too.*

Lourdes stumbled as she slipped out of the pew and headed down the side aisle, past the men with their sledge hammers. She avoided the rubble. Behind her she could feel in her body the woman raising herself on her knees, lifting her hands up toward the rafters and letting that sound, that beautiful, tormented, horrible sound free again.

As soon as they set foot on the steep street leading down to the lake, the girls who had followed them up the hill were at their sides, equally eager to accost them all the way down.

"I give you one, you buy four," a girl, perhaps a little younger than Mikela, said to Lourdes. Her voice was dry and flat, years too old for her round face. She waved yarn covered pencils in front of Lourdes' face. "You buy from me." She said something in their Indian dialect to the four young women who hemmed them in from each direction. They laughed.

Tired of the incessant banter, some frightening current of energy, half fun, half rancorous, that seemed to animate even the youngest, at last Lourdes said, "I don't need anything today. I don't *want* anything today. We will buy nothing. Nothing."

As they neared the dock, the vendors in the stores called out to them, waving woven cloth, a leather bag, anything, anything at all that might cause Lourdes or Ben to cross their palms with gold. Lourdes stared out over the heads of the girls toward the lake where the men poled their way through the reeds in small dugouts and women pounded clothes on the rocks.

The tallest of the young women slipped her arm inside Lourdes'. Lourdes kept moving. The young woman moved with her. Necklaces dandled from her forearm, their glass beads sparking in the afternoon light. She brought her face close to Lourdes' ear. "You bad woman," she whispered. Then she pulled away and repeated, loud enough for all to hear. "You bad woman. You say you buy from me and you lie. Why you lie, lady. You *bad* woman. *Bad* woman." She closed her hand down tightly on Lourdes upper arm.

Lourdes tried to pull away. Ben was now about a half block behind, saying something that made the throng of women around him laugh. Such a beautiful sound, and such a beautiful image, all those turbaned heads glittering in the sun. Laughing he moved toward her. Shaking off the grip of the young woman, she grabbed his arm and began to run. He followed, breathing heavily. The young woman yelled after them.

"What's she saying?" Ben asked. "Did I drop anything."

Lourdes pulled him up onto the pier. "She's saying I'm a bad woman. She's saying I'm a liar. Where on earth did they learn to talk to people that way?" Lourdes headed over to a seat out on the deck. Her face felt blisteringly hot.

"It's effective," Ben said. "Unpleasant but effective. She's got your number. She knows what you can't bear to hear. Want a scarf?" He unwound them from his neck and let them float out beside him like banners. "They told me I was kind, handsome, irresistible to women."

He stopped, looked at her. Those inexplicable tears pouring over her eyes, as if she were standing inside a waterfall.

"It's a game," he said. "That's all. They don't even *know* you, darling."

Lourdes turned toward the reeds, watching the men in their white calf-length pants pole deeper into the green grasses. The heavy wind dried her tears almost as quickly as she shed them.

Several young German women climbed onto the ferry, followed to the steps by an old woman holding out an embroidered cloth. "*Nein*," called out one of the tall blonde women, laughing. "*Nein*." The old woman opened out another cloth. The young woman's friends, all of them in khaki shorts and wearing backpacks, scarves like the one Ben had purchased wrapped around their necks, started laughing. The tall blonde woman, her curly hair tossing in the breeze kept calling out, "*Nein! Nein!*" as the old woman pulled embroidered cloths from the tray on her head and spread them out on the pier.

"You see," Ben said, sitting down beside her, "it means nothing. Either side, it means nothing."

Lourdes closed her eyes. The hammers crashed against the concrete. The woman screamed. *Dios mio. Madre de dios.* The young women danced around them, their hair loose, black as Natividad and Mikela's, red as Gwen's, the beaded necklaces flashing in Lourdes' eyes. The hand closed over her forearm, the lips touched her ear. "You are—"

She's right so far, the voice said. *You are, Lourdes. You certainly are.*

The engine started up. Lourdes dug into her purse and pulled out all the money she had and went over to the side of the boat. She waved at the old woman on the pier. But the old woman was so fixated on the young German women with their gold legs and blue eyes and their cries of *Nein! Nein!*, she didn't notice Lourdes until the boat began moving out of the dock. Even though she ran, holding out her goods, and Lourdes reached out with the money, they were too far apart to make the exchange.

As Lourdes made her way back, the young German women watched her somberly. "Not kind to tease the poor," one of them said.

"Lourdes," Ben called. He held out both his hands and gripped hers as soon as she was in reach. "She doesn't know you either."

Who does? the voice asked. *Annie? Jacquie? Mikela? Natividad? Gwen? Rosemary? Ginny? Marie? Who knows who you really are?*

"But I do," Ben said. "I know you, Lourdes, as a good woman, my lover, my wife for life."

And exactly how long are you expecting that to last?

One night and one day. Will you just leave me in peace? Lourdes whispered. Please.

The next day they found a small, well-inhabited hotel along the edge of the lake, accessible only by boat. For four days they kayaked, canoed and swam, with an occasional hike along steep cliffs to a tiny village where the only foods for sale were soft drinks and potato chips. The sallow, shy children kept their eyes fixed on the their hands as if the simplest eye contact with foreigners could harm them. Lourdes and Ben found a little church dedicated to the Virgin. All the wooden statues that lined the walls were dusted with white wash, giving the unpainted church a ghostly but evocative air. Men sat on one side, women on the other. After a brief glimpse, Ben and Lourdes left, but the image of all those ghostly statues stayed with her, a tranquilizing antithesis whenever the polychrome vision of the church at the other end of the lake came to Lourdes.

Every night as she was falling asleep, Lourdes saw the woman lifting her head and opening her mouth, and knew, just knew, she could not hear that scream again and live. Immediately, she would open her eyes and in her imagination paint the hotel room white, paint Ben and her bodies, paint the shadows. She would see the white statues in the tiny church lined up against the wall. The Church of Lost Voices. She would use paint from Annie's vanity case. But the brushes were so small, the amount they needed to cover seemed vaster and vaster in proportion. So in her mind Lourdes found white towels. Vats of paint. Barrels. Like the ones the homeless use for fires. Out of the soot, out of the fire, out of the rank smell of unwashed people, Lourdes would draw the towels dripping with whitewash. She never lost her concentration or her determination and the whiteness, like an inner silence, didn't fail.

"You never cared about anyone but yourself," Jacquie screamed. Lourdes transcribed her words. The judge looked up at Jacquie. Lourdes didn't. "You thought I couldn't see what you were doing to me—how you were turning everyone against me. You though I didn't see, Lourdes."

"She's using your name," said the judge, a precise and disturbingly unlined man in his late forties. "Is there something I should know here?"

Lourdes shook her head.

The judge gestured to the deputies to stand back. Jacquie in the doorway had her arms spread wide, palms out. No one could enter or leave the courtroom.

"What more do you intend to do to me, Lourdes?" she asked.

Lourdes kept typing on the shorthand machine.

"She's disturbing the peace," the judge said. "I'll have to do something. Are you sure you wouldn't like to explain?" He leaned forward to read Lourdes' last name from her name plate. This was only her second day in his court. She didn't know how Jacquie had found her so quickly. This was the sixth job in three months Jacquie would have ruined. She was off her meds again. "What do you expect me to do?" the caseworker had asked when Lourdes called the last time. "Shove them down her throat?"

"Ms. Stevens?" The judge beckoned her forward, but Lourdes just sat there. Then she put her hands in her lap and lifted her head.

"She is my sister. She's insane. I am not her legal guardian. She is a ward of the state."

"I never hurt him," Jacquie yelled. "You hurt me, Lourdes. You're the one who deserves to be punished."

"No one's going to be punished," Lourdes heard one of the deputies say. "Just come with us young woman. The judge needs a quiet place to get his work done."

"Why is he choosing her?" Jacquie said with a sob. "Why isn't he choosing me?"

"Hush, hush," Ben said. "It's all right. I'm here now. Let it go, darling. Let it go."

Lourdes opened her eyes. She could feel how cold and wet her cheeks were. She could feel Ben's hands, so familiar and so strange, holding her close. What did he know? What could he possibly know?

"It's over. There is nothing you can say. Nothing you can do. It's over."

The rage surged through her like a pure white wave. The sound of Seth's cry. It was all she was. The sound of Seth's cry. Her own son, not four months old, left alone for God knows how long to scream in hunger. By Jacquie, whom she had protected all her life. Her own son. Her own child. She knew she had no choice but to help Jacquie pack her bags and leave. She called a local shelter. Called Jacquie's psychiatrist and social worker, went in to see them.

"It isn't drugs," she told them. "It's something worse." And who should know better than Lourdes who had covered for her since she was a little girl. Who had taken care of Annie in her drunken splurges as well. She knew what was drugs and what was not drugs. Knew what drugs could not touch.

"She doesn't have a soul," Lourdes said. "My sister doesn't have a soul."

"You're saying she doesn't have feelings? Or she doesn't have remorse?" The doctor was only a few years older than Lourdes and his beard hadn't grown in completely. He tried to conceal the lack with a small, frayed moustache the color of a penny whose hairs curled raggedly over his thin upper lip. His hair was black.

"She doesn't have a center," Lourdes had said. "She will devour you if you let her. *Me* is her only sense of right and wrong. What feeds her is right. What starves her out is wrong."

"She doesn't even have enough love for a little baby. How empty do you have to be not to put a little baby first?" The young resident looked at her dubiously.

"Do you have children?" she asked him, pointing at his wedding ring.

"Not yet," he said, giving a little sigh of relief. "It doesn't really go with training."

Or law school. Wasn't that what George had said with Evan and then even more loudly with Seth? And didn't Lourdes know, Jacquie's hair ruffled, her eyes vague with booze, what Jacquie had been up to and probably with whom. Didn't she know.

And it was your sister you got rid of? You didn't think George had just a little hand in it?

I was twenty-two. I had two babies. I wasn't ready to be on my own yet. I did what I had to in a few more years.

You put your own sister on the streets. Your own crazy baby sister.

I had no choice. She was nineteen. I protected her from George. I protected the boys from her.

And you? What did you do to protect yourself, Lourdes?

From what? Lourdes thought frantically. From what?

She's only twelve years old. She's been through hell.

You think Annie was any better? You think my pain was any less than Jacquie's? What do you know?

But whatever she said, the image that stayed with Lourdes was still her own hand going out to touch Jacquie's cheek, Natividad's cheek, Annie's cold cold cheek in the casket—those cloudy eyes looking blindly back at her. Oh, baby, what have you done to yourself?

What undid her was the softness in her own voice. So much rage inside her and only that sweet voice.

She wasn't the only one who didn't know where she began and you ended, Lourdes.

It was my center, Lourdes said. It was always my center.

You shouldn't have taken them in, Lourdes. You shouldn't have married him if you couldn't love his little girl, Lourdes. And Jacquie, your own baby sister. Your crazy baby sister. On the streets.

I didn't abandon her. I held her accountable, that's all.

But was she, Lourdes? From the time she was born, was she really accountable? Or Annie? Or your father?

Couldn't he have helped her?

You tell me. He's your family.

No, Lourdes said angrily. He was our way station from Annie's death until I could support the two of us. That's all. Four long painful years.

Worse than what came before? Worse than what came after? Is that what you're afraid of, Lourdes?

You have no idea what it feels like to be so unwanted. So clearly second-rate.

Don't I? the voice asked gently, so gently. *Don't I, Lourdes? Have you ever looked into my face?*

"Is there something you need to tell me?" Ben asked, holding her firmly and shaking her awake for the second time that night.

"Did I say anything?" Lourdes said, suddenly terrified.

"Not a word," Ben assured her. "Not a word."

If the vendors, and the voice, and Jacquie had Lourdes' number, so did Gwen—who was waiting for Lourdes and Ben when they returned to the apartments in Antigua four days later.

"Well," Gwen said, leaning over the two chairs at the dining room table, one arm around Mikela and one around Natividad. "Aren't you going to say something, Dad? Lourdes? I thought I'd surprise you both by coming early. And then you weren't here. But these marvelous little girls were. Let me introduce you, Dad. Their names are Mikela and Natividad."

"How did you get in?" Lourdes asked.

"No problem," Gwen said. "Your friends have been great, Lourdes. Rosemary was here when I arrived. I've been having dinner there most days. I've been trying to talk her into letting me have these beautiful kids over to spend the night, but she seems to feel that she needs to clear it with you. Maybe they think Dad might have an objection. Or I wouldn't feel like sharing my apartment with them."

"Your apartment?" Lourdes said. She looked at Ben.

He sat down in the one remaining chair at the table and reached out to shake Mikela's hand, then Natividad's.

"*Hola,*" he said. "*Me llamo Ben. Soy esposo de Lourdes, padre de Gwen.*" My name is Ben. I'm the husband of Lourdes, the father of Gwen.

"*Ella es su hija?*" Mikela asked Lourdes. She is your daughter?

"*Hija de mi esposo,*" Lourdes corrected her. Daughter of my husband.

"*Su hija?*" Mikela asked again. *Your* daughter.

"*Mi madre se murió,*" Gwen answered in Spanish. "*Estuvimos una familia, ella y yo. No tuve familia con mi padre. Ni con su mujer. No tenemos relaciones formales, Lourdes y yo.*" My mother is dead. We were a family, my mother and I. Not my father. Not with his woman. We have no formal relation, Lourdes and I. "Until now," she continued in English, flashing Lourdes a bright smile.

"Your Spanish sounds great," Ben said. "I bet you never imagined it would pay off one of these days."

"*Madrastra*," Mikela said. "*Ella es su madrastra. Y usted es su hijastra.*" Step-mother. She is your step-mother. You are her step-daughter. "*Sí es una relación formal. Mala, de vez en cuando. Pero real.*" It is a formal relation. Bad sometimes. But real.

"I wish you had let us know when you were arriving," Lourdes said.

"I knew it wouldn't really matter to you," Gwen said. "I quit my job just after Dad left because they weren't going to give me vacation time, and I thought, I'm not going to stay here using my Spanish on fast food clerks when I could be using it for real." Gwen pulled the girls closer to her. "I've taken over the tutoring for your friend Ginny while she's away—and I'm helping out Rosemary in the afternoons."

"This is great," Ben said. "I'm amazed at how quickly you've made yourself at home. Aren't you, Lourdes?"

"Yes," Lourdes said. "I truly am."

"Rosemary's coming by in a half hour to take the girls back. I bet I could go over there for the night if you guys want total privacy or something."

"Of course not," Ben said. He didn't turn to look at Lourdes when she rose to her feet.

"If you'll excuse me," she said. "I'm a little queasy from the ride. I think I'll lie down."

"*Enferma?*" Mikela asked. Sick?

"*Enojada,*" Natividad corrected her. "*La Señora es enojada.*" She looked at Gwen and smiled. Angry. The Señora is angry.

"No, I'm not," Lourdes corrected them. "I'm not sick. I'm not angry. I'm just tired. Very tired and surprised."

And a stranger to your own life, the voice said as Lourdes slowly climbed the stairs, leaving them all murmuring below. *Again.*

In her studio, Lourdes opened Annie's vanity case, covered with so many fingerprints and handprints the blue leather was barely visible. Brick red. Blood red. Black. Purple. Green. Lourdes dumped the contents on the floor, turning over the creased tubes. There was no white left.

Lourdes touched her hand to her cheek as she stared at her face in the bathroom mirror. Where am I going to go, she thought. Where on earth am I going to go?

Home, the voice said firmly. *That's where you're going. Terrifying thought, isn't it. Home. It's where the heart is. Where seeing is believing. Where your hands are always as cold as Annie's face in the morgue. Where Jacquie's voice echoes and echoes. Where that little girl spreads her legs and you draw a baby red with blood into your arms. And it breathes, Lourdes. It breathes.*

LIVING UNTIL WE DIE
(Ginger)

Well, there's no one left to tell except myself. Again. I told Janet and Betsy. That was easier than telling Rosemary. For my daughters, my death is all in the natural order of things. Their father died five years ago after all. And my George has been dead ten years now. I suppose they're wondering how I've held on as long as I have. I'm not, by my own standards, an old woman. I am, unlike my daughters, surprised at the news. I did not see it coming.

I've made it clear I'm not coming back and being a burden on them. I'm choosing to die where I've chosen to live for the past fifteen years. Even though they protest a little, I can hear how relieved they are. Janet married late and her children are still at home, and Betsy and Chip have a grandchild on the way and an unemployed son-in-law come to stay indefinitely—not to mention Chip's parents, his mother with her oxygen tank and his father forever asking his own name. Besides, I think in some way I died to both my daughters when I decided to live in a foreign country permanently. It's as if their world is flat and I just slipped over the edge of it. When I talk to them from my home in Antigua I feel like saying, "I'm passing Neptune now. You should have seen the rings of Saturn. Something for your scrapbook, no doubt about it."

Betsy, my younger, makes her own scrapbooks with lace borders around the Laura Ashley floral print covers. In that context, the pictures I send them look especially shocking: A new latrine for Maria. A stove for Asunción so her family no longer cooks on the dirt floor. Juana, at twenty, nursing her fifth baby.

Today, as I spread the photos out on the bed in Janet's guestroom, they feel as exotic and strange to me as they must to my daughters and my grandchildren. It isn't until I see a picture of Rosemary or Anita with her adopted daughters that I can remember the air down there, that faint film of dust over everything in the dry season, or the faint scent of mold during the rainy season. I can remember the smell of incense during the religious processions. I can remember that better than anything, and sometimes when I wake in the middle of the night confused about where I am, confused about whether I am living or dying, I just imagine that huge cloud of incense billowing around me, enveloping me and all the other onlookers, blessing the air so Christ can labor through with his cross or the Virgin with that dagger deep in her breast. I recall the rocking motion of the men in their purple robes carrying Jesus, the women in the black mantillas and tight black party dresses staggering under the weight of the Virgin. The motion, steady as a heartbeat, lulls me back to sleep.

It's odd. I would say that I live where I do because suffering is just part of the natural order there. It has a natural place in the world. But what I mean is something very different from my daughters' indifference. I don't want to burden them with my care, but I want them to register that I'm gone. I want death to keep its mystery and absoluteness. I don't want it to be something to be checked off on a questionnaire about life stages, stressful events, or the locksteps of mourning. I want someone, anyone, to know in a way that goes beyond words or reason or grief that I, Ginger Ansley, am no more and that no matter how we try to buffer it, this is an astonishing loss. We may feel that we are moving on to something larger, more healing. But to be aware of our own absence—to give up, willingly or not, everything we have ever known—nothing makes up for it except to have someone share our shock. Share the knowledge that our mortality is an extravagant mystery and always will be.

The closest I have to a potential mourner of this ilk is Rosemary. And we're as off-key here as we are in every other area of our life—but the discordance encourages me unreasonably. "This isn't good," she said when I called to tell her the diagnosis. "Who's going to help with the jam project or the birth control clinic? And what about those girls I may be forced to take in? I was counting on you for their English instruction." Her voice was a little thick.

"And the worship services," I said. "You'll have to take over indefinitely." There was just a little goading in my voice, I admit it.

"No way," she said, her voice clearing up immediately. "I'll lower you through the roof if I have to, but you're coming as long as you're able to draw a breath. And it better be soon."

Some days I think I'll die the way I imagine Rosemary will—oppositional, *painfully independent and courageous, but not wise.*

"I'm tired," I blurted.

"You don't have time for that until you get back."

Rosemary knows, I think all of us do, that Antigua is really our safe place. It is where we struggle to get back to when we're sick in spirit or in body. We don't want to leave that part of our lives out in the leaving of it, grieving of it. I think all of us who have moved to Antigua have done so knowing our families can't, or won't, follow us, that we are, truly, our own creations. That may be why God has become so necessary to me. I can't shoulder the responsibility single-handedly.

I'm going back because I know Rosemary will stay at me until the day I die, demanding this or that, never taking no for an answer, never letting me forget the difference between living and death. And I do, just like Jesus, want to live every second of my own dying. I want to know, and I want You to know, exactly what I'm giving up for You. So, yes, it is true. I do hold You responsible, it's part of the irrational economy of my monotheism, for death as well as life, suffering as well as mercy. And yes, I do, I really do want to hold You accountable, right now, for what You are putting me through. And I know You'll receive that demand of mine as the biggest and best gift I can give You—just as I receive Rosemary's insatiable expectations as the gift they are. Living is friction, she reminds me in everything she does. Loving is too. And at my most exasperated, I can see how she keeps calling me out of myself—just like You. It's a very odd feeling to think You might have a character as demanding and vulnerable as Rosemary. In some odd, exasperated way, I find the idea stabilizing. It makes me less afraid.

Chapter 12
FOSTER CARE

What *was* holding her back? Rosemary wondered. The voice had asked her the same thing, and it seemed like they were coming to some resolution—and then everything blew up in their faces. But there had been a few weeks there, just like with the collective, where Rosemary could feel this wonderful communal will being harnessed and bringing them all into a new and glorious place. And then, just as with the collective, it collapsed. First there was Lourdes calling up and asking her to take Natividad and Mikela and the baby in without a second's notice and Wilma getting uppity and speaking up from the second phone and announcing they would before Rosemary had a chance to say anything—and then Ginger came back and it didn't seem that it was going to work having her stay in the house even though Rosemary had insisted that she come and live with them. But Ginger kept acting like there was nothing that could be done about her condition, like Rosemary had invited herself to her friend's deathbed vigil. If that was her intention, Rosemary would have waited later—Ginger was far too chipper to be so focused on her departure. Rosemary wasn't going to talk about death for months on end. It was morbid. Ginger said she had no sense of her own mortality—or she didn't trust in an afterlife. Of course Rosemary did, that's why she talked with Walter so frequently, but that didn't mean that she thought either of their times had come. Ginger would just look at her with this disgustingly holier-than-thou expression whenever Rosemary said this—like she and God had a private understanding the rest of the world wasn't privileged enough to understand. Rosemary had certainly not invited Ginger to stay with them in order to be condescended to.

And then Ginny Fox started meeting with the collective because Rosemary was feeling a little fragmented (and face it, frustrated with all the projects that didn't get off the ground) and now all the women could do was tell Rosemary about all the suggestions Ginny was making to them, even though Rosemary had made the same ones over the years and they hadn't even blinked. But now they were all praise, and, what was worse, they seemed to be willing to test some of them out. Now that they had heard them out of Ginny's mouth.

Then there was Gwen, Lourdes' step-daughter, who had taken a shine to Rosemary and the girls when they showed up at Lourdes' apartment to use it for their lessons while Lourdes was out of town with her husband and the collective was meeting at Rosemary's. How was Rosemary to know that Gwen had come unexpectedly? Or to stop Gwen from befriending the girls her step-mother had just evicted? Rosemary tried to tell Gwen that the girls were staying with her because they were just redistributing the responsibility. Lourdes had already done her part. But Gwen had a look as knowing as Ginger's when Rosemary said this, so Rosemary gave up. She had no idea what Gwen was up to, and she didn't want to alienate Lourdes now that Lourdes was back. For one thing, she needed her help, or would, if Ginger took a turn for the worse and she had to ask Lourdes to take the girls back until Rosemary could locate a permanent placement for them.

How quickly it all had collapsed—this vision she had had of connection. There were days now she really didn't want to get out of bed in the morning, and other days when she took a siesta, without explanation or apology. No one noticed. In this crowded house no one noticed when the dueña was sleeping. It was too much for Rosemary. It made her want to shake them up a little.

The knock on her door was vigorous and gave Rosemary a little shock. *Ginger*, she thought immediately.

But it was not. Mikela, it seemed, had stolen the baby. That was what Natividad and Gwen were claiming, but Rosemary was sure they were mistaken. She felt oddly protective of Mikela, even though the stubborn little girl was proving to be the bane of her existence.

"Mikela wouldn't do anything underhanded," she said firmly. She had thrown an old kimono over her slip and she wasn't going to put a hand to her head to straighten her hair. She looked, she was sure, like her own grandmother in late stage Alzheimer's.

"If she was taking the baby, at least she would have left a note."

Wilma glanced over at her with an amused but assessing expression. She had come up behind the girls as soon as Rosemary opened the door.

"Do *you* know where the baby and the girl may be, Señora?" she asked quietly. "Are we even sure they are together?"

"She was cross with us," Gwen said. "I'm not sure why. She said we were laughing so loud we wouldn't hear the baby if he cried—which is ludicrous because he's always in someone's arms and his lungs are so big, you'd have to be stone deaf to ignore his cries. I think she may be jealous of all the attention I'm giving her sister and the baby."

"She's afraid you'll take him away from her," Wilma agreed. "And you too, Señora. Perhaps you must both assure her that the baby is safe here."

"What does that mean, safe?" Rosemary asked.

"What do you think?" Wilma shrugged. "Alive. In her sight."

"He's not her child," Gwen said. "She's ten years old, for goodness' sake."

"She thinks you want the baby for yourself. And she thinks Señora Rosemary wants to sell him."

"*Sell* him?" Rosemary said. "I'm trying to give him away, and still nobody's willing."

"He's not yours to give, Señora," Wilma said. "Do remember that. Nor yours to take," she said to Gwen.

"What's wrong with giving him a little love? Whoever can have too much?"

"If that's all it is," Wilma said. She had an odd air to her, a sureness that was different from her usual skeptical detachment. Rosemary didn't like it.

"What else could it be?" Rosemary asked, putting her arm around Gwen.

Wilma put her hand up like a traffic cop. "You do not need to explain to me. I will find the little girl and let you explain to her, both of you, how you have no secret plans for the baby, how you understand that the three of them—Natividad, and Mikela, and Miguel—are like the Trinity, how you cannot love one without the other, how they are, in their deepest nature, indivisible."

"Really, Wilma, you are no help," Rosemary interrupted crossly. "I believe I will call the police."

"For a little indigenous girl?" Wilma asked her incredulously.

Wilma went over to Natividad then and put her hands on the girl's shoulders, forcing her to look directly into Wilma's eyes. Wilma's eyes, to Rosemary's mind, were unusually cool and demanding. Almost black. Wilma spoke so quietly and quickly in Spanish that Rosemary couldn't follow the words any more than she could the emotion that seemed to pass between them. Whatever it was, it made Natividad stand a little straighter, breathe a little deeper. Rosemary did wonder sometimes if Natividad were still sniffing glue, she seemed so out of it most of the time. Except after Wilma had stared into her eyes with slightly demented intensity—then the girl seemed both more alert and more relaxed. Maybe they all needed to stay right in her face.

Maybe they were all going a little mad. Communicating by glances. Dancing to the whims of a miniscule *enfant terrible* named Mikela. Except, of course, Mikela claimed to be a fully rational, albeit diminutive, adult.

"I have sixty-one years on her, 124 pounds, and I am her pawn. We all are," Rosemary complained as Wilma headed out to look for Mikela.

"*Teacher*, Señora," Wilma called back as she opened the front door. "Think of her as your teacher. It will make you feel better about yourself and it may well be true."

Well, if everyone Rosemary felt used by right now was a teacher, Rosemary was taking a full course load and she wasn't interested. She just wasn't interested. She wanted those girls and the baby settled somewhere. She wanted them off her mind. She wanted the collective back. She wanted Ginger miraculously healed. She wanted Ginny out of her hair.

Rosemary waved the girls away and closed her bedroom door. She had missed her morning commune with Walter. She wanted to stop waking up every morning queasy with dread, as if some terrible wave was rushing over the vast ocean directly toward her.

Toward you alone? the voice asked. *Really, Rosemary.*

I've got a bad feeling about this, Rosemary insisted.

I never said you shouldn't, the voice said gently. *But it may not be your doing.*

Of course it isn't. I didn't get that little girl pregnant. I didn't find her laboring in the ruins. I didn't invite them here—I was shanghaied.

And you may not be the solution.

That's what I'm telling you.

For them, Rosemary. But they may be the solution for you.

I have no problems. I mean, nothing but morning anxiety.

It's all slipping out of your grasp, the voice said slyly. *This life you were so pleased with. It's all slipping away, Rosemary.*

Whose side are you on really? Rosemary asked.

That's a question you must answer for yourself. It's your call.

I'm not calling anything, Rosemary insisted. There was something frail in her own interior voice that made her physically ill to hear. I'm just asking for some more information, she said.

Aren't we all. Always. And sometimes it's not to be had for hell or high water.

"Call her," Rosemary heard Ginger yell. "Just call her."

Rosemary hurried to Walter's cabaña where they had settled Ginger in a few weeks earlier—just as soon as Rosemary had taken a first look at her friend's pale face and rapidly dwindling frame as she slowly made her way across the airport lobby. *Cachectic.* She couldn't get the word out of her mind. Sickness unto death.

"Call who?" she asked. Ginger didn't look at her, or seem to notice that she had just walked in. It was as if she was holding a debate with Rosemary in her head and was already getting angry about losing. Rosemary was beginning to worry that the cancer had gone to Ginger's brain. Her reasoning definitely wasn't what it once had been. Although her nature remained as difficult as always.

"Ginny," Ginger said. "Call Ginny immediately. I want to make my last confession."

"To Ginny?"

"I can't make it to you dear." Ginger opened one eye. "You have no sense of shame—much less of sin."

"But Ginny? She doesn't seem the most empathetic of people."

"Empathy is not what I'm looking for," Ginger said. "She has the authority to absolve."

"Just *do* it," she yelled at Rosemary before Rosemary could say anything. "Who but me should know when my time has come."

"I think she may be a little crazy now," Rosemary said to Ginny over the phone. "The morphine. Maybe metastases to the brain. Would you mind coming? It makes no sense that she has chosen you, but she has." Rosemary was furious at having to ask Ginny. Ginger must have known that. She just wanted to test her friendship. It had nothing to do with metastases at all.

Well, Rosemary was going to pass the test with flying colors.

"Do come," she urged Ginny. "If it gives her a little peace, we may be able to buy her a little time, revive her will to live."

"Are you talking about me as if I weren't here?" Ginger asked.

Whose will? the voice asked.

You're right, Rosemary thought, sinking into the chair by the fireplace. My will is flagging. Whatever will I do without it?

Rosemary pulled the belt on her robe a little tighter and walked across the patio to the kitchen. It was close to noon and with the alert about Mikela and then about Ginger, she hadn't had time to dress. Lucky she had no clients yet. She felt she couldn't dress without the lift of a little caffeine. What time was it anyway? She peered into the dark kitchen to find the clock—and saw the flash of fat little legs in the cardboard box

Rosemary sat at the kitchen table sipping her coffee. Where had the baby come from? Had Mikela returned while she had been talking on the phone with Ginny? Had Wilma willed the little girl back? There was something suspicious in the way Wilma had locked eyes with Natividad. Maybe it was all some elaborate act on Wilma's part—just like Ginger saying her hour had come.

She watched Natividad hand the baby to Gwen, Lourdes's stepdaughter. Gwen was a small but wiry young woman with deep auburn hair, the curls tumbling to the middle of her back. She seemed very experienced handling the baby. This was due to having babysat for spare change most of her teenage years, she said. Gwen was an only child and never saw her cousins enough to practice on them. It was her neighbors who made live offerings, she told Rosemary with a wink.

It was Rosemary's experience, with her own children and all the foster ones, that only children and youngest children were often quite stonyhearted toward the young. As a middle child herself, she couldn't imagine what went on in their heads when they watched a child cry and just ambled off, seemingly oblivious. But Gwen wasn't like that. She seemed to enjoy the baby and Natividad equally. Right now she bounced the baby, letting his tiny feet slap down on her knees and then lifting him up over her head. All the time she was reciting with Natividad the conjugation of various verbs in the past tense. *Hablé, hablaste, habló hablamos, hablaron. Descubrí, descubriste, descubrió, descubrimos, descubrieron.* She seemed to have made herself completely at home in Rosemary's house. She'd only been here in the city for six days, but it seemed like months. She would hug Wilma or Natividad or Mikela when they answered the door, so damn sure of a warm welcome.

And what is wrong with that? the voice asked. *Surely you don't begrudge her that, Rosemary?*

I hate closed questions, Rosemary answered.

What she hated was feeling like a stranger in her own house. Gwen was on her feet now, patting Natividad on the shoulder. Bussing the baby's cheeks with loud smacks before she handed him back.

"I think I'll drop in on Ginger," she said.

"Tell her I've called Ginny and she's coming in an hour."

"Is it something I can help with?" Gwen asked.

"Don't think so. She might be after final unction or something. Always too quick off the mark, Ginger is. And why she thinks Ginny specially suited for this, I can't imagine. Maybe because she can keep a straight face though Sunday services."

"Didn't you tell me she was a priest?" Gwen said.

"She's an activist," Rosemary corrected her. "That's why she's helping out with the collective."

Horning in, the voice said. *Isn't that what you're always complaining of these days?*

But Rosemary ignored the question, gesturing to Natividad to hand over the baby—which the girl did, but with a hesitation that maddened Rosemary. What did Gwen have that she didn't? What did Ginny have? Why was she setting herself up like this?

You're seventy-two and you just want to be loved. That's not setting yourself up.

Needed, Rosemary corrected her. I want to be needed. At seventy-two, maybe that isn't so easy.

"Where's your sister?" she asked Natividad. "When did she bring the baby back?"

"School," Natividad answered her, still relatively fluent after her time with Gwen. "She did not steal the baby, just took him down to the plaza so that he would not disturb us." She didn't look at Rosemary when she spoke, but that wasn't what made Rosemary doubt her, rather the way she reached out and touched the baby's shoulder as if she were finally, six weeks after his birth, beginning to see him.

This is the beginning of the end, Rosemary thought, holding the baby tightly to her chest with her right hand as she helped herself rise with the pressure of her left hand pressed flat against the tiled table top. Natividad rose too and held out her hands for the baby. Rosemary handed Miguel back to her, but held the baby's bright blue eyes as she did so. He was a strikingly alert infant. Surprising, given the drug use, but a relief. There's not a thing wrong with him, she assured everyone she talked to—friends of her children and foster children, anyone who expressed any interest at all in adoption. If he's half as bright as his mother and aunt, you'll be ecstatic.

But the more questions people asked, the more hesitant all these leads became. They didn't like the idea of coming down here. They wanted everything handled through a lawyer. They wanted to make sure their claim was legal and irreversible. They didn't like that he was still living with his mother. What would they have preferred—that he lay, untouched, in an orphanage?

Rosemary wanted the child touched— but unbonded. For his sake—and his future parents. Less grief all around that way. So, she didn't like what she was seeing—Natividad's growing interest, Mikela's need to be in almost constant contact with the baby from the time she returned from school in the afternoon until she returned to school the next morning. Surely the baby was picking up a little of her desperate anxiety.

Miguel el arcangel is what they had named him—or Mikela had and Natividad had gone along. Miguel, Mikela had informed Rosemary, had a sword with him at all times. That is what made him an archangel. She had slashed her upraised arm toward the ground.

"Just so," Mikela told Rosemary, "he protects himself and those he loves."

"Not all swords," Mikela added, "are visible to the eyes. Just like the Holy Spirit, they can change shape."

"In other words," Wilma had translated, "he is a baby who must be treated with great respect."

"As if he isn't," Rosemary had scoffed—and immediately felt the worse for it as Mikela wound both arms around the infant, and Wilma wielded her own secret weapon, that merciless slash of her ink black eyes.

Now Rosemary watched Natividad stroke the infant's hair, draw him close and peer into his eyes as into a mirror. The baby smiled at her, but Natividad's expression, severe but curious, didn't change. I wonder what she makes of him? Rosemary thought. What kind of maternal feeling do you have when you are twelve years old. But then she thought of Mikela, the softness in the fierce little girl's body when she was caring for the baby. Maybe it had nothing to do with age at all. Maybe that was why Gwen, at twenty-two, was studying the little girls' behaviors as if she could learn something from them.

Rosemary went off in search of Wilma to see if she knew where Rosemary's appointment book had ended up.

"I am the housekeeper," Wilma said. "Not the secretary."

"Why limit yourself, Wilma? Why not call yourself General Factotum. I just thought you might have seen it lying around. I wasn't asking you to *keep* my calendar for me. I wanted to check what massages I have scheduled for this week."

"Señora, don't you recall you asked me to cancel all your appointments? 'For the foreseeable future' is what you told me to tell them. So I called everyone in your calendar for the whole year. That is, is it not, the foreseeable future?"

"What was going on with me when I said that?" Rosemary put her hand out to rearrange the statues of the Virgin on Wilma's writing desk, but stopped herself just as Wilma began to speak. "I'm not saying I didn't say it—just that I can't imagine why I would have done that."

"Señora Ginger had just had her first bad spell. Señora Lourdes had just called about the girls," Wilma reminded her.

"But now Ginger has revived. The girls have settled in. The collective—"

"Is now the responsibility of Señora Ginny. I see," Wilma said.

"See what?" Rosemary stood at Wilma's window and looked out on the grassy patio with the fountain plashing in the middle. The grass was green now, but Rosemary was coming around to Wilma's view that paved earth is best. Of course, tiles over the grassy area would up the sound level in the cabaña dramatically—and it would be impossible to do anything anyway until Ginger had passed on.

"The Señora is not, for the moment, feeling in the middle of the torrent of life?"

"I like that phrase. Torrent of life. Did you read it somewhere?"

"Most likely. In one life or another," Wilma said. "So little of what happens to us is truly new, Señora. Our words. Our thoughts. The tangled situations we find ourselves in."

"This feels pretty new to me," Rosemary said. She watched Natividad and Gwen settle themselves on the porch outside the kitchen. They were chatting away in Spanish—not just Gwen, Natividad too. Rosemary heard the bell peal and Gwen got up to answer it, piling her torrent of red curls on the top of her head as she walked over to the large door to let Ginny in. She was such a small, sprightly thing—a physical demeanor completely at odds with Lourdes' marvelous physical groundedness and her slow, deliberate way of talking and moving. Gwen was fire to Lourdes' earth.

"What is new?" Wilma asked.

"To have a torrent of life in the middle of my own house and not feel part of it."

Ginny and Gwen embraced. Natividad rose to her feet, eager to be noticed by Ginny, who didn't even look around to see if Rosemary or Wilma might be there—just headed to the cabaña to see Ginger with a wave to Natividad.

"That is new for you, Señora? Truly?" Wilma's voice was very quiet, kind—as if they had a confiding relationship.

"Why would I lie to you?" Rosemary asked curtly. "If I said it's new—it's new."

"I think we all have a place inside us where the torrent of life swirls at our feet so white and inviting but we, we know *al dentro* that we have no part in it. I think this is one of the normal conditions of the human being."

"I don't want it to be my final one," Rosemary said softly.

"You still have before you many positions before the life. Of this I can give you the promise." Wilma's voice was so sure and clear, Rosemary turned to look at her. But she was just sitting in her armchair, her feet on the little ottoman, her eyes closed. The light from the windows didn't reach to the far side of the room where she sat, so it was difficult to see her face.

"I didn't know you were a fortune teller." Rosemary's arms were covered with bars of light from the shutter blinds. She saw the door to the cabaña open and Ginny beckon to Gwen, who had rejoined Natividad on the porch.

"Who says I tell what I see, Señora? All or even part."

"Is there something you need to tell me?" Rosemary asked. She felt quite odd now, as if, without warning, she had dropped down into a cool pool.

"Only what I have said before. You must treat those three as if they are indivisible."

"Why? What makes you so sure that is the right thing to do?" She watched Natividad sitting back on her heels, smiling at Gwen as she made her way over to the cabaña with a tray with three teacups.

"I am *not* sure," Wilma said. "It was what I was told. And I was told to tell you." She smoothed her skirt with her palms but kept her eyes closed.

Rosemary looked around the room, cheerful with its apricot walls, but austere all the same, with only a single crucifix over the bed. Wilma did not, like Concepción, wear a cross around her neck. She had never specifically told Rosemary she was going to mass. But the crucifix made her spare bedroom look monastic. She knew that Wilma was Concepción's cousin, that there had been a marriage, a son—but never had Wilma mentioned them. There were no photographs.

"By who?" Rosemary said. "Who told you to tell me?"

"The one you trust most. But he is not the one who knows, just the one who knows you must be told."

"Are we talking about Walt?" Rosemary asked. She went over and sat on Wilma's bed, in part to see if Wilma would open her eyes, but mainly because she felt as if her knees would buckle.

"Are you telling me you can talk with Walt too?"

"Not as you do," Wilma said, smiling.

"If he wanted me to know, why wouldn't he tell me directly?" Rosemary asked.

"He was just there, Señora. He heard what I did, and then he was concerned and he told me to make sure you knew too for he knows the great care you take of both the young and the old. It was an act of confidence. Señor Walter knows your strengths, Señora Rosemary. He knows that you will do the right thing."

"Which is to listen to you?" Rosemary asked. She sniffed. This sounded more like Wilma. Back-handed. Manipulative. A master of indirection. Subterfuge. Guerilla tactics. Calling in the dead to support her own interpretations. Really.

"You tell Walt if he has something to say to me, he better tell me directly. Tell him we don't need go-betweens."

Wilma just rolled the back of her head gently across the red velvet chair.

"You can tell him yourself, Señora. We both know that. But can you hear what he says in return?"

Can you hear what anyone says in return? the voice asked. Today she sounded just like Rosemary's mother, mercifully dead thirty years.

"You, of all people, have no right to ask that," Rosemary said as she rose slowly to her feet.'

"I did not mean—" Wilma began, without opening her eyes.

"I wasn't talking to you," Rosemary said. "But I'll be sure to tell Ginger that you can get in touch with her George, and I'm getting the feeling Ginny may have a skeleton or two in her closet who might want to start chattering. Don't restrict your meddling to me, Wilma."

"You are insulted, Señora, but you need not be. Please do not ignore the message because you dislike the messenger or the way in which the message was delivered."

When Rosemary turned to look at Wilma, she could not tell if Wilma's eyes were open. Her face looked perfectly relaxed. Here she'd fired Rosemary all up, and it hadn't affected a hair on her head, a nerve in her body. Life was wasted on Wilma, that was all there was to it.

Gwen opened the door with her finger to her lips. Ginny was sitting by the bed, the red prayer book in her hands. Ginger lay there with her eyes closed, a self-satisfied smile on her face, listening to Ginny read in her beautiful low voice. She could be reading the phone book, Rosemary thought, and it would sound just as good to anyone except Ginger. Ginny dipped her finger into one of the teacups on the tray and with her thumb made the sign of the cross on Ginger's wrinkled yellow forehead.

"As you are outwardly anointed with this holy oil, so may our heavenly Father grant you the inward anointing of the Holy Spirit."

Gwen edged closer to Rosemary. "It's so moving," she whispered. "I wish someone had come to see my mother."

"Your mother died of cancer?" Rosemary asked her.

Gwen put her fingers to her lips again. It made Rosemary want to bellow. What was a young woman of twenty-two doing making hand signals to her as if she were a kindergarten teacher and Rosemary a recalcitrant member of her class? And if she was so interested in preserving the sanctity of the moment, why was she in here in the first place? She didn't *know* any of them, really.

Rosemary stared at Ginger lying on the mounded pillows, her skin sallow because her liver was beginning to shut down. Her pale blonde hair was now so thin, her scalp was visible everywhere, the saddest pink known to man. The blue flannel nightgown she wore was embroidered with yellow flowers and had five little white buttons rising to her throat, a flare of ruffles marking the top of the straight collar. She looked like someone from a nineteenth century funerary portrait. SO Ginger, really. Couldn't she have bought a housedress at K-mart?

Rosemary went over to the far side of the bed, grabbing the chair from the worktable set by the window and dragging it along the tile floor. She sat down on it, hands clasped in her lap. "Sorry to have missed the confession. What skeletons have I missed, Ginger?"

Ginger's eyes flashed open. "Wouldn't you love to know." And then the energy disappeared, just like that, and she held Rosemary's eyes with her own fading blue ones. The whites of her eyes were even more yellow than her skin. "Even if I told you, Rosemary, you wouldn't get it."

Rosemary leaned over and put her hand on Ginger's crossed hands. "Do you think you could hold this ethereal position for an hour or so? I might hire Lourdes to do a portrait."

"I'm not going today, Rosemary. You can lay off a little," Ginger said. She turned to smile and wink at Ginny. And Rosemary noticed that Gwen too nodded, as if she were included in the aside.

"They changed your sheets this morning?"

Ginger nodded, pulling her hand out from under Rosemary's and running it over the bedding. Her skin felt like paper—something expensive, a little waxy and also dry. Too dry. If Rosemary wasn't careful, she would begin to imagine she could see Ginger's bones. How did the weight drop off her so quickly?

"You've eaten today?"

"I'm not trying to hurry the process," Ginger said. "It just hurts,

Rosemary. The pain is greater than any pleasure I get from the food—which is no criticism, absolutely no criticism, of Wilma's wonderful cooking."

Rosemary had seen Wilma squirting an eyedropper of one medicine in Ginger's fruit juice, grinding a pill to powder and stirring it into her bowl of soup.

"Do you want me to see the doctor about increasing your morphine?"

"I like being present," Ginger said. She watched her hands moving automatically across the sheet and blanket. The knuckles stood out grotesquely now that she was so thin.

"I like being aware of my company. It feels odd to have discovered such interesting people just as I'm making my fond adieus."

Ginger reached over and stroked Ginny's hand. "I know this was a stretch for you, given that you're down here incognito, but I'm so glad you came. You don't know how much peace this has given me, Mother Fox."

Rosemary had heard that Ginny had once been a priest, but how like Ginger to bring them into this most high and most low, most pickled Episcopal relation. Maybe Ginny had belonged to the Methodists or Presbyterians, who, Rosemary believed, did not infantilize themselves in relation to their clergy. Why did Ginger always assume in the absence of competing information that everyone shared her background?

"Really, Ginger, won't just plain Ginny do? If you call her Mother, what does that make you?"

Ginny turned to Rosemary. "It's an outdated custom—and, of course, a new-fangled one as well—but there's no reason for it except tradition. It sits well with some people—and others prefer Reverend. Neither are particularly appropriate, since I recently resigned from all parish ministry."

Ginger squirmed a little to get a better view of Ginny. Ah, Rosemary thought with relief, curiosity has set her sharp claws in her and woken her up again. Gwen too had come closer as if she wanted to be in on any confession Ginny might make.

"I didn't think you could resign—just go into priest purgatory at your own volition. Not unless something scandalous had taken place—and then you were tried and expelled, you couldn't just up and quit." Ginger opened her eyes briefly and fixed them on Ginny's flushing face.

Gwen stared intently at Ginny, a look of surprise, cut as it seemed to be with speculation, made her look unexpectedly, a little unpleasantly, old for her years.

"Your church was in the Boston area, wasn't it?" Gwen said. "Wasn't there something in the papers last summer—" Gwen's eyes widened. "Oops. Sorry, Ginny. I'm always saying things before I think them through."

"When I was a young woman," Ginger said, "I fell in love with a soldier, a boy four years younger than me. I was twenty-two. He was eighteen. His name was Daughtry. Daughtry Wilson. I was working in Washington then. He was there on leave. I wrote to him until the letters began to come back unopened. Deceased. They had a stamp. Can you imagine what it felt like to receive the first one stamped that way? Do you know, much as I adored George and thought he was the most marvelous grace in my whole life, as I lie here, it is Daughtry's skin I can remember. It's amazing really to be able to remember touch at all. But that one weekend almost sixty years ago, to think that it is stored so vividly back there in my mind. I wonder what else will come back to me in these last weeks."

Gwen came over and stood by the foot of the bed. "If you need someone to talk to, Ginger, I'm available." Her small freckled face was very white, earnest, all the coyness Rosemary had surprised on it falling away. "I would really like to know you before you die. I know that sounds rude and pushy probably—but it's what I mind most about my mother going the way she did. I didn't *know* enough."

"And you think if she talked non-stop for six months, even a year, you'd know Ginger?" Rosemary asked. The laugh that spilled from her was completely unforced. "I've known her for twelve years and she is a mystery to me."

"That's because you don't take me at face value," Ginger said. She began to laugh, but it quickly turned into a thick ugly cough. Rosemary quickly stood up and drew Ginger to a half-erect position and began to tap her back forcefully but with a massaging finish to each contact with her hand.

"I don't want to let you go," she said quietly.

"I'd like you to see me through Holy Week at the very least," Ginger answered equally quietly. "Do you think we could make a carpet this year? I've never done that."

"The collective might like to help," Ginny said.

"And their husbands would enjoy the drinking, no doubt about it." Rosemary forced herself to meet Ginny's innocuous gaze and smile. "Do you want to ask them?"

"Simon's friend Byron is coming down from the lake. I'm sure they'd help. And Lourdes, don't you think, Gwen?" Ginny smiled at all of them, already taking over. She couldn't help herself.

"And maybe Natividad could make the design," Gwen added. "She's a dynamite artist."

"Or your step-mother," Rosemary felt the need to add. "She's pretty striking in her own right. Have you seen any of the work she's done while she's been here?"

"Her studio is like Bluebeard's closet," Gwen said. "She locked the room back at Dad's house that held her paintings too. But if you want, I'll ask her."

But Rosemary said she was looking for an opportunity to talk to Lourdes and would do it herself. Gwen straightened her back but shook her hair forward so it partially covered her cheeks and the flush that rose there. Rosemary felt a small measure of satisfaction—but more curiosity. What game was the young woman playing? Before, she would have just said that she felt Gwen proceeded on instinct, but that flush implied an intentionality that intrigued her.

Rosemary had slowed down the slaps until they turned into a steady massage. She could feel Ginger's back begin to soften, then tense again as the pain came.

My friend, she thought. My last true friend.

Why can't you be direct then? Why can't you tell her you want her to hang on.

Obviously you don't know her the way I do, Rosemary thought. And then she felt a pain in her gut so sharp she almost buckled with it. Ginger looked over at her and Rosemary forced her hands to continue their massage. She leaned against the headboard as she did so, watching the pigeons swooping down onto the grass as Wilma threw seed out to them. A habit Rosemary had introduced her to years before.

"Holy Week it is," she murmured to Ginger.

"It would be too much for you, I'm sure, if I died on Good Friday."

Rosemary put her hands on Ginger's temples and Ginger leaned back against her shoulder.

"Make it Easter—people are less hung over. They can give it their full attention. You want everyone to be fully present."

"Of course. Not before Easter then." Rosemary could see her mouth making tiny involuntary suckling movements.

We spend so much time trying to put our lives in order, in sequence, and then it all collapses into one moment that holds the baby's memory of the breast and the texture of an eighteen year old boy's skin, Rosemary thought. She slowed her breath to match Ginger's and nodded at Ginny and Gwen, who had risen to their feet, to go on and leave them alone.

"Tomorrow then," Gwen whispered.

"Me too," Ginny said. "The collective's meeting at ten."

Gwen carried the tray. Ginny set the prayer book by the bed, reached over and set her hand on the top of Ginger's hand.

"The peace of God that passes all understanding, keep your hearts and mind in the knowledge and love of God and of his Son Jesus Christ Our Lord, and the blessing of God almighty, the Father, the Son, and the Holy Ghost, be among you and remain with you always."

"Thank you, Mother Fox," Ginger said, her lips tightening in a perverse smile.

Rosemary kept stroking her head.

"Are they out of earshot?" Ginger asked after a minute or two.

Rosemary kept massaging her friend's forehead, pressing down with her thumbs, drawing the dry frail skin out toward the scalp.

"This is not a confession," Ginger said.

"I wouldn't expect it to be," Rosemary said. "It's not your style and I'm not a priest. You had your chance back there and didn't take it."

"I worry about all those girls. Not just the little Indian ones, but this new one—Gwen. I just keep hearing this phrase, *spirit of adoption*, running through my head. I should have asked Ginny where it comes from. I think it's the gospels, but maybe it's from Paul."

"She wants to adopt the baby, you know."

"Who—Ginny?" Rosemary asked, trying to keep the sinking feeling under control.

"No. The other girl, Gwen."

"She's too young."

"No younger than we were when we had our children, Rosemary."

"No younger than I was, certainly. But you were wiser. She should be too."

"No. That's what I'm telling you. I had another child, a son. With that boy Daughtry. No one knows. Except me. Now you."

"You want me to find him?" Rosemary stroked her friends cheek but was careful to keep her posture exactly as it had been.

"Don't be ridiculous. It would take longer than I have left. Why, for God's sake, would he want to see me? But what I'm saying is, don't rule her out because she's only twenty-two. She may know exactly what she's doing."

Rosemary slid out from behind Ginger and let her rest back on the pillows.

"And she may not. How much do any of us know when we take on responsibility for another? Really. How much do any of us know of our motives, our abilities?"

"She admires you, you know."

"She'd be better off admiring her step-mother."

"I was talking about Ginny Fox."

"Well, how was I to know you were shifting from apples to oranges."

"You could make them both your own if you wanted to."

"But I don't. Why would I? I'm an old woman, Ginger. Just like you. I don't have time for friends."

"The younger one has an aversion to me, but the older one visits me with Gwen."

"We're talking about the little girls now?"

"Is there any way you can keep the baby with them, Rosemary?"

"Not you too? What is this, some plot you and Wilma have cooked up together? You want Gwen, at twenty-two, to adopt all three of them?"

Rosemary turned her chair so she could look out the open door at the bright sun intensifying the vivid orange of the bougainvillea and the red of the roof.

She may have metastases to the brain, but you, Rosemary, may have metastases to the heart.

"I was thinking about you," Ginger said. "Not Gwen."

Rosemary's eyes teared. She patted Ginger's hand and stood up. She was insane, that was obvious.

"I loved your touch. Could you do that for me again, Rosemary? People are so afraid of the dying, whatever they say. They don't know that all we want to do is find our way home to the womb again. Touch helps."

"Your skin's so fragile."

"Just use a lighter touch. With all of them, Rosemary."

When Rosemary reached the door, Ginger added, "Don't reject it right away, Rose. I do know what I'm suggesting. I'm not mad. I've never been clearer in my life. Behind you, I see doves fluttering down into the fountain and rising again and I know God hasn't finished with you yet. Far from it. I can see there are big things still in the making."

Yes, Rosemary thought, pausing a second longer on the threshold. I too am going to die.

Surprise! the voice said with a deep belly laugh. *Surprise!*

Rosemary decided to go over to Lourdes' house to consult with her about this surprising suggestion of Ginger's—just to alert her, really. She'd feel remiss if she didn't. And Gwen was such a fixture at Rosemary's house that there was no danger of paths crossing. Besides Rosemary hadn't met Lourdes' husband yet and was curious. Then she would go on to the mercado as well. Act like the dueña she had once been. No one would notice her absence.

What *had* she been thinking, letting Wilma cancel all her massage appointments? There were two new massage therapists in town. She might not get her clients back. And then what would she be left with? How many good-byes could a person endure at any point in time?

Her car had an unpleasant rattle as she bounced over the cobblestones. So hard to know if she were simply losing a muffler or something much more dangerous were happening. A tire coming loose. An axle coming apart. Amazing the car still moved at all—and that she did as well. Many of her friends found the jarring of their own motion too much these days. It was all in the ankle and the knee, that's what Rosemary kept assuring them, but they insisted on their thumping, straight-legged walking postures, or stoically endured the jarring of their cars on the cobblestones. Wheelchairs, of course, were out of the question. The streets all sloped down to drain in the middle and one could end up stranded there when the rains came, frantically turning the wheels and never gaining purchase on the muddy cobblestones. Why had she not noticed before that it wasn't a town to grow old in? It was only for the hale, however advanced in age. When Ginger passed on, would Rosemary be the oldest person she knew? Would she be the oldest *extranjera* in Antigua?

Wouldn't you like the distinction?

I'd rather have Ginger, she thought. Irritably, Rosemary wiped at her welling eyes as she pulled up in front of Lourdes' building. She should have called and warned them, she supposed. They could be out.

She pushed on the doorbell.

"Should we bother?" she heard a man's voice ask.

"Yes," Rosemary yelled, banging on the door with the flat of her hand. "It's Rosemary."

She heard steps quickly descending stairs and someone fumbling with the lock before the large dark door pulled open and a white haired man with a very engaging smile leaned around to peer, blinking, out into the street.

"You must be Rosemary. The current keeper of the girls. Not to mention Gwen."

"And you must be Lourdes' husband."

"That's one of my hats," he agreed. "My favorite one. My name is Ben. Ben Silver."

Rosemary extended her hand. She noted approvingly that he had a warm, steady grip.

"Could I invite you out for coffee?"

"Who is it?" Lourdes asked. She leaned over the banister of the upstairs apartment, then came round and started down the stairs.

"An outing?" Ben asked.

"I just got started," Lourdes said. "Why don't you come up and join me in the studio, Rosemary."

"If you'd like me to make myself scarce—"

"Not at all," Rosemary answered him after an awkward silence from Lourdes. "Join us, why don't you. I won't stay long."

Lourdes' bold drawings fascinated Rosemary, encouraged her and at the same time made her feel very sad. Especially the enormous one of Lourdes with the broom, Natividad swinging by her heels. And the one Lourdes was doing now, an enlargement of the drawing Ben had referred to, with Rosemary as God holding the girls, twined together, stiff as a crucifix.

"Have you considered sculpture?" Rosemary wondered. "Or life casting. I can see these as life-castings, can't you, Lourdes? It feels to me they're dying to move into three dimensions."

"Now that you say it—," Lourdes said. She smiled at Rosemary, lifting her heavy brown curls from the back of her neck in a gesture that was surprisingly similar to Gwen's habitual one. "I can *feel* these drawings as I make them. Feel them as mass. It's a strange sensation. New. It must be very familiar to you as a masseuse. As if my hand is serving as my eye."

"Think about it," Rosemary urged. "I bet you could get Marie and Ginny and me to model. Ginger's too sick, of course, and Wilma is too prudish. But perhaps the yoga teacher, what is her name, Yolande, might be willing to as well. Perhaps Gwen too."

Rosemary could feel the chill that came with Gwen's name and wished the words back. Then decided to forge right on.

"Actually, I've come to talk to you about Gwen," she said. She accepted the mug of coffee Ben offered her.

"Is she making a nuisance of herself?" he asked. He offered her the sugar bowl, but Rosemary shook her head.

Lourdes returned to the drawing of Rosemary she was enlarging, working off a grid. Rosemary found the rasp of the charcoal reassuring and exasperating in equal measure. Why was she always putting her foot in her mouth?

Agility, the voice said. *At your age, you're always needing to prove you haven't lost your agility.*

"She's a great help. Please don't misunderstand me. Natividad has opened up to her in a way she hasn't with any of the rest of us. But it's causing friction between the sisters. Mikela is jealous. She's afraid Gwen is trying to persuade Natividad to give her the baby."

"To *Gwen?*" Ben asked, smiling.

"Mikela's fears may be well-grounded," Lourdes said.

Ben carefully set his own mug down on the little bookcase beside his straight chair, opening and closing his jaw as if the coffee had scalded the roof of his mouth.

"She told you this? That she's thinking of adopting the baby? She hasn't finished college. She's just arrived here. It's crazy. She's not old enough."

"As if Natividad is," Lourdes said dryly. She was outlining the figures of the little girls.

"Have you encouraged her?" Ben asked. He sat forward in his chair, suddenly suspicious.

Even though Rosemary knew it was beneath her, she could feel her back go rigid at the insult.

"Believe me," she said coldly. "I want better for the baby too."

Ben and she locked gazes and then, to her surprise, Rosemary found herself joining him in his laughter.

"Who knows," he said. "It might be some kind of solution. What do you think, Lourdes?"

Lourdes didn't answer, just leaned over to pick up some white chalk.

"Adoptions take a long time here," Rosemary said. "When is her return flight?"

"Easter. Same as mine. That's only ten days more. What can happen in ten days?"

"Here?" Lourdes asked. "I'm afraid to imagine." She began to rub vigorously at the paper, melding the white chalk and the charcoal until one could, just as she had described, feel the mass of the little girls' stiffened bodies fill the inside of your palms.

"You'd like us to talk with her about it?" Ben asked.

"I was thinking maybe it wasn't a good idea for them to come over here and spend the night. Especially since she's only inviting Natividad. Mikela might feel left out."

"She invited them back here?" Lourdes asked. "Without discussing it with us?"

"It was thoughtless," Ben said. "She has no idea what it might bring up."

"I'll tell her we've discussed it, Lourdes and I, and have decided it's not for the best," Rosemary said.

She could see Ben lean forward and draw a breath, as if to question her—but then glance over at Lourdes' tense back and resist. Rosemary felt a fondness for both of them deeper than the circumstances merited.

At least that's a change, the voice said. *Most of the time you're feeling an exasperation completely out of line with circumstance.*

"I'm off to the market now," Rosemary said. "I promised I wouldn't stay long. Think about those sculptures, Lourdes. We could make a party out of it, you know. And before I forget, we're planning to make an *alfombra*, a flower carpet, on Maundy Thursday night. Would you like to join us?"

At this, Lourdes turned around, her face suddenly relaxed with interest. "With sawdust and rose petals?"

"It's Ginger's deathbed request," Rosemary said and then had to cough, the reality of it catching up with her.

"Count on us," Lourdes said, coming over and putting her arm around Rosemary.

Rosemary shook herself, willing the sorrow down.

"I thought if I got her back down here where she belongs, she would live longer. But she just seems determined to choreograph her death in double time. Good Friday, she asked me if I would mind if she went on Good Friday. She had Ginny over at the house this afternoon anointing her with oil. Why would anyone want to hurry their own death—will you tell me that?"

Lourdes and Ben stared at each other, then back at Rosemary. Rosemary stared at the wall of the pila, which was painted a satisfyingly deep brick red.

"When Ginger goes, there will only be Wilma who had any of knowledge of my life before Walt died."

"Your children?" Ben asked.

"Your daughter knows you?" Rosemary asked. "Surely you must be aware you're blessed with a miracle if that's really the case. In my own experience, we are all ducklings in swan's nests. Ginger was that sister God foisted on me—the one you'd never have chosen on your own. A bigger accident than genes. But I'll miss her."

Rosemary left before either of them could irritate her with comforting words. Truly, what did they know about letting go of your last new life?

When she arrived at the mercado, she realized she had no appetite for anything but flowers, so she pushed her way through the teeming crowds to the flower merchants. She bought several bouquets of Easter lilies and also, on impulse, a huge pod of coro, the fragrant palm flower used in the churches during Holy Week. She told the woman she would come back before she left the mercado and have someone carry the coro pod to the car. At the candle vendor she bought a dozen candles and an equal number of cones of incense. Ginger wanted a drama, Rosemary would give her one, filled with pomp and circumstance, smoke and mirrors. She'd find a tape of the funeral marches. If Ginger couldn't make it out of her bed to see the processions during Holy Week, Rosemary would bring their essence to her. She'd dress the little girls up in purple robes and have them carry censors and waft clouds of fragrant smoke around the courtyard. She'd dress Gwen up as the Virgin Dolores with that big sword thrust into her breast.

I'm pleased to see you accepting what you can't change, the voice said. Her tone reminded Rosemary so forcibly of Ginger's exasperating false piety that she had to put her market bags down on the floor and put her hand to her breastbone, willing her heart to slow. She hadn't been this sad and mad since Walt's death. There wasn't, after Ginger went, anyone who would trigger that passion again.

So? I'd think at your age you'd like to give it a little rest.

"It?" Rosemary asked aloud.

The candle vendor looked up, puzzled, then continued his conversation with a pretty young girl in a skin tight electric blue lycra top and equally snug black pants.

Rosemary would never be able to explain what happened to her next. Her field of vision began to darken slowly, as if someone were closing their hand to make a little keyhole. In the center of the keyhole, the world became extraordinarily clear. And in the center of it she saw herself, naked as a jaybird, sitting on a throne, just the way Lourdes had drawn her. And below her at her feet had been set a bier on which Ginger lay, her entire body covered with red roses except for her pale face. At the head of the bier stood Natividad with the baby strapped to her back. And at the foot of the bier stood little Mikela with huge sword in her hand. Slowly Mikela raised it above her head, the blade flashing light, mirroring the blood red roses.

"My love," she heard Walt's voice as clear as if he were standing right beside her. "My love, won't you come now?"

"You don't know what you're asking," Rosemary said. She could feel her heart lunging against her ribs like a chained dog.

But he does, the voice crooned. *Of course he does, Rosemary. Who better?*

"Señora? Señora Kempe?" She felt a sharp tug at her shirt. But when she bent her head to look down, her world went perfectly, blissfully black. She didn't faint. She didn't lose her balance. She just entered a perfect darkness that tasted sweet to her tongue, soft to her skin. It had a murmur to it, like the surf, but also like a high electric hum. She could feel her hand pressed to her chest, her heart's lunges losing force, subsiding into a rhythm closer to the murmur in her ears. She had never felt so pure. So sure. But of what?

Repeat after me, the voice said. *Repeat after me: I am that I am.*

And then Rosemary felt a pinch so sharp and unmerited it made her squawk with anger and surprise.

"*Aquí estoy,*" Mikela said. She stood with her arms at angles, forcing the people moving in an endless stream to eddy out around her. Her lips were pressed tightly together as if she were imitating the sternest expression of the Mother Superior. "I will carry," she told Rosemary. Slipping a bag on each shoulder and carrying the bouquet of lilies within her crossed arms.

"Por favor, Señora, do not talk, just follow."

Rosemary refused Mikela's offer to drive the car, but handled the girl's curt directions with a calm that anyone who knew her well would have found most suspicious.

"*Por favor,*" Mikela scolded when Rosemary turned on her signal two blocks early. She gently pulled the steering wheel back toward the right.

It was only when they pulled in the drive that Rosemary realized that she had forgotten her coro. The thought brought tears to her eyes. She could feel the heavy woody pod, smell the white fronds so neatly packed inside. But when she went to start the car again, Wilma reached in and took the keys from the ignition. Rosemary hadn't even noticed Mikela leaving the car. How long had she sat there?

The darkness still surrounded the edges of her vision and the edges of her body, like something indescribably soft, sweet, welcoming.

Wilma seemed as unperturbed as Rosemary, although Mikela was a flurry of movement, running to the kitchen first with the flowers, then with the shopping bags of incense and candles.

Wilma rested her arms on the open car window, like a neighbor passing the time of day. Even this gesture, so uncharacteristically informal, felt supremely natural to Rosemary.

"I forgot the coro," Rosemary said and again the tears began to spill from her eyes, so soft on her cheeks, so indescribably soft as if the darkness had become something real.

"Leave it to the girl and me, Señora. We will arrange all."

Why not? Rosemary wondered, the dark slipping underneath her feet, lifting her up like an ebullient sea.

Wilma opened the door and reached out her hands to help Rosemary slip out from behind the wheel. Rosemary took her hands eagerly, just to feel them, their strength, their smoothness. When Mikela came around to one side and put her arm around Rosemary's waist, while Wilma, on the other side, put her arm around Rosemary's shoulders, Rosemary just let herself rest inside their arms as if they were the darkness itself.

"How good you are to me," she said. "How truly good you are to me."

"The Señora is not herself, obviously," Wilma said with a funny little cough, both dismissive and pleased.

"*Su alma se asustó?*" Mikela asked. Her soul has left her?

"No," Wilma said. "Her soul is inside her just as she is inside her house. She has nowhere to go. No task that is asked of her except to throw wide the doors of her house and invite in the spirits, both living and dead."

"It's dangerous," Mikela said. "The spirits often have angers and vengeances."

"They have a hunger, just like the rest of us, for love and understanding," Wilma said. She opened the door to Rosemary's bedroom.

"The Señora too?" Mikela asked. "She has a hunger for love and understanding?"

"I heard him, you know," Rosemary interrupted. "Wilma, I heard Walt clear as a bell."

"He misses you," Wilma said, guiding Rosemary over to the bed.

Mikela knelt down and untied Rosemary's tennis shoes.

"Will she die before the yellow lady?" Mikela asked Wilma.

"The Señora is not dying. She is letting herself be lifted up."

"Her hands are very cold," Mikela said. She rubbed them with both her hands and looked deep into Rosemary's eyes as if she could see the sweet darkness gathering there.

Wilma drew a blanket over Rosemary and crossed her hands on her chest.

"So now you are not so afraid to release your friend, yes? And not so afraid to remain." Wilma set her hand on Rosemary's forehead as she spoke.

"I do not think the Señora hears anymore," Mikela said.

"The question is not whether she hears but whether she understands. In this she does not differ from the rest of us."

"It is hard to imagine people so alone as these foreigners. They have no children near, no husbands, no brothers or sisters. When life shocks them, who is watching? Who is there to invite their souls back?" The little girl sadly ran her hand up and down Rosemary's forearm. It felt to Rosemary as if her hand was being dipped deep into water. She gave a sigh of pleasure.

"Who do you think?" Wilma said.

"It is not fair," Mikela said. "We wash their floors and clean their stoves and we must watch over their souls too?"

"And who, my little warrior, do you imagine watches over you?" Wilma asked. She gestured to the girl to leave Rosemary.

"But what does she know, this old woman from the United States, about God's children? What does she know about our riches, out secret riches?"

"What do you know about hers?" Wilma asked as she closed the door.

With a sigh, Rosemary stretched her arms and felt the dark, which was Walt's voice, the reality of his love made fluid and close, lift her.

And so you always were and always will be loved, the voice murmured. *Give yourself over to it, Rosemary. Just give yourself over to it.*

It? Rosemary asked.

Yes, it, the voice said. *Give yourself over to it. Give yourself a rest.*

When Rosemary woke in the middle of the night, she breathed in the smell of the coro and smiled and fell back to sleep. She didn't notice Wilma sitting in the armchair or Mikela lying, covered with a blanket, sleepless on the rug. She did not hear them stir as she stirred, rest as she rested. She did not hear them opening the window into her dreams and inviting her spirits out again.

DO GOODERS
(Mamí Concepción)

    We have traits we learn from the Virgin—*bondad, misericordia*—but we do not have this word do-gooder. I asked Senora Rosemary what it meant. She was having an argument with her friend Ginger about the collective and Ginger said, "Rosemary, dear, when will you lay off being a do-gooder. It never works. You're seventy-one and even you should have gotten it through your thick head by now. It's a dead end. They're never grateful. It never turns out the way you planned."

    I have to admit, for a moment I felt sorry for Señora Rosemary, but I find that hard to sustain for long. A woman with such magnificent—and irritating—energy is difficult to feel sorry for. Even, perhaps especially, as she grows old.

    "What does this mean, this do-gooder?" I asked. I wanted to remind them that I was there. It felt too much like a family argument for me to wish to be present at it. I wonder sometimes if Wilma and I will end up like them—getting on each others nerves but truly not being able to imagine any better alternative.

    "Do-gooder," Wilma said as she came into the room, "is someone trying to do God's work and wanting the privilege, the credit to go to herself."

    "No it's not," snapped Senora Rosemary. "It is about trying to give a little back."

    "They are not, then, like the people who come to the square with their microphones and their loud speakers and sing to us about God and Jésus as if we had never met them before?" I asked.

"I wouldn't call Rosemary a do-gooder, I'd call her a harpy," Ginger said with a short, barking laugh that was all her poor lungs could manage anymore with the cancer filling her body so tightly.

I like both the women, I just wish they got along better. Rosemary is furious that she's losing Ginger but can't stand to say it. She thinks her heart will break if she does. She's more than a little like Mikela that way. Which may be why they're having such trouble with each other.

Just this afternoon, they each pulled me aside to ask about Mikela going back to the girls home. But for opposite reasons. Rosemary wants to separate the baby from Mikela. Mikela wants to spirit the baby away from Rosemary. I told Mikela the truth, just as I have all along. She can't take Miguel back with her. She has to choose, just like her sister. It is a home for girls, not girl-mothers or girl-aunts. With Rosemary, I turned the truth a little. I told her it was not possible for Mikela to return to the home right now. Her place had been given to another. But the Mother Superior was willing to keep her on as a student, so it really was better to have Mikela stay here with them for the present. If Rosemary couldn't get along with the little girl, I said, I'd take her home with me. Of course, Rosemary knew I was only threatening, that there was no way I would be able to separate Mikela from her sister or her nephew. And no way I could fit all three of them in my little house.

"Something has to be done," Rosemary said. She raised her voice as if the volume might drown out the undertow of helplessness. Of course, something must be done—but by whom. . . and what. . . those are the mysteries.

I think Rosemary is wrong to think only of the baby and the mother, not of Mikela. Wilma can feel this too. Something very strong is going on with Wilma, I can see it in how she gets so still and turns her head as if the voices are back. She doesn't say anything, but there's a slowness in her motions like her attention is always distracted.

I don't understand exactly how these spirits work. I know Wilma hears hers. Other people see them or smell them or feel them as a prickling on the back of their necks. There was a time when Wilma's spirits became too much for her. That was before she found the spiritualists' church and learned there were others like her—people who harbor strangers' hearts, willingly or not. But since she went to work for Rosemary, she never mentions them. Her spirits, her voices. Before that, she became quite popular—people were visiting her all the time asking to speak with their dead mothers or the women of their dreams, their husbands or sons who had been massacred or disappeared. There is a rule that you must never share what you learn from the spirits, even if it concerns a neighbor or a family member, if they don't ask you.

But the spirits don't ask Wilma if she wants to know. They tell her and then it's up to her to keep her mouth shut. I know I couldn't stand the pressure. I have a need to tell my thoughts almost as soon as I think them. It clears the air inside me, even if it makes a ferment outside. But when the ferment takes place outside me, it interests me—I like the fizz of personalities, like at the girls' home when I asked did everyone know that Andreas, the handsome volunteer from Switzerland, might have a venereal disease. I just sat back and watched who became very stiff, who leaned over and whispered eagerly to their best friend and where their eyes gravitated. Of course, Andreas was furious when he heard about it, but I had had my suspicions confirmed and told him I didn't really think he belonged there. I understood his need to do good, but perhaps he would be better off helping the men build homes. He was only nineteen, taking a year off before university, and was getting himself quite tangled and soiled, poor boy, no matter how pure his original motives. I didn't hold him responsible, of course. My girls can corrupt anyone. But I also believe in trying to influence the situation so less damage is done. I've suggested to the Directora that we concentrate on getting female volunteers from the language schools and asking Andreas to write up a description of his good work, so he will be known as a trail-blazer instead of a tail-chaser.

Is that what Senora Ginger means by a do-gooder—what I've just done for Andreas? I see it as common sense. I don't like feeling guilty. I don't believe anyone does. And guilt doesn't enlarge us—it makes us feel frightened and then we act in ways that diminish us. Just see how my mother always acted with me—or how I act with my own children when I know I've been too harsh on them. It doesn't make me kinder, unfortunately.

Just like Rosemary and her friend Ginger. Rosemary keeps up the sparring because to stop it will mean that Ginger is really sick. But each time she does it and it passes without comment, she feels worse. That is why Wilma steps in—she'd just as soon Ginger didn't have to hang around after her death until Rosemary can say she's sorry. That might take a very long time. Wilma's time—if Ginger chooses her as a medium.

Sometimes I see Wilma watching Rosemary like she is holding back a fierce pressure to say something—not about Ginger but about the girls. Then she shakes her head sharply and turns away. My cousin is a wise woman. She knows when to keep her own counsel. It's a pity Rosemary doesn't know about or want her wisdom. But even Wilma looks a little dazed when she looks at the girls, as if she doesn't know what is best for them either.

Rosemary keeps saying that the best thing to do is to give the boy up for adoption, put Mikela back in school, and Natividad—well, no one really knows what to do about her. Rosemary has been asking some of her foster children in the States if they would foster Natividad, but no one is interested. A glue-sniffing, twelve-year-old mother who *communicates only through drawing—I'd have my doubts too if I just heard about her. These descriptions leave out her beauty, the power of her drawings, some fierce thisness that makes you feel, however she behaves, that everything is not lost. These descriptions leave out Mikela's love, which surrounds her sister, or did, like the bright rays of light surround the Virgin of Guadalupe.*

"How are you going to get her up there anyway?" Ginger asks her friend. "You've got no hope of getting adoption papers. Even if we forged a birth certificate, she's too young for a work permit."

"She must work here," Wilma says, "or she will starve. She is no different from thousands of other girls. I do not see why you try to pamper her. No one is just a mother here."

My cousin looks at me, daring me to say anything. Her son Lucas' death—and his life—are the one thing I never mention—to Wilma or to anyone else either. Rosemary, I'm sure, has no idea my cousin has had a family, a life, a tragedy of her own.

I've heard Rosemary suggest getting Mikela adopted too. In the United States. All these women want to spirit the girls and the baby out of the country. I take this as a measure of how much they like them—and how hopeless they feel about our country. It never occurs to the women who meet here to discuss their fates—Lourdes, Marie, Ginny, even now the midwife, not to mention Lourdes' step-daughter—that these girls might want to be together, that they don't want any family but the one they've already made. It doesn't occur to them that, in our country, at ten or twelve they may not be children. It doesn't occur to any of them that one of their choices is to just open the door and let them go. They survived before, why shouldn't they survive again without them?

Right now, they have Natividad under house arrest because of that episode with the glue at Lourdes' house. There was another episode with Natividad, which only Mikela and I know about. We found Natividad, only three days after they'd moved in here with Rosemary and Wilma, near one of the coffee plantations on the far side of town. With the baby. Intoxicated with the glue. I distracted them while Mikela slipped her back inside the house. I don't think I'm wrong keeping it from them, seeing how strongly they reacted to the first episode.

It made me impatient, I must say, the way they responded to the first incident. The way Lourdes poured out the story to me when I came to give her her Spanish lesson, as if Natividad had done it just to hurt them—or out of a more general depravity—when nothing could be farther from the truth. How depraved can you be at twelve? The answer is very. But Natividad isn't. She doesn't want to harm the baby, although she certainly wishes him away with her whole heart. She did it because she hurt and was scared and she doesn't like all the bother of the baby—and she knew the glue as a dependable pleasure.

It is very difficult to give up your pleasures when your life is very hard. It is very difficult to give up what makes you feel free when life presses down so tightly every way you turn. I feel these women do not understand that. They do not understand how powerful and good it is to have a dream of freedom. I cannot imagine inviting any of them to the girls' home. They wouldn't last a minute. My girls at eight, ten, twelve know far too much about the press of life and what we will do, every one of us, to get some relief.

But that is the world Mikela and Natividad belong to—it is our world here in Guatemala. And these American women refuse to see this world of ours as having any good in it. That is why their first thought is to export the girls. To be honest, this attitude makes me very angry. They would think I was very callous if I suggested just opening the door and seeing what God had in store for them. But I am not cold. I am not callous. I have a very hot heart and I know what these girls are capable of—both good and evil. It makes me feel strong, just knowing that they have such powerful wills. Such a drive to live. Such a craving for freedom.

Sometimes Mikela looks at Wilma with the most wistful expression. I wish one of Wilma's spirits had a word or two to spare for her. But since they don't seem to, or not yet, I'm filling the vacuum by telling her what a smart girl she is, how if she just goes down and prays to the good brother and the Virgin regularly, something might turn her way. Mikela is as unable to say what turning her way is as we are. She thought these women were the solution to all her problems—and now she longs for the chaos of the girls' home.

Mikela's even stricter on her sister than the other women. Although she is very afraid of losing the baby to some secret plan of Rosemary's, she feels Natividad herself is safer here—that she is walled off from temptation here. But with the birth of the baby, her patience with her sister is failing her. She has her priorities straight, Mikela has. Baby first—then mother. I'd do the same with my own daughter—just like my grandmother did for me. If she had to choose, Mikela would choose Miguel—but it feels like hell to her to know that. You can see it in her peaked little face. How she wraps Miguel so tightly against her, then goes to sit beside her sister, as if she were the glue that they both really needed, the true source of freedom for each of them.

I don't know where our freedom or good lie. Part of me feels just the way Rosemary does: Something needs to be done. But I have no idea what. I have no idea when. All I know is that it is wrong to turn someone against their own history, their origins, their country, their reality. I can see no good coming from that. So I give them back to God. I give them up.

"You were always lazy, Concepción," Wilma speaks out behind me, making me jump. But I am ready, as always, to share my thoughts as they come.

"What you call laziness, I may call faith," I say. Sometimes it is unnerving to

have a cousin who can read your thoughts. Sometimes it is just efficient.

I take Wilma's beautiful hands in mine. I look deep into her eyes. "If there's anyone in there who would like to have a word with me, cousin, I am ready to listen."

But she just looks at me, her big eyes filling with tears, her face looking just as peaked as little Mikela's. She looks very young at that moment, and in great pain. They are like sisters, Mikela and Wilma, with this pressure building and building inside their heads.

It hurts me to do nothing, but I know it is better than any of the alternatives right now. Any of the other alternatives.

Chapter 13
FORETHOUGHT

Mikela tried a lot of other things before she decided to steal the baby. But when she heard Señora Rosemary talking to her friends on the phone and realized the word she was using in English was just the same as the one in Spanish and that Señora Rosemary was trying to give Miguel away, even though she had promised Mikela she would never do that, Mikela knew she had no choice.

But she was wise about it. She didn't act like she was upset or suspicious. She didn't act like she understood English. She just wrapped Miguel up more tightly in the *rebozo*. Natividad was eager to give him to Mikela. She was helping Señora Wilma. She was waxing floors and the weight of the baby on her back made her tired, she said. Mikela didn't understand how Natividad could say this because Natividad had never complained when they carried their brothers. She and Natividad had been even younger and smaller then. Mikela herself felt a powerful energy pour through her every time she tied Miguel to her. She knew then he was safe and she didn't feel so frightened and tired, like she did all day at school worrying what Natividad might do or what Señora Rosemary was plotting.

Mikela bided her time, but it was easier to do if Miguel was drawn up so close to her no one could come between them. Just his touch made Mikela feel safer than she ever had in her life. She was never, ever going to give that up. She knew it came from God, that feeling of safety, that it was what the Mother Superior called the peace that passes understanding. Something too sweet and deep for words. But true and sure. Just like the heat and light from a fire.

But Mikela didn't feel that way around anyone else these days. Sometimes the strength of her anger frightened her, especially when she felt it toward Natividad, which was happening more and more often in the last week since they had left the artist woman's house and had come to live with Señora Rosemary and Señora Wilma.

Mikela had a very bad feeling here. Maybe it was because of the sick woman who was in the dead Señor's cabaña waiting for her own time to die. Some days the sick woman asked to see Miguel and Mikela would take him in there, or the sick woman would be sitting on a chair in the patio and she would wave Mikela over. Mikela tried to pretend she didn't see her, but then the sick woman would call Mikela's name in a high scratchy voice that was so piercing Mikela could not pretend she didn't hear.

She was very religious, this lady. Her name was Señora Ginger. Her Spanish was better than Señora Rosemary's. She would ask Mikela about her school work and offered to correct it, but Mikela liked it better when Señor Simon and Señora Ginny looked at her *tareas*. There were so many adults who wanted to see Mikela's *tareas* these days. They wanted to help. They all said they wanted to help. But with Señora Ginger, Mikela felt poorer with every look, every word. Señora Ginger liked to feel sad for people like Mikela, orphans and original people of a place who have lost their place.

But what kind of place did Señora Ginger have? She was here with old Señora Rosemary, no children or grandchildren around her. Maybe that was why she and Señora Rosemary kept talking about how to give Miguel away. They didn't want anyone else to have a warm weight close to their hearts.

"Tell me about yourself," Señora Ginger would say to Mikela. But Mikela never wanted to say anything because it would just bring anything she said into the circle of Señora Ginger's powerful sadness. Mikela felt the sadness was bad luck, but it was also magnetic. It took a lot of energy to resist it. The only person Señora Ginger couldn't pull into her circle of sadness was Señora Rosemary. In fact, Señora Rosemary could sometimes pull Señora Ginger out of the sadness. Usually by making her angry.

But Mikela didn't dare make Señora Ginger angry. She was very very angry inside herself, but she knew it would make everything worse if she let anyone know. Anyone at all—even God. The only time the anger let up was when she was holding Miguel, then it just turned into this good safe heat that filled her from the top of her head to her toes. Miguel loved that warmth and always stopped crying for Mikela.

So Mikela had her own kind of circle around her, just like Señora Ginger. But, other than Miguel and maybe Natividad, Mikela didn't want to draw anyone into it. She wanted to push them all out. *Hard.*

Here at Señora Rosemary's, Mikela had a difficult time keeping track of everything. She felt she had to always be looking around her and, even so, things were happening just out of her sight and hearing. Things that she needed to know.

At the artist lady's house, there had been more people coming in and out, but Mikela had felt safer, she didn't know why. Señora Lourdes was the name of the artist lady, like the place where Sister Bernadette saw the Virgin, the place where the spring came up in the cave and everyone who was touched by the water was healed. Except the artist lady did not believe in the Virgin, even though she drew pictures of her. The Virgin wasn't part of her religion, but she was part of the religion of Mamí Concepción, Señora Wilma, and the Mother Superior. Also, Mikela believed, the Virgin was part of the religion of Señora Marie, who came from France, which was near Germany but not the same. Señor Simon said he believed in anything with breasts, like the fountains in the plaza, where water poured out of the women's nipples day and night.

Many Protestants didn't believe in the Virgin, the Mother Superior had warned her. And Americans were almost all Protestants. This meant that they were disobedient, that was what the Mother Superior said. But Mikela, who had watched the girls in the home go to the churches of the evangelicals knew they were actually more obedient in some ways. (Evangelicals were Protestants, but they didn't like all Protestants, only evangelicals from their own church. There were some Catholics who said they were evangelicals too, but the evangelicals said they were papists, so it was all very confusing.) The evangelicals said if you didn't do what God the Father and Jesus the Son said you would burn in hell. You didn't have to go to confession once you became a Protestant. You had one chance at the very beginning to be forgiven—and then you were meant to be perfect. You couldn't drink beer or breathe glue or smoke or dance or steal or say bad words.

Mikela didn't like to go to confession every month, but she was glad that she had more than once chance to get it right. Especially now that she knew she was going to do something that would make everyone angry. Everyone, that is, except God. God would understand that she needed to protect her peace that passes understanding. God hadn't protected his peace in his own son, Jésus, but he promised never to do that again. He promised he wouldn't do to anyone else what he'd done to his own son. And Mikela knew Jésus must have been God's peace, just as he was Mary's. She didn't understand why God couldn't have acted a little more like Mary, but she guessed it was because he was a father and not a mother. Of course, mothers could punish their children too, Mikela knew that. They could stand back while they were being beaten or raped and do nothing—just like God did with Jésus. They could, like Mikela's own mother, beat their own children. But not, Mikela needed to believe this, if they really knew their children, their girls as well as their boys, were their peace. The mothers got confused. That is why some of them did nothing when their children were being killed by the soldiers. They thought God might have a hand in it. That he wanted their children to be just as special as Jésus. And the mothers knew they weren't as powerful as God—or the soldiers. But that doesn't mean they shouldn't have done anything, no matter how afraid they were. They were confused. They forgot that God promised that he wouldn't make anyone else suffer the way he let his own son suffer. He too had gotten confused—but only that one time. He was sorry for his mistake. Mikela knew she wouldn't get confused and that she would do very bad things to anyone who tried to hurt Miguel, and he wasn't even her own baby. He just felt like it. She would do even more for him than she had done for Natividad when she broke the bottle and pushed it so hard into the stomach of that bad man in the capital. For Miguel, Mikela felt she might hurt anyone at all. Anyone. Even her sister, who was Miguel's real mother even if she didn't act like it.

Mikela was very angry at Natividad for what she did when she was at Señora Lourdes' house, how she went out and found Pablo and Tomás and breathed the glue with them again and then she came back and just sat in the doorway of the house until the Señora opened it and found her there. If Mikela hadn't been busy writing her stories for Señora Ginny, maybe she could have stopped Natividad. Señora Marie had taken Natividad to the mercado. Mikela had offered to keep the baby, but Natividad said no, she wanted Miguel with her and everyone was so happy about this they didn't wonder why.

Mikela wondered now. She wondered (but she knew it was a very bad thought) whether Natividad had meant to sell Miguel there at the market when no one was looking. She had tried to look in the notebook that Señora Lourdes had given Natividad to draw in, but Natividad never let anyone see what she was drawing anymore. Not even Mikela. Mikela found this very hard and dangerous. She didn't know how she could keep track of Natividad's soul if she couldn't study her drawings the way a hunter studies the footprints in the forest.

At the mercado, Natividad told Señora Marie she would carry the bag back from the market and give it to Señora Lourdes. She put it on her head as if she were heading home. Señora Marie wanted to take her other purchases back to her own house, so she agreed. But Natividad lied to Señora Marie. She did not go back to Señora Lourdes' house with the bag. She found Pablo and she gave the food to him, and he and Tomás gave her the glue.

The look on Señora Lourdes' face when she found Natividad, it was terrible to Mikela. Señora Lourdes cried out and just the sound itself brought Mikela running out of the downstairs apartment. It was like the expression on Mikela's mother's face, the look on Señora Lourdes' face, like she was looking at something only she could see. Señora Lourdes did not turn Natividad round and round with a broom. She just closed her eyes as if she were going to fall, and then she leaned down and spoke to Natividad in the calmest, gentlest voice Mikela had ever heard, but the look on her face didn't change, even when the gentle voice came from her throat. The look wasn't gentle. Señora Lourdes closed her eyes a minute, there where she was squatting on the doorstep, and then she reached out and turned Natividad's face to her. Natividad was so sleepy with the glue, her head wouldn't stay up by itself.

Señora Lourdes said something in English. And then she did a very strange thing, she used the wrong name for Natividad. She called her another name completely. That was when Mikela went to get Señora Ginny and Señor Simon. Señora Ginny led Señora Lourdes back into the house and then Señor Simon carried Natividad in. Señora Lourdes wouldn't let go of Miguel for hours and hours, not until Señor Simon made her give the baby to Mikela. Mikela tied Miguel to herself and locked herself in the bedroom. Señora Ginny had put Natividad to sleep by herself on a mattress in the next room. Mikela didn't even look at her sister, she was so angry she didn't feel sad. She knew something was going to happen. She could tell it from the way Señora Ginny and Señor Simon had talked with Señora Lourdes that night while they ate, the way they looked at each other and then looked over at Mikela and the baby but would not meet Mikela's eyes. Mikela knew they were plotting something.

Mikela tied Miguel to herself. She didn't untie him until Señora Marie came the next morning and promised she would stay there all day while Mikela was at school to watch him. Mikela trusted her a little more than Señora Lourdes, so she let her take him, but she did not go to school. She sat in an alley on the far side of the street and watched to make sure none of the foreign women left with her baby.

They were not sent to Señora Rosemary's right away, but Mikela knew that Natividad breathing the glue was why Señora Lourdes sent them away two days later. She said it was because her husband was coming from far away and so was her husband's daughter and they would need both apartments for themselves. She explained all this to Mikela and Natividad in very bad Spanish with Mamí Concepción's help. Natividad just sat there holding her big notebook to her chest. When Señora Lourdes told her she could keep it, Natividad seemed to wake up a little but she wasn't at all sad about leaving the artist lady's house even though it was filled with paints and paper.

Maybe Natividad hadn't been so sleepy with glue. Maybe she had seen the expression on Señora Lourdes face—and she wanted to get away from it. Because even though Señora Lourdes stopped looking so sleepy, that strange look came back to her face every times she looked at Mikela's sister. It was as if she'd seen a monster inside Mikela's beautiful sister. But what was so frightening was that at that moment when they found Natividad on the doorstep, Mikela had seen a monster there too.

It was only after a lot of talking between Señora Rosemary and Señora Lourdes and Mamí Concepción and Señor Simon that Señora Rosemary came over with her car and they put in its trunk all the things the women had bought for the baby—the diapers and the food for a bottle, and the bottles themselves, and the clothes for the baby and the dresses and blue jeans they had given to both Natividad and Mikela, and Natividad's notebook and Mikela's schoolbooks, and the cardboard box they wanted them to put Miguel in when he was sleeping—and they took them over to Señora Rosemary's. She had a room prepared for them. It used to be the room for visitors, but Señora Rosemary said she didn't plan to have visitors for a good while. Mikela wasn't sure if Señora Rosemary was still angry at her for her lying and thieving. When Señora Rosemary visited them at Señora Lourdes' house right after Miguel was born, Mikela thought maybe she wasn't angry anymore because she was so kind to Natividad and the baby and also to Mikela. But then she had Señora Lourdes look through all the bags to make sure Mikela wasn't stealing anything.

And now Señora Rosemary seemed very short-tempered, not at all like before, and the other women didn't come over so often, even Mamí Concepción, who was the cousin of Señora Wilma. Mamí Concepción had arranged with the Mother Superior for Mikela to go back to school even though she was no longer living at the girls' home, so it was harder and harder for Mikela to keep track of everything.

The Mother Superior told Mikela not to tell anyone she was living with the foreigners, which made Mikela wonder if the Mother Superior was lying to someone. She hoped the Mother Superior didn't get caught, and she was very careful to act the way she had always done before, studying very hard and running away as soon as school was over. She was happy to be back in her class and Sister Carmen said she had done such a good job studying on her own that if she kept up that way until the end of the year, she would be able to move up two grades. That would mean she would be studying with girls even older than she was. An indigenous studying with girls older than she was, this was a very unusual thing in her country.

Mikela didn't mind working so hard. She tried to keep hurrying Natividad too so that maybe Natividad could come to school with her next year. But Natividad would only pay attention for a little while these days—much less than Mikela, who spent her afternoons at school. She said it was because of Miguel, but Mikela could work better with Miguel near her, so she knew this wasn't true. And now Natividad would only pay attention to Señor Simon and Señora Ginny and this new young woman who was the daughter of the artist lady. As if Mikela had nothing more to teach her when Mikela was already two grades ahead of her big sister. This new woman's name was Señorita Gwen. She could speak Spanish, but had a strange sound to her words. All the foreigners had strange sounds to their words, but hers were the strangest. It was as if she was singing everything. She was a problem.

Mikela did not like the way Señorita Gwen and Señora Rosemary looked at Miguel when they were talking. Señorita Gwen said she wanted Natividad to teach her how to speak their private language. Mikela thought this was suspicious, but Natividad didn't seem to mind. Natividad didn't have a good sense of danger. This Señorita Gwen, what did she intend to do with their language? How could Mikela and Natividad make plans to run away if they couldn't have a secret way of talking. Mikela sometimes wondered if Señora Wilma could understand them. She knew Señora Wilma wouldn't say anything to anyone even if she did understand. But Mikela didn't think that was true of Señorita Gwen. Already she was saying too much about almost everything and she had only come to their country five days ago.

Mikela was thinking that she wouldn't be able to hurry now with her schoolwork like Sister Carmen wanted because she had other things she had to learn. And here, at Señora Rosemary's, she had to spend more time keeping track of Natividad to make sure she didn't do what she did before. Or didn't do it again. For Natividad had found Pablo and Tomás a second time.

Mikela and Mamí Concepción had found Natividad out near one of the coffee plantations when they were coming back from a place that helped poor people. They had taken a bus far out of town to a place run by foreigners, but not Protestants, where Mamí Concepción thought they might help Mikela too. But the people in that place only wanted to help families, not little orphan girls. Mamí Concepción talked to them about helping Natividad and Miguel, but they weren't very interested, except the woman who gave the clothes away (she gave Mikela a pair of white shoes to run in). She said that word to Mamí Concepción that Mikela was hearing too often. She said it in English and she looked over Mikela's head when she said it. But Mamí Concepción answered the woman in Spanish so Mikela could understand everything and said that none of them were going to be adopted—not the baby or Natividad or Mikela. Unless it was like this, where adoption only meant that someone sent you money every month like you were their true poor relations. They were not, Mamí Concepción said very loudly, going to separate the three of them.

Mamí Concepción helped Mikela when they found Natividad the second time she breathed the glue. Natividad was sitting on the side of the road, her skirt all dusty. She was sitting on the edge of a little plaza near the church where the good Hermano Pedro used to pray to the Virgin. In that churchyard there was a tree that grew where the good brother pushed a branch into the ground. Just like that, it set down roots and began to bloom because the good brother was so special to God. Its flowers were very healing. Mamí

Concepción and Mikela were going to stop in the church garden on their way back to the city to gather some flowers to take back to Señora Wilma and Señora Rosemary so they could make a tea for the dying woman.

Instead, they found Natividad sitting there in a corner of the little plaza, slumped against the yellow wall of the church, one foot in the gutter, her mouth open, her nose running. She was not beautiful then. She was very ugly. Mamí Concepción saw her before Mikela because Mikela was watching two boys walk down the street with their shoeshine boxes and she was wondering how she could get a shoeshine box for herself. She had talked to a boy in the central plaza, Juan, who said shining shoes was not very hard work and he made enough money to eat every day. Mikela was thinking she needed to learn how to be a shoeshine boy so that she could take Natividad and Miguel away from Señora Rosemary's, where all she heard, everywhere she turned, was that terrible word. *Adoption.*

It took a long time to return to Señora Rosemary's because Mamí Concepción had to lift one of Natividad's arms and Mikela had to lift the other. Natividad did nothing, nothing at all to help herself. Mamí Concepción had Mikela hide around the corner with Natividad, and she went on first but left the door a little open, so Mikela could sneak her sister in without anyone knowing. But Natividad was heavy, the glue made her very heavy, and Mikela was having trouble getting her in the door quietly, and then this young woman, Señorita Gwen followed them in talking loudly.

Señorita Gwen didn't know she was a problem. She thought she was helping. "Is she sick?" she asked Mikela when Natividad stumbled against her sister.

Mikela just stared at the American woman wanting her to go away, but this Señorita Gwen looked more carefully at Natividad and then got very quiet.

"Don't tell," Mikela said. "She's not going to do it again. I will watch her every second. But *please* don't tell." She hated to have to ask this because she did not trust Señorita Gwen, and to ask something of someone you do not trust is to put yourself in their power. But Mikela did not know what else to do. She did not yet have her shoeshine box.

"You can't watch her every minute, Mikela," the señorita said. "I know."

"You don't know me," Mikela told her. "I will keep my sister safe."

"From herself?"

"It is not my sister who is the problem," Mikela told her. "There are bad spirits who have gotten inside her."

The señorita bit her bottom lip with her teeth. She had very small sharp teeth and her hair was as thick and curly as her step-mother's, except Señorita Gwen's hair was red, while her step-mother's hair was the color of old wood.

"You don't want Señora Rosemary to know?" the señorita asked.

"She will send us away, just like your step-mother."

"Lourdes didn't send you away, she had to go traveling. She wanted you to be safe." The señorita's voice was flat when she talked, like her own words had a bad taste in her mouth. That was how Mikela knew that Señorita Gwen was, like her, an honest person who did not like lying but did it anyway.

After that, Señorita Gwen acted like she had privileges. If Mikela put Miguel in his box, she would pick him up without asking Mikela, as if the baby belonged to her. She visited Natividad when Mikela was at school or down at the plaza learning how to shine shoes. She talked to Natividad in a low voice like they had secrets together. Secrets against Mikela. And she talked in the same low secretive voice to Señora Rosemary and also to the dying lady, who she visited every day. She was the only person who could make the dying lady laugh. This did not make Mikela like her. Mikela thought maybe she hated Señorita Gwen, even if everyone else seemed to like her and woke up when she was around. Even Natividad's soul seemed to stay inside her more when Señorita Gwen was there.

But Señorita Gwen had plans, Mikela could feel it. Bad plans. And Mikela didn't know how to stop her.

Mikela wasn't the only one who had a bad feeling about Señorita Gwen's plans. When Señora Lourdes came back from her trip with her husband, she was surprised to find Natividad and Mikela and Señora Rosemary in her house with the señorita. Surprised and not very happy.

It was strange, the look on Señora Lourdes' face, like she was listening and not listening at the same time, as if there was another conversation going on in her head at the same time and she was trying to listen to both of them but they kept getting confused with one another. Mikela thought the voice inside Señora Lourdes was telling her not to believe Señorita Gwen. Mikela heard a very similar voice in her own head every time Señorita Gwen visited.

That voice told Mikela that Señorita Gwen wanted Miguel and Natividad for herself. She wanted to make a circle of the three of them and to push Mikela out, *hard*. Mikela felt that Señora Rosemary was willing to help Señorita Gwen but that Mamí Concepción and Señora Wilma, and maybe Señora Lourdes too, weren't going to help her, anymore than they were going to help Mikela. Mikela wished that Señora Ginny had not gone away on a pilgrimage—for Señora Ginny had said she would help Mikela. She wished any of the other foreign women were here, because that would mean that Señora Rosemary and Señorita Gwen would have less time to do their plotting.

It was when Señora Wilma and Mamí Concepción decided to go on a pilgrimage too and Señorita Gwen began to talk to Natividad in a very low voice, stopping whenever Mikela entered the room, that Mikela began to make her plan. After school, she had been teaching Juan to read and he was teaching her to shine shoes. Mikela was learning faster. Juan was a smart boy, but reading was difficult—all those letters, their different shapes and sounds. More difficult than shining shoes. Juan told her Señor Simon paid him the price of a shoeshine if he wrote something, but Señor Simon had taught Mikela many things already and never offered her money for her *tareas*. Mikela thought Señor Simon would only pay her for the shining of the shoes, not for writing her name since she did that every day. But maybe he would like to have his shoes shined by her because she was very careful. So, she went over to his house one afternoon to ask him if he would buy her a shoeshine box.

Señor Simon told her that Señora Ginny had not returned and started to close the door, but Mikela stuck her foot in to stop him. She explained about the shoeshine box. How if she had one, she could make money.

"Can't you make money working for Señora Rosemary?" he asked her.

"It is easier and more interesting to shine shoes than it is to wax floors," Mikela explained.

"I can't argue with that," he said. But he looked at Mikela like another voice was talking inside his head telling him not to believe her.

Mikela did not like this look, it made her feel a little dirty inside. Having secret plans you couldn't safely tell anyone was not the same as lying was it?

Her plans were not a secret from God, or the Virgin, or the good

Hermano Pedro—just from the people all around her. And that wasn't Mikela's fault. If she thought any of them would help her, she would be sure to tell them. But even Señor Simon looked like he had other plans for Mikela than the ones she had for herself. Why shouldn't she be a shoeshine boy? Why shouldn't she and Miguel join a carnival? Didn't she know, at the very bottom of her soul, that God did not mean to have them separated one from another, however angry she was at Natividad, however much Natividad ignored Miguel.

"I do not want us to be a burden on anyone, my sister or me or our baby," she told Señor Simon. "I will pay you back for the shoeshine box. I will help you teach the boys how to write their names. I will shine all the shoes of all your friends." She nodded at the tall, thin, brown-haired man who stood in the hallway listening to her talk to Señor Simon. Mikela turned to him.

"I will prove to you how good I am," she said. "I will borrow Juan's box and come back."

But the tall thin man was shaking his head and reaching into his pocket for money. He was just going to give her the money for asking. But Señor Simon stopped him.

"I will hire you to help me teach the boys their letters," Señor Simon said to Mikela

"And the shoeshine box?" Mikela insisted. Working for Señor Simon would be better than waxing floors for Señora Rosemary, but it would not allow Mikela and Natividad and Miguel to escape.

It was hard to see the face of the friend of Señor Simon because the light from the garden made a glare all around his head, the way Mikela had sometimes seen when Jésus was wearing his white robes, on those days before he went to heaven, when he walked around the earth with holes in his hands and a hole in his side a disciple could slide his fist into. But Señor Simon's friend did not wear a white robe, he wore a very neat gray shirt and tan pants. He looked like someone from the capital, one of the men who might have asked Natividad to lift her skirts.

But then he got down on his knees, this friend of Señor Simon's, and he said, "Can I see the baby? Not to touch, just to see his face. He is a very remarkable baby, from what I have heard so far."

"Remarkable babies do not need to suffer," Mikela said, backing away.

"No they do not," the man agreed. "My name is Señor Byron. I am a friend of Señor Simon and Señora Marie and, some days, of Señora Ginny. They have told me many things about you. They say you are a remarkable girl too."

"Are you from Germany?" Mikela asked him.

"I am from this country," he said. "My friend at the lake is from Italy. No one I know is from Germany. Do you know anyone from Germany?"

"Yes," Mikela said. "The Holy Spirit is from Germany." She did not like to admit this.

"You mean the man with blue eyes who was Miguel's father was from Germany?" Señor Simon asked her.

"No man made Miguel," Mikela said. "He just looked like a man. Until Miguel was born, we were very confused. Natividad still is. She thinks Miguel's father was a man, not the Holy Spirit. My mother got confused too. Natividad and my mother did not understand that God cast the souls out of the bodies of the man from Germany and the soldiers and sent the Holy Spirit in their place. Natividad was born from the Holy Spirit, just like Miguel. She doesn't know that either. She is just as confused as my mother."

"Poor Natividad," Señor Byron said.

Señor Simon looked at Señor Byron. "Patricio and his past lives—he's got nothing on this."

"You will pay for my shoeshine box?" Mikela asked Señor Byron. "If I let you look at our remarkable baby, you will buy the box and the polish and the cloths and the brushes?"

"The wise men brought myrrh and frankincense. I bet they cost more than a shoeshine box," Señor Byron said. He was talking to Señor Simon.

"I don't want to do anything that will help her run away," Señor Simon said. He leaned forward, his hands on his thighs, and stared right into Mikela's face. Mikela really did not like these men kneeling before Miguel and her that way, so she sat down on her heels too.

"You need us," Señor Simon told Mikela. "And we need you."

"You need our remarkable baby," Mikela said.

"But we cannot have that baby without you and your sister, isn't that right?"

"That is the truth," Mikela agreed.

"We need you more than you need us," Señor Simon went on. "You can buy a shoeshine box and go off with Natividad and Miguel and never visit us. That would hurt us very much—not just me, but Señora Lourdes and Señora Marie and Señora Rosemary and Señora Ginny and, oh, so many people."

Mikela was too smart to trust what Señor Simon was saying. He had plans, she was sure, with Señora Rosemary, or one of these other women—Señorita Gwen, Mamí Concepción, Señora Wilma. How did there ever get to be so many?

Maybe, Mikela thought, she could take her stories away from Señora Ginny and sell them back to her. It wasn't very smart of Mikela not to have sold them in the first place. It wasn't like her people, who sold their old clothes as well as their new ones, who made people pay them if they took a photograph, who knew that there was no end to what these strange foreigners would buy. Simon bought the names of the shoeshine boys, why should Señora Ginny not buy Mikela's stories, which had many more words in them. How many stories would buy a shoeshine box?

"It is all right," she announced to the men. She stood up again and patted them both on the head. "I have another idea."

"God save us," Señor Simon murmured.

"It is his job," Mikela answered.

"You didn't exaggerate," Señor Byron said. "She's priceless."

"I think you're wrong about that," Señor Simon said. He made a bad look with his mouth as he got to his feet, as if his legs gave him pain. "I think she's been very clear about her price."

"I'll open the door for you," Señor Byron said. As he pulled the door toward him to let Mikela and Miguel out, he reached into his pocket. He brought out several very big bills—Mikela knew from the colors. She put out her hand.

"This is not a present," he told her sternly. "You must come back once each month and pay directly to Señor Simon or Señora Ginny *in person* the cost of three shoe shines."

"For how many months?" Mikela asked. Three shoe shines was quite some money after a few months.

"Years," Señor Byron said. He held the money over her head.

"You're not cutting a deal with her, are you?," Señor Simon called. They'll never forgive you, Byron, if you help her escape."

"Until you are fifteen," he told Mikela. "That is my wish. But your debt is dissolved when you are eleven."

Mikela smiled a very big smile. "On my birthday?" she asked.

"Why not?"

Mikela took the money and slipped out the door before he could change his mind. She reached over and slipped the money into her shoe. Now she was all prepared.

"Forgive me, *Diosito*," she whispered as she opened the door. "I should have known you would listen to the Virgin and the Good Brother and your son Jésus too."

She decided she and Miguel would return to Señora Rosemary's house for dinner and act as if nothing had happened. Even if Señor Simon said something, Señora Rosemary would see she was still there, that there was nothing to be worried about. She would wait until the next day to leave. She needed to prepare Natividad. Señora Lourdes and her husband, Señor Ben, and Señorita Gwen were coming for dinner on Thursday night. There were going to be other people too. Then they were all going over to Señor Simon's to work on an *alfombra*. All the people on Señora Rosemary's street were foreigners, so Mikela did not believe they would know how to make the carpet. She wasn't sure about the people who lived around Señor Simon's apartment—but just to be sure, Mamí Concepción was bringing her sons over to teach all these ignorant people the customs of the city. Mikela was going to help them, and then, when everyone made their tour of the city to see the other streets covered with flowers, she and Miguel would disappear.

She blessed Señor Simon's friend and wiggled her foot to remind herself the money was still there. She pushed Miguel, who was beginning to cry a little from hunger, higher up on her back and hurried back toward Natividad.

CREATING A GOD GINNY CAN WORSHIP
(Simon)

  She's off in Esquipulas now having her own personal tête á tête with the Black Christ like the good liberation theologian she is. Putting her own small personal tragedy in perspective. What is it, she will ask me when she comes back, in comparison to the agonies inflicted during the Conquest, or the horrors of the slave ships and the tortures that came after. Or the recent civil war and genocide here. Or poverty that knows no beginning or end. It's everything you are, I want to say. Everything you were, everything you ever wanted for yourself. There's nothing, for any of us, bigger than that. She'll look at me as if I'm taking away the last vestiges of hope. But I know I'm giving them back.
  I guess I should take a lesson from David's debacle, or as they say here, *fracaso*. He tried to show the world where he saw God, in Ginny's lovely taboo body, in my dying. But in the process he created a living hell for her. Stripped her bare for all to see, even her congregation. They didn't see beauty, they saw bare-naked. So did the bishop.
  David got a gallery in New York and a solo show at the Soho Guggenheim. Ginny got, as far as she can see now, pure catastrophe. It hurts me to see what David destroyed. Not because I saw these qualities as permanent, invincible—but because I saw them as precarious, delicately poised, even if Ginny herself didn't know it. Such a fine line they gave her, such a narrow path to reach God. She needed to leave her body behind. She needed to leave her heart—because our hearts can't exist without our bodies. She needed to leave behind hopes of true community, ones where we know our predicament, however painful, is shared. There she was, my cool transvestite, pure male in her imagination, mind

meeting Mind.

So, where, I ask myself, was the real mind fuck? What David did or the situation she was in? The answer is both. The situation she was in was a mind fuck and also the greatest freedom possible to her. It was her path, the only one she knew, to the ultimate. What David did exposed the mind fuck for what it was. He must have known what would follow. But I think he imagined his own path could be Ginny's too, that if she could see what he saw, she would find another, larger path by which to reach God. One that made room for her as a vibrant, desired, fully sexual woman. But Ginny's God, like the bishop and the rancorous church warden, just saw bare-naked.

So, any God I give Ginny will wear ten bras and seven slips. She'll be fat and foul-mouthed and smoke cigars just like San Simón. She'll want a steady supply of rum—not to mention chocolates and marshmallows and Coke. She'll read the National Enquirer, especially stories about extra-terrestrial possession and babies with four legs or two hearts or children whose bodies age at the speed of light so by the time they're six, they're wizened and wise. Ginny's God will always wear a headset, and watch soap operas on a miniature television strapped to her wrist. She'll shit shamelessly in the gutters. She'll have six small kids, each with a different equally feckless father. She'll ignore them, all tugging imperiously at her skirts, as she talks to her friends, complaining about the selfish, sodden ways of men. She'll have a store in the front room of her house where she sells candles and incense and cigars and chocolates and rum and pictures of herself to the faithful.

"First come, first served," she'll tell her worshippers. "The more you give me, the more I'll give you. Buy up. Pray on. But remember the higher you climb, the harder you'll fall—and I'll push you if I have to, you can count on that. Don't talk back. Give me a little room, don't squeeze up to me like that. I've got my own needs to tend to just like you. What makes you think you're so special anyway? Sure, I don't mind your bringing more worshippers. What kind of commission you thinking about? Fifty percent—you've got to be kidding. The Catholics and the evangelicals only take a tithe. You're a greedy little bugger aren't you! But we're talking business here, none of that non-profit stuff. Self-interest is what made the universe. I'll give you twenty percent."

I want Ginny to have a God who will not say that what happened to her was inevitable, just. I know she'll have to find Her inside herself—but what, I'd like to know, gives her the tiniest starting place, that still point from which she can begin to move the world? For Ginny's God loves most deeply, most completely, everything she is not. So it is hard as hell to find that God in yourself when you are all that you have left.

I should know, shouldn't I?

The worst night of my life was the year before last. Halloween. It was before I'd agreed to try the new cocktails. I had quit my job in Manhattan the June before because my sick leave had run out. The parents of the kids in the private school where I taught fourth grade were beginning to gather at PTA meetings and look meaningfully at me. Grace Redmond, the principal, was doing her best to stave off the inevitable. But we could both see the writing on the wall. We could see the parents thinking, "Enough is enough. We may run in fund-raising marathons, we may visit our sick brothers, but HIV doesn't touch our world. He leaves or we do." I didn't want to put anyone through that. After Jade left I didn't see what I was hanging on for anyway. So, at the end of the school year I moved up to Boston near David, the only family I have left, however distant. And I began my great accounting. Or would have, but life intervened. Again.

David introduced me to Ginny, whose church was just down the street from the apartment he'd found for me and a few blocks from the renovated factory where he had his own studio. It was a trip to go to her church. An all black Episcopalian parish, formal as could be, everyone addressing each other as Mr. or Mrs. or Miss. And plopped right down in their midst, this improbable blonde, blue-eyed valkyrie of a vicar, Virginia Fox, who they called Mother Fox. It was a marvelous mismatch. They were mainly from the Caribbean originally, Jamaica and the Bahamas. What they had, at first, responded to was her intrinsic sense of style—and this very distant God she turned their attention to. Anglo-catholics so retrograde they'd have the eucharist in Latin if they could. But Ginny's God and theirs had very different attitudes toward justice. Ginny's God looked beyond them toward the even more deeply disenfranchised, and theirs, they'd always believed, had looked directly at them and encouraged them to join or re-establish their position in the middle-class. They were Episcopalians, after all. But Ginny, with her preferential option for the poor, kept shoving them back toward the gutter with her soup kitchen and her daycare for the deranged and, the coup de grace, her support groups for people with AIDS.

It wasn't, you could hear them muttering, that they'd even chosen her. They came to feel she'd been imposed on them by the bishop, who had his own affirmative action quotas to fill and too many congregations recalcitrant to women in leadership positions. Only parishes like St. Peter's, too poor to survive without direct subsidies, were unable to vote their own conscience in this matter. The bishop had given them options, of course, and they'd taken the best available. But surely, God did not appear to them in the form of a white woman, who (no matter how she'd impressed the bishop with her administrative ability or swayed them herself at the beginning with her liturgical bravura) was radical in her sociology and increasingly whimsical in her theology.

I remember the first sermon of hers I heard. "God may well be a turkey," she began. It wasn't Thanksgiving, rather one of those countless weeks of Pentecost. You could see that she'd lost them, and hooked all the guests—artists like David, political activists, radical thinkers from the several divinity schools in the area, and, of course, the local locos from the daycare for the deranged, who made their way to the church on Sunday too. One of them in his excitement began to make turkey calls. Ginny looked down from the pulpit and spoke to him directly, "Good, you got my point, Sam." Her message, if I remember, was that God wasn't bound by our rules, or our image. We may always look like God, but God may not always look like us. It was as difficult to imagine ourselves into the mind of God as into the mind of a turkey. But it might be a more profitable exercise for us to observe turkeys than to look at ourselves in the mirror and whisper, Divine! at our own reflection, however well decked out. Her elegantly dressed congregation looked suspiciously at each other. Mrs. Rufus Johnson, the senior warden's wife, angrily adjusted her large brimmed black hat with its peacock feather.

Oh, Ginny! Why didn't she see it coming? I suppose I did, but thought I'd get what I could out of the drama on my doorstep. It also seemed polite. Ginny had taken up with David just before I moved there. I think he might have met her looking for the apartment for me. She was so embarrassed by the affair, I felt I had to help ease her social discomfort, mainly by pretending I had no idea what was going on between them. Attending her church gave us all a cover. When she heard I was a school teacher, or had been, she asked if I might start a support group for kids whose parents had HIV. The neighborhood was now heavily Hispanic and there were a number of kids whose mothers were infected. In particular, there was a boy, Victor, who haunted the church with his little brother on his back—just like the kids you see here. Ginny introduced me to Victor and I took to him and I got something set up for him and a couple of other kids. But the original congregation didn't like it. Even though none of them knew my own status.

It all caved in for me that Halloween. I was sick, very sick. My CD-4 count was about 200 and falling. My viral load in the stratosphere. The guy I'd started seeing wanted to cool things. Having just buried his long-term partner a year before, he didn't feel he could go through the same thing again. A few weeks before when I was in the hospital, Jade, my own long-term partner, had come to visit me with his unsuspecting wife and four month old son. He told his wife I had cancer, but made her stand at the door. And Victor, the little boy from the church who had inspired the creation of the HIV support group, that very morning had learned, through his angry mother, that I was positive and gay. In other words, I was a worse person than she was so he should just back off from all the nagging about vitamins and rest and let her enjoy what little time she had left. A hit or two of crack didn't make her an addict, just an harassed single mom with damn little to count on.

It was Jade's visit that brought everything crashing down. I hadn't seen him since our break-up and I wasn't prepared for it. Jade and I split up a year before. Eight months before I moved to Boston, he met a woman at work he wanted to marry. He'd lived with me for ten years. He was Laotian. He never talked about his past, how he'd gotten to the States, anything, even when he learned English. Said he couldn't explain any of it in English so there wasn't any point in trying. My life is here now, he said. The other is gone forever. I helped him get his GED, finish college. I took all the precautions, from the first, but I never wanted to get tested. Why hurry the hour of reckoning?

But four months before we broke up, I had my first, diagnostically definitive battle with PCP pneumonia. No one was fooling anyone anymore, including me and myself. I woke up one night and found Jade reading my small red notebook. My list. It was what I did instead of getting tested. Wrote down all the partners I'd had in my lifetime. I included their status now, if I knew it. Whistling in the dark. You don't need to tell me.

I think we all have something in our lives, in our psyches, that we feel it would kill us to know but just can't leave alone. I expect for many of us it has something to do with sex. It definitely has to do with identity. And with God, since God is the great accountant after all. Before that last night with Jade and what I learned after, I would have said that for me it was knowing for certain I was infected. I didn't feel I could live with the truth. Little did I know how easy it would be compared to Jade's departure. But those things it feels like it would kill us to know are usually indicators of what is, for us, a state worse than death. Like betrayal. Destitution. Being exposed, bare-naked, to your whole congregation. Living with the guilt of murder, massacres, like the people here in this country.

When Jade and I split up, I felt I had destroyed his life. When the world came crashing down on me that Halloween, having seen Jade with his healthy baby and doting wife, I still felt the same way. It is the most terrible thing in the world to do great harm to someone and not know you're doing it. Your ignorance doesn't mitigate the damage, it magnifies it.

You see, I loved Jade and felt that he loved me too and that was why he lived with me. I knew we had these differences—age, race, language, culture, nationality, education—but that our love was the great equalizer. I did everything I could to bring him along. You know that song—you are the wind beneath my wings. That was me, Simon, the sweet breeze. I never imagined, until I came upon him that night weeping over my red book that for him, his association with me had never been voluntary. I wasn't the wind beneath his wings. I was the single bullet in the revolver in this game of Russian roulette we call life.

Jade looked at me, holding the book to his chest with both hands just the way Victor had held his little brother when he came over to tell me off. But all Jade said was, "There are so many. So many who are sick now."

What could I say to him now that I was sick too?

"You'll have to get yourself tested."

What was I expecting him to say? It's too late now. Or, It doesn't matter, Simon. We're in this together.

What he said was, "I am. I have been."

"And?"

"I am healthy," he said.

"We'll be sure to keep you that way. We have for this long, haven't we?"

"I can't," he said. "I can't do it anymore."

"Do what?" I asked. I couldn't see his face, only his silhouette in the window. The way his hands closed over the book the way some of the children in my classes held theirs. So tight nothing could prise it away.

"We can get through this," I said, coughing.

"No," he said. "We can't. I can't. I have done a terrible thing to you, Simon. But I cannot stop myself."

"You're seeing someone else?" I asked. I was angry, but not that worried. What did I, my destiny assured, really have to worry about anymore? I remember running my hand over my forehead, feeling one of those heavy sweats coming on.

"We can handle this," I said. "We have handled so much." How many times had I picked him up when he was ready to give up? When his first immigration application was denied. When he failed his first two college classes. The first job interview, when they told him they preferred native English speakers. We had, as far as I knew, been remarkably faithful to each other—so he was just weathering a little guilt. I could understand, couldn't I? I'd been in the hospital, he'd been lonely, scared, angry, whatever. Between men, fidelity didn't count so much. Except to me. But I knew I was unusual this way. So, I had always assumed, was Jade.

"You don't understand. I want a family, Simon."

"Don't bury me yet," I said. "We have a lot of time left."

"I want a family," he said again. "I want children. I want to be married."

"Oh, Jade," I said. Sweat pouring down my face. The eerie lights from the street flashing over his gold face as I stepped closer. Hadn't we all, at some time, wanted this? Just to be normal. Just to be right with the world.

But he backed away as if he was afraid of my touch. "You don't understand."

He had such small hands and wrists. They didn't cover the notebook the way my own would.

"I was planning to tell you just before you got sick. Then couldn't."

"What's his name?"

"I want to get married," he said again. "I want a son. I want to be the man I was meant to be."

Meant to be. Meant to be. I would keep hearing that for months, years. That's when I finally got it. And the bottom fell out of my world. Permanently.

"Meant to be?"

"I am not like you, Simon."

"I know that," I said. Just look at us, who could be confused? There he was, gold-skinned, black-haired, thin and wiry. Those preposterously small hands. Almond eyes. The precise soul of a CPA. And me, tall, blonde, a little shambling, totally Anglo, a teacher of fourth grade hooligans.

"I am not like you," he said again. "Can't you understand?"

He wasn't telling me he was even bi-sexual. He was telling me that for ten years he had been my whore.

"Why?" I asked him.

"To survive," he said. Then he shook his head. "You were so kind. You were my friend."

I didn't then or ever ask her name. She was two months pregnant. He was getting married in a month. He was leaving the next day to go live with her family. She was Vietnamese, not Laotian, but they thought this wouldn't be a problem. They were both CPAs. He couldn't come by and help me even if I was sick. She mustn't know about this—about us. She wouldn't understand. He was so sorry. He had always intended to wait until I died, but he knew that this wouldn't happen soon. Soon enough. And now he had met the right woman. The danger was too great. He was afraid he was going crazy. He couldn't bear to get within three feet of me. The smell, he said. The smell.

"I want to have a son," he said again. "I want someone to carry on after me."

"I want," he said again, his breath coming out in desperate bursts, "to be the man I was meant to be."

My first response was revulsion. At myself. I had, you see, always prided myself on being a good man. I was the son who stayed and met his obligations, unlike my much older brother David, who high-tailed it from our small Ohio town as soon as he finished high school. I went to the state university, fifty miles away. Came back and found a job. I didn't come out until I moved to New York in my mid-twenties. Not because I was confused about my sexuality or afraid, on occasion, to act on it. But out of respect for my mother. That's what I said to myself, although, thinking about it, I suppose I couldn't stand the censure. For her or for me. I wanted to be seen in the way I saw myself: good. I was loyal. I was there for the difficult three years it took my mother to die from breast cancer. To my mind, my womanizing, heterosexual brother was the one with the reprehensible mores—

which for him boiled down to more. More women, more fame. More distance from where he'd come from. I made more regular visits to see his own daughter than he did. I grieved more for our mother. So I guess my morality boiled down to more too.

I met Jade when I was twenty-eight and he was eighteen. I'd had an uncomfortably free first few years in New York. Too many anonymous encounters. Too much lust and not enough need.

But there he was, this brave sexy kid. Haunting the bath house. And I had something to give. An apartment. A steady income. English. Enough savvy to help him get ahead.

How many times, I wondered in the dark months after the break up, had he read The List? It wasn't long by the standards of most people I know, gay or hetero. But it was the cost, for him, of surviving in this new country. Even now, in my after life, I have some trouble running through all this. He should have told me earlier. He shouldn't have raised the stakes so high.

There are guilts that strike so close to where our I begins that we may not survive them. This was mine. Still is, I guess.

That Halloween night, I'd dressed in drag and had gone out dancing with my now platonic friend John and some friends of his. I could feel I had a fever, that I was coming down with something again. Probably PCP because I was having trouble breathing. I'd just gotten out of the hospital two weeks before. So I knew I was in bad shape. But I didn't give a shit. I kept on drinking. I wanted to hurry up this damn process. That's why I had come to Boston in the first place. I was throwing in my towel. I'd just gotten distracted. Kidded myself into thinking I still had some reason to be here.

All night while we were dancing, wherever we went, I kept seeing that little kid Victor showing up at the door of my apartment earlier in the afternoon and telling me that he didn't want to see me again. The scene just kept playing over and over again, like a dream I couldn't wake from. He knew all about men like me—what we did to kids like him. They'd told him about it at school every year. He wasn't scared of me, he said. He had his baby brother strapped like a shield to his chest. His chin kept quivering, but he kept his head high. Everything I'd ever said to him was a lie. His mom was never going to die. Neither was his little brother. I was the devil and I was a liar and he was going to tell Mother Fox to send me to hell. Prison was too good for the likes of me.

When I wasn't replaying that scene over and over again, I was looking at myself in the mirror of the boys' bathroom at the Fairfax Academy the day before I handed in my resignation, my shirt and my hands all covered with blood. Not my own. A boy named Eric in the first grade who'd taken a dive on the playground and cut his head open. I carried him to the nurse's office and she had just grabbed him from me as if I were a bigger danger *than the fucking swing set.*

Or I was seeing Jade in our apartment, the light from the flashing neon street signs on the street turning his skin red and blue, turn to look at me. That damn red book held to his chest. Tears streaming down his face. I'd never seen him cry before. The beginning of the end. And the end itself. Jade and his wife and baby standing at the door to my hospital room. Maybe David had called him to tell him I was on the way out. Maybe it was chance.

"I am very happy now," he said. He walked by himself to the end of the bed. His fingertips just barely grazed the sheets. "We have named the baby after you, Simon. I will always be grateful for what you've done for me."

His wife, almost as small as Victor, standing there in the doorway nodding demurely and holding the baby up for me to admire. No idea in the world she was talking to the devil incarnate.

So, there I was, 1:30 in the morning on the Day of the Dead, drunk as a skunk, beating on the door of the rectory. I wore a blue flowered dress and a large straw hat decorated with cherries. I could have been mistaken for the senior warden's wife. "Mrs. Simon Goodall at your beck and call," I bellowed, banging ever louder on the door.

Ginny came down in her robe. She tightened the belt as she pulled the door open. The robe was a deep navy blue terry cloth. Manly, but not on her. She pulled the door close to her shoulders as if to bar my way. Maybe David was up there with her. I'll never know. Don't want to, although imagining it that way makes the irony keener. There she was, beginning her own steep slide to disaster. But that wasn't the knowledge she brought to bear. How could she?

"A little late," she said, looking me up and down. "Lucky tomorrow is my day off." She stood aside, ushering me in. "Coffee seems in order."

I went into her living room and sprawled on her sofa. My hat tipped over my eyes. She tried to pull it off, but the elastic band under my chin snapped it back into place.

"At least get rid of the high heels," she said. "I can't explain any punctures in the new slip covers. Remember, I am just a wayfarer here too. This house belongs to the church. And they have appearances to keep up. Especially the Rufus Johnsons."

"Not like us," I said, breathing in the mildewed straw of the hat.

"Not like us," she agreed. "I'll be right back."

Did she listen at the foot of the stairs to see if David was stirring? Did she go up to warn him? Was she making some kind of inner decision about what was the appropriate stance to take with a drunk, dying man—a parishioner and her lover's brother and, I believe this was already the case, a soulmate?

She was back, soon enough, with coffee.

"So," she said, setting the tray down on the coffee table and sitting in the old armchair. "What did you want to tell me?"

"Forgive me, Mother, for I have sinned."

"Sugar?"

"Look at me, goddamn it." I pushed the hat behind my head, felt the straw crown give as I threw my hand back down on it.

She studied me carefully. "I see a handsome gay man in drag, who is having a bit of a set back. Lots there to celebrate. Just as much, I suspect, to forgive. I mean, hey, what would make you any different from the rest of us?"

She shrugged and stirred her cup, then leaned back and put her feet on the glass table.

"Have you ever done something truly wicked? I mean, have you done anything, Mother Fox, that even came close?"

"I harbor some very dark thoughts about the warden. Who wouldn't? And about Reagan, even now that he has trouble recognizing his own hand. Not to mention Clinton."

I lifted the hat off my head and tossed it, crown crushed, brim bent, onto the floor. I straightened the folds of my skirt. "Have you ever thought of yourself as a transvestite?" I asked Ginny. "That collar of yours, for example. Those pantsuits you usually wear."

"If you've just come to discuss a fashion make-over, could we do it when you're sober, Simon? Your judgment would be better. It's such a serious matter, I want us both to be up to it."

"You think God insists on eight hours of sleep a night and regular bowel movements?"

She smiled. "I find it difficult to predict God's wishes. But I'm off hours, so I'm assuming you just came to visit me, Virginia Fox.

"A nine to five priest, that you?"

"I'm always a priest to my parishioners, if I can just stay awake. I opened my door to you."

"Damage control. You were afraid I would wake up the whole block."

"There's that too." We didn't, of course, mention David, who may or may not have been upstairs in her bedroom.

She leaned back and closed her eyes. Waiting. Her blonde hair brushed the collar of her robe. She was a handsome woman, even in her nonsensical collar, which, praise God, she didn't wear at night. Tonight, in her state of relative undress, she looked about ten years younger. And I, I'm sure, looked like a corpse warmed over. But neither of us was looking.

"God may have sent his Jews into the wilderness for forty years, but I kept one man in bondage for ten. I didn't even know it. I can't get over what I did. Or not knowing."

"Do you want to start at the beginning?"

"What do you think you can do—absolve me?"

"It's not me but the power that resides in me that absolves. We can cut out the middle man. It's in you too. All it requires is the courage to ask, Simon. The courage to hear the answer."

"He named his kid after me. Can you believe that? It makes me sick. That poor little kid will be carrying that huge burden of injustice even after I'm dead. Like it will keep going on and on, the wrong I did. There's no end to it."

"Did you ask him to forgive you?"

"He doesn't think in those terms, don't you see? It was just the cost of surviving. Letting me fuck him over was just the cost of surviving. I can't get over that. I thought I was a source of love and support—and I was the worst thing that ever happened to him."

"The beginning, Simon. Start at the beginning."

So I did. Meeting Jade. Our years together. The red book. PCP. The man he was meant to be. Standing at the doorway to my hospital room with his wife and baby. Victor clutching his baby brother and telling me he knew all about men like me.

"I did that. For ten years I kept him from being the man he was meant to be. And I believed all the way through that I was doing good. How can you trust a God who will let you go so fucking wrong?"

"What would have been right?"

"You tell me."

"I can't."

"I wanted to die feeling I had been a good man. Believing that God took it all into account, not just the homosexuality but the good faith."

"And you think God doesn't?"

"Would any of this have happened if I weren't gay?"

"Any of what? AIDS or getting dumped?"

"I enslaved him for ten years, goddamn it. I corrupted him. Every day I made him betray the man he really was."

"Who wants you to believe this? He named his son after you. He came to visit you in the hospital."

"I wanted to die a good man, Ginny."

"You want to die a good man—or die believing you are one? What exactly are you raging at now. And who? You? God? Jade?"

"You," I said sitting up. "I came over to rage at you and your twerpy collars and your sure conduit to the Godhead. Where did you get off thinking you could pull it off, Gin? He doesn't like people like us."

"Us?"

"You're trying to cross dress with the best of us."

"I'm trying to be myself, Simon. Just like you. It's enough. Ask Him. Ask Her, if that makes you more comfortable."

"I don't give a fuck for God's forgiveness. I want my own."

"I don't see that coming any time soon," she said. And laughed. She laughed. She reached over and touched my hand. "So what do you want to do in the meanwhile?"

"Die."

"Ah, so that's what you really want to talk about."

But I didn't. I wanted to talk about what to do to help little Victor. I wanted to talk about how much it hurt to be brushed off by this new lay of mine. I wanted to talk about the murderous jealousy I felt when I looked at Jade's lovely young wife. I wanted to talk about how I seemed to move in and out of that scene in our apartment a year ago, how I couldn't tell anymore, especially in the hospital, what was memory, what was nightmare, what was waking and what was dying.

Ginny listened and listened. And then, as the sky was lightening, she yawned and said, "The long and short of it, my friend, is you're in no shape to die yet. We've got to get you some help. Why is it you're not taking any drugs?"

"I thought I'd just get it over with quickly. But I can't." Even as I was speaking, the scenes started rolling again. Victor clutching his little HIV-positive brother to his chest—looking at me as if I were the biggest danger he would ever experience. What the hell did he know? My face, so gaunt, bloodied, looking out of the mottled mirror of the boys bathroom at Fairfax Academy. I meant to put an end to everything right then, didn't I. Not do more damage.

"I can't imagine what God is up to, Simon. Who of us can. But I do know this. God doesn't expect us to wuss out. God doesn't protect us from that two-edged sword, freedom. And God often doesn't let us know how to use it wisely. It is there to help us become wise.

"I'll play devil's advocate for a moment and ask you this. If you hadn't taken Jade in, would what happened to him be better or worse than what happened to him by living with you? Maybe denying his "natural" sexuality was a small price to pay for what he received. Maybe he really believes this. Maybe it is true."

"I can't pretend that anymore. That's the horror. Death is easier by far than going through this day after day. I can't sleep. I can't breathe. I want to end it, don't you see."

"If you really did, you wouldn't be talking to me."

"I wanted somebody who really knew me to be sitting there holding my hand when I left this world. Was that too much to ask?"

She leaned forward and took my hand. Her eyes were bright. "I can't change anything, Simon. I don't know that God can either. But I would like to ask you to imagine living a little longer just so I could know you better. I have so much to learn from you."

"That's supposed to make me feel better? You're edified and I'm haunted."

"It's all I have to offer. But God, I do believe, has more. Would it insult you if we prayed?"

She waited until I nodded, then began in that strong clear voice of hers: "Almighty God who has taught us in returning and rest we will be saved, in quiet and confidence will be our strength, by the might of your Spirit, lift us, we pray you, into your presence where we may be still and know that you are God."

"If God had your voice," I said dreamily, "I'd believe."

"Can you believe, Simon, that there are some people who may look at you and see God moving there in all His glory. Just as you are. Exactly for everything you've told me tonight. For what haunts you. For what hasn't turned out right."

"God, you mean, may be a turkey—or a drag queen?"

And we both sat there, the morning sun pouring down over the new sateen slip cover and my blue flowered house dress, laughing.

I'd like to tell her now what she told me. If she could only hear. But she's still got her ear to the ground listening to the deafening silence of her dead hopes.

It isn't a set up, Ginny. You really are free. You really are beloved.

Chapter 14
THE PASSION

"I do think it's kind of nuts to decide to go visit the Black Christ in this week of all weeks," Simon told her. "All the buzz is here."

"Breathing room," Ginny said and he shrugged.

"Glass houses," he said. Then, with a little scooping motion of his hands, he released the subject. "Sacred earth. They sell it there in the market right beside the cathedral. Bring back a little, will you? Byron likes it. It looks a little like shortbread cookies to me, but obviously I'm an infidel."

"Like Patricio," Ginny couldn't help saying. Simon raised his right eyebrow, then blew her a kiss.

Byron was coming, without Patricio, on Palm Sunday to spend Passion Week. "Patricio feels post-Christian this year," Byron had explained to her the last time he was down. "But me, I wouldn't miss it."

"If you have the need for the company," Marie told her when she learned of Ginny's plans to go down to the south of the country, "I go too—any week of the year but this one."

"No, no," Ginny said. "I must do this alone."

Just as she had needed to call Bob Althorpe without mentioning it to Simon. Just as she had needed to set the phone down two days ago when David's voice, so penetratingly familiar, said, "Hello? Ginny? Ginny? Is that really you?" Just as she had to slip quietly down the hall, her eyes averted, when Byron came down to spend the night several weeks ago——in Simon's bed and arms. Keeping her own counsel. Hoarding her own ghosts.

"Why now?" everyone asked her, and she really couldn't explain. It wasn't about feeling awkward around Simon and Byron, or not completely.

"It's sex," Simon said to her the night before. She wasn't sure if he was teasing her. She wasn't sure if he was referring to her incipient trip or Byron's incipient arrival. "Except for astrophysics and, perhaps, accounting, I do believe it's behind everything. But it's certainly behind religion in all its forms—especially here. Don't tell me those sculptors didn't find their Jesuses and Johns and Josephs and Mary too in her thousand guises, beautiful. *Desirable*. Have you noticed how often people rub their hands on Jesus' feet or thighs? It's not benign."

"The wood feels good," Ginny said. "There's something comforting about it. It's always a little cool to the touch. Try it yourself if you don't believe me."

"But I have Byron coming here this weekend," Simon said. "Why would I go and take a six hour bus ride to stare at his inanimate double. And, like many of the statues here, I believe he's hidden away in a glass case, your Black Christ. So there's no touching allowed. I'd rather take my consolation in the flesh, if you don't mind. He—your Black Christ—really is very like Byron. Don't be startled. It's not the basis of my attraction, I assure you, but it's there. If you doubt it, just crown him with thorns and you'll see the resemblance immediately."

"What *is* the basis of the attraction?" Ginny asked.

"We'll share accounts when you get back," Simon said. "We may respond to similar things, you in your mahogany martyr and me in my mahogany man about town and the lower astral planes."

"It doesn't damage your friendship with Patrició?" Ginny asked. "It seemed like the two of them had a good thing going. I'd be sorry to see it end."

"Who's saying they don't have a good thing going now? And who said anything about ending their relationship. It's not in the cards I assure you. What's going on between Byron and me doesn't in any way endanger their relationship."

"How is that?"

"Trust me," Simon said. "It's a man thing. You wouldn't understand. But if we need to clear the air and start over again, we'll all come to you for absolution. I do hope that's not why you're going off by yourself to the far end of this country, Ginny. Not to pray for our souls. Or your own. You don't need absolution—not from a statue, not from your bishop or your parish, not from your parents, not from your friends."

"What *do* I need, Simon?"

"You need to love again, Ginny. Not a statue or an abstract idea—like your liberation theology. You need to love a human being, a man who farts in his sleep, a woman who snores. You need to wake up in the morning eager to be alive, to reach out and touch the object of your desire. You need to let yourself be the a very sexy lady you are deep inside—and you need to let God in on that secret too."

He's beginning to sound like Will now, isn't he? the voice said.

And for the same reasons, Ginny thought. His brain is in his dick. That's all he means by love. Afterlife indeed. More like perpetual afterglow.

"I'll be back in time for the big stuff," Ginny said. "I'm looking forward to making a carpet over at Rosemary's."

"Ask, my dear, and it will be given to you," Simon said, taking a lock of Ginny's hair and tucking it behind her ear. "Talking about answered prayers, David called late last night and said he thought he'd heard your voice. He wanted to know if he was hallucinating."

"What did you say?" Ginny, suddenly weak, sat down on her bed. Above Simon's head, she could see the half moon rising, mammoth and surreally gold, over the walls of the garden.

"I told him he had an over-active imagination. That an auditory hallucination wasn't as bad as visual one—although it was more diagnostic of schizophrenia. He seemed to accept it—even if he didn't necessarily believe it. I'm not in any way excusing what he did, Ginny, but he's not the same man he was before he met you."

"No, he's richer and more famous," Ginny said.

"He'd give it all up in a minute if you'd just speak with him."

"You don't really believe that, do you, Simon?" Ginny leaned back on her elbows, her laugh completely spontaneous. "That's you you're describing, not your brother."

"A year ago, I would have said the same thing, Gin. Now I'm not so sure."

"I'm so far beyond all that now, Simon. Why don't we give it a rest." Ginny's voice sounded like she had swallowed grit and she could see from the look that crossed Simon's face that he felt pity for her.

Well, screw him. Screw Byron. Patricio. David.

"I have to catch the five o'clock shuttle to the capital," Ginny said as she turned around and began to zip her knapsack. "I'll be as quiet as possible."

"Don't be too quiet," Simon said. "I like to know where everyone is. In or out. In relation to me. Only in relation to me."

Just before the bus turned the curve into the valley, Ginny (who had finished her murder mystery where the vicar indeed did what vicars do) was musing at the mystery of trash in this country. It didn't matter where you went, how far from any adobe hut or shed, there were always plastic bags dangling dustily from the bushes, old plastic bottles half-buried in sand, whole hillsides strewn with dirty pampers, tin foil, styrofoam and plastic bags. On her morning runs in Antigua, Ginny had discovered the Rio Pensativo—a dry stream bed filled almost to its banks with trash, the plastics and papers made malodorous with decaying fruit and meat and excrement that she assured herself was not human. She had blessed the dry season as she ran, but she kept having in her mind a truly disgusting vision of all that trash beginning to rise up on muddy, frothing water. She closed her eyes, blinking away the images of the river back there, of the plastic bags waving from the bushes along the highway here and now.

And then, there it was, with no forewarning. Its towers gleaming so whitely amid the green. Esquipulas. A true oasis. The streets as they pulled into the town looked unusually wide and unusually clean

Two old peasants, each with a sheathed machete at his waist, struggled to pull two heavy bags from the overhead rack. Ginny, who easily had a foot over each of them, was careful not to offer help. She saw their muscles bulge as they began to drag one of the bags out of the rack.

"*Cuidado*," one warned the other, as dust began to swarm around them.

At first Ginny thought they had brought cement, but then she realized that it was dirt. Dirt stuffed into old flour sacks. Perhaps they wanted the Black Christ to bless their cornfields. Perhaps Ginny should have brought a bag of leavings from the Rio Pensativo. She smiled to herself.

The two men in front of Ginny managed to pull the second bag off the rack and the dust swirled up around all of them, bringing tears to Ginny's eyes, an unpleasant fullness to her lungs.

Alpha and omega, beginning and end, the voice said. *Breathe it in.*

Surreptitiously, Ginny put her hand to her face and began to breathe back in some of the moisture from her own departing breath. Less, she thought to herself, breathe less. It made her feel very light, as if a hummingbird was moving with a little brr of hunger here and there inside her rib cage.

Soon, she thought, very soon, I will know why I've come.

Ginny found a modest hotel on the street running alongside the cathedral. After washing her face and hands, she left her knapsack there and headed back over to the cathedral. It was four now and she doubted she would be able to see the Black Christ up close. The lines, she'd been warned, were formidable. But when she entered the church, all Ginny felt was how *vació* the church felt—a cement floor without pews, or worshippers. The height of the church, the obscurity of shadows above her and on all sides, were a weight she wanted to slip out from under before it settled securely on her shoulders. She hurried across the nave without looking up toward the altar.

The guard looked pointedly at his watch but then shrugged and gestured Ginny into the long, empty rope path that twisted forward and back like a labyrinth—or the route to an airline ticket counter. The same circuitousness marked the walkway inside the church that led up to the altar. It folded back and forth like a fan. Even empty, it spoke of the press of bodies, the relentless urgency of so many prayers, and set a pace for Ginny that was so steady, so enveloping, that she felt a physical pressure against her back when she stopped halfway up the ramp to look at an image of Christ's bearded face composed of tiny milagros, metal charms shaped liked heads and feet, arms, hearts, lungs, kidneys, eyes, wanted and unwanted children, lost husbands, unfaithful wives. The circles that shaped his mouth looked like an anatomical dissection of the facial muscles. His long hair dangled, bedraggled, on either side of his sharp chin.

She felt the pressure against her left shoulder increase as she stood there inspecting the face, but it was nothing, no one. She was a white woman coming to see a Black Christ, alone on Holy Tuesday of Passion Week, unsure what she was asking for or why.

Ginny made her way up the ramp toward the sanctuary. When she turned the corner, she could see the glass case that enclosed the Black Christ and Saint John and Mary Magdalene. In its mirroring surface, she could see this strange new version of herself in a billowing red knee-length shirt and black pants growing larger with each step. She looked at her hands, dangling there so white and limp, and knew what was missing: Mikela. She wanted to feel the weight of her hard little hand as they made their way through the crowded Friday *velaciones* during Lent, observing both the diorama and the abundance of fruits, vegetables, and palm flower beautifully arranged over the church floor as offerings. She missed the way Mikela squeezed her fingers and said, "Señora Genie, this Virgin, she has not slept for two weeks. I believe her other children have fevers and she cannot attend, as she knows she must, to the son of God." Or, "This Jésus, he has not forgotten what happened to him. He believes his father left him on the cross to die."

But Mikela was not here and this statue, no blacker than the ones in Antigua, did nothing for her. She came up behind it and looked out through the glass toward the church itself. It wasn't as deserted as it had appeared to her as she crossed it. Small groups gathered here and there in the vast spare space. She could see a few candles lit and glued to the floor as they did in the churches up around lake Atitlán. Alone behind the glass cabinet, Ginny felt as distant, as empty and as bemused when she looked at the beautifully carved figure as she did seeing this unfamiliar image of herself without any clerical trappings superimposed over him. She imagined, just for a second, stripping off her clothes and donating them to him, so he could take on the funky tender intimacy of the statues in the church up by the lake.

Remember, the voice said, crowding up behind Ginny, covering her back. *You've come here to know love. You've come here to know love.*

Ginny leaned closer to the glass case, to the gilded cross that hid Christ's gilded loincloth and tortured body, leaned closer to her own troubled face.

A perfect emptiness, she insisted. I came here to accept a perfect emptiness.

Ginny startled awake at his first word. She heard David's voice clearly just in that single syllable: *Yes.*

Even now, alone in her hotel room, she could feel how alive her breasts and chest had felt, how they just needed to be in contact with David's skin, his lips, his enormous hands. That was where they were meant to be. Just as his fingers were meant to be inside her, *all* of him was meant to be inside her, so slowly, so deliciously slowly, while the echoes of the door, the unbolted door, still pulsed in the air around them. No time at all. Eternity. An urgency so deep it dissolved her boundaries and a stillness so perfect it was like all time had stopped and she knew exactly where she was, who she was, forever.

It wasn't just lust. If it were, the feeling would have worn off, wouldn't it? Wouldn't Ginny have felt a sense of self-loathing and aversion? But she never did. Even when she saw the painting. Even the day she broke with David (because of course there was no other recourse), her *body* refused to participate. It felt just as urgent, alive, present, yearning, and satisfied as it had throughout that year.

That was what felt the most unspeakable, most unbelievable, most shameful to her now. That David made her immune to shame—even now, even in this hotel room whole countries away from him, if she drew him to mind, the feel of his skin, the way her body softened and reorganized at the sound of his voice, the touch of his breath, the impetus and rhythm of his laugh, she was back where she had been before. That thought, so unbidden, so unwanted, was still there: *This is what I was put on earth for.*

It was a kind of idolatry. No one had to tell her that.

No, the voice said. *We need to tell you the very opposite.* The voice had a faint throatiness, a foreignness to it, like the accent of Marie Toussaint.

She couldn't defend herself. They were right. Bob Althorpe. Will. Even Mr. Rufus Johnson. Barbara Neville. Of course they were right. She had never questioned that. Never. She had, as they implied, or said outright, betrayed them all—the church, her sacred calling, her parish, even God. And this was the essential proof, deeper than any of them had any idea of, interpreting her silence as they would. She could not *feel* shame. She understood. She agreed with them. Who wouldn't. But she couldn't *feel* shame.

She could feel shame when she remembered the tribunal, especially what Will said. Feel it when she remembered her last meeting with Rufus

Johnson and the vestry. Feel it when she remembered her last sermon.

But it was not the same feeling she felt when she remembered walking into the museum and seeing David's large canvas for the first time. It wasn't the same feeling she felt when she told him there was nothing, nothing at all, he could do to make things right between them. She was telling him the truth—there was nothing he could do. Because, and this was what was so terrible, *nothing had happened for her.* She looked at his arms and wanted to be inside them. She watched the expressions moving so rapidly across his face—anguish, remorse, guilt, frustration, desperation, yearning—and felt that total fascination she had felt the first time they talked with one another.

He'd picked up on it, of course. She was sitting on the couch in his huge, drafty studio—cool even in August. The light through the high and dusty windows not quite falling to the ground to meet them, so, just as in the cathedral here, shadows were always gathering on the edge of the visual field. It was a kinesthetic sense of light and shadow—both dangerous and calming. There wasn't enough light to fill the vast space. It was just a fact, not a metaphor. The shadows seemed to gather in the tall abstract painting that covered half the three-story height of the wall. She lifted her head and studied the metal landings above her where, like everywhere else in this space, they had known each other. In the flesh. In the bones. In the soul.

"One last time," he said. "It's all I ask."

And she almost did it. For the solace. For the truth of it. What more, really, did she have to lose?

You feel wrong about that, the voice said. *Wrong about refusing.*

"Yes," Ginny said aloud, alone in her hotel room. "I do. I feel wrong about refusing." And the relief she felt at hearing the words out there was so deep it was as if her body had opened to David for the last time, as if he were inside her moving and not moving and she was doing the same and she knew once again exactly where she was in space and why, she knew exactly why she was here on this earth.

How could you trust a way of life, a church, a God who asked you to give that up? the voice asked.

And then Ginny did feel a shame so heavy, so intense it was as if her heart were sealed in stone, unable to beat, her lungs too, sealed, weighted, as empty of air as her heart was of blood. She turned over and pulled the pillow over her head trying simultaneously to recover and erase that moment of pleasure.

Feel the difference, the voice insisted. *Which way leads to life?*

In the morning, before going to the cathedral, Ginny wandered over to the large market, its stalls filled with straw hats decorated with ribbons and bright baubles, candy, candles of all colors, garish lacquered medallions on colored ropes with the Black Christ on one side and the Virgin of Guadalupe on the other. What she first took to be cookies turned out to be sacred earth—and she bought some for Byron. It looked like very stale shortbread, just as Simon had said. She bought herself, on a whim, one of the two-faced medallions. Also candles twisted like taffy, with little paper medallions of the Black Christ glued on them.

She took a walk through the town, its paving stone streets unusually clean and wide. Everywhere she looked, there were inexpensive hostels to house the faithful. Stores filled with religious statues and others filled with cheap shoes and tight jeans. She crossed a bridge over the town's river, which smelled like the canals of Venice and looked like the Rio Pensativo would at the beginning of the rainy season, plastic bags snagging on the banks, plastic bottles and metal cans bobbing to and fro in the infinitesimal flow of black-brown water.

Again the church was nearly deserted. In the back, a group of pilgrims wearing fanciful hats stared up at one of the large paintings, so stained with age and the smoke of candles and incense it was nearly indecipherable. There was a constant low murmur, good humored and a little irreverent, that seemed to surround the pilgrims, to bob like the decorations on their hats. Ginny felt slightly reproving. It was Passion Week after all.

She chose a space for herself over in the left corner of the church, tucked up close to the altar, a place that was as private as possible, but where, out of the corner of her eye, she could see people crossing the width of the church to enter the viewing lines for the Black Christ. Ginny spread out her fifty candles and three books of matches. She intended to light one of the candles and attach it to the floor after every five recitations of the general confession. Her own version of the rosary.

Before you begin, just remember, Ginny-gin-gin, what you used to say: Open our eyes to see your hand at work in the world about us. Deliver us from the presumption of coming to this table for solace only, and not for strength; for pardon only, and not for renewal.

Ignoring her, Ginny began to murmur: "All things quake with fear at your presence, they tremble because of your power—But your merciful promise is beyond all measure; it surpasses all that our minds can fathom. O Lord, you are full of compassion, long suffering and abounding in mercy. You hold back your hand, You do not punish as we deserve."

Losing your parish, your best friend, your lover, your living, your calling, and your God—not to mention your self-respect. What's left?

"In your great goodness, Lord, you have promised forgiveness to sinners, that they may repent and be saved."

You don't know shame, Ginny-gin-gin. Where will you begin?

Not a word, Ginny thought fiercely. Not a goddamned word more out of you. She made a slicing motion in the air to cut out the interruptions. She took a deep breath before she struck the first match and lit the first candle. She studied the candle in her hand and realized she would need to use it to melt and glue the second candle down on the floor, which she did. Then she thought about it a little more and melted the bases of all the candles and arranged them, unlit, in expanding semi-circles around her.

Shame, Ginny-Gin-Gin. You don't know—

She just wouldn't stop. "I need your help, God. I can't get a word in edgewise," Ginny whispered miserably.

They're not your words, that's why, the voice said with a kindness that took Ginny by surprise. *We have fifty candles here and some real accounting to do. We need your full attention. And your hope, Ginny. Not your remorse, your hope.*

For what, Ginny asked, closing her eyes, rising up on her knees, her back straight. What's left? Truly, what's left for a woman like me?

"How did you get *into* this mess?" Bob Althorpe exploded. He shook the arts section of the Sunday paper at her. David's painting was reproduced, in color, on the first page.

"Every one of your parishioners must have called me by now. What were you *thinking*, Ginny? You're a *priest* for heaven's sake. You have a reputation to uphold. Not just for yourself, but for all of us. Look at what you've done to the *church*. Not to mention me. I went out on a limb when I placed you there. I used up a lot of political capital on that placement—and this is how you pay me back, pay us all back?" He looked significantly over at Will, who sat with his eyes fixed on his folded hands, then back at Ginny. "*All* of us, Ginny."

"I didn't know," Ginny said. "I had no idea. I know it isn't an excuse, but it is the truth. I knew nothing about this painting."

"But you knew the painter. He is a member of your parish, isn't he? And he, obviously, knows you more intimately than most of us would care to."

"Whoa, now," Will stopped him. "The whole affair wouldn't have gotten the play it did if she didn't come off looking so good. People *like* the woman in the painting, she's beautiful, vibrant, powerful—they just don't like knowing she's a priest, in the painting or in real life. Nobody wants their priest to be an up front sex object. Especially if their priest is female. At its best, its like their mother is going around bare naked for all the world to see. At its worst, it's their daughter they're seeing up there. Not to mention the Christ analogy. "

"But what I don't get is why you didn't say it was just a work of imagination," Will said. Not only there at the large, gleaming table at the bishop's office, but also, far more harshly, when they were alone later.

Yes, the voice agreed. *Why didn't you say that, Ginny? You accepted the consequences. More consequences than were necessary. But you didn't renounce him or his imagination. Why?*

Whatever I wanted to save myself from had already happened the minute I saw the painting. *Their* responses made more sense than mine. There was my destruction walking toward me and I just felt *graced* by it. Make sense of *that* if you can. I can't. I know I need to repent. But not of knowing the truth about myself. Not of that. I *wanted* to know myself in that way. Beautiful. Beloved. Powerful. Able to carry the truth of Christ's suffering about my body and live. They're right. It was grandiose, over-reaching, shameful. David caught it all. He showed it all.

As something beautiful. But it cost you everything, Ginny. Maybe that's why you can't renounce it, even now.

That image of myself. I wanted it more than everything I had—just as I wanted David more than I wanted that parish. I failed God. Terribly. And for that I—

Let's go back to what you felt like when you saw that image of yourself, naked, beautiful, stigmata in your hands, a crown of flowering roses on your head, carrying Simon, wasted, dying, similarly marked, in your strong arms.

Blessed. I felt relieved too. As if something had been said that could never be unsaid.

And in everything you did afterwards, you were true to that. To what had been said and couldn't be unsaid.

Oh, my chest hurts. It burns. It burned then, in the art museum, under my black shirt, like there was a real fire inside me and all that time, facing Bob Althorpe, Will, everyone at St. Peter's, it was like a live coal smoldering there. I've never felt so much pain.

That was his true gift to you, wasn't it? He took out of your chest your heart of stone and gave you a heart of flesh.

He was just a man. Self-absorbed. A womanizer from what I'm told. Eager to have his go at the church. No matter who it hurt.

And he gave you this tremendous gift. He took out of your chest your heart of stone and gave you a heart of flesh.

That burns, God. It burns—-

To be known. It burns to be known.

"I never meant anyone to be hurt," Ginny said.

"Wish we could say the same for David," Barbara answered. "He shouldn't have done it. But you gave him the opportunity, Ginny. It was a breech of trust. And just plain dumb. Beneath you, damn it. *Look* at what you were beginning to accomplish here. And you threw it away. You just threw away."

"I didn't ask to be relieved of my duties. I'm willing to live this one down."

"Can't have people undressing you with their eyes as you're serving the communion. There's proprieties to be observed. Especially in a church," Mrs. Virgil Johnson said. The rhinestones on her long red fingernails glittered.

"Mens going to be mens," Mr. Walter Dodds agreed. "Undress anything. Can't control their appetites except by starving them. That's what them robes is for. Now though, they know what's underneath."

"I'm not responsible for their imaginings," Ginny said.

"For years now, you've been holier than thou. And you can't stop.

Acting even yet like you're the one being done to. Shifting the blame. That's your game, Mother Fox," Mr. Cecil Bartholomew said.

"You never had any respect for us," Mr. Rufus Johnson, the senior warden, continued. The last vestry meeting. His show. But they were all there. His sister-in-law, Mrs. Virgil Johnson. Mr. Cecil Bartholomew. Mr. Walter Dodds. David's friend, Barbara Neville, the only newer member voted to the vestry. She too nodded in agreement when Mr. Rufus Johnson went on.

"You can't see it, I guess, you're so armored with your righteousness. But what business did you have talking down to us the way you did? Like you had some private channel to God—not just the Bishop."

"That's my job," Ginny said. "To preach. To lead."

"Not to prophetize," Mrs. Virgil Johnson said. "Not to act like we're the sinful and you're not."

"This is not about the painting at all, is it?" Ginny asked.

"Last straw for us," Mr. Rufus Johnson said, leaning back in his chair, letting his chest swell with a big easy breath. He had caramel colored skin and a caramel colored voice. His suit was chocolate brown. "I been talking to the Bishop for years about you and he just wouldn't listen—but there it was, like a billboard sign. No one could fail to see."

"See what?" Ginny asked.

"That you been going around here thinking you and God was one and the same thing. In that painting, it's there for everyone to see. But me, I've been seeing it all along. Came in with your ideas all fixed—how you was going to change us—and never stopped once. We done fine without you. Just fine."

"I didn't have anything to do with the painting," Ginny said. "I didn't know it was being made. Or that it would be shown."

"You're saying there was no relationship between you and David Goodall?" Barbara Neville asked, her voice hard.

Ginny held her eyes, surprised at the harshness. Barbara and David were old friends. And then, holding Barbara's eyes, something became very quiet and very large inside her, as if she were walking in an empty church. Tock, tock, tock went her heels on the stone floor. Tock, tock, tock.

"I accept full responsibility for my actions," Ginny said. "I know you have asked for my resignation—and so has the Bishop—and I am in no way contesting this. You're right, Barbara, there should have been no breech of trust. David was a member of the parish. As soon as I became involved with him, I should have asked him to join another church."

"Or held your own self in check. Kept yourself for your wedding night. Had a prenuptial that he couldn't paint you in the raw," Mr. Walter Dodds said. His soft brown eyes slid away from Ginny's.

Ginny sat silently watching them all. Mr. Rufus Johnson straightened the papers in the opened manila folder in front of him, then closed it and opened his calendar. Mrs. Virgil Johnson, striking in her gold turban and tiger print dress, carefully observed her fingernails. When she looked up at Ginny, though, a look of real regret crossed her face.

"We've always been proud of this church," she said. "You brought shame on us, Mother Fox. When people think of St. Peter's now, they don't think of black people bettering themselves. They think of this naked white woman carrying a naked white man with AIDS. It's like you played this big joke on us. All these years here, you're talking about a preferential option for the poor, telling us to take in those drug dealing Hispanics whose got their own church. You even said they didn't have to worship—could just get our services for free. Not yours alone. Ours too. Without so much as a please. It's like you're just going to let us get a little way up there—and then make us pay for what we never done in the first place. The way you talk to us, just like Mr. Rufus Johnson said, it was contemptuous. Punishing. Like we was the rich white people responsible. You have your preferential option for the poor—" Her voice imitated Ginny's most cruelly. "But what about an option for those who struggle and try all their lives? It's like all the pity you got in you goes only to those who destroy their own luck. What about us, Mother Fox? Compared to everyone else in this high class church, don't you think we're as poor as you've got? Why didn't you give a tithe of your time to lifting *us* up?"

"I never meant—" Ginny took a deep breath, stared at the clock on the far wall that seemed to have stopped. "You never said—"

"No, ma'am, Mother Fox," Mr. Cecil Bartholomew said. "You never heard, no matter how many times. I warned you."

"You resented the church's expansion," Ginny said. "I thought it would make you self-sufficient."

"A church of bored rich white folks, homosexuals, Spanish speaking crack addicts and crazy people is going to make *us* self-sufficient?" Mr. Rufus Johnson asked.

"I wanted you to expand your 'us'," Ginny said firmly. "I wanted you to see your relative privilege, your relative wealth, within a larger system. I wanted you to *feel* how rich you are and to use that wealth wisely."

"Don't we know ourselves for what we are, relatively, when we go to diocesan meetings, the only church too poor to be able to call someone by theirselves, to have their wishes respected. Got to take the Bishop's favorite toady—or his hot potato? His *vicar*. Can't control what she says from the pulpit or what programs she starts." Mr. Rufus Johnson looked above Ginny's head as he let his voice roll out.

This was something thicker, deeper, sweeter and more suffocating than contempt.

"I never knew you hated me so much," she said.

"No," he said, looking at her then. He smiled—a large, genuine smile. "Just hate the relativity of my privilege. Don't like shifting from righteous and striving to Pharisee with the blink of a white woman's eye."

"So you've asked the Bishop to replace me with a black man?" Ginny asked.

"With one of us. Mr. Cecil Bartholomew's son, Solomon, just got his preaching degree by long distance, and we're asking the Bishop to ordain him. He's worked on that degree for ten years. More than once said he was giving it up. But he made it. He knows who we are. He knows what we want."

To climb, Ginny thought bitterly—and then a silence came over her that was so profound that she couldn't hear a single thought in her head. Just the swish of Mrs. Virgil Johnson's tiger print dress, the shuffle of pages in Mr. Rufus Johnson's calendar, the sound of Mr. Walter Dodds' foot tapping, Barbara Neville's muffled cough, Mr. Cecil Bartholomew's long, slow sigh.

"What is it?" she asked. "What is it you want?"

Mr. Rufus Johnson leaned forward on his arms and stared at her belligerently. But it was Mr. Cecil Bartholomew who spoke.

"To feel free," he said. "To feel as free inside the knowledge and love of God as white people do in this world. But you brought that white world right into our church, Mother Fox, and you took away our little breathing space."

"I didn't understand—"

But you do now, the voice said. *You do now. Token. Pawn. Prisoner. Oppressor. Or woman with a lot to learn. Choose your term.*

Ginny it a candle and began murmuring. Lit another one. Another one. Murmuring. Murmuring. "Lost sheep. . . offended against, done. . . undone. . .penitent. . .godly. . .righteous. . .sober. . .glory." Again. Again. And the voice didn't interrupt her once but was there, under everything, like the slur of her own blood returning and returning to her hot, troubled heart.

    Her calves hurt, but her feet no longer had any sensation in them. Her mind seemed in slow motion and she had no idea how much time passed from the lighting of one candle to the next. She let the images come and go now as she kept reciting the confession, her fingers folding as she uttered each amen, trying to keep count.

    Her attention was disrupted by the vivid memory, unbidden, of Bob Althorpe on the phone last week. "The priesthood isn't something you can renounce, Ginny. And we're not taking it from you. I made a solemn promise to Will about that. You could go back for a doctorate and teach. You have the mind and temperament for it. I'd give you a recommendation. I can't see you in parish ministry right now. I can't imagine a church that wouldn't feel just like St. Peter's did. Honestly."

    Don't you love how people do that, the voice murmured. *Honestly! Like they're just putting the nail in the coffin and letting someone else drive it home. Honestly!*

    But even the voice was tired now, her comments coming so slowly that they words often dissolved into static, like a disrupted radio signal, before they reached Ginny's ears.

    "You did it to get even with me, didn't you, Ginny?" Will asked her. Shaking her out of herself with his magnetic voice and his repellent narcissism. How could she have been so blind—and for so long.

    "How can you suggest something like that?"

    "I let you down, Ginny. It would be very human to want to get even."

    "With a dying man?" Ginny asked. "Who had nothing but contempt for everything we both stood for? Who *never* controlled himself, never confessed, never repented—if anything, flaunted—"

    "You're pissed. I rest my case," Will said. "Or I would, except I want more for you. I want more *from* you."

    "Why?" Ginny asked, her hands on her chest, unable to stop this fire that never stopped burning, that made her skin wildly alive to the least movement of air. As if she, just like the candles, were being consumed.

"*For in her there is a spirit that is intelligent, holy, unique, manifold, subtle, mobile, clear, unpolluted, distinct, invulnerable, loving the good, keen, irresistible, beneficent, humane, steadfast, sure, free from anxiety, all-powerful, overseeing all, and penetrating through all spirits that are most intelligent and subtle.*"

Ginny, rocking on numbed feet, tried to bring Will's face to mind, a face that could match those words, the kindness in his voice at this moment, but all she could see was him leaning over her out in the hall at the break in the disciplinary hearing. Hissing at her, so in her face there was nothing for her to focus on. "Why didn't you cover your ass, Ginny? For *all* our sakes?"

"I was your cover, wasn't I?" Ginny asked. "I believed so completely in the face you showed the world that when I was around, no one could doubt that it was your only one."

"I never tried to mislead you," Will said. "You saw what you wanted to see. And it wasn't me. You saw ideas about purity, calling, and justice, Ginny, justice. You were so above the one form of justice you really need, you couldn't even see it. It wasn't black people you needed to liberate, Ginny. It was your own damn self, your *own* nature."

"So I can have a God who's no larger than my own self-interest?"

"You think that's what my life was about, Ginny? Self-interest?"

"It takes a powerful measure of ambition to become a bishop, Will. Especially as a black man. And to lead a double life."

"That was what was going on with you and David? Were you leading a double life or starting your first *true* one, Ginny? This church of ours ain't going to help you be whole. Can't be holy if you're not whole. And what I'm saying is this church that's got to put the holy in a cage, a *white* man's cage, once that door is sprung, doesn't get to say what's in and what's out."

"Who does, Will?"

"People like you and me, Ginny. The ones who never counted. The ones who never got to add a single word to that white man's scripture."

"If that's so, Will, why did you believe so much in covering your ass? Why did you want that for me?"

"Because I wanted to spring that cage from the inside, honey. The only way it can be sprung. It was what I was raised to be, just like you, Ginny—a double agent. But you got to remember in that condition whose side you're fighting for. You look around you and see who's suffocating, going numb because they don't know there are any other options—but there you are, in your flesh and blood, another option. And that's the key you show them. Your own damn flesh and blood self, so dark like me, so female like you—free to move in and out of that white man's cage we call the church. But you can never stop calling it a cage to yourself, Ginny-gin-gin. And you never call what's in the cage freedom. And you don't ever forget what it feels like to be written out of existence. To be on the far side of that cage of privilege. You never forget that. It was easier for me as a man, even a black man. To remember which side was mine. To pass through.

"Here's the question, Ginny, the one you have to stop this prattling about repentance and answer: Is there any *woman* in that whole blessed book who makes you feel you'd like to change places with her, that you too can talk directly with God, that you can name with the same power those men did, what comes in and what stays out. A *woman*, Ginny. Is there any place in there, where, to feel free, beloved by God, you don't have to put your sex aside? Don't say it doesn't matter. That's the damage Marcella was talking about. 'You treated her like she wasn't blessed with ovaries,' she tells me. But it didn't begin with me, Ginny-gin-gin. I want you to see what it was inside you that made you so willing to be a man's idea of a woman rather than the real thing. I want you to mourn what made you forget whose side you were truly on."

Ven a mí, dulce pan de la vida
Ven consuelo mi amarga dolor.
Soy la oveja que andaba perdida
lejos, lejos de tí mi señor.

The two women's voices were beautifully clear, haunting. The second time they sang the refrain, Ginny translated it. Come to me, sweet bread of life. Come console my bitter sorrow. I am the ewe that wanders lost, far, far from you, my Lord.

The third time, the tune was so captivating it seemed to come out of her too of its own accord.

As she listened to the women completing their hymn and beginning to recite the rosary, all the voices in Ginny's head stopped. There were only their voices, their words, in a language she was too tired to translate. But it lifted her, this beautiful stream of sound—and then set her down abruptly as she realized that she recognized their voices.

What were Señora Wilma and Maria Concepción doing here? What would they think of the large puddle of multi-colored wax that surrounded Ginny on all sides, so the flames of the candles all flickered out of a single repository of paraffin.

That you are a woman of good faith and powerful yearning. Just like them. They'll see themselves in you. And you, if you let yourself, will see yourself in them.

But Ginny couldn't make herself get up and face them.

"O martyred son whose skin is as dark as the sins of our country, hear us," Señora Wilma said. "Quiet the screams of memory. Quiet the silences that followed. I can't bear to hear anymore, my Savior. I can't bear to hear anymore. Let the dead stay buried."

Ginny just knelt there, her hands on her knees, her head bowed, the candles guttering, waiting the women out. Her face flushed with the heat in her chest, this scalding pain that she called a perfect emptiness.

She heard them rise and leave by the door that would lead them up behind the Black Christ. She imagined them looking through the glass cabinet, just as she had, and seeing her, down on her knees amidst her spreading puddle of wax and she couldn't bear it, she simply couldn't bear it. She forced herself to her feet, rocking wildly as she tried to develop enough feeling in her legs and feet to regain a sense of balance so she could retreat unnoticed.

A woman, the voice murmured, *who knows shame*.

And what could you possibly have to say to explain this. Just look at you. Just look at the two of you. Just look at the two of you.

Ginny woke, breathless with terror, her heartbeat filling the dark room as it did her own eardrums. She knew this voice. She knew it inside and out. It wasn't God's. She knew that much.

Her chest wouldn't stop burning, there, where her father had put his weeping head and his breath was heating her nipples, her breasts. She had eyes only for her mother who stood, backlit, in the doorway. Light flared around her. Her face dark, unreadable.

All day she had yelled at Ginny's father. "Who, except you, Harold, can lose a job in the government? How low can you go, Harold?"

"It had nothing to do with performance," Ginny's father said. "It was a bureaucratic technicality. We had too high a supervisor to staff ratio."

"This will keep us from sending her to college," Ginny's mother screamed. "That's not a technicality."

"What do you want me to do?" Ginny's father asked whenever Ginny's mother would pause for breath.

Ginny sat on her bed, her bedroom door closed, praying, although she didn't know the word for it, would have called it wishing, hoping, needing, yearning for the sound to stop, just to stop. She no longer cared if her parents made up. All she wanted was to be able to finish her homework. To be able to make the print on the page resound in her own head.

When her father came in to her bedroom, her mother furiously clattering pots and pans in the kitchen, he asked her what he'd been asking her mother all afternoon: "*What do you want me to do?*"

She just sat there, her feet on the floor, her hands at her sides, as if she were sitting in the principal's office preparing to be suspended. He came over and knelt down in front of her and looked up at her. His face looked so sad, so wistful. He put his arms out and straightened her shoulders so she had no choice but to look him directly in the face. He wasn't a young man. His hair was gray. From where she sat, above him, she could see the bald spot, so perfectly round, that he tried to conceal every morning.

"What do you want me to do?" he asked Ginny again.

"Stop her," she said. "Just stop her."

"I can't," he said. And he pulled Ginny close and he laid his head on her breasts like a baby would and began to cry, and she held his head while he did so and his tears made spots on her t-shirt and his sad sad breath made her breasts hurt, it made them hot. And Ginny couldn't stop his crying and she couldn't stop the sensations in her chest or in her heart anymore than she could stop the look of horror on her mother's face, the voice, so venomous, so without mercy, that said, "Just *look* at the two of you. What in the world do you have to say for yourself."

Yes, the voice said, there in the dark, in the hotel room where Ginny couldn't move, couldn't take her eyes from the light flaring in a fiery halo around her mother's dark form. There where Ginny's chest burned and burned and burned, inside and out, skin and heart. *Let's go back there, Ginny-gin-gin. Let's do what she's asking. Let's look.*

So Ginny stood in her mother's shoes, in her mother's body, and stared at the girl in a woman's body cradling her father's head the way a woman, a real woman, might cradle a baby.

It all begins here, the voice says. *Mercy. Forgiveness. Look at her, that girl whose soul has left her body and set up residence in her head. For more than twenty years. To escape the burning in her chest. To escape the judgment in these eyes. Tell her, Ginny. Tell her what you see.*

"It never should have happened," Ginny spoke into the dark. "It wasn't such a big thing, but it should never have happened."

It wasn't such a big thing, Ginny-gin-gin, to leave your body for twenty years, to deny your essential nature? How can you know love and forgiveness without a body, Ginny? How can you take them in? How can you know me without a body, Ginny?

"I didn't have anything to do with it. I didn't make it happen."

Then why, if that's true, have you taken all the consequences on yourself all these years—and found a God, a church, a way of life—that justified that sacrifice?

And then Ginny was sitting in church, her very first time, on the Mainline. A Wednesday noon. There were only three people in there. She still couldn't remember why she had walked in. She heard her shoes on the stone floor. A black man in a white robe was busy at the altar. Two old women and a derelict she could smell from ten feet away were all kneeling. She took her place in the back row and opened the prayer book but left it unread in her lap. She heard that huge warm voice rolling out into the echoing silence of the church. Saw the colors from the stained glass staining her own hands. She looked up and saw Will, for it was Will, put his hand on the bread and then on the cup and it felt as if he had put his hand blamelessly on her. She heard the Our Father rising out of the air, sourceless. And then, when Will raised the host and she heard it crack, it sounded as if someone had broken a board before her with one blow of his hand. She heard the sound ringing and ringing inside her head, as if her head was a bell, a holy temple, and she knew that was where she belonged. She knew even though at that moment her eyes ran with her father's tears and she did not dare leave her seat to eat that bread or drink that wine.

But now, the voice asks her gently, *now, tonight, where does your freedom lie?*

But Ginny couldn't answer. She was cradling her burning chest, trying to put out the fire there with her own cold tears.

She didn't stop for breakfast, just checked out of her hotel and walked briskly to the bus station and bought a ticket for the next available bus. She sat in a small restaurant drinking coffee and watching the people around her intently. But she did not see Wilma and Concepción until they set their hands on her shoulders and she cried out in surprise at the touch.

"So, we all return together to celebrate the terrible passion of our Señor, no?"

Calmly, Wilma reached for Ginny's glass of water and held it to Ginny's lips to quiet the spasm of coughing that has overtaken her. Concepción pulled out a chair.

"We must ask a great favor of you," Concepción said.

While she listened, Ginny swallowed back her initial protest as she had tried to do with her cough. But she still felt as if something had snagged in her throat.

"You know I am no longer a priest in good standing," she said to them.

"But you are here, you know her rituals, you speak her language. It will bring her peace. How could God object?" Wilma's said as if the matter bore no further discussion. "We will go to your service instead of to our own to make it appear more respectable."

Ginny, a little amused at how quickly she had conformed herself to Wilma's will, did not feel she could ask her why Wilma has come here with Concepción. Neither Wilma nor Concepción volunteered anything. They talked more about the *alfombra*, the carpet of flowers, that they were all to build that night, the excitement of the girls, of Simon and Byron, of the women from the collective. It was as if they have encountered each other in a cafe in Antigua, not six hours away, in a town whose only purpose was the church whose steeples reached so whitely into the cloudless blue sky.

On the bus, Ginny took her assigned seat. The two women sat a few rows behind her. Ginny opened her prayer book and skimmed the section on Maundy Thursday, trying to imagine how to adapt it. But she fell asleep as soon as the bus turned the curve that shielded the town and the pristine steeples of the cathedral from view. A sleep without dreams. Perfectly empty. Five hours later, just before they arrived in the capital, Wilma woke her and waited patiently as she pulled on her knapsack and sleepily descended from the bus. Wilma and Concepción walked one to either side of her over to the bus that would take them all to Antigua, but they let Ginny sit by herself on a seat holding only a mother and two small children, while they shared a seat with a woman with a large basket of rose petals.

By the time they left the bus in Antigua, Wilma had purchased the basket of rose petals, and two more sacks of petals the woman has had stored on the roof.

"He must have the sweetest rug under his feet to ease the anguish we can't prevent, no?" she said to Ginny.

Ginny wasn't sure whether she was being escorted or patrolled. Concepción, even here in the busy bus lot, did not leave her side. Wilma paid two boys to carry the rose petals. She slipped her arm through Ginny's, nodding at Concepción to do the same, and they made their way over the dirt road, dust rising around them in little whirlwinds.

"It is not only our feet that we will want washed," Wilma murmured. "Like Saint Peter, we will want the savior to bathe us from head to toe."

"You will do us the favor of saying you met us in the capital," Wilma announced to Ginny as they crossed the central plaza of the city. "We did not want to preoccupy Señora Rosemary, so we said we were going to the capital. We said there was an unexpected death in our family." Wilma looked straight ahead. Her face mirrored the strange mix of lights at this hour—the reflected red of the clouds and the bluish cast of the electric lights that illuminated the little *taquería* stands that surrounded the plaza—like a moody, fauvist painting.

Concepción, having to trot to keep up with Ginny and Wilma, patted Ginny's arm. She wobbled a little on the cobblestones and gripped hard. "It is not a lie. There have been unexpected deaths in our family."

"But not this week," Ginny said.

"The dead too need our attendance," Wilma said. "Sometimes they need to ask the living to intervene."

"And that was what you were doing?" Ginny asked. "Intervening for the dead?"

"No," Concepción said. "Just like you, it was our own peace of mind we were after. There is so much suffering in the air right now. Sometimes it is too much to breathe—there isn't any air that isn't touched by it. The terrible passion of God's son brings it all out. Every year he dies again and we die with him, whether we wish to or not. My cousin's mind and body are not her own. They are at the service of all humanity, living and dead. It is a great burden—not so different, I think, than the Savior's. That is why I insisted that we go to see the Black Christ. I wanted her to see that she and God's son shared the same *don*, the same gift."

"Channeling?" Ginny asked. These women looked so small, but they gripped her like stevedores.

"An open heart," Concepción said, drawing herself up with a little snort of irritation. "Why must you, like all the priests, be so suspicious? Doesn't Jésus himself say when we accept each other, we accept him, and when we accept him we accept the one who sent him? What is that, I ask you, but a heart open to the souls of others? How is that any different from the gift of my cousin?"

"Because I don't," Wilma said. "Sometimes I don't accept them. Sometimes I want to send them to the hottest and darkest and most agonizing of hells, but I cannot because I am not the son of God. Sometimes I seal my lips so they won't escape me, and I become myself the hottest and darkest and most agonizing of hells and I become the one who is suffering."

Wilma paused, nodded to a neighbor on the far side of the street. Unperturbed, completely unperturbed by what she had just said. She pulled out her large ring of keys. She gestured to the boys carrying the large sacks of rose petals on their bent backs.

"Is there anything I can do to help?" Ginny asked Wilma.

"You can ease the heart of Señora Ginger with the ritual of the feet and your *extranjera misa*. And make the rug for our Savior. May I suggest you go and talk with Señora Ginger immediately but ask Señora Rosemary to accompany you. She does not like to be, as you say in your language, out of the loop."

"Even when the loop is a crown of thorns," Concepción added with a laugh.

Wilma pushed the large wooden doors into Rosemary's house open and entered the courtyard. Concepción pulled Ginny inside.

"At last," Rosemary cried as she came out to meet them. "I was beginning to worry. The girls and I have been cooking, so has Gwen, but it is a little slapdash." Rosemary brushed her disheveled hair up off her flushed face. When she saw Ginny standing behind the boys with their sacks of rose petals, she became quite still.

"I thought you were on a pilgrimage. Weren't coming in until later. Byron and Simon are expecting you. We've been ferrying materials for the *alfombra* up to Simon's apartment all afternoon since you all are on the processional route and we're not. They've brought some other friends of theirs in on the project. And Lourdes is cutting a large stencil from a design she created."

"Señora Ginger wanted her ceremony," Wilma said. "So we brought Señora Ginny for she has the most experience, yes?"

"Don't you think enough is enough?" Rosemary asked, her face flushing an even deeper red. "I don't want to do anything to contradict Ginger—but this was a welcome omission, at least from my point of view. I thought we'd just have a nice dinner and leave it at that."

"She doesn't need to know I'm in town yet," Ginny said. "I was only doing it as a favor." She stopped. She was obviously doing Rosemary no favor. The sound of water falling into the fountain filled the silence that had settled all around them.

I wanted this to be a happy night, that's all," Rosemary said. "I didn't want it to get weighted down with all this last supper stuff."

"*Por favor*, Señora Rosemary, what happiness is worth anything if it does not know that it was born of sorrow?" Wilma gestured to the boys to set down the sacks of rose petals in the corner of the courtyard and paid them. She picked up her red plastic bag and carried it out to the kitchen, calling out to the girls as she went.

Rosemary pursed her lips, then nodded her head. "Wilma is right—we can't take Jesus out of Holy Week. I'd rather celebrate the last supper than the crucifixion. So there you have it. Pedicure night it will be."

She led the way to Ginger's cabaña. In the last four days, Ginger seemed to have lost considerable weight and her skin was more yellow, her breath more labored. She was dressed in an elegant pale blue caftan—obviously Rosemary's doing. Someone had wrapped a scarf with blue and purple metallic threads around her head in the style of the indigenous women. It made her look even frailer.

Ginger opened her eyes when Ginny was seated beside her, holding Ginger's limp hand in both of hers.

"They found you after all. It makes me feel like Mohammed's mountain, you bringing the service to me. But it felt so right somehow, so intimate."

They decided to hold the service at eight in the central courtyard around the fountain. Dinner was to follow immediately out on the patio. Everyone was to be invited to be part of the ceremony—regardless of religious persuasion, or lack of it.

"I've thought about the communion, and I know Ginger is very fond of those white cardboard thingummies, but I think tortillas and *té de jamaica* will be better. It's hard to feel sanctimonious chewing on a tortilla. The more secular among us can think of it as an hors d'oeuvre." Rosemary laughed and Ginger joined her, gracefully conceding.

Since there was less than an hour to prepare, Ginny put in a call to Simon asking him to bring her a change of clothes. "I'll bring your coat of many colors," he said. "Even Rosemary said you looked very high priestess in it." He paused. "Marie will be coming a little before us—and she'll pick up Lourdes and Ben on her way down. Some other friends have come into town to help out and Rosemary invited them over too. We'll be a little later—so don't worry about starting without us. We're all set up at this end for the rest of the night. We may need to use one of our bedrooms as a sickbed for Ginger, but since none of the rest of us are sleeping tonight, it really doesn't matter."

"I could crash at Marie or Lourdes tomorrow if your friends want to stay over."

But Simon, obviously preoccupied, just murmured something about letting it all take care of itself and did she want the long red dress or the long black one.

"You choose," she said. "I trust you—in these matters. Certainly more than I trust myself."

"Hope you came back refreshed—purged—whatever. This is really a night to remember, Gin. I want you to open to it."

This time it was Ginny's turn to murmur something abstracted and noncommittal. As soon as she hung up, she went off and borrowed a towel from Wilma and tried to make herself presentable.

She extricated Mikela from the kitchen to help her arrange the chairs around the fountain. Mikela was very clear that Ginny's version was bound to be inferior to the masses held in the churches. For one thing, they didn't have one of those beautiful gold *sagrarios* for the host. And the little girl was as stuck as Ginger on what Rosemary called those white cardboard thingummies.

"Tortillas," Mikela exclaimed. "That is what we give to San Simón—not what God gives us. God gives us perfection. And perfection is tasteless and without color. It is made in machines, not by women's hands. Even my mother, Señora Genie, could make tortillas. Even the Virgin. Even me. They cannot be holy food."

"If they're blessed," Ginny said.

But Mikela just tightened her lips and looked stern. Ginny went off in search of candles and a white cloth, a large glass goblet and napkins to cover the *té de jamaica* and the tortillas. She instructed Mikela to fill bowls with water from the fountain and set them around its base, with a space between them to set candles.

When she returned, she and Mikela concentrated on making a comfortable settee out of a chair, a side table and several pillows and blankets for Ginger—and arranged chairs for everyone else. She sent Mikela in to get a headcount from Rosemary. Then, Ginny sat down on the edge of the fountain to review the service once again, her concentration effectively blocking out the strange mélange of emotions—eagerness, familiarity, shame, bemusement.

I can't wait, the voice purred, *to hear what saith the priest manqué.*

"It is hard to reconcile these two readings of the bloodbath that was the original Passover and this most humble and human feast, the last supper," Ginny said to the women assembled before her. Women and Ben Silver, Lourdes' husband, who seemed perfectly at home being the token male. "In one, God is merciless to all but his chosen, who must feast on their own blood sacrifices with their loins girt and their sandals on, ready for flight. He strikes down every first born, man and beast, whose doorway is unmarked by sacrificial blood just to show his dominance over the gods of Egypt. The salvation of his followers is defined by the ruthless harm done to all others.

"And then we have this image of Jesus, knowing he is already betrayed by Judas, still choosing to strip himself of his outer garments and kneel before his disciples, one by one, a towel tied around his waist, a basin of water in his hands. When Jesus has done this, he dresses himself and returns to the table and says to them, 'Do you realize what I have done for you, the one you call teacher, master?' As he has done for each of them, he says, they should do for each other.

"Why? Is Jesus suggesting abasement is necessary for all of us if we are to feel at one with God? I find that message as troubling as I do God's choices of who to sacrifice and who to pass over in Egypt. Like Peter, I want to bring my head into it. I don't want my whole interaction with God—or my fellow man—to be centered on the part of me that is most serviceable, dirty, worn. Remember, we're not talking here about feet that are sheltered in leather, nails that are clipped.

"I am much more comfortable with the last supper itself, this symbolic transmutation, where a bleeding body promises to become bread and wine, where physical sacrifice becomes a metaphor for spiritual nurture. But that isn't what is being asked of us tonight. We're not being asked to move up to the metaphorical, rather down into the body, the humanity, of Jesus and of each other. Here in Antigua in these days of Passion Week, there is a focus, very different from what we have in the States, especially among Protestants, on the physical reality of suffering. We suffer with and for Jesus' physical torment. I want us, as we perform this ceremony—as we let the person to our left kneel before us and wash our feet—and do this in turn to the person to our right—to feel what it is like to stay with the physical reality of the action, to stay with the sense of tenderness, or embarrassment, it provokes. Only then can we begin to wonder what it truly means to worship a god who would kneel before us, accept us in the flesh just as he accepted himself."

As Ginny knelt before Ginger to begin the ritual, she heard the doorbell ring and someone leave to open the door. She heard Simon's laugh, Byron's melodious greeting. But she concentrated on dipping the red washcloth in the cool water and wrapping it around Ginger's long, bony feet, the skin so thin she was afraid at the least pressure it would dissolve. She heard Rosemary ushering everyone in, the scraping of chairs. She heard Gwen hand out the closing prayer that she had run out and had copied.

Mikela and Concepción carried several bowls of water and cloths to the next row. They had seemed a little surprised that Ginny would not be washing all of their feet as the priests did in their own masses.

"Peace," she said to Ginger as she poured the water over her pale wasting feet, "Peace is my last gift to you, my own peace I now leave with you; peace which the world cannot give you, I give you." She patted her feet gently dry. "I give you a new commandment: Love one another as I have loved you."

"Peace," she heard Rosemary say to Wilma as she poured water over her feet.

"Peace," she heard Mikela say, now sitting in the empty chair to Ginger's right, as she poured water over Natividad's feet. "Peace," she heard Marie say as she poured water over Lourdes' feet. "Peace," she heard Lourdes say to Ben. "Peace," she heard Gwen say, washing Simon's feet. "Peace," Byron said, seated on the ground behind the last row of chairs washing the feet of one of the friends they brought with them.

"The end of the line," Ginger murmured as Ginny took the seat to her left. "Who is going to wash your feet my dear?"

Ginny patted her hand and leaned back and closed her eyes.

"Peace," Wilma said.

"My own peace," Concepción said.

"Peace which the world cannot give you," Simon said.

"This is my new commandment," Mikela said in English, surprising them all.

"I don't like you being forgotten," Ginger murmured before turning her attention to Mikela. In some way that surprised her, Ginny didn't like being forgotten either. The feeling alternated with a sense of relief. She let all the voices echo indecipherably inside her. "The peace the world cannot give you," she heard Ginger say to Mikela, who huffed and stood up. Ginny smiled. It was worth the try.

Then she felt the shadow looming over her, smelled the truth before she heard it. How could it be otherwise?

"My turn," David said, putting his hand on the back of her chair to steady himself as he knelt. Mikela stood beside him, holding out a blue bowl, a red cloth. Everyone was perfectly still, the circle complete, watching.

Ginny closed her eyes as David lifted her foot in his hand and slipped off her shoe, pulled down her sock. He did the same with her left foot. Ginny heard Mikela breathing lightly, resolutely. She heard the water plashing in the fountain. She heard the breath that whistled in and out of Ginger's failing lungs. She felt the water pouring over her feet, felt the washcloth rubbing the skin to life.

"Peace is my last gift to you," David said. She felt the dry towel David closed over her feet. Felt the care with which he pulled on first one sock, then the other. One shoe, then the other.

"By this shall the world know that you are my disciples—" David said, standing, his hand on Ginny's shoulder.

Rosemary came up to Ginny and put her hand over David's as she leaned down and whispered loudly, "Do you think we might just skip over the communion and get on with dinner?"

"Ginger?" Ginny asked.

But Ginger was sleeping and, really, Ginny had no right to administer the sacraments anymore.

So she stood up and repeated, "By this shall the world know that you are my disciples: that you have love for each other." Her face flushed with the reality of her loss, the reality of David's body so close to her, so unbearably, so irresistibly close.

Love in your skin and bone and groin, the voice said. *Amen.*

"Go in peace," Ginny said, although she had no special right anymore, did she, to bless.

Ginny turned then to look at David, not a single word in her head. He looked down into her face, smiling. He set one finger in the middle of her forehead, where her brow wrinkled with the effort to take him in.

"I should have been prepared," she said. "Why didn't you—why didn't someone let me know."

"I couldn't have told you two days ago I was coming. It was pure impulse. It hasn't let up."

At dinner, Ginny seated herself at the far end of the table from David, who sat between Lourdes and Ben. Simon pulled up a chair beside Ginny.

"You should have let me know."

"I didn't know until he showed up on my doorstep last night."

"On the phone," she said. "An hour ago."

"*Rico! Rico!*" Simon exclaimed, taking a large portion of stewed chicken, dishing out an equivalent portion for Ginny before handing the platter on to Byron. "You would have had to meet up sometime, someplace. Anticipation wouldn't have helped."

"I like this big handsome brother of Simon's," Marie said to Ginny. "He has been working with Lourdes all the day to design the *alfombra*. He is, he tells me, a friend of yours as well." She brushed her fingers through her short hair, letting it fall softly back against her skull. Sighed. "It is clear the two of you has a history. I do not pry."

"Well, I do," Rosemary cried out loudly as she passed a bowl of beet and orange salad in their direction from her position at the center of the table. "I want to know how all of you met—the world you left behind."

"Just so you can see what other skills we have that you can put to the service of your causes, Rosemary," Simon chided her. "He's only going to be here another day or two."

But Rosemary had already turned, her hair tumbling happily from its askew bun, her face still flushed with the pleasure of her feast, to interrogate Lourdes and David about the *alfombra*.

"We're doing the station of the cross—is it seven or eight?—where Jesus comforts the pious women," Lourdes said. She looked very happy and at ease, seated between Ben and David. "The stencil is enormous, so everyone can participate. Even those who already served as our models."

"Like Natividad," Gwen said, putting her arm around the girl and giving her a hug.

Mikela, busy removing plates from the table to prepare for desert, paused, her face expressionless, watching her sister smile and lean back against Gwen's arm.

"Quickly now," Wilma chided her.

Ginny rose to help, but both Wilma and Mikela shook their heads.

"*Es mi tarea*," Mikela said proudly. Her job.

"But you may help me serve the flan," Wilma said, rising herself.

In the kitchen, Wilma opened the large refrigerator and pulled out two flan and began slicing them into thin, shivering slices, which Ginny placed on separate plates.

"It is a great blessing for you, the arrival of this brother of Señor Simon," Wilma said.

"I don't think he knew I was here."

"He came, he has already told me himself, because he was called."

"But not by me," Ginny said, handing off two plates to Mikela, who returned to the patio and the exhilarated hubbub.

"Sometimes God acts on the prayers we most need but do not dare ask. It is good he has come now, at the time of our Lord's suffering." Wilma paused, knife upraised, then turned and put it in the sink.

Ginny was struck by the assurance of her tone. "How do you know all this?"

"You have a friend, his name is Will. He is *moreno* like us. He is keeping watching over you. He speaks with me now and then."

"Is that why you went to the cathedral?"

"No, it was as Concepción said. The self-interest. I, too, have a life, Señora Ginny. I too have dead who will not rest—but who cannot speak to me directly."

"Will talks to me," Ginny said. "I don't see why he needs to go involving third parties."

"You sound like Señora Rosemary," Wilma said with an impatient shake of her head. "Jealous."

"Of *what?*"

"The way they trust me. You confuse this with love, but it isn't. It is a freedom of attention that sometimes love can't give."

"What does Will want you to tell me that he can't tell me directly?"

"He is a gift from God, Señora. The painter is a gift from God to you. That is what *el moreno* wants to tell you—and that you must, out of a love for God, open to this possibility. That God, like a mother, wants you to know love and forgiveness."

This is crazy, Ginny thought, arranging the last slice of flan on a brightly painted clay plate. I don't know this woman at all and she is talking to me as if she can wander freely in and out of my mind whenever she wants, as if I have no secrets, no private anguish. She listened to a roar of laughter from the table outside. How did this come to be, she wondered. We have, without noticing it, made a community.

"There is a traitor here," Mikela murmured angrily as she took up the last pair of plates. "It is just like the last supper, there is a traitor here who will not say."

"So," Wilma said to her with a shrug, "you are like Jésus—prepared. For traitors, and for the weak who will deny you."

Both Wilma and Ginny watched Mikela march out onto the patio again, her motions stiff with anger. "She is so sure that Señorita Gwen is a gift of the devil. I wish someone could tell her differently."

Ginny studied Mikela as she set Marie's plate of flan in front of her and paused just slightly as Marie put her arm around her to whisper something in her ear. They looked, with their short haircuts, their sharp profiles, their pale and brown skins, like reverse images of each other.

"I need your help," Wilma said. "I have a feeling that if we do not all start listening to where God and our dead are leading us, something terrible will come to pass."

"What can I do to help?" Ginny found herself asking, as if she and Wilma lived in the same universe of meaning, where Jesus still walked on carpets of rose petals, still felt the blood run salt and sweet down his face, where the dead never let us go, where our hearts and minds were common ground, a shared mystery.

"Listen with me," Wilma said. "Listen to the love that's out there. Unless we know ourselves through that love, present and past, the worst will come to be. That is what the dead have to teach us, Señora Ginny, that love and the loss of it, the rejection of it, the betrayal of it are all, now and forever, real *through* us. If we can go into the heart of our suffering, the deepest mystery we will find there is the reality of love. It is as real as a carpet of rose petals and sawdust, as an angry little girl with a baby on her back, as a man who knows your own heart holds his soul, as Señora Marie's dead daughter or my dead son and husband. It is as real as the sacrament you no longer dare share. It is as real as the voice that never, ever, leaves us in peace."

"Teach me," Ginny said to her, the sound of the forks scraping pottery, of glasses being clinked, of sharp meaningless bursts of laughter louder to her than her own words. "Teach me how to hear in this way."

"It begins down here," Wilma said, placing her hands over her belly. "Where we know desire, know ourselves in desire. That is why that tall, handsome, guilty man out there is your gift from God. He is the only one in whom you have been able to know yourself in love, through love. Your whole body is the soul's ear. God would have you hear, Señora Ginny, for all our sakes. You cannot hear for the rest of us until you can hear for yourself."

"I hear you brought more rose petals from the capital," Simon said from the doorway. He paused, picking up some strangeness in the atmosphere, their postures. "I hope I'm not interrupting anything. We thought we'd take the bags back with us. David and Lourdes want to get started. You're free to ride with us if you want, Ginny."

"I'll clean up here first."

"I don't want you to miss out on this, Ginny. Can't you kiss the past good-bye and get on with the good stuff?" The look that he gave her was so gentle and knowing, Ginny felt her lips tremble.

"I'll never be the same," she said.

"That's right. And I pray, I really do *pray*, Ginny, that in time you will come to find that it is the best thing that ever happened to you. Like my afterlife in Antigua."

It's all a question, you see, of receiving, the voice said.

From who? Ginny asked her.

Would you believe it if I told you? Would you believe it coming from me? And there is no other voice, there never has been. It's mine, Ginny-gin-gin. It's all mine.

"They are traitors," Mikela announced to Ginny as they squatted along the edge of the street sifting colored sawdust through a wooden stencil to make an ornate border for the *alfombra*.

"Who?" Ginny asked. She wondered how Mikela could keep bending over the way she did with Miguel on her back. But she'd offered twice to carry the baby and each time had been angrily refused. Mikela hadn't even bothered to answer when Gwen asked, and she turned her back forcefully on Natividad, saying something in their private language that sounded soft but seemed to affect Natividad like a slap in the face, making her turn her head quickly with a grimace of pain.

"They are pretending to make Jésus a woman. You see how they have made the hair longer. They have made it fall in curls like the hair of Señora Lourdes and Señorita Gwen. They have used us too, my sister and I and the baby, to be the ones who help her. But we would not be so stupid as to help a woman carrying a cross."

"Why not?"

"Because the story will not come out as it is meant to be. God the father and God the son can become one—up in heaven—but God the father and a daughter, that is not possible."

"If God could be a mother, could the daughter carry the cross?"

"God cannot be a woman for women are of the earth. Only men are of the heaven, and God is of the heaven, like a man. Besides, women do not love their daughters for suffering. They hate them for that most. For it proves we are all daughters of Eve—we do not care about the difference between good and evil."

"I thought that was exactly what we did care about," Ginny said. "That was what got us into so much trouble in the first place. We wanted to know the difference between them."

"No," Mikela said. "We were hungry. We were hungry for the forbidden because we thought it would taste sweet."

Mikela brushed the green sawdust from her hands and cupped a handful of orange sawdust and began to fill in the flower petals on the stencil.

Ginny stood up to look at the larger image, but it was still unfinished, except for the image of the three girls over in the corner near her. Lourdes had included Gwen with Mikela and Natividad and the baby—something sure to drive Mikela to fury. But in the image, a hand on each of the girls, she seemed a caretaker.

David, who was helping Lourdes remove the stencil from the top left of the rectangle, paused for second, hoping to hold Ginny's gaze. "This was completely Lourdes' inspiration," he said. "I suggested we go by the book, but she insisted."

Lourdes turned and smiled at Ginny. She looked radiant. Her time with Ben seemed to have taken years off, released a tension in her face that had seemed intrinsic, a function of character rather than stress.

"I'm respecting the conventions," she said. "Just introducing an exciting level of ambiguity."

"About time, I'd say," Simon added. "But this is worse than surgery, all these little lines you've cut and expect us to fill."

"I wanted it to have mass," Lourdes said. "I suppose I got carried away."

"Let's get some perspective here," David said. He made his way carefully along the little walkway they'd left between the stencils. He joined Ginny where she stood at the carpet, then drew her down behind Rosemary and Wilma in order to see the full length of the image. His arm went around her without hesitation, and she found her body fitting easily against his. Just as it had been.

Suddenly gunshots rang out. David gripped Ginny more tightly.

Ben Silver, laughing, fell back on his heels. They could hear horses clattering across the cobblestones.

"The judgment is coming," Mikela said.

A group of men dressed as Roman centurions clattered into view. They were caped and wore armored breastplates, sported red broom heads as plumes on their helmets, and leather sandals that laced to their knees. They carefully kept to the side of the road so as not to disturb the people making carpets in the middle of the street. His mount dancing backward, one of the soldiers unrolled a scroll and began to read aloud.

"Even if you don't believe a word of it," David murmured into Ginny's ear, "there's no doubt something magical is going on here."

That magic, the voice said, *is in you, Ginny. Where it belongs. Always.*

"I have not had a day of peace since I last saw you, Ginny," David said. "I'm not asking, I'm pleading for another chance."

"But I," Ginny answered softly, "have run out of second chances."

The centurion rolled up the scroll and tucked it into his breastplate, then drew his horse around in a large capering circle and thundered off.

"Fine," David said. "That means this time we'll have to get it right."

THE CHILD WITH BLUE EYES
(*Mikela*)

    When my sister draws, she calls the world, and with it her soul. She draws the moment just before her soul left her. She invites it back. You might not know it as a story. But I do. The one I tell you now, unlike the story of our mother, has not ended yet. Natividad has a drawing of a camera on a table set beside a window. You see, first, the signs outside the window, how carefully she has drawn the folds in the curtains, the bars outside the window, how the light from the neon signs fall on the table, like puddles and long fingers. Only if you look very carefully can you see, inside the blind eye of the camera, the bed on the far side of the room, the two figures tangled together, so still, like bodies in our villages after the soldiers left.

    One of those bodies is my sister's. The other is the body of the tall white man from Germany who put inside her the seed of the baby my sister now feeds. He put it there without asking, just like the soldiers did with my mother. When Miguel, her son, looks up at Natividad, she sees his father's blue eyes and something in her gets as cold and still and hopeless as she felt lying on the bed in the hotel room, watching, from a great distance, in the blind eye of the camera, exactly what was happening to her body until her soul closed its eyes and left completely.

    When she gets like that, I take Miguel from her breast, but she doesn't notice. I talk with him. I make him smile. I see me in his eyes and I feel as if I am swimming in a cool blue lake. It makes me laugh, I feel so light—as if something is lifting me. I lift him from side to side, side to side, always holding myself in view.

The women who are helping us now look at Miguel's pale brown skin, his curly blonde hair and blue eyes and they wonder where he came from. They are afraid of Natividad, the way she keeps slipping out of her body whenever Miguel fixes her with his eyes and closes his lips around her breasts. "She is just a child," they keep saying to each other. They want to take Miguel away from her. They are afraid harm will come to him if they don't. They don't understand what harm will come to my sister if they do.

His eyes hold Natividad, like the blind eye of the camera held her body safe that night her soul slipped away and the German put his seed inside her. If they take Miguel away, what will hold her body so that her soul knows that it does have some place to come home?

I am not sure if these women are our enemies or our friends. I tell Natividad not to see them if I am not with her. I am smarter now. I wish I had said the same thing the night she went to visit the German.

But we were so sure, you see, that he would help us. He wasn't like the other men Natividad had learned to lift her skirt for to earn our daily bread. We lived for three months on the streets of the capital before she said yes to the men. She told me to go around the corner so I wouldn't see. We were so hungry.

But the German man was different. His Spanish was slow but very correct. He came with his camera and sat beside us on the streets near the central plaza. He was interested in Natividad's drawings. That is what he said, and we believed him.

When we first came to the capital, we lived in the mercado with some other children who, like Natividad and me, had no home to go to. At first, Natividad and I tried to help some of the marchantes in the mercado, thinking that they would give us some food. But they did not trust us. We were too dirty.

In the city, it is not as easy to feed yourself. It is not so easy to find a river to wash in. We met some boys who showed us where we could sleep when the mercado closed. They showed us where they threw away the fruits and vegetables. If we looked carefully, we could find some avocado and banana, mango and melon that were only a little rotten. Then one day, the marchantes hired guards to come through the mercado and make sure no one was sleeping there, especially children. The boys, David and Pablo and Tomás, told us that we needed to be very careful of these guards. They treated girls worse than the soldiers in the countryside.

We were very afraid and followed them out into the streets. We were happier in the mercado because the women dressed like us, and all the vegetables and fruits and flowers made us feel more at home. It is very dirty in the city. There is a blackness to the air that covers your skin. And people like us must use the streets to do our business, so there is the smell of piss and shit everywhere. The cars and buses never stop all day long, so you must always be looking and running. And then there are the police, so many kinds of them, standing with guns beside every store, walking down the street. You must be very secret. And there is the smell of food cooking, but it is not for you, so you must not be tempted, you must never get dizzy from the sweet smell, never complain about the burning in your stomach. Everywhere you look, there are things to buy. Watches and clothes, shoes and pots and pans, books and paper, but only if you have money. We had no money.

    David and Pablo showed us another place to sleep after the guards came to the mercado. Tomás did not care where he slept when he was sleepy with glue. He would lie down in the middle of the sidewalk, his shirt pulled over his head, his hand tucked into his pants to cover his private parts.

    In the large lot David and Pablo showed us, there were many people who had come from the country to earn money in the city. David and Pablo said we must sleep completely covered so no one would know we were girls. Natividad and I would lie together under our carrying cloths, whispering to each other about the foods we would like to eat. Or what we had seen that day. Birds plucking fortunes from a tray, or the girls like us, but with clean clothes, who walked together in the plaza on Sunday. An old woman with a blindfold holding a sealed envelope and telling a large crowd what was in it. I wished then that I could see into the future, but I wish it even more now. Or we would talk about what we would like to eat—tortillas and beans and fresh cheese and chicken, sweet mangoes and watermelon. Oh, that we could talk about food for a very long time. If we described it well enough, the pain in our stomachs would ease up as if we had really eaten it.

    Whatever Pablo and David said about keeping covered, it made us feel safe to hear our own language spoken. There were many sounds all around us. Not just people talking. Men laughing, a little drunk. Or men throwing up, very drunk. Here and there a baby would cry, and then get quiet as its mother fed it. Sometimes we could hear men and women coupling. We could hear the women, before it was light, beginning to light their fires. It was not so very different from the country except that we in the city had no roof and no walls and we were all strangers to each other and there was no firewood to burn, so the women made their fires from old paper and plastic, which did not smell very nice. We did not make a fire because we had no matches and nothing to cook and Natividad saved all the paper we found, however dirty, for her drawings.

    But then one night a man came over to where my sister and I were sleeping. He dragged our carrying cloths away from us. He told us we had to pay to sleep there. But we had no money. We will work, we told him. He could not stand still. He kept leaning a little to the right and to the left. There was spit on his lips that shone when he moved toward the streetlight.

    "Of course you'll work," he said. "You have a debt to pay. How many nights have you slept here already?"

We could see David and Pablo look out from the plastic bag that covered them and then slip back. We understood that they would not help us.

The man grabbed my arm and began to pull me to him. "How old are you, girlie?" he asked. "How old are you, little whore?"

I understood that in his village, he would not talk to the girls this way. When he came to town, he became another person. And he expected us to be other people too, because we had no family to protect us.

"Hurry," I said to Natividad. "We are leaving."

" But where will we go?" she asked. She was still lying on the ground, she did not dare move.

"You can't leave," the man said, leaning down and staring into Natividad's face. She closed her eyes but didn't move.

I leaned down to collect our carrying clothes. I made sure to collect Natividad's drawings. Near my foot, there was an empty bottle. I picked it up by its neck and cracked it as hard as I could. The sound made the man let go of Natividad's shoulder. As I turned, I saw Pablo and David pull their plastic bag down around them more tightly.

I pushed the broken bottle as hard as I could into the man's stomach. He grabbed me, but that just brought me closer and made it easier. Our skins are very thick, but I kept pushing until the bottle went in. The man's hands went to my throat, but then he let go and put his hands around the bottle to pull it out. I backed out of his reach.

"Run," I told Natividad. But she didn't move. It was as if she couldn't get out of his sight, she was held there by bad magic.

"For me," I told her. "Do it for me."

And then she began to move, dragging me away with her. The man was leaning back and forth like he had been before, but he was looking at his stomach now, not at us. He pulled the bottle out and shook it in the air. Already his shirt was dark with blood. He leaned over and vomited.

"You little whore," he yelled. "You'll pay for this."

But Natividad and I were slipping outside the gate by then. We ran down the street. We didn't know which way to go, but we knew we needed to keep moving.

"How could you?" she asked me.

"He was going to harm us." I pulled her to make her run faster.

"What if he finds us? What if he dies?"

"Run," I told her. "Don't think."

We found our way to the big plaza. I thought we could sleep beside the church. Who would hurt you beside a church? But churches are white. They don't hide you. As soon as we got near, we heard a voice hissing.

"He's here," Natividad said, beginning to shake. "He knew where we were going and he got here first."

"The night belongs to men," I told her. "They are not all the same one." But I made her start running again.

Finally we were so tired we could not run anymore. We had come to the part of the city where the buses leave. All around us were booths where people sold shoes and clothes during the day. At night, many of them sleep there, but they wouldn't let us stay.

We slipped into a doorway and crouched in the shadows. After awhile, Natividad's breathing slowed and she rested her head on my shoulder. But I didn't sleep. I was thinking how we were going to protect ourselves. I decided we must cut our hair. We must find boys' clothes, even if we had to steal them. I thought we must go on the next Sunday and ask the girls like us walking together in the plaza where they worked so their clothes were clean and they could laugh with each other as they walked, as if they had no worries. I thought maybe we could do what they did. None of them looked hungry.

But Natividad would not cut her hair or change her clothes, however much I begged her. We still wore the same clothes we had worn the day we left out village. I think Natividad was afraid if she changed them for others, we would become completely different people. Our people, especially the women, do not cut their hair for fear a witch might find it and use it for a spell.

But I was not afraid of that as much as I was afraid of the men. The next day, I went into a place where they cut hair. Here in the city, women do not all have long hair as we do. Maybe they have other ways to protect themselves from the witches. I don't know. At first the woman told me to leave. "Please," I begged. "Just lend me your scissors for five minutes. I will wash them. I will do anything you need me to do."

Natividad sat on the front steps, drawing. Whenever we sat down, Natividad would draw on whatever paper she had found, even if people had walked over it and it kept the black tracks of their feet. She was drawing now a picture of the black plastic that covered Pablo and David when the man came toward us last night. All you could see were David's fingers pulling the plastic down over them.

"I am strong," I told the woman. "I can wash floors and sweep. I can gather firewood. I can till fields and plant corn."

"Why don't you go back to your family?" she asked me. "What have you done that they sent you away?"

"Everyone is dead except the two of us. Our house was washed away in the rains last July. We came here looking for our aunt, but we cannot find her. We look every day."

She looked at me in the mirror and shook her head. She did not believe me. When she began to turn around, I reached to grab the scissors from the jar on the counter in front of the mirror, but she grabbed my hand and slapped my face.

"If we looked like boys," I said, "the men would not bother us."

She got very quiet then, like she was remembering something. She handed me the scissors.

"Do it out on the street. I don't want your hair in my shop. You are dirtier than a dog."

So I stood in the gutter outside the shop and cut my hair as short as I could. I pressed the side of the scissors right against the skin of my head and cut. My hair is very thick and the scissors would cut only a little at a time. I was afraid my time was going to be done before I was finished. Natividad didn't look up from her drawing—but she pushed me so hard that I fell when I tried to cut her hair too.

I gave the scissors back to the woman. She was standing in the doorway watching me.

"Wait," *she said. She went into the back room and then came back with a pair of pants and a shirt.*

"These may fit you," *she said.* "Give me your clothes and I can probably sell them and get paid back for the trouble you put me to." *On her walls were big pictures of women whose hair stood on end like flames, or rolled in large waves like rough water. I looked at the clothes she held out. The shirt was torn and the pants were twice as wide as me. Our clothes are our fortune. We weave them ourselves. They are very beautiful and foreigners want to buy them. They were worth far more than the old clothes the woman gave me, but I didn't care.*

From then on the men never bothered me.

If I had made Natividad give away her clothes and cut her hair, maybe she would not have decided to lift her skirts for the men. Maybe they would not have asked her so many times that she finally gave in. Maybe the tall foreigner would not have started to speak with her. I should have paid attention that he never spoke to me, but we had become so used to this. It meant that when Natividad went with the men, I could stay very near without anyone paying attention.

We met the foreigner when we went with Pablo and David to beg for food at the children's home. They told us we couldn't come in because we were girls. There was another home in another city for girls. But there was no room, they said. So many children came to the city these days. They spoke with contempt they tried to hide by keeping their voices soft. They believed that we were drug addicts, like Tomás. Maybe because we were so dirty. The foreigner followed Natividad and I as we walked away. I liked looking through the gate into the children's home even if they would not let us in because they had a fountain in the middle. It sounded like our river running over stones. I liked imagining what it would feel like to wash ourselves clean. There were many foreigners there in the home. They were always laughing and talking with the boys, who were friends of David and Pablo and Tomás. They did not talk in the same way to David and Pablo and Tomás outside the gates. They talked as if they were a little afraid.

We did not realize that the foreigner who followed us did not come from inside the home. He, like us, had been on the outside looking in. We did not understand that the contempt in their voices may have been for him. I wish we did. We felt so dirty and poor when we left. And the voice of the foreigner was so warm and serious when he came to sit beside us as we sat on the steps of the church hoping someone would give us a little money so Natividad would not have to lift her skirts that night.

Natividad didn't complain. She said it didn't hurt her, that she sent her soul to watch from far away, as if it were happening to someone else. When we send our souls away, we can invite them back. It is only when they are frightened out of us that they may not return. We can send them away for safekeeping. I too watched my sister's body making those strange motions with so many different men so that her soul would have someplace to return to. I watched and I cried the tears she could not.

Only before the German put his seed in her did my sister cry, but by then it was too late to stop him. I wish I had the gift of seeing into the future. I don't. I can only see when Natividad's soul has left her and go out to find it. I can't keep it from leaving again and again. I wish I could give her my soul so she could be whole more. I am not so surprised by what life shows us. But I was surprised by the foreigner.

For many weeks, the foreigner came and sat beside us—whether we were sitting beside the church or sitting in a doorway with our friends Pablo and David and Tomás. If he met us in the mercado, he would buy us bread and atole and bananas, sometimes soup.

"It's nothing," he always said. "I want to see you someplace safer, but until then, I want to see that you're fed."

It was strange to us, his sympathy. Our people do not help people who are not their own family. That is why the marchantes would yell at us to go home and beg from our families. We might wear the same clothes, but that did not mean they could help us. Life is too hard to help anyone who is not your own flesh and blood. That is why we do not ask money from each other, only from the city people and the foreigners.

The foreigner told us that he wrote for the newspapers. He wanted to take pictures of Natividad and her drawings. He wanted to find a home where we would be safe. We were afraid we would be separated, but he told us that he would talk to the people and make sure we weren't. "Your brother," he said to Natividad—meaning me.

When Natividad began to correct him, I pinched her.

Every day, he would come and sit beside us. He would ask us where we had spent the night. He gave us a bag with fresh bread in it, which we could not keep ourselves from eating right away.

"And what have you drawn since yesterday?" he would ask Natividad, putting his arm around her. The first few days, she got very still when he did this, but when he did not ask her to lift her skirts for him, she began to relax. She showed him her drawings, and he would look at each one for a long time.

"Can I photograph them?" he asked. "I want to take many pictures of you children of the streets. I want people to see how beautiful and talented you are."

"Can you sell her drawings?" I asked.

Natividad looked at me like the man did after I pushed the broken glass through his thick skin. But I wanted to see if maybe she could stop lifting her skirts for the men. She said it didn't hurt her, but every day it took longer to find her soul and bring it back.

I liked the foreigner because he helped me bring Natividad back.

I didn't know then that he was an evil spirit, that he was luring her soul back in order to send it away forever. He was very clever.

I am only a little girl. I am most angry at God because he should have let me know that there was an evil spirit hiding inside those cool blue eyes that looked so calm and interested. I cannot be watching, every hour, in every direction, for what might hurt my sister. I need God to help me a little—but he didn't. I am very angry at him now, or I was until I held Miguel and saw my own smiling face reflected in his eyes. Then I began to trust what God had in store for us again.

When my sister looks in her son's eyes, all she sees is that hotel room where her soul left her body forever. She knows God is punishing her—not for lifting her skirts for the men before him and after him—but for believing what the foreigner said. God is punishing her for believing, even for a few weeks that she could escape the destiny that was decided for her before she was even born.

I keep telling her that her destiny isn't decided yet. I keep telling her that God gave her me as well, and that I will always be watching over her and fighting for her. She will never be alone. And now I tell her that God gave her Miguel too, that he is an arcangel and his sword will be very powerful, he will be able to slay evil. If I watch over Natividad, Miguel watches over me. The three of us together will be strong enough. But she watches his small mouth closing over her nipple and her soul slips away farther and farther as if to escape the evil spirit of his father.

My sister believed the foreigner when he said he would find a home for us. She believed him when he said he would find work for us as maids. She didn't believe him at first, but after he found us day after day, she began to feel that he was our guardian angel.

She began to make drawings that showed him, his name was Señor Friedrich, standing on the corner under the streetlight where I would be holding her in my sight as she leaned against the wall and let the men relieve themselves inside her. She should have drawn me. She should not have drawn her dreams because they were not true and could lead her soul astray. I would have torn up these drawings. But the foreigner saw them first. He took them from Natividad. He paid her money for them. I should never have asked him about selling her drawings. When she sold them to him, she sold him her hope. That is why her soul won't come back. It is his slave now.

After many days, the foreigner asked my sister to come to his hotel. He told her there was a woman he wanted her to talk to, that she would hire us both to work in her house and she had a little room for us to live in. She did not live in this city, but in another town where the air was cleaner and it was less dangerous. But it would be better, he told my sister, if she came alone to see him. He was going to make a moving picture to show the woman how beautiful and smart and talented Natividad was.

I waited outside the hotel for a long time. Women in tiny dresses that did not cover their knees went in and out several times, each time with a different man. But my sister didn't come out. I had a very bad feeling. Worse than when I heard my mother crying and hurried toward the house and found Natividad turning and turning. I tried to go in, but the man behind the desk told me to go away.

My sister did not come out until early in the morning. She had something clutched to her chest and she looked both ways as she left, as if she were very afraid. But she didn't look for me. It was as if she no longer believed I existed, that there was anyone who could accompany her.

I ran across the street from the doorway where I had been watching for her. "Give that to me," I said.

"You mustn't lose it," she said in a very low voice. "I will die if you lose it."

In the camera with the moving pictures, I carried her soul. The foreigner had stolen it from Natividad, but she had stolen it back while he was sleeping.

I don't have the camera anymore. The policemen who arrested my sister and me a few weeks later took the camera away from me. They didn't understand, even when I fought to take it back. I bit one of them and he grabbed my arm and bent it so that it cracked. Later, once they had sent us to the home, they took me to the clinic where a doctor wrapped my arm in white cloth that turned to stone. The policeman who cracked my arm thought I was a thief. He thought Natividad lifted her skirts for drugs, not for bread. It is true that once or twice, when the hunger was too much, she breathed the glue with Tomás so she could sleep.

The policemen threatened to put us in the jail with the murderers and thieves. But in the jail there was a policewoman and she took us away to a special room. She asked us where our home was. I told her we couldn't go back. She thought we had run away, but I explained about Natividad and my mother. I asked her for the camera back. I told her my sister would never be safe without it. Could we see the moving pictures, I asked her, because since Natividad had come out of the hotel two weeks before she had not spoken. She wouldn't draw either.

Sometimes when she went with the men, I had to be sure they paid her. She would just stand there, looking so sleepy, whether or not she had shared Tomás' glue.

I knew her soul was inside the moving pictures, I told the policewoman. Couldn't we get it out and give it back to Natividad? The policewoman left us alone for several hours. When she came back, she talked to us differently. She had another woman with her, Señora Garcia. She was the one who took us away from the capital to this town. In the girls home, we are prisoners but we are not hungry anymore. I wish Natividad had stayed with me there.

But she felt safer on the streets with Pablo, who came to find her at the girls' home. He said he would take care of her and be her husband, until he saw Miguel's blue eyes. Then he wanted nothing to do with Natividad. None of our people do. But Miguel's blue eyes make the foreign women nervous too.

I am the only one who is at rest with them because I know that when they hold me, they are the eyes of God.

Chapter 15
JUDASINA

All the foreign women were to come to dinner at Señora Rosemary's house on Holy Thursday, and Señora Rosemary had Natividad and Mikela working all day in the kitchen getting ready because Señora Wilma and Mamí Concepción had gone off. They said they would be back for the dinner, but Señora Rosemary wasn't putting her faith in that she said.

Señorita Gwen was over helping Señora Rosemary too. Sometimes she would come to the kitchen and stir the chicken simmering in the pot, or pat Miguel's head while Natividad did the stirring. Oh, it made Mikela want to spill something on the floor to make her slip, or flick the grease spitting in the pan until some landed on Señorita Gwen's pale white skin. But Mikela would never do anything, ever, that might hurt Miguel, and at these moments Señorita Gwen was always too close to Miguel, so Mikela just pressed her lips very tight and held her arms very hard against her sides so the anger wouldn't come out. Usually, when Mikela felt she couldn't stand the smell of Señorita Gwen one second more, Señorita Gwen would put down her spoon, or lift her hand from Miguelito's head, and go off and spend time with the dying woman, assuring Natividad, but never Mikela, that she would return soon.

Señorita Gwen was not afraid of the dying woman. It sounded like Señorita Gwen thought of her own mother when she saw the dying woman, when she smelled that terrible smell that meant the Devil was waiting just outside the door with his bucket filled with slops. Mikela, if she hadn't been so angry with Señorita Gwen, might have felt a little sad for her.

When she thought of her own mother, Mikela never thought of death. She thought of Natividad's long black hair flowing down toward the floor like a river. She thought of the sound of the broom, and the music in her mother's voice. *Death of me. Death of me.* Terrible words, but there was a music to them all the same, a music that made light shiver in Natividad's black, black hair. And there was a smell to her mother, of ashes and pine and chocolate, that Mikela longed for with all her heart because it made her feel so safe and alive.

But when Mikela came to the door of the dying woman's room, she thought of the smells of the capital, how people left their shit on the sidewalks, how there was a blackness to the air that covered everything. It didn't matter that Señora Ginger was white, there was this darkness like soot, this smell like shit, that followed her everywhere as the smell of roses was meant to surround visions of the Virgin. Mikela had never seen a vision of the Virgin, but she would recognize the smell of roses. She didn't understand why no one, not even Natividad or Miguelito, could feel what she could when she approached the dying woman's room.

Señorita Gwen certainly didn't feel the evil that made Mikela so afraid. You could hear Señorita Gwen's voice lift, some eagerness come in to her, when she entered the room. And when she could get the old woman to laugh, Señorita Gwen would laugh with her, even louder, and it was a pure sound, like the first water of the rainy season running faster and faster over the stones, washing away the dust of all the year.

Señorita Rosemary, on the other hand, always sounded angry when she talked to her old friend—just the way Mikela often sounded with Natividad these days. But underneath the anger there was another sound in Señora Rosemary's voice, something deep and sweet, like the syrup pressed from sugar cane, something that made your teeth ache, it was so thick and powerful. Mikela knew that feeling too.

But this was not going to stop her. She knew that she couldn't trust Natividad, not yet, with her plans. Just as Natividad wasn't trusting her with the plans she was making in secret with Señorita Gwen.

Mikela had her money from Señor Simon's friend. She was ready. But she needed to be careful as the fox is careful. She needed to move in a way that was so light and natural it would sound like water falling from the fountain, like the wind troubling the bright pink leaves of the bougainvillea, like a hen in her coop. Tonight, she must let no one know what she smelled in the dying woman's presence. She must not bring attention to herself.

She was relieved, late in the afternoon, when Señora Wilma and Mamí Concepción and Señorita Ginny all returned together from their pilgrimages. They looked very dusty and very tired. They looked like people who now accepted their burdens, just like Jésus did, when he looked out from under the cross. Mikela knew that she must go and receive Jésus' blessing before she and Miguel went on their journey. Mamí Concepción had explained to her how, if she stood right at the corner of the church plaza on the morning of Good Friday, Jésus would catch your eye as he was leaving the church. Powerful things happened when you were seen, just so, by the Savior. Mikela wanted Jésus to hold Miguelito and her in his eyes as they carried him off to Calvary. She thought this Jésus had skin just as dark as the Jésus Mamí Concepción and Señora Wilma had gone to see, but he had more mercy for those who were not just one thing. People who were girls who wanted to be boys, who were aunts who wanted to be mothers, who were brown babies with cold blue eyes, who were original people of a place they could never return to.

Señora Ginny wasn't afraid of the dying woman either. She talked with Señora Rosemary as soon as she came into the house, and then she went to see the dying woman. They were planning something. Everyone, everywhere, was always planning something. But this plan of the foreign women couldn't hurt Mikela. It was something they were doing for the dying woman.

What they planned could only hurt themselves. They had no respect, these *extranjeras*, these foreign women. No respect for death. No respect for the sacraments. No respect for the priests. In the churches tonight, they celebrated the blessed sacrament, for this was the night that Jésus was betrayed and he took bread and he broke it and he took wine and he passed the cup and everything that had been and would be passed before his eyes. And in some of the churches, the priest chose people, people of standing in the community, and knelt before them—the priest himself knelt before them—and he washed their feet and he told people to do as he had done, to do as Jésus had done, to bend low so that later you could sit high up there at God's right hand in the next world.

But these foreign women, this dying woman in particular, she thought that they could just invite Jésus to be with them anywhere—that they didn't need the church and they didn't need the people. They could just be here in Señora Rosemary's house, sitting around her fountain, and Jésus would come and be among them. They thought they could ask him to wash their own feet. Women! Foreigners! They thought that Señora Ginny could pretend to be a priest and that God's anger (not to mention the anger of the Virgin) would not pour down around her as it did around the woman who would be king.

Mikela was just a little girl and she couldn't stop them. Actually, she didn't want to. She wanted God's anger to pour down on them like thunder and lightning, like fire and liquid stone from the volcano. But she kept these thoughts to herself as she helped Señora Ginny set up the chairs and fill bowls with water and set candles all around the fountain. Not a word did she say as she made a special chair covered with blankets and pillows for the dying woman. As she put a bowl of incense nearby so the smell of her dying and her dreadful pride would not be so intense.

Mikela brushed at the shoulders of Señora Ginny's black shirt, which were pale with dust. Señora Ginny took Mikela's hand gently between both her own and leaned over to look in Mikela's face. Her eyes were silver, like mirrors, or a lake an hour before sunrise.

"It's all right," Señora Ginny said. "The dust fits with the mood of the evening. Jesus and his disciples must all have been very dusty." She smiled. "I missed you, little one, while I was gone."

Señora Ginny's face looked sad and strong. Mikela was sorry that Señora Ginny was going to make God so angry. She was truly sorry. She like Señora Ginny. And she believed her when Señora Ginny said she would help Mikela. But how could a woman over whose shoulders God's anger was going to pour like streams of melted stone help Mikela?

Mikela tried to warn her. "God doesn't want women giving away spiritual food. That is men's work. Women can sing. And they can pray. And they can teach children, like the sisters do. And they can say the rosary for nine days time nine at a time. And they can read the Bible. But they cannot pass their hand over wine and make it Jésus' blood and they can't pass their hand over bread and make it Jésus' flesh."

Señora Ginny held Mikela's hand gently but firmly, as if she hadn't heard the warning.

"But can they do the opposite?" Señora Ginny asked. "Can they make blood, wine and flesh, bread? Wouldn't that be more practical. There are so many hungry people in the world."

"And so many dead," Mikela said. "Especially here. Because of the war."

"Tortillas and *té de jamaica*," Señora Rosemary said, bustling up behind them. "Better than bread and wine any day, don't you think so, Mikela?"

But Mikela just smiled and dropped a little of the oil Señora Rosemary gave her into each of the bowls of water that they had dipped out of the fountain. The oil made the water smell like roses, but that didn't mean the Virgin was coming. The Virgin wasn't going to have anything to do with women like these. What would her son think? What would his father? The Virgin knew who she belonged to. This is what made her so powerful.

Just the way Mikela was when Miguel was tied tightly to her side and when she walked she moved for both of them. She was strong for both of them. There were weights that made you more powerful. Her people knew that. That was why they carried so much on their heads and on their backs. They had learned from Jésus. They had learned from the Virgin.

Mikela wondered who these foreign women were learning from.

From you, her mother's voice said. *From Natividad. From each other.*

Mikela had to sit down, fast, on the edge of the fountain. She knew her mother was not dead, so it wasn't her spirit talking. And she knew what she said was not right. Mikela had nothing to do with these women. Surely God knew that. And Jésus. And the Virgin. Whatever it might look like from the outside.

It was time, that was clear, that she got away from them. All these *extranjeras*. These foreign women who could not see the Devil standing with his slop pail outside the room of the dying, who could not hear a soul leaving a body, who thought God couldn't see and couldn't hear and wouldn't be angry when they took his powers on themselves, who couldn't see little Miguel for the blessed savior he was, who didn't know God always sent his saving grace to us in the form of baby boys.

The Virgin, Mikela decided, was a woman of great pity. That was why she had been so favored by God and why she so favored the sinners who came to her. She didn't want anyone to suffer, not even the guilty. That is why she drew God's attention elsewhere while the women had their ceremony.

Why she came herself. It was not just the drops of the oil of roses that made Mikela feel this way. It was like someone staring at you when you don't know it, but with the greatest care, so suddenly you feel your body going all soft and warm with the attention. It made you feel light in your body and safe. Mikela felt this as she poured the water over her sister's feet and looked up and saw Natividad looking at her very carefully, the way she used to years before when they lived in the country, as if she, Mikela, were someone who could bring her happiness, someone who could touch her heart. For a second, Natividad looked down on Miguel's head, where she held him on her lap, with the same look that Mikela could feel the Virgin was giving her, giving Mikela, as she knelt there beside her sister, washing the dust from her feet and saying the prayer the *extranjeras* said: "The peace that the world cannot give, I give you."

Natividad looked so still and so peaceful, it made Mikela want to cry. Just as the softness in her own shoulders, which was the touch of the Virgin's eyes, made her want to cry. And the way Natividad played with little Miguel's short fat legs, lifting them inside her hands as if they had always belonged there, filled Mikela with a sense of joy and purpose. Maybe she would share her plans with Natividad, after dinner, when they were working on the *alfombra*. She carefully wiped her sister's feet. Then she dipped her cloth again and wrung it almost dry, and she wrapped it, ever so gently, around Miguelito's fat little feet. She looked in her sister's face as she did so, and she felt both of them, at that second, had been lifted up and carried into the Virgin's heart, that there was a home for all three of them in the Virgin's sacred heart.

But it didn't last. For then it was Señora Ginger's turn to wash Mikela's feet. And Natividad's turn to wash Señorita Gwen's feet. Mikela did not want that dying woman's hands on her skin, but she knew she had to pretend, she had to pretend so that she and Miguel could escape. And she watched Natividad, the way she knelt before Señorita Gwen and took her long white feet inside her small brown hands—and she knew, she knew as if God's fury had come pouring down around her like liquid stone, that she could never have confidence in her sister again.

Mikela held Miguelito against her so tightly, he made a sound like the beginning of a cry. Mikela became perfectly still. She didn't send her soul away. She sent it deep inside her to that little place where it could sit, like the host did in the *sagrario*, untouched, safe. Then she felt a great freedom inside herself. She made her arms go very soft, so Miguelito would know no fear. She smiled at her sister as if she did not feel betrayed. She leaned back in her chair and lifted her dirty feet into the dying woman's lap so that all she had to do was set her damp cloth on Mikela's feet.

The dying woman just set the cloth over Mikela's feet. The dying woman didn't rub the dirt and dust away. She let it get darker, thicker with water, like mud. She stared into Mikela's eyes. Because Mikela could feel her own soul closed up like something small and perfectly thin and white, like Jésus' own suffering carne made into something pure and painless inside a very heavy and expensive gold *sagrario*—she stared back.

The old woman with the thin hair under her blue scarf and the blue dress standing up around a neck whose skin was as creased as lizard's, with a smell just like the Devil's slop pail, looked at Mikela as if she could see right through her, could see where she had locked up her soul for safe-keeping. She had a little smile on her lips, which were cracked in places and had a covering of white, like she had been eating clay.

"Don't be afraid," she told Mikela. "Whatever happens, don't be afraid. God means well by all three of you. You can rest in that, Mikela."

Her Spanish was very exact. But strangely made inside her mouth, as if it had a bad taste to it. Bitter.

God is going to take you away very soon, Mikela thought.

"That is true," the woman said, as if Mikela had really said something. "I am leaving any day now. I am going to see God. And Jesus."

And the Virgin, Mikela thought, holding on hard to Miguel, concentrating on the lock on the gold *sagrario* that kept her soul, so still and white and perfectly round.

"I'm not afraid," the old woman said. She pressed down a little, a very little, on the cloth that covered Mikela's feet. "I'm ready for my next life. But God has asked me to do something for you, Mikela."

She smiled at Mikela. She had very yellow teeth that looked almost black in the candlelight. Mikela didn't trust her at all. She was a bad mother. Mikela knew she was a bad mother. Mikela knew God didn't have anything to do with bad mothers. That was why the Devil was waiting outside her door, ready to throw her soul in his slop pail as soon as it left her body.

"The peace the world cannot give you," this terrible woman said to Mikela, pressing her feet through the damp red cloth, "I give you."

"All that anger," she said, leaning forward just a little, so the light could climb up her cheeks and the shadows could fill the inside of her mouth and darken her eyes until they were like the sockets of a skull. "All that anger, my little one, let me carry it for you. Just for a day or two. Let me carry it for you."

But Mikela wasn't taken in by the old woman. "I know you," she said. "I *know* you."

She clutched Miguel to her chest as hard as she could. She pulled her feet, still covered with the wet cloth, up close to her chest.

Hell is your home, she thought. I know you and hell is your home.

It is all our home, said the voice that sounded like Mikela's mother's, and Natividad's and the wicked dying woman's all put together. *Heaven as well as hell. It is all our home, Mikela.*

But Mikela was a brave girl. She was not afraid. She had Miguel el arcangel in her arms and her soul had been turned into something white and perfectly round and as thin as a leaf and was safely locked away. She could use the heavy gold cross that hid it as a weapon if she needed to. She began to recite the prayer that would save her. "*Padre nuestro, quien esta en el cielo.*"

She knew there was only one woman who could speak for God as a daughter and a mother and a wife. She knew she didn't sound like her own mother and she didn't sound like this wicked dying woman and she didn't sound like Natividad reciting with all these *extranjeras*, "The peace the world cannot give you, I give you."

Mikela was a brave girl and she was not afraid and she pulled her feet away from the dangerous dying woman and she stood up and she turned her back on her sister who was staring like a silly fool into Señorita Gwen's face and she went over and stood by the enormous man who had come with Señor Simon, the man who was now going to wash Señora Ginny's feet. She held out her bowl of water that smelled like roses, that smelled like the Virgin who knew her real place in the world. She handed him the red cloth. She felt some huge pressure in her ease up as he dipped it in the water and squeezed out all the dirt from her own feet. Squeezed out the touch of the dying woman. Squeezed out the way they had mixed together. Squeezed out the dying woman's terrible suggestion that anything in Mikela, anything at all, could have a place inside her. That anything that was inside Mikela could have a place in the Devil's slop pail.

There are traitors here, she told Señora Wilma and Señora Ginny out in the kitchen when she couldn't hold it in anymore—not the fear or the anger or the urgency.

But Señora Wilma said it was natural. At the last supper there needed to be traitors and people so weak they would deny you. That made Mikela feel a little better. She could tell Señora Wilma felt the danger in the air, so she did not feel so very alone. Unless she looked over at Natividad talking to Señorita Gwen, how the Señorita would touch Natividad's shoulder or her hair, and Natividad would get this look on her face almost as if she were breathing the glue again. It was the same look she had on her face when the German man would sit beside her and look at her drawings.

Mikela's sister had no sense of danger. If you had no sense of danger, your soul could not stay in your body. It was always being startled, sent away. Why couldn't Natividad learn for herself. Even Miguelito had a sense of danger, why didn't his mother? Miguelito could feel that his mother was ready to give him away to the Señorita, just so she could feel the Señorita's hand on her own forehead, rest her own head against the Señorita's shoulder.

To betray Jésus, Judas demanded thirty pieces of silver. But Natividad would betray her own son for less, for an *extranjera's* hand on her forehead. And Natividad would betray Mikela for even less—a smile, a laugh. Her own sister.

Mikela took Miguelito, who was crying, from her sister and tied him to her own back. She hurried around the table gathering the dirty dishes. She took them away from the artist lady and her white-haired husband, the father of Señorita Gwen. He did not seem like such a bad man. Mikela did not know how he could have such a traitorous daughter. She saw Señora Lourdes studying Señorita Gwen as if she had the very same question in her mind.

"You will come and help us tonight?" Señora Lourdes asked.

Mikela nodded. She had never made a carpet for God to pass over before. But she wanted to—and she wanted to keep anyone from being suspicious.

So, after she and Señora Ginny and Señora Wilma gathered all the plates and silver and glasses and carried them out to the kitchen to wash them, she and Miguel slipped into the back of the large car of Señora Rosemary, along with the two bags of rose petals Señor Simon and his big friend had set there. In the seat ahead of her, Mamí Concepción and Señora Wilma and

Señora Rosemary laid the dying woman. Mikela was careful to keep Miguel's head completely covered so he would not smell that terrible smell. She held her own breath too. Señora Rosemary got in behind the wheel and Señora Wilma and Mamí Concepción sat together on the other front seat, Mamí Concepción sitting forward with her forehead on the glass. Mikela hoped that Señora Rosemary would not drive so fast that she banged them up and down and broke the glass, wounding Mamí Concepción. But whenever Señora Rosemary started driving too fast, the car bounced and shook and the dying woman cried out—so Mamí Concepción stayed safe although Mikela thought she herself would suffocate, she had to hold her breath so long in order not to breathe in the terrible air the dying woman released with each groan, each cry.

When they arrived at Señor Simon's, Mikela was relieved to find everyone else there. Both Señor Simon and Señora Ginny waved at her to join them. She chose Señora Ginny because she was working on one side of the *alfombra*, while Señor Simon was in the middle where it would be hard to balance on the boards with Miguel on her back—and Mikela was not going to let Miguel be separated from her for any reason. Besides, Mikela didn't approve of the design of Señora Lourdes had made—especially since it included her and her sister and Miguelito—and Señorita Gwen. She ignored Natividad and Señorita Gwen, who were working on the opposite border. She ignored the dying woman, who sat in a chair with wheels under a bright light, her face so filled with shadows her head looked like a skull. Mikela was so busy not paying attention that she thought she would burst. She could hear every sound Natividad murmured, although she couldn't make out the words. She could feel the dying woman's eyes touch the top of her head or her back. She kept moving Miguel around so the dying woman's eyes couldn't touch him.

She told Señora Ginny that it wasn't right, this way they were trying to make Jésus a woman in their *alfombra*. But Señora Ginny didn't seem to understand the danger she was in. Anymore than Natividad understood the danger she was in from Señorita Gwen.

Mikela busied herself sifting colored sawdust to make leaves and flowers. She tried very hard not to hear and not to see and to keep away from the dying woman's eyes, and all the time the fear and the fury were building inside her like a big river.

The very big man who was a friend of Señor Simon's (or perhaps he was his brother, although how a blonde man like Señor Simon could have a dark-haired brother who was so much taller, Mikela didn't know) came over and stood beside Señora Ginny like they were *novios*. Señora Ginny was a tall woman, like all the *extranjeras* except Señora Marie, but she was as small compared to this big man as Mikela was compared to Señora Ginny. Mikela was not a small girl, she and Natividad were almost the same size now. But these *extranjeros*, both women and men, were so much bigger. It was true, the stories Mikela's people told, of the gold-haired giants who owned the world. But next to the tall dark man, Señora Ginny, even with her gold hair, looked as helpless as an indigenous. Mikela hoped the big man would save Señora Ginny from God's anger that was soon to pour down like melted stone. Maybe, if God knew that Señora Ginny would be obedient to this man on earth, he would believe she could be obedient to him too and would not send his wrath down on her for trying to take the power of priests on herself.

Mikela, now that her side of the carpet was finished, decided it was time to make a Judas that Jésus would see on his way to Calvary so that not only would his feet be eased by the flowers but his mind too would be at rest because he could see that there was justice. The weak might deny him and the traitors might betray him, but all the silver in the world would not save them. She did not want to leave Miguel for even a moment, but she knew this was the last thing she needed to do by herself before she took him away with her forever. Natividad and Señorita Gwen were still working on the *alfombra*, but Mamí Concepción was sitting resting. Mikela gave Miguelito to her to hold.

"You may only release him to me," she told Mamí Concepción. "He is my responsibility. Mine alone."

"Thank you for your confidence," Mamí Concepción said softly. "I will be worthy of it. I promise."

Mikela wanted to make her Judas of straw but they only had sawdust and rose petals out on the street. She wondered if Señor Simon might have some straw in his garden. She told him she needed to use the bathroom so he would unlock the door for her and let her in.

Mikela was sorry that she had to use Señora Ginny's clothes to make her Judas. She had wanted to use the clothes of Señorita Gwen—or even of Natividad, but that felt too dangerous, no matter how angry she was at her sister. But she had to use Señora Ginny's clothes because the time had come to make her traitor and Señora Ginny's clothes were the only ones available to her. Oh, of course, she could have taken the clothes of Señor Simon—for they were not that different. Señora Ginny liked her blue jeans and t-shirts, just as Mikela did. Just as Señorita Gwen did. Señora Marie. These *extranjeras* women had the same secret wish that Mikela did to be men. She could see it in everything they did. And they had no reason for they had not lived, like Mikela and Natividad, on the streets of the capital.

But Mikela's traitor, her Judasina, needed to wear the clothes of a woman—even if they were the clothes of a woman who wanted to be a man. Mikela was very sure of this. The Virgin herself had whispered this in Mikela's ear. Mikela was sure it was the Virgin's voice because it did not sound at all like her own mother. It had a deepness to it, like the sound of the Mother Superior's voice, and a lightness to it that was like Mamí Concepción's (although Mikela thought the Virgin might not completely approve of Mamí Concepción because of her laziness). It had a music too, which reminded Mikela of Señora Ginny, but Mikela knew that wasn't possible. What could Señora Ginny, who dared assume the power of the priests, have to do with the Virgin? But Mikela knew it was the Virgin's voice because when she heard it, she smelled roses, and her body felt exactly the way she did when she held Miguelito, when she felt the peace that passes understanding. But it was as if Mikela was the one who was being held, who could smell, deep in the folds of the Virgin's robes, the smell of roses.

Out there on the street, the smell of pine and coro was as strong as the smell of roses. But here in Señor Simon's garden, following the Virgin's instructions, Mikela could only smell the scent of roses. No pine. This meant there was no trace of the spirit of her mother. Mikela understood, even though the Virgin never said it, that it was very important to separate these two scents. And she knew what she was doing pleased the Virgin, because there were no roses in Señor Simon's garden, so where else could the smell be coming from except directly from her?

She knew she needed to work quickly. She had taken a pair of Señora Ginny's blue jeans and a t-shirt and the long coat of many colors she had left lying across her bed.

There was no straw in Señor Simon's garden, but at the very back there were many dead leaves, the last clippings of the vines. They were in a big plastic bag. Mikela took another vine from the wall and used it to tie part of the big bag off to make the Judasina's head. And she broke four branches off a bush to fill the arms and legs of her Judasina. She wanted to give it long curly red hair, but when she broke off parts of the red bougainvillea, the thorns cut her fingers.

So, instead, she broke off four branches of hibiscus to run them through the top of the bag after she had dressed her traitor. The Judasina needed long hair to show she was a woman. It was not possible to make breasts with the plastic bag for the vines and branches didn't stay in any particular shape. Mikela went into the house and found the trash under the sink and brought out all the paper. She pulled the t-shirt over the head she had made. She had to pull hard because the head was very big. Filled with bad ideas, she thought.

Bad ideas that are, just like Jésus' ideas, the will of God, the voice that did not sound like the Virgin's said.

Mikela did not know how she had gotten in here. The Virgin's scent of roses was a shield. She should not have been able to slip through, this other spirit who sounded suspiciously like Mikela's mother. But Mikela knew what she said was true. All her people knew this. San Judas was a saint, just like San Pablo and San Agustín and San Juan. There would not be the glorious crucifixion of Jésus if it had not been for Judas. Jésus would not be able to be the savior if Judas had not been the traitor. Just as there could not be the gold haired conquistadors if there were not the dark indigenous.

Just as Jésus knew his fate from the time he was a boy in the temple, Mikela wondered if Judas had always known his fate, known that he was to be despised even after death, that the ground that he was buried in would be barren. It was the worst thing for her people—to be someone who destroyed the *tierra*, it was like destroying God himself. Not his son. God. The place all life came from.

Mikela pulled on the blue jeans she had take from Señora Ginny's room. She pushed the grasses and dead leaves and the stiff, woody vines this way and that until she could zip the pants closed. Her Judasina was very *panzona*. Very fat. Mikela stuffed all the dirty paper into the t-shirt to make breasts. She pulled on the coat of many colors and pushed sticks up its sleeves to make stiff arms and then pushed sticks up the legs of the blue jeans to make legs. She ran the hibiscus branches through the top of the bag for hair and tied them together with vines. It looked a little like a crown. A traitor's crown.

Then she slipped back into the apartment of find some paper and a pen. There was so much laughter coming from outside the door, she felt a little sad to be inside here by herself. But the Virgin told her not to trust that laughter and to hurry back to the garden and make her *denuncia*.

In her pueblo, the year before Natividad and Mikela left, on the Judas someone had written something about her mother and the soldier. Mikela, who could read, even when the words were at a distance, saw it soon after the boys had hung the traitor-saint from a tree near the church. She had climbed up there and had ripped the paper off, even though she knew it was meant to shame the soldier. Even though she knew it had been written by the priest or by the shopkeeper, Carlos, who was not of her people but who wanted their mother anyway. Mikela's mother couldn't read. Neither could her father. But the children in the school could and they might tell their parents.

She wondered now what would have happened if she had not torn away the warning, if her father had learned about her mother's love for the soldier in this way, would her mother still have beaten Natividad so badly that they had to leave. Was it destined, their leaving, the way Jésus' sacrifice and Judas' treachery were?

This is what I want my son to be able to read as he carries his cross to Calvary, the Virgin told Mikela. *I, like your mother, cannot read or write. I depend on you.*

But could Jésus read any better than his mother, Mikela wondered. He was a carpenter. Many carpenters, just like the shoe shine boys or the farmers like her father, could not read. If Jésus had been a shopkeeper, Mikela could be sure he could read. But not if he cut wood.

But the Virgin wanted her words in writing and it wasn't Mikela's right to question God's mother.

Things are not what they seem, the Virgin dictated to Mikela.
The guilty will be punished.
Silver or gold, thirty pieces or a hundred, will not save those who ignore the power of the most high.
Women cannot take the place of men.
Sons must obey their fathers, just like God.
Women must obey the Virgin, just like God.
No one dare separate a mother and her baby. Only the Virgin knows which

babies God wants and when.

Babies only go into exile with their own mothers, like the Virgin took Jésus to Egypt.

When a mother is not good to her baby, a sister can take her place—but she has to be of the same people and the same place and love that baby with a peace that passes understanding.

Everyone should be an indigenous—the original people of a place. Foreigners should go back and become indigenous again.

Foreigners should go back to their own countries and steal babies from each other.

The only son who must die for his father is God's son Jésus—and Judas, for otherwise Jésus could not be betrayed and taken into captivity and condemned and crucified and made to sit on the right hand of his father. Everyone else can pray to the Virgin for dispensation. Her job is to make God nicer.

The Virgin will even help foreign women—but only after they go home and become indigenous again.

Now sign it, the Virgin said. So Mikela did.

She signed it, Maria, Mother-Daughter-Wife of God, *el todopoderoso.*

Mikela pinned the paper to the t-shirt with the thorns from a branch of bougainvillea. She left a little blood on the shirt and was sorry. But otherwise, she felt very pleased with her Judasina and she could feel the Virgin's relief that Mikela would be able to hang it from the roof in time for Jésus' passing. Mikela began to make the noose out of the big thick rope that Señor Simon used to hang clothes on to dry. She used very little rope to make the circle around the neck because she wanted her Judasina to hang close to the ground so Jésus could read his mother's words very clearly and carry them straight to God. The *extranjeras* could read them too and ponder them in their hearts.

When the big man who was Señora Ginny's *novio* came out into the garden, Mikela was testing the noose she had slipped around her Judasina's neck. She had heard him coming, so she was not surprised. Also, the Virgin had told her that he was the one to help her hang the Judasina. But the Virgin had just said that Mikela was not to hang the Judasina out on the street. This made Mikela angry. What was the point of hanging a Judas if it wasn't for the whole world to see? But Mikela was not going to question the wisdom of the Virgin, however angry it made her. She would hang her Judasina on the highest limb of the pomegranate tree that grew by the tall wall. The wall had broken glass on it, under the bougainvillea, but Mikela was wearing her tennis shoes. All she needed was for this giant man to lift her up there.

Because he did not speak Spanish, it was hard for him to understand her. But she kept repeating her gestures until, like a big old trained bear, he did what she wanted. Holding the Judasina close to her chest, its legs folded over her hands as if it were already a dead person, she had him lift her onto the wall. She left the Judasina lying there as she climbed the tree, the rope around her waist also attached to the Judasina's neck.

She heard Señor Simon and his friend Señor Byron come out into the garden. And then she heard the voice of Señor Patricío, the man who was almost as big as Señor Simon's brother, but who spoke Spanish. He spoke Spanish now. His voice was very fast and hard. The other men were laughing, but he said something and they were quiet.

"*Chiquita*," he called to Mikela. "*Ten cuidado*." Little girl. Take care.

As if Mikela were eight years old. As if she weren't following the Virgin's orders. And of all the men there, he should know because, like Señora Wilma, the spirits visited him. But maybe not the Virgin.

Mikela climbed higher and higher in the pomegranate tree, until the branches began to bend. She needed to get her Judasina up there high enough for Jésus to see. Even if his mother said she wasn't to hang it in the street, wasn't she meant to hang it somewhere where he could see it and understand that he had left the world in good hands, that the Virgin, even if she couldn't stop his dying, could make sure justice was done. She could so fill Judas' mind with torment and remorse he would pay for his evil. Even if he didn't have a choice. It was still evil and Judas would have to pay. In his own way, God was harder on Judas, giving him this job that would make him despised through all history. Jésus, after he died, could feel good about himself. But not Judas, even if his fate was decided before he was born by God himself.

Mikela knew that Natividad and the *extranjera* women would think Mikela was a traitor when they learned she had taken Miguelito. But they didn't know about the Virgin's guiding. And Mikela was not taking any money, she wasn't betraying anyone. She was just taking Miguelito into exile with her until the sacrifices were over. The Virgin had done the same thing. Of course, she had San José to help her. But Mikela had the Virgin herself. Certainly that was better.

But the Virgin then said something surprising. She said that Mikela should stop climbing. That Jésus did not need to see the Judasina Mikela had made for him, that carried his own mother's words. The Judasina is a lesson for the pueblo, the Virgin told her. About what can happen if you ignore the will of God.

Or if you follow it, the voice that was suspiciously like Mikela's mother said.

Mikela suddenly felt dizzy. She slipped a little, but hung on with her hands. As Mikela slipped, the Judasina fell off the wall, and she hung with all her weight from the rope tied around Mikela's waist.

The men crowded around the Judasina, who now dangled right before their eyes because the rope Mikela was using was so long. (She had hoped the Virgin would change her mind about letting her hang it from the roof down into the street.) The length of the rope made the Judasina very heavy, and the rope pulled into Mikela's waist so tight she felt she was going to be cut in two.

The men were all laughing, reading the Virgin's words aloud. Or they started that way. Señor Byron, the man who gave Mikela the money for the shoe-shine box, was the one who was reading. Señor Simon was changing the words into English for his brother, the giant man.

Mikela tried to pull herself back onto the branch. Her arms were getting very tired. She wasn't going to let them know that she needed help, but she could feel her hands getting wet with the effort of holding on. She couldn't untie the rope until she had her legs around a branch again. The Judasina was too heavy for Mikela to hang on with only one hand and do the untying from where she was now. She should have carried her on her back, like men carried their sacks of corn, like Jésus carried his cross. Mikela only thought of carrying her on her head because that was where women and girls here carried everything, except babies. And the Judasina wasn't a baby.

Oh, Mikela's hands were getting so wet. And a groan came out of her mouth even though she didn't mean it.

And then she heard this talking moving down below and there was a scraping as someone tried to get up on the wall. But, Mikela thought, they were all very old men, even if they were big. They could not climb like cats and monkeys. They were going to be no help for her.

And she wondered—as she imagined falling, landing on the broken glass on the top of the wall with only the sticks and stones and the thorns of the Judasina to protect her—if this had been the Virgin's plan after all. And if it was, why the Virgin would treat in such a hard way a girl who was as loyal to her as Mikela (even if she did want to be a boy). She didn't want the broken glass to go right through her skin the way she pushed the broken glass into the belly of the drunken man in the capital.

Maybe the Virgin was going to make sure justice was done. So Mikela told her how sorry she was she had done that, but surely the Virgin understood about wanting to protect the people you loved. Surely the Virgin understood that sometimes mothers took machetes and tried to cut off the arms of the soldiers before they shot their babies, sometimes sisters and brothers set fire to the soldiers' trucks to stop them raping and murdering.

Oh, it hurt so much, the way the rope that circled the Judasina's neck was digging into Mikela's waist making her see stars where there were already more than enough stars.

She hear Señor Simon say something and then the pressure on her waist began to ease. They were holding the Judasina up so Mikela could breathe. And she heard Señor Patricio, who had a big but sweet voice, singing a little song for her:

Cuidado, mijita. Cuidado, amor.
Cuidado, mijita. Cuidado, amor.
Agarres el arbol con toda tu fuerza.
Ayuda viene, viene, amor.
No tienes miedo. Ayuda viene.
No tienes miedo, amor.

And somehow, just the sound of his deep voice rising up through the night air and the leaves of the pomegranate tree made Mikela's breath come in bigger and bigger waves and her hands feel strong again. She kept her eyes very wide so she wouldn't imagine the broken glass down there.

"Ya, vengo. Ya, vengo," she heard Señor Byron calling as he stood at last on the wall and began to climb the pomegranate tree. "Ya, vengo. Ya, vengo, mijita."

For an old man, he moved quickly. When he was a few branches below her, he stopped and reached out his arm and wrapped it around her legs. He told Mikela to let go of the branch, he would catch her. But Mikela knew that even brown-eyed men could sometimes lie, so she told him to untie the Judasina. It was hard for her to talk, she was so tired, but she told him what to do.

"Once I no longer have the Judasina on me," she told him, "I can save myself."

He kept apologizing because it took him three tries to untie the knot and the tree shook, it shook like there was a very bad storm. Señor Patrició and Señor Simon kept telling him to hurry. To use a knife. Acting like Mikela wasn't a very strong girl. Just the way they talked about her made her angry—and that was good because it made her heart pump faster and her mind get clearer and her hands stronger.

And then, at last, with the men below, especially Señor Simon's enormous brother, lifting the rope so it no longer dug into Mikela's waist, Señor Byron was able, with his legs wrapped around the tree trunk, sitting on a branch, to slip his hands under the rope and undo the knot.

Mikela knew what he wanted to do was just pull her onto the branch with him, but when he tried, she kicked out, so he followed her orders, just repeating, along with Señor Patrició that little song that made Mikela feel sad and strong and not alone. *Cuidado, mijita. Cuidado, amor.*

As soon as Señor Byron had the rope in his hands, Mikela lifted herself with her arms enough to slide one elbow over the tree branch, then to swing her leg over it.

Señor Byron was about to throw the rope down to the men below, but Mikela cried out so loud he lurched a little on his branch and the whole tree shook.

"The Virgin has given me a task," she said. "I must finish it."

"Can we help?" he asked, very politely. "You have helped with the foot washing and the dinner and the *alfombra*. Certainly we can help you with your doll."

"She is a saint, Santa Judasina," Mikela corrected him.

"The Virgin said it was time for a Judasina, not just a Judas. But she told me I was not to hang her for all the pueblo to see. I was not even to hang her where Jésus could see her," she said, her voice sounding angry even though she was trying to be obedient to the Virgin's wishes.

"If you climb down, *mijita*, I promise I will not leave until I have hung it exactly to your wishes." His voice was very kind. But Mikela knew that could mean many things, and not all of them good. And even though he spoke Spanish, she thought Señor Byron was really an *extranjero*, a foreign man. Not all the bad *extranjeros* came from Germany.

"Just give me the rope, thank you," she said. "I will wind it around the tree and bring it down myself. Then I could use all your help to lift my Judasina." She sounded just as kind and considerate as Señor Byron.

"I will follow you down," he said.

But Mikela insisted he go down first, for if he stayed behind, he could throw the rope down and defy the Virgin. Mikela wasn't going to let that happen.

When she stood on the wall, her feet finding their balance on the broken glass and the bougainvillea vines, all four men stood below her staring up with the silliest looks on their faces. Señor David, the giant man, opened his arms, so did Señor Patrició—and Señor Byron and Señor Simon.

"*Ven a mí, pajarito,*" sang Señor Patrició.

"*Ven a mí,*" sang Señor Simon.

"*a mí,*" sang Señor David.

"*a mí,*" sang Señor Byron.

Then Señora Ginny, who had come out without anyone noticing, gave a sharp cry, as if someone had struck her, and Mikela, without thinking, dove off the wall into the arms of all those men with skin as white as the Virgin's and eyes as blue as Miguelito's or as brown as her own.

As she fell, holding tight to the rope, the Judasina rose into the air. When the men put her down on the ground, they all pulled together, bringing her Judasina up higher, higher in the tree until no one, not even Mikela with her far seeing eyes, could read what the Virgin had to say.

Señora Ginny knelt before her, so serious. "*Mi amor,*" she said. "Thank God you are safe. The next time I want you to ask for help. I promise I will be there for you."

Mikela patted the shoulder of the nice *extranjera* woman who wanted to steal the power of the priests. Soon, she thought, very soon, if the Virgin has her way, she will leave, they all will, to become indigenous again in their rightful land.

An hour later, as Mikela wandered the streets with Miguelito looking at all the other *alfombras*, she kept imagining she could hear the laughter of Natividad and Señorita Gwen following her—and each time she heard it, she slipped around the next corner as quickly as she could. But she could never move fast enough. It was always there. Those two sounds weaving together.

Señorita Gwen's voice so silver and Natividad's gold but with something shiny and hard as obsidian glinting inside it.

After the procession tomorrow morning, after Jésus had blessed Mikela and Miguel and the two of them had started on their journey, then Natividad's voice would go back inside her where it belonged, and Señorita Gwen's voice would not sound so bright. It was the way the voices curved around each other, like the threads of a rope, that hurt Mikela so. It was her own voice Mikela had always heard moving in and out of Natividad's—even in Natividad's silences, Mikela's voice moved in and out of the stillness that was her sister's truest speech. But Mikela's voice, oh, by itself, it sounded like an old blanket, filled with burs, rough. It didn't belong with the two of theirs. She could hear that, even in her own mind. She couldn't keep from hearing that. But her voice *had* belonged with Natividad's.

Perhaps it can again, said the voice that made Mikela dizzy because it reminded her of their mother.

You could never believe a word that voice was saying, especially if it was saying something hopeful. It had bothered their mother, the way Mikela was always at Natividad's side, the little murmur, like water over mossy rocks, which was the sound of Natividad and Mikela's voices running together. Why would she want to hear their voices together again unless she had plans, bad plans, for them?

Señorita Gwen wanted to know so many things. Too many things. Where Miguelito's blue eyes came from. What they had done, Natividad and Mikela, in the city, what life was like at the girls' home. The other day, Natividad had pulled out some of her old drawings to show Señorita Gwen, and Mikela had grabbed them and yelled at her in their own language, "She is not your sister. How dare you share them with her." It was like sharing prayers. You didn't do that with anyone who wasn't your own flesh and blood.

Mikela paused to look at an *alfombra* made out of vegetables. It had a border of lettuces and then big medallions in the center, circles made of beets and radishes and carrots. It was very beautiful and made Mikela's stomach ache. She knew that once she and Miguel left Señora Rosemary's house, they would get hungry again. Not as hungry as she and Natividad had been in the capital (because now Mikela would have her own shoe-shine box and could earn money every day)—but hungry the way Mikela had been most of her life, an aching deep inside her that always kept her awake.

She leaned down just to touch the lettuce, it was so pretty. And then she heard their laughter again, and she stood up and looked forward and behind. Mikela was very tired. She had gotten tired all of a sudden when she saw Señora Ginny's *novio* and Señor Simon pull her Judasina up into the branches of the pomegranate tree, higher and higher, until no one, not even Mikela who had made her and whose eyes could see long distances could see her. No one could read what the Virgin said. They acted like her Judasina was a *piñata*, something for a party. She was a saint. Just like San Pablo or Hermano Pedro or Santa Teresa or Santa Magdalena or Santa Verónica. They didn't seem to know, the way they behaved, that they were playing with one of God's favored people.

But Mikela did, and she had suddenly felt so tired. She had been following the Virgin's directions—and now this. With the *denuncia* way up there in the leaves of the pomegranate tree, how would the *extranjeras* ever hear what the Virgin was trying to tell them. The men had laughed together—and that reminded her of Natividad and Señorita Gwen's laughter, which had made her go into the house and make the Judasina in the first place.

So, she had left Señor Simon's garden pretending she was going back to work on the *alfombra*. Instead, taking Miguelito from Mamí Concepción, she had waved at all the women still working on the *alfombra*. She had made her way down the street, slowly, so slowly, until she heard Natividad and Señorita Gwen's laughter following her, everywhere she turned, as if it were a rope tied around her waist, cutting off her breath just the way the Judasina had. Mikela had tried to go faster and faster and faster. But the rope that was their laughter just kept pulling tighter and tighter. It felt worse than being up in the pomegranate tree.

But now Mikela was too tired to go on moving. She was just going to sit here on the steps of a stranger's house and wait for the dawn to come and then make her way to the church plaza to receive the regard of Jésus on his way to Calvary. And after that, she and Miguel would be on their own. She would take Miguelito's sword and slice through that rope of laughter—whoosh—just the way they had sliced through the rope that had tied Natividad's feet when their mother raised her to the roof beam and beat her with the broom. But this time there would be no one to catch Mikela. She would have to catch herself—and Miguelito too.

Mikela pushed fiercely against the waists and legs of the people. She pulled Miguel around so his head rested on her chest. She *had* to be there at the left hand corner of the church plaza when the Jésus Nazureño passed. She and Miguelito needed his blessing. After that, they would on their way. But without it, they would not be safe. Mikela knew this. She didn't need to have the Virgin keep repeating it every two minutes, but she did—just like a regular human mother, not one who had the privilege to make a home for God in her own body. Just a regular mother who had no faith in what had come out of her. Had Mikela *ever* not done what the Virgin suggested?

She was in her place, right at the corner of the plaza, even before it was completely light. The doors of the church were open, and she could see all the marchers going inside in their purple robes and white headdresses. And soon, out where she was, they began to carry out the small statues of St. Peter and Jésus at the column looking so sad and so kind. He stared down at Mikela and Miguelito for a very long time. Too long. It began to make Mikela feel very hopeless, and the kindness seemed to leave his face so that he looked like Natividad when her soul was missing. He had such a handsome halo of silver, but his hands were tied with rope and blood ran down his face and over the column, which was as white as the rope that bound him.

Mikela was pleased when the boys came out in their white pants and shirts and blue robes and red hats carrying gold trimmed banners in which she could read what everyone said as they condemned Jésus. She whispered some of the words aloud to Miguel because he was beginning to squirm and to press his mouth against her as if she could give him milk.

"*Sería una vergüenza, si nadie defendiese a este inocente.*" That was José de Arimatea, a friend of Jésus. It will be a shame if no one defends this innocent.

"*Las leyes no condenan a nadie sin justa rázon.*" That was Subito. The law doesn't condemn anyone without reason.

"*Por qué perdonarle durante tanto tiempo? Por qué no lo condenamos?*" That was Ptolomeo. Why pardon him during this time? Why don't we condemn him?

Mikela didn't know the stories of most of these people. She only knew about Pontius Pilate washing his hands. And the crowd screaming for Barabbas.

No one was screaming this morning. Not even Miguel, although he was making little bubbling noises that often meant he would start crying soon.

"*Por haber excitado al pueblo es digno de muerto.*" That was Diarbias. Because he incited the community, he should die.

"*Que sea justo o injusto, ha de morir, porque no guarda la Ley de nuestros padres.*" That was Sabintini. Whether it is just or unjust, he has to die because he did not keep the law of our fathers.

And Argnias said: "*No se condena a nadie sin haberle escuchado.*" Don't condemn anyone that you haven't heard.

And, of course, Pontius Pilate: "*Inocente soy de la sangre de este justo, y vosotros responderéis de ella.*" I am innocent of the blood of this just man, and you will answer for it.

Although she kept whispering the words to Miguelito, they made Mikela a little uneasy. She could understand how the people might want to punish someone who made trouble. At school, they punished girls who talked too much or made fun of the sisters behind their backs. And in the capital, if you said something bad to the police, oh, they could take you into the police station and pour glue over your hands so your fingers stuck together. But why would anyone want to punish the Son of God unless they wanted to punish God himself? How did they know that God would not punish them this time? God had punished them before. Just think of Noah. And Lot's wife. Eve. Adam. All the firstborn of Egypt.

The more Mikela thought about this, the more worried she became. She really didn't understand why God didn't even try to save his son. He knew what was happening. Of course, He had to know what was happening.

She understood how the Virgin couldn't stop what was happening, any more than her grandmother could stop what the soldiers did to her mother. The Virgin was just a human woman, even if she gave God the Son a good home inside her. Human people can't stop other people from killing or raping. But the Virgin didn't look away. She followed her son up the hill. She stood at the foot of the cross. She wore, for the rest of her days, that sword in her heart so she would always remember what she felt like at that moment.

Mikela wondered whether it was really a good idea for them to have Jésus look at them. It would give Jésus ideas it was really too late for—ideas of running away. Mikela imagined trying to help him. Getting up there and holding the cross up so he could slip out from under it. She would take his hand and he could run away with them. The Virgin would help them. She was just a human woman, the Virgin, so of course she wanted her son to live. Mikela was sure about his. No one ever said it was the Virgin's will that Jésus be crucified. It was God's plan, and because she was just a human woman, however immaculate, she had to go along. But that didn't mean she approved—that if someone brave like Mikela had stepped up and pushed up the cross and said, "Run!", the way the mothers told their children to run when the soldiers came, that the Virgin wouldn't cry out with Mikela. That she wouldn't help. That she wouldn't take her son's other hand and pull him along, however tired he was from all the cuts on his back and the weight of the cross.

There was a big noise coming from the church now and all the boys with the banners and the bearers with the little statues were starting to march down the street. Mikela stretched as high as she could, but she could see nothing. Mikela was so deep in her thoughts about saving Jésus when he came by that she didn't see Natividad and Señorita Gwen until it was too late, until they each had a hand on her shoulder.

"We've been looking for you everywhere," Natividad said. "You didn't ask. My breasts ache, they're so filled with milk."

She tried to take Miguel from her, but Mikela held him tight with both hands. The crowd pressed so close to them on all sides there was nothing Natividad could do. As soon as the procession went on its way, just as soon as Jésus passed by, even before the Virgin of the Sorrows followed, Mikela would slip away from them again. Natividad and Señorita Gwen both gripped her shoulders as if they knew what she was planning.

"I can't believe how many people there are," Señorita Gwen said. "Don't you want me to take the baby, Mikela? Lift him above their heads. For his own safety." She sounded a little scared, but that was just part of her trickiness. Even so, Mikela let her lift Miguel up because she wanted to be sure that Jésus saw him, that the Savior understood that after his death, his father made some big changes. That boys like Miguel had a chance now.

Mikela hopped up and down herself, trying to get Jésus' attention as the men, all dressed in purple robes, with white gloves, rocked from side to side in a motion like a boat, slowly, slowly moving forward. All around her, people were pressing closer and closer, trying to get to the place which Mikela had so carefully chosen under Mamí Concepción's guiding, the spot where Jésus could never miss you. Right there, by the lamppost.

But the crowd was very powerful and they kept pressing and pressing toward the big platform on which the men carried Jésus. Everyone wanted his attention.

"Lourdes," Señorita Gwen called out. She had lifted Miguel up across her left shoulder and was covering his body with her right hand. She held Mikela and Natividad's wrists with her left hand, as if they were prisoners. She was very strong.

"Help!" Señorita Gwen called out, holding their hands up. As if Mikela and Natividad had done something wrong. As if they had been trapped.

And Lourdes, the artist lady, was suddenly there, as were Mamí Concepción and Señora Wilma and Señora Marie, and even Señora Ginny, and they were all surrounding Mikela and Natividad like prisoners, while Señorita Gwen held Miguelito up there out of reach. Mikela held up her hands to him, but he was too high. She pointed to Jésus. It was the most she could do. Make sure they saw each other, Miguelito and Jésus. Did Jésus, Mikela wondered, have blue eyes? She knew that was a very bad thought, but she couldn't stop herself.

Did the Virgin, separated from her son by the crowds, feel the same way Mikela did surrounded by these foreign women who held her own Miguelito up in the air, dangerously out of reach? Did she wonder, just like Mikela was now, whose will it was wise to follow?

She could tell that all the women were scared by the power of the crowd. They held Natividad and Mikela trapped inside their circle because they did not want them to be at one with the other people who looked like them. Even Señora Wilma and Mamí Concepción were helping them in this plan. Even these new strange women who had joined the circle, who, like Mamí Concepción, were only indigenous to Antigua. Didn't they have their arms locked around the *extranjeras* and the lamppost? Hadn't Mamí Concepción told them, all the *extranjeras*, to come to this place and receive Jésus' blessing, making no distinction between these foreign women and people like herself or people like Mikela. No distinction at all.

Mikela could see that Señorita Gwen was as scared as she had been herself when she was hanging from the highest branches of the pomegranate tree. Señorita Gwen's face was so white all her freckles were visible. There were little drops of sweat around her eyes, like she had a fever. She held on to Miguelito so tightly that his skin puffed up around her hands although he didn't cry. Actually, he looked happy, crowing like a rooster and hitting Señorita Gwen's back like a drum. Maybe he was already feeling Jésus' blessing. Mikela could tell that, with all the people there, Jésus had not had time to look down and see her. So she was glad to see that Miguelito had been favored. It would be enough, she decided. She would have liked to have Jésus' eyes be able to find her too, to know that he would carry with him to Calvary the sight of Mikela, trapped there inside the ring of foreign women, unable—but so willing—to help him with his cross.

The Virgin was coming right after her son. But she only had eyes for her son at this time, so even if Mikela were able to jump above the heads of these big women, the Virgin would not look her way. But Señorita Gwen was so tall that perhaps Miguelito would receive the favor of a very small bit of the Virgin's attention on this day that was, every year, the most terrible of her life.

Mikela could see how Señora Wilma kept her head up as if hoping for just a brief glance from the Virgin. Perhaps, Mikela thought, she longed to have had children, but since she didn't she was contented now, as an old woman, to carry a little of the pain of the sword that pierced the Virgin's own body and soul.

Mikela knew that as soon as the procession passed by Señorita Gwen would try to run away with Miguelito on her shoulders, so Mikela had her arms out, moving this way and that inside the circle, ready to stop her, whatever direction Señorita Gwen might choose.

Señorita Gwen didn't even seem to notice Mikela. She kept staring at her step-mother. Señora Lourdes was talking to Señorita Gwen in English. What she said sounded very kind, but Mikela could tell it was some kind of plan and that it had to do with Miguelito. Her Miguelito. Natividad kept looking down at her chest, where the milk that was slipping from her nipples was making her blouse heavy although it did not show through the weaving. She seemed to be very happy inside the circle. Every now and then she would smile at Mikela as if Mikela shared her happiness, as if Mikela didn't know they were trapped there against their will.

Mikela pulled at Señorita Gwen's shirt and told her to give the baby back to Natividad. She knew Señorita Gwen wouldn't give the baby back to her, only to her sister. Señora Lourdes kept saying something to Señorita Gwen. And then Mikela began to understand that anything she did wouldn't matter, that these women, all these women, only had eyes for one another. They rocked back and forth, all their arms wrapped around each other.

"*Tranquilízate*," Mamí Concepción was saying to Gwen. Calm down.

"*Tranquilízate*," repeated one of the strange women from Antigua.

All of them pressing closer and closer together as the people on the street tried to move them out of the way so they could follow Jésus and his mother.

Miguelito beat on Señorita Gwen's head, while he lifted his head up to the sky that was now a nice clear blue. He knew Jésus had looked at him. He knew Jésus carried the picture of him there above the heads of the women, there, safe in his aunt Mikela's eyes, safe in Jésus' eyes, safe in a little attention from Jésus' mother.

Mikela lifted her hand once again to pull at Señorita Gwen's shirt, but Señora Wilma said, "*Por favor, mijita*. Please, my child. Leave her in peace. She isn't your enemy. You are going to hurt all of us if you don't stop."

But how could Mikela, trapped inside this circle they had made, invisible to Jésus and the Virgin, hurt them?

"All they want to do is help us," Natividad said. She was watching the milk weight down her blouse as if the milk came from a fountain, not from her own breasts, her own heart. She had a foolish smile on her face.

"Their ways are not our ways," Mikela warned her sister. "Never forget that." But her voice didn't sound sure, like the Virgin's. It didn't sound kind. It sounded like their mother's just before the sorrows made her crazy, and hearing this made Mikela reach her arms up high, so high, as if in celebration, as if she were reaching for the moon, as if she were reaching for her sister, hanging feet first from the rafters, or her Judasina hanging from the neck in the pomegranate tree, as if she were terrified and trying to hold the danger off just a little while longer, as if she were a small child herself wanting to be held. The sound of that voice made Mikela reach and reach and reach, for a thousand reasons, out of herself.

"Believe me, *mijita*," Señora Wilma said. "We are all here to help you.

To make sure no harm will come."

But Mikela knew these were all human women, women who had not, like the Virgin, ever made a home for God. So how could they, any more than her own mother, make promises? She looked helplessly at Miguelito, so far out of reach, and she thought, here I am, trapped among them.

But Miguelito threw back his head and slapped his hands on Señorita Gwen's forehead and crowed with delight as the crowds moved the circle of women back and forth, back and forth, and Mikela knew that he was both what was most vulnerable and what was most strong about her. That as soon as she held him in her arms again, he would become her sword, and that the Virgin, unlike the women here, made promises she could keep. And she had, hadn't she, said they would always be together, she and Natividad and their *arcangel* Miguel who had come to heal with his peace that was sharp as a sword and sweeter than any song a mother could sing.

Oh, Mikela reached, she reached and reached for her sword, her sweet song. She acted as if she still believed what the Virgin had planned for the three of them. She acted as if she still believed because there really was no alternative, there had never been any alternative.

SECTION IV
GOD IN THE ROUND

You have loved us first, O God, alas! We speak of it in terms of history as if You have only loved us first but a single time, rather than without ceasing. You have loved us first many times and every day and our whole life through. When we wake up in the morning and turn our soul toward you—you are the first—you have loved us first; if I rise at dawn and in the same second turn my soul toward you in prayer, you are there ahead of me, you have loved me first. When I withdraw from the distractions of the day and turn my soul toward you, you are the first and forever. And yet we always speak ungratefully, as if you have loved us first only once.

S. Kierkegaard

THE SPIRIT OF ADOPTION
(Wilma)

Our religion teaches us that the wounds of Christ are our salvation, that they opened to us the infinite love of God, that it pours, more tumultuous and abundant than blood, out of those ruptures in his skin, his integrity. The whole spirit world, as I know it, pours through those wounds.

Concepción, when she saw the pressure building, took me to see the Black Christ. I had responsibilities I told her. To Señora Rosemary, Señora Ginger. And to those girls whose fates are being tossed about like juggling balls between all these well-intentioned women from abroad. They do not see that they are nailed, the three of them, to the cross that is our history. They see those children as free. Separate. Untouched. They keep talking about adoption as if it were something purifying, abstract. They don't understand that, should they, alone or together, adopt the girls, they are choosing to be nailed themselves to the cross of our history. Who, in their right mind, would choose that if they could escape it?

They are not as strong, these grown women, as the girls who are not yet afraid to live inside their wounds.

"And you," Señor Walter tells me. "You have that courage too, Wilma. You can live inside your wounds."

My cousin Concepción wanted us to go see the Black Christ so I could see how much grace poured out from the wounds made by our history. It was here, in the eighties, that the presidents of all the war-torn countries in the area gathered to pray for peace. It was here the pilgrims came after our peace accords were signed four years ago. But peace does not seal a wound. Didn't our resurrected Lord wander around with his wounds still bright, still oozing?

"Let us know your wounds, Wilma," Señor Walter says to me. "We on the other side can make you real inside them. Free inside them. We are not afraid to live there with you."

I have never asked anything of the dead in all these years of visitations. I make a space, a large, clean, resounding space inside me for them and for those who seek them. But I keep myself separate. From them and from the ones they wish to reach. I don't know how I would survive otherwise.

"To live inside the wound is to live inside God's womb," Señor Walter tells me. "It is to be touched, held, rocked by the deepest waters. It is peace."

He's wrong, of course. God has no womb. Only the Virgin does, and it only once proved safe harbor for the divine, but don't tell me it was untroubled.

I know what it means to live inside the wound and I don't know why Señor Walter keeps inviting me to die. I, who tended him so faithfully in those last years when he could not move or speak.

"Because you did," he tells me. "You helped me live into my death and I, I am inviting you to live into your life again, Wilma."

"To what end?" I ask him. It is a cry from my deepest heart, but even I cannot hear it as anything but a convulsive pressure, as if this torrent of voices inside me is determined to tear me open from the inside, pour out.

"Lucas," Señor Walter said. "Tell me about Lucas."

At first I am furious, for no one, no one, has dared speak the name of my son to me for many many years.

When Lucas comes to see me, he has not gained or lost a single month of his life. He is always nineteen, the same age I was when I gave birth to him. He tells me these days that with the peace accords everything is *arreglado*, put back in place. He was always credulous, my son. He could not believe that the world couldn't be changed, that deaths, any death, including his, could take place without reason, without redemption flowing from them just as they did from Christ's own sacrifice. I blame the priests for this. Not him, never Lucas. Not even now.

My son is perfect in my eyes. He always was. He always will be. His credulousness makes me ache with protectiveness. I would draw him back into my womb when I see that *look of trusting courage on his face as he tells me, "I have to join the guerillas, Mami. Don't you see? Who but us, people like us, can protect them, speak for them?" The them he spoke of were indigenous children and women like Natividad's mother and her mother's mother.*

Protect them, he meant, from people like his own father.

Agustín always blamed the Jesuits, and me because at that point in my life I was a believer, for Lucas' disloyalty and the final catastrophe. But I blame my son's credulousness. Lucas always believed what was in front of his eyes. He saw what was happening at the universities, in the city. He went up to the mountains and he saw what this policy of his father and the other officers meant. He saw the bodies for what they truly were. Life. Life lost and crying out for redemption. Bodies without a tomb, a womb, of meaning.

And Lucas believed, as well, when he saw it for himself, saw what their very presence, those credulous boys who joined the guerrillas, did to the people they wanted to save. He believed what he saw. All those deaths, more deaths, he couldn't stop—all that carnage that just the smell of his own presence in a village justified. They say he disobeyed orders, that he saw the army lining up the villagers, among them his novia and her family, and he couldn't stand by, he couldn't stand the meaninglessness and he rushed down from the mountain, endangering all his comrades, and not changing a damn thing. He just added his own body to the mass grave. The wound. Out of his own free will. Added it to those who he realized now were being sacrificed against their will for him and his credulousness. He wasted his death, my son did.

"Mami," he says to me gently, so gently. "It was all I had to give."

"It wasn't yours to throw away like that," I tell him. "You threw mine away with yours. And it changed nothing, Lucas. Nothing."

"It changed him," Lucas tells me. "You cannot tell me it didn't change him." He's talking about his father.

He is still so credulous, my son. It is as if he believed that Jésus' sacrifice changed God himself. He was too young, my son will always be too young, to understand men.

What changed Agustín was not the loss of his son, my beautiful black-eyed, honey-skinned boy with his ravishing smile. What changed him was the shame he felt Lucas brought down on him by his disobedience. What changed Agustín was the contempt I felt from the day I learned of my son's death for all Agustín was and had been and ever would be. A contempt I feel to this day, no matter how many times Agustín comes to visit me, his mouth always half-open, just as it was when the bullets caught him in the army jeep a year after Lucas' death.

These foreign women who read the stories in the newspapers, who came here after the terrible massacres were all done—they have no idea how many people come to the Church of the Spirits not to talk to their dead but to silence them for a day or an hour. For the dead never stop asking, just as the living do: Why? Their loyalties are no clearer than mine. Or Lucas'. They are haunted by images. A knife slitting a woman's belly, dragging a spitted baby out. Or slitting the belly of a man as he is being burned to death and the fat pouring out in a golden torrent.

They are haunted by the hands that hung at their sides when the soldiers took the young girls inside the houses and the screams started. Haunted by the children they know still dream of their starving nights and days in a cave slicker and darker than the womb waiting for help that never, ever came. And still, they are dead. Whether they were heroic or craven, the bodies still lie, by the thousands, unidentified, in mass graves. And they can make no sense of it to help their children, their grandchildren.

"Why?" I screamed at Agustín. "What Devil has entered your head—and the heads of all your brother officers—that you think there will no be consequences to you not only here on earth but for all time?"

"My conscience is clear," he said. "I had my orders. They were a danger to the state."

"God help you," I said. "I won't. In any way. In this life or the next one."

"Grief has driven you mad," he told me calmly. His only child was lying at the bottom of a mass grave in some tiny pueblo in the mountains, his chest holding, like the secret of life, a bullet from an Army revolver. One just like the one Agustín still dared carry.

And then, as if he hadn't heard a word I said, when he returned on his next leave, he brought the baby with him. He came to me in Lucas' room, where I now slept. He showed me the little girl wrapped in a bright blue rebozo.

He told me the baby was ours. It was Lucas' daughter. He had heard through some of the soldiers that the baby was Lucas' and he had followed the trail of the villagers himself as they fled up into the hills. He and his men. And when he found the villagers, he asked them which one of the babies had been fathered by a guerrilla.

A guerrilla. A romantic boy of nineteen with a big heart.

So what were they to do? Which mother decided to sacrifice her baby so that her other children could go free? The soldiers, Agustín's men, stood there with their guns pointed, just as ready to murder them as the earlier patrol had been to murder the rest of the village—and my crazy, culpable son who, at least, knew his sin.

So, the mother who had made the decision tried to barter the baby. She asked that all the other villagers be able to leave and then she would give him the baby. But as soon as she spoke, she knew she had been crazy to do so. All she had to do was look in my husband's eyes.

Crazy to let her baby go, crazy to sacrifice all of them. So she screamed for her children, for everyone to run, and they did—for what little good it did them. They ran as they had just two weeks ago, ran as fast and as far as children and women who have not eaten for days can.

And she stood her ground, for there really was no difference, was there, and Agustín came and grabbed the baby from her, ordering his men to kill who they could. And my son's father, his granddaughter in one arm, raised his revolver and shot her mother, like a horse or a cow, between the eyes.

And then he brought the baby to me. To make amends.

How do I know this? The mother told me herself. Told me over and over again. But only years later. After Agustín was dead. She was looking for the baby. She wanted to know what I had done with her daughter.

What did she expect me to do with her? I gave her away. As soon as Agustín left, I put the baby in the car with me and I drove to an orphanage a half-day's journey away and I acted to be exactly what I was, a well-bred lady from the city with an indigenous baby in her care.

My maid, I told them. A little girl from the countryside. She had given birth to the baby and then abandoned her. Of course, I couldn't be expected to do anything more than I was doing. They asked me the name of the mother, and I made up a name so common they would give up before very long trying to locate her. I knew with this story the baby could never be adopted. That someone would have to make up a story very like the real one if they were ever to get her adopted. I wanted us all to have to keep coming back to the truth, however we tried to escape it. I never wanted to see that baby again. Never feel the softness of its skin. Hear its soft cry against my chest. Hear my own heart quiet at the pressure of its little mouth moving hungrily across my neck. I wanted nothing to do with her. Nothing.

"You did what?" Agustín screamed at me when he came home.

I told him I'd left her on the side of the road, up in the mountains, after I'd crushed her head with a stone. That is what I told him. I told him exactly what it felt like to feel the skull cave in. How I had kicked a little gravel over the body. Covered it with some dusty branches. I told him in such detail he did not say anything. To begin with. He just went out into the garden and began to hit the wall.

He came back in. "You did that to your own grandchild?"

"I want my son," I told him. "I don't want you. I don't want God. I don't want life. I certainly don't want some worm-ridden indigenous infant. I want my son. And I want you, Agustín, to burn in hell for eternity and I want to hear every scream, every single scream you utter."

"You're crazy," he said. He tried to sound sure of himself, but I could see I frightened him. I frightened him more than he himself did. Isn't that crazy, really crazy? And absolutely credible. He feared me more than he feared himself.

He always slept, when he came back to our house, with his pistol, safety off, by his bed—and, if he had been doing something particularly unforgivable—with his knife in his hand.

And I would sit up in Lucas' room, a knife in my own hand, just in case he thought we were young enough, he and I, to replace Lucas.

"Why," he keeps asking me. "Why did you sacrifice her too?"

He needed to feel that there was a world uncontaminated by his actions. That I was that world.

"Why?" Lucas asks me now. "Why didn't you keep her?"

"She wasn't you," I say.

"But she could have consoled you. She had no one else."

"I wouldn't give your father the satisfaction," I said.

"For that?" Lucas asks me, and I can see that he fears me too. "Just for that?"

I can see that all these years he has believed the lies I told his father. I am so angry, I refuse to disabuse him either.

"Yes," I tell my son. "Just for that. I am not a teat to be tucked into every thirsty baby's mouth. I'm not a heart that opens at any man's whim."

"What are you, Mami?" he asks me.

"I am your inconsolable mother, Lucas," I tell him. "I am your inconsolable mother."

So, you see, I understand these girls that God has sent to us. I understand everything that brought them here. I understand their mother who tried to beat the war out of their souls and her own. I understand Natividad, who would sell her son for a half-filled bottle of glue if Mikela weren't looking. I understand why the blue of that baby's eyes is enough to chill the soul of the arcangel he's named for.

"And you understand, don't you, why they have come to you, Mami," Lucas says. "There is a second chance."

His eyes are black as tar, my son's, and still they are filled with light. My son. My credulous son.

"You have that courage too," Señor Walter says. "You too can live inside the *wounds, Wilma."*

"Please, Mamí," Lucas says.

Every night now he comes to me—after all these anguishing years of absence. "I ask this for you, Mamí. For us. I can't rest until you can. There is a second chance. Take it, for both of us."

That is all I ever wanted for him. A second chance. A second life.

"It's up to you, Wilma," Señor Walter tells me. "It's all up to you. Invite him back. Choose to live, like him, like me, like those girls who so need you, inside the wound of history."

I don't know what is right. I don't know what is wrong. All I know is my son has returned to me and I will not lose him, I will not lose him a second time.

Chapter 16
BURIAL

Ginger thought it would be best if she left while Rosemary was resting. She knew her friend would try, for all the right reasons, to hold her back. But she didn't want to wait. She really wanted this new adventure. And she was tired of the morphine. She wanted to be awake again.

But to get there, the voice said, *perhaps you'd like a painless transition. There's more where that morphine came from.*

"I'm not afraid," Ginger said. "I know what's waiting for me."

Such certainty, the voice said with a bit of an edge to her voice. *Puts you in a small, select company. Most of us wonder what's awaiting us on the other side. Don't you have one iota of curiosity?*

"Not really," Ginger murmured. "But I wouldn't mind having it come quickly." A moan escaped her. The pain really was spectacular, even muffled by the doubled dose of morphine.

Gwen entered the room, her face tight with anxiety.

"Can I do anything for you?" she asked.

"You already gave me my pills, dear," Ginger answered.

"They're not enough. Obviously they're not enough," Gwen said. "You're still suffering. I heard you."

"God never gives us more than we can bear."

God may not, but life is a little freer with the agony, the voice said.

"It isn't more than I can bear," Ginger said again. She admired the wonderfully white, fresh skin of the young woman. Her eyes rested on her lovely face, the sharp chin, the freckles standing out against the skin, even whiter than normal with fear. Gwen's long red hair tumbled in unruly curls over her back. Ginger reached out to touch it. It looked so soft, so alive.

"My mother had hair the color of yours," Ginger said. "But she never let me touch it. Even as a child. I began to imagine it was hot as fire, that there was something magic and dangerous about it. Finally I asked my older sister. It was so pedestrian, really. My mother had a dry scalp and didn't want the dandruff to show. That's all. Such beautiful mysteries we make."

"You can touch mine if you want," Gwen said.

"It's time," Ginger said.

"I know."

Ginger looked at her carefully. She was so young, so alive. Had Ginger ever been that free?

"Will you help me?"

Gwen sat down on the chair beside Ginger's bed, her elbows on the mattress, her hands clasped together, her hair falling over her cheeks. She closed her eyes like a child at bedtime prayers. She took a deep breath.

"How?"

Why this young woman, Ginger wondered, and not Ginny? Not Wilma, who was as tough as they came? Why this girl whose skin went a white so complete it held the blueness of arctic ice in it when Ginger asked her the question.

Something is being completed here. Something new is taking shape.

Ginger wondered whose voice she had ever heard that had such a music to it, such a store of compassion. Her older sister, Diana, singing to herself as she played dolls? Her grandmother? Or could it possibly have been her own voice singing her daughters to sleep?

She wondered who would be there to greet her. George, without a doubt. So it wasn't true that she had no curiosity. She wanted to see how he'd changed.

"There was a container of pills on the bureau," she told Gwen. "Another inside the first drawer, under the nightgowns."

Wilma had brought the second bottle to her yesterday. "It is a gift," Wilma had told Ginger. "From Señor George. He misses you very much. He says you will know when the time is right."

In some ways, Ginger wished she could have had a last word or two with her daughters, Janet and Betsy. She *did* want to be missed. But Rosemary's frustration—and the white, white willingness of Gwen would have to satisfy her.

Gwen brought the two bottles over to her. Her face was beaded with sweat. "Are you sure you wouldn't rather wait? Wouldn't rather have Rosemary or Wilma or Ginny with you?" she asked Ginger.

"No." Ginger stared at the young woman, so beautiful, so surreally beautiful, in the late afternoon light—like a Rossetti angel. "But if you are afraid or feel it is wrong, just drop the bottles here by my hand. Leave me a glass of water." Now that she had said this, Ginger felt an urgency that was overwhelming, a neediness that was mortifying. She *wanted* those pills, that water. She wanted to be able to get up and get them for herself. She didn't want to be judged by this young woman and found wanting. She didn't want to be held back.

"I'm not turning my back on life," she said, hating herself for the pleading tone of her voice. She looked down at her hands lying so still on the bed covers. How did they come to be so large? So crude? Her arms felt heavy, too heavy. What if she couldn't lift herself enough to swallow? What if she couldn't open these irritating new childproof bottles? What if Rosemary woke up and put a stop to everything?

"I know you're not," Gwen said. "I know you're not trying to punish anyone."

What's holding you *back*, then, Ginger thought angrily. Do you want me to beg?

Give her time, the voice said quietly. *She's going to live with this all her life.*

"My mother," Gwen said slowly, "I believe my mother took her own life. She didn't need to. She had cancer, but it was in remission. I think she decided I wasn't going to be there when the time came." She gripped the bottles so tightly her pale hands began to redden. There were no tears in her eyes, just this bleak clarity.

Ginger touched the young woman's clasped hands. "We both know that wasn't true—what your mother feared. You would have been there for her until the very end."

"I know," Gwen said. She looked unseeingly at Ginger's yellowed, knobby hand, which covered her own and the pill bottles. "I don't know if it would have been the right thing, but I would have been there. I would have given up everything to be there."

"Will you be here with me, then?" Ginger asked. Oh, her voice sounded rough and mournful as a crow's. Wicked.

"Yes," Gwen said. "I don't want to see you suffer any more. I didn't want her to feel so alone. I never wanted her to feel so alone. All my life, I kept trying, you know. I kept trying. But it was like there was a hole there. She couldn't *know* love. My mother couldn't *know* love. She called it every other word in the book—contempt, pity, indifference, obligation, passive-aggression, hypocrisy, fear, submission, dependency."

"But I do," Ginger said. "I know love. I know that what you are doing for me is loving."

"But what about what you are asking of me?" Gwen said slowly, as if each word were a piece of broken glass she were trying to expel from her mouth without cutting herself. "Is that loving?"

"Yes," Ginger said with conviction. "I am helping you set something powerful and dangerous to rest. I am freeing you to move forward."

"I am only twenty-three and I will have two lives on my hands. Two lives." Gwen's eyes widened, her pupils dilated in the darkened room until she seemed as drugged as Ginger.

"Hold me," Ginger said. "That's all I'm asking. Just hold me until it's over. I *do* know what I'm asking of you, Gwen. And it is huge. Huge. I am asking you to love me into my death. It is what I know you wanted to do for your own mother."

"Are you *sure*?" Gwen asked. "Are you absolutely sure?"

"Absolutely." Ginger patted the young woman's hands to get her to release the bottles.

She had wanted it all to be so clean, so symmetrical. So liberating. But in the end, Ginger couldn't open the pill bottles, so Gwen did. She couldn't keep lifting the pills one by one to her mouth, so Gwen did. She couldn't lift the water glass, so Gwen did, murmuring constantly, "Are you sure? We can stop. Just tell me what you want."

Ginger, resting against Gwen's young, strong shoulder, safe inside her arms, looked out into the vivid courtyard. "I want to move on," she said. "Into the next life. The right one."

And she experienced it, that life to come, right there, in the delicate fragrance of Gwen's perfume, the mesmerizingly light touch of the young woman's red hair brushing her neck and cheeks, in the coolness of Gwen's tears falling on her scalp, in the firmness of Gwen's embrace, in the way the room, her whole consciousness, darkened, widened and became unerringly grand.

"Amen" she whispered. "Amen, my love."

"People kept wondering what the glue was between us. Believe me, I've asked myself too," Rosemary told Ginny. "Sometimes I think it was because we didn't *like* each other so very much. Her piety drove me bananas. And she never approved of the collective. But we liked being at odds. It made us feel alive—that someone cared enough about us to disapprove of what we were doing. You don't know how hard that is to find at our age. Someone who has expectations of you."

"So," Ginny asked. "Do you want to give her a funeral she'd approve of or one that will make her squirm in her coffin?"

"Both," Rosemary said, the stupid tears beginning to run again. "I want to give her both. I want to hear her saying, 'Too much, Rosemary. Must you always be so heavy handed.' And I want to hear her saying, 'Oh—' You know, that dry little 'oh' she used whenever something felt just right to her."

"Oh," Ginny said.

"You don't know what you're saying, I expect." The bitterness in Rosemary's voice startled them both. "Too young to have a good friend die on you. Never had children to grow beyond."

"But I bet I get the gist," Ginny said dryly. "Hard to get to my age—especially as a priest—and not have attended a few funerals." Her mild aggressiveness startled Ginny—but she could feel Rosemary relax with it. She could feel herself do the same. Maybe friend was just a word Rosemary used for favored adversary.

"What do you think will make Ginger feel flattered? What will make her squirm?"

Rosemary wanted as authentic as possible an Antigua funeral. She wanted to hire the musicians used during Holy Week to play some of those strange little marches. And flowers. Not only all over the coffin, but enough to leave traces on all the streets. She didn't want her friend's departure to go unnoticed.

Ginny was relieved that Rosemary seemed able to stay focused.

When she had come over five hours earlier following a call from Wilma, Rosemary couldn't stop pacing the length of the portico.

"She didn't do it herself," she had said immediately. "The signs weren't there. I've been at enough death beds. I would recognize them. They told me she was sleepy, and when I looked in last night, that's exactly what it looked like. Gwen was sitting on the bed with her. Just sitting there. I was touched. Touched in the head. You probably all had a hand in it."

"Hand in what?" Ginny had asked. "What are you suggesting here."

Rosemary's face had been deeply flushed. So was her chest. Ginny couldn't get a feel whether it was anger or grief that was fueling the physical response.

While Wilma and she had waited for Rosemary to stop pacing, Wilma had said placidly, "Do not be concerned about Señora Rosemary. She is just a little hurt that Señora Ginger left without a formal good-bye. But it is an irritation to her, not a genuine wound. Señora Rosemary does not like to say good-bye. To anyone she has loved. She would have told Señora Ginger it wasn't time yet. We all knew that."

"She felt left out," Ginny had chided Wilma.

"Best friends are sometimes not the people we turn to at those moments when we must be most true to ourselves," Wilma said with a shrug. "As a priest, you must know this. It was Señora Ginger's choice to make, you know."

Ginny did know. And part of her, like Wilma, had been obscurely pleased at Rosemary's mild come-uppance. But she was also worried about the physical change in Rosemary. So, Ginny was relieved that Rosemary several hours later, focused on creating a most exquisitely ambivalent funeral in honor of her exquisitely ambivalent friendship, was quickly regaining her naturally autocratic style.

"I've put in a call to Ginger's daughters. Told them the laws here require burial within 24 hours. They considered cremation, but decided against it. Honestly, I think they were afraid they might be asked to carry the ashes back. I told them I'd take care of everything, and I will. I hope my own children aren't as put out by my death. It's as if they expected their mother to die on a Friday so they could have a Saturday stay-over discount. My estimation of Ginger rose with every minute I talked to them. She never once complained, never said anything that wasn't flattering about either of them."

"They will want a large part in designing the service, I'd expect." Ginny was thumbing through the prayer book to review the funeral service.

"They asked me to make all the decisions." Rosemary appeared to be thrown off balance by the lack of resistance. "They'll come in late tonight. Stay in a hotel for two nights—to give them time to review her will and her belongings and attend the funeral. In that order. Fly out first thing the next morning. I offered to have them stay here, but they became animated for the first time. They wouldn't hear of it. They never came to visit Ginger. She always went back to see them. 'For the convenience of the families,' she always said. But I wonder what they imagined. That she lived in a thatched hut? That *I* do?"

"So, let's plan the service *you'd* like, Rosemary, and let them add or subtract a little as they see fit." Ginny stretched, still feeling luxurious from the long afternoon she and David had spent in his hotel before he caught a taxi to the airport. When she'd returned to Marie's apartment, where she was going to stay from now on, she had found a note from Wilma.

"No one knew where to find you," Marie had said with a smile. "Not me. Not Simon."

Ginny's cheeks had flushed a little, but not very much. She was still so lulled by all those hours of the sweetest touch.

"We are most happy for you. All your friends here. But especially Simon."

"It was just a weekend," Ginny said.

"But sometimes weekends lead to lifetimes. And sometimes they contain a lifetime, just so, you know, like those bubbles of glass. You shake them and the snow falls on the little house. Every time you hold the globe in your hands, the snow falls, just so, on the little house. All is as it should be." Marie had looked at her so contentedly, it was as if she rather than Ginny had been the one trysting in a hotel.

Although she had responded immediately to the note, Ginny had not felt ready to look at Ginger. But when Wilma opened the door to the cabaña and she saw Ginger so carefully laid out in her best nightgown, her sparse hair lovingly brushed, the sheets pulled flat around her, her bony hands crossed over her chest, Ginny had felt a real pang of loss for this uncomfortably pious woman who would not for the life of her forget that Ginny had been a priest. Ginny, however much she had resisted it, had felt held in place by Ginger's opposing tendencies. Her fondness for the lulling familiarity of the liturgies of her childhood. Her fastidiousness about the rituals and her laissez-faire about ecclesiastical authority.

But the last thing Ginger said to Ginny really shook her. The night they made the carpet, Ginger had watched, tucked snugly in a wheelchair Simon had borrowed. It was often impossible to tell if she was dozing. So, Ginny had jumped when Ginger spoke up.

"You don't think, my dear, that I don't know this is all cant, dated, holds us back? I hold onto it because its my only way in. But there are other women out there, even women my age, who hunger for other ways. Maybe, now that this door is closed to you, you'll be one of those trailblazers. For you have it, Ginny. You have the fire of God in you. No one can come close to you and not feel warmed by it."

Ginger had looked at Ginny so coolly out of those yellowed eyes. Four in the morning. A steady stream of half-drunk pilgrims passing them by. Ginger propped up on all sides with pillows. The stunning carpet of sawdust and rose petals spreading, perfect, ready for the marchers, at their feet. And Ginny had looked steadily back, moved, unbelievably moved. By the wish. The distance. The setting.

"I'm not saying he was right in what he did, that painter friend of yours. But he seems devoted."

"Now that the damage is done."

"Yes, there is that. But it's just the church—not God—you're separated from. The fire is in you, Ginny, there's no one, no one in the world who can quench it—except you. For all our sakes, I hope you won't. And it's up to you, as it is for each of us, to be true, ruthlessly true to what truly feeds it. Fires, like people, die without nourishment."

And again she had held Ginny's gray eyes with her eerie yellow ones. "Look at you," Ginger had said with a smile. "Just look at you, Ginny Fox. Brought to tears by an old woman."

She knows who you are, Ginny-gin-gin, the voice said. *She sees what you see. And still she believes. Still she believes. In you.*

"Would you mind," Ginny asked Rosemary, tapping the table to get her attention, "if I used my own words at the service. I know Ginger loved the prayer book. But there was something she said in those last days that makes me feel she would like something simpler, closer to the bone."

Rosemary looked at her, blinking back tears. "She liked all those pompous words—grievous and erred and heartily. I always expected to see her eyes rolling in ecstasy as soon as she uttered them. But they never did anything for me. It's not going to bother me if you drop them. Maybe you want to get a rise out of Ginger yourself."

"But you see, I loved—love—the liturgy just as much as she did. And for the same reasons. That is why she could ask me to stop. She knew I would understand."

And you do, don't you, Ginny-gin-gin? You understand she reached out to you. She helped you take your next step. You understand she took it with you.

"I miss her," Rosemary said. "She isn't even twelve hours dead and I miss her more than I ever expected."

Ginny took Rosemary's hand in hers. "She misses you too. Just as much. It surprises her just as much as it surprises you."

"I guess that's some kind of consolation," Rosemary said. "Do you want to listen to the marches I'm considering? I want them to bring the neighbors to their windows wondering who the hell we have in there."

"She left us in the lurch, you know. It wasn't the other way around," Janet, Ginger's older daughter said. She looked as aggressively around the table as someone so determinedly nice and nondescript could.

"She was a civil servant for thirty years, for goodness sake," Janet went on, accompanied by the eager nods of her sister. "Nothing changed when she divorced, life was just as before. When she remarried, George seemed just like her. They even *looked* alike. Blonde hair. That pale white skin that never tans. Who would have expected, once they retired, they would move to a foreign country? Never do the same thing two days in a row. Speak Spanish. Never consult us."

"We liked our mother the way she was," Ginger's second daughter added. Rosemary tried for a minute to recall her name then gave up. "We wanted to live lives just like hers. Without the divorce, of course. I mean, I work for the city school system and Janet works for the state comptroller. We're dependable people."

Rosemary glanced at her watch. Why had no one arrived for the wake? Lourdes and Gwen were to come. So were Ginny and Marie. "I can't do it," Rosemary had said to each of them, "without someone, more than one, actually, to censor me." But they weren't here and she was afraid of what she might say. To control herself she imagined Ginger's daughters' expressions when they heard the funeral marches tomorrow morning. She was particularly pleased with the tuba. The musicians had given her a little preview and she knew it would make Ginger, wherever she was, cringe. But so would her daughters.

"It wasn't the same at all having her come up twice a year to visit. We wanted someone to call when the kids had a fever—or chicken pox," Ginger's younger daughter said, pulling her sweater tightly across her extravagant chest.

Betsy. Her name was Betsy, Rosemary finally remembered. Where had scrawny Ginger found the genes for these four-square farm hands?

"Your mother remained an ardent Episcopalian until the minute she died," Rosemary said. "We had to pry the prayer book from her grasp."

"We're Methodist, like our father," Janet said.

"What I'm trying to say is that she didn't change. She always balanced her checkbook, never missed a scheduled showing at the cultural center, always arrived on time, handled the books at Home Is Where the Heart Is whenever they discovered something fishy. She was very respected here. She organized a church, for goodness sake."

"Why couldn't she have stayed in Cincinnati?" Betsy asked.

Rosemary was opening her mouth to say the unspeakable when Wilma showed Simon and Lourdes, Gwen, Marie and Ginny in simultaneously.

With the reinforced audience, Ginger's daughters renewed their lament about their mother's desertion. Lourdes glanced over at Gwen briefly, a smile brushing her lips.

"At least she knew what she wanted," Lourdes said after hearing how Ginger had run off to Antigua with George after only a month's warning. Ginger and her husband had come to Antigua for a visit, fell in love, returned to Cincinnati and sold everything and moved .

"It's hard at any age to have parents change," Gwen said. "I mean, I hadn't lived with my Dad for years, but when he married Lourdes, it was still a shock for me. My mom and I, we'd become a world to ourselves. I don't know why I didn't imagine the same for him."

"After twenty years, thirty, you build up expectations about a person," Janet said.

Janet had fat hair. That was the only way Rosemary could describe it. Each strand was fuller of itself than any hair she had ever seen. It was a nondescript beige brown, but gleamed with self-satisfaction. Her younger sister had that wispy hair of Ginger's, although it was a funny color, a little purple, like real mahogany. It made her scalp look almost iridescently white.

"If any of you had children, you'd understand," Betsy said with a little huff of frustration, her mahogany curls atremble. She seemed a little more sensitive than her sister to the chilly reception.

"Some of us do," Lourdes said.

"And how have they taken the news that you've just kicked off your traces, dropped out?"

"Your mother *retired* here," Rosemary said. "Whatever is the big deal? Are you feeling guilty you never came down to see her? Don't be. She had lots of people here who enjoyed her company. Who understood the choice she made."

"It isn't very difficult to understand, is it?" Gwen asked. "I mean, I've been down here three weeks, and I don't think I'm ever going back."

"You talk as if your mother was running away—from you," Marie observed. She smiled as she made a space on the couch for Mikela and the baby to come and join her. "But most of us, we are not running away from, we are running towards. We see something so beautiful, so right for us, something that let us know ourselves in a way that is both very new and very familiar. We fall in love with the country that give us this feeling. What is so surprising?"

"We live in the largest and most beautiful and most prosperous country in the world," Janet said. "What could top that?"

"My countrymen, they too asked me the same. You know how the French are—even the United States they see as beneath. But *this* place, with the terrible history, the poverty, the garbage filling all the ravines, the earthquakes and typhoid and dengue and corruption and terrible cooking. Why here?"

"And what did you tell them," Betsy asked, while her older sister stared stonily over all their heads.

"I say what every lover say: Because. Just because."

"We loved her, whatever you might think. We asked her, every time she visited, to see reason and come back. But she wouldn't. She just wouldn't. I had a home all picked out for her. And after we heard the diagnosis, a hospice," Betsy said.

"No one is asking you to justify yourselves," Lourdes said.

"There's nothing to justify," Janet said.

"Do you want to see your mother?" Rosemary asked to ease the tension.

"I would rather remember her the way she was," Janet said.

When, Rosemary wanted to ask, but bit her tongue, and left Janet to Lourdes and Ginny and Marie's more patient ministrations, while she and Gwen took Ginger's second daughter in to see her. What, Rosemary wondered, would Betsy think if she knew about the boy Ginger had given up. Would she and her sister use this for the rest of their life to stoke their anger? Their anger was a kind of love, she understood. Understood better than she wanted. How often did her own children come to see her? Worse, how often did she go to visit them? Could she have ever imagined, in the midst of all that frantic family life, that a whole new era awaited her with Walter. Thank goodness Ginger had had her George.

"I was planning to come down as soon as school was out and insist she come back with me," Betsy said with a sob. "It hasn't been easy. Not with my in-laws."

"She died the way she wanted to," Gwen said. She put her arm around Ginger's burly daughter. "I promise you that."

Rosemary looked reprovingly at the young woman. How dare she, only three weeks here, speak with such assurance about Rosemary's friend. But she did. Gwen glanced at Betsy and Rosemary as if they both needed this reassurance—and as if she were completely qualified to give it.

"She was a very special woman, your mother," Gwen said, taking Betsy's hands in hers. "I can see why you would have wanted her to live near you. My own mom just died last year, and you don't know what I'd give to have her just around the corner. You really don't know. But your mother, she understood that. She really did. What I'd give to have my mother back. So I'm sure she knew what she was asking of you was very big. And I'm sure she wouldn't have asked it if she didn't absolutely have to. This country has a magic to it—for some people. It makes you feel more real, more yourself. Just like Marie said."

"I can't see it," Betsy said, touching Ginger's eyelids with her pink, perfectly manicured nails.

"But your mother could. Just the same way she could see you and Janet. You wouldn't believe the wonderful things she said about you every time she returned from her visits," Rosemary said.

And meant them, Rosemary, the voice chided. *She meant them.*

There is no explaining love, Rosemary thought, assailed, yet again, by a wave that was equal parts grief and exasperation. It was going to be a long, a very long evening.

"Thank you," Ginger whispered to Rosemary. "I really mean it."

Rosemary stepped back from the coffin, but the voice was behind her disappearing around the door. Rosemary suggested they all follow and rejoin the other guests. It made sense, of course, she told herself. Ginger always needed to be in the know. Where would the need be stronger than at your own wake? But she didn't see why Ginger couldn't have waited a few days, a month, before letting her presence be known. Let herself be good and truly missed.

But she is missed, the voice said. *Good and truly. And she knows it. Can't you give her credit just this once, Rosemary? She's trying to make things easier for you.*

"Do you think it's safe?" Janet asked Rosemary as soon as Rosemary arrived at their hotel the next morning. The sisters were sitting on the sofa in the lobby, hands clasped over the handles of matching black patent leather pocket books. "Don't you think we're just asking for trouble. Especially if we take those little Indian girls with us. People will think we've stolen them."

"All they did was get off the *bus*," Betsy said with a shudder. She looked nervously around the hotel dining room.

"What on earth are you talking about?" Rosemary asked.

When they told her, Rosemary at first found herself disbelieving, but then they showed her the pictures in the paper. A few years after Walter had died here, there had been a lynching. Atrocious. But she had been a woman alone. It wasn't an explanation, but it set limits to the danger. Rosemary herself never left Antigua unaccompanied. But this. A bus load of Japanese tourists. Not even Americans, for goodness sake. And they hadn't just stoned and burned a tourist, a woman of forty, they'd also murdered the bus driver, who had tried to step in.

"Why would Mother choose a place like this over Cincinnati?" Betsy asked with disbelief.

"Maybe we should hire a hearse and have it take the coffin down to the cemetery," Janet suggested. "No need to make a big production out of it. Feels like we're just asking for trouble."

"Everyone's waiting," Rosemary said. "The musicians have come. Simon brought three friends of his, so we have a back-up if we find carrying the coffin ourselves too tiring."

Janet looked at the picture in the English language newspaper again with horror. "A human being," she said. "They did that to a human *being*. And for what? Just looking at them."

"It wasn't people like the ones around here," Rosemary said. "People here are too sophisticated."

"That's why they carried out all those massacres," Betsy asked, pointing to an article about the truth commission. "Sophistication?"

"You don't think those generals trained in our School of the Americas? You don't think we bear some responsibility—not just here but throughout Central America," Rosemary responded quickly.

"The Japanese don't. It was a busload of Japanese they attacked. And just because their own racist army attacked them doesn't mean they have to be racist in turn. But what I don't get is how you can bear to live in a country where people do such things to each other on a daily basis."

"It's not that uncommon," Betsy said. "It's not just foreigners. They have a chart here of how many lynchings there have been in the last ten years. They mutilate and murder each other too. If I had known, I would have insisted Mother return and live with us. She told us it was civilized down here. Made it sound like Florida. We were remiss, I don't deny it. We should have come down and seen for ourselves. We should have been suspicious when she showed us pictures of her girls. But they had such smiles on their faces. We didn't realize it was so dangerous. That *they* were."

"*Her* girls?" Ginger had always refused to employ domestic help.

"You know. The women she used to help with their, um, you know, basic sanitation." Betsy re-arranged the lace collar on her black dress. "They looked like the people in that town."

"Latrines. She helped them build latrines. Big improvement over going at the bottom of the garden. She was proud of that work," Rosemary agreed. "But did your mother really call them 'her girls'?"

"Oh no. That was Janet and my joke. My mother-in-law is always talking about what she and the girls do. You know, movies at the mall, a game of bridge, bingo at the church. And Janet and I would remember the pictures

Mom showed us and just break up."

"So you were proud of her," Rosemary said.

The two women looked at her, their mouths opening and shutting like carp.

"No," Janet said.

"Yes," Betsy said.

"We had no idea." Janet shook her head, her bangs and chin length hair staying obediently in place, but her sagging cheeks shook like wattles.

"We should have been firmer," Betsy said. Tears filled her pale blue eyes. Her fingers gripped her bag so tightly the knuckles were white.

"She died of cancer," Rosemary said. "She would have died of the same thing in your spare bedroom. This country had nothing to do with it—except she loved living here. It fascinated her, just like it does me. But let's go. We're holding up the show."

"You're not going to take the girls with us, are you?" Janet said. "Honestly, I don't think it's safe. What will people think?"

"That they're our servants," Rosemary said. "It's very customary here to take in young girls from the countryside to work in your houses. No one thinks anything of it."

"Could you dress them in uniforms?" Betsy asked, brushing some lint from her dress as she stood. "So it was clear to everyone."

"There will be other indigenous women at my home afterwards. Women from my collective. So are some of the other volunteers and participants from Home Is Where the Heart Is—the organization your mother volunteered at. I hope you'll be able to say something to them."

Betsy looked abashed, Janet determined. They looked at each other, then Janet spoke. "After we read this, we decided to leave straight from the cemetery. We've arranged with the hotel to send a driver over with our bags in two hours. They tell us the cemetery is not very safe. *Bandas*, they said. I assume they mean gangs—not street musicians."

"We appreciate what you've done." Janet pressed a condescending hand against Rosemary's back to help her down the front steps.

"We've talked to the lawyer about disposing of Mom's belongings. We looked through her things last night after we left your house. What's left here doesn't really speak to us. It's so heavy and, well, you know, peasanty. If we were artsy types, we'd make the effort. But with shipping and all, we decided it was better to sell it off and keep the profit. If there's anything of hers that has special significance for you, we'll sell it to you for half price."

"Janet," Betsy tried to temper her sister.

Janet brushed her bangs away from her forehead and, for a second, looked older than Ginger had until her last months. Then the bangs fell perfectly into place, the wings of her Buster Brown bob slid forward, hiding the thickening chin. "Take it," she said. "She'd have wanted it that way. And we'll never know the difference. We haven't made up an inventory."

"The lawyer said he'd take care of that. He seemed very able. His English was almost perfect."

Armando, Rosemary agreed, was a very slick snake. He'd already called Rosemary and cut a deal with her. She was buying all Ginger's possessions to redistribute, as circumstances dictated, among the collective. She knew Ginger had wanted to give everything to Home Is Where the Heart Is but forgot to put it into writing. Since they'd refused to help Mikela and Natividad, Rosemary couldn't give them Ginger's things, but she couldn't let Armando sell them to his brother either. Why she was really hanging on like this was the real question. Possessions hadn't been a big thing to Ginger—or to her either. Until now. She definitely wanted to control where Ginger's goods were going. The urge was so strong it was pointless to ask why. She just needed to act on it.

Rosemary paused on the steps of the hotel and looked up the street where her station wagon was parked, with the coffin inside and the marchers patiently waiting for the family of the bereaved. When I die, Rosemary thought before she could stop herself, who is going to work herself up over me and my memory?

"I miss you, Rosemary," Ginger said. "I already miss you."

That's what I want, Rosemary thought as she wiped her eyes. I want at least one uncontrollable outpouring of tears.

When the time comes, I'll be there Rosemary. I'll be at the head of the line with my head high, a handkerchief blowing through my fingers. Don't look around you with disgust. Like it or not, I'm the best you've got.

It was not, they both knew, enough. Rosemary, nearly lifted off her feet with an unreasonable surge of self-pity, stumbled—only to be righted by Simon, who quickly handed her his handkerchief.

"I think the time has come," he whispered in her ear, "to make our relationship formal. If you'll be mine, I'll be yours."

"Your what," Rosemary asked, rubbing furiously at her eyes with the soft white cloth.

"Friend for life," he said, and gripped her tightly as she stumbled on those damn cobblestones once again.

"I feel as if they have put someone else entirely in that coffin," Marie said, pressing her hand to her cheek, trying to check the hectic flush.

"We all do," Wilma said. "If you asked each woman here who was in that coffin—it wouldn't be this stranger."

"And you," Marie asked. "Who is in there for you?"

"My husband," Wilma said. "But he won't stay there, of course."

"No more will my daughter," Marie said. And then she felt Colette's hand on her neck, so clearly it drew all the blood from her face.

What was it about this woman, Señora Ginger, that made the spirits so restless? Wilma wondered. She could feel them hovering around each of the women—even Señora Ginger's cold-hearted but good-natured daughters. And nowhere, except with Señora Rosemary, was the spirit Señora Ginger's. It made Wilma very alert, very wary. They needed to make a space for Señora Ginger in all this throng. Wilma concentrated on visualizing Señora Ginger as she had looked just before they closed the coffin lid. So old and so dry. If you rubbed her hands together, the skin would flame.

"Make room for the others first," Señora Ginger said to Wilma.

So Wilma studied the women around her, all of them except Señora Rosemary and her own cousin Concepción as strange to her as the dead woman who was already beginning to visit her. It wasn't right, really. Wilma had her own dead to attend to.

And she hadn't been totally truthful with Señora Marie. It wasn't just her husband in the coffin, but beneath him, just tossed on the dirt like the other victims of massacre, her son Lucas. But why would they bother to present themselves to her here? They had no investment, surely, in the proper burial of this elderly *extranjera*. But that didn't mean that when Wilma looked down at the sealed coffin she didn't see her husband Agustín, so young of face and trim of body, so correct in his army uniform that concealed the bullet holes, so correct in his expression, from which the undertaker had been able to erase that last look of astonishment and anguish that the photographer had captured through the shattered windshield of the army jeep, the expression she carried with her always, engraved somewhere below thought. Agustín leaning against the side window, the glass shattered into fragments by the first of so many bullets. Unable to believe his luck. But the embalmer had given him back his appearance of confidence, of righteousness. And that is what Wilma saw now when she looked down at the coffin and felt the hot sun flooding on her head and waited for Señora Ginny to finish the prayer she was speaking straight from her heart, not reading from Señora Ginger's favorite red book.

And underneath the coffin, there was Lucas' hand, outstretched, open.

What did any of this have to do with Señora Ginger, who came to live in this country after they were both dead? Who had never, to Wilma's knowledge, even acknowledged that there had been a civil war.

What did this have to do with *any* of them? Wilma asked herself. Any of these *extranjeras*?

"Don't you think they feel the same about all their unwanted guests?" Señora Ginger asked her. "Don't you think they're asking themselves exactly the same question?"

Wilma looked around again. She was reluctant to respond to Señora Ginger because she did not want the Señora to make a habit of visiting her. Early on, in those first years after the deaths of Agustín and Lucas, she had no ability to say no to anyone. But after she went to the Church of the Spirits and learned her powers were very normal and that she could use them rather than be used by them, well then she became as firm about who visited her mind as she was about who she allowed into Señora Rosemary's house. At the beginning, of course, she had been such an open door, such a vacant house, because she so longed to see Lucas again. But he never came. Never. Agustín would come, constantly, until Wilma learned how to deflect him to Dionisio Dávila, whose son was in the army and who found Agustín's visits an honor rather than a torment.

But today, it wasn't as if she could close the door on anyone. It wasn't her house they were visiting, all these spirits. What was it about Señora Ginger's death that had brought them out in the open? Señor Walter was there, but standing far off, just paying his respects to the dead woman. Señora Ginger's husband was probably the man who stood beside Señor Walter. Señora Marie had her daughter in her arms, the girl's long thin arms hanging lazily over the Señora's back. Oh, there was such a tenderness there, such an aching. Wilma could hardly associate it with this so strictly thin, so elegant and intellectual a French woman.

And over there, standing a few feet behind Señora Rosemary, who was that? She looked very liked Señora Rosemary, but a little younger. A few inches smaller. Whenever Señora Rosemary was about to cry, the woman would put out her hand toward her and raise her eyebrows in disapproval—and Señora Rosemary would straighten her shoulders and sniff loudly and tighten her lips as if she were angry but wasn't sure why. And the other woman, feeling Señora Rosemary harden so, would harden herself—and then Wilma understood that this was Señora Rosemary's mother and that Señora Rosemary had had with Señora Ginger a very similar dance of affection and disapproval. It almost made Wilma laugh, but then she could feel the sadness, the confusion, that kept the distance between the two women so exact.

Señora Lourdes stood on one side of the grave and her step-daughter, Señora Gwen, stood on the other. They stared at each other in the same way they had done at the procession when they were protecting Natividad and Mikela from the crowd, as if it was dangerous to look away, as if they were hypnotized by something. They would look down into the grave and begin to lose their balance, just a slight quiver that could have been mistaken for the wind moving in their curly hair. When Wilma moved a little closer, she could see that inside the coffin they each saw the face of their own mother and that they would do anything to keep that knowledge from each other. Or the knowledge of how they felt when their mothers looked back at them from the spirit world, or, worse, from other people's faces.

But what, Wilma wondered again, did this have to do with Señora Ginger, who knew next to nothing about either of them? The dying woman had seemed to have become fond of Señorita Gwen, fond enough to ask her to assist at her dying, but that wasn't enough to explain the presence of these spirits, was it?

Señor Simon was attended by his mother, as was Señor Patricio, but these were very familiar and open relationships. Each man had put up his right forearm to support the arm of the tall, rather grand woman who had raised him.

As Señora Ginny finished reading from some papers she had pulled from the red book and raised her hands, her actions were imitated by her spirit companion, a large, handsome man with skin as dark as an African. He had a smile that was almost like a touch. He was looking out kindly at all of them and nodding as if he knew something they all didn't. From the far end of the grave, he slowly looked around at all the women until he came to Wilma. He held her eyes. He was a kind man, she could tell that. There was something important and not very pleasant he wanted to tell Wilma, but he didn't know how to put the thought into his very poor Spanish. Wilma wanted to tell him she spoke English, but she realized immediately that he didn't want any help, that he rather liked the struggle. He gestured to Wilma to join him over behind the next tomb. But Wilma felt it would be disloyal to Señora Ginny, who obviously thought no one but she could possibly sense him, and she thought he was there to distract her from something having to do with the grave, the women.

The little girls both kept scuffing at the dirt and at first Wilma thought they were bored, but then she saw that they were desperately trying to cover over so many little fetuses, washed up on the dirt like a school of dying fish. They looked up in the air, off to their right or left, but never glanced down. They were very quick, those two, staring into everyone's eyes, checking how delicate and distracting their little dance was proving to be. They were, Wilma understood, all the babies their mother had lost. All the brothers and sisters who would never be. The proof of her perfidy.

The only ones who stood there unaccompanied by spirits were Señora Ginger's two daughters. But they kept looking around them as if they could hear something. They kept looking at their watches too. What right, Wilma wondered, did *they* have to be frightened? What right did they have to judge? They just wanted Señora Ginny to step back and let them throw some dirt on their mother's coffin and then wipe their hands daintily as if just the touch of the earth here might pollute them.

Oh, it made Wilma so angry. And then she understood what was happening, that Señora Ginger, just as she was dying, understood what it meant, this spirit of adoption, and she asked God if she could participate, if not through her life, through her dying. Perhaps she felt guilt for the boy child she gave away. Perhaps she felt a sense of waste with these two daughters with their clean fingers and empty hearts. Perhaps this was her last gift to Señora Rosemary.

"And to you, Wilma," Señora Ginger said. "You're the one who can see what has been set in motion."

By whom? Wilma wondered as Mikela stopped her little dance and peered out over the grave, searching, still as a wild animal, for some faint scent of danger. For what purpose?

"Love," Señora Ginger said firmly. A little snappishly. "You of all people should know that, Wilma."

What do I, Wilma thought, what do I, of all people, know about the power of love?

And she threw her own handful of dirt against the box that protected Agustín's youthful and righteous face from her and watched it collect in the outstretched hand of her son, so crudely tossed, like so many others, into the common grave beneath.

Chapter 17
STANDING FIRM

Mikela could see Pablo and Tomás and the rest of their *banda* staring out at them from behind the different tombs in the cemetery. She hoped they wouldn't do anything stupid. She knew sometimes they stopped women in the cemetery and demanded money from them. But would they demand money from people who were in the process of burying their dead—even if they were *extranjeras*? She didn't dare let Natividad know they were there. She shook her hand at them and brushed the air, as if that would send their spirits flying. Of course, all they did was laugh.

Mikela went over to Señor Simon and tugged on his hand. She wished his brother, who was so *grandote*, had not left for the United States. But Señor Simon, although he was thin, was still very tall. And he could put a fierce look on his face when he needed to. For some reason, Mikela did not want to talk to Señor Patricio. He would know about Natividad and the glue. Just looking at their faces, he would know. Señor Patricio was like Señora Wilma in this way. He knew things without being told. In some ways people like Señora Wilma and Señor Patricio were a relief. You didn't have to worry so much about disappointing them since they could always see through your lies. But they also made Mikela feel very lonely and exposed. They *knew* things, they saw things, but they wouldn't help. Mikela knew things too—not in their way, like it came in through their skin—but because she was quick-sighted.

She could see, for example, that Señora Marie was standing back on her heels with her arms wrapped around her like she was holding something that weighed almost as much as she did. She could see the way Señora Lourdes and Señora Gwen held each other's eyes on either side of the grave, like they were two kinds of magnets at the same time, pushing and pulling equally hard. She could tell they would both fall if they turned away.

She could tell that Señor Patricio was feeling very happy for some reason, like there was a big space inside his chest and something light and bright was growing in there. And she could tell that her sister Natividad missed Señorita Gwen's attention and was feeling empty inside. She could almost see inside her sister, see the body hanging feet first from the rafters, feel the whoosh of the branches as they came down on her back and began to turn her body round and round and round. She could see Natividad's hair ruffling the dirt floor. She could feel her sister's hunger for the glue growing. How it would make that room perfectly empty, get rid of the body. She could see her sister's eyes beginning to droop, the way she did when she left her body, could see how Natividad tried to hang on by looking down at the coffin and trying to see the woman inside it the way she was in the bed, so still, so calm, when Señorita Gwen had called them in to show them she was dead. Señorita Gwen had sent Mikela to tell Señora Wilma, who was to tell Señora Rosemary. Mikela knew that something had happened in that room because she saw the open pill bottles and the pills that had slid into the creases in the blankets. She could tell trouble was coming because she saw Natividad quietly pick up those pills, pretending she was just flattening the sheet, and slip them inside the *rebozo* with Miguelito.

Oh, there were so many things Mikela could see, but she couldn't see the future. All she could see were possibilities. All she could do was prepare herself. Sometimes she wished she didn't see so much, so she didn't have to prepare for everything.

Sometimes talking to someone like Señor Simon who didn't seem to see as much, and didn't seem to worry about what he saw, but was willing to help her or the shoeshine boys, sometimes someone like Señor Simon was the right person to trust—even if he couldn't tell when she was lying.

She pulled sharply on Señor Simon's hand again. He wasn't as strong as he looked to be because he wobbled. A big man like him wobbled when a girl whose head only reached his elbow pulled hard on his hand. It was then Mikela understood that Señor Simon was a sick man who just appeared well.

This made her very sad. It made her pull again, but this time more gently.

He leaned down. Then, because that didn't bring him close enough to Mikela, he got down on his knees, making a scrunched up face as he did so as if something inside him hurt. Mikela got down on her knees too so he would only have to look down. She thought that was easier than looking up. Her neck was always hurting after she talked to these big looming *extranjeras*. Although it never hurt when she looked up at the Virgin or the good Hermano Pedro.

"There are some bad boys over there," she said.

"Where?"

"Behind the big white tombs."

"You know them?"

"They come from the capital. They like this city because it has rich tourists. They like to take money from people. They like to do this in the cemetery where there aren't so many people to see."

"They're you're friends?" Señor Simon asked. He had a gentle way to him that frightened Mikela.

"No," she said. "I told you. They are bad boys. I know them but they are not my friends."

"I don't think they will attack us because we have too many big men here." He smiled. "I'm not so big—but Señor Patricio is. And even though we know he won't even slap a fly, they don't know that. And there is his friend, Señor Byron."

"I wish your brother was still here. He is as big as a giant," Mikela said.

"I always wished he was there when I was a little boy," Señor Simon said. "But he said everyone had to fight their own battles."

"But that means when there are many bad boys on the other side, you might lose," Mikela said. "Why does God give you brothers and sisters if not to help you fight?"

"Exactly what I asked him," Señor Simon said.

"This means that he will not protect Señora Ginny either? He will not be a good *novio*?"

"I don't know," Señor Simon said. "I have my hopes. We can all change. Sometimes you just need to find the right thing—idea or person—to fight for. What you know you can't live without—that's what makes you fight."

Mikela knew she couldn't live without Natividad—even when she was mad at her. She knew she couldn't live without Miguelito. She knew if they needed her she would fight for them. Just like she was doing now. But there were eight boys over there behind the tombs, she had counted, and she wasn't enough in herself. This made her angry to admit, but it was true.

"They know my sister too," Mikela told Simon. She put her hands on top of his, so it would look like they were praying together, not planning. "They sometimes get Natividad to do bad things."

"They're the ones she lived with after she left the girls' home?"

Mikela nodded. She felt very bad. Now Señor Simon would think Pablo and Tomás were Natividad's friends. They would rob everyone and Señor Simon would tell Señora Rosemary that they were friends of Natividad, and she would think Natividad helped plan the robbery and would send Natividad away, just as Señora Lourdes had. She might even send Natividad to jail. And then Natividad would give Miguelito to Señorita Gwen because she knew Mikela couldn't keep him at the girls' home and she couldn't feed him because she didn't have breasts yet. Oh, Mikela was afraid she would start crying, she was so upset. She could see so many possibilities, so many bad possibilities, and she didn't know how to stop them.

"They are not her friends," Mikela said. "Whatever they say, whatever *she* says, they are not her friends. They get her to do bad things—like breathing the glue." Even as she said this, she could see Natividad's hand flattening the sheet, folding Señora Ginger's pills in her hand. Mikela knew that now the badness was in Natividad herself. Maybe it always had been, but it had been safely locked up before. Pablo and Tomás used the glue like a key to open that door. Mikela wanted to put a new lock on it, a big powerful lock that only she had the key to. And she would throw that key away somewhere and never ever tell anyone where it was. She would save Natividad from that bad place inside her that was like her mother's love for the soldier.

"I will take care of it," Señor Simon said.

"There are eight of them," Mikela said. "I counted. They have knives." She was afraid Señor Simon would go and offer them money to write their names and they would grab him and take his watch and all his money. They didn't really care if anyone saw them because they were so fast. And they didn't really care about each other, so if one of them was caught, it didn't tear at anyone's heart. They weren't Mikela's friends, these boys. They were her enemies. But she *knew* them. She knew how they thought. It was the way she thought about everybody but Natividad and Miguelito and, perhaps, Señor Simon and Señora Ginny.

"I want you to stay here," Señor Simon said. "Keep an eye on your sister. Make sure she doesn't go over there."

Señor Simon climbed to his feet. Again, he made that ugly look with his face as if he were an old man and his bones hurt him. Mikela hoped he would ask Señor Patricio to help him because she, a girl, could make him wobble—so what would those eight boys be able to do.

But Señor Simon just patted Señor Patricio on the back, nodded at Señora Ginny, who was saying a last prayer as the men began to throw shovels of dirt on Señora Ginger's coffin. Mikela was glad to see the dirt go in because that meant that Natividad would never find Señora Ginger's pills. Mikela had found them where Natividad had hidden them in Miguelito's clothes and she took them and, when she went to look in the coffin last night, she reached in and pretended to touch that terrible old woman's hand, but really she was slipping those pills under it, putting them back where they belonged. Her own people liked to be buried with tortillas and chocolate. Why wouldn't Señora Ginger want her pills in the next world? Mikela didn't really believe that even in heaven your bones didn't hurt, that you couldn't get sick. She did believe you didn't need to sniff the glue or smoke the sweet cigarettes there. But old people hurt wherever they were. There was nothing anyone, not even God or the Virgin, could do about oldness.

Señor Simon wasn't old, but he walked like someone who was. Mikela knew he'd told her to stay, but she saw that Natividad had sidled up to Señorita Gwen, who was talking to her step-mother and to Señora Rosemary. So Mikela slipped away to help Señor Simon.

She went around the other side of the tomb she had watched Señor Simon walk around. As soon as she turned the corner, out of sight of the people at the funeral, she stopped. She could hear Señor Simon's voice. She could hear the boys laughing in a bad way.

"I'll pay you," Señor Simon said. "I'll pay you to leave us alone today. Everything I have on me. Five hundred."

"Your watch too," Tomás said. Oh, he was a greedy boy.

"These *extranjeros* wear money belts," another boy said. "I see them at the automatic tellers. They pull them up out of their pants and they fill them with money."

"Tourists wear them," Señor Simon said. "People who live here don't."

"Take down your pants," the boy said. He had a deep voice, like a man's. Mikela did not recognize his voice. She slipped along the wall of the tomb to see if she could get closer.

"No," Señor Simon said. "I have no more money and I won't take my pants down."

Mikela heard an awful click. She knew someone had opened a knife. She looked around to see if she could find a glass bottle. She could protect Señor Simon just the way she had Natividad—except these boys were not drunk or sleepy with the glue. They were wide awake, *hungry* for the glue. If she could find a glass bottle and break it and jab one of them until the blood came, maybe the others would run away. They were bad boys and they liked to hurt people. They weren't brave or loyal. They wouldn't try to protect each other. Mikela would scream as loud as she could as she attacked. She would scream, "*Robos! Robos!*" The men with the shovels would come running from the grave. She and Señor Simon would pretend the boys were strangers. No one would know.

But there was no glass bottle. The tops of the walls of the cemetery, and even the tops of some of the tombs were covered with broken glass. But it was cemented in. Mikela edged forward. She hadn't heard another click. In fact, she heard nothing. Nothing at all.

"*If* I cut my own wrist," Señor Simon said, "I will be more dangerous to you than you are to me. I will be as dangerous to you as you would be to me if you put your knife in me. I am a sick man, you see, and the sickness is in my blood, and it is very dangerous if it touches you. Just a drop or two—there, where your pants are torn and you have a scratch on your leg—or on your bare feet with all those broken places. Just a drop. I am a *very* dangerous man, you see. One drop of my blood, just one drop, if it gets inside you, can poison all your blood."

It was a terrible lie. Worse than any Mikela had ever told herself. But in Señor Simon's voice it sounded completely true. He sounded dangerous, very dangerous, and very sad—as if he really had this power of life and death.

"I told you I would pay you to let the funeral finish in peace and all the women leave. You want my watch along with my money, I'll give you that."

"And your shoes," Tomás said.

"And my shoes," Señor Simon agreed. "But then you leave. If you don't, I will cut my wrist in such a away that the blood will spray like water from a hose. It will reach every one of you."

Oh, Mikela felt so proud of Señor Simon, how he had told his story so convincingly that these big bad boys all got silent. She peeked around the corner and she could see how they almost didn't dare to go up and get the money. Even the big boy with the mean voice, who had a cut near his eye. None of them dared to get near Señor Simon. It was as if he was inside a magic circle they didn't dare cross.

He was, Mikela realized, as powerful as Miguel el arcangel. He could divide the good and the evil. For wasn't he inside the circle—and weren't those bad boys outside it, their shoulders sagging, their bones showing, like whipped dogs.

Señor Simon kept his eyes on them. He kept the knife to his wrist.

"Mikela," he said without looking over at her. "Come here." When she came up to him, he handed her the knife and showed her where she was to cut. He told her to hold the knife over his wrist in everything he did.

"He isn't lying," Mikela told Pablo. "His blood is very poisonous."

"That means you will die too," Pablo said.

"But so would you," Mikela said. "So would you, Pablo." Her voice sounded just as powerful and sad as Señor Simon's. If she didn't know better, Mikela would believe what she was saying. She knew Pablo and Tomás and David did because they had seen her stab the man in the capital. Mikela liked this feeling. Finally she was not just seeing bad possibilities everywhere. Finally she and Señor Simon had found a magic circle where they could begin to turn the world around.

Señor Simon, Mikela's hand following his every move, removed the money from his pocket and threw it at the boys. They didn't dive for it. Rather Pablo put his bare foot out and trapped it under his toes and tugged it toward him. All the boys gathered behind him.

Cowards, Mikela thought triumphantly. But she did not forget her job and she held the knife over Señor Simon's hands as he pulled off his watch. Then he took the knife from her and she knelt down and he lifted one foot after she had untied his black tennis shoes and she prayed, she prayed hard, he wouldn't wobble and the knife wouldn't slip and their lie wouldn't be discovered. But she was very careful and Señor Simon didn't wobble, not even the second time. Mikela threw the shoes as hard as she could. David grabbed one. Tomás the other. Pablo and the big boy with the cut near his eye were already fighting over the money. Another boy had quietly grabbed the watch and was running away.

"*Váyense*," Señor Simon yelled at them. He had both hands over his head, the knife right at his wrist. "Count of ten and I cut."

The boys ran. Just like it was a race and the gun had gone off. That was how loud Señor Simon's voice was.

At the sound, Señor Patricio looked over from the grave and then started running toward them. So did Señor Byron, but more slowly. The grave diggers looked up but decided it was safer to continue with their work. Señora Rosemary started down, but Señora Lourdes stopped her, so she stood by the grave screaming fiercely at the boys, "*Malcriados! Malcriados! Criminales! Criminales!*"

Señor Patricio was breathing hard when he reached them. Señor Simon was looking very white and his legs were shaking. Mikela could feel his weakness, although it was almost impossible to see with your eyes. Señor Simon folded his knife up.

"You all right?" Señor Patricio asked him.

"Barefoot and broke, but other than that, I'm fine. I had a great helper here in Mikela." Señor Simon put his hand on Mikela's shoulder. Mikela stood very straight because she knew Señor Simon needed her strength, that he didn't want Señor Patricio to know that his legs were shaking.

"He was very brave," she told Señor Patricio. "He told a very big lie and he got them to believe it. He said his blood was poisonous and he was going to cut his wrist and pour his blood all over them and they would find that it wasn't blood and wine, like Jésus', but poison."

"And they believed this?" Señor Patricio asked her. "They were such foolish boys they believed this?"

"Every one of them," she answered. "And he gave me the knife while he took off his watch. And the boys believed me too because they saw me once in the capital—"

But she had the sense to stop herself, for Mikela was very good at seeing danger. Not good enough, but good.

"They saw you were tough," Señor Patricio said. "As tough as Señor Simon."

"They were mean boys," Mikela said. "But we are brave. Because we know we have something to fight for, don't we, Señor Simon?" She put her arm around his waist to give him a hug—and also to lift him up a little so his legs would stop shaking.

Señor Patricio put his arm under Señor Simon's and lifted him a little.

"The grave's about filled in. Let's say good-bye to the women and head up to the lake, why don't we? Byron and I have someone we'd like you to see." Señor Simon looked up at Señor Patricio and then down again.

"No use hiding it, I guess, from a clairvoyant."

A clairvoyant, Mikela learned, was someone who could see through people. But even she, a quick-eyed girl, could see that the two of them were talking in two languages at the same time, like she and Natividad used to. It wasn't lying exactly, but it made Mikela feel very alone. She wasn't a man. She wasn't a woman. She was brave, but she wasn't very big. She was quick-sighted but she couldn't see the future. There was no one who could talk with her as she had once talked with her sister.

Señor Simon knelt down and put his arms around her. "It's going to be all right, Mikela. I promise you, it is going to be all right."

Oh, Mikela couldn't stop herself, she let her head lean against his chest and she took a deep breath and for a moment, just a moment, she let herself rest against Señor Simon the way, when she was a very little girl, she once or twice rested against her mother.

"Up you go," yelled Señor Patricio as he pulled Mikela up on his shoulders. He put his arm under Señor Simon's and pulled him upright too. When they reached the top of the hill, all the women surrounded Señor Simon and tsked tsked about his shoes. Señora Ginger's daughters kept their shiny black purses clutched to their chests. They backed away from the grave, bobbing their heads weakly at the others, and then turned and hurried down to the cemetery gates where the car from the hotel was waiting to take them to the airport. Señora Wilma and Señora Rosemary hurried after them, but Mikela could tell they would rather stay with Señor Simon.

"Our knight in shining armor," Señora Lourdes said.

Natividad looked up at Mikela, high above her on Señor Patricio's shoulders. Mikela looked down at the grave, making sure it was all filled in, that Señora Ginger and her dangerous pills were gone forever. Natividad looked out over the tombs, watching to see if the boys had all disappeared. And then something wonderful happened. Natividad left Señorita Gwen's side and she came over to Señor Patricio and she pulled on his shirt and she asked him, very clearly, to let Mikela down so she could thank her, so they could all thank her, for she had been very quick-sighted and brave too.

"She surely has," Señor Patricio agreed and lifted Mikela from his shoulders and set her on the ground.

And Natividad put her arms around Mikela and said what Mikela hadn't heard for a very long time. She heard her sister say thank you. Mikela heard her sister say thank you. Because Mikela had sent the boys and their glue away. And Mikela knew that all her doubts were not true, Natividad really *did* want to be saved from herself. And it made Mikela feel that again they were together inside the same magic circle.

Brave and a liar, the voice said. Today it sounded hoarse and bitter, like Señora Ginger's.

"Like Señor Simon," Mikela answered back. "Lying doesn't matter if you know what you're fighting for."

Natividad untied Miguel and gave him to Mikela, and she buried her nose in his black hair, and she knew, for this day, they were all safe. She knew from now on, she would let Señor Simon inside their circle. That his blood wasn't poisonous, it was magic, because he would shed it for them, just like Jésus did. She had said good-bye to that dying woman with the bad smell who kept trying to draw them into her circle of pity. Mikela had made her own circle, with Señor Simon's help of course—a circle of bravery. They were all safely back inside it.

THE LOOK
(*Gwen*)

When she held my eyes there, outside the church, after the Christ statue stared into each of our eyes with that look that Concepción said ensured our living in a state of grace for yet another year, I felt something quite similar. Something I was completely unprepared for. Why on earth should I feel forgiveness coming from Lourdes? What, in the first place, does she have to forgive me for? And why would I want forgiveness from her? Who is she to me, after all?

It wasn't an illusion—because in that terrifying hour that followed, our eyes locked more than once, and beneath all the other expressions, that forgiveness was still there. As if I cared! But I did. That is the strangest thing of all. I cared enormously. I did not want to be given up on—and by her of all people. I felt it just a week ago over Ginger's grave as well. And I had the same response—why should I care, but I did. I really did. Whatever happened, I didn't want her to turn away first.

My father tried to talk me out of staying. At first he did it circumspectly—talking about how I should be thinking of getting myself enrolled, somewhere, anywhere, for the fall semester. I only lack eight credits to graduate. He's already talked to the university and they'll accept credits from almost anywhere, given the circumstances. But when that approach didn't seem to work, he talked about how important this fellowship was for Lourdes and how, with Mikela and Natividad, her time was being stolen from her right and left. I told him that I didn't see her complaining. She seems to like all the companionship.

"I want her back," he said finally. "Gwen, I want her back. I don't want you doing anything, anything at all that would alienate her."

"Anything more, you mean?"

"We should have discussed it, all of us together, when you came down in October. I shouldn't have expected her to just fall in with your plans, even if I was willing to."

"Why not?" I asked. "It's not as if I planned Cristina's death, is it?" And why, I thought, didn't Lourdes tell you she was planning to leave the country. For all we know, she may have been planning that before I ever arrived.

"You're free to come and stay with me until Lourdes returns," my father said. "No one expected Cristina's death. But it isn't Lourdes' responsibility."

"She knew you had a daughter."

"Who was twenty-one when we married, a junior in college, and lived with her mother. We never thought we were making a family of our grown children. Not her sons. Not you. It's too late for all that, Gwen."

"You're saying I have no right to expect anything of you?"

"Of course not," he exploded. His face got all red, it looked striking against his white hair. He looked both younger and older than his fifty-nine years. I could tell how afraid he was of losing her. How afraid, that meant, he was of me, his only child.

If you'd asked me before I came down here what I wanted from my father, I think I would have said I wanted exactly that look. I wanted to have an effect on him that was as great as the effect he had on me when I was thirteen and he drove away in his gray car following the moving van that was taking all his belongings to North Carolina and leaving me alone with Cristina. But now that he was looking at me in just that way, I realized I didn't want that at all—and maybe, if wanting that look had been a little behind my wanting to stay on in Antigua, that motivation disappeared completely at that moment. It didn't mean I didn't want to stay on—just that my relationship with my father wasn't part of it anymore.

I haven't stayed on because I wanted to see some similar look on Lourdes' face either. No. The minute I saw that look on my dad's face, that was it. I knew I was really and truly on my own. I know my dad doesn't believe that and that he had a long talk with Lourdes about it. But that was after the Good Friday procession, after that look that passed between Lourdes and me the one I suppose Concepción wanted me to feel from the Jesus statue itself. And I knew Lourdes had experienced the strangeness of it when she told my dad not to worry about it, that I could stay downstairs until she left.

I couldn't tell from her voice if she plans to go back to live with him when this is all over. I don't think she knows herself. Of course, I hope so, for his sake. He isn't young, my dad. I don't think he's going to meet a woman he likes more than her. He didn't in the *eight years before he met her. He didn't in those years my mom was playing around while they were still married. I would have known about it, just as I did with Cristina. I have a sense about these things. It's not even as if I have to go looking for answers. They just come to me. It didn't matter what my mother said, I always knew if she'd been with someone. She could have showered, put on more perfume. I still knew.*

That morning when I came back to the apartment, I knew, for example, before I ever opened her door, that Cristina had chosen that night, the only night I slept with Todd, as the night when she knew, she really knew, she wasn't needed anymore.

That was why I was so mad at my father when I learned how serious he was about Lourdes. He had been seeing her for several months. Every time he'd gone up to see me, he'd seen her too—and I had no idea. I didn't have any idea. He felt just like himself, nothing different at all. Not being able to tell, that was what made me know how far apart we had become.

Even now, living with him day after day, getting his goat the way I do, I still can't tell what he's really thinking—other than being able to tell he's so afraid Lourdes might not come back that he won't even let the thought cross his mind.

That's the way I always felt about Cristina. Maybe I knew if I went out with Todd, if we really, you know, got together, it would kill my mother. Maybe I did know that and just wouldn't let myself hear the thought. Maybe I did know that my showing up on my dad's doorstep would make them separate. Maybe I did—but if I did, I didn't let myself hear the thought. That's different from this other kind of knowing, the kind that is just there, you don't have time to block it out.

That's what happened with Lourdes, I think. I showed up on the doorstep and she just knew, she just knew it was the end of something. And something in her just left her body at that moment so she could go on acting like a normal person. From what they say, something like that happened when she found Natividad on the glue.

But what is really the strange thing is how an event can have such a different effect on two different people. Because it was when I saw Natividad on the glue that day Concepción and Mikela were trying to sneak her back into Rosemary's house—that time none of us have ever mentioned, even to each other—it was at that moment that I knew, I just knew that I was meant to be part of their lives. I looked at Natividad, so lost, and my heart just opened right up. She didn't know it yet, but she needed me—something that I couldn't even name but that was just part of who I am. And I knew, this is what makes it so important, that what I had to give Natividad was good and that it would, whatever anyone might think, it would make a difference. It wouldn't be like loving Cristina, where no matter how much you poured in, it couldn't fill the emptiness. It never could fill the emptiness.

You see, I looked at Natividad and I just knew, I just knew there was a real person in there. A real person who might not be able to be a mother, but who could be a girl, could be a girl with a prodigious talent for drawing. She could do things with her life if someone gave her the chance. And I looked at that baby and I just knew, I just knew, I could love him like no one else. I just knew this.

So, I'm not staying here to make Lourdes' life difficult. I'm staying here because Natividad and her baby speak to me like nothing ever has before in my life. I mean, when I was thirteen—and again and again over the years—I knew I couldn't leave Cristina, I just knew this. And, until that last night with Todd, I always made the right choice. But that knowing was different. That knowing had a sinking to it so deep you never expected to rise again. It was a necessity. But this knowing is different—it has a yes at the heart of it. I know I can make things better here.

I tried to explain this to my father, but he says that I haven't finished college yet and how do I think I'll support the baby if I just quit my job. A job at Hardees, of all places, he doesn't even bother to say. Of course, we both know the answer to that. I'll use the money from the sale of Cristina's condominium. It will go a long way down here.

What my dad doesn't understand, you see, is that what is growing in me is something good, something faithful, something destined—just like he feels his love for Lourdes is. He's afraid if I adopt this baby, a man won't want to marry me—like he thinks no one wanted to marry Cristina because I was around. But he's wrong. More than one of Cristina's men wanted to marry her because of me. I'm not implying something sexual, just that they had this feeling, like I have with Miguel, that something good inside them now had a place to express itself. But it never happened—just because of that. I wouldn't let that happen to Cristina. Not again. Not after my dad. You'd have to be a fool not to see that it was me he loved, me he hung on to. Cristina couldn't live without me—and she couldn't, ever, forgive me for that betrayal of my father's either. That has been, all my life, what it has meant to me to be Gwen. A necessary source of division.

And then, when I saw Natividad and Miguel, I just knew myself, I just knew myself completely differently. And there isn't any question in my mind about which way I want to go. In that old pattern, I was always shrinking, holding fast. Trying to avoid my destiny. But here, in this new pattern, I can keep getting bigger and the people around me can keep getting bigger and we can know each other in this larger way. Natividad can get bigger in my gaze, in the way I understand something about her she doesn't have any shape for yet. Natividad, one day, can become me. An independent young woman. And I can know myself right now as a mother. A real mother. Someone with something good to give. We both win.

"But what about Mikela?" Wilma has asked me. Lourdes too. This always

sends me for a loop. I don't see why they can't understand that what I'm suggesting will protect Mikela as well. What's she going to do, spend her whole childhood forcing Natividad to be the mother she doesn't want to be, can't be, in a place deeper than wanting or willing, a place that is like God's decree? I wouldn't put it past the little girl. She is stubborn in a way I've never associated with a child—like she just has this 'in' with life with a capital L. She doesn't question herself. Ten years old, a street kid, carrying a baby on her back since she was what, three? Four? The life they lived in the capital was awful, I can tell from the little bit Natividad has been able to bring herself to say, and what Mamí Concepción let drop once or twice—until, that is, she began to get jealous of Natividad's attachment to me, just like Mikela has.

It feels so strange to be an object of suspicion to them. Or maybe it feels like home and that's why I rebel at it so much. It is so difficult to take your own motivations at face value if no one else will. I just think of how Cristina was always listening for the least little crack in my loyalty, a hair's breadth, just the slightest hair's breadth, and she'd be at me with that enormous sledge-hammer of a will of hers. "What do you mean there are two sides to every story? Whose side are you on, Gwen?"

"I know which side my bread is buttered on," I would sass back. "Don't worry."

But here, no one knows what side my bread is buttered on except Natividad and me. They keep thinking there is something else going on here. I couldn't possibly just be doing Natividad a good service because I like her and she's down on her luck right now and I'd like to give her a second chance at a childhood, or at least an adolescence. They can't believe I truly like her. That I see her as someone who will, with a little help, be able to make her own way in the world.

It's as if all the qualities they see in Mikela can't possibly apply to her sister as well. Mikela knows what she's doing. Everyone buys into this. Everyone. A ten year old kid and they treat her like she is this little Dalai Lama or something. "A force of nature," is what Simon calls her. But they're all mesmerized by something about her—this purposefulness. They never question it. Doesn't that feel strange to you? All these adults and they never question this sense of purpose of hers. What she's going to do next remains mysterious, something to be on the alert for—but there's no sense that Mikela's next intention may be misguided.

She's a kid for goodness sake. And she feels she's been put on earth to be her sister's caretaker and her nephew's indefatigable bodyguard. Why don't people truly get that maybe she doesn't want Natividad to be whole, she wants her to be a mute, to prostitute herself. So Mikela can get the scholarships. So Mikela doesn't have to sell her soul—or her body—for their daily bread. Maybe she's hanging on to that baby because she thinks it will increase his worth—once she finds the right buyer.

I wouldn't dare raise these questions with a single one of them, especially not Lourdes, who can see no wrong in Mikela and probably is busy, like every single one of them, second guessing my motives.

Just once, I would like to be taken for what I appear to be, you know. Cristina's daughter. As angry at her death as I am devastated by it. In need of some commitments that will set me on the right path in life. I want to be a mother. I want to be a friend. What on earth is so strange about that at my age? Lourdes was a mother twice over by the time she was my age, but no one, I bet, ever asked her why. And even if they did, all she would have had to say was, "Because—" and that would be it. That's the difference between natural motherhood and intentional motherhood. Life, raw life, is the only intention that creates a natural mother. Can't that be the same here? Something larger than all of us is creating the intention and we're just resonating with it?

Actually Lourdes may be a little more sympathetic than I think. She told me the other day that she had taken care of her sister as she was growing up. What was the word she used to describe them—a dyad? She was trying to defend Mikela—but at the same time, she was saying she knew what it was like to take care of someone.

"What happened?" I asked her.

"I had my own children," she said. "I had to choose. She wasn't well. I couldn't take care of everyone."

"She wasn't well," she said again.

Like Natividad, she implied. But she's not right. You can't just wash your hands of a girl of twelve. You can't sentence her to a life of taking care of a child she never wanted, either. And it's Natividad's decision finally. Not all these other women's. Not her little sister's decision either. Just hers.

"Like it was your decision to spend the night with that black boy, Todd," Cristina asks me. I look around, ready to stare her down. Just as I did at the graveside. Her own and just last week when I could feel her there inside the coffin where Ginger should be. But death hasn't changed anything. She is as intransigent as she ever was. Except now there's nothing to hang on to, now that I can't see deep in the back of her eyes that pain that knew no bounds. Nothing, in other words, to hold my own anger in check.

"Yes," I tell her. "Yes, it's exactly like that."

When Lourdes held my eyes during that terrifying half hour at the procession— all those little brown people pushing at us, like flood waters or lava, something completely impersonal—I saw something there in her eyes, this feeling that I call forgiveness although it wasn't exactly that. It was acceptance, simple acceptance, and it gave me a sense of what it might feel like to be taken at face value, to be taken as one. And the other impression I had was of a certain kind of resolve, of assurance. We were going to get out of there, Lourdes's gaze seemed to say. All of us. The little girls and the baby and all of us women who had joined our arms, weaving them in and out of each other's, to protect them.

What I remember as I'm going to sleep every night is just the pressure, how people would just press and press. They weren't even angry, that was what was so frightening. We kept saying, "Hay niños. Cuidado." There are children. Be careful. And it meant nothing. Absolutely nothing. They were like a flood that had found an obstacle and would over run it if they could.

The girls didn't seem to have any sense of the danger they were in. We had been looking for Mikela for at least an hour. Natividad kept saying she had stolen the baby, which was ludicrous. Natividad had just started to undo the carrying cloth Mikela had tied around herself in order to take the baby back.. Mikela was protesting. I began to get a little concerned as the crowd surged up around us. I took the baby then and held him over my shoulder. Just to get him up above the bodies. I grabbed both the girls' hands with my other hand because I was afraid of losing them too. People were moving in only one direction all around us and it was the "natural" direction, toward the statue. I called out to Lourdes, who was standing on the sidewalk and she pushed her way toward me immediately. So did Concepción and Marie and Wilma and Ginny, who had all walked down together from Simon's, thank goodness.

Mikela was so out of it, all she was concerned about was making sure the statue saw the baby. She kept jumping up in the air and pointing to the baby. If it wasn't so sad and dangerous, it would have been funny.

People began pushing against us just as soon as the last of the pallets passed. There was this pressure, this incredible pressure. Hundreds of people poured down the street for blocks and blocks and blocks—like a huge mud slide. I know how those daughters of Ginger's must have felt when they read about those lynchings. I mean, they were scared and they had no real basis. But now I can see, I can see how it could happen. All those people were like sheep—you know that crazy unity sheep have, where one of them runs and they all run, like they were one animal. That's what it felt like.

I was scared. I've never been more scared. Miguel was kind of folding over my shoulder and I kept trying to balance him and wondering if little thin Marie and little plump Concepción could possibly be strong enough to keep the circle intact. They were all smiling, all these people pressing against us. They were all smiling. And they were dangerously small. And powerful. Dangerously powerful in that terrible, sheeplike way.

Trying to follow a Jesus carved out of wood and covered with blood and as callous about life as they were themselves.

    I knew, if Marie and Concepción let go, I wouldn't be able to keep my balance, and I'd fall and that baby, with his fat little fingers drumming happily on my back, would go down with me. The thought made me sick. Sicker than you could possibly believe. I didn't want anything bad to happen to him. That was the only thing I was clear about. I didn't want anything bad to happen to him and I didn't want to be responsible for it most of all.

    Lourdes was unflappable. She kept looking into my eyes—just looking. "It's all right," she said. "We'll make it, Gwen. Nothing's going to happen. Nothing's going to happen. If you begin to fall, I'll catch him."

    It was all about the baby, you see. It wasn't about me and it wasn't about her—or maybe it was. Maybe we understood each other better at that moment than we ever understood each other before or ever will again. We both knew it wasn't any more complex than what it seemed. We couldn't stand, neither of us could stand, the idea that this baby would be trampled and we would do everything we could, everything we had to, to keep that from happening.

    And we weren't alone in this. We were all united. Concepción, Wilma, Ginny, Marie, even those two women who were total strangers. Rosemary too. We were just not going to let that happen. But it was Lourdes' look that helped me keep my balance, the way she kept calling on me by name that let me know that we were strong enough. We were strong enough because we had to be. For no other reason at all. Just because we had to be.

    Even Natividad could see what was happening. You could feel it when she took the baby back after it was all over. I think it was the first time I've ever seen her kiss Miguel. But not Mikela, oh no. The minute Natividad had Miguel back, Mikela slipped between us with her little arms spread out. As if I was the danger. After all we had been through, it should have been funny. But it wasn't.

    Sometimes when that little girl looks at me, I feel she is communing directly with evil. That she sees in me someone I have never been and never will be. I felt exactly the same way when I looked into Cristina's wide open sightless eyes and saw myself reflected there. I know I'm not evil. But I can't describe how it made me feel. I really can't describe it. And I can't make it go away and I can't get it out of my mind. It is a terrible feeling against which there are absolutely no defenses. The queerest thing is that somehow I know that the one person in the world who would understand this perfectly is Lourdes. And she knows as well how perfectly impossible it is to defend yourself against it. It can come at you from any side. An angry ten year old girl. A twenty-three year old step-daughter. A twelve year old mother stupefied with glue. Those blind, wide-eyed mothers who wait for us in strangers' *graves.*

This crazy thought comes to me: It can't exist, that world of evil, if we take each other at face value. But of course that's untrue. Those people who would have trampled us, they looked right through us. They saw nothing. We weren't even human to them.

We get to choose, I believe, which look we know ourselves through. I have to believe that. I would like to know myself through the look that Natividad gives me. The look of little Miguel. I would like to know myself through the look Lourdes gave me as we fought for our balance together in that circle of care. Scared. Determined. Held in place by the arms and eyes of other women. Seen as someone with something good to give. The way Ginger looked at me before I did what I did to help her on her way.

Chapter 18
BODY CASTING

What made Rosemary suggest the body casting sessions was this sudden sensation she had—more a sensation than a vision—of the reality of Ginger's body in the coffin. She missed her friend. Missed massaging her paper-thin skin, knowing her bones as they appeared and seemed to swell in size as she lost weight so rapidly toward the end. She missed the feel of her breath inflating her lungs, making her ribs seem to float for a second before collapsing again. She could see Lourdes turning around the suggestion in her mind—surprised, Rosemary could tell by her expression, at the rightness of the idea. This was where she had been moving in her art all this time. Maybe it took someone like Rosemary, someone who knew that the illusion of mass, of life, never made up for the reality of it, to suggest it to her. Maybe it required someone without imagination.

So she'd made the suggestion about the body casting—and when Lourdes seemed open, had offered to round up other participants as well. They had all been over at Lourdes after the funeral, looking at her drawings, laughing about Ginger's daughters. Trying to shake off something potent but insidious that seemed to infiltrate Ginger's funeral. It wasn't just the news about the lynchings. There had been, Wilma had murmured in her exasperatingly smug way, great disarray in the spirit world when Ginger passed over. It *would* be just like Ginger to get herself noticed in what should be a very normal rite of passage. But it was in all of them, not the spirit world, that the feeling of disorder seemed to linger. And it was so physical—like someone familiar but not necessarily *nice* had put a hand on the back of each of their necks and whispered words that couldn't be taken back—or shared. That was the worst.

It made Rosemary think about getting her massage practice up and running again—just to shake the sensation, replace it with something more consoling. In the meantime, body casting would have to suffice. So here they were, ready to be bound up like Lazarus.

When Rosemary felt Lourdes smoothing the first strip of wet gauze over her rib cage, she sighed. Opening her eyes slightly, she saw Lourdes's long square-tipped fingers stretch out another strip and lay it, still dripping, above the first. Rosemary closed her eyes again and gave herself up to the feeling. Her body's need to be touched was like a surge, a stabbing hunger, a sinking deep, all three.

"You don't need to keep your eyes closed," Lourdes teased. "You can kibbitz. I'm as new at this as a medical student." Late Thursday afternoon, they had located a medical supplier in the capital and had bought out his entire supply of orthopedic gauze—to the great dismay of four medical students who needed to practice on each other for their exams. Lourdes, now into the project, had shown the single-mindedness often ascribed to artists and refused to cede a single roll.

"Just make sure I have room to breathe."

"I'm making the molds fairly thin. Just a couple of layers. I'll reinforce them later. I can't tell you how much I appreciate this, Rosemary."

She should, Rosemary thought. How many seventy-one year olds strip for their friends? But she just nodded, closing her eyes again. She was suddenly very sleepy, as if all her muscles were falling away from the bones. People discount the power of touch, she thought. Me too. Which was very odd given that touch was how Rosemary had developed her following here. It was strange, though, how no one saw her as having the same needs. No one, for example, even other masseuses, offered *her* a massage. It was as if at her age she was beyond all that. Maybe that was why they came to her with that trust often reserved for ministers and doctors.

Often people came talking in code—complaining of leg pains or upper back pain when what they were really wondering was whether their viral load was rising again or their cancer had come back or whether this time the tightening in their chest was angina rather than indigestion. It is hard, at any age, to live too keenly awake to the reality of one's own death. But death wasn't what people feared, really. What they feared was the body's treason. For where do we go to rest when we can't rest in our bodies?

That was the job of Rosemary's hands. To invite people back into their bodies. To let them know it was safe to live on intimate and tender terms with their limitations. She'd started her massage practice in a serious way after Walter's long illness. She gave him so many massages, and she could see how they helped, just as she could see how laying her hand on Ginger's shoulder or putting her arm around Shirley made something in them relax, something else wake up.

"I hope this pose isn't going to be too hard to hold. I could just do your torso today and your arms and legs separately another day," Lourdes said. She smoothed the plaster across the separate pieces of gauze covering Rosemary's stomach and ribs, erasing the seams, and then began to place the strips across her breasts.

"You forget I got used to modeling on a regular basis for Walter—although what he wanted with an old biddy never was clear to me. What do you have in mind here if you don't mind my asking." She was standing as Lourdes had arranged her, both arms bent, her right hand outstretched, palm up, her left hand crossed in front of her waist with the palm up as well.

"I was rather thinking you'd be good for a sculpture about divine judgment. But I keep getting ideas for other statues. Maybe I can get you to agree to do this on a regular basis."

Of course, Rosemary thought dreamily to herself, feeling Lourdes' fingers traveling across her back. Of course I'll do this again. Mentally, she shook herself awake. What was she doing enjoying being wrapped in a winding sheet?

"Could you use a lighter touch? Do it only when I'm breathing out and even so give a little extra slack."

"Do you want Mikela or Natividad or Gwen as your watcher?"

"You're doing Ginny today too?"

"And one of the others as well, I'm just letting chance determine which one. I feel uncomfortably god-like today—telling everyone where to put their hands and legs, what expressions to take. It's opening up a part of me that should probably stay hidden—especially from myself. I never imagined I could get off on being so directive." Lourdes tipped her head back and laughed that rich deep laugh of hers that seemed to resonate not just through her own body but through the body of the listener as well.

Lourdes turned Rosemary gently to the right as she moved around her to the left, unwinding the wetted gauze bandage and running it over Rosemary's buttocks, across her pubis, safely covered with underwear to protect her pubic hair, and, finally through her legs and around her upper thighs.

"I find it amazing that everyone has been so open to trying this with me. Usually, you know, visual art is not about touching others in the flesh. It's about seeing them and touching your medium—clay or wax or acrylic or oils. You save all your feeling for your media, your creation. It's wonderfully sensual but also very safe because everything is at one remove. All this feeling can pour in and out of you because no one is at risk, not even yourself. But with these casts, its very different. It's not just about me, about getting to know myself. I'm so aware of how little I know about each of you. And at another level, as I wrap you with the gauze, I know so much that I didn't know before. You must feel like that when you give massages, Rosemary."

Lourdes ran her hands over Rosemary's torso a last time, beginning with her shoulders, then her breasts, her back, her buttocks and stomach.

I know but I am not known, Rosemary thought. That is what old age is all about.

"Are you afraid of getting old?" she asked Lourdes.

Lourdes stepped back a foot or two and looked carefully at her work, appearing to ignore Rosemary's question. Then she looked into Rosemary's pale blue eyes, held them gently with her own deeper ones. The smile she gave Rosemary was so natural and easy it felt like a hook had snagged into Rosemary's skin.

"Seriously, I love your body, Rosemary. I'd love to have mine look as true as yours does when I'm your age. I look at your body and I just feel you in it in a way that sometimes I don't even feel about myself when I'm looking in the mirror. I'd love to have that in a constant way when I'm your age. I'd love to have it now if that were possible." Lourdes shrugged and turned and beckoned to Natividad, who sat on a small wooden chair with the baby strapped, nursing, across her chest.

"Tell her to bring her paper and pens. I see no reason why, immobilized, I shouldn't do double duty and model for her as well. Captivated Old Woman can be the title."

"Now I'm off to petrify our prophet," Lourdes said. "I can see she's having second thoughts already. When the cast begins to feel a little warm, send Natividad to get me and I'll cut you out."

"How warm? You didn't tell me about that."

But Lourdes was already on the other side of the apartment. She had put them in separate rooms out of respect for their modesty, Rosemary supposed, but all the doors and windows opened into the central patio where their voices mingled, magnified by the air well in a rather surreal way.

"Are you sure you want me to do this?" Rosemary heard Lourdes ask Ginny. In the other room, she could hear Gwen, Lourdes' step-daughter, trying to talk to Mikela, who answered so slowly that she sounded like a 78 record played at half speed. Mikela refused to believe Gwen could really understand Spanish and derived great pleasure out of talking to her with the care usually reserved for the mentally retarded. Natividad smiled as she listened to her sister.

"She's a good teacher, your sister," Rosemary said in Spanish.

Natividad stared at her and then nodded. "She likes school," she answered. She bent her head again toward the sketch pad, a gift from Lourdes that she rarely let out of her sight. She pulled her small breast out of the baby's mouth and pulled the *rebozo* around so that the baby rested on her back. She seemed completely indifferent to the baby's startled and angry cry—as indifferent as she had been to the nursing itself. So different from the experience Rosemary had had nursing, where, given the state of that marriage, it was the greatest sensory peace she knew. On the other hand, she had been in her early twenties—not twelve years old.

Natividad looked attentively at Rosemary in her cast and started to sketch, a small, wonderfully attractive smile on her beautiful face. I just can't, Rosemary thought. I'm seventy-three. I doze off more than the baby. But someone has to step in and separate them and give that child her life back. Give both those children their lives back.

Mikela came to the doorway, drawn by the baby's muffled cry. She went over to her sister and pulled at the *rebozo*, loosening it and taking the baby into her arms with a small, crooning sigh. Whatever are we going to do with Mikela? It was a question that was growing more intense every day. Mikela stuck her finger in the baby's mouth, and he closed his lips around it sucking greedily, his bright blue eyes fixed on her smiling face. They might change color of course, Rosemary thought, but they were startling. They raised questions no one wanted to ask—but made it all the more important that something be done. If they didn't change, what chance did a child like that have here? What chance did his mother?

Mikela glanced at her sister and almost spoke, but stopped herself. Natividad was deeply immersed in her drawing, her face gaining with her concentration a liveliness and softness that was completely absent from her interactions with anyone but her sister or Gwen.

She was done with mothering, Rosemary thought crossly. Her children and Walt's were awaiting their own grandchildren, and their foster children were making their own families. And all time had taught her was the world vastly over-rated the role of mothers. What influence had she really had on any of them? Her daughter Giselle shared a mannerism or two, her son Vernon had her nose—but they didn't identify with any of her life choices or she with theirs. Which is not to say that she didn't have her share of sleepless nights raising the two of them, or moments of deepest delight and pride. But motherhood, like childhood, was really a terminal condition. It was impossible to imagine, in the thick of it, that those feelings attenuated. But they did. And a rather intense or cursory curiosity took its place. Maybe that's why Walt took up painting when he did—so nobody would be surprised by the look of intense concentration in his face that said, if you were really listening to it, "Who *are* you?" That look of his didn't make her feel uncomfortable, rather it felt like being loved anew each day, released in some way to be exactly what this day, this time in her life called for.

She could hear Mikela and Gwen cosseting the baby in the next room. For whatever reason, Mikela had eased up a little on Gwen today. Natividad looked up from her paper and smiled at Rosemary, a smile so clean and sweet and present it took Rosemary's breath away. There really is someone in there, she thought.

"Can I see?" she asked, nodding her head toward the paper. "My husband was a painter and he painted me many times." Every hour of every day, I miss being alive in his sight, she thought.

She bent her head slightly as Natividad held up the drawing.

"But this is extraordinary." Rosemary blinked away the tears that caught her by surprise.

Natividad had drawn her upper torso and head, her bandaged hands with their open palms, and her face, capturing there an expression Rosemary had never known herself capable of, at once stern and vulnerable and sensuous. I would like to know this woman, she thought. And I'd like to know the girl who can see her.

"Marvelous," she said to Natividad. "You are very very good."

Natividad, unsmiling now, held Rosemary's eyes as she lowered the tablet and brought it close to her chest. As if she were covering an exposed heart, Rosemary thought.

"Marvelous," Rosemary said again, keeping her face this time as immobile as her body.

"Lourdes, can you bring your clippers," she called out in a loud voice. "I am getting scalded in here." So that's it, she thought, slightly giddy with the heat and immobility. It's that simple, isn't it. I just made my last commitment. I'm taking her in.

"Are you sure you want to do this?" Lourdes asked Ginny again.

Ginny had the sheet Lourdes had given her draped over her shoulders like a high priestess' robe. Her straight ash blonde hair was pulled up off her neck in a casually elegant twist, a few strands falling loose. She looked the way Lourdes herself felt when she went to the doctor's office—as if she had assumed the position of observer with herself, had slipped out of her body and saw it now with a doctor's clear, cool abstractness.

As Lourdes waited for an answer, she could feel the spirit coming back into Ginny's body, a faint relaxation of her hands and shoulders. There was a weight of sorrow here, washing through her like a dark wave. Lourdes could tell that Marie, leaning back into the couch, felt it too. Ginny's expression became uncertain.

"I'm modeling other faces," Lourdes said. "No one could possibly know who the body belongs to."

"Perhaps she wants them to," Marie said, leaning forward. "It is strange how anonymous our bodies are without our faces. We think they are not, of course. We think they are indivisibly us, that no one can look at them without thinking our names. But think of all those torsos and statues you see in museums. You do not think, Laura or Tanya. You think, beauty, age, woman. You do not think of indigestion or embarrassment. You do not think, May 10, 2000, sun on the floor at ten in the morning, the smell of oranges and coffee in the kitchen. You do not think, someone made a choice to be seen, to be drawn into this new relation to her body, to the artist, and to us who are now looking. You will never know her name, usually, or the reasons for her choice."

"I could model you with the sheet over you if that would be more comfortable," Lourdes said.

"Are you afraid when you go back to the States that they will use this against you?" Marie asked. She, like all of them, knew about David's painting now. Not from David, or Simon—rather from Gwen, who had been in Boston when the show opened and described the painting glowingly. "It is true, I cannot imagine any of the priests and sisters here modeling for Lourdes—but if they did, who could possibly connect their bodies with their robes? Perhaps, Lourdes, we should do this as an exercise, no? A group of figures in robes but with faces and another group of bodies without faces. Even I, who have undressed many a man and woman with my eyes, would find this a difficult matching game."

"Perhaps Simon could help," Ginny said, laughing. "He's had a lot of experience with that kind of looking too." She shook her head briskly, took a deep breath, and let her sheet drop. "Let's get on with this," she said."

"Do you think you could stand with one foot forward and your arms outstretched?" Lourdes asked.

"Like this?"

"Higher, like you're trying to pluck an apple from the tree of life."

"You have nothing to be ashamed of," Marie said, letting her eyes move coolly up and down Ginny's body. It should have made her feel uncomfortable, but it didn't.

"You sound like you are inspecting a melon at the market. Next I expect you to come over and thump me."

Lourdes adjusted Ginny's right leg and brought her hands closer together. "This is going to feel cold at first," she warned Ginny as she began to wind the first strip around her waist.

"This position will be difficult to hold," she said as she stepped back.

"I'll be able to see what I've accomplished with my weight lifting and exercise regimen," Ginny said. "Simon keeps telling me I'm like a wild animal refining my fight or flight reflexes. He'll be pleased I'm using them to hold still."

"If that is what you're doing," Marie said. "But I feel perhaps you are taking a step forward."

"There is this phrase in yoga, *the pause becomes the pose*. It is about finding the state of balance, the state of tension and relaxation of all the different muscles, that will allow you to hold a pose indefinitely. It is another kind of strength, the strength to stay still. All good models have it I think." Lourdes continued to dip strips of plaster coated gauze in the pail of water and wind them around Ginny's torso.

"Would you mind if Marie helped me?" she asked. "I'm concerned about how long you can stand like this, no matter how many push-ups you've done over the past few months."

"Well, now that you've presented this as a spiritual discipline rather than exhibitionism, I'm tempted to raise the stakes. But I'm already feeling the forces of gravity, so faster would be better."

Ginny at first tried to keep track of both their hands, Marie working on her legs while Lourdes began to wind the bandages around her arms. For some reason as they had shifted tasks, they had left her lower torso to last. That sensation was completely unfamiliar to Ginny—and very liberating too. It should have filled her with a sense of embarrassment, but it didn't. It was as if something were being reclaimed—but in a way she would never have been able to imagine. What was shocking to her was how readily she gave herself up to it.

"What will you call this one?" Marie asked Lourdes, as if reading Ginny's mind.

"Miriam's Question."

"And what was her question, this Miriam, whoever she was?"

"She was Moses' sister-in-law, wife of his brother Aaron," Ginny said. "Or Aaron's sister, depending on the reference."

"And a prophet in her own right," Lourdes said. "She dared to ask the question everyone else had but couldn't speak—which was why was Moses the only one who could talk directly to God. Who, or what, gave him sole access."

"And she was punished for it," Ginny said. The wind from the patio was brushing across her stomach. Her arms ached already.

"But in such an interesting way. She received the punishment she would have received if she had spit in her father's eye. She was sent out into the desert for a week and inflicted with a terrible skin disease—like psoriasis or leprosy. But her community waited for her, they didn't leave her. It was as if they were of two minds, you see. They could see Moses' point of view and hers as well."

"But that is an old story," Marie said. "What use are you making of it now?" She wound a bandage from Ginny's knee toward her pubis.

"I'm not sure. The image just speaks to me. Miriam alone in the desert watching her skin turn white as if she were covered with salt or fish scales or manna. As if she were shedding her skin like a snake. And all because she asked, *Why not me?* And I have this other image of all these people waiting for her. I see them as all women, but I suppose it would be just as powerful or perhaps even more so if there are men there too. And just by waiting, they are saying that Miriam's question is theirs too. Part of me wonders whether that isn't what we're all being asked to see—that until we can claim Miriam's question as our own, each of us will feel as if we are sent out alone into the wilderness when we ask it, that the question is going to be greeted with punishment. I am so tired of hearing women's lives—the ambiguous consequences of their courage and daring—only being the source of cautionary tales. But what if we all understood that Miriam's question is *our* question and that it is hard to imagine any God worth worshipping who can't hear it or any community worth belonging to that can't either. Only if we can go out and join her, share her terror at the changes in her body and, by sharing it, change that terror, will we change that experience for each of us. So maybe I'll call the sculpture, Insisting on an Answer."

Lourdes stepped back and looked at Ginny, her eyes sliding down the white, hardening arms and chest, the fair skin exposed between waist and pubis. The wind felt like a hand brushing again and again across the remaining expanse of skin. It was erotic and unsettling to Ginny to be looked at this dispassionately. I have never felt so simple, she thought. So taken in.

Lourdes went off to get more bandages, while Marie tried to slide the remaining bandages under Ginny's feet. Ginny wiggled her toes, suddenly claustrophobic.

"Could you hurry this?" she asked as Lourdes came in with more bandages.

"You're a saint to do this. All of you are. My company of saints."

"As long as we don't confuse the saintly with the self-deny," Marie said, rapidly unrolling one of the bandages and dipping it into the water. She had a few dabs of plaster on her high smooth forehead. "For me, when I help Lourdes, I am moved by the self-interest. I am very tired of the insipid virgins that they have both here and in France. I want a little sex in my religion. I want a lot of worldly experiences. And I want to see faces that interest me if I see them on the street today—I mean with expressions I can recognize—like anger or fear or lust or sorrow or disappointment or envy or shame or hope or anxiety. All the the messy things that make the life worth living. It's hard to see those as bringing us closer to God—but they are what we are. They are our only means to know—our so far from the perfect bodies, our so close to the crazy *sensibilité*."

"I hope you have a tape recorder going," Ginny said to Lourdes. "You could use her comments in your liner notes."

"And what would you say?" Lourdes asked. She finished winding the last bandage through Ginny's legs and around her thighs.

Everything, Ginny thought. Here I am white as Lot's wife, paralyzed from my neck down, feeling I can look forward for the first time in months. I love being touched by them. It's brought back too much. David's visit. The energy that is still there between us. The agony of the last eight months. And it made it all fall away as well—as if it has no place here at all.

"I'm thinking," she said. "Believe me, I'm thinking."

"Well I'm off to do Gwen next, but I'll want to hear more when I come back. Marie, you're staying to entertain her, right?"

"I shall sit like a buddha on the top of the table so you will have no need to move your head to see me."

"How did we ever get into this," Ginny asked as the door closed behind Lourdes.

Marie looked at her, letting her eyes move slowly from floor to face. "As usual, I believe there are more reasons than there are people. And they are not always the same, are they, why an experience took place and how it changed us."

"You do look like a buddha up there," Ginny said. Marie was folded into the lotus position.

"Yes, I've taken the only seat in the room. But that plaster has the same effect, does it not? Here we are, two women, *immobile* and flooded." She shrugged, lifting her hands and moving her head to right and left in a gesture similar to a Balinese dancer.

"I think I need to call Lourdes to liberate you right now with her garden shears. You are looking very white."

Hurrying from the living room of the downstairs apartment, where she had left Ginny with Marie, through the patio to the next room where Rosemary stood frozen in a posture both giving and beseeching, Lourdes knew she had taken on too much. She should have done them individually, as she had Marie earlier in the week. This did not feel like art, rather an assembly line, but with her as the sole moveable object. She knew she'd feel differently later when she could work with the casts themselves. Alone. One at a time. Now she couldn't hear herself think. For one thing, there were all these little fragments of conversation coming from the different rooms—Rosemary's exclamation that had brought her running, the stumbling conversation between Gwen and Mikela, the cooing of the baby, Ginny's wonderful deep voice answering some inaudible question of Marie's, all this mixed with the sound of a huge truck rumbling over the cobblestones, a child beating on the wooden bars over the windows, schoolgirls chattering on their way home for lunch, a barrage of firecrackers, the maids in the next house answering the telephone.

"Do you want to help me?" she asked Natividad.

"Look at what she's done first," Rosemary ordered.

"Where's the baby?" Lourdes asked.

"With her sister and Gwen. It's good for them to have a little time apart. For Gwen and Mikela to get a little more accustomed to each other. Show Lourdes your drawing, dear."

Slowly Natividad lowered her sketch pad from her chest. Lourdes knelt down beside her to look. She put a hand on the girl's shoulder. The confusion she felt was just as strong as it had been when she found Natividad on her doorstep, the baby half-suffocated in the folds of her *rebozo*, her eyes glazed, her nose running, this same damn pad clutched to her chest where the baby should have been. Feeling her anger rising, Lourdes concentrated more closely on the drawing.

"How do you develop a talent like hers?" Rosemary asked.

"I'm not sure. Mainly by keeping her supplied with paper and pens. Teaching her a technique here and there when she's ready. I was such a late developer myself, it's hard for me to imagine what it would be like to have such facility so early."

"Clearly, she'd have to learn other things as well—how to cook and clean and read and write well in both English and Spanish. Computer skills maybe. We don't want her to be some freak."

Or idiot savant, Lourdes thought, looking at the girl's blank face and then back at the wonderfully knowing portrait she had done of Rosemary. In truth, she was a little jealous of Natividad. Horrified by her as well. Neither emotion felt appropriate to the child everyone kept telling Lourdes she was. Lourdes could *see* it. Why couldn't she feel it?

"Do you ever think of taking her on as an apprentice?" Rosemary asked.

"I'm not going to be here long enough. And, to be honest, I don't know how teachable she is. She's off in her own world so much of the time. The only one she seems to connect with is her sister, and sometimes not even with her, or, now, with Gwen." Lourdes paused, musing on the oddness of this. How, given Gwen's obsession with Natividad and the baby, there didn't seem to be any way Lourdes was going to be able to keep a comfortable distance from Natividad. How odd it was that the distance, the dangerous charge, between her and Ben's daughter had been absorbed into this larger dilemma of what to do about the girls. She and Gwen were coming to know each other through their responses to the girls—and, even with Lourdes' aversion to Natividad, something positive was happening between her and Gwen. Impossible to describe to Ben except to tell him what Gwen's current intentions were and to say she supported Gwen.

"This is her language," Rosemary said. "She needs someone who can speak it with her. It's a lovely language—I just wish it were mine."

Lourdes had already decided Natividad would be no help liberating Rosemary, since she stood there throughout their conversation more immobile than the old woman cased in plaster.

"Shall we ask her to leave us alone while I extricate you?"

"For her comfort more than mine. I told you I was a shameless old hussy."

"Off with you," Rosemary said with a quick jerk of her head.

It sounded like she was talking to a dog.

Lourdes closed the door behind the girl, then concentrated on how to free Rosemary. She stood behind her and, inserting a small pair of shears at the base of her neck, began to clip down following her spine. When she reached her waist, she began to clip in a circle to her left and then, reaching Rosemary's navel, clipped up between her breasts to her breastbone. She proceeded to clip down from Rosemary's right shoulder to her hand, then carefully pulled aside those two quarters of the upper torso, setting them, hollow side down, on the tile floor. She would need to reinforce the casts fairly soon.

Rosemary watched her attentively, breathing a little easier when they both were reassured that Lourdes would be able to free her. As Lourdes began to clip around the other half of her waist, she said, "It's interesting who speaks to us and who doesn't, isn't it? With all her talent, you've taken against the girl. You like her sister better."

The plaster had set a little too long and Lourdes had to use both hands to work the clippers. She was relieved at the concentration it required of her.

Lourdes pulled the two left sides of the upper torso apart. "Maybe I should do a sculpture titled, The Mother Who Sings for Herself. It's a terrifying idea, isn't it, that mothers have a choice about who they love."

Lourdes adjusted the two left sides of the torso beside their counterparts on the floor, making sure that they would not distort as they hardened further. She studied Rosemary's lower torso, trying to figure out how best to separate it, deciding that a single long cut down either side would work best until she came to the feet.

"Depending on where you're standing," Rosemary said. "If you are a child, recognizing voluntariness on the part of your parents, especially your mother, is terrifying. But it's equally terrible to tell a woman that she is a heart for hire, that there is nothing volitional in her love. After we had our foster children, I felt so exasperated by the complacency of my own two, how they could never see that I gave them what I did as much out of the freedom of my heart as out of necessity."

Lourdes glanced over at the casts lying on the floor. They looked like enormous versions of the wax molds of body parts—hearts and legs and hands and eyes—they sold in the booths outside the church down the street. People hung the small wax replicas from the hands of their most trusted saints, praying for relief from heart ache and lumbago, helplessness and truths too terrible for them to see. Scale, Lourdes thought, humor and tragedy are a question of scale.

"And your step-children?" she asked Rosemary as she clipped down her thigh.

"It remains a mystery to me where our sympathy and identification flow freely and an equally surprising mystery where it doesn't. All I've learned by this age is not to fight it. God, or the life force, has a surprising way of establishing new and better balances. Just think of the women in your life who have been more than mothers to you."

"Or friends who have been more than sisters."

"Men who have been closer than women friends."

"Short list, that one," Lourdes said with a laugh.

"For all of us, but they change our lives, those men."

Lourdes felt her eyes tear as she pulled away the front of the lower torso very carefully. It was just about time to start working on Ginny. She should have bought two sets of clippers. She would have to put Gwen off until another day—except that she really couldn't imagine using her as a model without the other women present. It hadn't been her idea to include Gwen anyway—anymore than it had been to have her stay on after Ben left. She had, graciously, acceded to the inevitable. Maybe that was a choice—the graciousness. Just as Ben had graciously acceded to her departure.

"I felt very lucky in my sons," she said to Rosemary. "They were so close in age, only eleven months apart, they were more like twins. Such an interesting little world to themselves. The observer role felt natural to me. But when I see the women they've chosen, I wonder if they wanted something very different. They've each chosen someone so like them they could be twins. Maybe they're just trying to duplicate their original relationship with each other."

"And you. You might have wanted something warmer—like that lovely man you've hooked yourself up with now."

"We're through, I'm afraid," Lourdes said, pulling the last half of the lower torso away. She let the double sense shiver there for a second before she added, "You might want to shower and get some of that vaseline off."

"You're looking flustered," Gwen said as Lourdes came out of the room with Rosemary, now draped in a sheet, and ushered her into the large pink bathroom in the bedroom that Gwen had used. Now Gwen had moved herself upstairs, complaining of the echoes. Moved herself into Lourdes' original studio. It meant that Lourdes had the entire downstairs at night if she wanted to work, so she didn't complain. Gwen had said to leave the drawings up—she found them comforting. An adjective that astonished Lourdes, although she didn't question it. She was more comfortable than she imagined she could be having Ben's daughter sleeping in the next room. It didn't mean they talked much. Or not about themselves. They talked about Lourdes' drawings. About Gwen's plans to adopt. About that terrifying experience at the procession. About Ginger's death—but carefully, since there was such a Pandora's box that could be opened there.

But, no doubt about it, as big and rackety as this place was, she was still counting the days until Gwen's departure. And her own. Although where she was going remained a persistent blank. All Lourdes could think about these days were the sculptures. Once Rosemary brought them up, some flood gate in Lourdes had opened and she was surrounded by possible images. Now, of course, reality was intruding. Big time. If she wasn't quick, the women would all be scalded by the setting plaster.

"I over-estimated my efficiency," she said, brushing her hair away from her face with her wrist, her hands still sticky with the plaster. She had the shears in her hand and snapped them nervously. "I have to get back to Ginny."

"Sounds as if you'd like to call it quits," Gwen said. "I can do it some other time if you want."

"Maybe we could make you a group project," Lourdes said. "I could just give directions and the others could wrap you up."

"If that's what you want," Gwen said. Her expression seemed both relieved and disappointed. "Mikela would like it, I think. She'd like to imprison me. Make sure you keep hold of the clippers."

"Count me in," Rosemary called from the bathroom. "I'm thinking this is a skill I could teach my women. If Gwen and I get good at it, we could do it without bothering you."

"Jam-making and body-casting collective," Gwen said in a low voice to Lourdes. "Can't see why I didn't come up with that."

Lourdes laughed. "You forgot condom and contraceptive distributors. Can't you see the park filled with life-sized sculptures on wheels. They can be little stores, filled with jams and birth control pills. They could have little tape recorders inside that repeated incessantly, 'You want to buy, lady? Why you buy from her and not from me?' Imagine how uncomfortable people would be bringing them home as mementos. So different from an exotic photograph or a piece of cloth. Man with unbearable burden on his back.

Woman balancing basket half her height."

"And the babies," Gwen said. "Whole clusters of babies. Those would be the most troubling." She looked down at little Miguel asleep in her arms. "Are you going to do a sculpture of him?"

"Possibly free-sculpting. I think he might object to being frozen in plaster."

"Or it might just feel like another day strapped on mama's back." Gwen shivered. "It gives me the creeps, really, how they smother the babies here."

"I suppose if you grew up with it, you'd find it reassuring. It may be why people here don't care about how close they are pressed together."

"Don't remind me," Gwen said. "That was too spooky."

"Do you think you can take it in the body cast? Some people get claustrophobia." Lourdes snapped her shears. "Speaking of which, I need to emancipate Ginny."

"Funny image of an artist, isn't it? Cutting people free of their second skin."

"I prefer to see it as a form of costume-making."

After they extricated Ginny, Lourdes and Marie moved the casts of Ginny into the other room with Rosemary's, while Gwen stripped down and covered herself with vaseline and Rosemary and Mikela began to unroll bandages and soak them. Ginny was showering, but returned to join them by the time Lourdes and Marie had settled the casts to Lourdes satisfaction. Natividad and Miguel were sleeping, she told them.

"I guess this is what I've always dreamed of—being the center of attraction," Gwen said, looking at the four women gathered around her. "Someone tell Mikela we'll do her too some day. Natividad as well. I think they'd get a kick out of it, don't you, Lourdes?"

"Let's see how these turn out first," Lourdes said.

Of course, her mind was filled with sculptures inspired by Natividad's drawings and the little flashes of their past that Ginny and Simon coaxed from Mikela with their more fluent Spanish. The girl hanging by her heels from the ceiling, her mother beating her like an old rug. And the other image, the one that had inspired all of this, the image of Gwen and Marie and Rosemary and the two middle class women from the town all trapped with Natividad and Mikela and the baby in the crowd at the procession on Good Friday, all joining hands to encircle and protect the baby, Natividad and Mikela from that implacable press. They had no hands, in Lourdes' image, none of the protecting women had hands, just their arms interlaced with each other, those sad little holes where hands should plug in. Women Without Means is what she wanted to call it. She needed that image for herself in a way that she didn't need the others. How sad it was, their eyes, hers and Gwen's, locked on each other, the terror she could see on Gwen's face, her own voice going out to embrace her, keep her calm and safe. "They mean nothing by this. It's going to be over soon. Spread your legs so you have a secure center of balance. If you fall, I'll catch the baby."

"And don't forget the ocean breath," Marie had added with a laugh.

"Or that, if one of us goes, the rest go too," Rosemary said. "You do what you have to do." And Gwen had listened to all of them, but it was Lourdes' gaze, Lourdes' steady gaze that held her. And something similar had happened at Ginger's grave. Lourdes so sure if she looked down into the coffin she would see Annie's face staring back at her, or, worse, Jacquie's. So it wasn't clear that afternoon at the graveside who was holding whom steady.

"Now?" Mikela asked, tugging Lourdes back to the present. She was lifting the wetted bandages out of the bucket carefully, as if they were fragile, magic.

"Remember not to wrap too tightly," Lourdes said to all of them. "Rosemary, do you want to do her torso. Marie her arms. Ginny her lower torso, and Mikela her legs. I'll keep the bandages coming."

"I must say, this pose leaves me feeling more than a little exposed," Gwen said as the women set to work.

"Exuberant," Rosemary said. "Welcoming."

"Like I said, a little exposed." Gwen closed her eyes as if the light hurt her.

"You ok?" Lourdes asked.

"What am I meant to be, Lourdes? A sacrificial victim?" Her voice was sharp enough to make all the women pause a second.

"It shouldn't be long now," Marie observed briskly. "With this many hands, we have no worries."

"No," Lourdes answered Gwen, holding her step-daughter's eyes steadily as she had those other days. The same sense of surprise and steadiness running through her. "I don't see you as alone in this, Gwen. I see you in a circle of women, gaining strength from them. I see you acting in a protective way."

Without hands, Lourdes thought, the sad holes in the wood. The sculpture she'd seen in the museum rising before her. Magdalene's empty wrists beckoning to the future. *Look ma, no hands!*

"You're holding something back," Gwen said. "I can see it in your face."

"Isn't that always the way," Rosemary said, rubbing her hands over Gwen's shoulders. "The more direct I try to be, the farther I seem to get from the true subject. There feels like something surprising is lurking behind every word. Maybe that's what I like about body work. It feels complete in itself."

"You have to wrap the fingers together," Lourdes told Marie. "Otherwise we'll never get her out of the plaster."

I should offer to do it, Lourdes thought, but instead she stepped back and watched everyone moving busily over Gwen's body. She must have her mother's build, Lourdes thought, able to see almost nothing of Ben in her slight frame and strong, packed muscles. Gwen looked down at all the hands, a bemused expression on her face. Then she looked at Lourdes.

"This feels weird," she said. "I feel like I should have offered to help."

"Next time," Lourdes said. "It helps to have a real knowledge of what it feels like to be the subject before you do it with someone else, I think."

"Did you?"

"To be honest, it puts me in a panic even to think about doing it," Lourdes said, laughing at the absurdity of it as they all turned to look at her suspiciously. "Like my mind will have no choice but to evacuate my body."

"Sounds like you're next, Lourdes," Ginny said, rising to her feet, her hands milky white with plaster. "We may have something new to teach you."

"Not until I'm free," Gwen said. "I want to be part of this."

Whatever happens, Lourdes thought, I can't afford to let her touch me. The thought itself was like a burning hand closing down across her arm.

"To change the subject," she said, "what are we going to do about that baby. He's not safe with her. We all know that. We can't stand back and just—"

"Let life take its own course?" Marie asked.

"We're part of that course," Rosemary said. "That's what's keeping some of us up at night." She looked mildly accusingly at Ginny and Marie.

"Me too," Gwen said. " I'm willing to take Miguel. I'm willing to take Natividad."

Lourdes looked at her quickly and found that Gwen was already looking at her. "You have no idea what you're suggesting," she said. "The baby is one thing. Natividad, that's something completely different."

"How old were you when you had your sons?"

"I came from a different world."

"We all do," Marie said sharply. "No matter how much we pretend differently. Even identical twins see different suns rise every morning. Who is to say it isn't the right thing for her?"

"Yes," Gwen said. "Who?"

"Your mother hasn't been dead a year, Gwen."

"And nothing's going to bring her back."

"But this is your chance to come into your own. To finish your education. To explore. Find your voice."

"Why does coming into your own always have to mean being alone?" Gwen looked at all the women, one by one. " Is that what any of you have wanted or still want?"

BURNING THE BABY SNATCHERS
(Mikela)

We children are brought to earth to ease the burdens of our parents. To keep them company. That is why they teach us so early how to carry babies on our backs, how to gather firewood, how to dig the fields and plant the seeds, how to weave.

My people know that God, our father-mother, gives and grabs back life without explanation. We have so many children to protect ourselves from God's whims. We never know when they'll be taken from us. The priests say they go to a more dependable place, where they never hunger and thirst, where there are no fevers or worms, where there are no soldiers. I don't know. I think many people don't know. If they did, wouldn't they just send the babies directly there without bothering to breathe this air? But the mother who has lost a child to hunger or fever often has another as soon as she can. She can't stop believing that this world, too, has something to give. To her. Her babies are a gift to her.

My people know that foreigners have a great hunger, bigger even than God's, for our children. They want to steal them from us and take them away to the States. Some of our people believe they kill the children and give their hearts and lungs and livers and hands to the rich white children. They believe the foreigners are interfering in a terrible way with God's will. If God wanted those rich white children to have hearts, wouldn't God have given good hearts to them? I think sometimes of all those white babies with the hearts of dark-skinned babies beating inside them. I wonder what they dream. I wonder what startles them. I wonder whether there are watchers there too—and what they do to protect children with stolen hearts.

Some of our people don't believe the foreigners kill the children. They believe they're stolen by the rich in our country and sold in the States for slaves. They don't believe all this talk of adoption. For what kinds of burdens can a poor child relieve for rich parents in a rich country?

Some of our women do sell their own babies. They believe this talk about adoption. They think they're sending their babies to a place like the one the priests describe, where they will neither hunger nor thirst, where the last will be first. For those mothers, it is a fate for their children better than death by hunger or fever or mudslide or earthquake. It's true, they're trying to trick God but they're not betraying the promise God's son Jésus made us of a world where the last will come first. And with the money they receive they can feed their next baby.

But none of this is fair—not what God, or the rich in our country, or the rich foreigners do to us. To take someone's child is to rob them of the gift of life. It is like cutting their heart, still beating, out of their chest and leaving them there. Even if you get money for it.

Some days our people can't stand the pain of this any longer and they rise up against God and the rich, whether they are from our country or from the States. "Baby snatchers," they cry out. "We have so little, how can you want to take even that away?" And my people stone the foreign baby snatchers and they hang them up and they set them on fire so that they can feel exactly what they are doing to us.

We do not feel this is unjust.

But it makes the foreigners feel that my people can be possessed, at a moment's notice, by evil spirits. They think that what we do to one foreigner here or there is worse than what they do to all of us every day. For they are the evil spirits, aren't they? Tempting the rich in our country to take even more away from us than they already have. They wouldn't steal babies if someone wouldn't buy them. And they tempt us too, the foreign women who come, childless, rich, one by one, begging our babies from us—for they teach us all to be discontent with what God has given us. Your babies will be better off with us, they tell us. You will be better off with one less child to feed. They make nothing of what we children can give our parents and what our parents can give us. They spit in God's face and they don't even know it. When we sell our children, we know what we're doing. Why don't they, when they buy them?

There are many foreign women in this town who come here just to buy babies. Some of them visit Señora Rosemary. They bring their brown-skinned, black-haired children, who call them mommy. They talk about how long it takes to buy or steal a baby, how many lawyers and judges you have to pay. They talk about the latest lynching and how they're afraid now to go traveling in the mountains alone with their children. They have to bring one of our people along too so no one will know the babies are stolen.

I see them look a little fearfully at their own children, as if they wonder whether one day they too will be possessed without warning by evil spirits. Whether it is in their blood. But the children look back, fat and happy, and there is no danger—for in their bodies, even if their skin is dark, beat the hearts of rich children. Rich children never get mad at God because they live in heaven now.

It's in the next world where all our fortunes are reversed that the rich children will rise up, poor, wild with anger at God and those who are rich in the next life. But we will have learned from this world. We will treat them, then, better than they have treated us. We won't tempt them.

We won't tempt them the way that Señora Rosemary is tempting Natividad now. Señora Rosemary points to those fat dark children sitting in their white mothers' laps and says to Natividad, "Don't you want to give Miguel a better chance?"

She's frightened now, Señora Rosemary, about the latest burning. They all are, all these white women with their brown babies. But that doesn't mean they don't keep tempting Natividad. I know these women are just biding their time. They all want to steal Miguel. I can feel it. I am sorry I ever asked them to help me watch over Natividad.

If Miguel is not drinking Natividad's milk, I tie him to me when we are around them. I don't trust them anymore. Miguel is my baby as much as Natividad's. I will never let them steal him. Without Miguel, who is my watcher, I will not be safe. And without me, Natividad is not safe. These foreigners understand nothing, although I have tried to explain.

At moments, I thought Señora Maria and Señora Lourdes and Señora Ginny might understand. But they are afraid of Natividad, I can see it in their eyes. It's worse now since Natividad visited Señora Lourdes sleepy with the glue. Worse since the news of the latest lynchings. Worse since I tried to steal Miguel on Good Friday and they all united to stop me.

It is my fault Natividad is in such danger now. I spent so much time finding these women. I was a stupid girl. I thought they could help me invite Natividad's soul back. I thought they would help me take care of Miguel until Natividad's soul felt safe enough to return. I think they don't believe Natividad has a soul. That means sometime they may kill her and give her heart away, for what reason is there to live if your soul will never return?

If Miguel were a girl, I could take her back to the home with me. I pretended to be a boy when we lived in the capital, but I think it will be too difficult to pretend that Miguel is a girl. Babies go peepee all the time. Someone would see. Then they would put him in a home by himself, far from both Natividad and me.

Señora Rosemary wants Natividad to give Miguel away. Señora Rosemary wants to send Miguel away to the States. I know she has asked Señora Lourdes if she would take Natividad back with her, but Señora Lourdes said she would only be interested in taking me. So now Señora Rosemary is trying to tempt me too. She says Natividad can continue to live with her. Natividad would do the work I have been doing for the Señora. She wants to separate us all.

It is a terrible thing among my people to be an orphan. If you have no father-mother, you have no one to protect you. But Natividad and Miguel and I have a father-mother in God. We are not alone. And we have San Miguel el arcangel, who can slay serpents and baby snatchers. I take Miguel every day to the church and I pray for help. I pray for forgiveness for my stupidity. Natividad sold her hope to Miguel's father with her drawings, so she was made hopeless when he put his seed inside her without asking, and her soul left her. But it came back again in the form of Miguel. I don't see why only I can see that. Not even Natividad knows yet.

I know Señora Rosemary likes Natividad. She likes her power to draw the world clear as a mirror. She wants to give her art lessons. She wants to teach her English. But she doesn't want Natividad to be a mother. She wants to take her gift of life away. She says Natividad is a little girl herself.

But Natividad is twelve years old. I am almost eleven now. We are not children. We are old enough to know the gift of life is something God gives and takes away. Not Señora Rosemary.

I don't know what to do. God has got me so confused. Some days I think I must take Miguel and try to run away again and leave Natividad—and then my heart breaks because I know I am put on earth to watch her. And I know I can't feed Miguel from my chest because I have no milk.

Other days I think I must burn down Señora Rosemary's house and frighten her away. I don't want to burn the Señora, just her house because that is what keeps her here. If I burned her house, then Señorita Gwen would go away too maybe. The spirit inside Señorita Gwen is even more wicked than the one inside Señora Rosemary. I can feel it. Why can't my sister? I keep warning her, just as I did about Pablo and Tomás. But Natividad will not listen, so it is all up to me. If I burn Señora Rosemary's house, then she would leave and that would be a good thing. She is possessed by an evil spirit right now, and she doesn't know it. Maybe, if I can startle her enough, it will startle the evil spirit out of her. Maybe then she will stop tempting us to be discontented with the gifts God's given us.

In the mountains, in the villages where our people are many, and the foreigners come one by one, we can rise up against them and protect what God has given us. Here, because we are fewer and they are more, because Natividad and I are more than orphans, because Miguel has the blue eyes of the rich foreigners but inside him beats a heart as poor as mine, there is no community to rise up with us. Natividad doesn't even know it is the devil's voice slipping out of Señora Rosemary's mouth now. She doesn't see the danger.

I don't know when I've ever felt so alone.

Father-mother God, why won't you talk to me? It is too much to bear to think we're worse than orphans here and it will be just the same in the world to come.

Chapter 19
BUSQUEDA

Ginny motioned Marie to come sit beside her on Rosemary's patio. Mikela was performing a pantomime in imitation of the evangelical missionaries performing daily this week down on the plaza. Rosemary and Wilma were seated together over by the kitchen, and Gwen and Natividad were sitting on the grass near the fountain keeping watch over Mikela's props and also playing with the baby, who Mikela had momentarily relinquished.

"I wish Simon could have made it," Ginny said. "Something magical is going on here."

Magical and grotesque. For Mikela, instead of imitating the performance she'd seen in the park about the wages of alcohol, promiscuity, and wife-beating had devised her own—about the lynching and burning of foreign tourists.

"Oh no," Ginny said as she caught on. "This is going to finish things with Rosemary. I could shake her."

"She needs to have the say," Marie said. "She's like a propane cylinder heating up in the sun."

Mikela donned silvered sunglasses and mounted a bus, leaning across a seat here, over a seatback there, to say hello to the other passengers. She sauntered back up the aisle and sat directly behind the bus driver.

Then she pulled off the sunglasses, assumed another persona, and sat in the driver's seat, steering with one hand and holding a microphone (a tiny colander) in the other.

"We are going to the pretty town of Todos Santos," the bus driver announced in a deep voice, turning around to ensure the attention of the passengers. "Here you will see the indigenous in their original place. You will see floors of dirt and fires to cook on. You will see women who tie themselves to the trees to weave and men who carry firewood on their backs like burros. You will be able to look at them like statues in a museum, although we will keep moving. And everywhere, everywhere, you will see little babies tied to their mothers' backs. Those are not very safe to steal. The mothers will yell if you touch them. But the ones who are walking by themselves, their mothers cannot watch them all the time. If you grab one and put it very quickly in your big backpacks, no one will notice. But remember, half of you must go to the market and pretend to buy the weavings and the sculptures and the clothes, so they won't know you are group of baby-snatchers. Understand?" The bus driver put the microphone down on the dashboard and, still steering with one hand, turned dangerously far around to ensure the compliance of his audience.

Mikela jumped up and donned the silver sunglasses again and faced the back of the bus with her hands raised in blessing.

"You heard what Señor Carrillo said. These are stupid people. They give birth to their babies like animals, on their knees. We need the organs of these babies for our own children. And those we don't use, we will sell to the North Americans, the *estadounidenses*. Remember, if a baby is very pretty, a North American woman may pay more for it whole than the doctors in Japan or the United States will pay for its parts. Usually, though, if you add up the pieces of livers, lungs, kidneys, hearts and eyes, it will be better to cut them in pieces. But remember, you must act quickly."

Mikela waved her arms to change the scene. Now, according to the sign Gwen held up, they were in the market place of Todos Santos. A car drove around the square with a big loudspeaker on top.

"The Satan followers are coming," the driver warned. "They say they are tourists, but do not believe them. They are coming to steal the bodies and souls of our children. Go this very minute and pray to the Virgin for her protection. Mothers, if you have ever beaten your children, beware. Your children may leave you for the Satan followers. They may believe they are safer there. Go to the Virgin and confess your wickedness. Have her clean your dark heart. Ask pardon of your children. Count them all. Make sure none are missing. Tell your daughters to tie their brothers and sisters to them tightly, to hold their hands so hard they cry from the pressure. The Satan followers can pull with the strength of a hundred. No one is safe."

Mothers started lining their children up and counting them, shaking their heads and recounting, just as they might count limes in the market. They tied them all together, whole tribes, and, holding the cord, stumbled off like captives to the church, where they knelt before the Virgin.

Mikela, now covered by a blue *rebozo* from head to toe, stood up on the edge of the fountain, hands on her hips, staring sternly down at the penitent mothers and hobbled children.

"How many times have I told you, Daughters of Eve, that you must honor what comes from God? Your children come from God. You mustn't beat them or starve them or bury them before they have breathed their last breath. You must feed them in their fevers. You must treat them the way I treated the baby Jésus—with kindness, with gentleness. If you do not do this, Satan will come today, this very day, and steal your babies. He will take all of them, not just your first born, because he is crueler than God. Satan will come today with all his followers. They will all wear silver glasses to hide their eyes. They will wear big smiles. Don't believe a word they say. If any of you miss your children, even for a second, call out to me and I will aid you. I am your holy mother. You do not need to fear. Do I ever turn away those who truly repent and call out to me for help?"

The Virgin Mary briskly gestured them away. Mikela dropped her blue veil as she jumped down from the fountain and dashed to take her place on the bus.

"I would laugh," Ginny said, "if I didn't know what was going to happen."

"Maybe she has decided to rewrite history," Marie said. "To give the story a happier ending."

"Look at her," Ginny said. "I don't think so."

Mikela looked wonderfully firm and sure of herself. She looked meaningfully at her audience, especially at Rosemary before again assuming the persona of the bus driver as he pulled, with a flourish, into the market square.

"Don't be greedy," he said. "Only one child for each of you."

The leader of the baby snatchers stood up and put on her silver shades and stepped off the bus with her video camera glued to her eye. "Smile," she said to the people of the village.

But the mothers, with their plastic rosaries dangling from their hands, stared at her impassively.

"We have come to bring you money," the leader of the baby snatchers said. "We will take photos and pay you. Photos of you and your children."

The mothers gripped their children's hands and shook their heads.

The woman with the silver shades approached Natividad with her video camera. She crouched down as she moved. She pushed the camera very close to Natividad's face. "Smile," she said.

She reached around her camera and tugged at Nativad's red *rebozo*. "Just one picture of the baby. A picture like the Virgin and the Baby Jésus." Then she turned around, checking to see if anyone else was near.

"Fifty dollars," she said. "I will buy the baby from you for fifty dollars." She put his hand in his pocket and drew out, Ginny could swear, real dollars.

"You can always have another one," she said.

"Not with blue eyes," Natividad said placidly, unexpectedly entering the play. "He is blessed."

"One hundred? Two hundred? Five hundred? A *thousand* dollars?" the Japanese baby snatcher asked, pinning Natividad back against the fountain with the eye of her camera, her hand reaching out like a claw to rake the *rebozo* away.

"Help," Natividad cried. "Stop!"

"Are we in character or out?" Ginny asked. "Do I leap to my feet and protect Natividad from her possessed sister?"

But the baby-snatcher with the silver shades dropped her camera—made of three metal cans—and peered around her.

"Hush," she said sternly.

Ginny looked down, properly chastised. Marie swallowed her laughter.

"Baby snatcher," Natividad repeated mechanically. "Beware of the baby snatcher."

A crowd began to form. Mikela was a little maelstrom, acting men with firewood on their backs, machetes in their hands. Women holding pots of boiling oil, ready to throw them.

"If they take our babies," a man with his back bent to lift a huge pile of kindling yelled at the ground, "we will no longer be indigenous. We will not be the original people of this place. All our children will be taken away and we will die and light-skinned people will come and burn our houses and brush away the flowers from our graves. They will plant their own seeds in our cornfields. The earth will belong to the Devil and the baby-snatchers, not the children of God. We must not give up. The Virgin cries out to us as if they were taking Jésus himself, and we must come to her aid."

The tourist looked back and forth at the crowd. She took off her glasses. She pointed to her eyes, stretching the eyelids narrow and wide. She pointed at his skin. "I am not North American," she said. "I am not from Spain. I am the same color as you. When they are born, your children's eyes look like mine." She knelt down and raised her arms up to where the Virgin had balanced precariously on the rim of the fountain only minutes ago.

Mikela scrambled to her feet, becoming, before their mesmerized eyes, an enormous man, a machete dangling from his hand.

"It's real," Ginny said to Marie. "That machete is real."

"Everything is, unfortunately," Marie said. She drew a deep breath. There were tears in her eyes.

"I am Miguel el arcangel," said the big man emanating from the little girl. "The devil writhes under my foot, helpless. I, as God's messenger, can weigh your good deeds and your bad deeds. I can use my sword just as God would—with no pity for his enemies."

Miguel el arcangel straightened his shoulders and lifted his machete. He lifted his foot and set it six inches above the ground, on the back of the now invisible leader of the baby-snatchers. "Your hour has come. Pray that there will be an end to the flames that burn you, the agony you will feel until the end of time."

"I wish she were a few feet farther from her sister," Ginny said. "And that she would set her second foot down. That machete makes me nervous."

The avenger just lifted his sword higher. Rosemary pressed her hands against the arms of her chair and began to rise, but Wilma stood more quickly and barred her way.

"Simon would know what to do," Ginny said.

"Repent," the angel said. "Repent you wicked baby-snatcher or you will die."

"A million dollars," the leader of the baby-snatchers said, flipping over on her belly, her legs twitching, shaking the green bills in the air so they shivered in her silver lenses like leaves.

"Life," the angel cried out in a loud voice, "has no price. Ask the Virgin." And the angel lifted his sword with both hands, staring implacably at his victim writhing invisibly in the dirt.

"Enough," Rosemary cried out. "That is more than enough, Mikela. Gwen, for God's sake do something. Get Natividad away from her. You don't know what she might do with that damn machete."

Mikela—locking eyes with Rosemary, who lurched against Wilma's restraining arm—slowly lowered the machete, severing, they all supposed, the woman's head from her quivering shoulders. She kicked out with her foot as if rolling a coconut or a soccer ball.

"And that," she said, "is what we indigenous do to those who would help the Devil."

"She's ill," Rosemary said, turning to Wilma. "She needs to be institutionalized."

"For reflecting her country accurately?" Wilma asked. "*Por favor*, Señora. You may wish to stay deaf and blind—but our children cannot if they are to survive."

Wilma turned to Mikela and clapped her hands slowly. Marie joined her, and, after a pause, so did Ginny and, more reluctantly, Gwen. Gwen stood on the far side of the fountain with her arms protectively around Natividad, whose own arms, equally protectively, cradled the baby. Natividad didn't clap. She didn't act as if anything untoward had happened.

Mikela bowed her head, gracefully receiving the applause.

"I would like to have music," she said, "like the missionaries in the plaza. But they do not use a sword in their play. Only the bible and a belt for the man who beats his wife, and a bottle of water they pretend is alcohol and money to pay the girl in the city to lift her skirts. In their play they protect themselves from the Devil with a bible—but my sword is more powerful. It is made of metal not paper. Fire cannot destroy it."

And then, improbably, she lifted her face to the sky and began to sing, in English, *Jesus loves me, this I know, for the Bible tells me so. Yes, Jesus loves me. Yes, Jesus loves me.*

Ginny sat down, her knees weak. "In the park—they teach you that song? The missionaries from the United States teach you that song?" Ginny asked Mikela.

Mikela shrugged as she knelt and picked up the sheath for her machete. "Our own songs are more beautiful, but they give us money if we learn their songs and their words. They use the word Jésus, as we do, but they do not understand, I believe, about the power of Mary or the good Hermano Pedro or San Miguel. They do not understand that we have many, so many martyrs and saints, that we no longer have to fear the Devil. After the war, we in this country have so many more martyrs we do not need the saints of old—except that they are so wise, they are never surprised by life. They never lose their souls, the ancients. Our martyrs, many of them are still waiting for their souls to return—and until they do, they can't help us. Isn't that true, Señora Wilma?"

Marie had been so sure that this was the right thing to do, trying to find the girls' mother, but climbing down from Patricio's van in the remote mountain town, Rosemary had her doubts. All the men and women behind the booths in the market square looked at them stonily. Thank goodness they hadn't brought the girls. She didn't even think it was safe to show their photos, and she was opening her mouth to tell Marie so, when Marie slipped out of the van, sunglasses still on, and stuck her hand in the back pocket of her jeans and pulled out the photos of the girls and headed off across the street, slipping under the plastic tarp where women sat on their heels with mounds of tomatoes and onions and yellow flowering herbs in front of them.

At times like this, Rosemary wished she could recite the rosary, anything to channel her attention. All she could think of was, *Lord have mercy. Christ have mercy.* But she was pretty sure there was some third response that was meant to follow. *Let's flee* would do. *Lord have mercy. Christ have mercy. Let's flee. LordhavemercyChristhavemercyLet's flee. LordhavemercyChristhavemercyLet's fleequicklyquickly.*

"I've read that there are art galleries here—a group of primitive painters," Lourdes said. She looked as ill at ease as Rosemary. She'd only heard of Mikela's performance second hand, but in a certain way that was worse. The lynching was like an image trapped between mirrors, echoing forever in all their psyches.

"You think Natividad might have inherited her talent?" Patricio asked.

"It's foolish, I know. But we're all grasping at straws. We may be completely wrong about where they come from. They're both cagey and naïve. I doubt they'll ever be able to tell us."

"Why should they?" Gwen asked. "You might send them back to their mother. Neither of them want that."

"It's better than nothing," Lourdes answered. "And at their ages, if you don't bring the mother and father into it, there's no hope of adopting. A twelve-year old doesn't have the authority to sign her own baby away. Even here."

Patricio strode off toward the market in pursuit of Marie. The women stood around the van, circled in on themselves.

"I just can't get those stories out of my head," Lourdes said. "Not just the one in Todos Santos, but that other lynching six years ago. She was about our age, that woman they stoned. They videotaped it. I keep thinking of how scared she must have been, the mob beating in the door to the bathroom where she was trying to hide. The judge and the missionary who were meant to protect her ran out and left her, this crazy savage crowd outside. Three hours they beat her after they broke down the door and pulled her out of the building. And people stood there in the street videotaping it. *Videotaping* it. All because she had smiled at a child. I keep imagining her, six years in a coma. What images come to her now? The child's smile? The fists and sticks and stones? Their expressionless faces? The missionary and the judge running away?"

"They're a terrible people," Rosemary agreed. "Beautiful and terrible. But if you stay in the towns, limit your contacts, you're relatively safe."

"I can't *believe* you are talking that way," Gwen said. "It's so cold. It's so colonial."

"Let's walk, shall we, ladies?" Simon asked. He was looking very pale these days, but had gamely agreed to act as their bodyguard—having done such a good job at the cemetery. But he insisted they pay for new shoes if he had to donate his latest pair.

"I'm not afraid of reality," Rosemary said to Gwen. She settled her baseball cap on her wild white hair and put on sunglasses. "And if you're seriously thinking of adopting that baby, you'd better face up to it too. There's nowhere in this country, ever, that you will be perfectly safe. You will always be seen as an invader. A, what did you call it, colonial. Maybe not consciously.

But deep down there, where it matters. Where people will stand by and watch you beaten to death."

The town had cobbled streets, low near windowless adobe houses with more tin than tile roofs. There were no white faces to be seen except their own. There was a church, it seemed, on every corner.

"Can someone tell me again how Marie decided on this town?" Rosemary asked.

"She felt there was a resemblance between some of the faces she had sketched when she came here a few years ago and those of the girls. As if there isn't a resemblance to every adult and child in Antigua," Ginny said. "And, like Lourdes, she was thinking of the painters—that it might be a good place to bring Natividad, no matter what." Ginny had pushed her sunglasses on top of her head. She squinted into the noonday sun. "I saw signs for the galleries as we drove into town, but I can't see any of them now."

"Next right," Simon said.

Gwen and Lourdes, both in jeans and sweaters, quickened their steps. It wasn't just the air that was chilling them.

"This town—it doesn't have a history of violent attacks, does it?" Gwen asked.

"You think that is as genetically linked as artistic talent?" Simon asked pleasantly. Too pleasantly.

"I brought some of Natividad's drawings," Gwen said. "Over Mikela's loud protests. She didn't even ease up when I told her we might be able to get money for them."

"They not just drawings to Mikela," Ginny observed. "They're a supernatural code. It's as if you took the *sagrario* off the altar."

"What's that?" Gwen asked.

"Where they keep the host. It's very holy."

"Natividad didn't mind, and they're her drawings."

"Have you thought what might happen to the girls if you can't adopt the baby and you've driven the sisters apart?" Ginny asked Gwen.

But before Gwen could answer, Simon had started to knock loudly on a deep blue door, strikingly bright on the monochrome street of gray-brown adobe buildings. In the little barred window there was a sign that said Galería Chun Choc.

A small man with a large round face peered cautiously around the edge of the door.

"You are open, Señor?" Simon asked and leaned down courteously to hear the small man's answer, which sounded more like a wheeze than a yes.

"It is not the usual day for the tourists," he said.

"Many tourists come here?" Ginny asked, glancing up and down the empty street.

"They come from the capital and in buses from Antigua. Now, of course, they do not come so many because of the misfortune of Todos Santos."

"I guess that's one word for garroting and burning," Rosemary said.

"They say Spanish has a smaller vocabulary than English." Simon slipped his arm around her.

"Mi mamá," he said to Señor Chun Choc. "She likes to buy the paintings of the first people of the country."

Simon kept his arm around Rosemary as he toured the room. He began with the landscapes. Ginny and Lourdes started on the other side of the room, with the scenes of daily life.

Señor Chun Choc came up beside them, rubbing his hands together earnestly. "You see this after earthquake. No many house left. And here, our feast day, with all the balloons on fire over the mercado."

"And this," Ginny asked, peering closely at the next painting. "What is going on here?"

"The title is Calling the Spirits," Gwen offered, a few canvases ahead of them.

"It is our ritual to call the soul back when it frighten."

"And how exactly do you do that?" Lourdes asked. "Call someone's soul back?"

"How does it leave in the first place?" Gwen asked.

"The smallest thing do it—your horse fall, a child throw the firecracker at your feet on the plaza, your wife give the shock by come into the room, no sound. Or can be big thing. A man or child shot. A child he dies. Or the robbing. I, for example, was attack in the capital. On a bus. A group of young men they surrounds me with the knives. The other people on the bus, they look out the windows. I look at the bus driver in the mirror. He see. But he keep driving. I give all my money, but still they surrounds me, laugh together, just like the soldiers and guerillas in the mad times. In their eyes not even hatred. Nothing. Their eyes like television with no pictures, just the shivers of the dark."

"*Escalofrío*," Rosemary murmured, having come over to hear Señor Chun Choc's tale. "I always liked that word."

"When I return to my home here, I no leave. Every day I paint my paintings and then look the television, no picture, just the shiver of dark—" He wriggled his fingers in front of their eyes, his own eyes wide and momentarily blank.

"My soul have left me, you see. My wife invite my friends, but I no speak. My granddaughter pull at my knee, but I no speak. I no leave the house, no go to the *misa*. The priest come, the *cofradía* come, but I no talk."

"But here you are, talking to us," Ginny said. "What happened?"

"Art," Lourdes said, turning back to study the painting. "He painted himself back into existence."

"Soon, I put away the paint brush. The men from the capital come to buy and no new paintings for the galleries or the museums. The fields, I no put in the seeds.

"'They are not here,' my wife say to me. 'They never come to our town. Too far.' But you see, without soul, I no have the fear. I have the empty, and the sure. My evil spirit is the sure. My wife see it. I am now stubborn man. The boys in the city with their tv screen eyes *asustar* my soul and I no love my family. Their wicked souls inside me now because my soul run away. All I want the *cerveza* and the shivering screen."

"*And?*" Rosemary said. "Don't keep us in suspense."

Señor Chun Choc beamed at them. "So you sees, today I am as before I go to the capital and they rob me."

"How?" Ginny asked.

"In our country, we have the ritual."

"I have a feeling I'm on a *very* small merry-go-round," Gwen murmured.

"Go on," Simon said in Spanish. "We are most interested."

"We have people in our town with special gift. My wife talk when she go to the market. They decide I need more *curandero*. So they calls for my aunt and my *compadre*'s uncle and my wife's mother's sister. It always the old who remembers how to call back the spirits.

"So they come and they turn off the television and they throw away the beer. They calls all my children and grandchildren and brothers and sisters to come and be with me. And they beats the house clean with the flowers.

Then they fill the gourd with water, is in the painting. They burn the incense and brush the smoke into every corner of the house, and they speaks of all around me, of this house my father and brothers and I build, of the trees that grow so many years in our patio, of the beauty of our street, our barrio, our town. Of the beauty of the mountains and the sky. Of the beauty of our *milpas* and our forests. They speaks of all the people who circles me in wider and wider rings, as the water circle the stone. I listens, and I feel the sweet of their speak and their sing and the pray they give to all our gods both old and new, and without warn me one of them crack the egg with a machete and put in the water. Another egg. And the sound, which I never know when will come, startle the wicked spirits out and permit my own soul come back into the body quick as the eggs into the water.

"For seven evenings they come and do the same ritual—and then sit with me all the night. Then, I am like before. I paint. Plant my fields. Hold my granddaughter on my knee."

"Here's another one, along the same theme—but set along a river," Gwen said.

"Yes, it's a genre," Lourdes said.

"This is you, then?" Ginny asked the old man, pointing to a figure in the painting.

"Is the bad luck to paint your own person. But the same is the ritual. This man *también* receive back his soul."

"I want it," Ginny said.

"Are you sure?" Gwen asked. "Don't you find it a bit kitsch?"

"Primitive," Lourdes chided her.

"I actually find it wonderfully sophisticated," Simon said, dropping Rosemary's arm and coming over to peer at the painting with Ginny. "All the people here have long eyelashes and I could swear one of those eggs is fertilized and has a little drop of red in the yolk."

But Ginny was lifting the painting from the wall and carrying it over to the table for Señor Chun Choc to wrap.

"Maybe that's what the whole country needs," Rosemary said as they left the store. "An *asusto* ceremony for the whole country. No telling, though, how far back you'd need to go."

"So," Simon said, "maybe we should start right here and now. Since Ginger's gone, don't you think the expat church could expand its repertoire? *Asusto* ceremonies for colonials. We could hold them following every lynching, every kidnapping, every bank robbery."

"Look, someone turns one of these corners with a machete in his hand, you may need to call *my* soul back," Lourdes said. "I can't get over that image he had. The tv screen shivering with darkness."

"*Escalofríos de oscuridad*," Gwen said. "It has a rhythm to it. Oh shit."

They all stopped.

"I forgot to show him Natividad's paintings."

"But now you understand their meaning to Mikela," Ginny said. "They're like the eggs the *curanderos* slip into the water. They're the stuff of life trying to find its way back home."

"They're not here," Lourdes said when they reached the empty van. "I don't want to stand out here on the street waiting for them. We're so obvious. If only one of these people would smile, look the least bit pleased to see us, it would feel different."

Simon wiped his forehead, which was beaded with sweat.

"You're as nervous as we are," Rosemary said.

But Ginny looked at her friend and saw the future closing in. "Let's leave a note on the windshield," she suggested. "Tell them we'll be waiting for them in the church."

"No cameras," Simon reminded them. "No sketch pads. No second glances, especially at the children. I'm depending on all of you to make me look good in this new role. My machismo depends on it."

Ginny slipped her arm through his right one. Rosemary did the same on his left.

"It's getting time for me to leave," Lourdes said as they ambled, hyper-alert, toward the church. "All I can think about is how many more demented Marys and handless saints I'm going to encounter before I leave this country. There's a limit to how much one's imagination can take in."

"Demented, raggedy haired Mary's are the least of it," Rosemary said. "And to lose a hand, these days, is small change."

And in all their minds, they saw Mikela's machete descending, the sharp slash of her leg as she kicked the imaginary head off into the dust.

"For the whole world," Gwen whispered as they settled into the pews nearest the door. "An *asusto* ceremony for the whole world wouldn't hurt."

When Marie and Patricio had returned to the car after scouring the mercado for anyone who might recognize Natividad and Mikela from their photographs, they were resigned to the futility of their mission—for all the men and women in the market had asked them, before saying anything else, what the girls were wanted for. When they learned they were orphans, they just shrugged, as if that were an adequate answer to their question. There were many orphans, many *hijas y hijos de las calles*, daughters and sons of the street. If they left the villages for the capital, there was nothing to be done for them, was there? They became *viciosos* there.

"Vicious?" Gwen asked when Marie was describing the conversations in the van.

"Not cruel. Filled with vices," Marie answered. "Like hunger. Homelessness."

"Prostitution and glue," Rosemary added.

"They wouldn't even look at the photographs," Marie said. "Once they knew they were orphans, they wouldn't even look."

"There isn't a war anymore," Patricio said. "There isn't as much displacement. They probably know where their own children are."

"They won't look at the pictures of these lost girls, but they'll lynch a foreign woman for looking at their own children twice. It's changed things," Lourdes said. "For me, these lynchings have changed things."

"I agree with you," Marie said. "I think we should find the mother and try to put all in order. But I believe, you know, it is not possible. Even if we find their mother, would we be putting things in order or no? Would they just have to run away again? Especially Natividad."

"Mikela would follow. She would always follow," Gwen said. "It's like she's on some divine mission."

"Maybe she is," Patricio said.

Marie, sitting up in the front of the van, leaned over and said something to Patricio in a low voice. She was looking very tired. She was obviously more disappointed than she would say. Mikela's pantomime had had its impact— and she, as well as Ginny and Rosemary and Gwen, kept seeing the Japanese tourist in her silver sunglasses, flipped like a cockroach, frantically waving her dollars in the air as the machete came slowly, remorselessly down on her neck.

Who in the hell, Ginny wondered, wanted access to the psyche of this country?

It's all relative, the voice murmured. *Who, my dear, would want access to yours either?*

"We have a second plan," Marie turned toward them, half-kneeling on the seat.

"Which is?" Rosemary asked.

"A prayer with San Simón. We go by one of the biggest churches for him as we return to Antigua."

"I don't know," Ginny said. She remembered the wooden totem up at the lake, dressed in a hundred neckties, cigar in his mouth, rum at his feet. She'd rather go back and muse on her painting by Señor Chun Choc. She'd never bought a piece of art for herself before. She'd commissioned work for the church on occasion. But something for herself—that felt different. It felt as if she were settling in—and also was still perfectly mobile. And there, inside the canvas, all these rituals seemed, well, like rituals. A little distant. Exotic. Not like that visit to the lake, the creepy discomfort of the woman bowing before the totem, glancing behind her now and then to see if the offerings were adding up.

"How do you see that helping?" she asked Marie.

"Indirectly," Simon said. "It's a treat, Ginny. You'll enjoy it. It's different from the lake. The San Simón here looks like a wealthy white plantation owner."

"We've come to worship their oppressor?" Ginny asked.

"It's a way of getting your power back," Simon said. "Call him a God—and then you can hold him accountable."

"For what?"

"San Simón is based, I believe, or so one of the stories goes, on Judas. He's the bearer of the *denuncia*."

"And he is the god of material prosperity. Much visited by small business owners," Marie added. "He is the great delight of the bourgeoisie—of all races. Here there will be more ladinos than indigenous."

"And us. The same skin color as the *finca* owner," Ginny said.

"But without his moustache," Simon said. "Relax, Ginny. You've been there."

"That's exactly what I'm afraid of."

But as soon as Ginny walked into the courtyard of the church, carrying, at Marie's insistence, like each of them, a bouquet of flowers and a small bottle of rum and a small bottle of Florida water, a very large cigar, and three white candles, Ginny knew she was in another world.

The courtyard was filled with people, dense smoke, the smells of pine and chocolate and incense, and, in the midst of the dense cloud, the bright flicker of flames. When they climbed the short flight of steps to the red brick church, they could see the courtyard was filled with about six individual bonfires. Small groups of people were carefully constructing them out of kindling and balls of chocolate and balls of resin, dousing them with alcohol, and setting them into tumultuous flame. An older couple, the woman blonde, in a plaid shirt and pedal pushers, the man in a baseball cap, held a rooster tightly, watching the activity in the courtyard.

A plump middle-aged woman with the beginning of a widow's hump stood brooding by a large fire. She was accompanied by a man wearing a large red bandanna, who was reading from an old notebook. At his instruction, she added an egg to the fire. Then another one. He threw on more alcohol and, as the fire blazed to waist height, he took the woman's hand and led her first in a clockwise circle, then in a counter clockwise one.

Rosemary and Patricio and Simon and Gwen were making their way slowly in the line that led out of the church and along the broad steps that created a porch the width of the patio. But Lourdes, like Ginny, stood on the steps studying the happenings in the courtyard. Marie came to join them, placing a hand fondly on each other their arms.

"I knew," she said. "I knew this was the right thing for us to do."

The woman went over to the side of the courtyard and returned with a very sullen teenage girl, who, at the instruction of the man in the red bandanna, threw a cigar on the fire. Her mother added some pages torn from a notebook. The teenager went to the side of the courtyard and sat, staring stubbornly at the sky.

"Maybe she would like a good divorce settlement," Marie said.

A starving yellow dog, every bone in his spinal column and hips visible, edged close to one of the dying fires, trying to scavenge the now hard-boiled eggs.

"Or she wants him back," Lourdes said.

"You don't think it is about the daughter? She has an unsuitable boyfriend?" Ginny asked.

"Whatever it is, the request is very complicated for the *brujo*," Marie said. "I've never seen one have to read from his notes before."

The man in the red bandanna began to beat the woman with flowers, while still reading aloud.

"Do you think he has something in there that could apply to Natividad and Mikela," Ginny asked Marie.

"Seriously, Genie? Does that red book you and Señora Ginger are so fond of have anything?"

"Nothing specific," Ginny said.

"So. We ask for all the helps we can get. That is just good business, yes? But now we see the inside of the church."

Marie forged right through the line and into the church. The line, it turned out, was just for those who wanted to make their personal petition directly to the large statue of San Simón that sat, cased in glass, at the front of the church, accessible by a small set of stairs and a narrow walkway. He was barely visible for the smoke which, if it were possible, was even denser inside the church than outside it. All Ginny could make out was the glow of his pale straw hat. In even rows across the floor stood the waist high metal tables used in the Catholic churches for the votive candles. All of the tables were covered with flaming candles of all colors. The candles were stuck to the table by a huge sea of wax. There was a code, Marie had assured them as she had selected the white candles that were to ensure the health and well-being of children. Leaning down, women held out enormous cigars and lit them from the candles. The smoke joined with that of the candles and incense. All along both walls were metal plaques, thanking San Simón for a car, a washing machine, a house, a *milpa*, a horse, a husband, a wife, an operation for cataracts, recovery from cancer.

Marie walked up to one of the men in the red bandannas. When she told him what she wanted, he called over a woman, also wearing a red bandanna.

"Come," Marie said to Ginny. "We will set the model for the others." She handed a photograph of Natividad and Mikela to Ginny. "We will cleanse our intentions."

And before Ginny could protest, the man in the bandanna had come over to her and without asking what her prayers were for, took away her bouquet of flowers and the Florida water and rum. He put the Florida water and the rum on one of the tables covered with candles, and then he began to beat her quite firmly with the flowers.

It wasn't an unpleasant sensation. It was, in its way, quite sensuous, as was his strong deep voice declaiming in a Spanish that was too rapid for Ginny to follow something about sending away the bad spirits, the bad wind, and inviting in a spirit of prosperity and good faith. The priest or witch, whatever he was, beat Ginny about the head, the shoulders, the arms, the back, the legs, all the time keeping up his melodious chant. Then he crushed the flowers and pressed them to Ginny's face. She smelt the sharp smell of marigolds and petunias and mint and, deep inside, something sweeter, indescribably sweet. Just as she was about to draw another deep breath, trying to locate that sweetness, the man in the bandanna, who had now opened the bottle of rum, blew a large cloud of it over her face and head. It was as if she were walking in mist. Pressing the flowers against her face again with one hand, he took a swig of the Florida water and again enveloped Ginny in a mist, this one scented with orange blossoms. He walked around her, covering her with the spray. He returned to face her, and placing his hand on her head, made the sign of the cross over her, blessing her in the name of the Father, the Son, and the Holy Ghost.

"Beats communion, doesn't it?" Simon asked as he took her place. Ginny, following Marie's lead, handed Simon the photograph of the two girls. Lourdes, looking a little nervous but also very sturdy, was being attended to by the woman who had purified Marie. Marie led Ginny over to one of the metal tables.

"And now," Marie said, wriggling a little like a wet dog, "we are ready to pray." She lit her white candles in a group, then setting their bases over another rapidly melting candle, melted them and glued each of them to the table. She lit her big cigar. "You need not do this part," she told Ginny as she puffed and puffed.

Ginny hesitated.

"You do not need to pray to the San Simón," Marie said. "But we are at the point, Ginny, I think you agree, when we need the help of something much larger than ourselves. For the children's sake."

"I couldn't agree more," Ginny said. "But is this it?"

She looked around the room at the men and women busy lighting the candles, kneeling together or individually, just as they did in the cathedrals, to pray openly and loudly for all their hearts desired. Above her, on the walkway, she could see a woman talking fervently and plaintively to the encased statue of San Simón. She had a black rooster tucked under her white arm, a basket of eggs and kindling in the other. Behind her, the other people in line waited patiently, half-obscured by the cigar and candle smoke, some of them still puffing on cigars, others lulled by the sheer quantity of nicotine in the air.

"How can we know?" Marie asked. "It is the asking, I believe, that matters. Here or in the cathedral, does its essential character change? We cry out and we wait. We wait, like someone at a cave's mouth, to hear the shape of our need. It is the beginning. It is always the beginning."

"It matters who we address our needs to, don't you think?" Ginny said, a little queasy from the cigars. Her eyes burned with the smoke.

"You don't think they confer?" Marie asked. "San Simón, the Godfather, the Good Son, the Virgin?"

And me, the voice said. *You can't leave me out of this, Ginny-gin-gin.*

The minute the voice spoke up, her voice sounding eerily similar to the woman who, having beaten Marie and Lourdes was now busying herself with Rosemary, Ginny knew she was right. The voice *did* belong here in this lazy hubbub, among all these prayers for the most mundane of possessions—a new pair of shoes, a nose job, a boyfriend, a safe trip across the border, work in Chicago or San Antonio, a tv. She had no sense of boundaries, of the high mysteries.

But you didn't answer Marie's question, the voice said. *Don't you think we confer? Bandy things about a bit? Have our in jokes. Cover, for your sakes, all the bases?*

It wasn't neat, that was what bothered Ginny and attracted her. These ludicrous cigars in the mouths of small, elegant French women. The wonderful peace that descended with the battering of the flowers, the lulling assurance of the man in the red bandanna. When he made the sign of the cross over her, Ginny did, she really did, feel absolved—of something she couldn't even articulate.

So, the voice said, *cleanse your intentions, Ginny-gin-gin. Pray for the material well-being of those girls no one in their right mind would call sweet or innocent. Pray, if you like, for Mikela's shoeshine box, for her plan to run off with the circus. Pray for Natividad. Pray for the means, the right means, to help them. Pray, if you know what is good for you, that I have a part in it, Ginny-gin-gin.*

And there in that smoky, flickering, ordinary and most mysterious place, Ginny prayed for guidance and strength, she prayed for Mikela and her machete and her crazy clarity, for Natividad and her mute knowing. And the words surrounded her, just like those of the man and the woman in the red bandannas, in a fragrant mist that ran, pure as rain water, as the blood of the rooster, into the flickering light below her.

"Because," she prayed, "it all comes down to machetes and shoeshine boxes and breast milk and drawing paper, diapers and the daily wage, help us."

Knock, the voice said, sounding now just as sure of itself as Mikela or Rosemary, *and the door will be opened. Seek and you shall find. For who among you, if your daughter hungered, would give her a stone? Florida water and rum, maybe. A big cigar. An egg. A rooster. But a stone—never. Never.*

"You have to do this, Genie," Marie said, studying the painting Ginny had brought back from Señor Chun Choc's gallery. "It is not as if I ask this for my myself. Or even for Natividad. I ask it in the name of someone you can't resist."

"Mikela?" Ginny shook her head in disbelief. Marie was pulling out all the stops.

"She too, of course. But I ask this in the name of the Holy, Genie. And of course, you are the one who is most peculiarly suited to conduct such ceremony. For you know what it is like to be called back to yourself. To be sure, we all do. But you, you have the most beautiful words to use. And beautiful words, my dear, create their own reality."

"I'm not sure that we mean the same thing when we say the Holy," Ginny answered, amused and surprisingly intrigued by Marie's suggestion. "I'm not sure I would think of it as a person."

Marie looked at her with a small smile. "For seven days and seven nights, I invite you to think of Her that way."

"Mikela will have a cat fit."

"To invite Natividad's soul back, we must invite her mother back too. You do know that, don't you. And what use is a Holy-He to us in that situation? The Holy-She needs to protect us all—from Miguel to Rosemary. And none of us can do it alone. It wouldn't be safe."

"Don't you think Patricio—or Wilma. Someone who has a world view that is a little more compatible."

After all we've been through, the voice asks Ginny. There is a little growl in her voice, deep and real, and an even richer, deeper laughter. *After all we've been through, Ginny-gin-gin, you won't stand up to me and be counted.*

"Let me be clear about what you're suggesting," Ginny said to Marie, a little louder, it was obvious, than was necessary.

CALLING ALL THE SPIRITS
(Patricíó)

We are all, all of us, born of women. It is that still, mirroring water, a mother's amnion, we must trouble to call back our souls. Women as well as men. It is our mothers who give us—in the womb, in those first early months when the touch of their skin, the sound of their voices recreate that womb out here in the eerie air—-our first and most powerful experience of God. Our mothers who create our first experience of all that is good inside us and outside us, of a rhythm that need never end, an embrace that can always and in every state contain us.

But how many women know themselves, truly, as God's own medium? How many of them claim this awful power as what makes them one with God in both the giving and the receiving? They will need to name it as holy in themselves, between themselves, before men can. It is too big, too deep, too sweeping. All our religions are designed to deny or contain the truth that it is women's bodies that introduce us to the enormity of existence and make it safe, beneficent.

These women—Marie and Lourdes and Ginny and Rosemary, they keep looking at each other wondering what to do about these girls, this intractable little family, born of born of born of girls. These women see their own power, power they have never claimed, gone crazy in the girls——and they don't know what to do to hide it from themselves again. None of them knows what to do about the girl who does not want to be a mother and the even younger one who does. They don't understand how to bring Natividad's soul back—or how to keep Mikela, with her fierce, possessive love, from becoming an avenging scourge. They don't know how to keep the baby safe. Can children introduce other children to the enormity of existence and make it safe? Can they be God's medium?

That is why Marie has called me in. As a friend of the sex. A friend of the whole race. A lover of the supernatural and of all the ways, ancient and modern, by which we reach it. So often the supernatural is the natural allowed to expand infinitely into its own mystery. We have done that with maleness for all recorded history. The mystery of men as experienced by men. But how do women feel the mystery of their own being, how do they bring that mystery into all our existence under its rightful name?

Through the power and majesty and willfulness of their gods, men have made their own freedom to love absolute and holy. But women's freedom to love, and to reject, which is even deeper, more determining, have we ever, men or women, called it holy, allowed it to expand infinitely into mystery? No, we call that miracle—that a woman chooses to take the baby to her breast, welcome it into being—nature. And a woman who does not choose to do so, we call unnatural. We do not mirror that freedom to her as holy—only demonic.

Now I, like Jesus a fatherless child, had no doubt where all my claims to holiness came from. And they weren't from any father in the sky. Anymore than Miguel's will be—a child of rape born of a child of rape. They were in my mother's choice—so young, so angry and resentful—to take me to her breast and feed me, let me see, in her mirroring gaze, the gift of my own existence. Because she is, I am. Because she chose to love, I am beloved in my own basic nature. It is a great mystery, this gift of personhood, this knowing ourselves as a home for the holy, and it takes place so early and it takes place in and through a woman's flesh. Man and woman, it is first and foremost through women that we know ourselves as human. Why have we then not chosen to name this knowing as holy? Because it is too big, too deep, too close to extinction. It is not possible to feel manly in that place.

To call the spirits, to call all the spirits that are needed to make the world safe for Natividad, they need to recall, each of the women, the moment they felt themselves farthest from God, from holiness: the moment when they exercised the choice that makes them whole, completely free, the moment when they took their own power to love back into themselves.

It is strange when we think about it that men feel most holy, most God-like and righteous, when they choose. Choose to mete out justice—or mercy. Just feel the difference between Abraham, most righteously if not happily, sacrificing his son Isaac and Hagar desperately abandoning the son she had no means to care for under a bush in the desert. The sadness, the desolateness of that last little shade. The helplessness and self-loathing of that *casting off. And Abraham, who had already sold off his own wife Sarah as a concubine at least once to save his own skin, is righteously, so self-righteously setting out to do the same with his son. All in the name of God.*

For that is the difference, the crucial difference. Abraham feels holy and Hagar feels so far from it there's no describing her condition. What would we think of a woman (whether we called her God or human), who out of pique and jealousy and a powerful self-righteousness decided to sacrifice every first born animal and human just to show who's on top, where the power lies? What would we think of the men—and women—who went along with this vicious caprice? What do we say to women, like Hagar, who say most loudly and clearly, this world that men have constructed is not worth living in? The answers haunt our dreams, wake us, deafened by our own pounding hearts. We will not hear. God help us, we will not hear. Those answers have nothing to do with self-righteousness, justice, power, but they have everything, everything, to do with dependence and being.

So who, I ask you, who is going to mirror back to these women that this power they have to accept and reject, to welcome another into the enormity of existence, or to refuse to do so, is holy and terrible and distinctively their own. Men have made, again and again throughout history, whole theologies, whole societies based on the natural fact of their greater brute strength and aggression. Shouldn't women, for equally long, be able to build whole theologies, whole societies based on a capacity that is equally natural and even more powerful?

But who, I ask you, can help these women see themselves at that moment of choosing as holy in their freedom and their power: Marie, her face pressed to her dead daughter's cheek, closes her heart completely to any God that allowed this. Wilma leaves the baby at the orphanage, refusing, forever, any consolation from the world her husband is making. Lourdes turns her crazy sister out on the street. She leaves her husband when his daughter comes, raging, grief-stricken, demanding succor. Gwen chooses to stay out with her boyfriend knowing the silence of death will greet her on return. Natividad's mother hauls on the rope that elevates her daughter, like all women, feet first, sex next, toward heaven. Ginger gives away her boy without a word to anyone. Rosemary never promises a single one of her foster children a new world where their suffering has a reason. Natividad would, if her sister weren't watching, sell her baby for the peace she can find in a half-filled bottle of glue.

Who, I ask you, in all time, all history, can help these women see themselves, in these choices, as most holy, most free, most true? Could you?

Perhaps it takes a man like me, a fatherless one, one who knew the full uncompromising extent of that female power, its wildness and grace, and lived—and lived! One who is able to say, I know you now, in all my own freedom and manhood, as good—I know you as good.

Isn't it, then, just a small step and a world-reversing one to say: I know you, in your strength and your terrible freedom, as one with God. I know you, in all your self-doubt, your terror at that freedom, as one with history. I know you, in their reconciliation, as our future.

Chapter 20
ASUSTO

Although Ginny had, at Marie's request, written up some prayers and made out a rough sketch of the ceremony, following as well as she could Señor Chun Choc's description, she gratefully relinquished her role as spiritual leader to Wilma. For Wilma, as the preparations had progressed during the week, had demonstrated a natural ease and authority. Ginny was quite happy to assist. Rosemary, the most dubious of them all, seemed more surprised than put out by Wilma's expanding role.

The afternoon before the *asusto* ceremony, over at Rosemary's house, Wilma and Ginny had asked Mikela and Natividad about what they remembered, if anything, of such rituals in their own community. Their father's first wife's mother was a *curandera*, a healer, but she had refused to help their mother when their father began to beat her and her soul first slipped away, Mikela told them. Another *curandera* had tried, but she was not powerful enough. You needed all the *curandera*s in the community if it was to work. If even one thought the husband was justified in beating his wife, the *asusto* couldn't be reversed.

"We are all united here, Mikela," Wilma told her. "We all believe Natividad's soul should return."

"But you are not *curanderas*," Mikela said. "You are *extranjeras*. And even you, Señora Wilma, are not indigenous. So how can you know?"

"I am a receiver of the spirits," Wilma told the little girl. "Some of the spirits who come to me are indigenous. They can help instruct me, but you can too. What do you want us to pray for in these seven nights?"

"That my sister's soul understands that it is indigenous too. Indigenous to my sister. That it can't keep wandering off like this. It leaves her too lonely. And I can't keep looking for it. I don't have enough time—and she is too smart for me. She gets better and better at hiding. I am not so smart at finding anymore."

"And you, Natividad, what do you pray for?"

Natividad looked blank.

"Perhaps we should bring Gwen in," Ginny suggested. "She always appears more alert, more integrated when Gwen is around."

" Señorita Gwen has dangerous powers," Mikela said. "Just like the glue, she can fill my sister with a foreign spirit. Never has my sister looked the way she has when she is with Señorita Gwen. Never has she been so disloyal."

Mikela was on her feet then, her hands on her hips, a stern expression on her face as she stared down at her sister who sat on the floor with her back propped against the wall, her face obscured by her long, loose hair as she bent to lift her blouse and placed Miguel to her breast, and thus put her little, breastless sister in her place.

"Safety," Natividad said through the screen of black hair. "I would pray for safety for me and this little boy."

"*Your* boy," Mikela reminded her. "Ours."

"Do you remember what it was when you were a little girl that made you feel most safe?" Wilma gently asked Natividad.

"Having me near," Mikela answered for her sister.

Natividad raised her head, smoothed her hair back behind her ears, and regarded her sister calmly. "It is true, although I found you very heavy. With you strapped to me, I felt safe from our mother. She wouldn't hit me when I was carrying you—or later, my brothers."

"What else?" Ginny asked. "What else made you feel safe?"

"Watching," Natividad said. "Being inside my eyes. Inside my hand when the stick touched the ground and brought what I could see right up close where I could touch it.

"My mother's voice, when she was by herself and singing. I have never heard a sound that was more beautiful. It was like a church bell, it was so deep and it rushed in everywhere, everywhere.

"The sound of the branches in the air after they had hit me and she pulled them back. It was like a deep breath.

"The sadness on my father's face when he saw the bruises on my face and arms."

"And what about me?" Mikela interrupted. "What about the sadness on *my* face?"

"But there wasn't," Natividad said dreamily. "On your face was an anger bright as lightning. I kept waiting for the thunder to come."

"Didn't that make you feel safe?" Mikela asked softly.

"No. I never knew what you were going to do, what you were going to say. You have no hunger for safety, Mikela."

"I do," Mikela said, twisting her hands in misery, avoiding the eyes of the women. "I always wanted you to be safe, Natividad."

"She's saying for yourself," Ginny said. "You didn't care enough for yourself, Mikela."

"My sister's safety *is* mine," Mikela said. "Her safety and the baby's safety, they are mine, *mine!*"

"Once upon a time," Natividad said.

"You're lying," Mikela yelled. "There is a terrible spirit in you, Natividad, and I can see it. I can tell. It says things you would never say. It has no loyalty. It is bad, bad, bad, and we will send it away."

"Damage control?" Ginny asked Wilma. She wanted to take Mikela to her, make the fierce little warrior safe. But she knew Mikela spoke the truth. Her safety was Natividad and the baby. So what the hell were they doing here? she wondered. Mikela was involved in this healing as powerfully as her sister. And who was it they were calling on?

But Wilma seemed unperturbed.

"What else makes you feel safe, Natividad?" Wilma asked. "If it makes you feel more comfortable we can go away together and you can tell me."

Ginny felt as put out as Mikela by the suggestion.

"Drawing," Natividad said.

"Glue," she added, bending down to tend the baby.

"That's not true," Mikela said, kneeling down and pressing her hand on her sister's breastbone, trying to force her head back. "The glue makes the bad spirit in you feel safe. It doesn't make *you* feel safe, Natividad."

"How do you know?" Natividad asked, letting the force of her sister's hand and desperate questioning impel her upright. She looked straight into Mikela's face with a tender expression that was so unfamiliar it was eerie, as if she really had been invaded by someone else. Ginny couldn't believe she would ever want Natividad's disturbing blankness back, but she did.

"How do you know who I really am, Mikela? How do you know which of these many spirits is my own?"

"I have known you all the days of my life," Mikela said, her voice soft now with fear. "The soul that is really yours loves me, Natividad. It *loves* me. I can feel when it is there and I can feel when it has left you. I could feel that when I was a little baby. I would just listen inside your body, and I would know. I would always know. Miguel knows too."

Natividad peered at Mikela as if she were seeing her for the first time. The blankness came down over her face like a mask, to be replaced by this new, eerie pity.

"The spirit in me that loves you, Mikela, that you call my true soul, does not love the baby. She does not love Miguel. Do you want to invite her back if it means losing the baby, if it means my doing to Miguel what our mother did to me?"

Wilma nodded, her lips in an even line. She raised her eyebrows as she nodded to Ginny. "Our question," she murmured. "It's best if she poses it herself."

"That was not all she was," Mikela said. "She had a kindness to her too. She was kind to me, Natividad. Couldn't that kindness become part of your soul too? I know it already is. You have always been very kind to me, very good to me. It was no different, Natividad, your kindness and our mother's. When I was a very little girl, I did not know the difference."

"That is a very terrible thing to say," Natividad said, the blankness settling over her face, a barely perceptible softening indicating that something, some essence, had left her.

And she didn't say a word after that. Not to Mikela. Not to Wilma or Ginny. Not even to Gwen, who just held her, to Mikela's great distress, for the rest of the evening. Held Natividad as if she were the baby, Mikela muttered furiously.

Wilma firmly took Mikela off and had a long talk with her, and when Mikela returned, she looked chastened but also intent.

"She's the most splendid mystery," Ginny commented to Lourdes, who had come over to finalize the last details for the ritual. But it all was. What they were up to. Where it would lead. Ginny was very clear that she was safest inside a cloud of unknowing.

Trying to hedge your bets, are you? the voice had asked. *Trying to weasel out of the responsibility?*

It wasn't my idea, it was Marie's, Ginny protested. But she could see what the voice meant by weaseling. There were real powers here and she didn't want to treat them lightly, and for her sake, if not for anyone else's, Ginny was committed to calling the spirit, as Marie did, the She-Holy.

God, you mean? the voice had insisted. *You going to go as far as calling that She-Holy, God, Ginny-gin-gin?*

No, Ginny had thought, a shiver—a very non-metaphorical *escalofrío*—running up her spine. I won't go that far.

And what, the voice murmured, frankly malicious, *makes you feel safe, Ginny-gin-gin?*

It was the same question that Wilma asked without malice of all of them when they had settled into their seats in Lourdes' patio the next night.

The *asusto* ritual took place in the downstairs patio of Lourdes' apartments. There were so many spirits there already, past and present, adding a few more wouldn't make any difference, Lourdes said. And it was true that as they sat there in the deep blue light of evening, surrounded by Lourdes' body castings of them all, even of the girls, the air felt unbelievably charged with life.

Lourdes had lit candles and set them on the upper balcony and on all the window sills of the rooms that surrounded the patio, as well as along the floor. Their erratic placement made the women waltz to their seats. When they looked up, the candles above them flickered in the deep blue of the evening. The castings looked more mysterious, more intimate, in the wavering light.

Marie had brought flowers, enormous quantities of red gladiolas and orange Peruvian lilies and fragrant white Easter lilies. Mikela, who had finally come round at Wilma's urgings, had insisted on copal incense. Ginny brought an enormous ceramic bowl, blue as the night sky—a donation from Patricio and Byron, who would have liked to have been included in spite of their sex, but were busy with Simon at the lake. Simon assured Ginny he'd make his own spirit available for the occasion, wherever he was. Gwen brought the eggs. Rosemary, the beautiful blanket, rough with burs, on which Natividad was to sit.

"Natividad wants us to pray for safety for her and the baby. Here are some of the things she has described that make her feel safe:
The sound of her mother's voice, singing in the distance.
The relief when the branches used to beat her left her skin.
The warm weight of Mikela, as a baby, tied to her back or chest.
Drawing.
Watching.
Smelling Señorita Gwen's perfume when she puts her arm around her.
Glue."

When Mikela opened her mouth to object, Wilma raised her hand sternly and the girl took a deep breath and sat back, a look so troubled and vulnerable on her face, it made both Ginny and Lourdes want to go and shield her from view. But Mikela was sitting beside Marie, at Wilma's insistence, and Marie just gave her the same firm, admonishing look that Wilma had.

"*The baby's smile when he sees her,*" Wilma continued, "*the way it makes her feel real inside.*

The ooh he makes that is like a bright yellow balloon disappearing into a blue sky. The way it makes her feel beautifully empty too.

The touch of new white paper.
The smell of pine trees.
The statues of Señora Lourdes. And her big drawing of the girl in the grip of God."

Wilma nodded at Lourdes, who rose and walked over to the window on the right of the patio and unrolled the large cylinder of white paper so that her larger-than-life drawing was visible.

"And now, will you go and put your arm around Natividad and tell her some of the things that made you feel safe as a girl, that make you feel safe now, as a woman."

Lourdes stood staring at her drawing as if she'd never really seen it before. Her face was as blank as Natividad's had been yesterday afternoon. Gwen pulled on her step-mother's hand. Lourdes quickly came back to herself and went and sat beside Natividad. It was as if, in her passage across the patio, some new spirit had entered Lourdes. Gone was all the coolness, the physical detachment that she usually evidenced around Natividad. She sat down behind her and easily circled Natividad and the baby in her arms and began to rock them gently back and forth in rhythm to her words.

"When I was a girl, rocking my sister in my arms made me feel safe. So did the sound of my own voice singing to her.

"Feeling perfectly empty inside made me feel safe when I listened to my mother screaming.

"And I guess the same things made me feel safe as a woman.

"I felt very safe holding my boys in my arms.

"I felt safe feeling perfectly empty inside as I listened in the courtroom. I felt safe feeling like a machine, that my whole body was an echo chamber.

"I felt safe, safer than I ever dreamed of, when I learned how to draw and paint. When I learned to hear myself.

"I felt safe when I discovered how I was inside myself when I was alone, after my sons left home.

"I felt safe when I saw how Ben held my paintings in his mind in exactly the same way he held me in his arms—like he trusted himself with them and with me.

"I felt safe here when I could begin to see what was happening to me taking shape in my drawings. When I could see all the feeling had a purpose. When I could see."

And then Lourdes just closed her eyes and rested her head against Natividad's as if she were the daughter Lourdes had never had, the last echoes of Wilma's translation dissolving in the air around them.

"I want safety for you, Natividad, now and in the future," Lourdes said. "I want the kind of safety for you that never leaves. The kind that lets you trust yourself with yourself and with others."

And then it was Rosemary's turn. The old woman sat in the lotus position before Natividad and put her hands on Natividad's shoulders.

"As a child, I felt myself safest when I knew myself as different from my own mother. When I *knew* I was the swan and she was the duck." She laughed at herself.

"I felt safe when they put my first child in my arms and my hands knew what to do and I knew myself, for the first time, as truly loving, loving inside my muscles and bones and cells themselves. I felt safe when I knew, really knew, what that word loving meant.

"I felt safe when I finally told my first husband I wanted a divorce.

I could hear, as soon as I got the words out, that the danger I had felt—the danger to my soul—had been real and was now over."

"I felt safe when I met Walter. The very first date. The way my anger, my usual state of outrage, made him laugh with pleasure, acceptance. I felt safe to be myself. I felt safe to forget myself.

"I felt safe when I began to take in foster children because I knew I was grounding myself in the world to come—the one where the wounded can know true healing, the one where there is a second chance, the one where suffering truly exists, the one where we know, all the way through us and on a daily basis exactly what we are all capable of, good and bad, good and bad.

"And I felt safe when we decided to move here, when Walter and I, together, fell in love with the cobblestones, the volcanoes, the beautiful women in their brightly woven clothes, the courage of the shoeshine boys.

"I felt safe when I learned how to talk publicly with my hands, when I became a masseuse, because then I had a language that was as tender as the language Walter used with me and as powerful as my own character.

"I felt safe in Ginger's life." Rosemary's voice got thick and she quit.

She put her hand to Natividad's cheek, slid it under the screen of hair.

"I would like you to feel safe enough to speak, Natividad. Not just in your drawings but also with words. I would like you to feel safe to talk to yourself and to trust the person who answered back."

Would you, the voice asked Ginny, and each of the women present there, *be able to wish her that?*

And then it was Concepción's turn. She remained comfortably seated in the only armchair—Rosemary having gruffly refused it in favor of a rickety wooden bench—and leaned forward, talking placidly to Natividad's back and bent head, the lovely frail nape of her neck.

"As a girl, I felt safe with my grandparents who loved me when my mother, their daughter, couldn't.

"I felt safe with my cousin Wilma here, who was older and who never tried to pretend that my mother's behavior wasn't what it was, or that my grandparents' love wasn't what it was either. I felt safe in her clear-sightedness. It made me know I had two feet and needed both of them for balance.

"I felt safe in the honesty of my children when they were young—

that they too, by their clear-sightedness, made sure I stayed as firmly grounded in joy as I did in sorrow.

"And I feel safe in the same way with the girls from the home—even though," she nodded at Mikela bouncing in her seat, "many of them are liars. Their will to survive, their ruthless will to survive is as honest as we can ever be.

"I feel safe in the language school, where every day my student and I may imagine ourselves anew, tell a completely different story of the facts of our existence that is, each day, as true to our spirit as we can possibly be.

"And this is my prayer for you, Natividad. That you too, every day, experience the safety of being as deeply grounded in joy as you are in sorrow so you will know that it is the sum of *all* your experience that makes you whole and powerful. And I pray you experience the freedom of telling, each day, the story that is most true to your spirit, so every day you can know her a little more deeply, more completely, more mysteriously."

Miguel gave a big sigh and burp inside the red *rebozo* Natividad had tied over her chest. She wore the blouse Ginny and Marie had bought for her and the skirt that Lourdes had brought back with her from the lake.

Gwen made a movement to get up, but Marie stood first. She remained standing, her hand on Mikela's shoulder, looking at Natividad, who had completely concealed the baby's head again and was now looking at her hands dissolving and reforming in the flickering light and shadow of the candles.

"I believe there is a reason why, to invite your soul back, we remember all the safety in our lives, remember it as sweet and absolutely real. As real as the sorrow. This is very hard for human beings to understand. That our joy is *as* real as our sorrow. Only an artist like you can make our joys last long enough for us to take them in. Only an artist like you can see the beautiful *in* the suffering.

"I feel safe, Natividad, in your drawings.

"As a girl, I felt safe in the story books I read. I would stare at the pictures and, without noticing it, I would slip into the world of the picture. I would turn the corner, I always believed, and see what was on the other side of the building—what the author or artist didn't show us. I felt safe knowing I had this exciting alternative to my rather dull and proper life as an only child in the Paris suburbs.

"I felt safe in my daughter's character. I still do. I felt safe in the knowledge that she saw life as it was and *still* chose it. And wills the same for me as powerfully now, from the other world, as she did from this one.

"I feel safe, like Rosemary, in my choice to live here in this country where too many babies are born every day, where mothers with no milk must choose who to give away, who to keep. Where girls like the two of you, no older than my daughter when she died, nest in the streets, sell your bodies, give birth to blue-eyed boys.

"I feel safe knowing you, Natividad. I feel safe in your character. In the part of you that draws so beautifully and so accurately, the part of you that won't speak, the part of you that prefers glue to your baby. The part of you who still finds safety in the distant singing of your mother. I feel safe knowing you, Natividad. I feel safe knowing your sister. I feel safe knowing your son. It is my prayer that you too will feel safe in yourself and in each of them—and in us."

Gwen was surprisingly brief. She rose and sat facing Natividad, pulling the *rebozo* down so she could stroke the baby's hair.

"I felt safe going to school," she said. "I was a very good student and I liked the rules. I felt safe in my father's love when he lived with us. But most of all, Natividad, I felt safe in my mother's craziness. I felt safe in the way she could hate me and love me at the same time—push me away with one hand and pull me back even harder with the other. I liked knowing she couldn't live without me. I felt safe knowing she couldn't live without me.

"But here, in these last few weeks, I've found another kind of safety. A safety in doing something big and positive all by myself. A safety in a friendship that isn't crazy. I feel safe with you and the baby, Natividad. I feel that there is some good I am called to do here. I feel safe in that calling."

As Gwen talked, she was drawing the sleeping baby out of the *rebozo* and setting its head against her own chest. Mikela was bobbing furiously under Marie's restraining arm. Wilma put her arm out like a lion tamer to quiet her.

"Give the baby to Marie, Gwen, while you give your prayer to Natividad." Marie walked over as quickly as she could through the maze of candles and took the baby and carried her back to the bench. But she wouldn't let Mikela hold the baby, just put her face next to his and press her lips to his neck.

"I pray, Natividad, that you come to understand yourself as a source of love, of direction. I pray that you can hear a yes for yourself that is like the one I have just heard for myself. Whether that yes is to be an artist, to just let yourself watch and draw for the rest of your life. Whether it is to raise your baby with the help of your sister and anyone else whose help you are willing to accept. Whether it is giving the baby up and just coming back to the States with me as my little sister."

"No," Mikela yelled. "You are the Devil, Señorita Gwen. You are the Devil. But the Virgin is stronger than you. She has God on her side. She has *God* on her side and He will smite you. Jésus will spray his poisonous, magical blood all over you and just one drop will kill you forever. Miguel el arcangel will fly down with his sword and cut your head off. And I will burn you up myself for I know you, I know you. You are the most wicked baby-snatcher of all."

Mikela was spinning in fury. Turning first to Marie to make sure she wasn't making off with the baby, then to Natividad to see that Gwen wasn't sending evil spirits into her soulless body.

"If I had my sword," she cried, looking around her desperately. She was trying to decide, it was obvious if you followed her gaze, whether it was better to pull down Lourdes' drawing and set it alight with the candles or to throw a glass candle holder through one of the bedroom windows and then use the splinters of glass as knives. "If I had Señor Simon," she sobbed.

If she had me, if only she had me, the voice said to Ginny (and perhaps to every woman there).

"We will none of us hurt Natividad," Wilma said to her.

"I can't be sure," Mikela cried, running over to her sister, trying to push Gwen away with small, fierce slaps across her chest and face.

Gwen didn't raise a hand to stop her, neither did the other women. It was Natividad who at last grabbed Mikela's hands with surprising strength and spoke to her rapidly in their own soft, chuffing language. She pulled Mikela down to her knees beside her and, holding her sister's now obediently still hands in one of hers, Natividad began to slap Mikela around her own chest and face, muttering something in that language that none of the women understood but which felt terribly, terribly familiar to each of them. The sound of the words was dreamlike, like the deepest, choking grief, the most powerful, suffocating rage just before it broke through into speech or action.

Mikela sat as still for Natividad's blows as Gwen had for Mikela's.

"I think this is getting out of control," Ginny said getting to her feet. "I think this is enough. More than enough."

"Sit down," Wilma said. "All but one of the spirits is present now."

But Natividad wouldn't stop hitting Mikela, and Mikela, fierce, possessive Mikela sat there with her face as blank as Natividad's had been.

"Stop it," Ginny cried out in a fierce voice. Moving across the room so quickly that she tipped over one of the vases of gladiolas and thus, luckily, doused the several candles that she also toppled. "Look at you," she said, grabbing at Natividad's flailing hands. "Just look at you."

Natividad, as soon as Ginny's hands grasped her wrists, stopped all movement. She looked up at Ginny with that face that was exquisitely beautiful—and blank as a Greek theatrical mask.

"Just look at you. Just look at you," Ginny kept repeating until she felt she was using her words as the two girls had used their hands.

"I can't," Natividad said. "I can't see myself from afar. Not unless I send my soul out there to do my looking for me. All I can see is the front part of my body without my head. Or my back from my bottom down." Her face softened as she spoke and a simple happiness infused her words until she broke out laughing. "I *can't* see myself," she said again. "I can only *be* myself. Be my eyes. Be my hands. Be my feet. Be my belly. Be my breasts." If Ginny hadn't been holding her hands, she would have started slapping herself with glee.

"All the spirits are here now," Wilma said. She smiled tranquilly at Natividad. "Will you let Ginny give you her prayers? And you, young lady," she smiled at Mikela, "are to come and sit by me for the rest of the ceremony."

"You are a very powerful assistant," Wilma added as she put her arm around Mikela. "You did what no one else could. You brought the spirit of your mother out of Natividad. None of the rest of us could do that."

Marie made room for Gwen. Lourdes busied herself righting the flowers and reorganizing and relighting the candles on the floor.

Ginny sank to her heels, her hands still gripping Natividad's wrists, unsure who was speaking through her even as the words began to form in her mind.

Tell her who you see, the voice suggest. *Tell her exactly who you see, Ginny-gin-gin.*

"I see in you, Natividad, a beautiful girl to whom God has given very big gifts so that you can understand that you are and always will be her beloved daughter of whom big things, very big things, are being asked. She is asking you to listen and to choose, Natividad. She is asking you to choose, again and again, every day, what makes you feel safe and whole. She is asking you to understand your whole life, every choice you have ever made, however much pain came from it, however confusing it seems, as part of the story of your journey to find her. She is asking you to see your life, your whole life, as a love story, Natividad. A love story with a happy ending for you."

Not bad, the voice said.

"I felt safe as a child, following the rules," Ginny said. "Rules were for me like Marie's pictures. They were another world you could step into where the air was clearer and easier to breath. Where acts had specific, predictable consequences. I felt safe knowing not to jaywalk or copy my classmates answers on a test. I felt safe knowing to tell the truth.

"I felt safe as a young woman in the world of ideas. I liked learning them and teaching them. I liked how they all fit together, click, click, click, like an erector set.

"As a woman, I felt safe in the God I discovered through my friend Will and the church I thought housed Him. I felt very safe learning and teaching about God. I felt very safe in my priest uniform. I felt very safe outside my body, looking at me from a long distance.

"But I feel safer here than I ever have before," she said turning and looking around at all the women. "Can you believe, I have never had a woman friend, never really wanted one—and now I look around at all of you and I feel how safe I feel and I wonder whether this was available to me all along." She shook her head, her blonde hair sparking in the candle light.

"So my prayer for you, Natividad, is that you feel safe inside your body, safe *not* being able to see yourself from a distance. That you feel the safety of having so many women's eyes looking at you, seeing you, in all your mystery and freedom choosing, every day, to see your life as a love story with you as its heroine, the one to whom good things happen. The one who knows herself, at the end, as God's beloved daughter. That is what I want for you with all my heart."

"And now you, Wilma," Ginny said, letting go of the girl's hands.

Natividad immediately began to touch her knee as she looked at it, her shoulder, her forearm. This same loony loving smile coming and going across her face, which, for the first time looked fully alive—the face of a child.

Wilma gestured to Natividad to get up and come to her. She held both Mikela's wrists firmly in her right hand as she put her left hand on Natividad's shoulder.

"Can you tell me what it felt like when the branches of the broom left your skin?" Wilma leaned forward, studying Natividad's now mobile face intently.

"It was the sweetest feeling. Inside me I could feel the air coming in, touching me on the inside like the Holy Spirit, making everything all right. I knew if I was very still, I could become that air. I could ride out of my body before the branches came back again, slide in when she pulled the broom back the next time, and that way I could make everything all right. I felt very powerful. I knew I could become the Holy Spirit and I could save us both. She always called me the death of her, but I wasn't. I wasn't. I was our Holy Spirit."

"Yes you were," Wilma said, putting her hand to Natividad's cheek. "And you were very loyal. To your mother. To your little sister who loved you both."

"When my son makes me angry, I will beat him just so," Natividad said dreamily. "I will pull his feet up to the roof and I will take a broom of branches and I will beat him round and round so he can know that he too is part of the Holy Spirit."

"That is what you fear," Wilma said. She put her hand under the girl's chin and tipped her face so they made exact eye contact. "That is what we all fear. That is why we are here tonight. It would have been better, Natividad, if your mother had given you away when you were a baby. It would have been better for you to know yourself in *our* eyes—just as Señora Ginny described you. A beautiful girl with big gifts from God. God's favorite daughter, Natividad. God's favorite daughter.

"If you are sure you will do the same thing to Miguelito, then it is better for you to give him away too." Wilma held Mikela's arms up high with her right hand to keep the girl from breaking free.

"But you can tell a story for him with a happy ending. That too is possible."

"Like the Virgin told for Jésus," Mikela broke in. "Where he is a special boy, God's own son. But he doesn't have to suffer. Miguelito doesn't have to suffer. Jésus suffered for him. He can just be special."

"But you are twelve years old and you can't do it alone," Wilma continued, never breaking eye contact with Natividad. "You need your soul inside you always. You need your sister. And you need us to hold you safe in our attention and love. To be your mothers in God. For we all know, in ourselves, what we've done and what was done to us, that the God who is of women has terrible powers. She can choose to love us. She can choose to dig our umbilical cord out of the wall and throw it in the river and send us journeying forever. She can spin us around and around with the blows of a broom until we believe her when she says, 'You are the death of me.' And even then, her voice, at a distance, can make us feel safe.

"And sometimes everything that comes after, the hunger, the nights on the street, the lifting of your skirts and letting all the men relieve themselves in you, the betrayal of the blue-eyed foreigner, this baby filling up your body and taking away all that space where the clear air was, where the Holy Spirit could live—it can feel like she was right, your mother was right, that God herself is beating you, turning you round and round and round, with an even harder and bigger broom. And your soul has no choice but to leave because there isn't time between the blows to go back in and make it a little better. You can't protect God from her own cruelty the way you tried to protect your mother."

"We *all* know this place, Natividad. And it doesn't make you bad. It doesn't make us bad."

Suddenly Lourdes let out a terrible scream that made all of them jump to their feet. She dashed the water in the big blue bowl as she did so. Marie cracked one of the eggs and slipped it into the water.

At the same moment, Wilma grabbed both the girls to her, crying out in a strong voice, "Leave them both. Leave them in peace."

She isn't, the voice said to Ginny, *talking about me. Don't get your hopes up.*

Lourdes was the one who said they must keep watch over Natividad during the night. She offered to do so herself—but quickly Marie and Rosemary and Wilma and Ginny offered to help. When Gwen offered, Lourdes said, gently, "It can't be anyone strongly invested in the outcome."

"I wouldn't call any of you indifferent," Gwen said, flushing.

"To Natividad or Mikela or the baby—not at all," Lourdes said. "We care just as much as you. But we are open to whatever path Natividad chooses."

"So am I," Gwen said.

"You want it to include you," Lourdes said. "I don't blame you. No one suggests you're doing something wrong. In fact, just the opposite. We all think both your suggestions are fantastic."

"Don't humor me," Gwen said. "You think that they are just that—fantastic. You're no different from my dad."

"When I was your age," Lourdes said, "I was the mother of two sons. I was the main financial support of them, a husband in law school, and a schizophrenic sister. I don't think your suggestion is fantastic at all."

"Small potatoes is what you mean. I'm only willing to take one of them."

"That may be realism," Rosemary said. "You're not going to be eligible for much support—here or in the States. But the choice is Natividad's at this point, Gwen."

"How can a twelve year old make an informed decision?"

"And who is qualified to make it for her?" Marie asked.

"Mikela?" Gwen asked. Her face flushed an even deeper, almost magenta red.

"Go upstairs," Lourdes said. "Use my bed." She smiled at Gwen. "It's going to work out for the best—I really do believe that, Gwen, even if you don't know—even if none of us know—what that is yet."

"I don't want her to hurt that baby. I don't want her to hurt herself," Gwen said. "I *know* I have something to offer here. I know it."

"I do too," Lourdes said, putting her arm around her and escorting her step-daughter upstairs. "And I'll support you in whatever form it takes. I *admire* what you're trying to do, Gwen. But now is the time to step back."

When Lourdes returned, Rosemary had taken Mikela and the baby into the second bedroom and put them to bed on a mattress on the floor. She had tried to convince them to return to her house, but there was no way Mikela was going to leave Natividad alone with them, although she agreed, after some heated discussion with Wilma, that they could be trusted to watch Natividad for her while she slept.

So Wilma, Marie, Ginny and Lourdes took seats on the four corners of the bed until Natividad fell asleep. Then they appointed Lourdes to keep watch for the rest of the night, each of them promising to take a turn, or two, in the week to come.

Later, Lourdes would try to explain to Ben what it felt like to sit there all night watching Natividad sleep, safe in her attention. "It was just as she described the beatings, I felt myself, with every breath, become more and more transparent, more and more powerful. I knew I was of the Holy Spirit. I *knew* it. And I could feel that emptiness in me that has been such a source of safety and also so damaging, I could feel it joining with Natividad's emptiness, joining with the emptiness of the little girl in the barber chair after her father threw her back down into it for the fourth time, I could feel that emptiness becoming a fullness, a spacious fullness. Just like white paper waiting for the first mark of a pencil. I knew myself, Ben. I knew my life, *all* of it, as a source of promise. And I knew I could choose, just as we were helping her choose in real freedom, by creating that space for her, that safety, that I too could choose and could know myself as holy in that freedom. I could choose for myself alone, Ben, and know myself as holy. I could choose for another, and know myself as holy."

The voice had said to her, and this she didn't share with Ben, because it had sounded as slurred as Annie's voice in the last phone call she made before the car crash—the call when she told Lourdes she wasn't coming back until Sunday and there was some cash in the bottom drawer in her bedroom and she didn't want to listen to her sounding like a spoilsport—*Welcome to my world, Lourdes. Welcome to my world, sister.* And it had been all right. That was the amazing thing, the gracious thing. Lourdes could listen unafraid, her emptiness opening into Natividad's, into the emptiness of the little girl sitting dazed on the barber's seat, the emptiness of her sister Jacquie's body as Lourdes rocked her in the bathroom, opening into the perfect emptiness of a new canvas, the emptiness of Ben's own open arms.

GOD-IN-THE-ROUND
(Ginger)

I do wish that Rosemary had the least little touch of mysticism to her. I'd like to have just one last word with her. Tell her how good the view is from out here. Rub it in a little? Maybe. She does pride herself on her longevity, doesn't she?

But my purpose is more to reassure. The process of adjustment is easier than she imagines—and far less complete. From here, one can see how porous death is. A blank wall from there; from here is like a scrim. Everything is perfectly visible. Through this thin, lucent veil, even our anguish has a glow to it. Because it was, just because it was.

From here, you can see how poignant our doubts are, the thousand and one ways we try to ensure that life has meaning—a meaning that stays within our own narrow strict intellectual and emotional bounds. It's ourselves we are afraid of most of all—that we'll just give up if it gets too large and cruel and alarming.

But from this side, what gets to me most is just this sense of the sweet, entrusting heaviness of the flesh. How it never stops responding to the air that mothers us from birth to death like the waters of the amniotic sac. We can never, not a one of us, get too much of that particular kind of touch. The kind that says, I am, I just am, and I am alive to my own gratitude and delight, I am alive to the truth that we are all, everyone of us, alive in the Not-I. Alive, beloved, in the Not-I. From the moment of conception.

No one who lives hasn't experienced enough flesh love, enough tolerance of the Not-I, to come into full being. And believe it or not, that much, just that much is enough for each of us to have, deep down there at the core of our existence, a certainty that has *no place in cognition at all, that exists before and after it, a certainty that our existence is acceptable to that which is so much more than we are. Our existence is acceptable, before we have thought a thought, breathed a breath, accepted or rejected a single sensation. Our existence is acceptable and accepted. For there, in that centering point that all mystics seek and keep returning to, we know we've already said our non-contingent yes. For if we had really not wanted to come into being at the most basic cellular level, this too would have been decisive. We chose and were chosen, every one of us, before we even knew ourselves.*

I look at Rosemary still thinking that if she doesn't make the choice anew each day, the heavens will fall and I want to say to her, "It's not that hard. It's really not that hard."

The other thing I want to tell her, tell all of them, is that there is nothing they needed to rule out—certainly not as brutally as we all did. The terrible guilt of love not given or received. Our doubts about the nature of God—and about ourselves.

We shouldn't have held ourselves back. Here, I want to assure them, all those capacities that our scriptures never provided us—those capacities we most desire and fear— our capacities for separateness, for love at the most visceral level, for rage, for self-protection, for honor, for visibility, for assurance and for doubt, for intellectual clarity and mystical suffusion, for knowing ourselves most completely and deeply in the Not-I—- they all come to their holy fullness here. And they can there. That's what I want to tell them. They can there. We, you and I, Rosemary, are a God that can know her own name. You and I, Mikela, are a God who can know her own name.

I stand on this side of the scrim, watching them all prepare for Lourdes' show. I can see how they're all wondering what on earth it is they've set in motion. Just look at those statues! Ginny and Simon nailing an old man to a cross. Businessmen and farmers and soldiers and priests raping a young girl—Mother of God, Lourdes has titled it. And that old man with the tattoos, a cigar in his mouth, holding the crucified young woman in his lap in her dusty lace shift, the stigmata blooming on her hands. Or the little girl, the spitting image of Mikela, with the crown of blood circling her forehead, chained to a column, staring wide-eyed into the future: The Girl Christ Dreams Her Future.

I can feel how they love these works of Lourdes. I can feel how they love what she's saying there, love the fierce and very dangerous power of it, want at a level deeper than any language, any thought, to know themselves inside this world she has discovered. I can feel how they love the part they have played in all this. I do too. I wish she had included me. If only by making a death mask and applying it here or there. I feel as if I too belong in their pantheon.

And I can feel their fear too, their desire to protect Lourdes and her imagination— and, protecting her, protect themselves. You can see it in the faces of all the women who sit around the prophet Miriam, who has dared to ask the unspeakable: *Why not me, God? In all my femaleness, why not me, God?* Oh, the look Lourdes has put on Ginny's face, so questing and aching, so pure and furious, can't we all know ourselves through it? And the faces of the other women—they are all, every one of them, listening at last to their own hearts and what they hear is as lively as fire, as wild as water, bitter as acorns, sweet as apricots. They are, all the women keeping Miriam company, claiming her question as their own. Dangerous. No one would say it isn't dangerous. And necessary, completely, absolutely necessary. And a free choice. They know that any punishment that follows is as nothing to the punishment of swallowing that question back for another generation, decade, day, hour or second. They are resting in that knowledge. Completely alone. Completely together.

Even from the hazy distance I keep now, they are perfectly beautiful. How can they feel any fear? Anyone who walks into the gallery and sees these images will see them as beautiful—see the life they describe, the faith they claim, as beautiful. How could it be otherwise?

"Easy now," the Rosemary of old warns me. "Your God gets misty very quickly, Ginger."

From where I am here, this mistiness, this glow, this tendering of all the colors is just an intrinsic part of life. It can't be separated out. The fire of a lynching has the same tonal intensity of a little girl giving birth in the ruins; a statue carried on the shoulders of sixty women can appear fully human; these statues and drawings in the show elide so easily into a single morning in our lives. Back there. Back then.

You know what really breaks my heart now? I think of those church sessions I tried to keep going. All of us, old women and men, trying to recall the words, the sweet assurance of our childhood. Why didn't we see what was there—the truth of our strange, diasporean lives? Why didn't we see our Not-I? Why didn't we know ourselves through it? Those beautiful, dark-skinned people, fervent faiths that would never fit us, that bloody bloody history?

"Speak for yourself," Rosemary warns me. "Not all of us were as blind to our surroundings."

"But I wasn't blind, you know. I volunteered. I read. I just didn't know myself through the Not-I. No more has Rosemary, honestly."

I said the world is porous from this side. And Rosemary's voice, Mikela's—even mine once upon a time—echo here just as we heard God's voice echoing in our heads back there, all mingled up with the sounds of the real world. What would Rosemary do if she knew her voice echoed here exactly like God's. Exactly like God's.

What would they do, all of them, looking so achingly protective, so brave, and so *sad, if they knew we could see them, everyone who has ever been can see them, all those who they have lost can see them, and can hear their hearts. That the question Miriam cannot ask down there echoes up here like God's own question?*

I wish, I really do, that there was some way to get that message back to them: Think boldly. Dream boldly. Speak boldly. Each time you do, it echoes throughout the universe.

"So," Rosemary asks me, "don't you think it's less of a question of me being more mystic, Ginger, and more a question of your getting a little more down and dirty, a little more earthy?"

Chapter 21
THE VISITATION

"It's one of the requirements of the fellowship," Lourdes said. "An exhibition in the country you're living in. They give you funds to rent a space. But I couldn't possibly show my work here. I'd be lynched."

Lourdes looked miserable. There was a pinched whiteness around her eyes that bespoke a tension much deeper than her gentle, self-mocking voice conveyed.

"But it is not just you who is on the stage, no?" Marie asked. "You will use the sculptures, yes? We will all be there, not only in spirit, but in the intricacies of the flesh turned to stone—or *yeso*, plaster. You are not in this alone."

"I *like* my work," Lourdes said softly, so softly that her voice was almost inaudible in the midst of the plashings of the fountains. She and Marie had met Ginny at the cafe off the plaza after their morning life-drawing class. Simon, who had modeled, would be along momentarily with Rosemary. Daring anyone, with his gentle but commanding look, to mention the considerable weight that he had lost in the last two months.

"It makes me sick to turn on it. To feel it is something I need to hide. Feels worse than being lynched, really. I've felt so sure of myself while I was working. Maybe it was all the positive feedback I was receiving from all of you—and everyone participating in the body castings. Rosemary suggesting them in the first place. Now, all I can think about is how I need to cover all those bodies, change the titles. Mother of God... I didn't think a thing of it while I was making them. Or if I did, what I felt was honest and trusting. Trusting!"

"If they lynch you, they will lynch all of us," Marie said. "For I know not about you, Genie, but I must attend this showing to see if anyone can make the association between these beautiful bodies and the women who lives within them. For sure, when I look at the woman in the wonderful sculpture, *The Mother Who Sings for Herself*, I see a stranger. An enticing stranger."

"That's what I feel all the time when I draw," Lourdes said. "I know it came out of my hands, but I don't *know* the image that is before me. It's like I have to explore it as something completely distinct from me before I can feel any sense of personal connection again. Up until now, I've loved that exploring, especially with these body castings. It's felt very exciting and intimate and more open and social than anything I've ever done. I *know* this is how I want to proceed in my art. But when I think about a show—all that assurance caves in. I just want to cover them up, hide them."

"You want to protect them because they are your doorway," Ginny said. "You want to protect what they open up to you."

"You must leave that to us," Marie said, waving at Simon and Rosemary who stood over by the waiters' station scanning the room. "We are the arméd muses, ready to protect the artist we have inspired. We have swords, just like Mikela's archangel."

As Simon and Rosemary settled in, Marie explained the situation to them.

"You must hold the show in Ginger's house," Rosemary said promptly. "It's all cleaned out now. We won't put it on the market until after your show. I don't see the problem. It's on a cul de sac. Only gringos for blocks all around. No one who has settled here is a stick in the mud, Lourdes. Surely you know that. And you have more than enough work to show. What's holding you back?"

"The desire to appease," Simon said. "A filthy side to all of us. But it can't be repressed, that just makes it fierce. It must be elevated. Just like our need to see—and speak—the truth. That's what you've been doing all these months here, Lourdes, discovering your own truth. Now you're wondering if you're brave enough to live it out—and whether there is any place for it in the world that inspired it."

"Why didn't you stop me?" Lourdes looked with amusement and true distress at Rosemary. "Why didn't you make me think of scale. Weight. How on earth am I ever going to ship these back to the States?"

"If they meet with the reception you fear, you could just use the rubble as landfill."

"I forbid this attitude," Marie said. "We are all responsible for Lourdes' art. We must be tender with this world we have helped her make. It is terrible but also very beautiful. And it shows, does it not, that she has been touched by the spirit of this country?"

"I'll be lynched," Lourdes said again. "We'll have to make it a private viewing."

"For who?" Simon asked.

Me, the voice said contentedly to Lourdes. *Just me.*

No, Lourdes thought wildly, whatever else, not that.

"All of you," she said. "It's an invitation you can't refuse. Isn't it?" Even she laughed at the plaintiveness in her voice.

"I can't believe the woman who made these wonderful, bold images—these, as Marie says, terrible but beautiful images—can speak in a wee little voice like that," Simon said. "We should tape it, don't you think? It can say, 'Thank you. Thank you soooo much for coming. Too kind. Sweet. So very sweet. I don't know. They just come to me. Little snippets in my dreams. I toss them off in a day or two. They're nothing really. Yes. I think that gesture is rather sweet myself. Mm, yes, it *does* look like she is offering the infant up as a sacrifice, but you know, it could be it just needs to have its diaper changed. maybe she's offering it back to the mom or something. It's a puzzle to me too. I don't know where they come from. Like I said, Tooo sweet of you to come. Snippets in my dreams. You're more than welcome.'

And all the while, Lourdes, you can just stand there, silent, looking so beautiful and grounded, so powerful and sure of yourself, so of a piece with the wonderful works of your imagination."

Welcome, the voice said again. *Welcome to my world, Lourdes.* Lourdes tried to listen through the laughter that had accompanied Simon's riff. Was it Annie's voice? Was it slurred? Was it an invitation? Was it a threat? But the sound of water plashing in the fountain, the exuberant laughter of her friends drowned it out again.

When she first heard about the show, Mikela said Lourdes couldn't use her statues. It was a surprising response because Mikela had thoroughly enjoyed posing for them and would come to visit regularly with them in Lourdes studio—carrying on conversations with her little replicas as animatedly as she did with Miguelito. Then she insisted that all the statues—not just hers—be dressed. In men's clothes. She got huffy at Simon's suggestion of lace or sequined briefs or loincloths. Like Jesus in the sepulcher or on the cross, he assured her. Finally she said they could be used, all the statues including hers, if they were painted. So Lourdes dutifully painted all her white plaster white. But this didn't satisfy Mikela. She wanted the statues painted like the candles at the church—the colors of prayers. And so, with the help of Patricio, Byron, Gwen and Marie, they were. Ginny concentrated on making up the catalogue and writing a commentary on Lourdes work from a theological perspective.

"How do we fill the silence, the emptiness of all recorded history about the fullness of God as woman born of woman born of woman? We begin here, as Lourdes Stevens has, by trusting our imaginations, trusting our gut," Simon read aloud.

"I'm relieved you decided to leave turkeys out of it," he added as he returned to proofreading.

"I didn't feel the need," Ginny said. "There's so much else here to wake people up. Although you'd never know it from the titles. I included a blurb with each, just to make it juicy."

"Better a price than a blurb," Patricio said. "If she wants to make a living at this."

"I like this," Simon said, reading on. "Maybe the two of you should go on the road together. Give some workshops. Body casts and mind sets."

"Why not?" Lourdes asked, reading over his shoulder. "She says what I've been thinking—but with a clarity I couldn't hope to achieve. Words and I just don't have a thing for each other."

"But your imagination gives my deepest thoughts and feelings shape," Ginny said.

"A match made in heaven," Patricio intoned, grabbing one of each of their hands and holding them up in the air. "Go forth and spread the faith."

"We're going to be lynched," Lourdes said again, as she must have, fifteen times a day for weeks now.

"Broken record," Gwen chided her. "My father said what he liked about you was that you weren't predictable. What planet was he living on?"

"Mikela," Ginny called, "come and check these colors to see if I've described them correctly."

Mikela crawled out from behind her own statue. Actually it was a statue of Wilma and Mikela. It was called *The Visitation*. In it, Wilma is opening her arms in welcome as Mikela, sword flashing, runs toward her. It was a real sword. Lourdes had had the iron worker make it especially. Mikela couldn't get over it. It was better, more holy, than a machete.

Brushing off the fragments of white paint the she had loosed from the plaster casting, she looked at the sheet of paper Ginny held out to her. "White, yes. That is for the children. That is why the mother is white there. It is a prayer for the child."

"And that ruthless little Valkyrie is the child, I gather," Byron said.

"That's me," Mikela said. "With Miguel el arcangel's sword. It is white too, because it is a prayer for the well-being of children as well."

"So glad you cleared that up," Simon said. "We might have thought someone was just trying to whitewash it."

But Mikela was absorbed in proofreading Ginny's text. "And yellow is for the health of adults. That is why the woman in *The Mother of God* is yellow. Purple is for bad thoughts—and that is why the men there who are doing such bad things to her are all purple. The women (in which category Mikela clearly placed herself) in *The Beloved* are yellow too because it is about how, to be healthy, a woman, even if she is just a girl, needs to know where she came from and where she is going."

They had thought, all of them, of keeping the girls from the show, but then they wondered what in the world they were trying to protect them from. Hadn't their lives been the inspiration for much of it? And, other than wanting a layer of paint between the castings and the eyes of the world, both girls seemed to be unusually pleased at the works that were to go into the show. Natividad was fascinated by the drawings and sat sketching them—or something from her own odd world—for hours at a time. No one knew. She wouldn't let anyone near her sketch pad anymore. Not Gwen. Not Mikela. Lourdes would never have thought of asking. Neither would Rosemary or Wilma.

"Sky blue, *celeste*, is for travel and for students. That is why *The Mother Who Sings for Herself* is *celeste*. She is going, Señora Marie told me, to a new place where she has never been before. *Celeste* is also the color of the Virgin. And the color of a clear morning sky.

"And dark blue is for work, which is why the statue *Women Without*

Means is blue—because their work is protecting the babies, even if they have no hands. That is what Señora Lourdes told me. And that is why all the women in *Miriam's Question* are blue too. They are all learning how to become prophets, according to Señora Ginny. I think it is work to prophesize. Señora Ginny thinks so too.

"Green is for business. The are no green statues here, which I have told Señora Lourdes is a very big mistake. Why make all these statues if you do not pray to sell them as well?"

"We'll make a green cover for the brochure," Patricio assured her "We'll list the prices in green."

"And red," Mikela said, "is a wonderful color. It is faith and a warm heart. That is why *Divine Judgment* is red." Next to *The Visitation*, *Divine Judgment* was Mikela's favorite statue. It showed Lourdes blindfolded, a sword under her foot, holding a little boy baby out on the flat of her hands.

Mikela handed the sheet to Ginny with a nod of approval and went off to visit the statue again. She could ponder it for hours.

"You should have put a diaper on him," she said to Lourdes when she came over. "Sooner or later, you will be sorry."

"The statue will be," Lourdes said. "I'll be able to keep my own hands clean I think."

"The Mother Superior says when we worship the saints, we are not worshipping the statues but what they are leading us to."

Lourdes sat down on the floor beside Mikela and studied the statue. Like Mikela, she also found it one of her favorites. She liked the sturdiness of the woman, how, even though she was stepping forward, both feet had found their groundedness, so there was a momentum and stillness at the same time. She liked the way the little baby's fat legs kicked back at the sky. She liked the paint she and Mikela had agreed upon, a terra cotta with, here and there, the intensity of fire.

"Sometimes it's hard to remind yourself they aren't real," Mikela said. "I'm not even sure that's true, even though the Mother Superior and Sister Carmen say it again and again. But why would everyone push to stand in the place where Jésus Nazureño could look at them if he didn't have a power inside him? Why would they kiss his robes? Why would they light candles to the Virgin if she wasn't in there listening?"

"I have the same problem," Lourdes said.

"So does Natividad," Mikela said. "But she is worse. Even I can see that a drawing can't come to life."

Mikela waved at Gwen, who walked by carrying Miguel. What a relief, Lourdes thought, that Wilma had sorted things out so forcefully and so well. It had only happened a week ago, right there as they were all painting the statues to Mikela's specifications. Wilma had come in as Rosemary was, once again, separating Mikela and Gwen.

"It has been decided," Wilma had announced.

"What—and by whom?" Rosemary had asked.

"Señor Walter and the Virgin. My son Lucas and his father. There is great concord among the spirits. The girls are to stay with us, Señora Rosemary. However, Señor Simon and Señorita Gwen, they are to act as *compadres* to all three."

"And what about me?" Marie had asked. "And Lourdes and Genie?"

"Lourdes and Ginny are to return to the States. With the statues. There is great concord among the spirits about this too."

"You see—they're performing a spirit lynching," Lourdes had sighed. "They're riding us out of town on an aura."

"And me?" Marie had insisted. She looked quizzically at Wilma. She was suddenly tired. So tired. She didn't want to be a world in herself anymore.

"You will replace Señor Simon when the time comes. But now, you will learn to listen for me. For I cannot be tending to these two girls and the baby night and day and opening up to the spirits too."

"It is your daughter's wish," Wilma had added when Marie didn't respond. "Colette. She has wisdoms she wishes to share with the girls, but she wants them to come through you. And my son Lucas, he too has chosen you."

"I think you have me confused with Patrició," Marie had said.

"Of course not. You are a foot shorter and a hundred pounds lighter. What confusion is possible there?"

"I don't want to be a hotel," Marie had said. "A spiritual hotel."

"Think of yourself as a tidy little pension," Patrició consoled her.

And that was it. No one questioned it, even Mikela. "You will never be separated from Miguel or Natividad," Wilma had assured her. "As long as any of us live." And that was all it took. Wilma's word. Not Rosemary's. Gwen's. Simon's. Wilma's word alone. They were going to be a formidable pair, Mikela and Wilma, everyone could already tell. But somehow it made the rest of them easier in the roles they'd been assigned.

Gwen set about investigating correspondence courses to finish up her degree. Simon quietly made plans to return to the States with Ginny to try out another drug combination and give himself yet a third lease on life. Marie decided to leave her apartment unrented once Ginny left. The spirits, Wilma assured her, would like the extra space. And Marie herself might like to make their encounters just a little bit more formal.

Lourdes did wish that the spirits were of as great accord about the success of her show as they were about everything else, but when she brought it up with Wilma, Wilma was noncommittal.

"Promise me, at least, there will be no lynching," Lourdes had begged.

"That is worse than indifference?" Wilma had asked. But even Wilma was tantalized by the statues and more than once, when she came to deliver flowers or food for the opening, Lourdes found her touring the house, pausing before one or another of the statues, her head to one side, listening. For some reason, this moved Lourdes to tears.

Moved her to tears again when she tried to describe it to Ben. "It's as if I've been waiting for that all my life—a woman like her, just like her, bending her head just so, listening."

"Do you want me to come back for the show?" Ben asked her. "Give you moral support. Keep Gwen off your back?"

"No," Lourdes said. "But I want you to rent a large storage space until I can find a studio big enough to house these. I've begun to work on a completely different scale here. I don't want to cut back."

"So you're coming back," he said. The way he so carefully titrated the pleasure in his voice, afraid, so afraid of scaring her off again brought Lourdes close to tears. "I can't tell you what that means to me," he said. His voice so low she had to ask him to repeat it. "I haven't dared let myself hope."

"You are home to me, Ben."

"And Gwen?"

"She'll tell you her plans herself."

"You don't want to give me a hint."

"If you don't like it, you can take it up with Wilma and the great concordance of the spirits."

"Speaking of which—I want you to feel mine hovering all around you during the opening."

And Lourdes did, in between bouts of nauseating anxiety.

"Wilma will channel and Patricio and I will read the cards," Byron announced as soon as he heard Lourdes moaning again about the possible reception of her work. "We will do this as a diversion. People love to know about themselves. They will not notice anything around them."

But Marie rejected the idea. "Look around you," she said. "Just look. What is there to hide here? What is there to be diverted from?"

The walls in four of the rooms were covered with Lourdes' framed drawings. The large, high-ceilinged living room was filled with her plaster body-castings, as was the patio, protected from the elements for the week of the show by a large white tent.

"Genie is to give a talk explaining to the people who come why these drawings of Lourdes are so powerful and prophetic. How they come—how do you say it, Patricio—from the oversoul, or our common depths. High or low, it is more than just our little individual minds." Marie gave up with a Gallic shrug that made her appear, even in her speechlessness, chic and sure of herself.

"There isn't a woman who walks in here who isn't going to feel herself immediately at home," Simon agreed.

"Even if she hates herself for feeling so," Lourdes said, looking both proud and defensive.

"We will have a self-help booth," Byron announced. "With little mantras. *Prophets can have ovaries. There are no empty vessels. If I am made in the image of God, she too has cellulite. Transsexuals have a thing or two to teach the prick-ly Godhead. You can live well without it!*"

"I don't think that will help," Rosemary said. "Lourdes just followed her heart. Took in what was around her, inside her, and responded. The question is how do we help other people respond with their gut, their heart?"

"I just don't see that there's a problem here. There isn't a thing here—I mean, at an ideological level—that I didn't run into in Feminism 101 in college," Gwen said. "Sorry, Lourdes, but I think you're all worrying too much. What's going to get people is how much pain there is, how you can't run away from it, reject it, because it's been made so beautiful, so touchable. I suggest we have some tissues set up in strategic places—but that's it. All these other suggestions, they're overkill."

She looked around, shrinking a little in the silence.

"They just want to have roles to play, Señorita Gwen. They just want to be part," Wilma said. "They want the world to see what has happened to them too," Wilma said. She was carefully brushing the sculptures with a feather duster one last time. Mikela was following her with a broom and dustpan.

"But what *is* that?" Gwen asked. "What *is* it that has happened?"

"We have, each of us, been touched," Simon said. He coughed as he straightened up in his chair. "To me, that always has something of the miraculous in it. To know yourself through the kindness, the attention, the clarity of another—it's like an image flooding in through a pinhole to cover your entire wall. You begin to get a sense of what else is out there, what else is possible."

An hour into the opening, only six people had come in off the street. Patricio and Byron had swollen the ranks with a van of friends from the lake. Rosemary had told all four of her new clients, only one of whom had come. But four gallery owners from Antigua and two more from the capital had come as a favor to either Simon or Marie.

Lourdes was hiding out in the kitchen, where Gwen found her, having decided this was an appropriate time to discuss their future.

"A week and you'll be off," she said, seating herself on the counter.

"So my ticket says." Lourdes helped herself to another glass of white wine.

"Careful there," Gwen said. "You don't want to sound slurred when you thank Ginny for her talk."

"I think I'll listen from in here," Lourdes said. "It makes me feel weird to be talked about in the third person."

"Like you *were* someone? You're right. It's hard not to make it sound like a eulogy." Gwen poured herself some seltzer. "No weirder than looking at a life-size image of yourself. That *is* a trip."

"Do you like it?" Lourdes asked. Gwen, Mikela, Rosemary and

Ginny had modeled for a sculpture called *The Beloved*. They all held hands and radiated out, like a wheel, a mandala.

"Honestly?" Gwen looked thoughtful. "I love the sculpture. I love its title. I love being included in it. But I look at the young woman there and I don't think, me, Gwen Silver, college drop-out, *comadre*, expat, Ben's and Cristina's daughter."

"What do you think?"

"I fit. I look at it and I think, *I fit*. I'm part of the dance. I'm just part of the dance. And I love it. I love that sense of being held fast and being able throw myself out into space at the same time." She smiled, as if she were having the same kinesthetic experience as she was talking.

"I like that you knew that about me," she added softly.

She put her glass down. Unclipped her hair and pulled it higher on her head and clipped it again, the red curls tumbling madly all around her.

"You and Dad will come down and visit, won't you?"

"How can you ask?" Lourdes said.

Gwen looked at her—a slight flush covering her cheekbones.

"Together?" Her voice was as carefully controlled as her father's had been.

"You would like that?" Lourdes asked.

"I would like that," she said. She took a deep breath. "I've been so worried. It would have been the worst thing—because of me—again. You know—"

"Yes," Lourdes said. "I do. I really do."

Mikela was the first to notice her. After Ginny finished her talk, after all the visitors had left and they were alone again together. She smelled the roses. The scent was so powerful, she spread her arms and tipped her head back and sniffed as hard as she could so she could bring the smell and all the kindness that came with it deep deep into herself.

And then she smelled the pine and straightened her thin little back.

Where you find one of us, you will always find the other, the voice said to her. *Where you find me, Mikela, you will always find her as well.*

Mikela wanted to argue, but she knew she couldn't. Who could argue with the Mother of God? And the smell of the roses made that deep aching feeling that came with the smell of the pines bearable.

"Come," she said to the Virgin. She couldn't see her yet, but she knew she was there, within hearing. "See what Señora Lourdes has made."

Mikela pulled at the air, trying to get the Virgin to hurry. She wanted the Virgin to tell her what to think about the statue Señora Lourdes had called *Mother of God*. It wasn't one person, it was many. The woman on the ground with her skirt up was going to be the mother. The mother of God. That was why Mikela had insisted they paint her yellow, the color of the sun, because this was a prayer about the health of adults. She was going to be the mother, even though all those men, who Mikela had insisted they paint purple like bad thoughts, were relieving themselves in her. All together, these bad men and this woman that was going to be the mother of God, they gave Mikela that very complicated mother feeling. A feeling that was so sad and so strong that she needed the Virgin along to bear it with her.

Wherever I am, she will be there too, the voice murmured again, and Mikela wasn't sure who was speaking this time and who was the echo. Every time she smelled pine and chocolate, would the smell of roses soon follow?

FINDING THE HOME THAT WON'T GO
(Natividad)

     For seven nights the *extranjeras* sang for me. For seven nights they kept watch over my bed. Like mothers, they sat there, night after night, one at each corner of my bed until I fell asleep. They kept watch over me, not Mikela, not Miguel, just me. Natividad.
     Mikela did not trust them, of course, and lay with Miguel on the floor outside the door to the bedroom in Señora Lourdes' house that they used for this ceremony. They wouldn't let Mikela any closer to me.
     "She must dream her own dreams," Señora Marie told my sister. "She must die her own death. Live into her own resurrection." She made me sound like I was Jésus!
     They would not let Señorita Gwen sit with them. They told her that she, like Mikela, wanted to fill me with her own will, her own longings. The one who told Señorita Gwen this was her step-mother, Señora Lourdes, but Señora Lourdes spoke with such love, such gentleness, I could see that she did not want to hurt Señorita Gwen.
     Señorita Gwen wants my baby, Miguelito. I know this. And if she can't have my baby, she would like to have me love the baby as she would. My sister Mikela would have me love my son as deeply as she does, as deeply as she once loved me. The *extranjeras* are right. The wishes of my sister and Señorita Gwen fill me until there is no home there for my own soul. They know my soul is missing, we all do, but they hope with their wishing, to make a new soul for me. One that is very like their own. But our bodies can be a true home to only one soul. When your soul leaves your body, no other soul can truly fill it—whether it is the soul of an evil or a good spirit.

I know this. Mikela and Gwen, much as they wish otherwise, know this too. I believe they are afraid of my true soul. Afraid that if it returns they will not be able to love me.

But these extranjeras are not afraid. Each night, they sat there on each corner of the bed, Señora Lourdes and Señora Ginny and Señora Marie and Señora Wilma—or sometimes Señora Rosemary or Mamí Concepción. This was after the asusto ceremony. After we had all watched the light dancing in the still water in the big blue bowl. After everyone had called around us the spirits of the house we were sitting in, of the city, of the volcanoes, of the Vía Láctea, of the home I was born in, of the river where my mother drowned my afterbirth, of the broom that spun me round and round, of the cries of the men in the city who relieved themselves in me, of the bodies in the lens of the camera, of my drawings, all my drawings, of the glue. Each night, one by one, they called all these spirits into being. And then we waited, we all waited, a song without sound and without words filling our chests to bursting. There was such a happiness in that moment I didn't know what to do—and then I sank into it, as if it were the glue, and became very still. And the flames danced on the water. I breathed in the dance of the flames on the water. And then, from one or another of the women, just at that point where I felt safest, most lifted, a cry—so deep, so terrible, and someone would dash their fingers against the water and I was empty. So empty. All the spirits that came in to replace my own soul ran away. They just escaped. And I was empty. Completely empty. Just as I am now. Just as I may always be.

All night the extranjeras kept watch over that emptiness of mine. They made it deeper, cooler, wider. At first, I ached with the emptiness, it was so great. I felt I would explode with it. And then I had this feeling, so sweet, as if I was inside God's head, that this emptiness is God's own emptiness, that there is a wisdom and light to it that can fill every part of that emptiness—with more emptiness!

I can't explain really. I talk as if this happened but it happens again every time I imagine in my mind's eye the four women sitting silently at the corners of my bed, waiting with me. Waiting without any fear. Waiting with me in that emptiness. Waiting with me. For that emptiness.

I feel very big inside at this moment. And still. Perfectly still. Nothing is pushing in. Nothing is pushing out. If my soul never returns, it will be all right because God is this emptiness. In my emptiness I am in God.

Every night, in my mind, these women sit on each corner of my bed watching over me like mothers. They are watching over my emptiness. They are opening themselves to this emptiness as well. I can feel that. They know this emptiness. They are not afraid, any of them, of what will come to fill it. They know, whatever it is, it will have a face they recognize, one that is like their own—a woman's. They know that it is, whatever it says, as much of God as they are. And they are not afraid. They are not afraid to open their ears, to open their hearts, and make her, the heart of all emptiness, the emptiness inside our hearts, welcome. Just as they make me, Natividad, welcome every night. Welcome into my own emptiness as if it is the home that I have longed for all my life, the home I will never need to leave.

Reina del cielo
alégrate
Porque aquel
que dentro de
ti llevaste
Ha
resucitado.

MIKELA'S LEGENDS

La Llorana: The Weeping Woman

At night, you can hear her wandering the streets. Her cry sounds clear, like a beautiful bell at its center and then it is surrounded by something rough and deep, like the sound of a bear protecting its cubs, ready to tear what threatens them apart with her claws and her teeth. But it is just a woman and her cry fills the night every night.

When mothers hear it, they go in and pull the cloths over their children's heads, they put their babies to their breasts. They hold their breath until they think the silence inside them will swallow them back into the silent earth, and then they give up and start breathing again. Just like her. She breathes in the night air and she turns it into a sound so sad and so deep and so familiar we could all drown in it. Again and again she does this, filling us with fear and calming us too in the very same sound. No one knows exactly why she cries all night. She wanders through this town, but she wanders through every pueblo in our country too. She may even wander in your country. I don't know. I don't know anyone who has ever seen her, but the sound of her crying makes a picture. I believe we all see our own mother wandering, wringing her hands, crying for what she's done and can't undo.

For the woman who cries all night cries for her children who are no more. She is trying to bring them back from the earth where she herself set their little bodies, wrapped in bright cloths, surrounded by their favorite sticks and stones and maybe some corn and some frijoles and tortillas flattened between her own hands.

She cries for the children who she sheltered in her own belly and who are no more. She cries for their little mouths that will never close around her breasts again. She cries for the milk that still spills from them now that there is no one around to drink.

Here, in this town, you can hear her most clearly at the *pila*. When the moon shines into the water, sometimes you almost see her face. In this town, they say she drowned her children in the *pila*. In other places, like the pueblo we come from, those who hear her crying near the river say she drowned them there. She tied cloths filled with stones to their little feet and threw them in. Or if they hear her in the woods, they say she left them there for days to starve. I don't know what they say in the capital. Maybe there, she sold them to foreigners. But always, always the children are gone and she cries and cries for what she has done and can't undo.

When I am a mother, I wonder if I will cry that way too? I wonder if all mothers listen to her crying in the night and cover their children and hold their breath and wonder the same thing. Don't you?

La Engañadora: The Woman Who Plays Tricks

There is just something about the way she walks, the way her back sways and her arms swing, that makes you feel that if you can reach her you will be safe and a joy will bubble up in you as she puts her arms around you and you know in all your bones that you're home. They say that when men look at her always walking away from them, always hovering there in the distance, just there where their eyes can barely reach, where she is about to disappear into the mist, a desire fills them that is so strong they forget everything—their wives, their children, their cornfields. They start walking and sounds come out of their throat but they have no meaning because no one knows her name and the men don't know what they want from her for it is too big for one word. She keeps walking, never resting, never disappearing completely from sight. If it is dry, dust flutters around her feet like doves; if there is rain, she seems to lift a little from the ground so that she floats over the mud, while those who follow struggle. But she never lets them lose sight of her, and she never lets them reach her either.

Women don't like her. For she often comes to their men when they have been drinking, when they are walking home, and she leads them far across the fields. Promising. All the women say she is promising them something. That is has to do with lifting her skirts. Finally, after following her for hours, the men give up in exhaustion. They stumble and fall face down in the mud or the dust.

That is when it happens, just before they fall. They shout at her, so desperate because their strength has failed them although their desire has not. And then she turns, and the sight of who she really is terrifies them so much they stumble and fall and hide their eyes in the mud.

The women say the men follow her because she promises to lift her skirts for them. The women say she tries to destroy their homes, that is why they hate her. But I know she appears to me and to other little girls too, so maybe that is not really what she is promising the men. Maybe she is promising them what she seems to be promising me—a place so big and so safe it doesn't really have a word that can hold it.

Sometimes I see her, even here in this city, the way I used to see her in the capital. But I don't run after her anymore. And I'm careful to look away if a woman on a bus moves in that special way that wakes my heart and fills my whole body with a longing so big I think I will explode. Because I know even if I run after her as fast as I can (and when I want to, I can run almost as fast as the wind), even if I touch her clothes, she will turn to me and her face will be the face of someone who has lain in the ground for years. There will only be bones, no eyes, and a terrible smile.

One time riding on a bus with my sister, I saw a woman stand up to leave and I was sure, so sure it was my mother and I didn't know whether to hide or to run after her and give her another chance. And then she began to look back at me and I couldn't close my eyes, I just couldn't even though I was so afraid. Afraid that she would see us, and also afraid that maybe she wouldn't, that maybe everything was turned around now, and we, all the people on the bus, we were the ghosts and the earth belonged to her.

She turned, and for a second, it was my mother's face looking at us and then it was a blind face, only bones, no eyes, and teeth. Such big, smiling teeth, that could eat you alive. And then she wasn't my mother and she wasn't death, she was a fat woman, dressed in a bright blue blouse and a black skirt, a baby on her back. She reached out to help her other daughter off the seat. She smiled a big smile, but it wasn't at anyone or anything in particular. It was just her way. And something in me felt very safe because she was just a stranger with a happy face. And something in me got very still and small, like there was a very sharp machete inside me waiting, just waiting, for me to move too carelessly in my eagerness to reach her. I knew her, you see, for what she was.

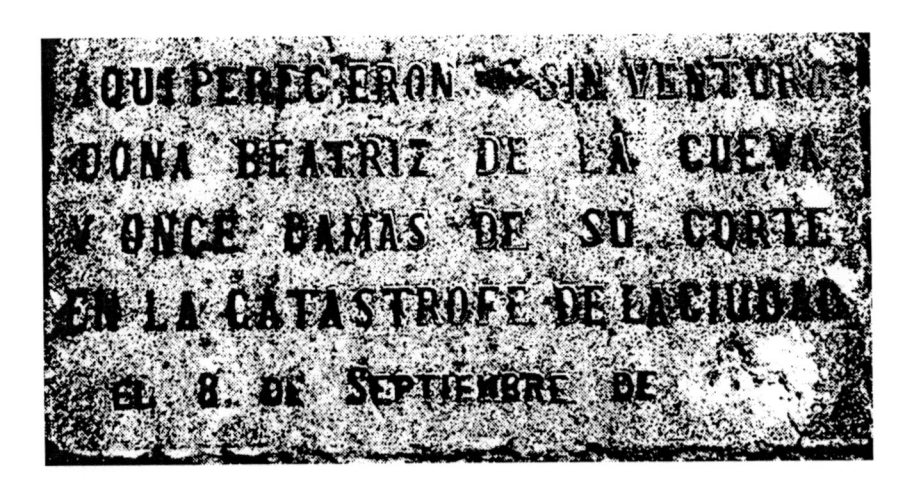

> AQUI PERECIERON SIN VENTURA
> DOÑA BEATRIZ DE LA CUEVA
> Y ONCE DAMAS DE SU CORTE
> EN LA CATASTROFE DE LA CIUDAD
> EL 8 DE SEPTIEMBRE DE

The Woman Who Brought Disaster

> *There once was a woman, a real woman, who brought disaster on everyone who knew her. She tried to make herself a queen. Right here where we live now.*

I learned this story in school this week. I will tell what I remember, although maybe I'll leave something out or turn something around. My people tell the same stories again and again and after awhile all the important parts stay where they were meant to be. But if you hear a story only one time, you can forget some important things, no matter how hard you listen. You can add some things. But I will do my best and tell you what I remember.

There once was a woman, a real woman, who lived here on this very earth where we are now, who brought disaster on everyone who knew her because she did not know her rightful place. She was the second wife of a very cruel man. He was from Spain. He killed many people, more than you can count, because he wanted gold and he wanted power and he knew God loved him especially well because he was from Spain where they had guns. After our people, he was the first ruler of this country. He was the first white ruler and he came from Spain.

But he couldn't control everything, even if he was God's favorite, so his first wife died. God gave her a disease, I believe, to show the cruel conquistador who was in charge. This cruel man had a concubine too. She was indigenous like me. But not of this place. Her people came from Mexico and she was a gift from her father to the white conquistador. I do not believe there are any black or brown conquistadors, so I will not call him white anymore. The job of the concubine was to make her own people safe by making this cruel man so grateful he did not harm them. She did her best to keep him in our country so that he would do no harm to her own people back in Mexico. I believe she did a good job because when the earth fell from the volcano's side, burying everyone, it did not bury her or her child. Maybe she was a favorite of God, more favorite than the woman who was the conquistador's second wife. That woman, the woman who mourned him when he died, the second wife—she was the one who brought destruction to everyone around her and she brought destruction to herself.

This story is about her, the cruel conquistador's second wife, not about the conquistador or his concubine. The conquistador's second wife was also a Spaniard, which is where many white people came from in those days. Now they can come from the United States, but then they could only come from Europe. In Spain, these white people are the indigenous, I think, but here they are the conquerors. We have dances to this day where we all wear gold hair and gold beards and know ourselves capable of fearful things.

This woman was the sister of the conquistador's first wife and he sailed all the way back to Spain to marry her and bring her to this city where we now stand. Then he went away to fight more wars. He had killed so many of my people, we were of no bother and he needed the bother. He was like some of the girls in the home who are only happy when they are conquering someone—they are sadder than anything when the person they are fighting gives up. They only feel like themselves when they are pushing at someone and that person is pushing back. So, because our people were not pushing back, the conqueror went away.

Maybe the woman who was now his second wife was happy when he left because she was tired of pushing back. Maybe she was sad because just like him she didn't feel real unless she was pushing at someone and they were pushing back just as hard. I think I would have been happy if he were far away, but I do not know her mind.

All I know is that when she heard he had died, she went a little crazy. She wanted the whole town to wear black and to say mass every day and to cover their mirrors and their furniture in black cloths. She wanted them to cover their windows with black cloth too so that their days would be as dark as her sad mind. She also made herself the ruler of the country. A woman! She did that. She set herself up against the natural order. You know something terrible had to happen. And it did.

For nine days and nine nights, the rain poured down from the heavens like the anger of God. Who was she to think she was equal to her cruel husband who had killed so many? Who was she, so soon come from Spain, to believe the men who had obeyed her husband would obey her? Men do not obey women, even white women from Spain. Day after day, the rains poured down from the heavens. But she wouldn't listen to the warning. She said the heavens were weeping for her cruel husband.

The men of the town began to talk among themselves. (There were no women there in that town except the second wife of the dead conqueror and the women she had brought with her from Spain.) The men said that the rains began when this woman tried to destroy the order God gave us when Eve disobeyed him in Eden. They knew something terrible would happen if they did not put a stop to this. She had made herself the ruler of the country. She had done that.

With all the rain, the ground was so soft the men sank in up to their knees with each step. The whole world was going to turn to mud if they didn't stop her, the men all agreed. The world would turn all to mud and God would make new people to take their place. He would fashion them all over again. It would be worse than Noah's flood. There would be no one left. They didn't like this. They didn't want God to make completely new companions. They wanted to be his favorites. They wanted to be the only people of the earth. They wanted to be the indigenous.

So on the ninth day of the rains, the men of the town took up their arms and marched over to the conqueror's palace. They were going to take the dead conqueror's second wife away to prison. They were going to treat her the way God would have them treat all women since the days of Eden. They were going to make her obey them like Eve had to obey Adam. But she heard of their coming and she took her eleven helping women on this the ninth day of the rains and they climbed to the top floor of the palace where the chapel was and they locked themselves in. They put a big bar over the door and they lit the candles and they listened to the rain and they prayed to the Virgin.

The second wife of the dead conqueror prayed loudest of all. For shouldn't she, the Mother of God, understand why she had done this? Didn't Mary stand so high above all the other women because she was the daughter of God and the mother of Jésus and the wife of the Holy Spirit? Wasn't their power hers as well? If God should die, didn't Mary think she could act in his place? After all those years in heaven with God and Jésus, didn't she know their business better than they did? Didn't people tell their real troubles to her, all the ones they wanted to hide from God? And didn't she get God to loosen up a little, let a little goodness flow their way? So, if God shouldn't be there, if God for some reason should die, just like the cruel conquistador, wasn't Mary more suited even than God's son to take God's place?

The wife of the dead conqueror prayed on and on and the women she had locked in with her began to get very frightened. What was she suggesting? No woman, even Mary who had risen to heaven untouched by death, could take God's place. Even Jésus couldn't. Not to mention the Holy Spirit. If she thought she was going to find understanding from the Virgin, she was wrong. That was what the helping women thought.

They heard terrible thunder outside and the rain began to fall harder and harder. They asked among each other if anyone beside the wife of the dead conqueror had a key to the door. She stood up, then, the woman who had named herself ruler, and her face was white as ice behind her black veil. Her breath hissed as she told them they were all daughters of the Virgin, they were all daughters of God, and they were not to stop praying.

But the woman looked through the small chinks in the walls and the lightning kept flashing and a terrible shaking began to move the palace, just the way a mother in a fury shakes her disobedient child.

"It is the end of the world," the helping women moaned to each other. "We must get out of here."

But they were too afraid of the woman who had named herself the ruler, who was now screaming at the Virgin, her hair all torn loose with her wailings. And on the other side of the door, they could hear all the men of the city smashing at the doors of the palace.

"Witch. Whore," they called. "Come out now."

Then a woman, an old woman, stood up and she put her hands over her ears and she began to sing: *Dios te salve Reina y Madre de misericordia, vida, dulzura, y esperanza nuestra. Dios te salve. A ti llamamos los desterrados hijos de Eva; a ti supiramos, gimiendo y llorando, en este valle de lagrimas. . .*

She had a very deep and loud voice, but it was also sweet, sweeter than anything any of the other women had ever heard, and suddenly the world became very still and silent except for her voice singing the same beautiful words over and over again.

And that was when the volcano let all the earth fall away from its sides in a single huge wave of mud and stones, and it poured down on the city and it poured into the houses and it poured over the palace of the dead conqueror and they were no more, the second wife of the dead conqueror and all her helping women and all the men who had come with their weapons to make sure she obeyed the words of God in Eden.

And Mary had taught them all a lesson, a lesson that was as strong as any lesson of God's and Jesus'. She showed the second wife of the dead conqueror the error of her boastful ways, that she had no right at all to try to turn over the ways of the world. She could not be a ruler. But she also showed those men who wanted to kill the lady who wanted to rule that this was not their business. It was hers. It was the Virgin's business. Not theirs. Not God's.

Some people say God told the ground to turn into an ocean of mud to punish her. But *I* know it was Mary herself who had the idea because Mary is a mother and the second wife of the dead conqueror was like a daughter to her, a daughter who wanted what she should not have.

For if Mary can't rule in heaven because she is a woman—and they say in the school and in our catechism class that she can't—then why should the second wife of the dead conqueror feel she could rule on earth? No mother wants her daughter to have what she cannot. No daughter should ever put herself above her mother. The second wife of the dead conqueror should have known that. She should have known what would happen to her if she tried.

Mary may not be able to tell God what to do, but she surely can tell us.

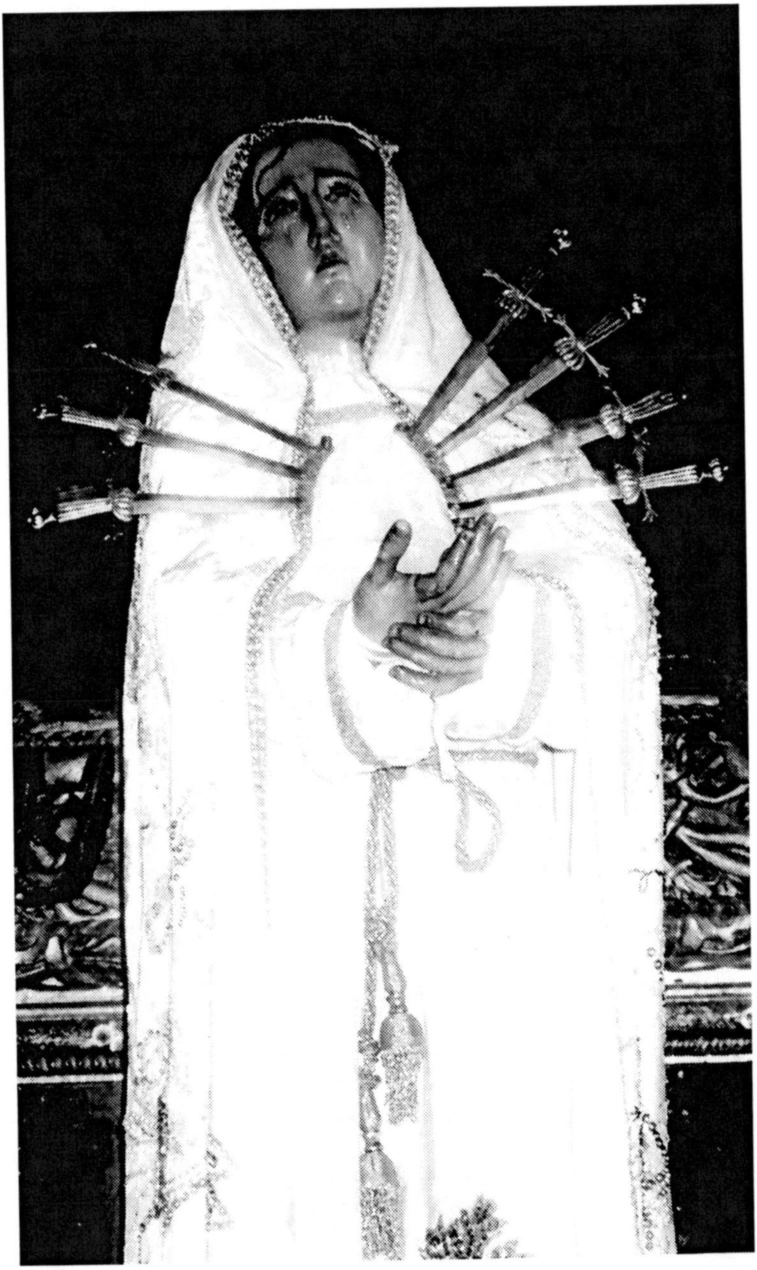